THE WORKS OF
Sir Thomas Malory

THE WORKS OF
Sir Thomas Malory

EDITED BY

EUGÈNE VINAVER

SECOND EDITION
IN THREE VOLUMES
· VOLUME I

OXFORD
AT THE CLARENDON PRESS
1967

Oxford University Press, Ely House, London W. 1

GLASGOW NEW YORK TORONTO MELBOURNE WELLINGTON
CAPE TOWN SALISBURY IBADAN NAIROBI LUSAKA ADDIS ABABA
BOMBAY CALCUTTA MADRAS KARACHI LAHORE DACCA
KUALA LUMPUR HONG KONG TOKYO

FIRST PUBLISHED 1947
REPRINTED WITH CORRECTIONS 1948
SECOND EDITION 1967

PRINTED IN GREAT BRITAIN

PREFACE TO THE SECOND EDITION

THE wealth of new ideas and facts brought to the study of Malory since these volumes first appeared in 1947 would have sufficed to justify a new and thoroughly revised edition. An even stronger reason for undertaking one was my own sense of dissatisfaction with some features of my earlier effort. I have now collated the text afresh both with the Winchester MS. and with Caxton's *Morte Darthur*, revised the critical apparatus and incorporated a good deal of new matter in the Commentary. A version of the French source of Malory's *Tale of King Arthur*, discovered while the first edition was going through the press, has supplied a new basis for editing and interpreting that work. Above all, the problem of determining the conditions under which an editor can emend the text without diminishing its critical value has had to be thought out afresh, and while it would be fair to say that I have not departed from the principles of emendation which I had adopted in the first edition, I have found many cases in which these principles had been interpreted in what now seems to me to be far too rigid a manner. I still think that the only legitimate way to correct a text is to discover in the first place how the supposedly faulty reading or readings could have arisen. Considerations of what the author is likely to have said, conclusions based upon what we feel he ought to have said are only valid if they can be related to the evidence supplied by the extant texts. But this approach permits various degrees of initiative on the editor's part, and as our knowledge of scribal technique grows, the limits of our legitimate intervention become at once more extensive and more precise.

One of the characteristics of the first edition which met with general approval was the endeavour to produce the text in a form similar to that of a modern work of fiction, divided into relatively short paragraphs, with the dialogue set out in modern fashion. In this respect, however, the first edition was far from consistent, and most of the first volume had to be reparagraphed accordingly. The result is,

I hope, sufficiently pleasing to the eye to repay the labour involved for users of the first edition in adjusting the page- and line-references throughout the work.

Some sections of the Introduction have been rewritten and a new section added in an attempt to elucidate the problem of the supposed unity of the works to which Caxton had attached the title of *Le Morte Darthur*. I remain convinced that Malory never wrote the 'single book' with which critics in recent years have endeavoured to credit him; and I am also convinced that had he written such a book his importance as a writer would not have been as great as it is. But the final verdict must rest with the readers.

Whatever may be valid in these pages is due in large measure to the co-operation of a number of friends and colleagues. I am indebted to Dr. Alan Fedrick for check- ing my collation of the text with the Winchester MS., to Dr. Arthur D. Sandved and to Mr. Shunichi Noguchi for many useful *corrigenda*, to Dr. Fanni Bogdanow for much important source material concerning especially the *Tale of King Arthur* and the *Book of Sir Tristram*, to Professor Jan Simko for allowing me to use the results of his study of the alliterative portion of the text, to Professor Roger S. Loomis for his help with textual difficulties, and to Mr. John Stoneham for checking the revised portions of the Glossary. Many of my reviewers have helped me to remove blemishes which I might otherwise have missed. Among them I owe a special debt of gratitude to Professor J. A. W. Bennett, Professor R. H. Wilson, and the late C. S. Lewis. There are besides a number of debts of which I am keenly aware, even though I can no longer exactly apportion them among those very close friends with whom I have had the privilege of discussing my problems. I can only hope that they will not fail to recognize how much this work owes to their constant interest and inspiration.

E. V.

December 1965

PREFACE TO THE FIRST EDITION

SIR Thomas Malory's Arthurian romances are a remarkable example of literary revival. 'Loved deeply, darkly
understood' by English readers of today, they are in all
essentials the product and the consummation of a movement
initiated by early French writers. They transform the legacy
of one nation into a cherished possession of another and by
the same token effect the transition from the medieval to the
modern conception of the novel—from early romance to a
type of fiction able to carry its message to the modern world.

How this was achieved is a problem which to a large
extent remains unsolved, but perhaps the chief obstacle to its
solution is the state in which Malory's writings have been
allowed to remain ever since they left his desk 'in the ninth
year of the reign of King Edward IV'. Of his numerous
editors none but the first, William Caxton, had access to his
work in manuscript form, and all the editions that have appeared since Caxton's time are based—directly or indirectly
—on his *Morte Darthur* published at Westminster in 1485.
What is more, modern editors, while differing only in the
degree of closeness with which they follow Caxton's text,
have so far made no attempt at a critical treatment of it.
Intent on presenting it in an 'accessible' form, they have in
most cases made it superficially intelligible by modernizing
the spelling, removing obsolete words, and occasionally
rewriting obscure passages. An exception to this practice
is H. O. Sommer's reprint, which, in the editor's own words,
'follows the original impression of Caxton with absolute
fidelity, word for word, line for line, and page for page'.[1]
But 'fidelity' in a reprint, especially if it is 'absolute', can
at best facilitate reference to an already existing printed
version; it can throw no fresh light on the work itself.

In 1931 I was asked by the Delegates of the Clarendon
Press to prepare a critical edition of Malory based on the two

---

[1] *Le Morte Darthur by Syr Thomas Malory, the original edition of William Caxton
now reprinted and edited with an Introduction and Glossary* by H. Oskar Sommer,
London, Nutt, 1889–91, vol. ii, p. 17.

extant copies of Caxton's volume. My work was nearing completion when, in the early summer of 1934, a startling discovery was made in the Fellows' Library in Winchester College by the then Librarian, Mr. W. F. Oakeshott. While the contents of the library were being examined for another purpose, a fifteenth-century manuscript of Malory's romances unexpectedly came to light. It had lost a gathering of eight leaves at each end, and probably for this reason had remained unidentified for the best part of a century since its first definite entry in the catalogue of the library in 1839. Further inquiry showed that, while the manuscript was not that used by Caxton, it was in many respects more complete and authentic than Caxton's edition and had the first claim to the attention of any future editor of Malory. My task was thus clearly outlined for me. Without undue regret I abandoned my original project and undertook to edit Malory's works from the newly discovered text.

The most obvious merit of this text is that it brings us nearer to what Malory really wrote. Less obvious but no less vital is the fact that it enables us to see Malory's work in the making—not as a single book such as Caxton produced under the spurious and totally unrepresentative title of *Le Morte Darthur*, but as a series of separate romances each representing a distinct stage in the author's development, from his first timid attempts at imaginative narrative to the consummate mastery of his last great books. And as we observe not merely what he achieved but how he achieved it, we become aware that his methods bear a close relation to the processes operating in the whole field of early fiction. No such approach has so far been possible: the 'static' view which, thanks to Caxton, prevailed in all critical works on Malory (my own monograph of sixteen years ago is no exception) precluded any study of his evolution. In the Introduction to this volume I have made an attempt to suggest how the omission may be remedied. But the problem is vast, and my essay is but an outline of what in abler hands may yet form a new and revealing chapter of literary history.

The method I have adopted in establishing the text is described in another section of the Introduction. Suffice it to say here that I have endeavoured to treat the Winchester

MS. with all the care due to a copy whose original is no longer extant: not to reconstruct that original in its entirety by means of hypothetical readings, but merely to lessen as far as possible the damage done to the work by its copyists. To discard emendations which cannot be justified on objective grounds may seem, in theory, an obvious procedure. In practice it is surprisingly uncommon, for while it is easy enough to lay down the rule *conserver le plus possible, réparer le moins possible*, it is less easy to apply it at the expense of editorial initiative and to retain awkward readings when more attractive conjectural ones come to mind. The temptation to accept these is such that I may occasionally have yielded to it against my better judgement. But throughout my work, and in face of every doubtful passage, I have borne in mind that the proper attitude to a text should be that of an archaeologist to a monument of the past: an attitude of respect for every detail that may conceivably belong to the original structure.

There is a vital corollary to this view. Where emendation ends, interpretation must begin, and while punctuation, paragraphing, and the like are often its most effective means, no 'conservative' edition can safely dispense with a commentary. Hence the bulky sequel to the text in Volume III. It deals in the first place with textual problems; but it is also concerned with Malory's method of work as seen against the background of his sources: with his reactions to the texts he used, his rejections and selections, and the extent and character of his contribution. Like any *Quellenforschung* this type of annotation runs the risk of defeating its purpose, for it can make our reading of the text so thoroughly 'source-ridden' that we no longer see it as it is in itself, but only as it contrasts with its models. Against this error there is no safeguard beyond a sympathetic insight into the infinite complexities of assimilation and growth which make a product of the mind resemble a living organism. But given such an insight, a knowledge of the author's mind and method has an attraction all its own. There may be other ways of reading enjoyably, but none of reading constructively, of following the process and seeing its completion as a human achievement.

On my inability to do justice to my task I need not dwell at any length, but one of my handicaps should perhaps be made clear at the outset. My long acquaintance with Malory's Arthurian romances does not alter the fact that, as one of my most generous critics has pointed out, I came to him with a memory 'too full and too recent' of his French antecedents. *Nous ne voyons jamais qu'un seul côté des choses*, and my natural tendency has been to place Malory, not against his native English background, but against that of medieval French fiction. I have resigned myself to this inevitable one-sidedness with the less regret because I know that I leave whatever lies beyond my grasp in better hands than mine, and because the anomaly of an English classic being edited by a French scholar is in this case almost a necessary evil. For not only are most of Malory's works 'briefly drawn out of French', not only is their inspiration and texture essentially French, but the establishing of the text cannot be attempted without the aid of such records of Malory's sources as are found among the French Arthurian romances. Yet the anomaly remains, and the inevitable risk of misinterpretation. Nothing has been more welcome to me, therefore, than the help and advice I received in the early stages of this work from a scholar-friend, the late Professor E. V. Gordon, whose supreme competence was equalled only by his generosity to fellow workers and his selfless devotion to learning. His untimely death put an end to a collaboration which I valued above all else and to which this edition owes more than words can acknowledge. Fortunately his successor, Professor G. L. Brook, was good enough to step into the breach and lend me a helping hand at a time when I needed it most. He is the sole author of the Glossary —the only section of these volumes which I can unreservedly describe as being worthy of the text. For this and for his invaluable assistance in the clearing of numerous textual difficulties I cannot thank him enough.

It was my good fortune to find among my former pupils, who had already left their own mark in the province of French studies, as many willing helpers as I could reasonably ask for. I should like to record my especial gratitude to Dr. F. Whitehead for his important contribution to my commentary on the *Tale of King Arthur*; to Mr. E. S. Murrell for having collated with infinite care the two extant copies of Caxton's edition; to Dr. J. A. Noonan for valuable bibliographical information; to Mr. J. P. Collas for transcribing with extreme accuracy several sections of the Winchester MS.; and to Dr. Gweneth Hutchings, who not only assisted me in the transcription of the text with the skill of an expert palaeographer, but supplied original material for the study of Malory's romances of Lancelot.

Several friends, including Sir Edmund Chambers, Professor M. K. Pope, and Professor T. B. W. Reid, were kind enough to read my Introduction in manuscript and give me the benefit of their advice on points of fact and interpretation. Of the libraries which provided me with the essential material I have incurred a particular obligation to the Winchester College Fellows' Library for generously allowing me to use and publish their newly discovered manuscript of Malory's text; to the Pierpont Morgan Library for permission to reproduce part of the unique complete copy of Caxton's edition; and to the John Rylands Library which in the person of its eminent Librarian, Dr. Henry Guppy, has done everything possible to facilitate my work at every stage.

The great institution under whose imprint this edition is privileged to appear is responsible for more than its outward form. To have seen a text of this magnitude through the press at a time of the greatest national emergency is in itself a unique achievement; but my debt to this self-effacing agency extends to every page of this book, to every detail of its presentation, and indeed to all the innumerable improvements which will, I hope, make it, in Caxton's phrase, 'for to pass the time pleasant to read in'.

As much of this work as belongs to me I dedicate to the memory of Joseph Bédier whose encouragement and example have been my lifelong inspiration. I wish for no higher reward than the knowledge that he would have recognized it as the work of a disciple.

December 1945

CONTENTS

VOLUME I

Complete

Contents

VOLUME III

Contents

LIST OF PLATES

VOLUME I

VOLUME III

LIST OF TEXT-FIGURES

INTRODUCTION

CHAPTER I

THE KNIGHT-PRISONER

1. *Sir Thomas Malory*

EVER since 1485, when Malory's romances first appeared in print, the only clue to their authorship has been the following paragraph at the end of the book:

I praye you all Ientyl men and Ientyl wymmen that redeth this book of Arthur and his knyghtes from the begynnyng to the endyng praye for me whyle I am on lyue that god sende me good delyueraunce and whan I am deed I praye you all praye for my soule for this book was ended the ix yere of the reygne of kyng edward the fourth by syr Thomas Maleore knyght as Ihesu helpe hym for hys grete myght as he is the seruaunt of Ihesu bothe day and nyght.

Apart from the author's name, three points emerge from this passage: he was a knight; he completed his work in the ninth year of the reign of Edward IV, i.e. between 4 March 1469 and 3 March 1470; and he was then in prison: the 'deliverance' for which he asks his readers to pray can only mean deliverance from prison.[1] A Sir Thomas Malory,[2] knight, of Newbold Revell (Warwickshire) and Winwick (Northamptonshire), is known to have lived at that time:[3] he died on 14 March 1471. But whether he was in prison in the ninth year of the reign of Edward IV remains uncertain.[4] It is known that he was excluded from at least

[1] Cf. my *Malory*, p. 115.

[2] The variants of spelling are: *Malore, Mallore, Mallere, Malery, Malorie, Malarie, Malorey, Malory.*

[3] Cf. G. L. Kittredge, *Who was Sir Thomas Malory?* Boston, 1897. The discovery was first announced in *Johnson's Universal Cyclopaedia* in March 1894.

[4] Malory's imprisonment in 1469 has so far been taken for granted. Cf. my *Malory*, p. 116.

four successive general pardons granted by Edward IV to the Lancastrians in 1468[1] and in 1470,[2] but exclusion from a general pardon is in itself no evidence of imprisonment.[3] It is also known that in the course of an eventful life Sir Thomas Malory of Newbold Revell was imprisoned several times and that the length of his detention varied from a few days to three years;[4] but his last recorded imprisonment ended not later than November 1462, and there is no conclusive proof that he was arrested at any time after that date.

The manuscript of Malory's romances discovered in Winchester in 1934 helps to some extent to dispose of this difficulty. One of the passages not found in the printed version of the work reads as follows:

And I pray you all that redyth this tale to pray for hym that this wrote that God sende hym good delyveraunce sone and hastely. Amen.[5]

These lines, obviously written in prison,[6] occur at the end of the *Tale of Sir Gareth*, long before the end of the last book. On the most conservative estimate the writing of the intervening matter, which in the present edition covers some nine hundred pages, could not have taken less than a year. Hence at least a year before he concluded his work, i.e. in February 1469 at the latest, the author must have been a prisoner. Still more helpful is the statement found on f. 70 of the manuscript, at the end of the *Tale of King Arthur*:[7]

And this booke endyth whereas sir Launcelot and sir Trystrams com to courte. Who that woll make ony more lette hym seke other bookis of kynge Arthure or of sir Launcelot or sir Trystrams; for this

---

[1] On 14 July, 24 August, and 1 December 1468 (cf. *Liber Albus*, ii, ff. 199–200, and iii. ff. 227–8) and on 22 February 1470.

[2] The first and the last of these have recently been discovered by Dr. Gweneth Whitteridge.

[3] Sir Humphrey Nevill, similarly excluded, was not in prison at the time when the pardon was granted.

[4] Cf. E. Hicks, *Sir Thomas Malory, his Turbulent Career*, Cambridge, Harvard University Press, 1928, and A. C. Baugh, 'Documenting Sir Thomas Malory', *Speculum*, vol. viii, pp. 3–29.

[5] F. 148.

[6] *The Book of Sir Tristram* (*v. infra*, p. 540) contains some remarks on the hardships of imprisonment, but it is not certain that they refer to the author's own experiences.

[7] See Plate I.

stronge þ he myght but feaw knyghtes stoode hym a buffette wt
a spere   And at þe nexte feste sir Pelleas and sir Marhalt
were made knyghtes of þe rounde table. ffor þ were ij. segis
voyde for . ij. knyghtes were slayne þ xij. month. And grete
joy had kynge Arthure off sir Pelleas and off sir Marhalte. But Pelleas loved nev after sir Gawayne. But as
he spared hym for þe love off þe kynge. but offtyn tymes at
justis & at turnementes Sir Pelleas quytte sir Gawayne
for so hit rehersyth in the booke off frensth. So sir Trystrams many dayes after foughte wt sir Marhaute in an
ylande and þ they dud a grete batayle. But at þ laste sir
Trystrams slew hym. So Sir Trystrams was so wounded þ unnethe he myght recov and lay at a nunnerye
halff a yere   And sir Pelleas was a worshypfull
knyght and was one off þe iiij. þ encheved þe Sankgreal.
And þ damesel off þe laake made by her meanes þ nev
he had a do wt sir launcelot de laake ffor where sir launce
lot was at ony justis or at ony turnemente. she wolde
not suffir hym to be þ þat day but yff hit were on þ syde
off Sir launcelot. here endyth this tale as þ ffreynsshe
booke seyth fro the maryage off kynge Uther unto kynge
Arthure þ regned after hym & ded many batayles
  And this booke endyth whereas sir launcelot And
Sir Trystrams com to courte. who þ woll make
ony more lette hym seke oþ bookis off kynge Arthure
or off Sir launcelot or Sir Trystrams ffor this was
drawyn by a knyght presoner Sir Thomas Malleorre
þ god sende hym good recov Amen ⁊ cᷓ

Explicit

was drawyn by a knyght presoner sir Thomas Malleorré, that God
sende hym good recover. Amen, etc. EXPLICIT.

Here at last we have, instead of a mere allusion to the
author's experiences, a plain admission that the *Tale of King
Arthur*—the second in date of his romances[1]—was written
by a *knight-prisoner*. Scarcely less definite is the indication
that when he finished writing it he had little hope of finding
'any more books of Arthur, Lancelot, or Tristram'.
Between this *explicit* and the resumption of the work there
must have elapsed an interval of time long enough to enable
him not only to change his mind but to lay his hand on fresh
material. His captivity, whether continuous or intermittent,
must, then, have begun long before he wrote the concluding
sentence of the *Tale of Sir Gareth* and at least a few years
before he completed his last work.

The bearing of this on the author's identification is clear.
Until now the only relevant passage in his work has been
his appeal for deliverance written six or seven years after the
last recorded imprisonment of Sir Thomas Malory of
Newbold Revell. The passages quoted above help to
reduce this gap. No doubt the identification is still a little
less than certain, for it depends upon the not altogether
impregnable assumption that between 1460 and 1470 there
was no other 'knight-prisoner' of the name of Thomas
Malory. But in the absence of any known alternative[2] it
would not seem out of place to relate in chronological order
the few ascertainable facts of his life.[3]

Sir Thomas Malory belonged to an old Warwickshire

[1] Cf. *infra*, Ch. II, section 3. *The Tale of Sir Launcelot, The Tale of Sir Gareth,
The Book of Sir Tristram, The Tale of the Sankgreal, The Book of Sir Launcelot and
Queen Guinevere* and *The Morte Arthur* were all written after *The Tale of King
Arthur*.

[2] A book suggesting one such alternative was announced by Professor William
Matthews in a paper read at the annual meeting of the Modern Language Association of America in Chicago in December 1965. But there is no evidence that his
candidate was either a knight or a prisoner.

[3] Unless otherwise stated my narrative is based on the records published by
G. L. Kittredge, E. Hicks, and A. C. Baugh, and on some of the materials contained
in Appendix I of my *Malory*. The late Sir Edmund Chambers wrote to me at some
length while I was engaged upon this work and made many useful suggestions. In
connexion with the present edition I have received substantial help from Dr.
Gweneth Whitteridge whose study of Malory's biography, still unpublished at the
time of writing, will certainly throw new light on the problem of Malory's identity.

family. As a young squire he is said to have served in the train of Richard Beauchamp, Earl of Warwick, 'with one lance and two archers'.[1] In 1433 or 1434 he succeeded to the ancestral estate. Between 1441 and 1449 he acquired the estate of his sister's husband, Robert Vincent,[2] and in 1445 served for his shire in Parliament then held at Westminster. The fact that as early as 1443 a Thomas Smythe charged him with the theft of goods and chattels is no proof that he committed any such offence.[3] Nor is it necessary to assume with one of his latest biographers that 'in view of the orgy of lawlessness on which he is in full career when we next meet him' he must have been engaged in criminal activities for several years before the 'orgy' began.[4] There is in fact no proof that the orgy ever took place. He was accused, but not convicted, of several major crimes alleged to have been committed in the course of eighteen months, from January 1450 to July 1451. These crimes included a robbery, a theft, two cattle-raids, some extortions, a rape, and even an attempted murder. It is claimed on the strength of the charges brought against him that on 4 January 1450 he lay in ambush with other malefactors for the purpose of murdering Humphrey, Duke of Buckingham; that on 23 May he 'feloniously raped' Joan Smyth and stole some property belonging to her husband,[5] Hugh Smyth of Monks Kirby; that a week later

---

[1] According to Dugdale (*Antiquities of Warwickshire*, London, 1656, p. 56) Thomas Malory served in the train of Richard Beauchamp, Earl of Warwick, *at the siege of Calais*, in Henry V's time, but as there was no siege of Calais in Henry V's time Sir Edmund Chambers suggested (*English Literature at the Close of the Middle Ages*, p. 200) two alternative corrections: 'Possibly he (i.e. Dugdale) wrote "Caleys" for "Harfleur" (1415) or "Rouen" (1418). But an easier slip would be to write "K.H.5" for "K.H.6" .' There was in fact a siege of Calais in "K.H.6" (1436) by the Burgundians; it was relieved by the Duke of York. Since, however, Beauchamp did not arrive in Calais until a year later, that is to say in 1437 and not in 1436, the correction of K.H.5 to K.H.6 does not help. The error in Dugdale's statement may be the reference to the siege. A roll in the Cotton collection (C.P.R. XVII, 1437–45, p. 324) states that a Thomas Malory was in Beauchamp's retinue when Beauchamp went to Calais in 1414: 'retenuz a une lance et deux archers'.

[2] Cf. my *Malory*, p. 121.

[3] It is not known what came of this charge, but it seems probable that it fell through.

[4] A. C. Baugh, op. cit., p. 4.

[5] He is also alleged to have made a return visit to Hugh Smyth's house on 6 August 1450 and repeated the offence.

he extorted money from Margaret Kyng and William Hales, and on 31 August dealt in like fashion with John Mylner. According to the same indictment, on 4 June 1451 he extorted with the help of five other men 7 cows, 2 calves, a cart, and 335 sheep from William Rowe and William Dowde of Shawell.¹ Another document states that on 20 July of that year he broke into a park at Caludon, carried off 6 does, and inflicted considerable damage on the property.² On 23 July he was arrested as a result of a dispute with the Carthusian monks at Axholme Priory. Sixty yeomen had been summoned to meet the Duke of Buckingham at Atherstone and secure the arrest.³ Malory was delivered into the King's custody at Coleshill, but two days later escaped by swimming across the moat. On 28 July, so our records tell us, he broke into the Cistercian Abbey of Blessed Mary Coombe by staving in its doors with battering rams, opened two of the abbot's chests, and stole various *jocalia* and *ornamenta* as well as two bags of money. The next day, according to the same records, he repeated the assault with the help of numerous accomplices, broke eighteen doors, insulted the abbot to his face, forced open three iron chests, and stole more money.⁴ With this the most eventful period of his life was, as far as we know, at an end. Soon after his alleged second attack on Coombe Abbey he was arrested again, and his detention lasted until May 1454, with at least one interval of freedom, for he was at liberty on 26 March 1453 when, according to an entry

---

¹ All the charges so far mentioned were brought against Malory at an Inquisition held at Nuneaton on 23 August 1451. The relevant documents have been published by E. Hicks (op. cit., pp. 93–102), but in dating the events to which they refer I have taken into account the corrections proposed by A. C. Baugh in an article in the *Journal of English and Germanic Philology*, vol. xxix, pp. 452–7.

² Cf. Baugh, 'Documenting Sir Thomas Malory', *Speculum*, vol. viii, pp. 20–22. The document referring to this offence is *Coram Rege Roll* 763, Hilary, 30 Hen. VI, m. 23 *dorso*. The plaintiffs are the Archbishop of Canterbury, Humphrey, Duke of Buckingham, and the Duke and Duchess of Norfolk. The damage done to the property is said to amount to £500—clearly an impossible figure in the circumstances.

³ K. B. McFarlane, *The Wars of the Roses* (Proceedings of the British Academy, 1964), p. 91, note 3.

⁴ This is one of the items in the Nuneaton Inquisition. It gives the names of fourteen men who accompanied Malory on his second attack on the abbey and states that about a hundred others took part in it. Cf. Hicks, loc. cit.

in the Patent Rolls, the Duke of Buckingham, Sir Edward Grey of Groby, and the Sheriffs of Warwick and Leicester were directed to arrest him 'to answer certain charges'.[1]

On 5 May 1454 he was released on bail to Roger Chamburleyn and nine others for six months. If we are to believe a complaint by a Katherine Peyto, he promptly took advantage of his freedom to carry off some oxen from a manor belonging to her in Northamptonshire.[2] At the same time he seems to have used his experience of cattle-raids to assist his friend and accomplice, John Aleyn, who on 21 May broke into the grounds and buildings of John Abot of Tilty at Great Easton in Essex to steal two horses. On 27 June Aleyn stole another horse from Richard Skott, vicar of Gosfield in the same county, and five days later carried off two more: one belonging to Thomas Bykenen and the other to Thomas Strete.[3] Malory is reported to have 'feloniously' given shelter to Aleyn a few days later at Thaxted and again at Braintree, and to have plotted with him an attack on the property of William Grene of Gosfield. The attack failed, but on 16 October Malory was committed to the custody of Thomas Cobham, keeper of the jail at Colchester, and so was unable to appear at the expiration of his bail (29 October). A writ was issued to the custodian of the jail to bring him to court, and although on the next day (30 October) Malory broke out of jail,[4] the custodian succeeded in producing him on 18 November. Malory was then committed to the Marshal. For the year 1455 no records are available, but when in February 1456 Malory was produced in King's Bench by the Lieutenant of the

---

[1] The date of this commission is wrongly given in my *Malory* (p. 6, note 3) as 1452.

[2] The petition of Katherine Peyto was found by A. C. Baugh (op. cit., pp. 19–20) among the *Early Chancery Proceedings* (C/1/15/780). Its dating presents some difficulty, but of the alternatives suggested by Baugh the more likely seems the period 1452–6, not 1442–50.

[3] A full account of these offences is given in a record of the *Ancient Indictments*, K.B. 9/280 m. 43. Cf. Baugh, op. cit., pp. 22–25.

[4] The record describing Malory's escape from Colchester prison (K.B. 9/280, m. 44) specifies that 'predictus Thomas Mallory . . . eandem gaolam sive prisonam domini Regis . . . vi et armis, videlicet gladiis, langodebeves et daggariis felonice fregerit et sic extra eandem gaolam felonice adtunc et ibidem evaserit et ad largum exierit'.

Tower, he offered a royal patent of pardon granted on 24 November 1455, presumably by the Duke of York.[1] On 3 July 1456 he was able to borrow money from Thomas Greswold, but was subsequently rearrested and detained in Ludgate (normally a prison for debtors), perhaps because of his failure to repay the debt, which could be regarded as a breach of the conditions of his pardon. On 19 October 1457 he was released on bail for two months,[2] and at the end of this time returned to the Marshal.

A year and three months later, at Easter 1459, he was reported at large in Warwickshire, and so far as can be ascertained remained free until the Hilary term of 1460, when he was committed to Newgate. We know neither the reason for this arrest nor the exact length of the imprisonment, but on 24 October 1462 'Thomas Malory, miles, alias dictus Thomas Mallorry de Newebold Ryvell' was included in a general pardon granted by Edward IV. This might explain why his name—assuming that it is his and not someone else's—occurs in a list of fifty-nine 'milites' who went with the forces of Edward IV to Northumberland in November of that year.[3] Whether Malory was present at the siege of Bamborough until its surrender on Christmas Eve and at the siege of Alnwick, which ended on 30 January 1463,[4] we cannot tell; but there is a strong likelihood that as a Warwickshire man he 'took the side of Neville, Earl of Warwick, in the dynastic struggle'[5] and accompanied him on this expedition. When later on the long pending breach between Warwick and Edward IV occurred and Warwick joined the Lancastrians Malory probably did so too. Hence his exclusion from the general pardons granted by Edward IV to the Lancastrians in 1468

[1] The King's incapacity lasted from 12 November 1455 to 25 February 1456, and during this period York acted as Protector. The pardon seems to have been disregarded in later proceedings.

[2] To William Neville, Lord of Fauconberg. The bail expired on 28 December 1457.

[3] *Brief Notes of Occurrences under Henry VI and Edward IV from MS. Lambeth 448*, in *Three Fifteenth-Century Chronicles*, etc., ed. by James Gairdner, Camden Society, 1880, p. 157.

[4] The references to Bamborough and Alnwick in his last book (*infra*, p. 1257 are perhaps not without significance.

[5] Cf. E. K. Chambers, op. cit., p. 203.

and 1470. The first of these pardons, dated 14 July, 1468,[1] states that it shall not extend to 'Thomas Malarie, kt.'; the second, similarly worded but referring to 'Thomas Malorie, miles', is dated 24 August; the third was issued on 1 December 1468 and the fourth on 22 February 1470. If Malory was in prison at that time he probably had to wait for his release until Henry VI's restoration on 9 October 1470. He died soon after, on 14 March 1471, and 'lyeth buryed under a marble in the chapel of St. Francis at the Grey Friers near Newgate in the suburbs of London'.[2] The inscription on his tomb said simply: *Dominus Thomas Mallere valens miles obiit 14 Mar. 1470 de parochia Monken-kyrkby in comitatu Warwici.*[3] In the monastery of the Order of the Grey Friars, across the road from Newgate, was a library from which another famous prisoner, Charles d'Orléans, released in 1440 after a long period of captivity, had borrowed many a manuscript book.[4] It was possibly there that Malory found his 'books of French'.

Biographical interpretation has done so much harm to literary criticism that it is a relief to find how very little room there is for it in Malory's case. No one will seriously attempt to read his life into his works or associate these with any phase or aspect of his curious career. The danger lies the other way. To those who think that criticism has some relevance for biography it may seem hardly credible that a man whose behaviour showed so little respect for conventional morality should have written a book which, according to Caxton's Preface, was designed 'for our doctrine and for to beware that we fall not to vice or sin, but exercise and follow virtue'. The book, the Preface tells us, describes 'the renowned acts of humanity, gentleness, and chivalry'; and it may conceivably be felt that while a mere portrayal of such 'acts' need have no relation to the author's own record, the moral teaching, the 'doctrine' which they purport to illustrate makes singularly bad sense in the context of his life. It can be argued on strictly historical grounds that the

---

[1] Discovered by Dr. Gweneth Whitteridge and described by her in her forthcoming article on *Sir Thomas Malory, Knight-Prisoner*. See above, p. xx, note 2.

[2] Dugdale, loc. cit.

[3] *Collectanea Topographica et Genealogica*, vol. v, p. 287.

[4] Cf. Richard D. Altick, *The Scholar Adventurers*, New York, 1950, pp. 75-76.

few facts summarized above refer to two different Malorys:
the felon from Fenny Newbold, and the political rebel from
Newbold Revell, the two place-names not being strictly
synonymous.[1] But whether this is true or not cannot be
decided on grounds of the 'moral' qualities of the work; and
lest there be any temptation to do so, it might be worth
while inquiring whether there is in fact in Malory's case a
moral cleavage between the book and the man to whom it
has been attributed.

The moral qualities of the 'noble histories' have been
variously assessed by the critics. Ascham thought that 'the
whole pleasure' of the book 'stood in two specyall poynts,
in open manslaughter and bold bawdrye'; Tennyson found
that Malory's work was 'touched by the adulterous finger of
a time that hover'd between war and wantonness'; Sir
Edward Strachey, while admitting that it exhibited 'a
picture of a society far lower than our own in morals', was
convinced that Malory had made a real effort to distinguish
between vice and virtue and 'morally reprobate the former'.[2]
This last view, with certain qualifications, has prevailed, and
Malory has become associated in our minds with such
qualities as 'humanity' and 'gentleness'. Few critics have
realized that this traditional image is based not so much on
Malory's work as on Caxton's preface to it.[3] The confusion
is the less excusable because Caxton clearly distinguishes
between the purpose of the work and his own object in
bringing it out. While insisting that his readers should
learn the 'noble acts of chyvalrye' and the 'jentyl and
vertuous dedes that somme knyghtes used in tho dayes', he is
truthful enough to admit that those are by no means the only
'dedes' recorded in the 'noble histories': 'for herein may be
seen noble chyvalrye, curtosye, humanyté, frendlynesse,
hardynesse, love, frendshyp, cowardyse, murdre, hate'.
From this miscellaneous array of virtues and vices Caxton
begs his readers to choose all that is good and reject the rest:
'doo after the good and leve the evyl, and it shal brynge you

[1] This is the line of argument adopted by Dr. Gweneth Whitteridge in the article referred to above (p. xxvi, note 1).
[2] *Le Morte Darthur*, ed. Strachey, p. xxiii.
[3] One example of this misconception is the chapter on *The Genius of Chivalry* in my monograph on Malory. See especially p. 59.

to good fame and renommee'. But he does not say that this choice is necessarily implied in the text or that Malory himself intended his 'noble histories' to serve as a means of moral improvement.

Nor does Malory's work, in so far as it is original, betray any such intention. No doubt, as long as he follows his sources he cannot help reproducing certain passages which suggest an idealistic inspiration; but his own additions to the text are of a different nature. His Tristram complains of having abandoned for the sake of his beloved 'many lands and riches'; his Guinevere gives her knights 'treasure enough for their expenses'; and on several occasions Malory makes King Arthur's knights acquire substantial sources of revenue 'through might of arms'. *The Book of Sir Launcelot and Queen Guinevere* includes a whole chapter of Malory's own composition which Caxton has entitled 'How true love is likened unto summer'. If, we are told, 'every lusty heart beginneth to blossom and bring out fruit' in May, it is because 'all herbs and trees renewen a man and woman, and likewise lovers. . . . For winter with his rough winds and blasts causeth man and woman to cower and sit fast by the fire.' This is Malory's counterpart to the idealistic doctrine of courtly romance. The escape from the oppressive atmosphere of *courtoisie* was made easier for him by the fact that a similar change of attitude had already occurred in some of the French romances which he used. Most of them belonged to the most advanced stage in the development of the French Arthurian tradition and preserved few traces of its original courtly inspiration. Knight-errantry as treated by the prose writers of the thirteenth century was less of a school of courtly service than a peculiar mode of living, characterized by a constant search for new adventures. It would not be surprising if in fifteenth-century England a man whose moral and psychological outlook was very different from our own, and different also from that of the early courtly writers, had been attracted by tle Arthurian novels of this type. If any background of actual experience was needed to awaken interest in them, it was certainly not one of moral and sentimental refinement; and there is no real reason why a man totally unaffected by the accepted code of behaviour should not have been as sensitive as Malory was to their poetic and human appeal.

There may be more to it than that. 'What manner of man was he', asks Mr. R. D. Altick,

with his flamboyant criminal record, that he could write a book cele- brating many articles of knightly behaviour which he himself had honoured far more in the breach than in the observance? We cannot, at this distance of time, answer the question with assurance. . . . But we cannot doubt that under the spell of the books he read and the tales he found coming to life again under his hand he was deeply stirred by the meaning of the ideals he had violated. He was great enough to know them as impossible in a frail and tempting world, but he also knew how truly the fact that we cannot follow them is the stuff of human tragedy: Lancelot caught to the very end in his unhappy tangle of divided loves, Guinevere afraid to accept a final kiss, Bedivere fumbling between love for Arthur and greed for Excalibur—these are the final pictures of a man whose vision of reality simply transcended the vulgar counsel of Caxton.[1]

This is as far as one can go in speculating about the miracu- lous play of character and circumstance which had brought the obscure knight-prisoner to his high theme: as far perhaps as any biographer should go in endeavouring to show how a life inevitably small can be graced with an unrivalled achievement. And when all is said we must gratefully abide by Caxton's dictum: 'For to passe the tyme thys book shal be pleasaunte to rede in, but for to gyve fayth and byleve that al is trewe that is conteyned herin, ye be at your lyberté.'

2. *The High Order of Knighthood*

The fairest specimens of what may be called Malory's 'morality' in the widest sense of the term are the remarks he occasionally inserts to describe the practice and the ideals of chivalry. Some of these remarks refer to principles of chivalric behaviour as distinct from the mere art of fighting. A knight, he says, should be courteous and gentle, for then 'he has favour in every place'. Nor should he indulge in useless fighting: his bravery and skill are to be subordinate

[1] Op. cit., pp. 83–84.

to a higher purpose, and those who abuse their physical superiority forfeit their claim to perfect knighthood. On the strength of such utterances Malory has been described by some as a belated but sincere exponent of the moral ideals of chivalry,[1] while others have suggested that he embodied these ideals 'in actual personages and so influenced the national character of his countrymen in the best way'.[2]

The text of Malory's writings preserved in the Winchester MS. throws new light on what chivalry really meant to him. The beginnings of his 'doctrine' are found in his earliest work, *The Tale of the Noble King Arthur and the Emperor Lucius,* of which the Winchester MS. alone gives a complete version. Caxton's rendering is not only a drastic abridgement, but a new work, and to reprint it as some publishers still do[3] under Malory's name is at best misleading. Puzzled by the archaic character of the *Tale,* Caxton, 'simple person', reduced it to less than half its size, and while doing so rewrote it from beginning to end,[4] with the result that until now it has not been possible to form an accurate idea either of the content of the story or of its position among Malory's romances. The narrative is based upon the English alliterative *Morte Arthure.* While shortening his original and modernizing some of its vocabulary, Malory treats it with far more respect than most of his other sources. The chief attraction of the poem lies for him in the record of Arthur's heroic exploits, which he expands and elaborates as best he can, so as to make Arthur appear as the true embodiment of heroic knighthood. Arthur is the 'Conqueror', the English counterpart of Charlemagne, and he claims by right the possession of the Roman Empire. He is the champion of the weak and the oppressed, witness his fight with the giant who had caused so much distress to the people of Brittany. But he has some of the characteristics of the primitive type of warrior. He does not shrink from a wholesale massacre of the Romans, and his cruelty in battle

[1] Cf. my *Malory,* pp. 55–69.
[2] Strachey, op. cit., p. xxi.
[3] Cf. Everyman edition of *Le Morte Darthur,* 1953.
[4] He even added some place-names and a few proper names. Cf. *infra,* p. 1666.

is equalled only by his enormous strength. Malory is careful to emphasize, however, that in spite of this cruelty to the enemy Arthur has human qualities which endear him to his own people. The implacable conqueror of the Romans mourns the death of his own knights as an irreparable loss and forgets for a moment his grim and glorious task. The Roman Emperor's challenge grieves him because he cannot tolerate unnecessary bloodshed. He is wise and prudent, anxious to take counsel with his knights, and generous in rewarding them for their services. The noble king is above all a political and military leader, conscious of his responsibility for the welfare and the prestige of his kingdom.[1]

This idealized portrait of Arthur may well be interpreted as a tribute to Henry V. As if to strengthen the analogy Malory adds several details which make Arthur's expedition against the Romans resemble Henry V's triumphant campaign in France. Just as Henry appointed two men to rule the country in his absence—Henry Beaufort and the Duke of Bedford—so in Malory's version of Arthur's campaign Arthur appoints two chieftains for the same purpose: Baudwen of Bretayne and Cadore of Cornwall. The king's itinerary through France is altered so as to resemble the route followed by Henry.[2] Just as the latter became virtually King of France after Agincourt (by the Treaty of Troyes Charles VI had agreed to let Henry succeed him on his death), so Malory's Arthur, after his victory over the Romans, is 'crowned Emperor by the Pope's hands, with all royalty in the world to weld forever'. Nor is it without significance that Malory brings his *Noble Tale* to an end at this point and dismisses for the time being the rest of the story which he found in the English poem: Mordred's treachery and Arthur's downfall. His intention is clear: he is anxious that the story of Arthur's triumph should remain uppermost in the reader's mind as a record of the greatest English victory of his age and that the reader should know *how* this victory was won. Caxton hits the mark when he

---

[1] Cf. my article on 'Malory's *Morte Darthur* in the Light of a Recent Discovery' in the *Bulletin of the John Rylands Library*, vol. xix, No. 2, July 1935.

[2] For details of these changes cf. *infra*, pp. 1368 and 1396-8.

says that in Malory's book his readers will see how those who 'used gentle and virtuous deeds' came to 'honour', but he mistakes—perhaps deliberately—Malory's practical intention for a moral one. *The Tale of Arthur and Lucius* is the first in date of Malory's extant works;[1] it was written at a time when the author's recollections of the great king were made particularly vivid by a dynastic dispute directed against Henry V's legitimate heir. Whether as a Lancastrian or as a follower of Warwick who had sworn allegiance to Henry VI while fighting his advisers and even resisted the Duke of York's attempt to assume the crown,[2] Malory had every reason to remember Henry V as the model of the 'crowned knight'.[3] His often quoted remark—'this is a great default of us Englishmen, for there may nothing please us no term'—may well be taken to refer to those who had forgotten not only the sanctity of the royal title[4] but the illustrious deeds of the great English monarch they had once acclaimed as victor. Malory's first 'noble history' is a clear reminder of those deeds and of the man who had taken pains 'to gather about him the trappings of the chivalric hero'.[5] Conceived in the midst of the greatest political upheaval of the century, the work was an attempt to show what had been and what could still be achieved 'through clean knighthood'.

Chivalry was, then, to Malory, at that initial stage of his work, the *faculté maîtresse* of a brave warrior-king and of his faithful knights; it was man's heroic devotion to a great cause. As Malory's work advanced, and as he ventured deeper and deeper into the vast labyrinth of Arthurian fiction, he found himself following the tracks of innumerable 'warriors wrought in steely weeds', some of whom had

---

[1] Cf. *infra*, ch. II, section 3.

[2] On 16 October 1460.

[3] Cf. Arthur B. Ferguson, *The Indian Summer of English Chivalry*, Durham, North Carolina, 1960, p. 52.

[4] In the thirteenth-century French version of the Tristan romance which Malory followed very closely there is a story of a rebellion against King Mark. In trying to persuade the rebels to lay down their arms Mark says that the land they have invaded belongs to the Pope and that their action might jeopardize 'la saincte terre de Jerusalem'. In Malory's otherwise faithful rendering of this incident Mark offers, as a price of peace, to go to war against the infidels and says, 'I trow that is fayrer warre than thus to areyse people agaynste youre kynge' (p. 680).

[5] A. B. Ferguson, op. cit., p. 44.

distinguished themselves in Arthur's victorious campaign. But as their fellowship grew their chivalric ambition, as Malory understood it, steadily decreased. They were no longer concerned with the practical business of warfare; they still wore their glittering armour and were eager to use their spears and swords; but their battles seemed to be fought in the void, and there was no discernible object in their exploits. Malory soon realized that the 'great books' of the French Arthurian Cycle failed to provide a worthy continuation of his first Arthurian work, and proceeded to supplement them with remarks of his own on the art and meaning of chivalry. Faithful to his original conception of knighthood, he treated it not as a vague background of adventures but as the principal function of the 'High Order of Knighthood'—a well-established order with its headquarters fixed in the household of a great prince. In most of the French Arthurian romances Arthur's court had been but the conventional starting-point of knightly quests and Arthur himself a benevolent and passive king of Fairyland. Malory makes him into an accomplished champion of chivalry and the founder of its great traditions. Under Arthur's leadership chivalry becomes a useful discipline which, if properly practised, can make its adherents into 'the sternest knights to their foes'. The technique of fighting, and more particularly of single combat, is Malory's favourite topic; he speaks of it with confidence and authority. If, in addition to this, chivalry is also a matter of good breeding, gentleness, and loyalty, it is because these qualities, as shown by the example of Arthur, equip the perfect knight for his task and make him conscious of the importance of his calling. This was what Malory must have learnt both from real life and from reflection, and what he endeavoured to convey in his early work, not as a doctrine, but as a rule of conduct, more vital than ever in times of stress and struggle. The issue as he saw it was essentially a practical one, and so far as we can judge it was in the same earnest spirit of practical heroism that in his later writings he so often attempted to commemorate in terms of imaginary knight-errantry some of the great declining traditions of his own age.

For indications of their inevitable decline Malory did not have to look beyond some of his French sources. Dinadan, a friend and companion of Tristan's, was given by the author of the French Prose *Tristan* the task of calling in question the wisdom of Arthurian chivalry.[1] Malory describes him as 'a scoffer and a japer', but cuts down to a few sentences his humorous speeches about the chivalric code of duty, the rules of knight-errantry, the etiquette of single combats and the 'love that punishes its servants for their folly'. For where the High Order of Knighthood is concerned Malory's aim is not to entertain the reader, but to express his own simple faith in actual and serious personages. He upholds knighthood, not as an ideal remote from reality, nor as a moral doctrine in Caxton's sense, but as an issue of immediate interest, related to memories of a recent past. And so his work has neither the light-heartedness of romance nor the doctrinal poise of a moral treatise: its dominating feature is the kind of earnestness one usually associates with early epic. He was from first to last in earnest about knighthood as a fellowship controlled by the authority and the example of a great king, and out of his miscellaneous material he succeeded in extracting a tale of heroic chivalry which, like so many of the legacies of medieval France, was destined to become inseparable from the form it assumed in the British Isles.

---

[1] On the character of Dinadan see my *Roman de Tristan et Iseut*, etc., pp. 134–7, and my recent article on *Un chevalier errant à la recherche du sens du monde* in *Mélanges de linguistique romane et de philologie médiévale offerts à Maurice Delbouille* (1964) and *infra*, pp. 1447–8. For a more detailed account of Malory's conception and treatment of this remarkable character see my *Malory*, pp. 67–69, and the relevant section of the Commentary where I have reproduced *in extenso* most of Dinadan's speeches as they appear in the French prose *Tristan*. Cf. also A. B. Ferguson's remarks in *The Indian Summer*, etc., pp. 47–48.

CHAPTER II

THE STORY OF THE BOOK

1. *Caxton's 'Morte Darthur'*

AS long as Caxton's edition—'enprynted and fynysshed in thabbey of Westmestre the last day of July the yere of our Lord MCCCCLXXXV'—was the only available record of Malory's writings there could be little or no reliable evidence as to how Caxton dealt with Malory's text. That he was no mere printer has never been doubted. But in the absence of any other version of his 'copy', his *Morte Darthur* has been tacitly accepted as a genuine reproduction of the original. 'I have', he writes in his Preface, 'after the symple connynge that God hath sente to me, under the favour and correctyon of al noble lordes and gentylmen, enprysed[1] to enprynte a book of the noble hystoryes of the sayd kynge Arthur and of certeyn of his knyghtes, after a copye unto me delyverd, whyche copye Syr Thomas Malorye dyd take oute of certeyn bookes of Frensshe and reduced it into Englysshe.' It is only now that the damage due to Caxton's 'symple connynge' can be partially repaired.

The essential difference between Malory's treatment of the *Noble Histories* and Caxton's was the difference between the methods of a medieval author or scribe and those of a modern publisher. A medieval 'book' could vary indefinitely in size and in content; it could be either a treatise of any size or a collection of different treatises under one cover.[2] There is evidence to show that in their original form Malory's works were in keeping with this traditional medieval connotation of the term. The first indication to this effect

---

[1] = 'undertaken'.

[2] Cf. *Oxford Eng. Dict.* s.v. 'book', 1a and b. The other possible meaning of the term was 'a mechanical or logical sub-division of a treatise'. Both meanings were, however, often confused with that of 'volume'. Cf. Horman (*Vulg.* 84): 'A whole boke is comenly called indifferentlye a volume, a boke, a coucher.' Horman attempts to distinguish between them by saying that 'a volume is lesse than a boke, and a boke lesse than a coucher'. Caxton's reference to Malory's 'noble volumes' and to the fact that he made them into a 'book' is a good example of this distinction.

occurs in Caxton's Preface immediately before the reference
to his 'symple connynge'. Speaking of the various Arthurian
romances known to him and of his own project, he remarks:
'And many noble volumes be made of hym and of his noble
knyghtes in Frensshe, which I have seen and redd beyonde
the see, which been not had in our maternal tongue; but in
Walsshe ben many, and also in Frensshe, and somme in
Englysshe, but nowher nygh alle. *Wherfore, such as have*[1]
*late ben drawn oute bryefly into Englysshe, I have ... enprysed
to enprynte',* etc. If this description is correct, Caxton's copy
must have consisted of *many noble volumes.* At no point does
he refer to them otherwise than in the plural, and the conclusion naturally suggests itself that what he published was a
collection of works, not a single composition.

The inference can now be substantiated with the aid of
the Winchester text. Although the manuscript is bound in
one volume, it is clearly divided into several sections and
each section, with the exception of the last which lacks a
gathering of eight leaves at the end, is concluded by an
explicit. The first *explicit* is the most significant of all. In it
the author bids farewell to the reader and suggests that
someone else might continue his work: *Who that woll make
ony more lette hym seke other bookis of kynge Arthure or of sir
Launcelot or sir Trystrams.*[2] The works which follow claim no
continuity of narrative, still less of composition. The following remarks, mostly deleted by Caxton, make this
abundantly clear:

(1) F. 70. (*The Tale of King Arthur*): And this booke endyth
whereas sir Launcelot and sir Trystrams com to courte.
Who that woll make ony more lette hym seke other
bookis of kynge Arthure or of sir Launcelot or sir
Trystrams; for this was drawyn by a knyght presoner
sir Thomas Malleorré, that God sende hym good recover.
Amen, etc. Explicit.

(2) F. 96. (*The Tale of the Noble King Arthur and the Emperor
Lucius*[3]): Explicit the Noble Tale betwyxt kynge Arthure
and Lucius the Emperour of Rome.

(3) F. 113. (*The Noble Tale of Sir Launcelot du Lake*): Explicit a
noble tale of sir Launcelot du Lake.

---

[1] = 'in so far as they have'.   [2] See above, pp. xx–xxi.
[3] See p. lvi, footnote 5.

and pitt vp in almeryes at Galyschiry / And anone Sir Bors seyde
to Sir launcelot Sir Galahad yonde dvne sonne saluteth yon by
me and aftir yon my lorde kynge Arthure and all the hole courte
And so ded Sir Pavale for I buryed þem both myne dvne hondis
in the cite of Sarras Also Sir launcelot Sir Galahad prayde
yon to remembir of thys vnsyker worlde as ye be hyst kynd whan
ye were to gydyrs more þan halffe a yere Thys ys trew seyde S launce
Now I truste to god hys prayer schall avayle me Than S launcel
toke Sir Bors in hys armys and seyde consen ye ar ryst welcom
to me for ye and I schall nevir departe in sundir whylis once lyvys
may laste Sir seyde he as ye wolt so wolt I Thus endith þ tale
of the Sankgreall that was breffly drawyn oute of freynsshe
which ys a tale cronycled for one of the trewyst and of ye holyest
that ys in thys worlde By Sir Thomas Malory knyght
O blessed ihu helpe hym throw hys myght. — Amen.

II. F. 409ʳ of the Winchester MS.

(4) F. 148. (*The Tale of Sir Gareth of Orkeney*): And I pray you all that redyth this tale to pray for hym that this wrote, that God sende hym good delyveraunce sone and hastely. Amen. Here endyth the tale of sir Gareth of Orkeney.

(5) F. 346. (*The Book of Sir Tristram*): Here endyth the secunde boke off syr Trystram de Lyones whyche drawyn was oute of Freynshe by sir Thomas Malleorré, knyght, as Jesu be hys helpe. Amen.

(6) F. 409. (*The Tale of the Sankgreal*): Thus endith the tale of the Sankgreal that was breffly drawy[n] oute of Freynshe, which ys a tale cronycled for one of the trewyst and of the holyest that ys in thys worlde, by sir Thomas Maleorré, knyght. O, Blessed Jesu helpe hym thorow Hys myght! Amen.[1]

(7) F. 449. (*The Book of Sir Launcelot and Queen Guinevere*): And bycause I have loste the very mater of Shevalere de Charyot I depart frome the tale of sir Launcelot and here I go unto the *Morte Arthur*, and that caused sir Aggravayne. And here on the othir syde folowyth the moste pyteuous tale of the *Morte Arthure Saunz Gwerdon* par le shyvalere sir Thomas Malleorré, knyght. Jesu, ayedé ly par voutre bone mercy! Amen.

The last of these passages is in a category of its own: it forms a link with the work which follows (*The Morte Arthur*) and suggests no interruption in the process of writing. Nor are the second and third *explicits* of any great significance, since they may well have been inserted in the course of continuous composition. Of the remaining four, however, two (1 and 4) contain an appeal for 'good deliverance' or 'good recovery'; and the other two (5 and 6) give the author's name and appeal for God's mercy. No doubt the works to which these endings were attached may eventually have been combined—either by the author or by a scribe—into a composite 'book', but each work must originally have been conceived and written as a distinct 'volume'.

It was probably for this reason that Malory's romances were allowed to retain certain peculiarities which would have been difficult to justify in a continuous narrative. Arthur's expedition to Rome is related twice: first, at great length, in Book V, and again, much more briefly and in a different

[1] See Plate II.

context, in Book XX. The story of Lancelot is split into two groups of episodes—Book VI and Books XVIII–XIX—but the first group refers to a later period of his life than the second. Some of the characters appear as fully fledged knights before they are born, while some others reappear after their deaths. Tristram is an example of the former anomaly: he is a prominent character in Caxton's Book VII, although his birth is not related until Book VIII. Breunis Saunz Pity is killed in Book VII and Tarquyn in Book VI; yet both return to life in the subsequent books. Similar incongruities occur throughout the collection; their most significant feature is that they are never found within any one of Malory's romances, but invariably between two different works separated by at least one of the *explicits*. An author who regards each of his works as a separate 'tale' or 'book' would hardly think it necessary to make them consistent in every detail with one another.

When these volumes fell into Caxton's hands he realized that, as a matter of practical expediency, he had to make them into a single 'book of King Arthur', not only for reasons of editorial economy, but because in such a form the work would best answer the demand of 'many noble and dyvers gentylmen of thys royame of Englond' for a 'history of the moost renomed crysten kyng, fyrst and chyef of the thre best crysten and worthy, Kyng Arthur'. He was thus led by force of circumstance to attempt a 'book' in the modern sense, i.e. a homogeneous literary composition 'of sufficient length to make a volume'.[1] Malory's collection seemed at first sight uniform enough to lend itself to such an experiment, and when Caxton undertook to print it he probably did not suspect the difficulties he was to encounter. His first stumbling-block must have been the farewell to the reader signed by the 'knight-prisoner Sir Thomas Malleorre'. Not only was the reference to the author's imprisonment undesirable in a book intended for moral edification, but the passage in which it occurred betrayed the composite character of the work. Naturally enough Caxton deleted the whole passage and dealt in the same way with all subsequent *explicits* except the very last which conveniently wound up

---

[1] Cf. E. Littré, *Dictionnaire de la langue française*, s.v. 'livre'.

the collection. It is, moreover, highly probable that the wording of this last *explicit* suggested to Caxton his most ingenious device: that of publishing the book under one general title. Malory clearly referred to the *last* of his romances when he wrote: *here is the ende of the deth of Arthur*; and neither Caxton nor anyone else who saw Malory's ending could have thought that it applied to any other work. Nothing daunted, Caxton added a colophon saying, *thus endeth this noble and joyous book entytled le morte Darthur*.

Of all the things we know about Malory this is the one that has taken us longest to discover—and to understand; and even now critics are not really fully aware of it. The discovery happened in a curious way. Such is the inertia of dogmatic literary history, and so powerful the conventional idiom of criticism, that we should probably have gone on by-passing the essential things in Malory but for a sensational event which occurred in 1934 in the Fellows' Library of Winchester College when a hitherto unknown manuscript of Malory's romances unexpectedly came to light. I need not relate here the circumstances of this discovery except to say that its importance did not become apparent until later, when it was realized that whoever produced the work contained in this manuscript, clearly never thought of it as a *single* work, but as a series of eight separate romances. This was the conclusion I finally came to, and on the strength of it I published not *Le Morte Darthur*, but a book in three volumes called *The Works of Sir Thomas Malory*. It was Caxton's idea, not Malory's, to publish these works under one general title, a title borrowed from Malory's last romance, *The Tale of the Death of King Arthur*. That the title was inappropriate as a general description of the various stories about Arthur and his knights Caxton knew full well, and to forestall any criticism he added his famous apology: 'Notwythstondyng it treateth of the byrth, lyf, and actes of the sayd kyng Arthur, of his noble knyghtes of the Round Table, theyr mervayllous enquestes and adventures, th'achyevyng of the Sangreal, and in th'ende the dolorous deth and departyng out of thys world of them al.'

The apology was soon to be forgotten, but the subterfuge proved successful. Ever since Caxton's time Malory's works have been published as a single work and considered not only 'long enough to make a volume', but continuous enough to claim a unity of design and structure. True, only nineteenth-century editors have allowed themselves to be misled by the title *Le Morte Darthur*: Wynkyn de Worde (1498 and 1529), Copland (1557), East (*c.* 1585), and Stansby (1634) had consistently rejected it, and the first to use it after Caxton was F. Haslewood in his 1816 reprint of Stansby's text. In the following year Southey had the good sense to describe the work by the list of contents which in Caxton's colophon follows the word *Notwythstondyng*, but although his example was followed in Dent's edition of 1893–4, all the modern 'standard' texts (Wright, Strachey, Sommer, Gollancz, Pollard) have confidently adopted Caxton's fanciful heading with occasional attempts to correct the gender of *mort*. This in itself is immaterial. But it is an indication of the extent to which Caxton's stratagem has affected the modern conception of his 'noble book'. It has been assumed that the author was responsible for the attempt to make all Arthurian romances into a single work, and on the strength of this he has been praised by some and blamed by others in a way which now seems totally irrelevant. In his admirable essay on Malory Sir Edmund Chambers pointed out some defects in the 'structure' of the *Morte Darthur* and suggested that Malory 'would have done better to have left the *Tristan* alone'.[1] R. W. Chambers, while admitting that much of the charm of Malory lay in the 'variety of ideals animating the different stories which he has taken over', remarked that 'this variety does not make for elaborate or consistent drawing of characters'.[2] At the other end of the scale Malory's readers have endeavoured, with varying degrees of success, to find in the *Morte Darthur* a dramatically developed plot[3] and to credit Malory with the intention of producing

[1] Op. cit., p. 5.
[2] *On the Continuity of English Prose from Alfred to More and his School*, London (E.E.T.S.), 1932, p. clii.
[3] Cf. my *Malory*, pp. 93–95.

an epic of Arthur—a vast composition commemorating the rise and fall of Arthur's kingdom and thus presenting, as Andrew Lang puts it, a 'very complete and composite picture of a strangely inherited ideal'.[1] Saintsbury even went so far as to say that although sometimes Malory 'may put in what we do not want' (*sic*), 'what is certain is that he, and he only in any language, makes of this vast assemblage of stories one story, and one book'.[2]

In writing this, Saintsbury, 'Malory's keenest advocate',[3] was far from realizing that he was paying a compliment to Caxton, not to Malory. Nor did it ever occur to him or for that matter to anyone else that if this view of the *Morte Darthur* were correct the greater part of what Malory wrote would be out of place. Judged as a continuous composition, the work would be 'better' not only without the *Tristram*, but without at least two other romances—*The Noble Tale of Sir Launcelot* and *The Book of Sir Gareth*—altogether some 600 pages out of a total of 1,260. The *raison d'être* of these romances is precisely that which has been consistently denied them: the distinctive character of each one. Instead of a 'single work' subordinate to an imaginary principle of all-embracing dramatic 'unity', what we have before us is a series of works forming a vast and varied panorama of incident and character. What their 'assemblage' may lose in harmony it gains in diversity and richness of tone, expressive of the author's real design.

2. *The Problem of 'Unity'*

The preceding section is printed here in much the same form as in the first edition, despite the fact that in the last fifteen years it has come in for much adverse criticism. Most of the objections have been summarized in a book published in 1964 under the title of *Malory's Originality* by a group of American scholars who deny that 'Malory wrote eight separate romances'.[4] The book contains eight chapters,

---

[1] *Le Morte Darthur*, ed. H. O. Sommer, vol. iii, p. xix.

[2] *The English Novel*, London, 1913, p. 25.

[3] R. W. Chambers, op. cit., p. cxxxviii.

[4] *Malory's Originality, a Critical Study of 'Le Morte Darthur'*, edited by R. M. Lumiansky, The Johns Hopkins Press, Baltimore, 1964.

one on each romance; four of these chapters were published in various learned periodicals between the years 1950 and 1957;[1] and one obvious weakness of the volume is that no attempt seems to have been made to bring these chapters up to date[2] or to include in any of the other four some consideration of the work done in this field in more recent years.

United in their rejection of my 'claim', the contributors to *Malory's Originality* vary greatly in their formulation of their own; but the variations are clearly designed to strengthen rather than weaken the overall case. Some hold that the unifying factor in *Le Morte Darthur* is consistent characterization;[3] others that it is Malory's constant concern with a particular moral issue resolved in the final cataclysm of the Death of Arthur story;[4] others again would regard the occurrence of cross-references from one romance to another as sufficient evidence of the unity of the book.[5] All these are important critical considerations; but the mere fact that they are being used as arguments in this particular debate shows that the problem itself requires careful redefinition. The view that Malory wrote eight separate romances does not imply that there are any serious discrepancies in their portrayal

[1] Ch. II (by Miss Mary E. Dichmann) in *PMLA* for 1950; ch. III (by R. M. Lumiansky) in *Modern Language Notes* for 1953; ch. VI (by Charles Moorman) in *PMLA* for 1956; and ch. VII (by R. M. Lumiansky) in *Medieval Studies* for 1957. The other contributors are Thomas L. Wright (ch. I), Wilfred L. Guerin (chs. IV and VIII) and Thomas C. Rumble (ch. V).

[2] In particular the authors seem to have taken no account of the volume of *Essays on Malory* edited by J. A. W. Bennett (Oxford, 1963), which contains an important study of the problem of the 'connectedness' (as distinct from 'unity') of Malory's romances by D. S. Brewer (pp. 41–63) as well as an essay by C. S. Lewis (pp. 7–28) in which the following statement is well worthy of note: 'I do not for a moment believe that Malory had any intention either of writing a single "work" or of writing many "works" as we should understand the expressions. He was telling us about Arthur and the knights. Of course his matter was one—the same king, the same court. Of course his matter was many—they had had many adventures' (p. 22). I have dealt in some detail with the various arguments advanced by the partisans of 'unity' in the relevant sections of the Commentary. Cf. especially pp. 1275–6, 1288, 1367–8, 1394, 1395, 1413–14, 1432 *n.* 1, 1446, 1470, 1493–4, 1500 *n.* 2, 1537 *n.* 3, 1584, 1591 *n.* 2, and 1613.

[3] The best example of this approach is Miss Dichmann's essay on *The Tale of King Arthur and the Emperor Lucius* in *Malory's Originality*, pp. 67–90, previously published in *PMLA* for 1950.

[4] Cf. W. L. Guerin's, Thomas C. Rumble's and Charles Moorman's contributions to *Malory's Originality*.

[5] Cf. chs. I (Thomas L. Wright) and VIII (W. L. Guerin).

of characters or that there are no links and similarities to be found between them. All it means is that the eight romances are not structurally unified, either in the way in which a thirteenth-century cycle normally was by its 'tapestry' technique or in the manner of a play or a novel built on the Horatian principle of *simplex et unus*; and that in so far as there was a principle of 'singleness' in the composition of these romances it operated within the limits of each individual romance, not for *Le Morte Darthur* as a whole. Unity of characterization and even unity of moral purpose there may well be. There is consistency in Shakespeare's treatment of Falstaff in the plays in which he appears, as there is in the handling of certain characters in the novels which constitute Balzac's *Comédie Humaine*; but who would suggest that *The Merry Wives of Windsor* and the two parts of *Henry IV* are one play or that *La Comédie Humaine* is one novel? The romances of Chrétien de Troyes, copied more than once in medieval times one after another in the same order, also show some consistency of characterization; it has in fact often been said that the figures of Arthur, of Gawain, and of Kay are recognizably the same throughout; but if there is one thing about which all Arthurian scholars are in agreement it is that Chrétien de Troyes wrote at least five separate romances.

Why, then, in Malory's case this passionate attachment to the 'unity' of the entire volume? The most likely reason is that, as C. S. Lewis once said in a somewhat different connexion, 'we largely make what we read', and what generations of readers have made of Malory is very different from what he made. Until the discovery of the Winchester MS. Malory's text had remained in the form in which the 'simple cunning' of the first English printer had left it, that is to say in the form of a single 'book' in the modern sense of the term. In this form it established itself in the readers' minds, and some of its acquired characteristics, such as its physical shape and its title, *Le Morte Darthur*, became after a while inseparable from the work itself. What a magnificent title it was! So delightfully inaccurate that even Caxton, who had deliberately applied it to the book as a whole instead of to the last work in the series, felt he had to apologize for its inaccuracy. It was one of those titles that assume an existence of their own: it became a poetic concept in its own right, the starting-point of a whole tradition of 'fine fabling'. For the critics it became a challenge—an occasion to speculate on the intention of the book and on the meaning of the great event which these curiously anglicized French words seemed to summarize.

And there was only one way in which the challenge could be met. When modern literary scholarship seeks to rehabilitate a literary masterpiece it invariably resorts to the favourite classical criterion of perfection which is, of course, 'unity'. We take it for granted that unity is not only a supreme artistic merit, but a feature without which no work of literature, regardless of its date and character, has any claim to recognition. To show that *Le Morte Darthur* was 'one book' and not several was therefore not simply to add to its value: it was to establish its *existence* as a work of art. No wonder, then, that when I ventured to suggest that *Le Morte Darthur*, as the Winchester MS. seemed to me to show, was not one book, but several, people in various parts of the English-speaking world felt that something precious was being taken away from them—not just a particular aspect of the book, but the book itself: an English classic was being destroyed, pulled to pieces by an insensitive critic whose ear was not attuned to the inner harmonies of the text. What puzzled them was that my apparent disability was of such recent date, that what they were saying was exactly what I used to believe myself: I too used to be convinced, and tried to convince others, that before Malory Arthurian romance was in a state of chaos, that it was a formless medley of incoherent stories, and that Malory alone made it into one great story and one book. The discovery at Winchester altered all this; not so much because of what it contained, but because of what it suggested, because of a hitherto unsuspected structural principle which it revealed.

One important piece of evidence, for long obliterated by a curious scribal error, could easily have been discovered before 1934; but it is only in the light of the Winchester MS. that it acquired its real significance. Of the two surviving copies of Caxton's edition only one—that which is now in the Pierpont Morgan Library—has preserved Malory's last colophon. It reads as follows:

Here is the ende of the hoole book of kyng Arthur and of his noble knyghtes of the Round Table that when they were hole togyders there was ever an hondred and forty. And here is the ende of the Deth of Arthur.

In the copy which is now in the John Rylands Library the last pages of the text are missing, and before the copy was acquired by the Library they were replaced, like all the other missing pages, by Whittaker's manuscript facsimiles. These, however, are not free from errors. In the above passage Whittaker misread *hoole* for *booke*, and wrote:

Here is the ende of the booke book &c.

Sommer reproduced the sentence as he found it,[1] and all subsequent editors using Sommer's reprint naturally thought that *booke book* was a printer's error for *book*. They therefore reduced the two words to one, and the word 'whole' (*hoole*) simply disappeared from the Malory canon. With this something of vital importance was lost: the implied contrast between the 'whole book' and the romance with which the series is concluded—between the work containing various romances or 'tales' about King Arthur and his knights on the one hand and the Death of Arthur story on the other. What we now have in most modern editions of the text is a statement which equates *The Death of Arthur* with the 'Book of King Arthur and his knights' and so provides what may well be construed as a valid argument in favour of *Le Morte Darthur* as a general title. But Malory's own terminology is crystal clear: the 'whole book' is the series which is here concluded; *The Death of Arthur* is a 'book'—the last part of the series; it is part of a larger *ensemble*, but it is also a distinct and recognizable unit, with a title of its own which is not that of the series. Perhaps not while he was composing his first five or six romances, but while he was writing his seventh or his eighth, the idea of putting them together and letting them be read one after another did occur to him; and there are some signs of this

[1] He did not record the error until a year later (op. cit., vol. ii, p. 28).

in the final sections of the series. Professor R. H. Wilson has described this dual character of the collection with admirable precision:

The desire for consistency in his cast of characters and other details of the Arthurian world, providing an explanation both for the added names near the end and for the smaller number earlier which may be partly the result of revision, is different, and yet hard to distinguish, from a concern that the series of tales be read as a unit. The strongest evidence that Malory did have such a concern when he was listing proper names is the allusions to previous stories, the presence in the Urré list of at least one representative from each tale, and the correlation of the increased use of lists in the last two tales with other indications that, after a good part of his work was done, he formed a conception that his tales were to fit together into a 'hoole book'.[1]

This, however, is something totally different from 'unity of composition' in the accepted sense of the term. The builders of the great thirteenth-century cycles of romances sought a certain sense of *relationship* between the work and the accompanying or the preceding tradition. Any Arthurian romance was in this sense part of a series, some of which might not even be in existence at the time when the romance appeared. An Arthurian 'cycle' was the place where the linking up of the various parts of the series took concrete shape and where complete cohesion ensued, productive of further growth. Malory is not in any way concerned with this growth: he is trying his hand at something different—at the unravelling of the threads of which the cycle is made, at reducing the entire narrative to relatively small self-contained units. Naturally this process cannot be carried to the point at which *all* connexions between the different parts of the cycle disappear; and so the resulting series retains perforce connecting links here and there. Many of them survive in his text in the form of accurately phrased reminders of earlier occurrences and of subtle anticipations of forthcoming events; and even where the source of such reminders and anticipations is not available they usually bear the stamp of his 'French books'. His own additions are of a different kind. From time to time he inserts of his

---

[1] Cf. 'Addenda on Malory's Minor Characters', *Journal of English and Germanic Philology*, 1956, pp. 574–5.

own accord a reference which does not in fact tie up with anything that happens in another work of his, but which gives the reader the *feeling* that he is reading part of a larger history—the kind of feeling that any medieval story-teller wanted his readers to have, and which has nothing whatever to do with a structural unification of the material. In the story of the Dolorous Stroke Malory refers, possibly without any prompting from his source, to the bed once occupied by the Maimed King, but says that the occupant of the bed was Joseph of Arimathea. Critics quote this remark as though it could be used to substantiate the theory of 'unity':[1] but it could only be so used if we forgot the role assigned to Joseph of Arimathea in Malory's own version of the *Quest of the Holy Grail* and in the French *Queste del Saint Graal*. Whatever Joseph of Arimathea may have done in history and legend, he was certainly not in Malory the Maimed King or even one of the 'Maimed Kings'. In the same way, when in the *Tale of King Arthur* Merlin prophesies Arthur's 'conquest of Scotland, Ireland and Wales' and the critics triumphantly declare that this is an indication of Malory's 'plan for *Le Morte Darthur*' as a whole,[2] one can say, of course, that there is in this passage a certain feeling of a 'plan' for the subsequent sections of *Le Morte Darthur*; but the feeling only lasts until we realize that no such plan exists in *any* of the romances which follow the *Tale of King Arthur*. Nowhere except in this *Tale* is there as much as an allusion to Arthur's conquest of Scotland, Ireland or Wales: a fact inexplicably concealed from the readers of *Malory's Originality*.

More serious than these errors of fact is the apparent

---

[1] *Malory's Originality*, p. 45. Mr. W. L. Guerin (op. cit., p. 254) makes a distinction between 'pervasive' links which can exist between separate stories and specific links which presuppose a unified design. Of these he gives seven examples for the *Tale of the Death of King Arthur*. Three of these are retrospective and do not therefore prove that Malory had intended to lead up to the Death of Arthur story; two (nos. 6 and 7) are parallels rather than links, and doubtful parallels at that. The two cases of possible anticipation are the survival of Bedwere in the *Tale of King Arthur and the Emperor Lucius* and the fact that Lancelot knights Gareth. On the first of these cf. *infra*, pp. 1394–5; as for the second, there is every reason to suppose that it occurred in Malory's source.

[2] Op. cit., p. 25: 'Here Malory's plan for *Le Morte Darthur* as a whole is implicit in Merlin's speech.'

inability to appreciate Malory's characteristic method of alluding to past and future events. A typical example is the way in which he predicts the advent of Galahad.[1] In the French romance there are two prophecies, each concerning a sword. Balin's sword, we are told, was to be handled by Lancelot: it was the sword with which he was to wound his best friend, Gawain, to death. The other sword was the one which Merlin fixed in a floating stone: it was to be drawn by Galahad, to whom the French romance refers as 'the best knight in the world'. The first prophecy is not fulfilled until the cycle has reached its last branch, the *Mort Artu*, but the second comes true in the *Queste del Saint Graal*, to which the Balin story serves as a prelude. The significance of these prophecies and of their fulfilment lies precisely in the contrast they suggest: the contrast and the tension between the dark forces of destiny which cause the tragic deaths of Balin and Gawain and the light of salvation and redemption which is brought to the kingdom of Logres by Galahad, and by Galahad alone. To say as Malory does that 'there shall never man handyll thys [i.e. Balin's] swerde but the beste knyghte of the worlde, and that shall be sir Launcelot *other ellis Galahad, hys sonne*' is to equate Galahad's virtue with Lancelot's and ignore the symbolism of the two swords, the opposition between the light of divine grace which shines in Galahad and the evil fortune which not only pursues the unhappy Balin but foreshadows the tragic climax of the entire cycle—the fatal encounter between Lancelot and Gawain leading to the destruction of Arthur's kingdom.[2] In this instance can be seen at one and the same time a characteristic desire on Malory's part to see the pattern of the story in clear outline and an equally characteristic reluctance to follow the profound and indispensable complexities of the cyclic model.

One of the major obstacles to any theory of 'unity' is the presence, in the middle of the volume, of the largest of

[1] *Infra*, p. 91. See Commentary, note 91. 23.

[2] Professor R. H. Wilson in his comment on this passage in 'Malory's Early Knowledge of Arthurian Romances' (*The University of Texas Studies in English*, vol. xxix, pp. 37–38) makes the point that 'the combination of the two prophecies is clearly a remodelling of the authentic version. As such, it is better attributed to Malory than to a copyist of the *Suite* who did not have his habit of compression.'

Malory's works, *The Book of Sir Tristram*, which is also the least relevant to any of the themes found in the earlier and later sections. What indeed has this romance to do with the history of Arthur's kingdom? The answer supplied by another contributor to *Malory's Originality*, Mr. Rumble, is disarmingly simple: Arthur's kingdom collapsed as a result of moral degeneration, the story of Tristram being primarily a 'story of adultery'. Thanks to the Tristram romance 'we see more clearly than would otherwise have been possible not only the essential inadequacies of the chivalric society, but the way in which those inadequacies bring about the fall of Arthur's realm'.[1] Thus *Le Morte Darthur* turns out to be in the end what Caxton hoped it might be and what Ascham thought it was not: an edifying tale showing how a 'potentially perfect kingdom' could be destroyed 'as a result of moral degeneration'. Was Malory, then, an early Victorian in disguise? Was he deliberately misleading his readers by saying as he did on many occasions that Tristram was a perfect knight and that everything Tristram did was 'through clean knighthood'? But there is more to it than that. A distressingly unreal conception of the Arthurian epic emerges as a result of this desperate attempt to establish a 'moral' link between the *Book of Sir Tristram* and the *Tale of the Death of King Arthur*. Not only is the Death of Arthur story made to serve as a moralizing sequel to an imaginary tale of 'moral degradation', but it loses in the process its whole meaning. The feud between Gawain and Lancelot, upon which in Malory's last romance the fortunes of the Round Table finally break, is attributed to an intrigue which in the prose *Tristan* centres upon Lamorak's illicit relationship with Gawain's mother, the Queen of Orkney: Lancelot sides with Lamorak and so becomes an enemy of Gawain's, and this, we are told, is the way in which 'the ground is prepared for the final disaster'. The truth is that if this were the case and if in reading the *Tale of the Death of King Arthur* we were to believe for a moment that

---

[1] Op. cit., p. 180. Cf. also the remark on the next page: 'We are somehow never allowed to forget that that relationship is, after all, an adulterous one.' The reverse is the case: what we are 'never allowed' to do is to think of the situation in those terms.

Gawain and Lancelot were enemies before the Death of Arthur story began, the entire basis of the tragedy of Arthur would be destroyed: the tragic conception requires that the depth of friendship between Gawain and Lancelot and the strength of their ties of loyalty should stand up to the severest tests until the final blow falls and turns passionate affection into mortal, all-destroying enmity.

This 'single book' that the critics are convinced Malory wrote, how fortunate it is for us that he never wrote it! The all-important fact about him is that he was able to see the drama of Arthur, of Gawain, and of Lancelot in stark isolation and not as part of a cyclic structure—as a *single* event with all its terrible finality. And to discover the truth about this great book we ought perhaps to remember what T. R. Glover said in the Preface to a now famous work: 'I find that the more I enjoy books, the harder becomes the task of criticism, the less sure one's faith in critical canons, and the fewer the canons themselves.' A medievalist would perhaps have said 'the more numerous the canons' instead of 'the fewer'. Our modern canons certainly have the effect of blinding us to Malory's real achievement, to the great innovation due to a writer who alone among the moderns had perceived in the dusty Arthurian world the springs of fresh discoveries and the promise of new poetic values. For in the history of prose the natural outcome of cyclic romances was not the long novel of today but the *nouvelle*, or the short novel, of the last centuries of the Middle Ages.[1] Even at a later period the *romans à tiroirs*—those curious modern replicas of the medieval prose cycles[2]—did not themselves become novels in the modern sense of the term, but produced, by a process of differentiation, short prose

---

[1] Cf. C. S. Baldwin, *Medieval Rhetoric and Poetic*, p. 268: 'Such singleness as the middle age cultivated in romance must be sought in the parts considered as separate stories, and will be found oftener in the shorter romances that remained by themselves.'

[2] Hence their inordinate size and the absence of proper endings. 'Le roman s'est donné pour loi, pendant tout le XVIIe siècle et une partie du XVIIIe, de n'avoir aucune loi de composition. . . . C'est pour cela que les romans paraissent en six, dix, douze volumes, dont la publication s'espace sur un certain nombre d'années et parfois (comme pour *l'Astrée*, la *Marianne* de Marivaux, etc.) ne s'achève pas. Personne n'est pressé de connaître la fin, puisqu'il n'y a pas de fin' (Daniel Mornet, *Histoire de la clarté française*, p. 135).

works, each centring on a particular theme or episode.[1] The
fact that Malory anticipated this development ensured the
survival of his rendering of Arthurian romances, just as
the inability of French writers to turn the Cycle into a series
of *nouvelles* was one of the causes of its eclipse in France.
'Au XVe siècle', writes Paul Morand, 'avec Sir Thomas
Malory, dans la *Morte d'Arthur*, la nouvelle sert à traduire,
sous une forme portative, ces traditions celtiques et chevaleresques dont l'influence devait être si grande sur Tennyson
et les Préraphaélites.'[2] Barring the somewhat contra-
dictory reference to 'Celtic chivalric traditions', this remark
aptly sums up Malory's position, much more accurately, it
may be said, than does E. A. Baker's elaborate account of
the 'growth of Arthurian romance, from its hazy beginnings
in myth and folk-lore to its embodiment in a single orderly
narrative by Malory'.[3] Like Thomas Nash in his *Unfortunate
Traveller*,[4] Malory gives us mere *disjectae membra novellae*,
and for this very reason stands in a direct line of descent
from the 'cyclic' technique of his medieval predecessors to
the individualized *nouvelle*—the real, if unacknowledged,
starting-point of modern fiction.

3. *The Sequence of Malory's 'volumes'*

If, as the foregoing account seems to suggest, there is no
strict continuity in the series of works which Caxton published under the title of *Le Morte Darthur*, is there any need
to assume that they were originally written in the order in
which we find them? Admittedly, the order is the same in
Caxton and in the Winchester MS. and was presumably the
same in their common source; but that common source was

---

[1] Perhaps the most famous example is *Manon Lescaut*, originally the seventh
volume of Prévost's *Mémoires et Avantures d'un homme de qualité*.
[2] *L'Heure qu'il est*, Paris, 1938, p. 211.
[3] *The History of the English Novel*, vol. 1, p. 304.
[4] Cf. J. J. Jusserand, *Le Roman au temps de Shakespeare* (Paris, 1887), pp. 123–4:
'Il a le défaut de tous les romans du temps, aussi bien en Angleterre qu'ailleurs: il
est incohérent et mal composé. Mais il présente des fragments excellents, deux ou
trois bons portraits d'individus bien observés et quelques scènes, comme la vengeance
de Cutwolfe, solidement construites, qui permettent de prévoir qu'un jour la
puissance dramatique du génie anglais, exténuée sans doute par une longue carrière
sur le théâtre, pourra, au lieu de s'éteindre, revivre dans le roman.'

not necessarily identical with Malory's original text; and even if it was, the order in which he arranged his works need not have been the same as the order of their composition.

A possible approach to the problem is suggested by Malory's habit of reproducing passages and scenes from his own work. An example is found in the episode of the *Tale of King Arthur*.[1] An earl offers hospitality to Marhalt and asks him to challenge a redoubtable giant who 'destroys all his lands'. Marhalt wonders whether the giant would fight on horseback or on foot. 'There may no horse bear him', says the earl, and Marhalt, leaving his own horse behind, sets out the next morning to fight the giant. Their battle is described thus:

> So on the morne sir Marhaute prayde the erle that one of his men myght brynge hym where the gyaunte was, and so one brought hym where he syghe hym sytte undir a tre of hooly, and many clubbis of ironne and gysernes about hym. So this knyght dressed hym to the gyaunte and put his shylde before hym, and the gyaunte toke an ironne club in his honde, and at the fyrste stroke he clave syr Marhautis shelde. And there he was in grete perell, for the gyaunte was a sly fyghter. But at the laste sir Marhaute smote of his ryght arme aboven the elbow. Than the gyaunte fledde and the knyght affter hym, and so he drove hym into a watir.

All that Malory's French source can offer by way of parallel to this episode is a story of how Gaheriet fought with a giant to rescue a damsel. But the circumstances and the nature of the battle are entirely different: Gaheriet strikes the giant down, rides over his body, crushing it with the horse's hoofs, and, finding that he is still alive, cuts off his head.[2] To discover the real model of Malory's description we must turn from his 'French book' to his own work, the

---

[1] For other examples see my *Malory*, pp. 39–41.

[2] MS. B. N. fr. 112, f. 54ᵛ: 'Quant Gaheriet voit le jayant a la terre, il n'est pas esbais, ains met la main a l'espee et li court sus tout a cheval. Et la ou il se vouloit relever a quelque paine, il le fiert si du pis du cheval qu'il le fait revoler a terre, et li met le cheval tantes fois par dessus le corps que tout le debrise. Et cil se pasme de la grant angoisse qu'il sent, et est tel atornés qu'il ne puet traire a soy ne pié ne main. Et lors descent Gaheriet et li trenche les las du heaume, et trouve que cil estoit en poismoison. Et il pense qu'il en delivrera le païs maintenant. Si dresse l'espee contremont et fiert a deus mains si durement qu'il li fait la teste voler plus d'une ance loing du but.'

Tale of the Noble King Arthur and the Emperor Lucius, and the curious account of Arthur's fight with the giant:

'Now, felow,' seyde Arthure, 'wouldist thow ken me where that carle dwellys?' . . . 'Sir conquerrour', seyde the good man, 'beholde yondir two gyrys, for there shalte thow fynde that carle.' . . . Than he paste forth to the creste of the hylle and syghe[1] where he sate at his soupere alone. . . . And therwith sturdely he sterte uppon his leggis and caughte a clubbe in his honde all of clene iron. Than he swappis at the kynge with that kyd[2] wepyn. He cruysshed downe with the club the coronal[3] doune to the colde erthe. The kynge coverde hym with his shylde and rechis a boxe evyn infourmede[4] in the myddis of his forehede, that the slypped blade unto the brayne rechis. Yet he shappis at sir Arthure, but the kynge shuntys[5] a lytyll and rechis hym a dynte hyghe upon the haunche. . . . With that the warlow[6] wrath Arthure undir, and so they waltyrde and tumbylde over the craggis and busshys . . . and they never leffte tyll they fylle[7] thereas the floode marked.

The analogies are obvious. They are found both in the general trend of the two passages and in several important details including the manner of the giant's death. Just as Arthur *coverde hym with his shylde,* so Marhalt *put his shylde before hym,* and although Marhalt puts his opponent to flight while Arthur drags him down the hill, in both cases the giant meets with his doom 'in a watir'. But perhaps the two most striking points in the first passage are the vision of *many clubbis of ironne,* a typically epic weapon which Malory could not have found mentioned in any French romance, but which figures prominently in his adaptation of the alliterative *Morte Arthure,* and the alliterative phrase *syghe hym sytte,* paralleled by *syghe where he sate* in the second passage.

Similarities such as these cannot be accidental. Either one passage must have been modelled on the other or both must have had the same source. Now it is known that for the second passage Malory used the English alliterative *Morte Arthure.* If he had used it for both passages it would have been difficult to account for the fact that in both cases he made exactly the same choice of words and phrases and adapted them in the same way (cf. *where he syghe hym sytte*

---

[1] = 'saw'.   [2] = 'famous'.   [3] = 'crown'.   [4] = 'well-aimed'.
[5] = 'steps aside'.   [6] = 'traitor'.   [7] = 'fell'.

in the first passage, *syghe where he sate* in the second, and *the syghte had he rechide how unsemly pat sott satt sowpande* in the *Morte Arthure*). The only reasonable theory seems to be, therefore, that the first passage was modelled on the second, i.e. on Malory's own version of the *Tale of Arthur and Lucius* which must, then, have been written *before* the *Tale of King Arthur*.

This would explain several other features of the *Tale of King Arthur*. The knights appointed by the Archbishop of Canterbury to attend on Arthur include 'Bawdewyn of Breteyne', a character belonging to Malory's own version of the *Tale of Arthur and Lucius* and modelled on Bishop Beaufort who shared the government of the country with the Duke of Bedford during Henry V's absence.[1] The appearance of this character in the *Tale of Arthur and Lucius* is justified by the analogy of the situation, but there is no such motivation for it in the *Tale of King Arthur*. Again, when in the latter work Arthur proudly rejects the Roman Emperor's claim and offers to pay his tribute 'with a sharp spear', his speech is a clear reminiscence of the alliterative text, as is the phrase 'brake the bushment' which occurs in a passage otherwise identical with its French source.[2] But perhaps the most important confirmation of the suggested chronology of Malory's first two works is to be found in their vocabulary and syntax, as has recently been shown by Professor Jan Šimko and other scholars.[3]

The interruption in the composition of the romances to which Malory refers in his first *explicit* (see facsimile facing p. xx) must have occurred, then, after he had written two romances—one borrowed from an English, the other from a French source. The exact order of the subsequent works can only be surmised. *The Noble Tale of Sir Launcelot* (Caxton's Book VI) refers to 'Sir Pelleas the good knight' as one of the three strongest knights, the other two being Tristram and Lancelot. The character of Sir Pelleas belongs exclusively to the *Suite du Merlin*[4] which Malory used for his

---

[1] Cf. *infra*, pp. 16 and 195. [2] Cf. *infra*, pp. 48 and 190.

[3] *Word-Order in the Winchester Manuscript and in William Caxton's Edition of Thomas Malory's Morte Darthur (1485)—A Comparison*, by Jan Šimko, Halle, 1957. See especially pp. 111–12.

[4] The relevant portion of the *Suite* is found in MS. B.N. fr. 112. On Malory's

Tale of King Arthur: until he had read it he could not have thought of Pelleas as being the equal of Tristram and Lancelot. In the *Tale of Gareth* the hero's mother is erroneously called Morgawse;[1] the error goes back to a passage in Malory's adaptation of the French *Merlin* in *The Tale of King Arthur*. He resorts to this work again in the *Book of Tristram*, in the *Grail*, and in the *Book of Launcelot and Guinevere*.[2] As for his *Morte Arthur*, one of the *explicits* quoted above[3] makes it clear that it was written immediately after the *Book of Launcelot and Guinevere*.[4] The four preceding romances may well have been composed in the order in which they appear in the extant copies but there is no clear proof of this.

We can, however, in the light of what we now know about the background of the work, see how the collection grew in Malory's hands. His *Tale of the Noble King Arthur and Emperor Lucius*,[5] the least 'romantic' of his works and the least polished, had a decisive influence both on the formation of his style and on his subsequent choice of material. It induced him to 'seek other books of Arthur' and to 'draw

treatment of it see the introductory remarks in the first section of my Commentary and Dr. F. Whitehead's article in *Medium Aevum*, ii, pp. 199 ff.

[1] In all French versions Gareth's mother (the wife of King Lot of Orcanie) is anonymous; *Morgan* is the name of her sister, wife of King Nentres of Sorhaut.

[2] In the episode of the healing of Sir Urry which has no counterpart in Malory's sources.

[3] The *explicit* of the *Book of Launcelot and Guinevere*, p. xxxi.

[4] In using Malory's borrowings from his own works as indications of the chronological sequence of his romances I have attached no importance to the frequent enumerations of Arthur's knights which the scribes seem to have lengthened at will. A good example is the inclusion, in the Winchester version of the *Tale of Arthur and Lucius*, of Ector de Mares and Pelleas among the knights who fought on Arthur's side against the Roman Emperor (p. 221). Pelleas belongs to the *Tale of King Arthur*, Ector de Mares first appears in the *Tale of Sir Launcelot*. But if on the strength of this we put the passage in question later than these two works, we should be unable to explain either the story of the fight with the giant in the former or the reference to Arthur's Roman campaign in the latter (p. 253: 'Sone aftir that kynge Arthure was com from Rome,' etc.). The Winchester scribe who had the whole collection of Malory's works before him must have added these two names, as well as some others, of his own accord. The examples of 'self-imitation' quoted above are in a different category: they occur in Caxton as well as in the Winchester MS. and bear the unmistakable stamp of Malory's workmanship.

[5] I have adopted this title and its abbreviations in order to avoid confusion with the *Tale of King Arthur*. The title given in Malory's colophon is the *Tale of the noble kynge Arthure that was Emperoure hymself thorow dygnyté of his hondys*. Cf. *infra*, p. 247.

from the French' part of the *Suite du Merlin*. Malory was clearly sensitive to the appeal of this type of romance even though he could not fully accept its 'cyclic' structure, and in his *Tale of King Arthur* he evolved, as it were by reaction, his own narrative technique. When, after an interval, he came back to his task with *The Noble Tale of Sir Launcelot* and *The Tale of Sir Gareth* he was able to apply this technique with great effect. Next he turned to the *Tristram* and the *Grail*. In spite of the vast amount of spurious episodic matter which had clustered round the basic themes of the French prose *Tristan* and the *Queste del Saint Graal* these romances had preserved the essentials of the two greatest medieval stories. Through them and with their aid Malory was able to discover what he needed above all: his own method of conveying sentiment through fiction. And so his last two works—*The Book of Sir Launcelot and Queen Guinevere* and the *Morte Arthur*—could reach a degree of independence unparalleled in his earlier books, or indeed in any earlier prose version of Arthurian romance, and retain their appeal long after their models had been forgotten.[1]

[1] Dr. D. S. Brewer sums it all up by saying that 'here the noble simplicity of theme, the moral earnestness, the firm conception of the roles of Lancelot and Arthur and Guinevere, the fertile invention of story and dialogue, the magnificent prose, all unite in a richness of feeling unparalleled in Arthurian literature before or since' (*Essays on Malory* edited by J. A. W. Bennett, Oxford, 1963, pp. 62–63).

CHAPTER III

THE WRITER'S PROGRESS

1. *Style*

PERHAPS the most significant conclusion to be drawn from the previous chapter is that Malory began his work with the *Tale of King Arthur and the Emperor Lucius*. It would be tempting to dwell at length on the implications of this change in the traditional idea of the order of his romances. For it suggests that, contrary to the generally accepted view, he first became familiar with the Arthurian legend not through 'French books' but through an English poem, the alliterative *Morte Arthure*. The epic mood of the fourteenth-century poet, so characteristic of the alliterative revival, his combination of stirring realism with heroic feeling, and above all the consistent archaism of metre, manner, and spirit—these were indeed worthy models for a writer who endeavoured to raise the romantic tales of Arthur to a heroic level. That Malory's whole conception of his theme was formed under the influence of the English epic of Arthur now seems certain, and it is a new and helpful sidelight on the continuity of the English tradition that by the time Malory came to 'reduce' his French books into English his attitude to Arthurian knighthood had been fixed in his mind by his reading of native poetry.

No less decisive was the effect of the alliterative poem on the formation of his style. Historians of English prose used to put him 'out of the general line of progress', both as regards matter and form.[1] 'The world to which the *Morte Darthur* belongs', writes R. W. Chambers, 'had passed away before the book was finished', and 'there was little room for Arthurian knighthood in the England of the Paston Letters.'[2] And yet—'such is the power of style that Malory, at the eleventh hour, was able to go over the old ground, and make it live once more'. Is this revival of a long-forgotten world to be regarded simply as a miracle performed

---

[1] G. Saintsbury, *A First Book of English Literature*, 1914, p. 60.

[2] R. W. Chambers, *On the Continuity of English Prose from Alfred to More and his School*, 1932, p. cxxix.

by a genius without antecedents, by a writer 'out of the general line of progress', who wrought his language in the void? Such a thought would be contrary to all we know of the history of prose, for whatever individual greatness it may achieve, literary prose, unlike poetry, is, in the noblest sense of the term, an 'institution', 'part of the equipment of a civilization, part of its heritable wealth, like its laws, or its system of schooling, or its tradition of skilled craftsmanship'.[1] At one time much emphasis was placed on the continuous development of English prose from the earliest times to the Renaissance. Yet the critic to whom we owe the best account of this development had found no room for Malory in the lineage of English writers and left him in complete, if enviable, isolation. The achievements of Peacock, of Fortescue, of Tyndale and Coverdale, and the succession of translations of the Bible closed by the Authorized Version of 1611 could all be, according to him, properly understood 'when we saw them against the continuous background of English devotional prose';[2] but no such background exists for Malory, or indeed for the other secular prose writers of his time. More recent critics tend to ascribe the comparative proficiency of these writers to more immediate influences: the resources of the common speech and the impact of French literary prose; and Professor Davis goes as far as to say that English fifteenth-century prose could not have made its halting steps without a helping hand from the already self-assured French which was so well known.[3]

Granted the importance of all such influences, it still

---

[1] J. S. Phillimore, 'Blessed Thomas More and the Arrest of Humanism in England', *Dublin Review*, vol. cliii, p. 8.

[2] R. W. Chambers, op. cit., p. cxxxv.

[3] Norman Davis, *Styles in English Prose of the Late Middle and Early Modern Period*, in *Langue et Littérature, Actes du VIIIe Congrès de la F.I.L.L.M.*, Liège, 1961, p. 177. Cf. also Professor J. A. W. Bennett's remark in the Preface to *Essays on Malory*, p. vi: 'no one has yet attempted a detailed comparison of [Malory's] prose with that of the French texts . . . nor with that of the English *Merlin*'. This still seems to be the case. Malory's style has been consistently praised and as consistently neglected. For observations on its place in the history of English prose cf. H. S. Bennett, 'Fifteenth-Century Secular Prose', *Review of English Studies*, vol. xxi (1945), p. 257; A. A. Prins, *French Influence on English Phraseology*, Leiden, 1952, pp. 17–18; and R. M. Wilson, 'On the continuity of English Prose', *Mélanges [. . .] Fernand Mossé*, Paris, 1959, p. 493.

remains doubtful whether they could have fashioned any great author's style, and whether the real beginnings of it are not to be sought in his own experience of *writing* and in the conditions which determine the nature of this experience. The all-important fact in Malory's case is that his first work was an adaptation of an English poem, the alliterative *Morte Arthure*. His object in adapting it was to rewrite it in a form accessible to contemporary readers. To do this it was not enough to reduce the amount of alliteration and modernize the vocabulary. The whole texture of the poem had to undergo a radical change, similar to that which occurred in the transition from verse to prose romances in thirteenth- and fourteenth-century France. Of the numerous devices which facilitated this transition one was of particular importance: the reduction of rhetorical matter. It is perhaps best illustrated by the opening paragraph of the French prose romance entitled *Le Chevalier au Cygne*. The author states that he has unrhymed his verse original *for the sake of brevity*: poetry, he adds, is 'very enjoyable and very beautiful, but very lengthy'.[1] At first one may wonder why he should blame poetry for its 'length' when it is well known that in nearly every case the prose renderings of early poems far exceeded them in volume. The answer is that by 'length' he means something other than volume. What he dislikes is not the size of the poem, but the rhetorical elaboration which had become an integral part of the art of poetry. To 'shorten' a work means to him and to his contemporaries to relieve it of such unnecessary burdens as ornaments of description, the artificial lengthening of speeches, and the inflated phraseology used in descriptions and speeches alike. The total length of the work need not be reduced; it may in fact be considerably increased by the addition of fresh narrative material, provided that the story is told, as another anonymous prose writer puts it, 'in clearer and more intelligible language'.[2]

Malory no doubt thought likewise, for his problem was similar to that which confronted all late medieval prose

---

[1] 'moult plaisans et moult bele, mais moult est longue' (MS. B.N. fr. 781).

[2] 'en plus cler et entendible langaige' (*Maugis d'Aigremont*, Paris, Michel le Noir, 1518, f. LVII^r, col. A).

writers. The stylistic and narrative patterns of the *Morte Arthure* must have appeared to him too ornate and too diffuse —'too lengthy', as the author of *Le Chevalier au Cygne* would have said. This type of 'length' could not have been remedied by sheer omission of complete passages. The simplification had to be both more radical and less mechanical: it had to be applied on a strictly selective principle to the entire text of the poem. And the most remarkable result of it was that the word-material of the alliterative epic aided by the author's instinctive choice produced a new and powerful prose style, a style 'too straightforward to be archaic',[1] and yet 'just old enough to allure and mark the age'.[2]

Placed side by side with its source, the newly discovered text of Malory's *Tale of King Arthur and the Emperor Lucius* reveals the nature of this process and the subtle working of the stylistic genius which directed its application. A few examples will suffice.[3] As Arthur approaches the walls of a beleaguered city, 'without shield save his bare harness', he is warned by Sir Florence that it is folly to face the enemy unarmed. In Malory's version this is his reply:

'And thow be aferde', seyde kyng Arthure, 'I rede the faste fle, for they wynne no worshyp of me but to waste their toolys. For there shall never harlot[4] have happe, by the helpe of oure Lord, to kylle a crowned kynge that with creyme is anoynted.'

The 'longer' version—that of the poem—is as follows:

'*Ife thow be rade*', *quod the kyng*, '*I rede thow ryde vttere*,
Lesse þat þey rywe the with theire rownnd wapyn.

---

[1] *Cambridge History of English Literature*, ii. 337.

[2] Andrew Lang, *Le Morte Darthur* (Introduction to Sommer's edition), vol. iii, p. xxi.

[3] In his *History of the English Prose Rhythm* (London, 1912) G. Saintsbury has given interesting examples of Malory's treatment of the stanzaic *Morte Arthur* and of the way in which 'out of the substance of verse he has woven quite a new rhythm, accompanying and modulating graceful and almost majestic prose of the best type'. But as Malory did not discover the stanzaic *Morte Arthur* until he had begun his very last work, comparisons with this poem are of little value for the study of the genesis of his style. The alliterative *Morte Arthure* and Malory's adaptation of it provide far more significant instances of his method of 'patching in' some of the bright stitches of his predecessor, 'not fearing but welcoming, and mustering them into a distinct prose rhythm—treating them, in fact, just as Ruskin does his doses of blank verse'.

[4] = 'rascal'.

Thow arte bot a fawntkyn, no ferly me thynkkys!
Þou will be flayede for a flye, þat on thy flesche lyghttes.
I am nothynge agaste, so me Gode helpe!
Þof siche gadlynges be greuede, it greues me bot lyttill;
They wyn no wirchipe of me bot wastys theire takle;
They sall wante, or I weende, I wage myn hevede!
Sall neuer harlotte haue happe, thorowe helpe of my Lorde,
To kyll a corownde kynge, with krysom enoynttede!'[1]

Out of the ten lines of the poem Malory has only taken
four, but with what a remarkable sense of stylistic emphasis!
The choice alone suffices for his purpose, and he need make
no change in the lines he borrows: they fully convey the
sense of the speech, and more. *And thow be aferde I rede the*
faste fle does not only cover the meaning of the first six lines,
but gains enormously from being relieved of epic ornamentation. Malory's Arthur need not say that he is 'nothynge
agaste'; his fearlessness is brought home more forcibly by
his proud retort to the coward. Nor is there any room in
Malory's context for such nerveless phrases as *I wage myn*
hevede. And while the last two lines of the speech, which
bear the full weight of Arthur's unflinching faith in the
sanctity of his crown, remain intact, they are thrown into
greater relief: in the *Morte Arthure* they are but the tail end
of a long discourse; in Malory they sound like a call to arms.

But the selection of complete lines is by no means Malory's
only method of 'reduction'. Some of his sentences consist
of words and phrases which in his source are scattered over
long passages. When, after his victory over the giant,
Arthur divides the spoils among his people he says: '*Looke*
that the goodys be skyffted,[2] *that none playne of his parte*'—a
perfect example of Malory's sentence-structure with its
characteristic cadence and crisp idiom. And yet it is but a

---

[1] *Morte Arthure*, ed. Björkman, 2438–47. Here is a literal translation: 'If you are
afraid', said the king, 'I advise you to ride away, lest they wound you with their
round weapons. You are but a child and no wonder, as it seems to me. You would
be afraid of a fly if it alighted on your flesh. I am not afraid, so may God help me!
I do not mind if such worthless creatures come to grief. They will gain no honour
from me, but they will waste their weapons. I will wager my head that before I go
away they will fail. The Lord will never allow a rascal to succeed in killing a
crowned king who has been anointed with chrism.'

[2] = 'divided'.

mosaic of words borrowed from half a dozen lines of the poem:

> He somond þan þe schippemen scharpely þeraftyre
> To schake furthe with þe schyremen to *schifte þe gudez*:
> 'All þe myche tresour, þat traytour had wonnen,
> To comouns of the contré, clergye and oþer,
> *Luke* it be done and delte to my dere pople,
> *That none pleyn of theire parte*, o peyne of ʒour lyfez.'[1]

Used in this way the words and phrases lifted from the text cannot always preserve their original meaning, but from the prose writer's point of view this is not too high a price to pay for brevity. Malory's *doleful dragon* which Arthur sees in his dream is a contraction of two alliterative lines in which the two words stand far apart,[2] while the description of the 'careful widow' who '*sate* sorowyng' is but an adaptation of a passage relating how the king greeted the widow with *sittande wordez*.[3] Such transpositions are, however, much less frequent than genuine abridgement, by means of which words and phrases selected from the poem are woven into the most astonishing tissue of pure and straightforward prose. *Than the kyng yode up to the creste of the cragge, and than he comforted hymself with the colde wynde*. Few masters of style have matched the descriptive force of this sentence.

---

1 'Thereupon he quickly summoned the sailors to go with the sheriffs to divide the treasure: "See to it that all this great treasure which that traitor gained is divided among my dear people, whether they be commoners, clergy, or others, so that no one complains of his share, on peril of your lives" ' (ll. 1212–17).

2 . . . a *dragone* engowschede, dredfull to schewe,
Deuorande a dolphyn with *dolefull* lates (*Morte Arthure*, 2054–5).

3 = 'fitting words'. Further examples will be found in the Commentary. From this method of transcription there is but one step to another device which may be illustrated by the following parallels:

Morte Arthure	*Malory*
LAUGHTE hym vpe full louelyly (2292):	LYFFTE hym up lordely (p. 225)
sette thane appon oure SERE knyghttez (1847):	sette SORE on oure knyghtes (p. 216)

When Malory applies this device to his French sources the result is even more startling. On one occasion the French *entre* becomes *under*, and on another Balin and his companion '*stable* their horsis' because the French has *la feste estoit par tel maniere establie*. The mysterious adjective *amyvestyall* which no commentator has yet been able to explain (p. 151: *his amyvestyall countenaunce*) is a compound of three French words, totally meaningless outside their context: 'Nous n'aviens nes poissanche de metre fors nos alainnes, *ains estions del* tout aussi comme mors' (see Commentary, note 151. 34).

But to see how it was made we need but glance at the corresponding lines in the *Morte Arthure*:

> *The kyng* coueris *þe cragge* wyth cloughes full hye,
> *To the creste of* the clyffe he clymbez on lofte;
> Keste vpe hys vmbrere, and kenly he lukes,
> Caughte of *þe colde wynde*, to *comforthe hym seluen*.

Every now and then, allured by the cadence of the poem, Malory reproduces complete groups of three or four lines with few, if any, alterations; but he never abandons his real task for more than a brief spell. With a persistence amounting to genius he manufactures out of a somewhat commonplace web of alliterative verse a language endowed with a simplicity and power all its own. And when towards the end of the *Tale* he abandons his source, his prose retains all the robust eloquence of epic and all the natural freshness of a living idiom:

'Ye say well', seyde the kynge, 'for inowghe is as good as a feste, for to attemte God overmuche I holde hit not wysedom. And therefore make you all redy and turne we into Ingelonde.' Than there was trussynge of harneyse with caryage full noble, and the kynge toke his leve of the holy fadir the Pope and patryarkys and cardynalys and senatoures full ryche, and leffte good governaunce in that noble cité and all the contrays of Rome for to warde and to kepe on payne of deth, that in no wyse his commaundement be brokyn.

It has been said of Goldsmith that he was 'Augustan and also sentimental and rural without discordance', because he had 'the old and the new in such just proportion that there was no conflict'.[1] It is a similar kind of harmony that we find in Malory when by a judicious arrangement of word-material he creates the new out of the old.[2] The secret of it

---

[1] T. S. Eliot, Introduction to *London*, by Samuel Johnson.

[2] The most elusive aspect of Malory's style is, of course, its rhythm. Saintsbury's attempt to reduce it to metrical patterns has led him to the unsatisfying conclusion that 'you may resolve sentence after sentence into iambs pure, iambs extended by a precedent short into anapæsts and iambs, or curling over with a short suffix into amphibrachs, and so getting into the trochee' (*A History of English Prose Rhythm*, p. 90). This leaves singularly few metres into which Malory's prose could *not* be resolved. More helpful is the remark that 'the dominant of Malory's rhythm is mainly iambic, though he does not neglect the precious inheritance of the trochaic or amphibrachic ending' (ibid.). Malory's use of the alliterative *Morte Arthure* may well account for this. In the poem the metre most frequently used in the first half of the line is the amphibrach, and in a number of cases Malory either preserves it intact or shortens it to an iamb.

escapes analysis; but in the light of the new text of Malory we can at least observe the beginning and the end of the process, gauge the distance between them, and so approach, with a keener sense of its magnitude, the unexpounded miracle of style.[1]

2. *Structure*

Next after the *Tale of Arthur and Lucius* came the *Tale of King Arthur*—a retrospective account of the early history of Arthur's kingdom, *from the maryage of Kynge Uther unto Kyng Arthure that regned aftir hym and ded many batayles*. But when Malory opened his first 'French book' in the hope of finding some material for the story, he encountered difficulties for which the simple technique he had so far acquired offered no solution. His English source was, in spite of its 'length', a straightforward account of certain pseudo-historical episodes placed in their natural order, and it was comparatively easy, by a mere process of 'reduction', to quicken its pace and remove some of the ornaments of epic style. The problem Malory now had to face was of a totally different kind.

His French romance was a combination of the prose *Merlin* with its sequel, the *Suite du Merlin*.[2] Its main attraction for Malory was that it supplied the natural beginning of the Arthur story by elaborating some of the episodes recorded in the chronicles of Wace and Geoffrey of Monmouth. But he soon found to his dismay that the treatment of the chronicle material was singularly unlike what he had seen in the *Morte Arthure*. Adventures were piled up one

[1] Of the numerous attempts to account for the survival of Malory's work the following is the most worthy of note: 'Le hasard voulut qu'il fût bon écrivain, si bon que sa prose n'a presque pas vieilli. Aussi cette ample composition, la *Morte d'Arthur*, comme il l'avait intitulée, imprimée d'abord en 1485 par les presses vénérables de Caxton, maintes fois réimprimée au temps d'Elisabeth et jusqu'en plein dix-septième siècle, et tout au long du dix-neuvième en des éditions sans nombre, demeure-t-elle un livre classique, l'un des joyaux du trésor qui forme, en Angleterre, le patrimoine spirituel de la nation. . . . Mystérieux pouvoir du goût, d'une langue saine, d'un bon style! Ce Malory ne fut qu'un traducteur, un adaptateur: sans lui pourtant, dans l'Angleterre d'aujourd'hui, ni la poésie, ni la pensée, ni l'art ne seraient tout à fait ce qu'ils sont' (Joseph Bédier, Préface aux *Romans de la Table Ronde nouvellement rédigés par Jacques Boulenger*, pp. iv–v).

[2] For details see the relevant section of the Commentary.

upon the other without any apparent sequence or design, and innumerable personages, mostly anonymous, were introduced in a wild succession. Every now and then they stopped to lay lance in rest and overthrow one another, and then swore eternal friendship and rode away.[1] The purpose of their encounters and pursuits was vague, and their tasks were seldom fulfilled: they met and parted and met again, each intent at first on following his particular 'quest', and yet prepared at any time to be diverted from it to other adventures and undertakings. As a result, 'the basic thought became subsidiary, the episode increasingly prominent, the slowing of the action defeated any attempt to reach an end, and the story lost all purpose'. In these words Gustav Gröber described three-quarters of a century ago the methods used by medieval prose writers.[2] But there is reason to believe that at a much earlier date their methods were condemned on similar grounds, and the often quoted remark of the Canon of Toledo in *Don Quixote* remains to this day the most characteristic expression of the modern view: 'I have never yet', he says, 'seen a book of chivalry complete in all its parts, so that the middle agrees with the beginning and the end with the beginning and the middle; but they seem to construct their stories with such a multitude of members as though they meant to produce a monster rather than a well-proportioned figure.'[3]

The real question is, however, whether neglect of *structure* in the modern sense of the term necessarily implies the absence of a *method of composition*. Gröber may have blamed the cyclic works for their lack of a *Grundgedanke*, and Cervantes may have thought them 'monstrous' because they formed no consistent whole; but it remains to be seen whether the criteria of a *Grundgedanke* or of a 'well-proportioned figure' are not in this case misleading,

---

[1] Cf. E. K. Chambers, *Sir Thomas Malory*, p. 6.

[2] *Grundriss der romanischen Philologie*, vol. ii, p. 726.

[3] *Don Quixote*, Part I, ch. xlvii. M. Jean Frappier, in his edition of the French *Mort Artu* (Paris, 1936), enters an eloquent plea for this work: 'Le judicieux chanoine de Tolède ne connaissait pas notre *Mort Artu*; sinon, il est permis de penser qu'il aurait volontiers donné l'absolution à ce livre de chevalerie en vertu de l'unité et de la robuste structure de son plan.' For a statement of the opposite view see F. Lot, *Étude sur le Lancelot en prose*, pp. 268–76.

and whether behind the apparent deformity and incoherence of the prose romances there is not to be found an architectural design so unlike our own conception of a story that we inevitably fail to perceive it. One *a priori* reason for suspecting the existence of such a design is that if each branch of the Cycle were a mere collection of episodes haphazardly put together, the Cycle would naturally fall into as many independent sections. In reality, the reverse is the case: none of the branches of the Cycle can be conveniently subdivided, and no subdivisions exist in the manuscripts. Apart from certain interpolations which can easily be detached from the main body of the work, few of the episodes, if any, appear as self-contained units. 'Aucune aventure', writes Ferdinand Lot, 'ne forme un tout se suffisant à lui-même. D'une part, des épisodes antérieurs, laissés provisoirement de côté, y prolongent des ramifications; d'autre part, des épisodes subséquents, proches ou lointains, y sont amorcés.'[1] Judged by our standards this would seem to be a strange paradox. On the one hand, the prose romances are admittedly the very negation of the classical principle of composition: the beginning does not 'agree' with the middle, nor the middle with the end; on the other, they seem to obey the age-long rule that no part can be removed without affecting the whole. There must, then, be something which binds them together, invisible though it is to the modern eye: some peculiar device which, while making the various parts of the Cycle inseparable from one another, fails to weld them into an harmonious whole.

Perhaps the easiest way to discover the nature and the working of this device is to draw an analogy with the technique of tapestry. Just as in a tapestry each thread alternates with an endless variety of others, so in the early prose romances of the Arthurian group numerous seemingly independent episodes or 'motifs' are interwoven in a manner which makes it possible for each episode to be set aside at any moment and resumed later. No single stretch of such a narrative can be complete in itself any more than a stitch in a woven fabric; the sequel may appear at any moment, however long the interval. But the resemblance goes no

[1] Ferdinand Lot, *Étude sur le Lancelot en prose*, Paris, 1918, p. 17.

further, for unlike the finished tapestry a branch of a prose romance has as a rule no natural conclusion; when the author brings it to a close he simply cuts the threads at arbitrarily chosen points, and anyone who chooses to pick them up and interweave them in a similar fashion can continue the work indefinitely. Hence the 'multitude of members' and the prodigious growth of the Arthurian tradition enlarged at each stage of its progress by continuations of earlier works.

The origin of this process may be sought in the combination of two rules of literary composition laid down by contemporary theorists: the *ordo artificialis* and the *digressio*. The former goes back to classical rhetoric;[1] the latter is a characteristically medieval invention and has no exact parallel in classical treatises. Geoffroi de Vinsauf insists on its usefulness and subdivides it into two categories: *Unus modus digressionis est quando digredimur in materia ad aliam partem materiae*; *alius modus, quando digredimur a materia ad aliud extra materiam.*[2] It is doubtful whether Geoffroi de Vinsauf or any other medieval rhetorician had in mind anything approaching the methods of thirteenth-century romance writers,[3] but as long as theoretical precepts were applied literally, without much regard for their purpose,[4] the advice to proceed both *ad aliam partem materiae* by way of anticipation, and *ad aliud extra materiam* by way of

---

[1] Cf. Horace, *Ars poetica*, 42–45; Martianus Capella, *De Rhetorica*, 30 (ed. Halm, *Rhet min.*, p. 472); Sulpicius Victor, *Institutiones oratoriae*, 14 (Halm, p. 320). For the medieval treatment of *ordo artificialis* see *Scholia vindobonensia ad Horatii artem poeticam*, ed. Zechmeister (1877); Mathieu de Vendôme, *Ars Versificatoria* (ed. Faral, *Les Arts poétiques du xiie et du xiiie siècle*), vol. i, pp. 3–13; Geoffroi de Vinsauf, *Poetria Nova*, 101–25.

[2] *Documentum de modo et arte dictandi et versificandi* (ed. Faral, op. cit.), ii. 2, 17. The first kind of digression is further explained as follows: 'A materia ad aliam partem materiae, quando omittimus illam partem materiae quae proxima est et aliam quae sequitur primam assumimus.'

[3] The second kind of digression—*ad aliud extra materiam*—was primarily intended for purposes of comparison or simile (cf. loc. cit. ii. 2, 21: 'Digredimur etiam a materia ad aliud extra materiam, quando scilicet inducimus comparationes sive similitudines, ut eas aptemus materiae'), but it was applied on a larger and more varied scale. Its extreme form was, and still is, 'the story in the story'.

[4] Cf. Faral, op. cit., p. 60: 'L'enseignement des arts poétiques, qui ne brille pas par l'envergure des conceptions, paraît avoir agi précisément par ce qu'il contenait de plus superficiel et de plus mécanique; mais ç'a été une action très réelle, dont la littérature porte les marques.'

digression proper, combined as it was with the various
prescriptions of the *ordo artificialis*,[1] could well induce the
romance writers to build up their narrative in such a way
that each episode appeared to be a digression from the
previous one and a sequel to some earlier unfinished story.
There are good examples of this technique in the poems of
Chrétien de Troyes; in the works of his successors—
particularly in the continuations of his *Conte del Graal*—it
assumes still greater importance; and with the *Lancelot-
Graal* it asserts itself as the dominating feature of the genre.[2]

Malory's handling of his sources shows how strongly he
reacted to this type of composition. With varying degrees
of success, but with remarkable consistency, he endeavoured
to do two things: to reduce the bulk of the stories and to
alter their arrangement. Of the processes he employed the
simplest was mechanical reduction: he seldom reproduced an
episode in full.[3] More elaborate was the device of 'telescoping', which consisted in making either two different scenes
or two characters into one.[4] But Malory's most successful
and historically most significant contribution to the technique of the prose tale was his attempt to substitute for the
method of 'interweaving' the modern 'progressive' form of
exposition.

The source of his *Tale of King Arthur* contained three main
groups of episodes interspersed with various adventures of
Arthur's knights: Arthur's wars against the enemies of his

---

[1] Cf. Geoffroi de Vinsauf, *Poetria Nova*, 101 ff.:

> Ordinis est primus sterilis, ramusque secundus
> Fertilis et mira succrescit origine ramus
> In ramos, solus in plures, unus in octo.
> Circiter hanc artem fortasse videtur et aer
> Nubilus, et limes salebrosus, et ostia clausa,
> Et res nodosa. Quocirca sequentia verba
> Sunt hujus morbi medici: speculeris in illis;
> Invenietur ibi qua purges luce tenebras,
> Quo pede transcurras salebras, qua clave recludas
> Ostia, quo digito solvas nodosa. Patentem
> Ecce viam!

[2] Cf. F. Lot, loc. cit.: 'De ce procédé de l'entrelacement les exemples se pressent
sous la plume. Ils sont si nombreux qu'à les vouloir énumérer on raconterait le
Lancelot d'un bout à l'autre.'

[3] The rate of condensation varies from 1:2 to 1:8. Cf. my *Malory*, pp. 30–31.

[4] Cf. ibid., pp. 34–38. Numerous other illustrations will be found in the
Commentary.

kingdom, the life and death of Merlin the enchanter, and the treacherous machinations of Morgan le Fay, Arthur's half-sister. How these three themes were interwoven with one another may be seen from the following brief summary of the middle portion of the story (*Huth Merlin*, ff. 184–220):

While Merlin and Nivene—'la damoisele chaceresse', with whom Merlin is in love—are visiting the land of King Ban of Benoic, they discover the Lake of Diana. Merlin tells Nivene how the great huntress disposed of her unfortunate lover Faunus by shutting him up in a tomb, and how she was afterwards punished for it. He also tells Nivene that Arthur is in imminent danger from his foes. Nivene urges him to return to Great Britain and rescue the king. Meanwhile Arthur repulses the attack of five hostile kings who have invaded his lands and massacred his men. One day he goes hunting in the forest of Camelot with Urience and Accolon; as they are busy quartering the stag by the side of a river, they see a beautifully decorated ship approaching the bank. Twelve damsels welcome them on board and offer them hospitality. The next morning the three hunters find themselves transported by enchantment to three different places: Urience to his own bed, Arthur to a prison, and Accolon to a meadow, where he is met by a dwarf who brings him Arthur's sword, Excalibur. Arthur's fellow prisoners tell him that their captor, Domas, would release them if he could find among them a champion ready to fight his brother. Arthur takes up the challenge. Nivene having rid herself of Merlin by shutting him up in a rock, 'qu'il ne fu puis nus qui peust veoir Merlin ne mort ne vif', goes to watch Arthur's battle with Domas's brother. But Morgan le Fay has in the meantime substituted Accolon for Arthur's original opponent. Armed with Arthur's sword, Accolon at first proves the stronger, but Nivene casts a spell upon him and makes him drop the magic weapon. Arthur picks it up and defeats Accolon with a few strokes. Morgan then attempts to murder in his sleep her husband Urience who is saved by his son, Ivain. At long last she success in stealing from Arthur the scabbard of his sword. But she and her men are put to flight, and Ivain is banished from the court: 'Car certes', says Arthur, 'je ne porroie pas cuidier que vous peuussiés estre preudom ne loial, pour le dyable dont vous estes issus.' This is the beginning of a new series of adventures in which Ivain, Gauvain, and Morhout play the leading parts.

It will be observed that the three basic themes alternate here in the following order: Merlin and Nivene (a^1), Arthur's wars (b), Morgan le Fay (c^1), Merlin and Nivene (a^2), Morgan le Fay (c^2). Now in Malory's account these themes, instead of being interwoven, are separated from one another and related in strict sequence. The order of events is not $a^1\ b\ c^1\ a^2\ c^2$, but $a^1\ a^2\ b\ c^1\ c^2$; the three threads of the narrative are unravelled and straightened out so as to form in each case a consistent and self-contained set of adventures. The same process can be observed on a smaller scale in each important subdivision of the story. After the story of the magic ship the French source gives a brief account of the situation of the three hunters, Urience, Arthur, and Accolon, on their awakening, and then deals with their particular adventures in the reverse order: Accolon, Arthur, Urience. Malory, on the other hand, first disposes of Urience, then combines two series of Arthur's adventures into one (the awakening and the resolve to fight for Domas), and lastly deals in a similar fashion with Accolon. Thus a simple narrative, with each sequence of events beginning when the other is at an end, is substituted for the elaborate chain of interlocked episodes.

The unravelling of a fabric such as that of the French romance is, however, no easy process, and every now and then, having failed to disentangle the full length of the thread at the proper time, Malory finds himself with the loose end of it on his hands. The story of Morgan le Fay may again be used as an example. In the French version Morgan's attempt to murder Urience is a natural sequel to the adventure of the magic ship. In Malory the connexion is broken, and the scene of the attempted murder is introduced without any reference to its antecedent:

The meanewhyle Morgan le Fay had wente kynge Arthure had bene ded. *So on a day* she aspyed kynge Uryence lay on slepe on his bedde; than she callyd unto hir a mayden of her counseyle and sayde, 'Go fecche me my lordes swerde, for I saw never bettir tyme to sle hym than now'.

Malory was well aware that in the original story Morgan le Fay did not discover Urience in his bed by chance 'on a day', but caused him to be brought there from the ship in order to murder him. The deliberate removal of the connecting link between the adventure of the ship and the attempted murder shows how anxious Malory was to avoid what the French romance writers valued above all: the impression that each episode either anticipated or continued *aliam partem materiae* with long intervals of extraneous matter between them. When this had not been achieved by means of a rearrangement of material, that is to say, when one or more elements of a sequence still remained separated from the rest, Malory either omitted them altogether or presented them as independent episodes: the pattern $a^1 b c^1 a^2 c^2$, if not already simplified by a consistent grouping of its component parts, was reduced to either $a^1 b c^1$ or $a^1 b c^1 d e$, thus closely approximating to the conventional modern technique of exposition.

The *Tale of King Arthur* was but the first attempt in this direction, highly characteristic of Malory's attitude to his task, yet hardly comparable to his ultimate achievement. His next two 'tales'—the *Noble Tale of Sir Launcelot du Lake* and the *Tale of Sir Gareth of Orkeney*—reveal a greater mastery of the same technique. In the opening chapters of the *Noble Tale* Lancelot, accompanied by Lionel, starts on his quest of adventures. As they lie asleep under a tree on a hot day there begin two distinct series of episodes: Lionel is captured by Tarquyn, and Lancelot by four queens who keep him prisoner in one of their castles. There Lancelot finds himself faced with the choice of either remaining a prisoner to the end of his days or becoming a paramour of one of the queens. Aided by a damsel he escapes, and to reward her for her service goes to a tournament and defeats the opponents of her father, King Bagdemagus. At this point the French romance introduces a digression equal in length to 500 pages of the present edition. Malory boldly dismisses it and, determined as he is to keep to the initial episode of his *Tale*, passes straight on to Lancelot's quest of Lionel: Lancelot kills Lionel's captor, Tarquyn, releases the other prisoners, disposes of Perys de Foreste Savage, an enemy of knights-errant, and rids the people of the Castle of Tintagel of the tyranny of two giants by cleaving the head of one and cutting the other in two. All this forms a consistent account, with 'a beginning, a middle and an end'. Some traces of 'interweavings' still remain, for Malory cannot altogether dismiss all the allusions, anticipations, and 'cross-links' which abound in his source; but he succeeds in disentangling from his material the outline of a continuous narrative without depriving the story of its essentially adventurous character. The result is a *roman d'aventure* rebuilt in accordance with a new principle of composition, and more palatable to the modern reader than any part of the original *Lancelot-Graal*.

A similar result was sometimes achieved by the French writers themselves. As the threads of the narrative lengthened and its pattern grew both in size and in complexity, the tendency arose to isolate certain episodes from their context and to treat them as 'stories in a story'. This was primarily the result of an excessively elaborate use of the 'tapestry' technique; but it was also the beginning of a new genre. Each composition as a whole became more and more unwieldy, but its various parts gradually acquired more shape and sequence. The cohesion which was no longer discernible in the larger works occasionally reappeared in what remained of their component elements; and so by a mere process of internal multiplication the over-developed varieties of medieval romantic fiction gave rise, and eventually yielded their place, to simpler and more enduring forms of narrative art.

There is reason to believe that the source of Malory's *Tale of Gareth* was an example of this process. It formed a branch of the prose *Tristan*,[1] but was virtually independent of it. Like Malory's *Tale of Gareth*, it was to all intents and purposes a self-contained account of the progress of a young nobleman who on his arrival at Arthur's court was ridiculed by Kay, the traditional jester, but soon distinguished himself by a series of daring exploits and finally achieved a degree of fame equalled only by Lancelot and Tristram. In the development of prose fiction this was a transition type inasmuch as it still retained some connexion with the romance of which it was a branch. By separating it from the *Tristan* and giving it an independent place Malory or the author of his source merely went a step further in the direction suggested by his French models. But the result was a story with a well-circumscribed plot,

---

[1] Cf. my article on the 'Romance of Gaheret' in *Medium Aevum*, vol. i, pp. 157–67 and the relevant section of the Commentary.

a real sense of completeness, and an harmonious working out of the central theme; a story which can serve as a genuine example of the technique of a modern tale applied to medieval romance.

3. *Interpretation*[1]

'Make use of the emotions. Relate the familiar manifestations of them. . . . These details carry conviction.' Aristotle, *Rhetorica*, iii. 16.

It is a commonplace of literary history to describe medieval romance as the prototype of the modern novel. Courtly romance writers, we are told, introduced into the realm of fiction the analysis of the mental reactions of the characters to the story and by so doing laid the foundations of the story of 'character and motive'. 'There is little incident,' writes W. P. Ker, 'sensibility has its own way, in monologues by the actors and digressions by the author on the nature of love. It is rather the sentiment than the passions that is here expressed in the "language of the heart", but however that may be, there are both delicacy and eloquence in the language. The pensive Fénice who debates with herself for nearly two hundred lines in one place (Chrétien de Troyes' *Cligès*, 4410–4574) is the ancestress of many late heroines.'[2] Gaston Paris states the case less enthusiastically but no less strongly. Referring to the immediate successors of Chrétien de Troyes in the twelfth and thirteenth centuries he remarks: 'L'analyse psychologique parfois très fine à laquelle, d'après l'exemple de Chrétien, ils soumettent les sentiments et surtout les conflits de sentiments de leurs personnages, ils l'expriment dans des monologues, souvent d'une subtilité fatigante, d'une forme recherchée et d'une fastidieuse longueur, mais qui souvent aussi joignent à une certaine profondeur une vraie naïveté. Par là ces romans sont les véritables précurseurs du roman moderne.'[3] And a more recent critic, Alfons Hilka, asserts with equal

---

[1] I have refrained from any extensive revision of this section in the hope of bringing it up to date in a wider context in a forthcoming book. Meanwhile some additional material will be found in my essay entitled 'From Epic to Romance' in the *Bulletin of the John Rylands Library*, vol. xlvi, No. 2, pp. 476 ff.

[2] *Epic and Romance*, p. 358.

[3] *Histoire littéraire de la France*, t. xxx, p. 16.

conviction that Chrétien's method of characterization through reflective monologues is identical with that used in the modern novel.[1]

If there is any truth in these statements, two cardinal questions come to mind: how did the poets of the courtly school, with no background of narrative literature other than the epic, come so near the modern conception of the novel? And if the similarity is no mere accident, if one genre is descended from the other, what were the stages of its descent? Neither question can be answered here fully; but as Malory's contribution to the 'story of character and motive' can only be seen against the background of these wider issues, it seems necessary to give some account of them, even at the risk of a digression *ad aliud extra materiam*.

(a) The origins of 'sentiment'

Perhaps the most obvious difference between Old French epic and romance is that the latter, not content to *narrate* events, endeavours to *interpret* them.[2] That this procedure should have been adopted in what was essentially a 'learned' type of work—and French courtly romance was primarily *un genre savant*—is not unnatural, but what made it inevitable was the intellectual background of courtly poets.[3] The search for the unexpressed meaning was perhaps

---

[1] Cf. *Die direkte Rede als stilistisches Kunstmittel in den Romanen des Kristian von Troyes* (Halle, 1903), p. 64: 'Im Volksepos bestehen sie (die Reflexionen) in der kurzen Andeutung der Gedanken der vor einem schnellen Entschlusse stehenden Person, so recht passend zur reflexionslosen Plastik des alten Liederstils; bei Kristian aber haben wir lang fortgesponnene, in spitzfindigen Betrachtungen des eigenen Ich sich gefallende und zugleich kunstvoll durchgebildete, nicht selten sogar dramatisch gestaltete Monologe. Bei ihm sind die Monologe immer ein beliebtes Kunstmittel, um uns neben seinen subjektiven (oft gleichfalls sehr ausgedehnten) Reflexionen einen Einblick in das Innere seiner Personen zu geben, die selbst ihre innersten Gedanken zergliedern und sich von ihrem quälenden Zustande voll auf- und abwogender Gedanken Rechnung ablegen, gerade wie dies in den modernen Romanen geschieht.'

[2] Cf. Joseph Bédier, *Les Légendes épiques*, t. iii, p. 418: 'Un romancier a le droit d'intervenir pour expliquer ses intentions. Homère, Virgile interviennent sans cesse; non pas Turold. Son art, sobre, elliptique, s'interdit toute glose.'

[3] The theory which holds the field at present is that the 'explanatory' lyrical monologue came from Ovid. Suggested by Gaston Paris (*Journal des Savants*, 1902) and adopted by A. Hilka (op. cit., pp. 62 and 71 ff.), this view has been substantiated with reference to the *Enéas* by Edmond Faral (*Recherches sur les sources latines des contes et romans courtois du moyen âge*, pp. 150–4). The influence of Ovid is

the principal feature of twelfth-century thought, almost equally noticeable in all spheres of learning. It may have been considered by some a waste of time to indulge in such subtleties as the attempt to find in the statement that Hyllus was the son of Hercules the inner meaning that a valid argument comes from a bold and vigorous disputant, or in the five vowels the five pleas of the crown, the names of which happened each to have a different vowel in the second syllable;[1] interpretation remained none the less the most widely recognized intellectual pursuit. Excellent practice in it was provided by *grammatica*, the first member of the Trivium, which had pride of place in the schools of Gaul from the seventh century to the eleventh and reigned supreme in the heyday of the school of Chartres, from 1050 to 1150. According to the classical definition formulated by Donatus (*scientia interpretandi poetas atque historicos et recte scribendi loquendique ratio*), repeated almost word for word in the ninth century by Rabanus Maurus,[2] and amplified by John of Salisbury in the twelfth, *grammatica* was primarily concerned with the elucidation of authors; the proper use of language, both spoken and written, was a means to this end.[3] John of Salisbury's famous chapter *De usu legendi et prelegendi* shows how the subject was taught at Chartres. Pupils were encouraged above all to develop and perfect the crude substance (*rudem materiam*) of a story or an argument 'with such abundance of learning and such elegance of composition and ornament that the work, brought to the highest perfection, seemed as it were the image of all arts'.[4] The practice of *grammatica*, *dulcis secretorum comes*,

undeniable, but it does not suffice to account for the complex processes involved in the technique of courtly narrative. What follows is but a brief summary of some of the salient points which have not so far received enough attention and with which I hope to deal more fully in a forthcoming study.

[1] John of Salisbury, *Metalogicon*, ed. C. C. J. Webb, 829 *a* (p. 10): 'Ylum esse ab Hercule, ualidum scilicet argumentum a forti et robusto argumentatore, potestates uocalium quinque iura regnorum, et in hunc modum docere omnia, studium illius etatis erat.'

[2] *De Clericorum Institutione*, III. xviii, in Migne, *Patrologia latina*, vol. cvii, col. 395 *b*.

[3] On the origin of this conception of Grammar see Karl Barwick, *Remmius Palaemon und die römische Ars Grammatika*, Leipzig, 1922.

[4] *Metalogicon*, ed. C. C. J. Webb, 854 *a–b*, p. 54: 'Illi enim per diacrisim, quam nos illustrationem siue picturationem possumus appellare, cum rudem materiam

thus instilled in the pupils' minds what few, if any, French epic poets possessed: the habit of expounding and elaborating a narrative or a discourse, of bringing out its significance, and so giving it new weight and attraction.[1] This was at first a habit of mind; but it soon became a habit of conception, equally prominent in religious and secular writings. The 'otherworldliness' of medieval preaching was not an attitude of indifference to physical facts, but a call to see through them: in St. Bernard's words, to conceive of the visible world as 'full of supernal mysteries, abounding each in its special sweetness, if the eye that beholds be but attentive';[2] and in the opening lines of the twelfth-century *Livres des Rois* the promise of a similar benefit was held out to readers of any 'simple' story:

Servants of God, listen to the story: it is very simple and seems unadorned, but it is full of meaning (*sens*) and matter. The story is chaff, the meaning wheat; the meaning is the fruit, the story the branch. This book is as a chest in which are locked the hidden things of God.[3]

Applied to narrative poetry, this attitude of mind produced at first a strangely inflated form of explanatory digression such as is found in the early *romans d'antiquité*: Ovid's story of Pyramus and Thisbe became in its twelfth-century French adaptation a series of redundant soliloquies; and in the French *Roman de Troie* Achilles, the silent lover of Polyxena, was made to describe at unnecessarily great length the devastating effects of his passion.[4] But less than two decades later, in the romances of Chrétien de Troyes,

historie aut argumenti aut fabule aliamue quamlibet suscepissent, eam tanta disciplinarum copia et tanta compositionis et condimenti gratia excolebant, ut opus consummatum omnium artium quodammodo uideretur imago.'

[1] Cf. ibid., 856 *d*, pp. 58–59: 'Ne quis tamquam parua fastidiat grammatices elementa; non quia magne sit opere discernere a uocalibus consonantes, easque ipsas in semiuocalium numerum mutarumque partiri, sed quia interiora uelut sacri huius aduentibus apparebit rerum multa subtilitas, que non modo acuere ingenia puerilia sed exercere altissimam quoque eruditionem ac scientiam possit.'

[2] *De Laudibus Virginis Matris*, in Migne, *Patrologia latina*, vol. clxxxiii, col. 56.

[3] 'Fedeil deu, entend l'estorie: asez est clere e semble nue, mais pleine est de sens et de meule. L'estorie est paille, le sen est grains; le sen est fruit, l'estorie raims. Cist livres est cum armarie des secreiz Deu' (*Livres des Rois*, ed. Curtius, p. 5). Cf. Professor W. A. Nitze's comment on this passage in his article on 'Sens et Matière', *Romania*, xliv, pp. 25–26.

[4] *Le Roman de Troie par Benoît de Sainte Maure*, ed. L. Constans, vol. iii, pp. 151 ff., ll. 17638–746.

the same method led to some truly remarkable results: in recording their reactions to each important turn of events the characters of Chrétien's stories were able to display a subtlety of thought and feeling far beyond any earlier attempts at characterization. The 'hidden things', once skilfully revealed, ceased to be a mere subject of school exercises; they became a vital element of a new form of narrative art.

But it is doubtful whether the literary genre thus created would have prospered as it did if it had not inherited at an early stage another feature of contemporary learning. If *grammatica* can be said to have shown how a given set of incidents could be explained and expanded, *rhetorica*, the second part of the Trivium, taught poets and story-tellers the proper use of imagination. The discipline which in the later Middle Ages was to be largely reduced to mere stylistic ornamentation[1] had not at that time lost its original composing function. In a number of important works embodying the doctrine of the rhetoricians from Quintilian onwards the term *colores rhetoricae* refers, as in Cicero, not so much to formal elaboration as to the 'treatment of the matter' from the speaker's or the writer's point of view. There is a significant agreement in this respect between Quintilian and the three great medieval scholars closely connected with the Gallic tradition of rhetoric: Sidonius Apollinaris, Martianus Capella, and John of Salisbury. Sidonius Apollinaris insists on the use of 'colours' because they 'provide boys' themes with pieces to weave in' and enable the orator to display his talent despite the meagreness of his case.[2] Martianus Capella in his allegorical description of the seven arts speaks of rhetoric as *rerum omnium regina* who has shown 'the power to move men whither she pleases, or whence, to bow them to tears, to incite them to rage, to transform the mien and

---

[1] Cf. Brunetto Latini, *Tresor*, ed. Chabaille, p. 486: 'Tout ce que l'om porroit en iii moz ou a moult po de paroles dire il (*le aornement*) les acroist par autres paroles plus longues et plus avenans qui dient ce meisme.' For less humorous definitions of rhetorical amplification see *Rhetorica ad Herennium*, iv. 28, and Edmond Faral, *Les Arts poétiques du XIIe et du XIIIe siècle*, pp. 61–85 *et passim*.

[2] 'Sic adulescentum declamatiunculas pannis textilibus comparantes intellegebant eloquia iuvenum laboriosius brevia produci quam porrecta succidi' (ed. Mohr, I. iv. 3). 'Sic et magnus orator, si negotium aggrediatur angustum, tunc amplum plausibilius manifestat ingenium' (ibid. VIII. x. 3).

feeling'.[1] And John of Salisbury goes so far as to attribute to rhetoric the function normally assumed by *dialectica*: he uses the term *probandi colores* in the sense of 'amplification of proof', and like his predecessors looks to rhetoric for means of persuasion.[2] Rhetoric provided prospective romance writers with three main types of exercise. First they were shown how to paraphrase some speeches in the *Aeneid* (*loci Vergiliani*); next came the *dictiones ethicae*, or soliloquies with which persons in history or mythology could be credited on certain occasions.[3] The third and most advanced stage of rhetorical training was reached in the *controversiae*, or disquisitions on general subjects, of which there are many striking examples in the letters of Sidonius Apollinaris.[4] All this was, of course, originally intended for use in discourses, not in works of fiction, but the common confusion between the notion of *narratio* ('statement of facts in a discourse') and 'narrative',[5] which can be traced as far back as Quintilian, helped to transfer to imaginative literature what was in reality a method of declamation, and the process was further facilitated by the fact that, as some passages in Sidonius clearly suggest, *declamatio* was itself treated as a literary form alongside the *epos tragoediarum*, the *comoedia*, and the *satira*.[6] Nothing seems more natural,

---

[1] 'Nam ueluti potens rerum omnium regina et impellere quo uellet et unde uellet deducere, et in lacrimas flectere et in rabiem concitare, et in alios etiam uultus sensusque conuertere tam urbes quam exercitus proeliantes, quaecumque poterat agmina populorum' (*De nuptiis Philologiae et Mercurii*, ed. Dick, vol. v, pp. 426–7).

[2] 'Siquidem Gramatica Poeticaque se totas infundunt, et eius quod exponitur totam superficiem occupant. Huic, ut dici solet, campo Logica, probandi colores afferens, suas immittit rationes in fulgore auri; et Rethorica in locis persuasionum et nitore eloquii candorem argenteum emulatur' (*Metalogicon*, ed. C. C. J. Webb, 854 *b*, p. 54).

[3] e.g. Juno's words when she saw Antaeus matched with Hercules or Thetis before the body of Achilles. Ennodius (*Dictiones* xxvii) gives as examples of this type of exercise *Verba Didonis cum abeuntem videret Aeneam*, *Verba Menelai cum Troiam videret inustam*, etc. A similar purpose was served by *sermocinatio*, one of the nineteen *colores sententiarum*, which is given considerable prominence by Geoffroi de Vinsauf in his *Poetria Nova* (1210), ll. 1265–6 and 1305–24.

[4] See also Ennodius, op. cit., xx.

[5] Johannes de Garlandia places *fabula* and *historia* among the kinds of *narratio* 'remote from legal pleading' (ed. G. Mari, *Romanische Forschungen*, xiii, p. 926).

[6]   Et nunc inflat epos tragoediarum,
    Nunc comoedia temperat iocosa,
    Nunc flammant satirae et tyrannicarum
    Declamatio controversiarum (VII. xi. 3).

therefore, than that rhetorical devices should have been used for purposes of original composition. And so, after having been trained by the grammarians to react in an articulate manner to works of Latin antiquity, romance writers were able to acquire from the rhetoricians the habit of expressing through a *fabula* or a *historia* a point of view of their own.

This habit more than any other single factor helped to shape courtly romance. Whatever the subject of the narrative, its function as conceived by twelfth- and thirteenth-century poets is to serve as an expression of a certain view of life which we usually describe as 'courtly' to translate in terms of actions and characters certain subtle varieties of sentiment and a highly sophisticated code of behaviour. A romance might recall the legendary exploits of King Arthur's knights, or some imaginary event at the court of Byzantium, or again some episode placed in a contemporary French setting; what it primarily endeavours to do is not to give an impression of life in the lands and the times to which its subject-matter ostensibly belongs, but to use this subject-matter as a means of conveying a coherent system of ideas. Hence the distinction between thought and matter so clearly expressed in the opening passage of Chrétien's *Conte de la Charrete*:

> Matiere et san l'an done et livre
> La contesse, et il s'antremet
> De panser si que rien n'i met
> Fors sa painne et s'antancion.[1]

With a modesty characteristic of contemporary etiquette Chrétien here credits his patroness, Marie de Champagne, with both the matter (*matiere*) and the spirit (*sen*) of the work. *Matiere* and *sen* are to him the two distinct constituent elements of courtly fiction. *Sen* is no longer used in the sense in which it is found in the extract from the *Livres des Rois* quoted above: it is not 'meaning' or *signification*, but the 'theme', or 'purpose', or 'intention' of the work;[2] not

---

[1] 'The countess having given him (= the poet) both the matter and the spirit [of the work], he undertakes to proceed with it adding nothing but his own labour and exertion.'

[2] *Grundidee*, according to the editor of the text, W. Foerster; *la nature de la thèse*, according to Gustave Cohen: 'la thèse qui consacre le pouvoir absolu, despotique, tyrannique de la dame sur l'amant' (*Chrétien de Troyes, sa vie et son œuvre*, pp. 226

part of a given matter, or a sense inherent in the story, but an idea brought in as it were from outside and expressed through the story, or the way in which the story has been remodelled by the poet to suit his purpose. Just as the colours of rhetoric were a means of developing and conveying the orator's conception of a case,[1] so *sen* stands here for the intellectual, emotional, and sometimes material content added by the author in accordance with his own interpretation of the original matter.

This conception of narrative had a far-reaching effect on its evolution. Superimposed as it was on the *matiere*, the *sen* was naturally regarded as something extraneous to it and therefore easily replaceable. A further consequence was this typical medieval phenomenon: the frequent recurrence of the same narrative theme with varying and sometimes conflicting 'colours' supplied by individual *remanieurs*. There is in the French twelfth- and thirteenth-century romances a striking contrast between the continuity in the transmission of the *matiere* and the corresponding degree of instability in the position of the *sen*. Lancelot's sacrifice of his knightly honour in the attempt to save Guinevere from captivity, as described in Chrétien's *Conte de la Charrete*, has a clear and unequivocal motivation: the service of love must come before all else. When Lancelot has to choose between being driven in a cart like a convict and failing to rescue his lady, he does not hesitate for more than 'two steps'; but even this momentary hesitation is enough to arouse Guinevere's anger: after rescuing her from Meleagant, Lancelot finds himself rebuked by her in spite of all the humiliations and trials he has faced for her sake, and his grief is the greater because for a long time he does not know, and cannot even guess, the cause of her displeasure. It was

and 276). In the Prologue to her *Lais* Marie de France says that 'it was the custom of the ancients to speak obscurely so that those who came after them and were to study them might construe their writing (*gloser la letre*) and add to it as they thought fit (*de lur sen le surplus metre*)'. The two processes correspond to the two varieties of *sen* noted above: the meaning implicit in the matter, and such fresh meaning or thoughts as may be added to it by the author or the *remanieur*.

[1] Gaston Boissier defines them as 'la façon dont l'orateur comprend la cause qu'il va plaider et le tour qu'il lui donne, sa manière de présenter les événements, l'attitude qu'il attribue aux personnages' ('Les Écoles de déclamation à Rome', *Revue des Deux Mondes*, 1902, t. xi, p. 491).

only natural that Chrétien's successors should have found this somewhat far-fetched; but while they objected to Chrétien's highly artificial *sen*, they found his *matiere* attractive enough to be used again. And so in the next version of the story—the thirteenth-century prose *Lancelot* —the *matiere* was reproduced and expanded, while the *sen* was altered beyond recognition. The Guinevere of the prose romance still rebukes Lancelot: this is part of the *matiere*. But she rebukes him for a very different reason. She is no longer the haughty lady of Chrétien's story with a logic that makes her actions seem unreal. Instead of blaming Lancelot for his would-be offence against the courtly code, she sends him away because she thinks that she has reason to be jealous. The readers of the prose romance no doubt preferred this simple motive to the one which had prompted Guinevere's action in Chrétien; but judged impartially, it does not blend with the narrative any more effectively than did the original theme. In nearly every important instance the same essential weakness can be observed: the *sen*, this cherished product of learning, appears as a superstructure, often attractive and significant in itself, but invariably detachable from its foundation.

If, in spite of this, courtly poetry, through its survivals and adaptations, became the ancestor of the psychological novel, it was because the two cardinal elements of modern fiction were there, even though they were lacking in cohesion and unity of purpose, as were the non-harmonized voices before the discovery of plural melody; and perhaps the main importance of Malory's work lies in the fact that it is an example of their gradual harmonization. It was in writing his two longest romances—the *Tristram* and the *Grail*— that he discovered and learned the medieval art of reinterpretation and began to discover his own way of blending matter and sentiment; and it was in his last two works— the *Book of Launcelot and Guinevere* and the *Morte Arthur*— that he was able to make the component elements of early fiction into an organic whole. This was not only, as Saintsbury and other historians of the novel have described it, a transition 'from the story of incident to the story of character and motive'; it was a new and significant attempt to

overcome an aesthetic anomaly inherent in the very foundations of medieval romance. All that made it possible is part
of a process which is well worth our understanding, for it
affects the whole development of imaginative literature. In
these pages we can do little more than notice its bare
outline, and that only so far as it is visible in Malory's great
books of Tristram, of the Grail, of Lancelot, and of Arthur.

(b) *Experiments in the use of 'sen'*

Caxton's remark that Malory took his 'copy' out of
'certain books of French' and 'reduced it into English' is a
paraphrase of two passages from Malory's book, neither
of which was intended to refer to the entire collection of his
romances. At the end of the *Book of Sir Tristram* Malory
says that it was 'drawyn oute of Freynshe'; and he con-
cludes the *Tale of the Sankgreal* by the words, 'Thus endith
the Tale of the Sankgreal that was breffly drawy[n] oute of
Freynshe'.[1] The fact that the author himself never uses the
phrase 'drawn out of French' except in reference to these two
works is no mere accident: none of his other compositions is
as fully accounted for by its sources, and none can provide
a better illustration of the twofold principle of condensed
translation.[2] This is not to say that in 'reducing' his *Tristram*
and his *Tale of the Sankgreal* from the French Malory
abandons the narrative technique which he evolved in his
earlier works; if anything, he uses more consistently, and
on a larger scale, the devices which he had occasion to
practise before, such as the telescoping of scenes and characters, the unravelling of interwoven motifs, and the division
of large compositions into smaller narrative units. But on
the whole he seems to be more inclined than ever before—
with the possible exception of the *Tale of Arthur and Lucius*
—to treat his sources as material for translation. His additions are timid in character and few in number. Never in
the whole of the *Book of Tristram* or, for that matter, in the

---

[1] Plate II. Caxton adds in each case: *in to Englysshe*.

[2] Caxton's 'to reduce' is obviously a synonym of Malory's 'to draw briefly', and
this alone should suffice to dispose of E. Brugger's suggestion that the former must
be taken to mean, in Caxton's context, 'to bring into another language without any
idea of shortening' (*Zeitschrift für französische Sprache und Literatur*, vol. li,
pp. 133–69).

Tale of the Sankgreal does he use his inventive powers as freely as he did at the end of the *Tale of King Arthur*; nor does he ever select his material with as little respect for the original as he showed in the *Tale of Sir Launcelot*. Patiently and consistently he 'draws briefly' upon the French prose *Tristan* and the *Queste del Saint Graal*. Scott's remark that 'the collection called the *Morte Arthur*' was 'extracted at hazard, and without much art or combination, from the various French prose folios',[1] is as true of these two works as it is inapplicable to most of the others.

But while doing a translator's work, Malory had neither the attitude of mind nor the temperament of a translator. However slight his alterations and additions may appear compared to the bulk of the narrative, they are enough to show that he read his sources with the inquisitiveness of an artist. He was not merely observing their manner: he was gradually and consistently fashioning his own.

One peculiarity of the French *Tristan* and of the *Queste* seems to have made a particularly strong and lasting impression on his mind. The *Queste* was a series of seemingly simple incidents which served as illustrations of a theological doctrine, and most such incidents were followed, with remarkable regularity, by a discussion of their significance. The prose *Tristan* was less consistent and correspondingly less monotonous. Its author was on the whole more concerned with the stories he had to tell than with any significance they might possess. But he could neither ignore nor indeed escape the tradition which lay immediately behind his work, the tradition of courtly romance with its characteristic use of direct speech and digression as a means of organizing and elucidating the narrative matter. And so the vast store of material which Malory found in the principal branches of the Arthurian Cycle and in the prose *Tristan* brought him face to face with the main issue of narrative art: the relation between matter and meaning. In reading the French *Tristan* and the *Queste* he realized— perhaps for the first time—that a story was incomplete without some account of its human motives or some emotional content; he also realized that neither the 'glosses' nor the

---

[1] Introduction to *Sir Tristrem*, 4th edition, Edinburgh, 1819, p. lxxxi.

themes contained in those two works were necessarily the
most appropriate or the most acceptable that could be found.
When his English predecessors—the poets who wrote
Ywain and Gawain and *Sir Gawain and the Green Knight*—
were faced with similar difficulties they generally took the
line of least resistance and dismissed the comments which
they thought unsuitable without replacing them by their
own.[1] They were, as W. P. Ker rightly remarks, 'plainly
unable to follow the French in all the effusive passages'.[2]
Malory must have experienced the same difficulty. But what
he disagreed with was not the 'effusiveness' of the French
romances, nor indeed their insistence on sentiment; his quarrel
was with the content and orientation of some of the 'effusive
passages' and with the treatment of some of the traditional
romantic themes. And so he proceeded, at first very tenta-
tively, but in the end with a genuine sense of purpose, to
remodel their *sen* and amend what Villon would have called
their *mesfait*. The most striking example of his endeavour
to reinterpret the story of Tristan and Iseult is his account
of how their love began. It will be remembered that in the
earliest version of the legend the lovers were the victims of
a magic potion which they drank by mistake on their
journey from Ireland to Cornwall, where Iseult was to marry
King Mark.[3] A later and more rationalistically minded

---

[1] The following parallel is an instance in point:

Chrétien's *Yvain*	*Ywain and Gawain*
(2639-50)	(1551 ff.)

Chrétien's *Yvain* (2639-50)	*Ywain and Gawain* (1551 ff.)
Mes sire Yvains mout a anviz	
S'est de la dame departiz	
Einsi, que li cuers ne s'an muet.	
Li rois le cors mener an puet,	No lenger wald syr
Mes del cuer n'an manra il point;	Ywayne byde,
Car si se tient et si se joint	On his stede sone gan
Au cuer celi, qui se remaint,	he stride,
Qu'il n'a pooir, que il l'an maint.	And þus he has his
Des que li cors est sanz le cuer,	leue tane.
Donc ne puet il vivre a nul fuer;	
Et se li cors sanz le cuer vit,	
Tel mervoille nus hon ne vit.	

[2] *English Literature: Mediaeval* (Home University Library), p. 108.

[3] When the hermit urges the lovers to repent Tristan says:

'Sire, par foi,
Que ele m'aime en bone foi,

[*Footnote continues on opposite page.*

poet, Thomas, seeking to avoid this purely supernatural explanation, added a new beginning: once, while Tristan was still at the court of the King of Ireland, 'Iseult beheld him with enamoured eyes'; and, in the words of Thomas's German *remanieur*, Gottfried von Strassburg, 'everything about him pleased her well, and she approved of him in her heart'.[1]

The author of the French prose romance of Tristan knew both these versions, but adopted neither. In order to account for the love motif he resorted to an expedient which was in keeping with the 'adventurous' spirit of his work, but singularly incongruous in the context of a Tristan romance: as Tristan was about to take part in the tournament of the *Château de la Lande* he realized, according to the prose writer, that another knight, Palomides (*Palamedes*), was in love with Iseult. Out of sheer love of rivalry he promptly decided to become Iseult's knight.[2] The same story reappears in Malory who knew no other version of it, but with a curious difference: Tristram's rivalry with Palomides, instead of being the motive which prompts Tristram's decision, is described as a consequence of his love for Iseult. In a passage which precedes the description of the tournament Malory remarks that Tristram 'cast great love to La Beale Isode',

for she was at that tyme the fayrest lady and maydyn of the worlde.

Vos n'entendez pas la raison:
Q'el m'aime, c'est par la poison.
Ge ne me pus de lié partir,
N'ele de moi, n'en quier mentir' (Béroul, *Tristran*, ll. 1381–6).

[1] '... gevíel ir allez an im wol und lobte ez in ir muote' (Gottfried von Strassburg, *Tristan*, ed. R. Bechstein, ll. 10006–7). The Norse Saga (*Tristrams Saga ok Isondar*, ed. E. Kölbing) describes the scene in similar terms: 'leit hun þá á hit fríða andlit hans með ástsamligum augum' (ch. xliii). Thomas's own rendering of this scene is not extant, but it can be reconstructed with tolerable certainty from these two adaptations.

[2] 'Tant regarde Palamedes Yseult que Tristan s'en aperchoit a son semblant qu'il l'ayme de tout son cuer. Tristan si l'avoit par maintes fois regardee, maiz ce n'estoit pas pour amour qu'il y eust. Et puis qu'il vist que Palomedes la regardoit si merveilleusement, il dit qu'il l'avra ou qu'il mourra, ne ja Palomedes pour povoir qu'il ait n'y avendra' (MS. B.N. fr. 103, f. 39ʳ, col. 1). Paraphrasing this passage, E. Löseth (*Le Roman en prose de Tristan, analyse critique d'après les manuscrits de Paris*, p. 22) writes: 'Tristan, qui jusque-là n'avait guère éprouvé de sentiments pour elle, s'éprend sérieusement en voyant l'amour de Palamède.'

And there Tramtryste lerned hir to harpe, and she began to have a grete fantasy unto hym.[1]

It is not until the next paragraph that we are told how Palomides 'drew unto La Beale Isode and proffered her many gifts', and how Tristram 'espied' him:

And wete you well sir Tramtryste had grete despyte at sir Palomydes, for La Beale Isode tolde Tramtryste that Palomydes was in wyll to be crystynde for hir sake. Thus was there grete envy betwyxte Tramtryste and sir Palomydes.

In this way the normal sequence of incidents is re-established and the true 'colour' restored. The love motif, instead of being a mere adjunct to chivalric contests, becomes once more the dominating theme. Nor is this the only instance of Malory's preference for emotional motivation. The first parting of the lovers,[2] Tristram's madness, his life in the wilderness,[3] his recognition by Isode in the garden of Tintagel, when she begs him to leave her and 'grant King Mark his will' in order to save his own life,[4] all these and other similar episodes acquire in Malory's rendering a new meaning. They are among his finest contributions to the otherwise uninspired matter of his *Book of Sir Tristram*.[5]

[1] *Infra*, p. 385.   [2] *Infra*, p. 392.

[3] *Infra*, p. 496: 'So thys lady and damesell brought hym mete and drynke, but he ete lityll thereoff. Than uppon a nyght he put hys horse frome hym and unlaced hys armoure, and so yeode unto the wyldirnes and braste downe the treys and bowis. And othirwhyle, whan he founde the harpe that the lady sente hym, than wolde he harpe and play thereuppon and wepe togydirs. And somtyme, whan he was in the wood, the lady wyst nat where he was. Than wolde she sette hir downe and play uppon the harpe, and anone sir Trystramys wolde com to the harpe and harkyn thereto, and somtyme he wolde harpe hymselff. Thus he there endured a quarter off a yere, and so at the laste he ran hys way and she wyst nat where he was becom.'

[4] *Infra*, p. 502. Isode adds these words, 'And ever whan I may I shall sende unto you, and whan ye lyste ye may com unto me, and at all tymes early and late I woll be at youre commaundement, to lyve as poore a lyff as ever ded quyene or lady.'

[5] It is of course possible to set against these passages a number of equally 'effusive' ones which Malory has mercilessly cut out. In describing the days when the lovers were free from suspicion and restraint the French prose-writer says: 'oncques mes ne furent tant aise com si sont orendroit, car, quant il vont ore recordant les maux et les paines que chascun a souffert endroit soi, et il se voient ensemble, que il poent fere toute lor volenté, il dient que il fussent buer nes s'il peussent toz jor mes vivre et mener tel joie et tel feste.' Malory writes instead: 'Than sir Trystram used dayly and nyghtely to go to quene Isode whan he myght.' But this only goes to show that while adopting the French author's method Malory used it in his own way and for his own purposes. For further examples see Commentary, notes 592. 4–14 and 779. 16–18.

But perhaps the type of 'colour' that Malory uses most effectively is the half-humorous dialogue—his favourite form of narrative ornamentation. Its purpose is the same as that of a digression or a monologue, namely to give the narrative some human interest. Here is one example out of many. Tristram tells Isode that they must both attend a gathering at Arthur's court 'at Pentecost nexte folowynge'. ' "Sir", seyde dame Isode, "and hyt please you, I woll nat be there, for thorow me ye bene marked of many good knyghtes, and that causyth you for to have much more laboure for my sake than nedyth you to have" '—a surprising thought for a courtly lady: instead of encouraging her knight to perform feats of prowess on her behalf she seems to object to any excess of 'labour for her sake'; she is clearly more concerned about Tristram's safety than about his fighting record. But she is by no means indifferent to his reputation, and when Tristram refuses to go without her ('Than woll I nat be there but yf ye be there') she urges him to do his social duty:

'God deffende', seyde La Beall Isode, 'for than shall I be spokyn of shame amonge all quenys and ladyes of astate; for ye that ar called one of the nobelyste knyghtys of the worlde and a knyght of the Rounde Table, how may ye be myssed at the feste? For what shall be sayde of you amonge all knyghtes? "A! se how sir Trystram huntyth and hawkyth, and cowryth within a castell wyth hys lady, and forsakyth us. Alas!" shall som sey, "hyt ys pyté that ever he was knyght, or ever he shulde have the love of a lady." Also, what shall quenys and ladyes say of me? "Hyt ys pyté that I have my lyff, that I wolde holde so noble a knyght as ye ar frome hys worshyp." '

'So God me helpe', seyde sir Trystram unto La Beall Isode, 'hyt ys passyngly well seyde of you and nobely counceyled. And now I well undirstonde that ye love me.'[1]

Chrétien de Troyes uses a very similar 'colour' in his *Erec et Enide*[2] to motivate the subsequent adventures of his hero. Here it has no such purpose. The dialogue is

[1] *Infra*, pp. 839–40.
[2] Cf. lines 2561–5:

Blasmee an sui, ce poise moi,
Et dïent tuit reison por quoi,
Que si vos ai lacié et pris
Que tot an perdez vostre pris,
Ne ne querez a el antandre.

designed merely to throw some light on Isode's character. She is neither the 'Iseut douloureuse et forte' of the old poems, nor the sophisticated courtly queen of the French prose romance, but an affectionate and ingenious *amie*, devoted enough to put Tristram's comfort and safety before excessive bravery, and yet thoughtful enough to protect his and her good name. It is she who begs Tristram, on another occasion, to carry arms when he goes hunting in the forest, a precaution which in the French romance he takes of his own accord.[1] Such details are few and far between; but they suggest important possibilities.

As for the *Book of Sir Tristram* as a whole, it remains true that in reinterpreting the story in his own way, as each medieval writer had done before him, Malory failed to give it a meaning, a *sen*, capable of supporting its complex and delicate narrative frame. He failed above all to grasp and bring out the tragic theme, essential to any coherent form of the Tristan legend and still discernible in its prose version.[2] Mark is Tristan's overlord whom he respects, as he respects the bond of feudal service. 'Il ne conteste pas', writes Joseph Bédier, 'la loi de l'honneur vassalique, il la viole et, la violant, il souffre.' Without this notion of an involuntary breach of a sacred tie the traditional *données* of the legend cannot survive. Already in the French prose romance an important change takes place: love, instead of being the cause of an insoluble conflict, becomes the sacred obligation of a knight-errant; from being *un pechié* (the word in Old French characteristically combines the meanings of 'sin' and 'misfortune') it becomes a virtue, and the story of Tristan and Iseult degenerates into a much protracted heroic comedy, in which the heroes successfully outwit the villains. Mark, instead of being an intensely human and almost likeable character, turns into a traitor, and the whole moral weight of Arthurian knighthood is thrown against him. In opposing him Tristan violates no sacred trust; he merely upholds

---

[1] Cf. *infra*, p. 757, and MS. B.N. fr. 99, f. 409ʳ, col. 1.

[2] Cf. the remarks on the love potion (MS. B.N. fr. 103, f. 56ᵛ, col. 1): 'Yseut boit. Ha! Dieu! Quel boire! Or sont entrez en la rote qui ja mais ne leur fauldra jour de leur vies, car ilz ont beü leur destruction et leur mort. Cil boire leur a semblé bon et moult doulz, mais oncques doulceur ne fu si chier achetee comment ceste sera.'

his own honour and the rights of 'true love'. In all this Malory whole-heartedly follows his source; it is with genuine delight that he relates the blissful retirement of the lovers to Joyous Gard and leaves them there at the close of the romance so that, in his favourite phrase, they may live 'cheerfully' for ever after. The happy ending is achieved here as in the *Tale of King Arthur and the Emperor Lucius* by the omission of the concluding portion of the original: 'Here endyth the secunde boke off Syr Trystram de Lyones whyche drawyn was oute of Freynshe by Sir Thomas Malleorré, knyght, as Jesu be hys helpe. Amen. But here ys no rehersall of the thirde booke.' The 'thirde booke' contained, among other things, the story of the death of the lovers,[1] but Malory prefers to end the work with a picture of their happiness in their peaceful abode: 'And than sir Trystram returned unto Joyous Garde, and sir Palomydes folowed after the ques-tynge beste.' In all essentials, then, Malory's *Tristram* is but another example of a medieval romance in which the author's *sen* fails to harmonize with the *matiere*, and the fairest approach to it is to regard it not as an achievement, but as an experiment: as the first and necessarily timid attempt at reinterpreting a traditional narrative.

When, after the *Tristan*, Malory turned to the *Queste del Saint Graal* he found himself more out of his element than ever before. With the *Tristan* he may have occasionally disagreed, but the story was not in itself alien to his tastes and tendencies: it belonged to a world in which he could live and move freely, even though it was not his own. With the *Queste* he entered a totally unfamiliar sphere. It was not merely a work of religious inspiration: it was a dogmatic exposition of a doctrine. In a long series of sermons to which the characters patiently listened in the intervals of their monotonous wanderings, it put forward and illustrated the

---

[1] That Malory knew this ending is shown by his reference to it in the *Healing of Sir Urry* (p. 1149): 'Also that traytoure kynge slew the noble knyght sir Trystram as he sate harpynge afore hys lady, La Beall Isode, with a trenchaunte glayve, for whos dethe was the moste waylynge of ony knyght that ever was in kynge Arthurs dayes.' This is not, of course, the 'pathetic and imaginative story of the black sail', but a reminiscence of its more realistic rendering in the French prose romance. On the prose writer's attitude and method see my *Études sur le Tristan en prose*, pp. 17–20.

notion that the coming of the Grail was the final and irre-
vocable test of good and evil and the triumph of heavenly
over earthly chivalry. For this kind of 'interpretation'
Malory had little use; but instead of replacing it by his
own, he simply 'reduced' all doctrinal comment, shifted
the emphasis from theological disquisitions to poetical re-
presentation, and so made the Grail quest appear as a mere
pageant of picturesque visions. Such at least is the immediate
impression one gets from a comparison of his work with the
French *Queste*, and to some readers it may be a relief to
find that Malory spares them the unnecessary elaboration
of 'symbolic adventures and still more symbolic visions, with
a hermit waiting at every road-side to expound the symbolism
in the bitterest detail'.[1] 'Do not our hearts,' asks Sir Edmund
Chambers, 'in these long books, sometimes go down the
hill with Gawain?' There is, perhaps, more to it than that.[2]
It may well be, as C. S. Lewis pointed out in a memorable
essay,[3] that Malory is not simply *for* the Round Table
and *against* the Grail, that he has 'a three-storeyed mind
—a scale of bad-good-best (Mark—Lancelot—Galahad)'.
The fact remains that while he is perfectly serious about
the nobility of Lancelot and of Arthurian chivalry, he
is simply not concerned with the yet higher law which cuts
across the courtly world in the Grail books. In the French
Queste Lancelot appears as a sinner who has offended God
in his earlier life by adopting the standards of *courtoisie*: if he
is more favourably treated than some other sinners, it is not
because his former life was better than theirs, but because he
is willing to repent. He is a clear illustration of a dichotomy
of worldly and spiritual, pointing 'from the way of earthly
achievement to the way of spiritual illumination'.[4] With this
point of view Malory has little sympathy. He reproduces
both the condemnation and the contrition of Lancelot, but

---

[1] E. K. Chambers, *Sir Thomas Wyatt and Some Collected Essays*, p. 32.

[2] Possibly more than I imagined when I wrote in my monograph on Malory
that 'faced with two main themes and forced to subordinate one, Malory made
Corbenic a province of Camelot' (*Malory*, p. 84). See Arthur B. Ferguson, *The
Indian Summer of English Chivalry*, pp. 51–56, for a careful and balanced reassess-
ment of Malory's 'secularity'.

[3] Review of *Sir Thomas Wyatt*, etc., in *Medium Aevum*, vol. iii (1934), pp. 238–9.

[4] E. K. Chambers, loc. cit.

sets them against the background of Lancelot's glorious
deeds in the days before the Quest, so that his former fame
may be constantly borne in mind. When Lancelot is told
that he will 'never see of the Sankgreall more than he has
seen', his answer is, 'Now I thanke God for Hys grete
mercy of that I have sene, for hit suffisith me. For, as I
suppose, no man in thys worlde have lyved bettir than I
have done to enchyeve that I have done.' This does not
mean that a triple scale of values is introduced where the
French author is using only a double one;[1] it means that if
there were a conflict, it would be between 'good' and 'best',
not between 'good' and 'bad'. But no such conflict exists
in Lancelot's mind. He is not seen in Malory, as he so often
is in the French *Queste*, in an attitude of abject humiliation.
He knows that his former life was 'good'; and it matters
little to him that because it was not 'best' the supreme reward
of the Grail is denied him. Hence a significant misrepre-
sentation of the theological issue, and a new treatment of the
character of the protagonist. The author of the *Queste*,
imbued with Cistercian mysticism, would no doubt have
severely censured Malory's frequent confusion of *chevalerie
celestienne* with 'virtuous living'[2] and denounced as sacri-
legious the scene in which the sick knight goes on his hands
and knees 'so nyghe that he towched the holy vessel and
kyst hit'.[3] But all this helps to place the action on a human
level. While in the French the singing of the birds is but
a means of bringing home to Lancelot his sense of wretched-
ness,[4] in Malory the same experience 'comforts' him: 'So
thus he sorowed tyll hit was day, and harde the fowlys synge;
than somwhat he was comforted.'[5] And when in the adventure of the magic ship he achieves what by the standards of
the *Queste* is a state of grace, Malory sends him off 'to play

[1] I cannot follow C. S. Lewis in his attempt to attribute the triple scale of
values to 'mediaeval writers' generally (loc. cit.). There is no such scale in the
French *Queste*. Cf. A. Pauphilet, *Études sur la Queste del Saint Graal*, p. 17.

[2] Cf. Commentary, notes 886. 18 and 891. 32–33.

[3] Cf. *infra*, p. 894. According to the *Queste*, no one can touch the Grail, and
the sick knight only touches the table on which the Grail stands: 'fait tant qu'il
baise la table d'argent *et touche a ses yeulx*.'

[4] The bright spring morning and the sunshine make him realize that 'Nostre
Sire s'est courrouciés a lui'.

[5] *Infra*, p. 896.

by the watirs syde, *for he was somwhat wery of the shippe*'.[1] The most striking 'colour' in Malory's treatment of Lancelot is, however, the concluding passage of the *Tale*, deliberately added to make him appear in all his human greatness, undiminished by his experiences in the course of the Grail-quest:

. . . than sir Launcelot tolde the adventures of the Sangreall that he had sene. And all thys was made in the grete bookes and put up in almeryes at Salysbury. And anone sir Bors seyde to sir Launcelot, 'Sir Galahad, youre owne sonne, salewed you by me, and aftir you my lorde kynge Arthure and all the hole courte. And so ded sir Percivale. For I buryed them both myne owne hondis in the cité of Sarras. Also, sir Launcelot, sir Galahad prayde you to remembir of thys unsyker worlde, as ye behyght hym when ye were togydirs more than halffe a yere.' 'Thys ys trew', seyde sir Launcelot, 'now I truste to God hys prayer shall avayle me.' Than sir Launcelot toke sir Bors in hys armys and seyde, 'Cousyn, ye ar ryght wellcom to me! For all that ever I may do for you and for yours, ye shall fynde my poure body redy atte all tymes whyle the spyryte is in hit, and that I promyse you feythfully, and never to fayle. And wete ye well, gentyl cousyn sir Bors, that ye and I shall never departe in sundir whylis oure lyves may laste.'[2]

This, like most of Malory's additions, contradicts both the letter and the spirit of the French. Not only does the *Queste* omit to mention Lancelot at this point, but the part which it assigns to him throughout the story would preclude him from joining the Grail knights—Galahad, Perceval, and Bors—and placing on record the events of the holy quest. No such obstacle exists in Malory's version: Lancelot remains to the end the dominating figure, and because he is spared the impersonal fate of a condemned sinner, he develops into something approaching a living character. No doubt, he speaks like a man who knows the significance of the mysteries which have been revealed to him. But his last promise to Bors—'never to depart in sundir' while their lives last—comes primarily from a faithful friend, from a true champion of all the good and noble knights of King Arthur, more conscious than ever of the bond which unites him to the other heroes of the great adventure, 'redy atte all tymes' while the spirit lives in his 'poure body'. These may

[1] *Infra*, pp. 1011–12.   [2] *Infra*, pp. 1036–7.

be but occasional glimpses of character; but the rudiments of the art are there, and the sentiments brought into play are sufficiently true and delicate to remain attached to the story and its protagonist. They are of the order of those 'familiar manifestations of emotions' which, in Aristotle's words, 'carry conviction'.

(c) The Tragic Conception

If Malory's rejection of the theology of the *Queste* set him free to attempt a delineation of character, it led to an even more striking result in his adaptation of the next and last branch of the Cycle, the *Mort Artu*. The decisive factor in his approach to this work was his drastic simplification of the spiritual tangle in which the traditional story of Arthur had become involved. In the chronicles of Geoffrey of Monmouth and of Wace the downfall of Arthur's kingdom had no relation to any religious or moral doctrine: it was a typical epic story of the 'defence of a narrow place against odds'. But when in the second quarter of the thirteenth century French prose writers introduced it in the Arthurian Cycle and placed it immediately after the *Queste* they found it necessary to read a new meaning into it. The *Queste* condemned the Round Table in no uncertain terms: 'In this quest your knighthood will avail you nothing if the Holy Ghost does not open the way for you in all your adventures.' The knights destined to achieve the holy quest —*li encerchemenz des grans secrez et des privetez Nostre Seignor*[1]—were those who had hitherto had little or no part in the adventures of the Round Table: Galahad, Bors, and Perceval. The great heroes of Arthurian chivalry were disqualified either wholly, like Gawain, or partly, like Lancelot, who was permitted to enter the Grail castle, but not to see the Grail or even cross the threshold of the sanctuary. It was only natural, therefore, that the compilers of the Cycle should have imagined that in the end the Round Table perished because it had offended God. Thus a link was established between the religious teaching of the *Queste* and the events related in the *Mort Artu*. The issue was complicated rather than clarified by the addition of the 'wheel of

[1] 'The seeking out of the high secrets and hidden things of our Lord.'

Fortune' motif. To this the author of the *Mort Artu* gave considerable prominence. The idea of the relentless motion of the fatal wheel causing the downfall of those who rise too high—a christianized conception of *Fortuna*—had been common enough throughout the Middle Ages,[1] but it was quite distinct from the doctrine of the *Queste*. As, however, it provided an additional reason for the fall of Arthur it was tacked on to the story with the result that in the *Mort Artu* the disaster was interpreted partly as a retribution for the sins of Arthur's knights and partly as a sequel to their rise: 'Tel sont li orgueil terrien qu'il n'i a nul si haut assiz qu'il ne le conviegne cheoir de la poesté del monde.'[2]

Of this elaborate attempt to give the story of Arthur's death a spiritual background nothing of importance remains in Malory's version.[3] Despite the French Cycle he treats the *Queste* and the *Mort Artu* as self-contained works and suppresses the most important links between them.[4] To understand his account of the tragedy of Lancelot and of the destruction of the Round Table it is enough to read his last two romances, *The Book of Sir Launcelot and Queen Guinevere* and the *Morte Arthur*, which seemed to be closely linked in his mind.[5] The *Morte Arthur* is built round a theme which

[1] On its diffusion see R. Patch, *The Goddess Fortuna in Mediaeval Literature*, Harvard University Press, 1927. On the treatment of the theme in the *Mort Artu* see Jean Frappier, *Étude sur la Mort le Roi Artu*, pp. 258 ff.

[2] *La Mort le Roi Artu*, ed. Frappier, p. 201. Cf. also the editor's remark in his *Étude*, etc., p. 288: 'L'auteur a repris à sa façon l'idée de la fatalité antique: il ne pouvait guère l'envisager que dans les limites de la religion. Mais cette contrainte relative n'a peut-être pas nui à la richesse psychologique de son œuvre, car elle ajoute des nuances chrétiennes au vieux thème du Destin.'

[3] The description of the wheel of Fortune seen by Arthur in his dream is reproduced, but all comment is omitted, and no attempt is made to relate the symbolism of the wheel to Arthur's fate.

[4] C. S. Lewis (loc. cit.) thought that it was an 'essential part of the tragedy of Launcelot that he should be given the chance of escaping from this human level on which tragedy is foredoomed, and should have failed to take it'. This is probably true of the French Cycle, but there is no evidence that Malory held any such view or that he regarded Lancelot's return to Guinevere as a 'relapse'. Rightly or wrongly he refrained from relating the tragedy of Lancelot to his condemnation in the *Queste*, and the references to the *Tale of the Sankgreal* in the opening paragraphs of the *Book of Launcelot and Guinevere* have no 'moral' significance.

[5] This is partly the effect of Malory's choice and arrangement of the material he found in his sources. The *Book of Launcelot and Guinevere* is based on two French romances: the *Mort Artu*, and a still undiscovered version of the prose *Lancelot*. It was also probably influenced by the English stanzaic *Le Morte Arthur*. The

is suggested in the seemingly disconnected episodes of the *Book of Launcelot and Guinevere*: in the opening dialogue between Lancelot and Guinevere, in the story of the maid of Astolat, and in the adventure of the Knight of the Cart. On the familiar bright landscape with its smiling meadows, on the glittering armour of knights riding in search of adventure, dark and ominous shadows begin to fall. We no longer see Arthur's companions perform endless feats of bravery; we hear less of their glorious record, of their ultimate reward. Lancelot is still the greatest of all knights; but with each new episode he seems to lose something of his early enthusiasm, of his faith in the glory of knight-errantry.[1] 'Do ye forthynke yourselff of youre dedis?' Guinevere asks him. There is a strange foreboding in these simple words. The last adventure in the *Book of Launcelot and Guinevere* shows Lancelot at the height of his knightly renown. Of all the knights of the Round Table he alone is privileged to heal the wounds of Sir Urry. But when the adventure is over, 'Sir Launcelot wepte as he had bene a chyld that had bene betyn'. The peripety, the final reversal of fortunes, is now upon us.[2] It is brought to its climax in the terms of the traditional story of the downfall of Arthur's kingdom, reinterpreted and reshaped in accordance with Malory's own *sen*.[3] Geoffrey of Monmouth had been the first to describe how Arthur, having subdued the peoples of the British Isles, was crowned in Caerleon upon Usk, how he then extended his sway to Norway, to Gaul, and to Rome,

Morte Arthur is derived partly from that poem and partly from the French *Mort Artu*. Malory used these two texts simultaneously, with a degree of freedom and independence unparalleled in his earlier works.

[1] There is a similar development in the *Mort Artu*, but it is treated as a consequence of Lancelot's experiences in the quest of the Grail. 'Il n'ose pas recommencer au su de tous ses exploits chevaleresques ni se montrer publiquement soucieux de cette gloire mondaine si contraire à l'esprit de la *Quête*. Amour-propre, pudeur morale, scrupule religieux peut-être, Lancelot éprouve à la fois tous ces sentiments' (Jean Frappier, *Étude sur la Mort le Roi Artu*, p. 230).

[2] E. K. Chambers, loc. cit.

[3] In my monograph on Malory (Oxford, 1929) I took the view that Malory merely disengaged the dramatic curve from unnecessary ramifications and by so doing produced his 'New Arthuriad' (pp. 95 ff.). This no longer seems to me to do him justice. Mere condensation of narrative is too mechanical a process to account for what appears to be, in the light of a more detailed study, the essential quality of his rendering. The difference between him and his predecessors is not in the *matiere* alone; it lies predominantly in the *sen*.

how during the Roman campaign his nephew Mordred started a rebellion, and how on his return to England Arthur fell in the final contest with the traitor. French prose writers had endeavoured to give this story a deeper significance by complicating both its narrative content and its motivation, and above all by linking it up with the spiritual doctrine of the Grail and with the symbolism of the 'wheel of Fortune'. Malory went further. Outwardly his *Most Piteous Tale of the Morte Arthur Saunz Guerdon* may seem to be a mere abridgement of the French *Mort Artu*, supplemented by drafts on the English stanzaic *Le Morte Arthur*; in actual fact it is a work of striking originality. Its dominating theme is neither a mere accident of warfare as in the Arthurian chronicles, nor as in the *Mort Artu* a spiritual ideal enhanced by the vision of the fatal wheel, but a tragic conflict of two loyalties, both deeply rooted in the medieval conception of knightly service: on the one hand, the heroic loyalty of man to man, 'the mutual love of warriors who die together fighting against odds', a loyalty 'more passionate and less ideal than our patriotism',[1] more sacred even than the ties of nature;[2] on the other, the blind devotion of the knight-lover to his lady, the romantic self-denial imposed by the courtly tradition and inseparable from any form of courtly romance. The clash between these conceptions of human love and service is neither an accident nor a caprice of destiny; it is inherent in the very structure of medieval idealism. And in Malory's rendering of the story of Arthur's death it brings about, for the first time in the history of the legend, a clear and convincing interplay of emotions, infinitely more significant than any encounter with chance.

This result is achieved by subtle, yet simple, means. The essential motif—the breach of one sacred trust through a whole-hearted acceptance of another—was already implicit in the French *Mort Artu* and in the English *Le Morte Arthur*. But each of the two conflicting forces—the power of the love of man for man and the power of courtly devotion—had to be brought out more emphatically. It was not enough that

---

[1] C. S. Lewis, *Allegory of Love*, p. 10.
[2] Cf. A. J. Carlyle, *Mediaeval Political Theory in the West*, vol. iii, p. 25.

in rescuing Guinevere Lancelot should have unwittingly killed Gawain's half-anonymous brothers as he does in Malory's sources; one of his victims had to be Gareth, the noble knight who loved Lancelot 'bettir than all hys brethirn and the kynge bothe'.[1] This is part of Malory's own narrative design, of a *sen* unknown to his models, as original as Lancelot's premonition of the coming disaster: 'And peradventure I shall there destroy som of my beste fryndis, and that shold moche repente me. And peradventure there be som, and they coude wel brynge it aboute, or disobeye my lord kynge Arthur, they wold sone come to me, the which I were loth to hurte.'[2] But Lancelot's duty is clear, even though 'that ys hard for to do'.[3] When the news is brought to Gawain that his brothers Gaheris and Gareth have been killed by Lancelot, he at first refuses to believe it. He is bound to Lancelot by ties of friendship and comradeship which have so far stood the hardest tests. He has forgiven him the deaths of Agravain, of Florens, and of Lovell, even though Arthur had told him that he had 'no cause to love Lancelot'. But when he knows for certain that his two beloved brothers, Gaheris and Gareth, are dead, he makes a vow upon which eventually the fortunes of the whole of Arthur's kingdom will break: 'From thys day forewarde I shall never fayle sir Launcelot untyll that one of us have slayne the othir.'[4] The fratricidal struggle then begins, with each opponent keenly conscious of his profound attachment to the other. 'I requyre and beseche you', says Lancelot,[5] 'sytthyn that I am thus requyred and conjoured to ryde into the fylde, that neyther you, my lorde kyng Arthur, nother you, sir Gawayne, com nat into the fylde.' And when he is forced to fight his dearest friend, Gawain, to throw him off his horse and wound him, he still refuses to put him to death, for it is shame 'to smite a wounded man that may not stand'.[6]

---

[1] *Infra*, p. 1185.
[2] *Infra*, p. 1172.   [3] *Infra*, p. 1173.   [4] *Infra*, p. 1186.
[5] There is no counterpart to this speech in Malory's sources.
[6] The reason given in the French *Mort Artu* is slightly different: 'De ce est Lancelos trop dolenz, car il ne volsist en nule maniere que messire Gauvains moreust par lui; car il l'avoit tant esprouvé qu'il ne cuidoit pas au matin qu'il eüst en li tant de proesce comme il i avoit le jor trovee; et ce fu li hom del monde qui plus ama bons chevaliers que Lancelos' (ed. Frappier, pp. 176–7).

But the harm is done. Gawain dies of his wound, repenting on his death-bed of his 'hastiness and wilfulness': 'For I am smyten upon the old wounde the whiche sir Launcelot gave me, on the which I fele well I muste dye. And had sir Launcelot bene with you, as he was, this unhappy werre had never begonne, and of all thys I am causar.' The 'unhappy war' is not at an end, and the 'piteous tale' goes on until the Round Table becomes a mere memory. Early in the day Arthur knows that disaster is at hand: 'Wyte you wel, my herte was never so hevy as hit ys now. And much more I am soryar for my good knyghtes losse than for the losse of my fayre queene; for quenys I myght have inow, but such felyship of good knyghtes shall never be togydirs in no company.' Only Malory's Arthur can say with such characteristic abruptness, 'quenys I myght have inow'; but perhaps for this very reason only Malory's Arthur can gauge the full depth of his grief at the destruction of his fellowship, the equal of which has not been seen in any Christian land, and the significance of his own defeat by the traitor Mordred in that last of all battles when 'of all the good knights are left no more alive but two', and a hundred thousand lie dead upon the down. The action which leads to this ending is swift, inevitable, relentless; the circle of fear and pity is complete. And the aftermath brings home the profound humanity of it all. When Lancelot comes to avenge the King and the Queen he finds that the Queen has retired from the world. To share her fate he becomes a hermit; not for the love of God, but for the love of the Queen: 'And therefore, lady, sithen you have taken you to perfection I must needs take me to perfection of right.' A year later he is allowed to bury her. And although it may be as a hermit that at first 'he wepte not gretelye, but syghed', it is as her faithful lover that 'when she was put in the erth syr Launcelot swouned and laye longe stylle'. To the hermit who reproves him for thus displeasing God he replies:

'My sorow may never have ende, for whan I remembre of his beaulté and of hir noblesse that was bothe wyth hyr Kyng and wyth hyr, so whan I sawe his corps and hir corps so lye togyders, truly myn herte wold not serve to susteyne my careful body. Also whan I remembre me how by my defaute and myn orgule and my pryde that they were bothe layed ful lowe that were pereles that ever was lyvyng of Cristen people, wyt you wel,' sayd syr Launcelot, 'this remembred of there kyndenes and myn unkyndenes sanke so to myn herte that I myght not susteyne myself.'

He repents not of the sins he has committed against God, but of the griefs he has caused his lady and King Arthur. And so there is no relief to his pain: 'Ever he was lyeng grovelyng on the tombe of kyng Arthur and queen Guenever, and there was no comforte that the bysshop nor syr Bors nor none of his felowes coude make hym, it avaylled not.' Death alone brings him comfort, and as he lay on his death-bed it seemed as though 'he had smyled, and the sweetest savour aboute hym'. In the earlier scene of Arthur's last farewell there is the same sense of unrelieved loneliness. 'Comfort thyself', Arthur says to Bedwere, 'and doo as wel as thou mayst, for in me is no truste for to truste in. For I wyl to the vale of Avylyon to hele me of my grievous wounds.' There is no remedy for Arthur's wounds, and no truth in the belief in his eventual return. 'I wyl not say that it shal be so.' And when night falls on the plain of Salisbury there is no 'trust left to trust in', no comfort to be found in religious explanations; all doctrine shrivels before the conflict of 'two goods' and the desolation it brings. It is not through sin or weakness of heart that this comes about, but through the devotion of the truest friend and the truest lover, through a tragic greatness which fixes for ever the complex and delicate meaning of Arthur's epic. And in the noble close of Malory's final chapter, in the threnody of Hector over Lancelot's dead body, the pure and passionate chord is struck again, enriched and sustained by harmonies unknown to lesser writers: 'Thou, sir Launcelot, there thou lyest, that thou were never matched of erthely knyghtes hande! And thou were the curtest knyght that ever bare shelde, and thou were the truest frende to thy lover that ever bestrade hors, and thou were the trewest lover of a synful man that ever loved woman, and thou were the kyndest man that ever strake wyth swerde.'

CHAPTER IV

THE METHOD OF EDITING

1. *The Texts*

FOR four and a half centuries the nearest any reader could get to Malory's text was Caxton's edition 'enprynted and fynysshed in thabbey of Westmestre the last day of Juyl the yere of our Lord MCCCCLXXXV'. The edition was based on a 'copye' which Sir Thomas Malory had 'taken out of certeyn bookes of Frensshe and reduced into Englysshe'. In his Preface, where this remark occurs, Caxton does not say that he received the 'copye' direct from Malory, and the chronological gap between Malory's death in 1471 and the publication of the work in 1485 would seem to suggest that he did not. Nor does it follow from Caxton's statement that the 'copye' he used was Malory's original manuscript. But as until recently no manuscript of Malory has been known to exist, all the editions published from the fifteenth century to the present day had to depend either directly or indirectly on Caxton's. Their history is uneventful. Only two copies of Caxton's print are extant: one in the Pierpont Morgan Library in New York, the other, wanting eleven leaves,[1] in the John Rylands Library in Manchester. Each of these, however, represents a slightly different 'state' of the text: corrections at Caxton's printing house were not limited to proofs, but were made in the formes after printing off had begun, with the result that in the two extant copies of the *Morte Darthur* there are four folios in which conflicting readings occur in practically every line.[2] In addition to this, there are thirty-two minor variants elsewhere, mostly in small batches. It was some such 'state' of the work that Caxton's disciple and successor Wynkyn de Worde used for his 1498 edition of the *Booke of the Noble Kyng, Kyng*

---

[1] Sig. li, rvi, rvii, Nii, Nvii, Tiiij, Tv, eeiii–vi. These have been replaced by Whittaker's somewhat imperfect facsimiles. See Bibliography.

[2] For a fuller account of the problem see Bibliography.

Arthur. In 1529 he issued another, which was used by the two subsequent editors, William Copland (1557) and Thomas East (*c.* 1585). A 'newly refined' version of Thomas East's text appeared in 1634 at William Stansby's press. This was the last of the black-letter editions, and in spite of its obvious remoteness from the original it held the field until the second half of the last century[1] as 'the latest of the old prints', 'with a sprinkling of obsolete words, not sufficiently numerous to be embarrassing'.[2] A radical change in editorial practice was made in 1868 by Edward Strachey.[3] Realizing that 'nothing could justify the reprinting of the most corrupt of all the old editions when the first and the best was within reach', he went back to Caxton, and his example was soon followed by H. Oskar Sommer. The word-for-word reprint of the Rylands (then Spencer) copy which appeared in Sommer's monumental work on the *Morte Darthur* (1889–91) has since been used by the vast majority of Malory's editors.[4] Their return to Caxton was certainly welcome in that it helped to remove from the text the alterations introduced by Wynkyn de Worde and his successors. But the text still provided no answer to these vital questions: How different was Caxton's 'copye' from Malory's? And how far did Caxton alter it when he prepared it for the press?

Such was the position until 23 July 1934 when Dr. W. F. Oakeshott announced in *The Times* the discovery of a hitherto unidentified paper manuscript of Malory's writings belonging to the Fellows' Library of Winchester College.[5] In an article published a month later (*The Times*, 27 August 1934) Dr. Oakeshott stated that the manuscript contained no indication of early ownership, its binding being comparatively modern, that the 1630 catalogue of the College library made no mention of it, and that the first entry was found in the

---

[1] The only exception is Southey's edition (1817) based partly on Caxton and partly on Wynkyn de Worde.

[2] Cf. *La Mort d'Arthure*, &c., ed. Thomas Wright (1856 and 1866), Introduction.

[3] *Morte Darthur*, &c., ed. Edward Strachey, p. xxxiv.

[4] A reprint of Wynkyn de Worde's first edition was published by the Shakespeare Head Press in 1933.

[5] The discovery was first announced in the *Daily Telegraph* by H. D. Ziman, at that time Secretary of the Friends of the National Libraries. On the circumstances of the discovery see Dr. W. F. Oakeshott's own account in *Essays on Malory*, ed. by J. A. W. Bennett, Oxford, 1963, pp. 1–6.

catalogue of 1839.[1] Palaeographical evidence suggested, however, that the manuscript was roughly contemporary with Caxton's edition, if not a little earlier. It is the work of two different scribes.[2] The finer of the two hands (see Plate II) is similar to that from which some English type of the late fifteenth century was designed.[3] Both hands show affinities with the Chancery hand of the period,[4] and one of the watermarks is identical in design and almost identical in size with that on a document dated 1475.[5] More important still is the fact that while the manuscript is neither Malory's own 'copy' nor the one used by Caxton, it is at least as reliable as Caxton's text and quite independent of it.[6] It supplies some of Caxton's obvious omissions, particularly in the *Tale of Arthur and Lucius*,[7] and often agrees with Malory's sources where Caxton is at variance with them. On the other hand, there are numerous readings in Caxton which, on the evidence of Malory's sources, appear to be more authentic than the corresponding readings in the

---

[1] The manuscript may originally have belonged to the Cathedral library, in which case it must have been transferred to the College in 1645 when Cromwell had dissolved the chapter. Cf. W. F. Oakeshott, 'Arthuriana at Winchester' (Bibl. No. 18), p. 75.

[2] Dr. Oakeshott has pointed out (*The Times Literary Supplement*, 27 September 1934) that 'hand A was probably in charge of this job, for in two instances he has started off hand B on a new book, and hand B has taken over after six lines or so'. The two instances are ff. 35ʳ (Plate III) and 45ʳ. Plate I (facing p. xx) is another example of hand B. Apart from ff. 35ʳ and 45ʳ the text is divided between the two hands as follows: ff. 9ʳ–44ᵛ, 191ᵛ–229ʳ, 349ʳ–484ᵛ are in hand A, ff. 45ʳ–191ʳ, 229ᵛ–346ᵛ in hand B. Ff. 1–8, 32–33, 347–8, and 485–92 are missing. A manuscript of the Arthurian section of the so-called 'English *Brute*' in the Library of Alnwick Castle (no. 457 A) belongs to a hand very similar to B.

[3] e.g. that used by Machlinia in London about 1486. Cf. W. F. Oakeshott, 'Caxton and Malory's Morte Darthur', *Gutenberg-Jahrbuch*, 1935, pp. 113–14.

[4] This has been established by J. A. Collins (cf. *Times Lit. Sup.*, loc. cit.), who also read a phrase in blind scratches twice repeated at the top of one page as 'Know all men by these presents'. It seems likely that the manuscript came from a scriptorium where legal documents were familiar.

[5] Cf. *The Times*, 27 August 1934. Another detail of some interest is that a vellum fragment used to repair a tear in the manuscript has on the gummed side part of an indulgence granted by Innocent VIII in 1489 and printed by Caxton. This suggests that the manuscript was at one time, probably somewhere about 1500, in the hands of a London binder.

[6] See my article on 'Malory's Morte Darthur in the Light of a Recent Discovery' in the *Bulletin of the John Rylands Library*, vol. lxix, No. 2, July 1935.

[7] Cf. *supra*, p. xxx. In my critical apparatus *C*'s readings inconsistent with the evidence supplied by Malory's sources are marked with a dagger (*C*†).

IN the begynnyng of Arthure .ffor he was chosyn kynge
by adventure and by grace for the moste pty of the barovns knewe nat he was
Uther Pendragon son but as Merlyon made hit opynly knowyn. But
yet many kyngis and lordis hylde hym grete werre for that cause. But well
Arthur ou com hem all the moste pty dayes of hys lyff he was ruled by y counceile
of Merlyon So hit felle on a tyme kyng Arthur seyde unto Merlyon my ba
rovnes woll let me have no reste but nedis I muste take a wyff & I wolde none
take but by thy counceile and advice hit ys well done seyde Merlyon that
ye take a wyff. ffor a man off youre bounte and nobles scholde
nott be w^t oute a wyff. Now is y ony seyde Merlyon that
ye love more than a noy ye seyde kyng Artqure I love Gwe
nyvere the kyngs doughter of Lodegrean off y londe of Came
lerde the whyche holdyth in his house the table rounde that ye
tolde me he had hit off my fadir Uther And this damesell is the
moste valyaunte and fayryst that I know lybyng or yett that ever
I conde fynde Sertis seyde Marlyon as off her beaute and fayre
nesse sha is one of the fayrest on lyve. But and ve loved hir not
so well as ye do I scholde fynde you a damesell off beaute and
of goodnesse that scholde lyke you and please you and youre
herte were nat sette. But there as mannes herte is sette
he woll be loth to returne. that is trouthe seyde kyng Artqur
But Marlyon warned the kyng covertly that Gwenyver was nat
holsom for hym to take to wyff. ffor he warned hym that Laun
celot scholde love hir and sche hym agayne. And so he turned his
tale to the aventures off the Sankegreall. Than M desyred off
the kyng for to have men w^t hym y scholde enquere off Gwenyv
and so the kyng graunted hym and so Merlyon wente forthe
unto kyng Lodegrean of Camplerde and tolde hym off the desire
of the kyng y he wolde have unto his wyff Gwenyvn his doughe
That is to me seyde kyng Lodegreauns the beste tydyng y y
ev I herde. that so worthy a kyng off prowesse & noblesse wol wedde
my doughe. And as for my londis I wolde geff hit hym yf I wyste

Winchester MS.[1] The two texts are, then, collateral versions of a common original, and each contains at least some elements of it which are not otherwise extant. Thus Malory's '*bole* of the tree' becomes *body* in the Winchester MS. and *hoole* in Caxton;[2] of the phrase *launcis and speres* the former preserves *launcis*, the latter *speres*;[3] and *a ryver that hyght Mortays* ('l'iaue grant que on apeloit Marcoise') becomes *a ryver and a Mortays* in the manuscript and *a ryuer and an hyhe montayn* in the printed text.[4]

There is reason to believe, however, that neither Caxton nor the Winchester scribes had access to the original form of Malory's work. The following sentence in Caxton—totally unintelligible as it stands, but reproduced without comment by all modern editors—should suffice to prove this:

And the mean whyle word came vnto sir Launcelot and to sir Trystram that sire Carados the myghty kynge that was made lyke a gyaunt that fought with sir Gawayn and gaf hym suche strokes that he swouned in his sadel (VIII. 28).

This reading is the result of two mistranscriptions: the words *made lyke a gyaunt that* are clearly a corruption of some such phrase as *made lyke a gyaunt whyght* (or *whycht*); some early scribe, mistaking the final *t* for *e*, made *whyght* (or *whycht*) into *whyche*, and a later redactor, probably Caxton himself, changed *whyche* to *that*. The first of these two errors is found in the Winchester MS.; hence it must have occurred in the common source of our texts, and this source (*X*) could not, therefore, have been Malory's own manuscript.

The same conclusion is suggested by the remarkable story of Maris de la Roche who after being killed in battle reappears unscathed. 'Sir Lucas', writes the Winchester scribe, 'saw kynge Angwysshaunce that nyght had slayne Maris de la Roche.' Finding some such remark in his original, Caxton, in an attempt to improve its grammar, replaced *nyght* by *late* and printed: 'Thenne lucas sawe kyng Agwysaunce that late hadde slayne Morys de la roche.'[5]

---

[1] For examples see, in my critical apparatus, any of the readings introduced by the sign *C** and followed by references to Malory's sources.

[2] Cf. *infra*, p. 255, line 7.   [3] Cf. *infra*, p. 229, line 17.

[4] Cf. *infra*, p. 934, line 27.   [5] Book I, ch. 15.

Malory's reading was obviously *nyghe* ('almost'),[1] mistaken for *nyght* by one of his copyists. This error, like *gyaunt whyche*, was, then, one of the features which distinguished the common source of *C* and *W* from the primitive text.[2] The following stemma would account for the filiation of variants in both these cases:

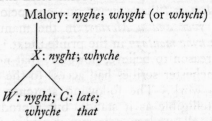

Malory: *nyghe*; *whyght* (or *whycht*)

X: *nyght*; *whyche*

W: *nyght*; *C*: *late*;
whyche   *that*

Needless to say, the straight lines connecting *X* and *W* on one side and *X* and *C* on the other do not imply that *X* was the *immediate* model of either *C* or *W*. There is, in fact, good reason to believe that it was not. A number of passages in *W*, such as the one analysed on p. cxiii, can only be accounted for as a result of two or more successive scribal errors. When, for instance, the two texts offer these two readings:

C (= *X*)	*W*
anon sire Tristram *redde them and wete ye well he was gladde for theryn was many a pyteous complaynte* Thenne sir Tristram said lady Brangwayne ye shalle ryde with me	anone seyde lady dame Brangwayne ye shall ryde with me

the discrepancy between them can best be explained if two successive transcriptions are assumed: one in which the recurrence of *sire Tristram* caused the omission of the italicized words, and the other in which *anon sire Tristram said* was contracted to *anon said*.[3] As the second of these

---

[1] In Malory's French source Maris is nearly killed, but escapes thanks to the timely assistance of Lucas the Butler. Cf. Commentary, note 308–9.

[2] Such errors are not easily detectable without the help of *F*. *Ye ar ryghte wyse of these workes* (989. 31–32) could pass for *M*'s own reading, if we did not know the French original: 'de ceste parolle avés vous bien dit que sages.' The change from *wordes* to *workes* must have occurred in *X*.

[3] This type of error, induced by the recurrence of the initial letter, usually occurs between words standing close to each other. It is not likely to have occurred until *sire* and *said* had been brought close together by the omission of the italicized words.

errors swept away the very words which had caused the first, the two could not have occurred simultaneously. Hence the first error belongs neither to X nor to W but to some state of the text (T) intermediate between the two.

There are equally strong grounds for assuming at least one intermediary between X and C. In the episode of the 'dolorous stroke' C describes the collapse of King Pellam's castle in most unusual terms: the castle, we are told, 'that was fall doune through that dolorous stroke lay vpon Pellam and balyn for thre dayes'. C then remarks that at the end of the third day Pellam still suffered from some minor injuries while Balin recovered. This incredible story, like so many of C's incoherences, has reappeared in all the modern editions of the *Morte Darthur*, and no editor or critic has so far questioned its cogency. Fortunately, with the aid of W, we can discover what Malory—and X—really wrote. *For the moste party of that castell*, writes W, *was dede thorow the dolorouse stroke. Ryght so lay kynge Pellam and Balyne three dayes*. In other words, Pellam and Balin did not lie buried under the castle, but lay wounded for three days. To make this simple statement into C's preposterous account at least two, possibly three, successive copyists must have been at work. Thus the same scribe may have omitted the words *Ryght so* and inserted *upon* between *lay* and *kynge Pellam*; but it was not until this was done that some grammatically minded reviser, probably Caxton himself, could have tried to make the previous sentence into a subordinate clause by adding *that* after *castell*. We must, then, assume at least three stages of transcription.

X: . . . castell was dede thorow the dolorouse stroke *Ryght so* lay kynge
Pellam

Z: . . . castell was dede thorow the dolorouse stroke lay upon kynge
Pellam

C: . . . castell *that* was fall doune through that dolorous stroke lay upon
Pellam

Z and T may, for all we know, each represent several states of the text along the lines connecting X with W and X with C respectively. With this qualification the foregoing conclusions may be graphically expressed thus:

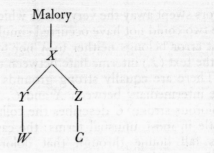

2. *The Principles of Reconstruction*

Since the primary aim of any critical edition is a text which would approach as closely as the extant material allows to the original form of the work, the real question before us is how far the material now available for the study of Malory's text will allow us to go in this direction. It stands to reason that, barring coincidence, whatever is common to *C* and *W* can and must be credited to *X*, but *X* is not, after all, Malory's own text, and even if we were content to edit *X* instead of Malory, we should still have to decide what we should do with the numerous passages in which its two derivatives differ.

The problem is similar to that which confronts a critic attempting to edit a text from two different families of manuscripts—a common, if distressing, occurrence in textual criticism. The traditional method consists in selecting from each of the two texts or groups of texts the 'best' readings they can offer so as to produce what is often inappropriately called a 'critical' text. Admittedly the value of such a text depends on the clear understanding that what is 'best' is not what seems best to the critic, but what is attributable to the author. And it so happens that it is not humanly possible for any critic, however cautious and competent, to maintain this distinction. The more he is bent on his task, the less he can conceive of himself and the author as two distinct individuals whose ways of thinking and writing are inevitably unlike, who are both liable to err, each in his own unaccountable way, just as they are capable of choosing two equally 'good', but conflicting, forms of expression. There may be various degrees of skill in the handling of the situation, and various degrees of accuracy in the results; but the procedure proves in the end just as disastrous in the case of, say, Wendelin Foerster compiling from several manuscripts, with his unique knowledge of twelfth-century French, a composite and totally unreal text of Chrétien de Troyes, as it did in the case of Pope who took from the various Quartos any readings which pleased him and inserted them into his edition of Shakespeare; for the fault lies not with individual editors, but with certain habits of mind inseparable from any practical application of the method, habits which broadly speaking amount to the belief that whatever satisfies one's taste and judgement must be 'good', and that whatever is 'good' belongs to the author.

The growing realization of this inevitable fallacy has induced some of the leading scholars of our time to adopt a totally sceptical attitude towards any attempt at editing and indeed to condemn any critical treatment of manuscript material beyond a mere reproduction of the extant tradition or of one of its representatives. The reaction has been a beneficial one in that it has helped to save a number of texts from unwelcome interference. But its real importance lies in the fact that it suggests a different attitude to criticism and imposes new and vital tasks upon the critic. The line of least resistance in textual studies is to declare a reading corrupt and substitute one's own. Refusal to emend the extant tradition on mere grounds of preference carries with it the obligation to spare no effort in interpreting each unemended reading. Now interpretation may mean two things: the elucidation of what is there, and the explanation of how it came to be what it is. And should what is there defeat all attempts at understanding, it might still be possible to explain how it arose, in other words, to detail the processes which have produced it. The problem of editing, far from being brushed away as it often is by the less thoughtful followers of the 'conservative' school, would then arise in a new form. Instead of the unanswerable question, 'What is the author, as we know him, likely to have said?' we should ask ourselves, in the first place, 'What does the extant reading mean?' and if no satisfactory answer is forthcoming, go on to ask: 'Can it be shown to be a scribal error?' Answers to this last question may not, and most probably will not, yield a complete reconstruction of any single text preserved in copied manuscripts; but only such answers can serve the true purpose of textual criticism: they alone can lessen the damage done to the text by its copyists and so produce a result similar to that recognized as the aim of restoration in the realm of the fine arts, namely a *partial* reconstruction of the original from what is extant. To go as far back as we can towards the original without necessarily reaching it is all that we profess to do. Our task so defined may appear unduly limited. It may be more pleasing to the mind to aim higher, more tempting to borrow the author's pen and venture to speak for him. But as long as our respect for the work is greater than our power of guessing the truth, we can but adopt the humbler course.

(*a*) *Textual evidence* (π)

To the question, 'Can this reading be shown to be a scribal error?' there is often no answer, for there is no general rule as to how a scribe should behave in any given circumstances, and the most common type of scribal error is the unaccountable one, that which occurs through one word's coming into a scribe's mind and being written down in place of another. But there are, on the other hand, 'definable' and, consequently, emendable errors—those which are typical of the process of copying as distinct from that of original writing. The reading of the text, the passage of the eye from the text to the copy, and the passage of the eye from the copy back to the text—these are the actions which constitute the technique of copying, and emendable errors are those which occur as a result of their imperfect performance. In an empirical fashion such errors have long been known to critics; but they cannot be properly dealt with, and sometimes cannot even be recognized, without a clear understanding of their nature and origin.[1]

Reading of the text. A scribe may either inadvertently or

---

[1] For a more detailed analysis see my 'Principles of Textual Emendation' in *Studies in French Language and Literature presented to Professor M. K. Pope*, Manchester, 1939, pp. 351–69.

deliberately misread his text. Examples of unintentional misreadings have been quoted in another connexion in the previous section of this chapter (*nyght* for *nyghe* and *whyche* for *whyght*). Mistaken contractions account for such misspellings of proper names as *Barcias* for *Bracias* (in *C*) and *Traquyn* for *Tarquyn* (in *W*), while failure to notice a contraction in a manuscript no doubt explains *C*'s utterly unintelligible remark in Book XX, ch. 7: 'the lawe was suche in the dayes that what someuer they were of what estate or degree yf they were fonde gylty of treson there shold be none other remedy but dethe and *outher the men or the takynge with the dede* shold be causer of their hasty Iugement.' The original reading was, of course, not *men*, but *menour* (= behaviour), as in *W*.[1]

The Winchester scribes copy their text mechanically and seldom, if ever, attempt to correct it. Caxton, on the other hand, is an editor rather than a scribe. He often tries to improve on his original where the latter seems to him to be deficient, although, as has already been shown, he is rather apt to be content with a mere appearance of sense.[2] His more sweeping corrections are prompted either by his sense of editorial economy or by his general conception of the form and structure of the book or occasionally by his peculiar moral bias. The curiously expurgated version of the oath taken by Arthur's knights may be an example of this last variety:[3]

W	*C*
and allwayes to do ladyes, damesels, and jantilwomen and wydowes [socour]: strengthe hem in hir ryghtes, and never to enforce them uppon payne of dethe	and alweyes to doo ladyes, damoysels and gentylwymmen socour vpon payne of dethe

From the copy to the text. After writing down a word or a group of words (sometimes only a letter or a group of letters) the scribe has to go back to the original and find the 'right

---

[1] *v. infra*, p. 1174.
[2] His attempt to 'correct' the description of the death of Maris de la Roche (*v. supra*, p. ciii) is an instance in point.
[3] *v. infra*, p. 120.

place'. To do this he must carry in his mind the last letter, word, or words he has written down, or sometimes the letter or word that he has to copy next. If, as is often the case, the word or letter he is looking for occurs more than once within a comparatively small space, he may easily pick up his text at some later point and omit the intervening matter. All such omissions can be described as *sauts du même au même* and subdivided into *homoeoteleuta* and *homoeoarchies* according as the identical letters or words occur at the end or at the beginning of the two neighbouring words or groups of words. In *W* accidents of this kind occur at the slightest provocation: sometimes the mere recurrence of the final *e* is sufficient to cause them. In the extract from *W* quoted at the end of the previous paragraph the recurrence of the initial *s* in two neighbouring words—*socour strengthe*—caused the disappearance of the first.[1] Nor is it necessary that the recurrent element should be a word or a letter. It may be any feature of the text that the scribe happens to use as a point of resumption. He may, for example, remember that to find the right place he must look for the beginning or the end of a line, or he may have a rough recollection of having copied say half or three-quarters of a line and look for the remaining half or quarter as the case may be. He would then be in danger of omitting a passage equal in length to one or several complete lines of his original. In *C* such cases are not only less frequent, but less easily detectable than in *W*. *C*'s remark that 'syre Bellangere reuenged the deth of his fader Alysaunder and *syr Tristram slewe Kynge Marke*' has so far been taken on its face value, and critics, including myself,[2] have tried to reconcile it with the traditional prose version of the Tristan story by making 'syr Tristram' the direct object of 'slewe'—an ingenious, but highly unsatisfactory interpretation. The real explanation is found in the corresponding place in *W*: 'Sir Bellyngere revenged the dethe of hys fadir sir Alysaundir and sir Trystram, *for he* (i.e. Sir Bellyngere) slewe kynge Marke.' Misled by the close resemblance between the *f* of *for* and the long *s* (ſ) of *slewe*, the printer's eye must have travelled

---

[1] The words *and wydowes* may have been omitted at an earlier stage.

[2] Cf. my *Roman de Tristan et Iseut dans l'œuvre de Thomas Malory*, p. 220.

straight from *Trystram* to *slewe,* and the vital words *for he*
were lost in the process.[1]

An 'eyeskip' of this kind does not necessarily presuppose
the presence in the original of two neighbouring words
with an identical beginning or ending. It is enough for
them to bear a certain general resemblance to each other in
size or shape for one of them—either the first or the second
—to disappear. If it is the first, the process is essentially the
same as in the case of a *saut du même au même* except that the
identity is more apparent than real—as when *after ester* is reduced to *ester.*[2] When the second of the two words is omitted,
what the scribe does is to mistake the word he is about to
copy for the one already copied. As a result, *He pulled hym
undir his hors fete* becomes *He pulled hym undir his fete,*[3] even
though the resemblance between *his* and *hors* is superficial.

The recurrence of similar or identical elements within a
comparatively short space may cause yet another type of
error. This may be described by the formula $M N O N P >
M N O N O N P$. Having copied $M N O$ the scribe
would return to the first N instead of going on to the second,
and in this way would duplicate $N O$. A curious instance of a
duplication complicated by a *homoeoteleuton* occurs in the
following extract from the *Tale of the Sankgreal* (the duplicated passage is reproduced in italics, and the passage affected
by the *homoeoteleuton* in square brackets):

And there kynge Hurlaine was discomfite and hys men slayne.
And he was aferde to be dede and fledde to thys shippe, and there
founde this swerde, and drew hit, and cam oute and founde kynge
Labor, the man of the worlde of all Crystyn in whom there is the
grettist faythe. And whan kynge Hurlaine *was discomfite and hys
menne slayne and he was aferde to be dede and fledde to thys shippe and
there founde thys swerde and drew hit and* [cam oute . . . And whan
kynge Hurlaine saw kynge Labor he dressid this swerde and] smote
hym upon the helme.[4]

The scribe's eye may occasionally wander off the line and

---

[1] By the same process 'Joseph[e], the son of Joseph of Arimathea' has become
in *C* 'Joseph of Arimathea' (Book XVII, ch. 22; *v. infra,* p. 1034, line 33).
[2] *v. infra,* p. 1119, line 1.
[3] *v. infra,* p. 524, lines 10–11. For a closer definition see below, pp. cxix–cxx.
[4] p. 987.

so bring into the copy parasitic elements from any neighbouring part of the original, thus producing what may be
called *contamination*. The strange remark in *W* to the effect
that 'sir Bagdemagus tyll another tyme was wondirly wrothe
that sir Tor was avaunced afore hym'[1] is an example of such
an error: it is due to the fact that four lines above King
Arthur declares that he will 'leve sir Bagdemagus tyll
anothir tyme'. Similarly in the question put to Lancelot by
the people of the castle of Corbenic—'Why have ye sene?'—
the scribe substituted *Why* for *What* because the previous
paragraph, which accidentally came into his field of vision,
began with the words: 'Why have ye awaked me?'[2] Sometimes—though comparatively rarely—contamination may
result from a purely mental confusion, as in the compound
corealme—a mixture of *countrey* and *realme*.[3]

From the text to the copy. Part of the process of transcription
consists in transmitting from the mind to the hand each word
and letter of the text. A slight acceleration in the movement
of the hand or a slight slowing down of the transmission can
easily upset their co-ordination and produce what is known
as *dittography*; a letter, a syllable, or a word, or even a whole
group of words, would then appear twice in the copy. Con-
versely, a slowing down of the movement of the hand or an
acceleration in the transmission may cause part of the text to
drop out. The omission of monosyllabic words, frequent
in *W*, is an example of this variety of *arrhythmia*.

Combined errors. Most editors tacitly—perhaps uncon-
sciously—assume that if they are dealing with one manuscript
they are concerned with one scribe only. In reality, however,
most of the manuscripts which have come down to us from
medieval times were copied not from the originals but from
earlier copies, and contain therefore numerous readings
resulting from two or more successive mistranscriptions of
the same passage. The discovery of such readings or 'combined errors' has already helped us to establish the degree
of proximity of our two texts to Malory's original manuscript.
But it can also help us to establish the text. An instructive
example, with which I have dealt at some length elsewhere,[4]

---

[1] pp. 131–2.   [2] p. 1017.   [3] p. 866.
[4] *Principles of Textual Emendation*, pp. 363–4.

occurs in one of the early sections of Malory's *Book of Sir Tristram*. Blamor, having been defeated by Tristram, says that he prefers death to dishonour and asks Tristram to kill him. Tristram appeals against this request to the kings who act as judges. The kings, however, refer him to Blamor's brother, Bleoberis, who, much to their dismay, declares that Blamor must die. In *W* his reply is as follows:

My lordys seyde sir Bleoberys thoughe my brother be beatyn and have the worse in his body thorow myght of armys he hath nat beatyn his hearte.

In *C* the same speech reads thus:

My lordes said Bleoberys though my broder be beten and hath the wers thorou myghte of armes I dare saye though syre Trystram hath beten his body he hath not beten his herte.

If we place the two readings side by side *his body* will appear in *W* roughly a line above the same words in *C*, and most of the intervening matter will be found missing in *W*. This suggests that originally *his body* occurred twice (once as in *W* and again as in *C*) and that its recurrence caused a *homoeoteleuton*, i.e. the omission of the words *thorow myght of armys I dare saye though syre Trystram hath beten his body*. How, then, is it that the first four of these—*thorow myght of armys*—still occur in *W*? The only reasonable explanation seems to be that at the time when the *homoeoteleuton* occurred they stood outside its sphere of action, and that the reading of *X* was:

. . . the worse thorow myght of armys in his body *I dare saye though syre Trystram hath beten his body*, &c.

In the next copy the italicized words dropped out, but it was not until the third stage of transcription that the order of words could have been changed and the two phrases, *thorow myght of armys* and *in his body*, placed in reverse order, as in *W*. In *C*, on the other hand, the original reading appears to be intact except for the omission of '*in his body*' before '*I* dare'—another case of 'eyeskip' or *saut du même au même*. The real interest of this example lies in the fact that neither *C* nor *W* offers here any apparent difficulty: both seem to give readings which any 'rational' critic would accept without a murmur, but which on our present showing turn out to be corrupt.

All the processes outlined above may in the course of the transmission of a text contribute to 'combined errors'. These may either be distributed over two or more successive copies as in the example just given, or occur simultaneously in one. In the former case their discovery supplies the missing links in the evolution of variants: sometimes a *saut du même au même* can only be traced if the 'key-word', lost at some subsequent stage of transcription, is restored to its proper place; or again, a hopelessly corrupt reading may turn out to be the result of a 'duplication' superimposed upon an omission. More obvious but no less vital are the 'simultaneous' combined errors such as the curious omission of the direct object in *W*'s remark: *the Pope called unto hym a noble clerke . . . and the Pope gaff undir leade and sente hem unto the kynge.*[1] Here a plural noun is clearly missing after *gaff*, but it can be restored once it is realized that in fifteenth-century manuscripts the word *bulles*, written with a stroke across the two *l*'s and an abbreviated *es*, looked very much like *buff* and was therefore apt to be omitted by any copyist after a word ending in *ff*. To make *gaff bulles undir* (or, as in *C*, *gaff hym bulles undir*) into *gaff undir* the scribe had to commit an 'unconscious misreading' and a *homoeoteleuton*, and both these errors must have occurred simultaneously.

(b) External evidence (F)

The preceding observations apply to almost any text preserved in copied manuscripts. But Malory's works offer yet another, much less common, approach to the problem. Among the great prose writers of all time he is perhaps the one who 'invented' least. He may sometimes disagree with the very spirit of his 'French books', alter their character and purpose, and introduce an atmosphere and a manner of his own; for all that, the greater part of his narrative is made of the material 'drawn briefly out of French'. In so far as this material is extant, it can, therefore, provide useful clues; for, barring accident, whatever either of our two texts has

[1] *v. infra*, p. 1194.

in common with the French must have reached it through Malory and can be safely ascribed to him. The following examples are among the simplest cases of this kind:

C	W	F (*Malory's source*)
(*the asterisk denotes the correct reading*)		
*he shotte hym thorou the sholder *with an arow*	he shotte hym thorow the sholdir[1]	cil le fiert *d'une saiette* envenimee
*toke his *hors* aboue the hede	toke hys swerde[2] *abovyn the bed*[3]	vient a son *cheval* et monte en milieu du *lit*
I am passyng heuy for your sake For ye wil not byleue that swerd shall be youre destruction	*I am passynge hevy for youre sake for *and ye woll nat leve* that swerde hit shall be youre destruccion[4]	Et je vous di fait elle que *se vous l'emportés* qu'il vous en mal averra

The more closely Malory follows his source the more often such cases appear in our texts and the easier it becomes to use the evidence of *F*. Nor can it be said that *F* merely confirms the validity of readings which would be recognized as genuine on other grounds: indeed the choice it suggests is sometimes contrary to most critics' 'rational' preference. In describing preparations for a tournament *C* remarks (Book VI, ch. 6) that *there were scaffoldis and holes that lordes and ladyes myghte beholde*. This has usually been taken as a hopelessly corrupt passage, and when Dr. Oakeshott first disclosed some of the features of the Winchester MS. he claimed to have found the correct reading of it: *scaffoldis and towrys* instead of *scaffoldis and holes*.[5] *Towrys* may indeed seem preferable to *holes* in this context, although on further reflection the building of towers for the benefit of spectators at a tournament would probably strike the reader as an odd proceeding. All 'rational' conjectures as to this, however, are made unnecessary by the reading found in *F*. The French prose writer states that on the occasion of the tournament stands were erected and *windows (fenestres)* made (presumably in the woodwork) so as to enable the ladies to watch the fighting: *Celui jour firent li doy roy*

[1] *v. infra*, p. 433. [2] *v. infra*, p. 1004. [3] *v. infra*, p. 990.
[4] *v. infra*, p. 64. As a result of the substitution of *ye wil not byleue* for *and ye woll nat leve* the sense of the speech has undergone a radical change. In *W* the damsel expresses her concern about Balin (*hevy* = worried) because unless he abandons his sword it will cause his death; in *C* she is displeased with him (*hevy* = angry) because he refuses to believe that the sword can do him any harm.
[5] 'The Text of Malory', *Times Literary Supplement*, 27 September 1934.

drechier loges en mi les prés, ou il avoit fenestres as dames et as damoiseles.[1] That *C*'s *holes* is Malory's rendering of *fenestres* is evident; and this is confirmed by the fact that the *Catholicon Anglicon* gives *holes* as an equivalent of *fenestra*. The seemingly corrupt reading thus turns out to be Malory's and the seemingly 'better' one a corruption.

But the formulae $C+F = M$ (Malory) and $W+F = M$ are subject to one important qualification: they cannot be applied where there is a reasonable possibility of an *accidental* agreement between *C* and *F* or *W* and *F*. We can be certain, for instance, that in the following passage[2] *F*'s reading could have reached *C* only through Malory:

W	C	F
he behylde sir Lyonell that wolde have slayne hys brothir sir Bors which he loved ryght well	he beheld Lyonel wold haue slayne his broder *and knewe* syre Bors whiche he loued ry3t wel	si *congnoist* maintenant que ce est Boors que il amoit de moult grant amour

But when *C* gives the variant *euensonge tyme*, *W evynsonge* and *F heure de vespres*, the possibility of *tyme* dropping out in Malory and reappearing by accident in *C* cannot altogether be ignored.[3] Much less uncertain is the series: *chemise blanche (F) > whyte shert (C) > whyght sheete (W)*.[4] Some notion of where the boundary between certainty and uncertainty should lie may perhaps be derived from a comparison of two groups of quotations, in the first of which the evidence of *F* is just enough to tip the scales in favour of *C*, while in the second an emendation of *W* would fall just below the 'safety line':

W	C	F
that one way defendith the that thou ne go *that day*[5]	. . . *that way*	. . . *que tu n'y entres*
I charge the that . . . ye hyre masse dayly and ye may *com thereto*[6]	I charge you that . . . ye here masse dayly and ye may *doo hit*	. . . se vous *estes en lieu* que vous le puissiés *faire*

(c) $\pi + F.$

Our two main witnesses, then, are π (textual evidence) and *F* (Malory's sources). In the examples quoted so far each has appeared independently and has sufficed for the

---

[1] MS. Add. 10293, f. 284 *a*.   [2] *v. infra*, p. 971.   [3] *v. infra*, p. 927.
[4] *v. infra*, p. 925.   [5] *v. infra*, loc. cit.   [6] *v. infra*, p. 833.

reconstruction of the text. But it may happen that while neither is strong enough in itself to supply an emendation, their concurrence would clinch the evidence and change a mere hypothesis into a virtual certainty. To take a simple example, Lady Columbe's reproach to Balin ('whan she aspyed that Launceor was slayne'): *two bodyes thou haste slayne one herte and two hertes in one body*, can be conjecturally emended, on textual grounds, by the insertion of *in* after *slayne*, for it is probable that in some earlier copy *slayne* was spelt *slain*, and *in* fell out by *homoeoteleuton*. But this is a mere conjecture; what makes it acceptable and, indeed, worthy of inclusion in the text, is the fact that in the corresponding place *F* gives the exact equivalent of the reconstructed reading:

F: deus cuers avés *ochis en un* et deus cors en un
M: two bodyes thou haste *slain in one* and two hertes in one body[1]

Another interesting case is the remark *thou hast resembled in to thynges*,[2] alleged to have been made by Josephe, son of Joseph of Arimathea, to Galahad. The sense clearly requires the insertion of *me* after *resembled*, and it is arguable that the word may have dropped out before *in* owing to the likeness between *m* and *in*. But the emendation would not be certain without the support of the corresponding reading in *F*: *tu m'as resemblé en deus choses*. On similar grounds, when *W* writes *ye ar ryght wyse of thes workes*, we can safely replace *workes* by *wordes* because the French has *ceste parolle*.[3]

The formula $\pi + F = M$ can yield even more striking results; it can help to restore readings absent from both our texts, as in the following two cases:

C	W	F	M
so these thre felawes and they thre were there no mo	so thes three knyght and these three elles were no mo	et avecques ces troiz *demourerent* lez trois compaignons	so⟨*there abode*⟩ thes three knyght⟨*es*⟩ and these three; elles were no mo[4]
in suche payne and in suche anguysshe I haue ben longe	in such payne and in such angwysh as I have suffird longe	en telle paine et en telle angoisse que *nus aultres homs ne la pourroit* souffrir longuement	in such payne and in such angwysh as I have ⟨*no man elles myght have*⟩ suffird longe[5]

[1] *v. infra*, p. 69.   [2] *v. infra*, p. 1035.   [3] *v. infra*, p. 989.
[4] *v. infra*, p. 1028.   [5] *v. infra*, loc. cit.

In the first of these two passages *F* supplies the verb *demourerent* for which there is only one normal equivalent in *M*: *abode*. π, on the other hand, suggests a reason for its disappearance: the word *abode* would most easily be lost if it belonged to a phrase the first three letters of which were identical with the first three letters of the next word (*thes*). Hence the reconstructed reading: *so there abode thes three*, &c. In the second passage there is a characteristic discrepancy between *C* and *W*: while the latter accurately reproduces an incomplete sentence, the former tries to restore the sense by deleting the word *as*. *F* shows, however, that *as* belongs to the original construction, and that a vital phrase corresponding to *nus aultres homs ne porroit* must have dropped out after the word *have*. But since on grounds of π it is reasonable to assume that that phrase disappeared because it ended with the word *have*, the conclusion naturally suggests itself that it read *no man elles myght have*.

A sentence already referred to in passing may be quoted as a last example. In relating Lancelot's adventures in the quest of the Holy Grail, Caxton tells us (Book XV) that as Lancelot rode through a deep valley he saw a *ryuer and an hyhe montayn*. *W*'s reading is *a ryver and a mortays*.[1] *C*, as usual, seems more plausible, but only superficially so, for while 'high mountain' may be more intelligible than *mortays*, there is no justification for it in the context, and the sudden appearance of a mountain at this point is totally inexplicable. *F* again provides the clue. It says: *Et lors regarda devant lui et voit l'iaue grant que on apeloit Marcoise, qui la forest departoit en deus parties*.[2] The whole process at once becomes clear: Malory must have written *a ryver that hyghte Mortays*; one of his early copyists misread *that hyghte* as *& an hyghe* and the resulting phrase *& an hyghe mortays* was preserved in *X*. Caxton, unable as he was to understand the word *mortays*, ingeniously replaced it by the only palaeographical equivalent that could go with the adjective *hyghe*. Thanks to *F* we can at long last get rid of that adjective and of the misplaced mountain—hitherto one of the many unsolved mysteries of the Grail.

---

[1] *v. infra*, p. 934.
[2] MS. B.N. fr. 120, f. 545ʳ col. 1.

(d) Hitherto neglected varieties of textual evidence

Without in any way departing from the principles formulated above it has been possible to add over one hundred emendations to the ones made in the 1947 edition of the text[1] simply by examining more closely the evidence supplied by our two texts and their sources. If the essential causes of scribal confusion are to be defined by some such terms as retreat from a word or a letter *believed to be* the last to have been copied or attraction to whatever follows such words or letters, the area of legitimate emendation can be considerably extended; it can include such cases as the confusion between the Roman numeral ii and the long *s* (p. 194, lines 24–25), between *deme you* and *were ye* (p. 514, line 17), between *now* and *not* (p. 948, lines 15–17) or between *at* and *al* (p. 1086, line 32). Generally speaking, whenever similar, as distinct from identical, words or groups of letters occur next to each other they can just as easily be assumed to have caused the scribe to mistake the 'point of resumption' and so miss a whole word or a phrase: *had ben* can become *had*,[3] *thys thre yere* can be reduced to *thys yere*,[4] *hys hors fete* to *hys fete*,[5] and *man may heale hym* to *man heale hym*.[6] The opening sentence of the fourth section of the *Book of Sir Launcelot and Queen Guinevere* (*The Knight of the Cart*), as printed in the 1947 edition, shows a curious disregard of the place of Easter in the Roman calendar: 'And thus hit passed on frome Candylmas untyll Ester, that the moneth of May was com.'[7] The word *after*, omitted in the

---

[1] Cf. 31. 22–25, 40. 6, 41. 25, 45. 4, 102. 8, 105. 5, 105. 18–22, 126. 1–2, 165. 7–8, 170. 4–5, 173. 5, 255. 28–29, 272. 5, 294. 2, 313. 3, 313. 33–34, 316. 18–19, 334. 8, 378. 3–4, 426. 9, 442. 30, 464. 21–22, 468. 14–15, 485. 18, 19–21, 497. 2, 500. 10, 540. 26, 550. 22, 613. 20–23, 675. 26–27, 677. 15, 715. 25, 727. 26, 735. 5, 743. 27–28, 769. 24, 795. 30, 807. 25–28, 825. 16–17, 839. 6, 887. 2–4, 893. 30, 916. 33, 942. 29, 961. 8–10, 964. 22–25, 994. 17, 1031. 19, 1032. 17, 1032. 21–22, 1051. 26, 1071. 28, 1077. 21, 1078. 27, 1111. 8, 1128. 19–20, 1161. 32, 1166. 23, 1169. 13, 30, 1170. 12, 20–21, 1175. 11, 1176. 11, 1184. 14, 1187. 10–11, 15, 1189. 19, 1219. 21, 1221. 8, 1233. 8, 1239. 14, &c.

[2] Cf. *Will's Visions of Piers Plowman and Do-Well, an edition in the form of Trinity College, Cambridge MS. R. 3.14 corrected from other manuscripts, with variant readings* by George Kane, London, 1960, pp. 121 ff., where the same concepts of retreat and attraction are applied to whatever is assumed by the scribe to have been previously copied.

[3] p. 24, line 9.   [4] p. 37, line 12.   [5] p. 524, line 11.
[6] p. 1146, line 24.   [7] Cf. *supra*, p. cxi and *infra*, p. 1119, line 1.

Winchester manuscript between *untyll* and *ester*, but preserved in Caxton, should be supplied to restore sense.

Another characteristic of scribal practice not fully recognized in the 1947 edition is the frequent disappearance from the text of monosyllables, without any visible motive other than their brevity: words such as *all, am, be, for, (h)it, hym, in, me, the* and even the abbreviated form of *never* can vanish simply through the scribe's mistaken impression of the text he is copying.[1] To restore them where they belong is as legitimate as to correct any other error of scribal origin. Hence a number of new minor emendations which, I hope, will improve the condition of the text without in any way detracting from its authenticity.[2]

No one is likely to discover all the accidents that have taken place in the course of the transmission of our text; all we can hope to do is to advance a few steps in the direction of the original. Our critical text will never be exactly like the one first produced by the author, no matter how much care we expend upon it. This is to some extent a measure of our own limitations; but it is also a consequence of the method of editing advocated and used in these pages—a method which always leaves room for further approximation to the authentic form of the work.

3. *The Present Edition*

Since we do not profess to reconstruct the original work in its entirety but merely to do the best we can with its two extant copies, the choice of our base text will imply no outright recognition of its excellence. The principles which should govern such a choice have been admirably formulated by Joseph Bédier in the Introduction to his edition of the *Lai de l'Ombre*:

Nous avons choisi, entre nos sept manuscrits, le manuscrit *A*, pour servir de 'base' à notre édition. Ce n'est nullement que nous le tenions pour le plus voisin de l'original, puisque, comme nous l'avons vu, il se

---

[1] Cf. 302. 30, 340. 25, 355. 24, 571. 29, 745. 24, 781. 25, 802. 5, 810. 35, 839. 7, 941. 20, 960. 29, 964. 14, 991. 3, 1161. 8, 1193. 26, &c.

[2] In a number of cases earlier emendations have been removed or altered. Cf. 27. 19, 28. 12, 40. 25, 105. 22, 125. 5, 176. 10, 195. 6, 260. 4, 343. 22, 608. 3, 721. 33, &c. For new readings see 18. 6, 23. 1, 87. 9, 107. 37, 145. 3, 172. 17, 1136. 5, &c.

peut fort bien que *D*, ou *E*, représente le dernier état du texte, tel qu'il plut à Jean Renart de le constituer. Si nous avons choisi le manuscrit *A*, le précieux manuscrit 837 de la Bibliothèque nationale, c'est de façon tout empirique, et simplement parce que, offrant d'ailleurs un texte à l'ordinaire très sensé et très cohérent, et des formes grammaticales très françaises (à part quelques 'picardismes'), et une orthographe très simple et très régulière, il est, entre nos sept manuscrits, celui qui présente le moins souvent des leçons individuelles, celui par conséquent qu'on est le moins souvent tenté de corriger. L'ayant une fois choisi, nous avons pris le parti d'en respecter autant que possible les leçons.

It is on similar grounds that the Winchester MS. has been adopted for the present edition of Malory's works as well as for that of 1947: not because it is in every respect the nearest to the original, but because it is so in some parts, and because as long as absolute 'truthfulness' is not aimed at, the less well known of the two versions, which is at least as reliable as the other, is as fair as any choice can be.

L'ayant une fois choisi, nous avons pris le parti d'en respecter autant que possible les leçons. This again is largely true of my two editions, though I may have placed on the words *autant que possible* a somewhat wider interpretation than that which Bédier had in mind. The principle I have endeavoured to follow resolves itself into two simple propositions: (*a*) that readings which can be shown to result from scribal errors or those which are condemned on grounds of external evidence must be emended; and (*b*) that all the rest, good or bad, 'probable' or 'improbable', must be retained and, as far as possible, elucidated. The astonishing fewness of what in the last analysis may be termed *loci desperati* in a text established in this fashion is another indication that the conservative use of the editor's discriminating faculty does little injustice to the author and imposes no undue burden upon the reader. A few passages, left unemended in the 1947 edition, have been emended in the present one without reference to any particular scribal process. They are, as it were, concessions to the reader, more concerned with the readability of the text than with strict adherence to a particular method of editing. Instead of 'Sir Tristram may be called a knyght' the text now has 'Sir Tristram may be called a noble knyght', as in Caxton, even though it is difficult to say exactly why

the adjective 'noble' dropped out before 'knyght'. Apart
from the cases where the emendation is supported by
Malory's sources, there are in the whole of the present text
not more than four or five such cases, and in each one of
them the emendation consists simply in borrowing Caxton's
reading.[1]

To enable the reader to see the emendations at a glance
I have distinguished them from the body of the text by
placing in square brackets the readings borrowed from
Caxton without the support of *F*, in half brackets (⌐ ⌐)
Caxton's readings confirmed by *F*, and in caret brackets (⟨ ⟩)
the words and letters which occur neither in Caxton nor in
the Winchester text. Square brackets have also been used
for *lacunae* in *W* (ff. 1–8, 32–33, 347–8, and 485–92) supplied from *C*, and for matter borrowed from *C* to fill the gaps
in some of the torn pages. Wherever the emendations are
not self-explanatory, the reasons for them will be found
either in the critical apparatus or in the Commentary.

The critical apparatus is the product of a collation of the
Winchester MS. with Caxton's edition, of both these texts
with Malory's sources, of the two copies of Caxton's edition
with one another, and of H. O. Sommer's edition with the
Rylands copy. The material it contains falls into four main
categories: (*a*) readings from the Winchester MS. not included in the text; (*b*) Caxton's readings, exclusive of differences of spelling and minor differences of wording such
as the use of the prefixes 'Sir' and 'King', variations in the
uses of *there, so, and, for, thenne, anone, afore* (for *before*), &c.,
and insignificant differences of word-order; (*c*) readings from
Malory's sources which have a bearing upon the reconstruction of his text; and (*d*) variants of the two extant copies of
Caxton's edition. Some of Sommer's departures from Caxton
and all the errors in Whittaker's facsimiles have also been
recorded.[2] For the purpose of the present edition all these
texts have been collated afresh and the choice of variants

---

[1] Cf. 433. 28, 535. 6, 763. 24, and 1199. 12–13.

[2] The variants are quoted with as much of the context as is necessary to find the
corresponding reading in the text. For example, if the text reads *longe hit was or he
myght welde hymselff* and Caxton has in addition the word *ever*, his variant is quoted
as *or ever he*. The words *see note* refer to the Commentary.

revised throughout with a view to achieving greater consistency. Caxton's readings which are either clearly preferable to those of the base text or likely to throw some light upon it are marked with an asterisk (*). The dagger (†) is used to denote less acceptable variants. All quotations are introduced by line-numbers and by one or more of the following abbreviated references:

C = Caxton's edition.
F = Malory's French sources as represented by the extant MSS.
MA = The alliterative *Morte Arthure* (Thornton MS.).
O¹ = *The Works of Sir Thomas Malory*, Oxford, 1947 (reprinted in 1948).
P = The Pierpont Morgan copy of C.
R = The John Rylands copy of C.
S = Sommer's edition of R.
W = The Winchester MS.
Wh = Whittaker's facsimiles in R.

The 1947 edition and its successors are the first attempts to produce the entire text of Malory in the old spelling with modern punctuation and word-division. Certain features of late fifteenth-century orthography which represent purely palaeographical conventions have, however, been removed: the modern use of *i*, *j*, *u*, *v*, and of capitals has been adopted throughout,[1] contractions and numerals have been expanded, *u*'s occasionally interpreted as *y*'s and vice versa, þ has been transcribed as *th*, and ʒ as *y*, *gh*, or *z*, according to its position in the word. The expansions, like the emended readings based on Caxton, follow as far as possible the normal spelling of the manuscript, but where the latter is inconsistent the convenience of the modern reader has been taken into account. Thus the sign ſ has been interpreted as *es* and the sign ꝰ as *er*,[2] despite the fact that the scribes of the Winchester MS. prefer as a rule *is* and *ir*. The acute accent has been used in polysyllabic words to distinguish the vocal *e* from the mute.

---

[1] Except in such words as *sir*, *kynge*, and *quene*.
[2] Except in the word *sir*.

Contrary to the practice which used to prevail in editions of old texts, light punctuation has been adopted, particularly in the case of noun or adjective clauses introduced by *who*, *which*, *that*, *what*, *where*, and the like. But wherever punctuation could clarify the construction it has been resorted to liberally, and no commas have been spared before adverb-clauses introduced by conjunctions signifying cause or purpose (e.g. *that* = 'so that', *for*, *because*, &c.).

In a text such as Malory's, punctuation can do more than clarify his meaning: it can help to bring out the rhythm and movement of his prose. The frequent occurrence of compound sentences strung together by innumerable *and*'s is apt to obscure the fact that Malory's favourite period is a short one, falling into not more than three parts, and that, although he sometimes uses a wider pattern, his natural preference is for crisp and compact construction. Punctuation can make this apparent and so reveal the real cadence of Malory's sentences, a cadence which achieves point and appeal and escapes the tendency to 'watering down', so prominent in medieval prose:

Than they fewtred their spearis in their restis and com togidirs as muche as their horsis myght dryve. And the Irysh knyght smote Balyn on the shylde that all wente to shyvers of hys spere. And Balyne smote hym agayne thorow the shylde, and the hawbirk perysshed, and so bore hym thorow the body and over the horse crowper; and anone turned hys horse fersely and drew oute hys swerde, and wyst nat that he had slayne hym. (p. 69.)

Than sir Launcelot unbarred the dore, and with hys lyftte honde he hylde hit opyn a lytyll, that but one man myght com in at onys. And so there cam strydyng a good knyght, a much man and a large, and hys name was called sir Collgrevaunce of Goore. And he wyth a swerde streke at sir Launcelot myghtyly, and so he put asyde the streke, and gaff hym such a buffette uppon the helmet that he felle grovelyng dede wythin the chambir dore. (p. 1167.)

Another characteristic of Malory's style—the substitution of dialogue for narrative—can be displayed by the even simpler method of paragraphing. The unfortunate habit of printing Malory's text in solid blocks of prose with scarcely more than one fresh line on each page has caused modern readers to lose sight of this vital aspect of his work. For my part I had no hesitation in giving it, as far as possible, the appearance of a modern novel and avoiding at all costs that of a learned treatise. How else, indeed, could one adequately render the brisk exchange of repartees in such passages as the dialogue between Sir Gareth and the haughty lady who resents his acts of heroism,[1] or the well-known scene of Gawain's despair at the discovery of his brothers' death?

'But where are my brethirn?' seyde sir Gawayne, 'I mervayle that I se nat of them.'

Than seyde that man, 'Truly, sir Gaherys and sir Gareth be slayne.'

'Jesu deffende,' seyde sir Gawayne, 'for all thys worlde I wolde nat that they were slayne, and in especiall my good brothir sir Gareth.'

'Sir,' seyde the man, 'he ys slayne, and that ys grete pité.'

'Who slew hym?' seyde sir Gawayne.

'Sir Launcelot,' seyde the man, 'slew hem both.'

'That may I nat believe,' seyde sir Gawayne, 'that ever he slew my good brother sir Gareth, for I dare say my brothir loved hym bettir than me and all hys brethirn and the kynge bothe. Also I dare sey, an sir Launcelot had desyred my brothir sir Gareth with hym, he wolde have ben with hym ayenste the kynge and us all. And therefore I may never belyeve that sir Launcelot slew my brethern.'

'Veryly, sir,' seyde the man, 'hit ys noysed that he slew hym.'

'Alas,' seyde sir Gawayne, 'now ys my joy gone!'

One of the distinctive features of the present edition as compared to the first is a more consistent use of this method of setting out dialogue. This has involved, especially in the first volume, a considerable amount of re-paragraphing and consequent changes of pagination. References to the text in the Commentary, the Index and the Glossary have had to be revised accordingly.

For reasons explained above[2] I have abandoned the traditional general heading of Malory's works—*Le Morte Darthur*—and have given each work the title which Malory himself assigned to it in his colophon. I have not, however, thought it necessary to alter the traditional sequence of the eight romances, since this sequence is confirmed by the Winchester MS. and may well represent the arrangement of the material in the author's own final copy.

I have naturally ignored Caxton's division into books and

---

[1] *v. infra*, pp. 305–6.　　　　[2] *v. supra*, pp. xxxix–li.

chapters, but have divided the five longest romances—*The Tale of King Arthur*, *The Book of Sir Tristram*, *The Tale of the Sankgreal*, *The Book of Sir Launcelot and Queen Guinevere*, and *The Morte Arthur*—into sections which in most cases correspond to subdivisions indicated in the text. Caxton's *Table of Rubrysshe* has been split accordingly and used as a substitute for the table of contents at the beginning of each section. To facilitate reference to Caxton's edition his book-numbers appear at the top of each page, and his chapter-numbers are given in brackets in the outer margin.

Caxton's Preface is reproduced in full as one of the finest essays ever written on the *Morte Darthur* and as a fitting and indeed indispensable prelude to the 'noble and joyous book'.

BIBLIOGRAPHY

I. THE FIRST EDITION[1]

THE first edition of Malory's works is a small folio volume[2] without a title, produced by William Caxton at Westminster on 31 July 1485. The first leaf is blank. Caxton's Preface begins on sig. ii recto and is followed on sig. iiij verso by *The table or rubrysshe of the contents of chapytres*. The text itself begins on sig. a i recto and ends on sig. ee 6 recto. The colophon reads as follows:

❡ Thus endeth thys noble and Ioyous book entytled le morte ‖ Darthnr │ Notwythstondyng it treateth of the byrth │ lyf │ and ‖ actes of the sayd kyng Arthur │ of his noble knyghtes of the ‖ rounde table │ theyr mer-uayllous enquestes and aduentures │ ‖ thachyeuyng of the sangreal │ & in thende the dolorous deth & ‖ departyng out of thys world of them al │ whiche book was re ‖ duced in to englysshe by syr Thomas Malory knyght as afore ‖ is sayd │ and by me deuyded in to xxi bookes chapytred ‖ and │ enprynted │ and fynysshed in thabbey westmestre the last day ‖ of Iuyl [*sic*] the yere of our lord │ M│CCCC│LXXXV│ ‖

❡ Caxton me fieri fecit

The black-letter type used in this edition[3] (No. 4* according to Blades) was first introduced by Caxton in 1483 when he published the *Confessio Amantis*, the *Festial*, and the *Four Sermons*. The lines are spaced to an even length of 118 mm.; 38 lines (190 mm.) make a full page, but some of the pages have 39 lines and some are a few lines short. There are no head-lines or catchwords. Initials are in wood of 3 to 5 lines in depth. The volume has 432 leaves divided into 54 gatherings. Two gatherings are taken up by Caxton's Preface and Rubrics; the first has four folio sheets, the second five. The gatherings containing the text proper have four sheets each, with the exception of the last which has only three; they are numbered from a to z &, from A to Z[4], and from aa to ee.

[1] For a description of the unique surviving manuscript see above, pp. ci–ciii.
[2] 281 × 200 mm.
[3] For a detailed description see William Blades, *The Life and Typography of William Caxton*, vol. ii (London, 1863), pp. 176–8 (reproduced with slight altera-tions in the same author's *Biography and Typography of William Caxton*, London and Strasbourg, 1877, pp. 301–3). Seymour de Ricci (*A Census of Caxtons*, Oxford, 1909) and E. Gordon Duff (*Fifteenth-Century English Books*, Oxford, 1917) have supplemented and rectified Blades's description.
[4] There are two misprints in the signatures: R iii for S iii and S ii for T ii.

Only two copies of the edition are known: one in the Pierpont Morgan Library in New York (*P*), and one in the John Rylands Library in Manchester (*R*).[1] One leaf of a third copy has been found in the binding of *Vitae Patrum* (1495) in the Lincoln Cathedral Library.[2]

A word-for-word comparison of *P* and *R*[3] shows that they represent two distinct 'states' of the text. The third sheet in gatherings N and Y has undergone thorough revision,[4] and in addition there are thirty-two variants scattered all over the text, mostly in small batches. Some of these variants (marked in the list below with a dagger) are due to accidents of imposition such as flaws in the paper, displacement of letters, or loss of loose type drawn out by ink-balls; others (marked with an asterisk) represent deliberate corrections made by the printer after the printing off had begun:

		Line	Rylands copy (R)	Morgan copy (P)
1*	sig. a 4^v	9	Now	N now
2†	„ d iii^r	..	*sig. omitted*	d iii
3*	„ k 8^v	27	best	hest
4*	„ n iii^r	18	loue	boue
5†	„ o 5^r	33	o	of
6*	„ o 6^r	33	Arthurle te	Arthur lete
7†	„ p 4^r	..	p iiii	*sig. omitted*
8†	„ p 6^v	38	kynges and quenes	*omitted*
9†	„ t 8^v	..	¶ Capitulum primum	„
10†	„ u ii^v	9	myssa	myssay
11*	„ u 7^r	1	sarche	serche[5]
12†	„ y ii^v	1	thre	thɔɪ[6]
13†	„ y 4^r	14	si	sir[7]
14†	„ z 7^v	7	bo	body[8]
15*	„ A ii^r	34	& fayne	and fayne
16*	„ „	35	what	*omitted*[9]

[1] The John Rylands Library also possesses a complete photostat of the Pierpont Morgan copy.

[2] Cf. Seymour de Ricci, op. cit., p. 76. The reference in the British Museum Bagford collection (vol. viii, n. 58) to another fragment is an error, as there is no original leaf in the volume (now 469 f., Ames Collection, vol. i), while no. 58 is a manuscript transcript.

[3] For this I am indebted to my friend and former pupil, Mr. E. S. Murrell, who collated the two copies from beginning to end for the purpose of the 1947 edition.

[4] Both are reproduced in full in my critical apparatus, cf. *infra*, pp. 856–61, 866–72, 1090–5, and 1105–9.

[5] u ii^v and u 7^r belong to the same forme.

[6] The ligature *re* is upside down in *P*.

[7] Flaw in the paper in *R*.

[8] Only the final loop of *y* remains in *R*.

[9] This is the result of a previous correction: *what* occurs at the end of a line, and there was no room left for it when *&* had been expanded to *and*.

ye haue made / For thurgh yow ye haue berafte me the fayrest
felauship and the truest of knyghthode that euer were sene to
gyders in ony realme of the world / For whanne they departe
from hens I am sure / they alle shalle neuer mete more in thys
world / for they shalle dye many in the quest / And soo it for
thynketh me a lytel / for I haue loued them as wel as my lyf
wherfor hit shall greue me ryghte sore the departycyon of this
felauship / For I haue had an old custome to haue hem in
my felauship /

Capitulum Octauuum /

And ther with the teres fylle in his eyen / And thenne
he sayd Galwayne Galwayne ye haue sette me in grete
sorowe / For I haue grete doubte that my true felauship
shalle neuer mete here more ageyne / A sayd syr Launcelot com
forte your self / for hit shalle be vnto vs a grete honour & mo
che more than yf we dyed in ony other places / for of deth we
be syker / A launcelot said the kyng the grete loue that I haue had vn
to you al the dayes of my lyf maketh me to say suche dolefull
wordes / for neuer Crysten kynge had neuer soo many worthy
men at this table as I haue had this daye at the round table
and that is my grete sorowe / ¶ Whanne the Quene ladyes &
gentilwymmen wyst these tydynges / they had suche sorowe &
heuynesse that ther myght no tonge telle hit / for tho knyghtes
had holde them in honour and chyerte / But amonge all oth
er Quene Gueneuer made grete sorowe / I merueylle said she
my lord wolde suffre hem to departe from hym / thus was al the
Courte troubled / for the loue of the departycyon of tho knygh
tes / And many of tho ladyes that loued knyghtes wold ha
ue gone with her louers / and soo had they done had not an
old knyghte come amonge them in Relygyous clothyng / and
thenne he spake alle on hyghe / and said fayre Lordes whiche ha
ue sworn in the quest of the Sancgreal / Thus sendeth you na
cyen the hermyte word that none in this queste lede lady nor
gentylwoman with hym / for hit is not to doo in so hyghe a ser
uyse as they labour in / for I warne yow playne he that is not
clene of his synnes / he shalle not see the mysteryes of our lord

iv. Sig. N 6ʳ of the Rylands copy of Caxton's edition

		Line	Rylands copy (R)	Morgan copy (P)
17*	sig. A ii	..	A ii	ii A
18†	„ A iii^r	33	dy e	dyde
19*	„ B iii^v	6	with in	within
20*	„ B 4^r	2	these	thefe
21*	„ B 5^v	1	sure	fure[1]
22†	„ D 1^r	21	Ma ke	Marke
23†	„ I 5^v	30	nyghtes	tn yghtes
24†	„ N 8^r	5	yghte this	yghte | this
25*	„ „	33	[gre-] to	[gre-]te
26†	„ O 4^v	34	eyth r	eyther
27*	„ P 4^r	9	for to	sor to
28†	„ T ii^v	20	fay u	fayu
29*	„ V ii^r	3	Soo a fter	Soa ofter
30†	„ X 5^r	4	lenynge	lenyng[2]
31*	„ cc 7^r	31	full	sull
32*	„ ee ii^v	21	forsake	sorsake

It is clear that the variants marked with an asterisk represent corrections made sometimes in *R* and sometimes in *P*. Hence each copy contains some corrected and some uncorrected sheets (no doubt because the binder did not trouble himself to sort them out), and neither can be regarded as representing a fully revised 'state'.

The accident of binding probably also accounts for the inclusion in *P* of two fully revised sheets, the first of which contains sig. N iii and N 6, the second sig. Y iii and Y 6.[3] The frequency of the variants in these four leaves is such as to suggest that the whole matter was reset from beginning to end. The alterations of spelling are fairly consistent: in *R* preference is given to such forms as *shalle*, *wille*, *alle*, and *soo*, whereas *P* distinctly favours *shal*, *wyl*, *al*, and *so*—forms which are less common in Caxton's edition as a whole. This added to such variants as *this he* in *R*, *this is he* in *P*, *assaye to take the suerd and at my commaundement* in *R*, *assaye to take the suerd & assaye at my comandement* in *P*, shows that in this instance *P* represents the revised issue. The most interesting variant occurs in the passage describing Galahad's magic sword which he was to draw from a stone found floating on the river. *R* says that when Gawain had failed to draw the sword there were *moo* (= 'more knights') who ventured to try it. Such is also the reading of the Winchester MS.: 'Than were there mo that durste be so hardy to sette their hondis thereto.' Caxton must have noticed the error and inserted a negation before *moo* when

---

[1] B 4^r and B 5^v belong to the same forme.
[2] The word occurs at the end of a line.
[3] The fact that in both cases the sheet is the third sheet of the gathering is probably a mere coincidence.

the text was already in the press, with the result that in P the correct reading *were there no moo* was restored, while R preserved the corrupt reading of Caxton's copy.

Cases such as this might explain why Caxton undertook the revision while the book was being printed. It has been suggested, as a possible reason, that having distributed the type he found that he had not printed a sufficient number of copies of two of the sheets and so had to produce a few more.[1] But this would not account for the fact that in resetting the type of the two sheets he made nearly seven hundred corrections, some of which represent improvements on the earlier issue. A more plausible theory would seem to be that he reset the type because he wished to make certain alterations, and that the occasion for making them arose when he had to wait for freshly printed sheets to dry.[2] Knowing that he would have some time to spare he could interrupt the printing of, say, the inner forme of one of the sheets, reset the two pages comprised in it, and so produce another issue. By that time the first issue would presumably be dry, and he could print the outer forme on it. But as he would come to the end of it before the revised issue was dry, he would naturally take the opportunity of resetting the outer forme as he had reset the inner one. In this way the two issues would remain distinct throughout, and each copy would come out of the press with either a completely revised or a completely unrevised sheet, as is in fact the case in the two extant examples of Caxton's text.

The Pierpont Morgan copy is the only complete one.[3] The John Rylands copy[4] wants eleven leaves (98, 152-3, 307, 312, 357-8, and 418-31). These have been supplied in facsimile by Whittaker, whose

---

[1] Cf. Curt F. Bühler, 'Two Caxton Problems', *The Library*, vol. xx (1940), pp. 266-8. I am grateful to Dr. Bühler for correcting an error in my 'Note on the Earliest Printed Texts of Malory's Morte Darthur' (*Bulletin of the John Rylands Library*, vol. xxiii, no. 1). The correction does not, however, seem to me to affect the substance of the argument summarized above.

[2] On the importance of this process in early printing see R. McKerrow, *Introduction to Bibliography*, p. 210.

[3] It was originally one of the twenty-two Caxtons which were dispersed in 1698 with the library of Francis Bernard, Physician to James II. In the course of the eighteenth century it was sold several times, and belonged successively to Thomas Rawlinson, the Earl of Oxford (Robert Harley), Bryan Fairfax, and Francis Child, maternal ancestor of the Earl of Jersey. It was in the Earl of Jersey's Osterley Park collection until 1885 when it was bought by Mr. and Mrs. Norton Q. Pope, of Brooklyn, N.Y. Its next owner was Robert Hoe. At the sale of Hoe's library in 1911 J. Pierpont Morgan bought the volume for $42,800. It is bound in old red morocco. The blank leaf (sig. i), preserved in the Rylands copy, is missing.

[4] It was bought by Earl Spencer at John Lloyd's sale for £300 and remained in the Spencer library at Althorp until 1892, when Mrs. John Rylands bought it for the John Rylands Library. It is bound in olive morocco by C. Lewis.

ye haue made / For thorugh you ye haue berafte me the fayrest
felaushyp and the truest of knyghthod that euer were sene to
gyders in ony royalme of the world / For whan they departe
from hens I am sure they alle shal neuer mete more in thys
world / For they shal dye many in the quest / And so it for
thynketh me a lytel / for I haue loued them as wel as my lyf
Wherfore hit shal greue me ryght sore the departycyon of thys
felaushyp / For I haue had an olde custome to haue them in
my felaushyp /

¶ Capitulum Octauum

ANd ther wyth the teres fyl in his eyen / And thenne
he sayd Galwayne Galwayne ye haue sette me in grete
sorow: / for I haue grete doubte that my true felaushyp
shal neuer mete here more ageyn / A sayd syr Launcelot com
forth your self / for hit shal be vnto vs a grete honour & moche
more than yf we dyed in ony other places / for of deth we be
syker / A Launcelot said the kyng the grete loue that I haue had
vnto you al the dayes of my lyf maketh me to say suche dole
ful wordes / for neuer cristen kyng had neuer so many worthy
men at his table as I haue had thys day at the rounde table
and that is my grete sorowe / ¶ Whan the Quene ladyes &
gentilwymmen wyst these tydynges / they had suche sorowe &
hewynesse that there myght no tonge telle it / for tho knyghtes
had holde them in honour and chyere / But emonge al other
Quene Gueneuer made grete sorowe / I meruaylle sayd she
my lord wold suffre hem to departe from hym / thus was al the
courte troubled for the loue of the departycyon of tho knygh
tes / & many of tho ladyes that loued knyghtes wold haue
gone wyth her louers and so had they done had not an olde
knyght comen emonge them in Relygyous clothyng / & thenne
he spake al on hyghe / And sayd fayre lordes whyche haue
sworn in the queste of the Sancgral / Thus sendeth you na
cyen the heremyte word that none in this queste lede lady nor
gentylwoman with hym / for hit is not to do in so hyghe a ser
uyse as they labour in / for I warne you playne he that is not
clene of his synnes / he shal not see the mysteryes of our lord

v. Sig. N 6ʳ of the Pierpont Morgan copy of Caxton's edition

work is, however, more remarkable for its artistic finish than for its accuracy: there are no fewer than seventy-two mistakes in the transcription,[1] some of which, left uncorrected by Sommer in his reprint of the Rylands copy, are still to be found in later reprints.[2]

The Rylands copy has no foliation. In the Morgan copy the first 132 leaves are numbered in a modern hand, but the first leaf is left out of account and no. 19 is duplicated. In Sommer's reprint the first leaf is likewise ignored for purposes of foliation. To avoid confusion, however, Sommer's numbering has been adopted in the present edition for all folio references to Caxton's text.

Among the early printers[3] Wynkyn de Worde alone used Caxton's *Morte Darthur*. His first edition appeared in 1498, his second in 1529.[4] William Copland (1557) was content to use the second, Thomas East (*c.* 1585) used both that edition and Copland's, and William Stanby (1634) used Thomas East's. No edition of Malory's works appeared in the eighteenth century, and Caxton's text did not come to light again until 1817 when Robert Southey produced his reprint of it under the title of *The Byrth, Lyf and Actes of Kyng Arthur*. But it was only when Edward Strachey published the text 'revised for modern use' in 1868 that its superiority over all the other early editions was generally recognized. Sommer's reprint of the Rylands (then Spencer) copy published in 1889 has for the last three-quarters of a century been used by most editors as a convenient substitute for the original Caxton.

[1] These are recorded in my critical apparatus under *Wh*.

[2] Sommer's edition is responsible for many other inaccuracies in modern reprints. When Sommer published his text in 1889 he declared that it 'followed the original impression of Caxton with absolute fidelity, word for word, line for line, page for page, and with some exceptions . . . letter for letter'. The exceptions are the normalizing of the three different kinds of *w*, the use of *I* for *i* and *j*, the distinction made between ȝ and z, the addition of the hyphen where words are divided at the end of the line, and the attempt to avoid the confusion, frequent in Caxton's text, between *n* and *u* and between f and ſ. In collating the reprint with the Rylands copy I found over a thousand mistakes, some of which, though by no means all, I have recorded in my critical apparatus under *S*. The mistakes range from a confusion between f and ſ to a complete distortion of the original, e.g. *on day* for *or day* (p. 37, l. 20), *this syde of the Iland* for *this syde the Iland* (p. 99, l. 19), *I am* for *I cam* (p. 233, l. 4), *ye* for *he*, *wold* for *wolt*, &c. No doubt the dimensions of the work, as any editor of Malory knows to his cost, make absolute accuracy humanly impossible; but the unfortunate thing about Sommer was that he belonged to that tradition of German scholarship which did not regard modesty as a virtue.

[3] For a list of subsequent editions see my *Malory*, pp. 190–6.

[4] These editions are at least as scarce as Caxton's. Only one copy of each is known, the first (1498) in the John Rylands Library, the second (1529) in the British Museum. In 1933 the Shakespeare Head Press produced a reprint of the first edition from the Rylands copy. The British Museum copy of the second edition has manuscript notes by Archdeacon Wrangham to whom it once belonged.

II. CRITICAL WORKS[1]

A. BIOGRAPHY

1. BAUGH, A. C., 'Documenting Sir Thomas Malory', *Speculum*, vol. viii (1933), pp. 3–29. [See also no. 4.]
2. CHAMBERS, E. K., *Sir Thomas Malory* (English Association, Pamphlet no. 51), London, 1922, p. 16, note. [Reprinted in revised form in the same author's *Sir Thomas Wyatt and Some Collected Studies*, London, 1933, pp. 44–45. Cf. no. 90.]
3. —— *English Literature at the Close of the Middle Ages*, Oxford, 1945, pp. 199–205.
4. HICKS, EDWARD, *Sir Thomas Malory, His Turbulent Career: A Biography*, Cambridge, Harvard University Press, 1928. [Reviewed by A. C. Baugh, *Journal of English and Germanic Philology*, vol. xxix (1930), pp. 452–7.]
5. KITTREDGE, G. L., *Who Was Sir Thomas Malory?* Boston, 1897. [Reprinted from *Studies and Notes in Philology and Literature*, vol. v, pp. 85–106; announced in Johnson's *Universal Cyclopaedia*, March 1894.]
6. —— *Sir Thomas Malory*, Barnstable, 1925. [Privately printed.]
7. MARTIN, A. T., 'Sir Thomas Malory', *Athenaeum*, 1897, pp. 353–4.
8. —— 'The Identity of the Author of the *Morte Darthur*', *Archaeologia*, vol. lvi, pp. 165–77.
9. MATTHEWS, WILLIAM, *The Ill-Framed Knight, A Skeptical Inquiry into the Identity of Sir Thomas Malory*, Berkeley, 1966.
10. VINAVER, EUGÈNE, *Malory*, Oxford, 1929, pp. 1–9 and 115–27 (*Materials for Malory's Biography*).
11. WILLIAMS, T. W. [Letter to] *The Athenaeum*, no. 3585 (11 July 1896), pp. 64–65. [On Malory's exclusion from a general pardon.]
12. —— *Sir Thomas Malory and the 'Morte Darthur'*, Bristol (J. W. Arrowsmith), 1909. [Privately printed.]

B. TEXTUAL HISTORY

13. BÜHLER, CURT F., 'Two Caxton Problems', *The Library*, vol. xx (1940), pp. 266–8. [Criticism of no. 28.]
14. OAKESHOTT, W. F., 'A Malory MS.', *The Times*, 23 July 1934.
15. —— 'The Text of Malory', *The Times Literary Supplement*, 27 September 1934. [First detailed account of the Winchester MS.]
16. —— 'The Manuscript of the "Morte Darthur"', *Discovery*, vol. xvi, no. 182 (February 1935), pp. 45–46.
17. —— 'Caxton and Malory's "Morte Darthur"', *Gutenberg-Jahrbuch*, 1935, pp. 112–16.
18. —— 'Arthuriana at Winchester', *Wessex, An Annual Record of the Movement for a University of Wessex*, vol. iii, no. 3 (1 May 1936), pp. 74–78.

---

1 Nos. 9, 74, 115, 116, 123a and 130 in this list came to my notice too late to be used in the revision of the Introduction and the Commentary.

19. OAKESHOTT, W. F., *The Finding of the Manuscript* (*Essays on Malory* ed. by J. A. W. Bennett, pp. 1–6), Oxford, 1963.
20. POLLARD, A. W., 'Bibliographical Note', [Preface to] *Le Morte Darthur: Sir Thomas Malory's Book of King Arthur and of His Noble Knights of the Round Table*, London (Macmillan), 1903, vol. i, pp. vii–viii.
21. SHAW, SALLY, *Caxton and Malory* (*Essays on Malory* ed. by J. A. W. Bennett, pp. 114–43), Oxford, 1963.
22. ŠIMKO, JAN, 'Malory a Caxton', *Časopis pro Moderni Filologii* (Prague), xxxv (1953), pp. 213–19. [For an English summary entitled *Malory and Caxton* see ibid., pp. 254–5.]
23. [SOMMER, H. OSKAR], *Le Morte Darthur by Syr Thomas Malory, The Original Edition of William Caxton Now Reprinted and Edited by H. Oskar Sommer*, London, 1889–91. Vol. ii (1890). *Introduction*: Sir Thomas Malory and the various editions of 'Le Morte Darthur' (pp. 1–14); Relation of the different editions of 'Le Morte Darthur' to one another (pp. 15–17); List of errors, omissions, and orthographical irregularities in Caxton's impression (pp. 21–25); Collation of Whittaker's facsimiles with the original pages (pp. 26–28); Caxton's and Wynkyn de Worde's editions (pp. 43–145).
24. STRACHEY, EDWARD, [Introduction to] *Le Morte Darthur, &c.*, London (Macmillan), 1919, pp. xxxi–xxxvi (*The Text and its Several Editions*).
25. VINAVER, EUGÈNE, *Malory*, Oxford, 1929, pp. 189–90. [List of editions of *Le Morte Darthur*.]
26. —— 'Malory's *Morte Darthur* in the Light of a Recent Discovery', *Bulletin of the John Rylands Library*, vol. xix, no. 2, July, 1935. [On the Winchester MS.]
27. —— 'New Light on Malory's *Morte Darthur*', *Yorkshire Society for Celtic Studies*, Session 1935–6, pp. 18–20. [On Caxton's treatment of Malory's text.]
28. —— 'A Note on the Earliest Printed Texts of Malory's *Morte Darthur*', *Bulletin of the John Rylands Library*, vol. xxiii, no. 1, April 1939. [Now superseded by the account of the first edition in Section I above.]

C. LANGUAGE

29. BALDWIN, CHARLES SEARS, *The Inflections and Syntax of the 'Morte d'Arthur' of Sir Thomas Malory*, Boston, 1894. [Reviewed in *Anglia, Beiblatt* v, pp. 323–4, and *Englische Studien*, vol. xxii, pp. 79–81.]
30. —— 'The verb in the "Morte d'Arthur"', *Modern Language Notes*, vol. x (1895), no. 2, pp. 46–47.
31. BENNETT, H. S., 'Fifteenth Century Secular Prose', *Review of English Studies*, vol. xxi (1945), p. 257. [. . . 'Professor Chambers . . . rightly saw that the main stream could not flow through the prose of Pecock, Fortescue, or Malory. . . . It would be nearer the truth to look on them as backwaters, or inland lakes which we may admire for their many beauties, but which do not feed the main stream.']
32. BENNETT, J. A. W., [Preface to] *Essays on Malory*, Oxford, 1963, pp. v–vii. [One of the suggested desiderata in Malory research is 'a

detailed comparison of his prose with that of the French texts that were the bases of the greater part of his book and with the English *Merlin*——the only prose romance known to us that could have been known to Malory'.]

33. CHAMBERS, R. W., *On the Continuity of English Prose from Alfred to More and his School*, London, 1932, pp. cxxxviii–cxl. [Cf. no. 31.]

34. DAVIS, NORMAN, *Styles in English Prose of the Late Middle and Early Modern Period* in *Actes du VIIIe Congrès de la Fédération Internationale des Langues et Littératures Modernes*, Liège, 1961.

35. DEKKER, ARIE, *Some Facts Concerning the Syntax of Malory's 'Morte Darthur'* (*according to the edition of H. Oskar Sommer*), Academisch Proefschrift, Amsterdam, 1932.

36. DUBOIS, M. M., [Introduction to] *Le Roman d'Arthur et des chevaliers de la Table Ronde*, Paris (Aubier), 1948, pp. 44–48 ('La langue') and 254–5 ('Glossaire des mots anglais').

37. FROMM, CHARLOTTE, *Ueber den verbalen Wortschatz in Sir Thomas Malorys Roman 'Le Morte Darthur'*, Marburg, 1914.

38. KEMPL, GEORGE, 'The Verb in the "Morte d'Arthur"', *Modern Language Notes*, vol. ix (1894), no. 8, pp. 240–1.

39. KURIYAGAWA, FUMIO, 'The Language of Malory's *Tale of Arthur and Lucius*' [in Japanese], *Studies in English Literature*, vol. xxxiv, no. 2 (The English Literary Society of Japan, 1958), pp. 253–69.

39a. MATTHEWS, WILLIAM, *see* no. 9 (pp. 76–98 and 177–238).

40. NOGUCHI, SHUNICHI, 'Malory's English: An Aspect of its Syntax', *Hiroshima Studies in English Language and Literature*, vol. vii, no. 2 (1961).

41. —— 'Notes on the linguistic differences between Caxton's edition and the Winchester MS. of Thomas Malory's Works' [in Japanese], (*Fukui University Studies in the Humanities*, no. 12, 1963.)

42. PRINS, A. A., *French Influence in English Phrasing*, Leiden, 1952, pp. 17–18. [Comment on *M* 13. 18–32: 'For all the gallicisms in vocabulary, this kind of prose is far less gallicized in phraseonomy or latinized in syntax than either Nicholas Love's or More's'.]

43. RIOUX, ROBERT N., 'Sir Thomas Malory, créateur verbal', *Études anglaises*, vol. xii, pp. 193–7.

44. SANDVED, A. O., 'A note on the language of Caxton's Malory and that of the Winchester MS.', *English Studies*, vol. xl (1959), pp. 113–14.

45. SHAW, SALLY, *Caxton and Malory* in *Essays on Malory* ed. by J. A. W. Bennett, Oxford, 1963, pp. 143–5 (*Linguistic comparison of the texts*).

46. ŠIMKO, JAN, 'A linguistic analysis of the Winchester manuscript and William Caxton's Edition of Sir Thomas Malory's *Morte Darthur*', *Philologica*, vol. viii (1956), pp. 1–2.

47. —— *Word-Order in the Winchester manuscript and in William Caxton's Edition of Sir Thomas Malory's* Morte Darthur (*1485*): *A Comparison*, Halle (Max Niemeyer), 1957. [Reviewed by T. F. Mustanoja in *Neuphilologische Mitteilungen*, 1960, vol. lxi, no. 4, pp. 391–2.]

48. SMITH, GEORGE GREGORY, *The Transition Period*, Edinburgh, 1900, pp. 330–3 (*The Prose Experiment in England*).

49. [SOMMER, H. OSKAR], *Le Morte Darthur by Syr Thomas Malory, The Original Edition of William Caxton Now Reprinted and Edited by H. Oskar Sommer*, London, 1889–91. Vol. ii (1890). *Introduction*, pp. 28–42: 'Notes on the Language of *Le Morte Darthur*'.

50. WILSON, R. M., 'On the Continuity of English Prose', *Mélanges de linguistique et de philologie, Fernand Mossé in memoriam*, Paris, 1959, p. 493.

D. INTERPRETATION AND CRITICISM[1]

51. ACKERMAN, ROBERT W., 'Malory's Ironsyde', *Research Studies* (Washington State University), vol. xxxii (1964), pp. 125–33.

52. ANGELESCU, VICTOR, 'The relationship of Gareth and Gawain in Malory's *Morte Darthur*', *Notes and Queries*, vol. viii, pp. 8–9. [Cf. Commentary, note 360. 34–35.]

53. ARNOLD, IVOR D. O., 'Malory's Story of Arthur's Roman Campaign', *Medium Ævum*, vol. vii (1938), pp. 74–75. [Criticism of no. 156.]

54. AURNER, NELLIE SLAYTON, 'Sir Thomas Malory—Historian?' *PMLA*, vol. xlviii (1933), pp. 360–91.

55. BAKER, ERNEST A., *The History of the English Novel: The Age of Romance*, London, 1924, pp. 190–207.

56. BALDINI, GABRIELE, *Storia della letteratura inglese*: I. *La tradizione letteraria dell'Inghilterra medioevale*, Torino (Radio Italiana), 1958, pp. 301–17.

57. BARBER, R. W., *Arthur of Albion, An Introduction to the Arthurian Literature and Legends of England*, with a Preface by David Jones, London, 1961, pp. 122–35.

58. BARTHOLOMEW, BARBARA GRAY, 'The Thematic Function of Malory's Gawain', *College English*, vol. xxiv (1963), pp. 262–7.

59. BOGDANOW, FANNI, 'The Rebellion of the Kings in the Cambridge MS. of the *Suite du Merlin*', *Texas Studies in English*, vol. xxxiv (1955), pp. 6–17. [Criticism of no. 170; cf. *infra*, p. 1281, n. 2.]

60. BRADBROOK, M. C., *Sir Thomas Malory* (published for the British Council and the National Book League), London, 1958.

61. BREWER, D. S., 'Form in the *Morte Darthur*', *Medium Ævum*, vol. xxi (1952), pp. 14–24.

62. —— [Review of] *The Tale of the Death of King Arthur* ed. by E. Vinaver [and of] R. M. Lumiansky, 'The Question of Unity in Malory's *Morte Darthur*', *Medium Ævum*, vol. xxv (1957), pp. 22–26.

63. —— '*the hoole book*' (*Essays on Malory* ed. by J. A. W. Bennett, pp. 41–63), Oxford, 1963: ['If I were contending that there was a modern organic unity of design in Malory's work, the *Tristram* would in itself be enough to refute me. But my contention is more modest: the tales are structurally connected and fit into a particular order.']

---

[1] I have listed under this heading whatever seemed relevant to the study of Malory's works and their sources. The list does not include publications dealing with Malory's influence on later writers, textbooks of literary history, prefaces to popular editions, or, except in a few cases, any unpublished 'dissertation abstracts'.

64. BRUCE, J. D., 'The Middle-English Metrical Romance *Le Morte Arthur* (Harleian MS. 2252): its Sources and its Relation to Sir Thomas Malory's *Morte Darthur*', *Anglia*, vol. xxiii (1901), pp. 67–100. [Cf. *infra*, pp. 1585 n. 2 and 1615 ff.]

65. —— [Introduction to] *Le Morte Arthur, a romance in stanzas of eight lines* (E.E.T.S., Extra Series, no. 88), London, 1903, pp. xiii–xx. [Summary of no. 64.]

66. —— 'A reply to Dr. Sommer', *Anglia*, vol. xxx, pp. 209–16. [Criticism of no. 135.]

67. CHAMBERS, E. K., *Sir Thomas Malory* (English Association, Pamphlet no. 51), London, 1922, pp. 1–15. [Reprinted with a few modifications in the same author's *Sir Thomas Wyatt and some Collected Studies*, London, 1933, pp. 21–43. Cf. no. 90.]

68. —— *English Literature at the Close of the Middle Ages*, Oxford, 1945, pp. 185–99.

69. CHILD, CLARENCE GRIFFIN, *The Book of Merlin; The Book of Sir Balin. From Malory's 'King Arthur'*, London (Harrap), Boston and New York (Houghton Mifflin), 1904; *Introductory Sketch*, pp. xiii–xvii.

70. DAVIES, R. T., 'Was Pellynore Unworthy?' *Notes and Queries*, N.S., vol. iv (1959), p. 370. [Cf. *infra*, p. 1333.]

71. —— 'Malory's Lancelot and the noble way of the world', *Review of English Studies*, N.S., vol. vi (1955), pp. 356–64.

72. —— 'Malory's Vertuouse Love', *Studies in Philology* (North Carolina), vol. liii (1956), pp. 459–69.

73. —— 'Gawain's Miraculous Strength', *Études anglaises*, vol. x (1957), pp. 97–108.

74. DAVIS, GILBERT R., 'Malory's *Tale of Sir Launcelot* and the question of unity in the *Morte Darthur*', *Papers of the Michigan Academy of Science, Arts and Letters*, vol. xlix, pp. 523–30.

75. DICHMANN, MARY E., 'Characterization in Malory's *Tale of Arthur and Lucius*', *PMLA*, vol. lxv (1950), pp. 877–95. Reprinted in revised form in *Malory's Originality*, ed. by R. M. Lumiansky, pp. 67–90. [Cf. *infra*, pp. 1367 n. 2 and 1368 n. 3.]

76. DONALDSON, E. T., 'Malory and the Stanzaic *Le Morte Arthur*', *Studies in Philology*, vol. xlvii (1950), pp. 460–72. [On the English source of *The Book of Sir Launcelot and Queen Guinevere*. Cf. *infra*, pp. 1585 and 1596.]

77. DUBOIS, M. M., [Introduction to] *Le Roman d'Arthur et des chevaliers de la Table Ronde*, Paris (Aubier), 1948, pp. 22–44 (Introduction: V. *L'œuvre de Malory*; VI. *L'art de Malory*).

78. FERGUSON, ARTHUR B., *The Indian Summer of English Chivalry: Studies in the Decline and Transformation of Chivalric Idealism*, Duke University Press, Durham, North Carolina, 1960, pp. 42–58.

79. FOX, MARJORIE B., 'Sir Thomas Malory and the "Piteous History of the Morte of King Arthur"', *Arthuriana*, vol. i (1929), pp. 30–36.

80. GÖLLER, K. H., *König Arthur in der englischen Literatur des späten Mittelalters*, Göttingen, 1963, pp. 144–65 (*Arthur im Werke Sir Thomas Malorys*).

81. GORDON, E. V., and VINAVER, E., 'New Light on the Text of the Alliterative *Morte Arthure*', *Medium Ævum*, vol. vi (1937), pp. 81–98.

82. GOSSMANN, A., and WHITING, G. W., 'King Arthur's Farewell to Guinevere', *Notes and Queries*, N.S., vol. vi (1959), pp. 446–8.

83. GUERIN, WILFRED L., 'Malory's *Morte Darthur*, Book VII', *Explicator* (University of South Carolina, Columbia S.C.), vol. xx, no. 8 (April 1962), 64.

84. —— '*The Tale of Gareth*': *The Chivalric Flowering* in *Malory's Originality*, ed. by R. M. Lumiansky, Baltimore, 1964, pp. 99–117. [Cf. *infra*, p. 1432 n. 1.]

85. —— '*The Tale of the Death of Arthur*': *Catastrophe and Resolution*, in *Malory's Originality*, ed. by R. M. Lumiansky, Baltimore, 1964, pp. 233–74.

86. HIBBARD, LAURA A., 'Malory's Book of Balin', *Mediaeval Studies in Memory of Gertrude Schoepperle Loomis*, Paris and New York, 1927, pp. 175–95. [Reprinted in *Adventures in the Middle Ages* by Laura Hibbard Loomis, New York, 1962.]

87. JACOB, E. F., *The Fifteenth Century* ('The Oxford History of England'), Oxford, 1961, pp. 656–8.

88. KER, W. P., *Essays on Medieval Literature*, London, 1905, pp. 22–27 (*The Earlier History of English Prose*).

89. LANG, ANDREW, '*Le Morte Darthur*' in *Le Morte Darthur by Syr Thomas Malory*, ed. by H. O. Sommer (see no. 134), vol. iii, pp. xiii–xxv.

90. L[EWIS], C. S., [Review of] E. K. Chambers, 'Sir Thomas Wyatt and Some Collected Studies', *Medium Ævum*, vol. iii (October 1934), pp. 238–9. [On the Grail theme.]

91. LEWIS, C. S., *The Allegory of Love: A Study in Medieval Tradition*, Oxford, 1936, p. 300. [On narrative technique.]

92. —— *The Morte Darthur* (front-page article in *The Times Literary Supplement* of 7 June 1947).

93. —— *The English Prose 'Morte'* (*Essays on Malory*, ed. by J. A. W. Bennett, pp. 7–28), Oxford, 1963. Cf. no. 154.

94. LOOMIS, ROGER SHERMAN, 'Malory's Beaumains', *PMLA*, vol. liv (1939), pp. 656–68. [Cf. *infra*, pp. 1430–1, 1438, and 1440.]

95. —— 'Onomastic riddles in Malory's *Book of King Arthur and his Knights*', *Medium Ævum*, vol. xxv (1956), pp. 181–90. [Cf. *infra*, pp. 1294–5 and 1667 n. 2.]

96. —— *The Development of Arthurian Romance*, Hutchinson University Library, London, 1963, pp. 166–85 (*Sir Thomas Malory*).

97. LÖSETH, E., *Le Roman en prose de Tristan, le roman de Palamède et la compilation de Rusticien de Pise, analyse critique d'après les manuscrits de Paris*, Paris, 1890, pp. xxii–xxiii. [On the source of *The Book of Sir Tristram*.]

98. LUMIANSKY, R. M., 'The Relationship of Lancelot and Guinevere in Malory's *Tale of Lancelot*', *Modern Language Notes*, vol. lxviii (1953), pp. 86–91.

99. —— 'The Question of Unity in Malory's *Morte Darthur*', *Tulane Studies in English*, vol. v (1955), pp. 29–39. [Cf. *infra*, pp. 1364–5.]

100. LUMIANSKY, R. M., 'Tristram's First Interview with Mark in Malory's _Morte Darthur_', _Modern Language Notes_, vol. lxx (1955), pp. 476–8. [Cf. _infra_, p. 1457.]

101. —— 'Gawain's Miraculous Strength: Malory's Use of _Le Morte Arthur_ and Mort Artu', _Études anglaises_, vol. x (1957), pp. 97–100. [Cf. _infra_, p. 1645.]

102. —— 'Two Notes on Malory's _Morte Darthur_: Sir Urry in England— Lancelot's Burial Vow', _Neuphilologische Mitteilungen_, vol. lviii (1957), pp. 148–53.

103. —— 'Malory's Steadfast Bors', _Tulane Studies in English_, vol. viii (1958), pp. 5–20. [See Commentary, notes 1036. 19–1037. 7 and 1249. 30–1250. 2.]

104. —— 'Malory's "Tale of Lancelot and Guinevere" as Suspense', _Mediaeval Studies_ (Toronto), vol. xix (1957), pp. 108–22. [On the persistence of the Lancelot–Guinevere theme and the presence in the 'Tale' of a 'pattern of suspense' repeated in each one of its various sections. Cf. _infra_, p. 1591 n. 2.]

105. —— 'Arthur's Final Companions in Malory's Morte Darthur', _Tulane Studies in English_, vol. xi (1961), pp. 5–19. [On the symbolical parts played by Morgan, the Queen of North Wales, Nineve, and the Queen of Waste Lands in the scene of Arthur's departure for Avalon.]

106. —— [ed. of] _Malory's Originality, A Critical Study of Le Morte Darthur._ The Johns Hopkins Press, Baltimore, 1964, pp. vii–viii (_Foreword_); pp. 1–7 (_Introduction_); pp. 91–98 ('_The Tale of Lancelot': Prelude to Adultery_); pp. 205–32 ('_The Tale of Lancelot and Guinevere': Suspense_). [The first of these essays first appeared in the _Modern Language Notes_ for 1953, the second in _Mediaeval Studies_ for 1957- See nos. 98 and 104.]

107. MACNEICE, LOUIS, 'Sir Thomas Malory', in _The English Novelists: A Survey of the Novel by Twenty Contemporary Novelists_, edited by Derek Verschoyle, London, 1936, pp. 19–28.

108. MATTHEWS, WILLIAM, _The Tragedy of Arthur—A Study of the Alliterative 'Morte Arthure'_, Berkeley and Los Angeles, 1960. [Cf. _infra_, pp. 1369–70.]

109. MEAD, WILLIAM EDWARD, _Selections from Sir Thomas Malory's 'Morte Darthur'_, Boston, 1897, pp. xxix–xxxviii (Introduction), 293–5 and 304–10. [On the sources of Books XVIII and XXI of _Le Morte Darthur_.]

110. MOORMAN, CHARLES, 'Malory's Treatment of the Sankgreall', _PMLA_, vol. lxxi/3 (June 1956), pp. 496–509. [Cf. _infra_, p. 1537 n. 3. Reprinted in revised form in _Malory's Originality_, ed. by R. M. Lumiansky, pp. 184–204.]

111. —— 'The Relation of Books I and III of Malory's _Morte Darthur_', _Mediaeval Studies_, vol. xxii (1960), pp. 361–6.

112. —— 'Courtly Love in Malory', _Journal of English Literary History_, vol. xxvii (1960), pp. 163–70.

113. —— 'Internal Chronology in Malory's _Morte Darthur_', _Journal of English and Germanic Philology_, vol. lx, no. 2 (April 1961), pp. 240–9. [Cf. _infra_, p. 1500 n. 2.]

114. MOORMAN, CHARLES, 'Lot and Pellinore; The Failure of Loyalty in Malory's *Morte Darthur*', *Mediaeval Studies*, vol. xxv (1963), pp. 83–92.

115. —— *The Book of Kyng Arthur: The Unity of Malory's* Morte Darthur, Lexington, University of Kentucky Press, 1965.

116. MORGAN, HENRY GRADY, 'The Role of Morgan le Fay in Malory's *Morte Darthur*', *Southern Quarterly* (University of South Miss.), vol. ii, pp. 150–68.

117. MUECKE, D. C., 'Some Notes on Vinaver's Malory', *Modern Language Notes*, vol. lxx (1955), pp. 325–8. [Cf. Commentary, notes 163. 20 and 615. 33.]

118. PARIS, GASTON, [Introduction to] *Merlin, roman en prose du XIIIe siècle*, Paris, 1886 ('Société des Anciens Textes Français'), pp. lxx–lxxii. [On the source of *The Tale of King Arthur*.]

119. PARSONS, C. O., 'A Scottish "Father of Courtesy" and Malory', *Speculum*, vol. xx (1945), pp. 51–64. [Cf. Commentary, note 1237. 16–18.]

120. PULVER, JEFFREY, 'Music in Malory's "Arthur"', *Musical News*, 9 December 1916, pp. 377–8. [Reprinted with slight alterations in *The Monthly Musical Record*, 1 January 1929, pp. 3–4.]

121. RAY, B. K., 'The Character of Gawain', *Dacca University Bulletin*, no. xi, Oxford University Press, 1926, pp. 8–11.

122. [READ, HERBERT], 'Sir Thomas Malory and the Sentiment of Glory', *The Times Literary Supplement*, 21 June 1928, pp. 457–8. [Reprinted in the same author's *Sense of Glory: Essays on Criticism*, 1929, pp. 33–56, and in *Collected Essays in Literary Criticism*, 1938, pp. 168–82.]

123. REID, MARGARET J. C., *The Arthurian Legend: Comparison of Treatment in Modern and Mediaeval Literature*, Edinburgh and London, 1938, pp. 24–29, 87–90, 191–203.

123a. REISS, EDMUND, *Sir Thomas Malory*, New York, 1966.

124. RHYS, JOHN, *Studies in the Arthurian Legend*, Oxford, 1891, pp. 20–23, 70 (note 2), 278–99, 357–8, 361–2.

125. ROBINSON, FREDERIC W., *A Commentary and a Questionnaire on Selections from Malory* (edited by H. Wragg), London, 1927, pp. 11–26. [On style and characterization.]

126. RUMBLE, THOMAS C., 'The First *Explicit* in Malory's *Morte Darthur*', *Modern Language Notes*, vol. lxxi (1956), pp. 564–6.

127. —— 'Malory's *Works* and Vinaver's Comments: Some Inconsistencies Resolved', *Journal of English and Germanic Philology*, vol. lix (1960), pp. 59–69. [Cf. Commentary, note 668. 20–25.]

128. —— 'The Tale of Tristram': Development by Analogy, in *Malory's Originality*, ed. by R. M. Lumiansky, Baltimore, 1964, pp. 118–83.

129. SAINTSBURY, GEORGE, *A History of English Prose Rhythm*, London, 1912, pp. 82–92.

130. SCHMIDZ, C. C. D., *Sir Gareth of Orkeney, Studien zum siebenten Buch von Malorys Morte Darthur*, Groningen, 1963.

131. SCHOFIELD, W. H., *Chivalry in English Literature: Chaucer, Malory, Spenser, and Shakespeare*, Cambridge, Harvard University Press, 1912, pp. 75–123, 262–3, and 284. [Cf. *infra*, p. 1440.]

132. SCUDDER, VIDA D., *Le Morte Darthur of Sir Thomas Malory: A Study of the Book and Its Sources*, London and New York, 1921.
ŠIMKO, JAN, *see* nos. 22, 46, and 47.

133. SNELL, F. J., *The Age of Transition*, 1400–1580. Vol. ii: *The Dramatists and the Prose Writers*, London, 1905, pp. 83–90.

134. [SOMMER, H. OSKAR], *Le Morte Darthur by Syr Thomas Malory, The Original Edition of William Caxton Now Reprinted and Edited by H. Oskar Sommer*, London, 1889–91, vol. iii (1891): *Studies on the Sources*.

135. SOMMER, H. OSKAR, 'On Dr. Douglas Bruce's Article "The Middle-English Romance *Le Morte Arthur*"', &c., *Anglia*, vol. xxix (1906), pp. 529–38. [Criticism of nos. 64 and 65. Cf. *infra*, pp. 1585 n. 2 and 1615 n. 3.]

136. STEWART, GEORGE R., Jr., 'English Geography in Malory's *Morte D'Arthur*', *Modern Language Review*, vol. xxx (1935), pp. 204–9.

137. STRACHEY, EDWARD, [Introduction to] *Le Morte Darthur: Sir Thomas Malory's Book of King Arthur and of his Noble Knights of the Round Table* [First impression, March 1868], London, 1919, pp. ix–xxiii (*The Authorship and Matter of the Book*) and xxxviii–lvi (*An Essay on Chivalry*).

138. THORNTON, SISTER M. M., *Malory's Morte Darthur as a Christian Epic*, Urbana, Ill., University of Illinois, 1936.

139. *The Times Literary Supplement*, [Front-page article on] 'Sir Thomas Malory', 21 June 1930.

140. TUCKER, P. E., 'The Place of the *Quest of the Holy Grail* in the *Morte Darthur*', *Modern Language Review*, vol. xlviii (1953), pp. 391–7.

141. —— 'A source for "The Healing of Sir Urry" in the *Morte Darthur*', *Modern Language Review*, vol. l (1955), pp. 490–2. [Cf. *infra*, p. 1591.]

142. —— *Chivalry in the 'Morte'* (*Essays on Malory*, ed. by J. A. W. Bennett, pp. 64–103), Oxford, 1963.

143. URGAN, MINA, [Introduction to] *Arthur ün Ölümü* (in Turkish), Istanbul, 1948.

144. VAN DER VEN TEN-BENSEL, ELISA FRANCISCA WILHELMINA MARIA, *The Character of King Arthur in English Literature*, Amsterdam, 1925, pp. 139–54 (*Malory's 'Morte Darthur'*).
VERSCHOYLE, DEREK, *see* no. 107.

145. VETTERMANN, ELLA, 'Die Balen-Dichtungen und ihre Quellen', *Beihefte zur Zeitschrift für romanische Philologie*, Halle a. S., 1918, pp. 52–84.

146. VINAVER, EUGÈNE, *Le Roman de Tristan et Iseut dans l'œuvre de Thomas Malory*, Paris, 1925, pp. 91–129 (*Matière et Sens*), 131–47 (*L'Idéal chevaleresque*), 149–52 (*Malory traducteur*), 155–220 (*L'Originalité de Malory*).

147. —— *Malory*, Oxford, 1929, pp. 14–114, 126–54.

148. —— 'Notes on Malory's Sources', *Arthuriana*, vol. i (1929), pp. 64–66. [On *The Tale of King Arthur* and *The Book of Sir Launcelot and Queen Guinevere*.]

149. —— 'A Romance of Gaheret', *Medium Ævum*, vol. i (December 1932), pp. 157–67. [On the prototype of *The Book of Sir Gareth*.]

150. —— 'Le Manuscrit de Winchester', *Bulletin Bibliographique de la Société Internationale Arthurienne*, no. 3 (1951), pp. 75–82.

151. VINAVER, EUGÈNE, [Introduction to] *The Tale of the Death of King Arthur* by Sir Thomas Malory, Oxford, 1955.

152. —— [Introduction to] *King Arthur and his Knights, Selections from the Works of Sir Thomas Malory*, Houghton Mifflin Company, Boston, The Riverside Press, 1956.

153. —— *Sir Thomas Malory* in *Arthurian Literature in the Middle Ages*, ed. by R. S. Loomis, Oxford, 1959, pp. 541–52.

154. —— *On Art and Nature: A Letter to C. S. Lewis (Essays on Malory*, ed. by J. A. W. Bennett, pp. 29–40), Oxford, 1963. Cf. no. 94.

155. —— *Epic and Tragic Patterns in Malory*, in *Friendship's Garland, Essays presented to Mario Praz on his seventieth birthday*, Rome, 1966, vol. i, pp. 81–85.

156. VORONTZOFF, TANIA, 'Malory's Story of Arthur's Roman Campaign', *Medium Ævum*, vol. vi (1937), pp. 99–121. [Cf. no. 53.]

157. WECHSSLER, EDUARD, *Ueber die verschiedenen Redaktionen des Robert de Boron zugeschriebenen Graal-Lancelot Cyklus*, Halle, 1897, pp. 22–23. [On *The Tale of King Arthur, The Tale of Sir Launcelot du Lake*, and *The Knight of the Cart*. Cf. infra, pp. 1322–3.]

158. WESTON, JESSIE L., *The Legend of Sir Lancelot du Lac*, London, 1901, pp. 155–8. [On *The Tale of Sir Launcelot du Lake*.]

159. WHITEHEAD, F., 'On Certain Episodes in the Fourth Book of Malory's *Morte Darthur*', *Medium Ævum*, vol. ii (October 1933), pp. 199–216. [On the final section of *The Tale of King Arthur*. Cf. infra, pp. 1361–4.]

160. —— *Lancelot's Penance (Essays on Malory*, ed. by J. A. W. Bennett, pp. 104–13), Oxford, 1963.
WHITING, G. W., see no. 81.

161. WILLIAMS, CHARLES, 'Malory and the Grail Legend', *Dublin Review*, no. 429 (April 1944), pp. 144–53.

162. WILSON, ROBERT H., 'Malory and the *Perlesvaus*', *Modern Philology*, vol. xxx (August 1932), pp. 13–22. [On the source of *The Tale of Sir Launcelot du Lake*. Cf. infra, pp. 1423–4.]

163. —— *Characterization in Malory: A Comparison with his Sources* ['Essential Portion' of a University of Chicago dissertation], Chicago, 1934.

164. —— 'Malory, the Stanzaic *Morte Arthur* and the *Mort Artu*', *Modern Philology*, vol. xxxvii (1939–40), pp. 125–38. [Cf. infra, p. 1585 n. 2.]

165. —— 'Malory's Naming of Minor Characters', *Journal of English and Germanic Philology*, vol. xlii (July 1943), pp. 364–85. [Cf. infra, p. 1665 n. 1.]

166. —— 'Malory's French Book Again', *Comparative Literature*, vol. ii (1950), pp. 172–81.

167. —— 'The "Fair Unknown" in Malory', *PMLA*, vol. lviii (1943), pp. 1–21. [On the source of *The Book of Sir Gareth*.]

168. —— 'Notes on Malory's sources', *Modern Language Notes*, vol. lxvi (1951), pp. 22–26. [Cf. infra, pp. 1410 n. 1, 1411 n. 1, 1423 and 1585 n. 4.]

169. —— 'How many books did Malory write?' *Texas Studies in English*, vol. xxx (1951), pp. 1–23.

170. WILSON, ROBERT H., 'The Rebellion of the Kings in Malory and in the Cambridge *Suite du Merlin*', *Texas Studies in English*, vol. xxxi (1952), pp. 13–26. [See no. 59 and *infra*, pp. 1281 n. 2, 1289–90 and 1295–6.]
171. —— 'The Prose *Lancelot* in Malory', *Texas Studies in English*, vol. xxxii (1953), pp. 1–13.
172. —— 'Malory's Early Knowledge of Arthurian Romance', *Texas Studies in English*, vol. xxxii (1953). [Cf. *infra*, p. 1407 n. 1.]
173. —— 'Some minor characters in the *Morte Arthure*', *Modern Language Notes*, vol. lxxi (1956), pp. 475–80.
174. —— 'Addenda on Malory's Minor Characters', *Journal of English and Germanic Philology*, vol. lv (1956), pp. 567–87. [Cf. *infra*, p. 1665 n. 1.] WRAGG, H., *see* no. 125.
175. WRIGHT, THOMAS L., '*The Tale of King Arthur*': Beginnings and Foreshadowings, in *Malory's Originality*, ed. by R. M. Lumiansky, Baltimore, 1964, pp. 9–66. [Cf. *infra*, pp. 1276 n. 2, 1288, 1297, 1317, 1333, and Chapter II, section 3 of the Introduction.]
176. WROTEN, HELEN I., *Malory's Tale of King Arthur and the Emperor Lucius compared with its source, the alliterative 'Morte Arthure'*, University Microfilms Publications, no. 2231 (1950).
177. WUELCKER, RICHARD PAUL, *Die Artursage in der englischen Literatur*, Leipzig, 1895, pp. 16–21.

III. TRANSLATIONS

French

1. DUBOIS, M. M., *Le Roman d'Arthur et des chevaliers de la Table Ronde, extraits choisis d'après l'édition originale du* Morte Darthur *de Caxton avec les principales variantes du manuscrit de Winchester*, Paris (Aubier), 1948.

German

2. LACHMANN, HEDWIG, *Der Tod Arthurs*, Leipzig, 1923.

Italian

3. BALDINI, GABRIELE, *Le più belle pagine della letteratura inglese*, Milano, vol. i, 1958 (*The Fair Maid of Astolat*).

Turkish

4. URGAN, MINA, *Arthur ün Ölümü*, Istanbul, 1948.

CAXTON'S PREFACE

AFTER that I had accomplysshed and fynysshed dyvers [Sig. Aij] hystoryes as wel of contemplacyon as of other hystoryal and worldly actes of grete conquerours and prynces, and also certeyn bookes of ensaumples and doctryne, many noble and dyvers gentylmen of thys royame of Englond camen 5 and demaunded me many and oftymes wherfore that I have not do made and enprynte the noble hystorye of the Saynt Greal and of the moost renomed Crysten kyng, fyrst and chyef of the thre best Crysten, and worthy, kyng Arthur, whyche ought moost to be remembred emonge us 10 Englysshemen tofore al other Crysten kynges.

For it is notoyrly knowen thorugh the unyversal world that there been nine worthy and the best that ever were, that is to wete, thre Paynyms, thre Jewes, and thre Crysten men. As for the Paynyms, ther were tofore the Incarnacyon 15 of Cryst, whiche were named, the fyrst Hector of Troye, of whome th'ystorye is comen bothe in balade and in prose, the second Alysaunder the Grete, and the thyrd Julyus Cezar, Emperour of Rome, of whome th'ystoryes ben wel knowen and had. And as for the thre Jewes whyche also 20 were tofore th'Yncarnacyon of our Lord, of whome the fyrst was Duc Josué whyche brought the chyldren of Israhel into the londe of byheste, the second Davyd, kyng of Jeru-salem, and the thyrd Judas Machabeus, of these thre the Bybl reherceth al theyr noble hystoryes and actes. And 25 sythe the sayd Incarnacyon have ben thre noble Crysten men stalled and admytted thorugh the unyversal world into the nombre of the nine beste and worthy, of whome was fyrst the noble Arthur, whos noble actes I purpose to wryte in thys present book here folowyng. The second was 30 Charlemayn, or Charles the Grete, of whome th'ystorye is had in many places, bothe in Frensshe and Englysshe; and the thyrd and last was Godefray of Boloyn, of whos actes and lyf I made a book unto th'excellent prynce and kyng of noble memorye, kyng Edward the Fourth.   35

20 *C* kno (*end of line*)

The sayd noble jentylmen instantly requyred me t'emprynte th'ystorye of the sayd noble kyng and conquerour kyng Arthur and of his knyghtes, wyth th'ystorye of the Saynt Greal and of the deth and endyng of the sayd Arthur, 5 affermyng that I ought rather t'enprynte his actes and noble feates than of Godefroye of Boloyne or ony of the other eyght, consyderyng that he was a man borne wythin this royame and kyng and emperour of the same, and that there ben in Frensshe dyvers and many noble volumes of his actes, and 10 also of his knyghtes.

To whome I answerd that dyvers men holde oppynyon that there was no suche Arthur and that alle suche bookes as been maad of hym ben but fayned and fables, bycause that somme cronycles make of hym no mencyon ne remembre 15 hym noothynge, ne of his knyghtes.

Wherto they answerd, and one in specyal sayd, that in hym that shold say or thynke that there was never suche a kyng callyd Arthur myght wel be aretted grete folye and blyndenesse, for he sayd that there were many evydences of 20 the contrarye. Fyrst, ye may see his sepulture in the monasterye of Glastyngburye; and also in Polycronycon, in the fifth book, the syxte chappytre, and in the seventh book, the twenty-thyrd chappytre, where his body was buryed, and after founden and translated into the sayd monasterye. Ye 25 shal se also in th'ystorye of Bochas, in his book DE CASU PRINCIPUM, parte of his noble actes, and also of his falle. Also Galfrydus, in his Brutysshe book, recounteth his lyf. And in dyvers places of Englond many remembraunces ben yet of hym and shall remayne perpetuelly, and also of his 30 knyghtes: fyrst, in the abbey of Westmestre, at Saynt Edwardes shryne, remayneth the prynte of his seal in reed waxe, closed in beryll, in whych is wryton PATRICIUS ARTHURUS BRITANNIE GALLIE GERMANIE DACIE IMPERATOR; item, in the castel of Dover ye may see Gauwayns skulle and 35 Cradoks mantel; at Wynchester, the Rounde Table; in other places Launcelottes swerde and many other thynges.

Thenne, al these thynges consydered, there can no man resonably gaynsaye but there was a kyng of thys lande named

6 *S* ony the　　13 but *not in S*　　18 *S* kynge　　21 *C* Glastyugburye
35 *S* mantle

Arthur. For in al places, Crysten and hethen, he is reputed and taken for one of the nine worthy, and the fyrst of the thre Crysten men. And also he is more spoken of beyonde the see, moo bookes made of his noble actes, than there be in Englond; as wel in Duche, Ytalyen, Spaynysshe, and 5 Grekysshe, as in Frensshe. And yet of record remayne in wytnesse of hym in Wales, in the toune of Camelot, the grete stones and mervayllous werkys of yron lyeng under the grounde, and ryal vautes, [*sig. Aiij*] which dyvers now lyvyng hath seen. Wherfor it is a mervayl why he is no more 10 renomed in his owne contreye, sauf onelye it accordeth to the word of God, whyche sayth that no man is accept for a prophete in his owne contreye.

Thenne, al these thynges forsayd aledged, I coude not wel denye but that there was suche a noble kyng named 15 Arthur, and reputed one of the nine worthy, and fyrst and chyef of the Cristen men. And many noble volumes be made of hym and of his noble knyghtes in Frensshe, which I have seen and redde beyonde the see, which been not had in our maternal tongue. But in Walsshe ben many, and also 20 in Frensshe, and somme in Englysshe, but nowher nygh alle. Wherfore, suche as have late ben drawen oute bryefly into Englysshe, I have, after the symple connynge that God hath sente to me, under the favour and correctyon of al noble lordes and gentylmen, enprysed to enprynte a book of 25 the noble hystoryes of the sayd kynge Arthur and of certeyn of his knyghtes, after a copye unto me delyverd, whyche copye syr Thomas Malorye dyd take oute of certeyn bookes of Frensshe and reduced it into Englysshe.

And I, accordyng to my copye, have doon sette it in 30 enprynte to the entente that noble men may see and lerne the noble actes of chyvalrye, the jentyl and vertuous dedes that somme knyghtes used in tho dayes, by whyche they came to honour, and how they that were vycious were punysshed and ofte put to shame and rebuke; humbly 35 bysechyng al noble lordes and ladyes wyth al other estates, of what estate or degree they been of, that shal see and rede in this sayd book and werke, that they take the good and

4 *C* boookes   12 *S* worde

honest actes in their remembraunce, and to folowe the same; wherin they shalle fynde many joyous and playsaunt hystoryes and noble and renomed actes of humanyté, gentylnesse, and chyvalryes. For herein may be seen noble
5 chyvalrye, curtosye, humanyté, frendlynesse, hardynesse, love, frendshyp, cowardyse, murdre, hate, vertue, and synne. Doo after the good and leve the evyl, and it shal brynge you to good fame and renommee.

And for to passe the tyme thys book shal be plesaunte
10 to rede in, but for to gyve fayth and byleve that al is trewe that is conteyned herin, ye be at your lyberté. But al is wryton for our doctryne, and for to beware that we falle not to vyce ne synne, but t'exersyse and folowe vertu, by whyche we may come and atteyne to good fame and renommé in thys
15 lyf, and after thys shorte and transytorye lyf to come unto everlastyng blysse in heven; the whyche He graunte us that reygneth in heven, the Blessyd Trynyté. AMEN.

Thenne, to procede forth in thys sayd book, whyche I dyrecte unto alle noble prynces, lordes, and ladyes, gentyl-
20 men or gentylwymmen, that desyre to rede or here redde of the noble and joyous hystorye of the grete conquerour and excellent kyng, kyng Arthur, somtyme kyng of thys noble royalme thenne callyd Bretaygne, I, Wyllyam Caxton, symple persone, present thys book folowyng whyche I have
25 enprysed t'enprynte: and treateth of the noble actes, feates of armes of chyvalrye, prowesse, hardynesse, humanyté, love, curtosye, and veray gentylnesse, wyth many wonderful hystoryes and adventures.

And for to understonde bryefly the contente of thys
30 volume I have devyded it into twenty-one bookes, and every book chapytred, as hereafter shal by Goddes grace folowe:

The fyrst book shal treate how Utherpendragon gate the noble conquerour kyng Arthur, and conteyneth xxviii chappytres.
The second book treateth of Balyn, the noble knyght, and con-
35 teyneth xix chapytres.
The thyrd book treateth of the maryage of kyng Arthur to Quene Guenever, wyth other maters, and conteyneth fyftene chappytres.

The fourth book, how Merlyn was assotted, and of warre maad to kyng Arthur, and conteyneth xxix chappytres.

The fyfthe book treateth of the conqueste of Lucius th'emperour and conteyneth xii chappytres.

The syxthe book treateth of syr Launcelot and syr Lyonel and 5 mervayllous adventures and conteyneth xviii chapytres.

The seventh book treateth of a noble knyght called syr Gareth and named by syr Kaye 'Beaumayns' and conteyneth xxxvi chapytres.

The eyght book treateth of the byrthe of syr Trystram, the noble 10 knyght, and of hys actes and conteyneth xli chapytres.

The ix book treateth of a knyght named by syr Kaye 'Le Cote Mayle Taylle' and also of syr Trystram and conteyneth xliiij [*sig. Aiiij*] chapytres.

The x book treateth of syr Trystram and other mervayllous 15 adventures and conteyneth lxxxviii chappytres.

The xi book treateth of syr Launcelot and syr Galahad and conteyneth xiiij chappytres.

The xii book treateth of syr Launcelot and his madnesse and conteyneth xiiij chapytres. 20

The xiii book treateth how Galahad came fyrst to kyng Arthurs courte, and the quest, how the Sangreall was begonne, and conteyneth xx chapytres.

The xiiij book treateth of the queste of the Sangreal and conteyneth x chapytres. 25

The xv book treateth of syr Launcelot and conteyneth vi chapytres.

The xvi book treateth of syr Bors and syr Lyonel, his brother, and conteyneth xvii chapytres.

The xvii book treateth of the Sangreal and conteyneth xxiii 30 chapytres.

The xviii book treateth of syr Launcelot and the quene and conteyneth xxv chapytres.

The xix book treateth of quene Guenever and Launcelot and conteyneth xiii chapytres. 35

The xx book treateth of the pyteous deth of Arthur and conteyneth xxii chapytres.

The xxi book treateth of his last departyng, and how syr Launcelot came to revenge his dethe, and conteyneth xiii chapytres.

The somme is twenty-one bookes whyche conteyne the 40 somme of fyve hondred and seven chapytres, as more playnly shal folowe herafter.

21 *C* kyug   24 *C* boook   36 *C* pyetous

THE TALE

OF

KING ARTHUR

[*Winchester MS., ff. 9ʳ–70ʳ; Caxton, Books I–IV*]

I

MERLIN

[Winchester MS., ff. 9ʳ–22ʳ
Caxton, Book I]

---

* S sodenly   † S garded   ‡ C gives no rubric for Ch. 16

* *C* 27   † *C* 28

[H]IT befel in the dayes of Uther Pendragon, when he was
kynge of all Englond and so regned, that there was
a myghty duke in Cornewaill that helde warre ageynst hym
long tyme, and the duke was called the duke of Tyntagil.
And so by meanes kynge Uther send for this duk, chargyng 5
hym to brynge his wyf with hym, for she was called a fair
lady and a passynge wyse, and her name was called Igrayne.

So whan the duke and his wyf were comyn unto the kynge,
by the meanes of grete lordes they were accorded bothe: the
kynge lyked and loved this lady wel, and he made them grete 10
chere out of mesure and desyred to have lyen by her. But she
was a passyng good woman and wold not assente unto the
kynge.

And thenne she told the duke her husband and said,

'I suppose that we were sente for that I shold be dis- 15
honoured. Wherfor, husband, I counceille yow that we
departe from hens sodenly, that we maye ryde all nyghte
unto oure owne castell.'

And in lyke wyse as she saide so they departed, that neyther
the kynge nor none of his counceill were ware of their de- 20
partyng. Also soone as kyng Uther knewe of theire departyng
soo sodenly, he was wonderly wrothe; thenne he called to
hym his pryvy counceille and told them of the sodeyne
departyng of the duke and his wyf. Thenne they avysed the
kynge to send for the duke and his wyf by a grete charge: 25

'And yf he wille not come at your somons, thenne may ye
do your best; thenne have ye cause to make myghty werre
upon hym.'

Soo that was done, and the messagers hadde their ansuers;
and that was thys, shortly, that neyther he nor his wyf wold 30
not come at hym. Thenne was the kyng wonderly wroth,
and thenne the kyng sente hym playne word ageyne and
badde hym be redy and stuffe hym and garnysshe hym, for
within forty dayes he wold fetche hym oute of the byggest
castell that he hath. Whanne the duke hadde thys warnynge 35
anone he wente and furnysshed and garnysshed two stronge
castels of his, of the whiche the one hyght Tyntagil and the
other castel hyght Terrabyl.

So his wyf dame Igrayne he putte in the castell of Tyntagil, and hymself he putte in the castel of Terrabyl, the whiche had many yssues and posternes oute. Thenne in all haste came Uther with a grete hoost and leyd a syege aboute the
5 castel of Terrabil, and ther he pyght many pavelyons. And there was grete warre made on bothe partyes and moche peple slayne.

Thenne for pure angre and for grete love of fayr Igrayne the kyng Uther felle seke. So came to the kynge Uther syre
10 Ulfius, a noble knyght, and asked the kynge why he was seke.

'I shall telle the,' said the kynge. 'I am seke for angre and for love of fayre Igrayne, that I may not be hool.'

'Wel, my lord,' said syre Ulfius, 'I shal seke Merlyn and he shalle do yow remedy, that youre herte shal be pleasyd.'
15 So Ulfius departed and by adventure he mette Merlyn in a beggars aray, and ther Merlyn asked Ulfius whome he soughte, and he said he had lytyl ado to telle hym.

'Well,' saide Merlyn, 'I knowe whome thou sekest, for thou sekest Merlyn; therfore seke no ferther, for I am he. And
20 yf kynge Uther wille wel rewarde me and be sworne unto me to fulfille my desyre, that shall be his honour and profite more than myn, for I shalle cause hym to have all his desyre.'

'Alle this wyll I undertake,' said Ulfius, 'that ther shalle be nothyng resonable but thow shalt have thy desyre.'
25 'Well,' said Merlyn, 'he shall have his entente and desyre, and therfore,' saide Merlyn, 'ryde on your wey, for I wille not be long behynde.'

(2) Thenne Ulfius was glad and rode on more than a paas tyll that he came to kynge Uther Pendragon and told hym
30 he had met with Merlyn.

'Where is he?' said the kyng.

'Sir,' said Ulfius, 'he wille not dwelle long.'

Therwithal Ulfius was ware where Merlyn stood at the porche of the pavelions dore, and thenne Merlyn was bounde
35 to come to the kynge. Whan kyng Uther sawe hym he said he was welcome.

'Syr,' said Merlyn, 'I knowe al your hert every dele. So ye wil be sworn unto me, as ye be a true kynge enoynted, to fulfille my desyre, ye shal have your desyre.'
40 Thenne the kyng was sworne upon the four Evangelistes.

'Syre,' said Merlyn, 'this is my desyre: the first nyght that
ye shal lye by Igrayne ye shal gete a child on her; and whan
that is borne, that it shall be delyverd to me for to nourisshe
thereas I wille have it, for it shal be your worship and the
childis availle as mykel as the child is worth.'   5

'I wylle wel,' said the kynge, 'as thow wilt have it.'

'Now make you redy,' said Merlyn. 'This nyght ye shalle
lye with Igrayne in the castel of Tyntigayll. And ye shalle
be lyke the duke her husband, Ulfyus shal be lyke syre
Brastias, a knyghte of the dukes, and I will be lyke a knyghte 10
that hyghte syr Jordanus, a knyghte of the dukes. But wayte
ye make not many questions with her nor her men, but saye
ye are diseased, and soo hye yow to bedde and ryse not on the
morne tyll I come to yow, for the castel of Tyntygaill is but
ten myle hens.'   15

Soo this was done as they devysed. But the duke of
Tyntigail aspyed hou the kyng rode fro the syege of Tarabil.
And therfor that nyghte he yssued oute of the castel at a
posterne for to have distressid the kynges hooste, and so
thorowe his owne yssue the duke hymself was slayne or   20
ever the kyng cam at the castel of Tyntigail. So after the
deth of the duke kyng Uther lay with Igrayne, more than
thre houres after his deth, and begat on her that nygh⟨t⟩
Arthur; and or day cam, Merlyn cam to the kyng and bad
hym make hym redy, and so he kist the lady Igrayne and   25
departed in all hast. But whan the lady herd telle of the
duke her husband, and by all record he was dede or ever
kynge Uther came to her, thenne she mervelled who that
myghte be that laye with her in lykenes of her lord. So she
mourned pryvely and held hir pees.   30

Thenne alle the barons by one assent prayd the kynge of
accord betwixe the lady Igrayne and hym. The kynge gaf
hem leve, for fayne wold he have ben accorded with her; soo
the kyng put alle the trust in Ulfyus to entrete bitwene them.
So by the entreté at the last the kyng and she met togyder. 35

'Now wille we doo wel,' said Ulfyus; 'our kyng is a lusty
knyghte and wyveles, and my lady Igrayne is a passynge fair
lady; it were grete joye unto us all and hit myghte please the
kynge to make her his quene.'

Unto that they all well accordyd and meved it to the kynge. And anone, lyke a lusty knyghte, he assentid therto with good wille, and so in alle haste they were maryed in a mornynge with grete myrthe and joye.

5   And kynge Lott of Lowthean and of Orkenay thenne wedded Margawse that was Gaweyns moder, and kynge Nentres of the land of Garlot wedded Elayne: al this was done at the request of kynge Uther. And the thyrd syster, Morgan le Fey, was put to scole in a nonnery, and ther she
10 lerned so moche that she was a grete clerke of nygromancye. And after she was wedded to kynge Uryens of the lond of Gore that was syre Ewayns le Blaunche Maynys fader.

(3, 4, 5)   Thenne quene Igrayne waxid dayly gretter and gretter. So it befel after within half a yere, as kyng Uther lay by his
15 quene, he asked hir by the feith she ought to hym whos was the child within her body. Thenne was she sore abasshed to yeve ansuer.

'Desmaye you not,' said the kyng, 'but telle me the trouthe, and I shall love you the better, by the feythe of my body!'
20 'Syre,' saide she, 'I shalle telle you the trouthe. The same nyghte that my lord was dede, the houre of his deth as his knyghtes record, ther came into my castel of Tyntigaill a man lyke my lord in speche and in countenaunce, and two knyghtes with hym in lykenes of his two knyghtes Barcias
25 and Jordans, and soo I went unto bed with hym as I ought to do with my lord; and the same nyght, as I shal ansuer unto God, this child was begoten upon me.'

'That is trouthe,' saide the kynge, 'as ye say, for it was I myself that cam in the lykenesse. And therfor desmay you
30 not, for I am fader to the child,' and ther he told her alle the cause how it was by Merlyns counceil. Thenne the quene made grete joye whan she knewe who was the fader of her child.

Sone come Merlyn unto the kyng and said,
'Syr, ye must purvey yow for the nourisshyng of your child.'
35 'As thou wolt,' said the kyng, 'be it.'
'Wel,' said Merlyn, 'I knowe a lord of yours in this land that is a passyng true man and a feithful, and he shal have the nourysshyng of your child; and his name is sir Ector, and he is a lord of fair lyvelode in many partyes in Englond
40 and Walys. And this lord, sir Ector, lete hym be sent for

for to come and speke with you, and desyre hym yourself, as
he loveth you, that he will put his owne child to nourisshynge
to another woman and that his wyf nourisshe yours. And
whan the child is borne lete it be delyverd to me at yonder
pryvy posterne uncrystned.'   5

So like as Merlyn devysed it was done. And whan syre
Ector was come he made fyaunce to the kyng for to nourisshe
the child lyke as the kynge desyred; and there the kyng
graunted syr Ector grete rewardys. Thenne when the lady
was delyverd the kynge commaunded two knyghtes and two   10
ladyes to take the child bound in a cloth of gold, 'and that
ye delyver hym to what poure man ye mete at the posterne
yate of the castel.' So the child was delyverd unto Merlyn,
and so he bare it forth unto syre Ector and made an holy man
to crysten hym and named hym Arthur. And so sir Ectors   15
wyf nourysshed hym with her owne pappe.

Thenne within two yeres kyng Uther felle seke of a grete
maladye. And in the meanewhyle hys enemyes usurpped
upon hym and dyd a grete bataylle upon his men and slewe
many of his peple.   20

'Sir,' said Merlyn, 'ye may not lye so as ye doo, for ye
must to the feld, though ye ryde on an hors-lyttar. For ye
shall never have the better of your enemyes but yf your
persone be there, and thenne shall ye have the vyctory.'

So it was done as Merlyn had devysed, and they caryed   25
the kynge forth in an hors-lyttar with a grete hooste towarde
his enemyes, and at Saynt Albons ther mette with the kynge
a grete hoost of the North. And that day syre Ulfyus and
sir Bracias dyd grete dedes of armes, and kyng Uthers men
overcome the northeryn bataylle and slewe many peple and   30
putt the remenaunt to flight; and thenne the kyng retorned
unto London and made grete joye of his vyctory.

And thenne he fyll passynge sore seke, so that thre dayes
and thre nyghtes he was specheles; wherfore alle the barons
made grete sorow and asked Merlyn what counceill were best.   35

'There nys none other remedye,' said Merlyn, 'but God
wil have His wille. But loke ye al barons be bifore kynge
Uther to-morne, and God and I shalle make hym to speke.'

So on the morne alle the barons with Merlyn came tofore
the kyng. Thenne Merlyn said aloud unto kyng Uther,   40

'Syre, shall your sone Arthur be kyng after your dayes of this realme with all the appertenaunce?'

Thenne Uther Pendragon torned hym and said in herynge of them alle,

5 'I gyve hym Gods blissyng and myne, and byd hym pray for my soule, and righteuously and worshipfully that he clayme the croune upon forfeture of my blessyng,' and therwith he yelde up the ghost.

And thenne was he enterid as longed to a kyng, wherfor the 10 quene, fayre Igrayne, made grete sorowe and alle the barons.

Thenne stood the reame in grete jeopardy long whyle, for every lord that was myghty of men maade hym stronge, and many wende to have ben kyng. Thenne Merlyn wente to the Archebisshop of Caunterbury and counceilled hym 15 for to sende for all the lordes of the reame and alle the gentilmen of armes, that they shold to London come by Cristmas upon payne of cursynge, and for this cause, that Jesu, that was borne on that nyghte, that He wold of His grete mercy shewe some myracle, as He was come to be 20 Kynge of mankynde, for to shewe somme myracle who shold be rightwys kynge of this reame. So the Archebisshop, by the advys of Merlyn, send for alle the lordes and gentilmen of armes that they shold come by Crystmasse even unto London; and many of hem made hem clene of her lyf, that 25 her prayer myghte be the more acceptable unto God.

Soo in the grettest chirch of London—whether it were Powlis or not the Frensshe booke maketh no mencyon—alle the estates were longe or day in the chirche for to praye. And whan matyns and the first masse was done there was 30 sene in the chircheyard ayenst the hyhe aulter a grete stone four square, lyke unto a marbel stone, and in myddes therof was lyke an anvylde of stele a foot on hyghe, and theryn stack a fayre swerd naked by the poynt, and letters there were wryten in gold about the swerd that saiden thus: 'WHOSO 35 PULLETH OUTE THIS SWERD OF THIS STONE AND ANVYLD IS RIGHTWYS KYNGE BORNE OF ALL EN⟨G⟩LOND.' Thenne the peple merveilled and told it to the Archebisshop.

'I commande,' said th'Archebisshop, 'that ye kepe yow within your chirche and pray unto God still; that no man 40 touche the swerd tyll the hyhe masse be all done.'

So whan all masses were done all the lordes wente to beholde the stone and the swerd. And whan they sawe the scripture som assayed suche as wold have ben kyng, but none myght stere the swerd nor meve hit.

'He is not here,' said the Archebisshop, 'that shall encheve 5 the swerd, but doubte not God will make hym knowen. But this is my counceill,' said the Archebisshop, 'that we lete purvey ten knyghtes, men of good fame, and they to kepe this swerd.'

So it was ordeyned, and thenne ther was made a crye that 10 every man shold assay that wold for to wynne the swerd. And upon Newe Yeers day the barons lete maake a justes and a tournement, that alle knyghtes that wold juste or tourneye there myght playe. And all this was ordeyned for to kepe the lordes togyders and the comyns, for the Archebisshop 15 trusted that God wold make hym knowe that shold wynne the swerd.

So upon New Yeres day, whan the servyce was done, the barons rode unto the feld, some to juste and som to torney. And so it happed that syre Ector that had grete lyvelode 20 aboute London rode unto the justes, and with hym rode syr Kaynus, his sone, and yong Arthur that was hys nourisshed broder; and syr Kay was made knyght at Alhalowmas afore. So as they rode to the justes-ward sir Kay had lost his suerd, for he had lefte it at his faders lodgyng, and so he prayd yong 25 Arthur for to ryde for his swerd.

'I wyll wel,' said Arthur, and rode fast after the swerd. And whan he cam home the lady and al were out to see the joustyng. Thenne was Arthur wroth and saide to hymself, 'I will ryde to the chircheyard and take the swerd with me 30 that stycketh in the stone, for my broder sir Kay shal not be without a swerd this day.' So whan he cam to the chircheyard sir Arthur alight and tayed his hors to the style, and so he wente to the tent and found no knyghtes there, for they were atte justyng. And so he handled the swerd by the 35 handels, and lightly and fiersly pulled it out of the stone, and took his hors and rode his way untyll he came to his broder sir Kay and delyverd hym the swerd. And as sone as sir Kay saw the swerd he wist wel it was the swerd of the stone, and so he rode to his fader syr Ector and said, 40

'Sire, loo here is the swerd of the stone, wherfor I must be kyng of thys land.'

When syre Ector beheld the swerd he retorned ageyne and cam to the chirche, and there they alighte al thre and
5 wente into the chirche, and anon he made sir Kay to swere upon a book how he came to that swerd.

'Syr,' said sir Kay, 'by my broder Arthur, for he brought it to me.'

'How gate ye this swerd?' said sir Ector to Arthur.
10 'Sir, I will telle you. When I cam home for my broders swerd I fond nobody at home to delyver me his swerd. And so I thought my broder syr Kay shold not be swerdles, and so I cam hyder egerly and pulled it out of the stone withoute ony payn.'
15 'Found ye ony knyghtes about this swerd?' seid sir Ector.

'Nay,' said Arthur.

'Now,' said sir Ector to Arthur, 'I understande ye must be kynge of this land.'

'Wherfore I?' sayd Arthur, 'and for what cause?'
20 'Sire,' saide Ector, 'for God wille have hit soo, for ther shold never man have drawen oute this swerde but he that shal be rightwys kyng of this land. Now lete me see whether ye can putte the swerd theras it was and pulle hit oute ageyne.'
25 'That is no maystry,' said Arthur, and soo he put it in the stone. Therwithalle sir Ector assayed to pulle oute the swerd and faylled.

(6) 'Now assay', said syre Ector unto syre Kay. And anon he pulled at the swerd with alle his myghte, but it wold not be.
30 'Now shal ye assay,' said syre Ector to Arthur.

'I wyll wel,' said Arthur, and pulled it out easily.

And therwithalle syre Ector knelyd doune to the erthe and syre Kay.

'Allas!' said Arthur, 'myne own dere fader and broder,
35 why knele ye to me?'

'Nay, nay, my lord Arthur, it is not so. I was never your fader nor of your blood, but I wote wel ye are of an hyher blood than I wende ye were.' And thenne syre Ector told hym all how he was bitaken hym for to nourisshe hym and
40 by whoos commandement, and by Merlyns delyveraunce.

Thenne Arthur made grete doole whan he understood that syre Ector was not his fader.

'Sir,' said Ector unto Arthur, 'woll ye be my good and gracious lord when ye are kyng?'

'Els were I to blame,' said Arthur, 'for ye are the man in the world that I am most beholdyng to, and my good lady and moder your wyf that as wel as her owne hath fostred me and kepte. And yf ever hit be Goddes will that I be kynge as ye say, ye shall desyre of me what I may doo and I shalle not faille yow. God forbede I shold faille yow.'

'Sir,' said sire Ector, 'I will aske no more of yow but that ye wille make my sone, your foster broder syre Kay, se⟨ne⟩ceall of alle your landes.'

'That shalle be done,' said Arthur, 'and more, by the feith of my body, that never man shalle have that office but he whyle he and I lyve.'

Therewithall they wente unto the Archebisshop and told hym how the swerd was encheved and by whome. And on twelfth day alle the barons cam thyder and to assay to take the swerd who that wold assay, but there afore hem alle ther myghte none take it out but Arthur. Wherfor ther were many lordes wroth, and saide it was grete shame unto them all and the reame to be overgovernyd with a boye of no hyghe blood borne. And so they fell oute at that tyme, that it was put of tyll Candelmas, and thenne all the barons shold mete there ageyne; but alwey the ten knyghtes were ordeyned to watche the swerd day and nyght, and so they sette a pavelione over the stone and the swerd, and fyve alwayes watched.

Soo at Candalmasse many moo grete lordes came thyder for to have wonne the swerde, but there myghte none prevaille. And right as Arthur dyd at Cristmasse he dyd at Candelmasse, and pulled oute the swerde easely, wherof the barons were sore agreved and put it of in delay till the hyghe feste of Eester. And as Arthur sped afore so dyd he at Eester. Yet there were some of the grete lordes had indignacion that Arthur shold be kynge, and put it of in a delay tyll the feest of Pentecoste. Thenne the Archebisshop of Caunterbury by Merlyns provydence lete purveye thenne of the

best knyghtes that they myghte gete, and suche knyghtes as
Uther Pendragon loved best and moost trusted in his dayes.
And suche knyghtes were put aboute Arthur as syr Bawdewyn of Bretayn, syre Kaynes, syre Ulfyus, syre Barsias; all
5 these with many other were alweyes about Arthur day and
nyghte till the feste of Pentecost.

(7)   And at the feste of Pentecost alle maner of men assayed
to pulle at the swerde that wold assay, but none myghte
prevaille but Arthur, and he pulled it oute afore all the
10 lordes and comyns that were there. Wherfore alle the
comyns cryed at ones,
      'We wille have Arthur unto our kyng! We wille put hym
no more in delay, for we all see that it is Goddes wille that
he shalle be our kynge, and who that holdeth ageynst it,
15 we wille slee hym.' And therwithall they knelyd at ones,
both ryche and poure, and cryed Arthur mercy bycause
they had delayed hym so longe. And Arthur foryaf hem and
took the swerd bitwene both his handes and offred it upon
the aulter where the Archebisshop was, and so was he made
20 knyghte of the best man that was there. And so anon was the
coronacyon made, and ther was he sworne unto his lordes and
the comyns for to be a true kyng, to stand with true justyce
fro thens forth the dayes of this lyf.
      Also thenne he made alle lordes that helde of the croune
25 to come in and to do servyce as they oughte to doo. And
many complayntes were made unto sir Arthur of grete
wronges that were done syn the dethe of kyng Uther, of
many londes that were bereved lordes, knyghtes, ladyes, and
gentilmen. Wherfor kynge Arthur maade the londes to be
30 yeven ageyne unto them that oughte hem.
      Whanne this was done, that the kyng had stablisshed alle
the countryes aboute London, thenne he lete make syr Kay
sencial of Englond, and sir Baudewyn of Bretayne was made
constable, and sir Ulfyus was made chamberlayn, and sire
35 Brastias was maade wardeyn to wayte upon the Northe fro
Trent forwardes, for it was that tyme the most party the
kynges enemyes. But within fewe yeres after Arthur wan
alle the North, Scotland, and alle that were under their obeis-
saunce, also Walys. A parte of it helde ayenst Arthur, but
40 he overcam hem al, as he dyd the remenaunt, thurgh the

noble prowesse of hymself and his knyghtes of the Round
Table.

Thenne the kyng remeved into Walys and lete crye a (8)
grete feste, that it shold be holdyn at Pentecost after the
incoronacion of hym at the cyté of Carlyon. Unto the fest 5
come kyng Lott of Lowthean and of Orkeney with fyve
hondred knyghtes with hym; also ther come to the feste
kynge Uryens of Gore with four hondred knyghtes with
hym; also ther come to that feeste kyng Nayntres of Garloth
with seven hundred knyghtes with hym; also ther came to the 10
feest the Kynge of Scotland with sixe honderd knyghtes with
hym, and he was but a yong man. Also ther came to the feste
a kyng that was called the Kyng with the Honderd Knyghtes,
but he and his men were passyng wel bisene at al poyntes;
also ther cam the kyng of Cardos with fyve honderd knyghtes. 15

And kyng Arthur was glad of their comynge, for he
wende that al the kynges and knyghtes had come for grete
love and to have done hym worship at his feste, wherfor the
kyng made grete joye and sente the kynges and knyghtes
grete presentes. But the kynges wold none receyve, but 20
rebuked the messagers shamefully and said they had no
joye to receyve no yeftes of a berdles boye that was come of
lowe blood, and sente hym word they wold none of his yeftes,
but that they were come to gyve hym yeftes with hard
swerdys betwixt the neck and the sholders; and therfore 25
they came thyder, so they told to the messagers playnly, for
it was grete shame to all them to see suche a boye to have
a rule of soo noble a reaume as this land was. With this
answer the messagers departed and told to kyng Arthur
this answer, wherfor by the advys of his barons he took hym 30
to a strong towre with fyve hondred good men with hym.
And all the kynges aforesaid in a maner leyd a syege tofore
hym, but kyng Arthur was well vytailled.

And within fyftene dayes ther came Merlyn amonge hem
into the cyté of Carlyon. Thenne all the kynges were passyng 35
gladde of Merlyn and asked hym,

'For what cause is that boye Arthur made your kynge?'

'Syres,' said Merlyn, 'I shalle telle yow the cause, for he
is kynge Uther Pendragons sone borne in wedlok, goten on
Igrayne, the dukes wyf of Tyntigail.'
40

917.44   c

'Thenne is he a bastard,' they said al.

'Nay,' said Merlyn, 'after the deth of the duke more than thre houres was Arthur begoten, and thirtene dayes after kyng Uther wedded Igrayne, and therfor I preve hym he is no
5 bastard. And, who saith nay, he shal be kyng and overcome alle his enemyes, and or he deye he shalle be long kynge of all Englond and have under his obeyssaunce Walys, Yrland, and Scotland, and moo reames than I will now reherce.'

Some of the kynges had merveyl of Merlyns wordes and
10 demed well that it shold be as he said, and som of hem lough hym to scorne, as kyng Lot, and mo other called hym a wytche. But thenne were they accorded with Merlyn that kynge Arthur shold come oute and speke with the kynges, and to come sauf and to goo sauf, suche suraunce ther was
15 made. So Merlyn went unto kynge Arthur and told hym how he had done and badde hym fere not, but come oute boldly and speke with hem, and spare hem not, but ansuere them as their kynge and chyvetayn, 'for ye shal overcome hem all, whether they wille or nylle'.

(9) 20   Thenne kynge Arthur came oute of his tour and had under his gowne a jesseraunte of double maylle, and ther wente with hym the Archebisshop of Caunterbury, and syr Baudewyn of Bretayne, and syr Kay, and syre Brastias; these were the men of moost worship that were with hym. And whan
25 they were mette there was no mekenes but stoute wordes on bothe sydes, but alweyes kynge Arthur ansuerd them and said he wold make them to bowe and he lyved, wherfore they departed with wrath. And kynge Arthur badde kepe hem wel, and they bad the kynge kepe hym wel. Soo the kynge
30 retornyd hym to the toure ageyne and armed hym and alle his knyghtes.

'What will ye do?' said Merlyn to the kynges. 'Ye were better for to stynte, for ye shalle not here prevaille, though ye were ten so many.'

35   'Be we wel avysed to be aferd of a dreme-reder?' said kyng Lot.

With that Merlyn vanysshed aweye and came to kynge Arthur and bad hym set on hem fiersly. And in the menewhyle there were thre honderd good men of the best that

16 O¹ hym, 'Fere not

were with the kynges that wente streyghte unto kynge
Arthur, and that comforted hym gretely.

'Syr,' said Merlyn to Arthur, 'fyghte not with the swerde
that ye had by myracle til that ye see ye go unto the wers;
thenne drawe it out and do your best.'   5

So forthwithalle kynge Arthur sette upon hem in their
lodgyng, and syre Bawdewyn, syre Kay, and syr Brastias
slewe on the right hand and on the lyfte hand, that it was
merveylle; and alweyes kynge Arthur on horsback leyd on
with a swerd and dyd merveillous dedes of armes, that many 10
of the kynges had grete joye of his dedes and hardynesse.
Thenne kynge Lot brake out on the bak syde, and the Kyng
with the Honderd Knyghtes and kyng Carados, and sette
on Arthur fiersly behynde hym.

With that syre Arthur torned with his knyghtes and 15
smote behynd and before, and ever sir Arthur was in the
formest prees tyl his hors was slayne undernethe hym. And
therwith kynge Lot smote doune kyng Arthur. With that
his four knyghtes re⟨scow⟩ed hym and set hym on horsback;
thenne he drewe his swerd Excalibur, but it was so bryght 20
in his enemyes eyen that it gaf light lyke thirty torchys, and
therwith he put hem on bak and slewe moche peple. And
thenne the comyns of Carlyon aroos with clubbis and stavys
and slewe many knyghtes, but alle the kynges helde them
togyders with her knyghtes that were lefte on lyve, and so 25
fled and departed; and Merlyn come unto Arthur and counceilled hym to folowe hem no further.

So after the feste and journeye kynge Arthur drewe hym (10)
unto London. And soo by the counceil of Merlyn the kyng
lete calle his barons to counceil, for Merlyn had told the 30
kynge that the sixe kynges that made warre upon hym wold
in al haste be awroke on hym and on his landys; wherfor
the kyng asked counceil at hem al. They coude no counceil
gyve, but said they were bygge ynough.

'Ye saye well,' said Arthur, 'I thanke you for your good 35
courage; but wil ye al that loveth me speke with Merlyn?
Ye knowe wel that he hath done moche for me, and he
knoweth many thynges. And whan he is afore you I wold
that ye prayd hym hertely of his best avyse.'

Alle the barons sayd they wold pray hym and desyre hym. Soo Merlyn was sente for and fair desyred of al the barons to gyve them best counceil.

'I shall say you,' said Merlyn, 'I warne yow al, your
5 enemyes are passyng strong for yow, and they are good men of armes as ben on lyve. And by thys tyme they have goten to them four kynges mo and a myghty duke, and onlesse that our kyng have more chyvalry with hym than he may make within the boundys of his own reame, and he fyghte
10 with hem in batail, he shal be overcome and slayn.'

'What were best to doo in this cause?' said al the barons.

'I shal telle you,' said Merlyn, 'myne advys. Ther ar two bretheren beyond the see, and they be kynges bothe and merveillous good men of her handes: and that one hyghte
15 kynge Ban of Benwic, and that other hyght kyng Bors of Gaule, that is Fraunce. And on these two kynges warrith a myghty man of men, the kynge Claudas, and stryveth with hem for a castel; and grete werre is betwixt them. But this Claudas is so myghty of goodes wherof he geteth
20 good knyghtes that he putteth these two kynges moost parte ⟨t⟩o the werse. Wherfor this is my counceil: that our kyng and soverayne lord sende unto the kynges Ban and Bors by two trusty knyghtes with letters well devysed, that and they
W begins, wil come and see] kynge Arthur and his courte to helpe hym
f. 9ʳ in hys warrys, that he wolde be sworne unto them to helpe
26 hem in theire warrys agaynst kynge Claudas. Now what sey ye unto thys counceyle?' seyde Merlyon.

'Thys ys well councelde,' seyde the kynge.

And in all haste two barownes ryght so were ordayned
30 to go on thys message unto thes two kyngis, and lettirs were made in the most plesauntist wyse accordynge unto kynge Arthurs desyre, and Ulphuns and Brastias were made the messyngers; and so rode forth well horsed and well i-armed and as the gyse was that tyme, and so passed the see and
35 rode towarde the cité of Benwyk. And there besydes were eyght knyghtes that aspyed hem, and at a strayte passage

---

21 *C* do the   24 *W begins* (kynge Arthur *etc.*)   *C* so helpe   25 *C* he wil
28–31 *C* the kynge & alle the Barons right so in alle haste ther were ordeyned to goo two knyghtes on the message vnto the two kynges Soo were there made letters in the plesaunt

they mette with Ulphuns and Brastias and wolde a takyn
them presoners. So they preyde them that they myght passe,
for they were messyngers unto kyng Ban and Bors isente
frome kynge Arthure.

'Therefore,' seyde the knyghtes, 'ye shall dey othir be 5
presoners, for we be knyghtes of kynge Claudas.'

And therewith two of them dressed their sperys unto
Ulphuns and Brastias, and they dressed their sperys and ran
togydir with grete random. And Claudas his knyghtes brake
theire spearis, and Ulphuns and Brastias bare the two knyghtes 10
oute of their sadils to the erth and so leffte them lyynge and
rode their wayes. And the other six knyghtes rode before to
a passage to mete with them ayen, and so Ulphuns and
Brastias othir two smote downe and so paste on hir wayes.
And at the fourthe passage there mette two for two and bothe 15
were leyde unto the erthe. So there was none of the eyght
knyghtes but he was hurte sore othir brused.

And whan they com to Benwyke hit fortuned both the
kynges be there, Ban and Bors. Than was hit tolde the two
kyngis how there were com two messyngers. And anone 20
there was sente unto them two knyghtes of worshyp, that
one hyght Lyonses, lorde of the contrey of ⌜Payarne⌝, and
sir Pharyaunce, a worshipfull knyght; and anone asked them
frome whens they com, and they seyde frome kyng Arthure,
kynge of Ingelonde. And so they toke them in theire armys 25
and made grete joy eche of othir. But anone as they wyste
they were messyngers of Arthurs there was made no taryynge, but forthwith they spake with the kyngis. And they
welcommed them in the most faythfullyst wyse and seyde
they were moste welcom unto them before all the kynges 30
men lyvynge. And therewith they kyssed the lettirs and
delyvird them. And whan kynge Ban and Bors undirstoode
them and the lettirs, than were they more welcom than they
were tofore.

And aft[i]r the haste of the lettirs they gaff hem thys 35 **9ᵛ**

5 *C* the viii knyghtes   7–8 *C* their sperys and Vlfyus and Brastias dressid
10 *C* speres and ther to hylde and bare†   18–19 *C* fortuned ther were both
kynges Ban and Bors   19, 20 two *not in C*   21 *C* were   22 *W* Bayarne
C* payarne   *F (Camb. f. 210ʳ, col. 1)* Paierne   23–24 *C* they asked from
26 *C* as the ii kynges wist   28 *C* with the knyghtes†   29 most *not in C*
31 men *not in C*†   32 them. And *not in C*   34 *C* were before

answere that they wolde fulfille th[e] desire of kyng Arthurs wrytynge, and bade sir Ulphuns and sir Brastias tarry there as longe as they wolde, for they shulde have such chere as myght be made for them in thys marchis. Than Ulphuns
5 and Brastias tolde the kynge⟨s⟩ of theire adventure at the passagis for the eyght knyghtes.

'A ha,' seyde Ban and Bors, 'they were oure good frendis. I wolde I had wyste of them, and they sholde nat so [have] ascaped.'

10 So thes two knyghtes had good chere and grete gyfftis as much as they myght bere away, and had theire answere by mowth and by wrytynge that the two kynges wolde com unto Arthure in all the haste that they myght. So thes two knyghtes rode on afore and passed the see and com to their lorde and
15 tolde hym how they had spedde, wherefore kyng Arthure was passyng glad and seyde,

'How suppose you, at what tyme woll thes two kynges be here?'

'Sir,' they seyde, 'before Allhalowmasse.'

20 Than the kynge lette purvey a grete feste, and also he lette cry both turnementis and justis thorowoute all his realme, and the day appoynted and sette at Allhalowmasse. And so the tyme drove on and all thynges redy ipurveyed. Thes two noble kynges were entirde the londe and comyn ovir the see
25 with three hondred knyghtes full well arayed both for the pees and also for the werre. And so royally they were resceyved and brought towarde the cité of London. And so Arthure mette them ten myle oute of London, and there was grete joy made as couthe be thought.

30 And on Allhalowmasse day at the grete feste sate in the hall the three kynges, and sir Kay the Senesciall served in the halle, and sir Lucas the Butler that was Duke Corneus son, and sir Gryfflet that was the son of God of Cardal: thes three knyghtes had the rule of all the servyse that served

1 *W* thy   5 *CWO¹* kynge   5–6 *C* of the aduēture at their passages of the
7 *C* my †good   8–10 *C* not haue escaped so So Vlfius & Brastias had   13 *C*
the two   16–17 *C* gladde At what tyme suppose ye the ij Kynges wol be
20–25 *C†* feeste and lete crye a grete Iustes And by all halowmasse the two kynges
were come ouer the see with thre honderd kyn3tes wel arayed   26 also *not in*
C   26–27 And so royally . . . London *not in C†*   29 *C** ioye as coude be
thou3t or made   33 of God *not in C†* (*see Index*)

the kyngis. And anone as they were redy and wayshe[n], all
the knyghtes that wolde juste made hem redy. And be
than they were redy on horsebak there was seven hondred
knyghtes. And kynge Arthure, Ban, and Bors, with the
Archebysshop of Caunterbyry, and sir Ector, Kays fadir, 5
they were in a place covirde with clothys of golde lyke unto
an halle, with ladyes and jantillwomen for to beholde who
dud beste and thereon to gyff a jugemente.

And kyng Arthure with the two kyngis lette departe the (11)
seven hondred knyghtes in two partyes. And there were 10
three hondred knyghtes of the realme of Benwyke and Gaule
that turned on the othir syde. And they dressed their shyldis
and began to couche hir sperys, many good knyghtes. So sir **10ʳ**
Gryfflet was the first that sette oute, and to hym com a knyght,
hys name was sir Ladynas, and they com so egirly togydir 15
that all men had wondir, and they so sore fought that hir
shyldis felle on pecis and both horse and man felle to the
erthe, and both the Frensh knyght and the Englysh knyght
lay so longe that all men wente they had bene dede. Whan
Lucas the Butler saw sir Gryfflet ly so longe, he horsed hym 20
agayne anone, and they too ded many mervelous dedis of
armys with many bachelers.

Also sir Kay com oute of a bushemente with fyve knyghtes
with hym, and they six smote othir six downe. But sir Kay
dud that day many mervaylous dedis of armys, that there 25
was none that dud so welle as he that day. Than there com
Ladynas and Grastian, two knyghtes of Fraunse, and dud
passynge well, that all men praysed them. Than com in sir
Placidas, a good knyght, that mette with sir Kay and smote
hym downe horse and man, wherefore sir Gryfflet was wroth 30
and mette with sir Placidas so harde that horse and man
felle to the erthe. But whan the fyve knyghtes wyst that
sir Kay had a falle they were wroth oute of mesure and therewithall ech of them fyve bare downe a knyght.

Whan kynge Arthur and the two kynges saw hem be- 35
gynne wexe wroth on bothe partyes, they leped on smale

---

1 *W* waysher   1–2 *C** they had wasshen & rysen al knyȝtes   6 unto *not in C*
12 that *not in C*   14–15 *C* that mette with a knyghte one ladynas and they mett so
16 sore *not in C*   17 *C* to pyeces and hors   20 *C* Gryflet soo lye he
25 many *not in C*   29 *C* knyghte and mette   33 *C* out of wyt And

hakeneyes and lette cry that all men sholde departe unto
theire lodgynge. And so they wente home and unarmed
them, and so to evynsonge and souper. And aftir souper
the three kynges went into a gardyne and gaff the pryce
5 unto sir Kay and unto sir Lucas the Butler and unto sir
Gryfflet. And than they wente unto counceyle, and with
hem Gwenbaus, brothir unto kynge Ban and Bors, a wyse
clerke; and thidir wente Ulphuns, Brastias and Merlion.
And aftir they had [ben] in her counceyle they wente unto
10 bedde. And on the morne they harde masse, and to dyner and
so to theire counceyle, and made many argumentes what were
beste to do.

So at the laste they were concluded that Merlion sholde
go with a tokyn of kynge Ban, that was a rynge, unto hys
15 men and kynge Bors, [and] Gracian and Placidas sholde go
agayne and kepe their castels and theire contreyes, for kynge
Ban of Benwyke and kynge Bors of Gaule had ordayned them
all thynge. And so passed ⟨they⟩ the see and com to Benwyke.
And whan the people sawe kynge Bannys rynge, and Gracian
20 and Placidas, they were glad and asked how theire kynge
10ᵛ fared and made grete joy of their welfare. And accordyng
unto theire soveraigne lordis desire, the m[e]n of warre made
hem redy in all haste possible, so that they were fyftene
thousand on horsebacke and foote, and they had grete plenté
25 of vitayle by Merlions provisions. But Gracian and Placidas
were leffte at home to furnysh and garnysh the castel[s] for
drede of kyng Claudas.

Ryght so Merlion passed the see well vitayled bothe by
watir and by londe. And whan he com to the see he sente
30 home the footemen agayne, and toke no mo with hym but
ten thousand men on horsebake, the moste party of men of
armys; and so [s]hipped and passed the see into Inglonde
and londed at Dovir. And thorow the wytte of Merlion

2 *C** vnarmed *W* unharmed   3–4 *C* after the   7 *C* syr Ban   14 *C*
Ban and that was   15 [and] *not in O*¹   16–17 *C* countreyes as for kynge
Ban of Benwick   *W O*¹ contreyes and as for kynge Ban of Benwyke   20–21 *C*
how the kynges† ferd   21–22 *C* welfare and cordyng† and accordynge vnto the
souerayne   22 *W* desire and the man   *C* desyre the men   24 *C* on hors
25 *C* vytaylle with hem by Merlyns prouysyon   26 at home *not in C*†
26 *C** the castels   *W* the castell   31 *C* mooste parte men of   32 *W* so hipped
C so shypped

he ledde the oste northwarde the pryvéyst wey that coude be
thought, unto the foreste of Bedgrayne, and there in a valey
lodged h[e]m secretely. Than rode Merlion to Arthure and
to the two kynges, and tolde hem how he had spedde,
wherof they had grete mervayle that ony man on erthe 5
myght spede so sone to go and com. So Merlion tolde them
how ten thousande were in the forest of Bedgrayne well
armed at all poyntis.

Than was there no more to sey, but to horsebak wente all
the oste as Arthure had before provyded. So with twenty 10
thousand he passed by nyght and day. Bu[t] there was made
such an ordinaunce afore by Merlyon that there sholde no
man of warre ryde nothir go in no contrey on this syde
Trente watir but if he had a tokyn frome kynge Arthure,
wherethorow the kynges enemyes durst nat ryde as they dud 15
tofore to aspye. And so wythin a litill whyle the three kyngis (12)
com to the forest of Bedgrayne and founde there a passynge
fayre felyship and well besene, wherof they had grete joy,
and vitayle they wanted none.

Thys was the causis of the northir hoste, that they were 20
rered for the despite and rebuke that the ⌜six⌝ kyngis had at
Carlyon. And tho six kyngis by hir meanys gate unto them
fyve othir kyngis, and thus they began to gadir hir people.
And ⟨now⟩ they swore nother for welle nothyr wo they
sholde nat lyve tyll they had destroyed Arthure, and than 25
they made an othe. And the first that began the othe was the
deuke of Can⌜benet⌝, that he wolde brynge with hym ⌜fyve⌝
thousand men of armys, the which were redy on horsebakke.
Than swore kynge Brandegoris of Strangore that he wolde
brynge with hym fyve thousand men of armys on horsebacke. 30
Than swore kynge Clarivaus of Northumbirlonde [that he]
wolde brynge ⌜three⌝ thousand men of armys with hym.
Than swore the Kynge with the Hondred Knyghtes that was

1 *C*† he had the hoost   3 *W O*¹ lodged hym   5 ony *not in C*
6 *C* soone and goo   7 *C* how *not in C*   16 *C* lytel space the   17 *C*
Castel of Bedegrayne   *F* (*Camb. f. 215ᵛ, col. 2*) foreste de Bedigran; (*ibid. f. 216ʳ,
col. 2*) en la praierie del chastel de Bedigran   20 *C* the cause of   21 *W* vii
*C** syx   *F* sis   24 *WC* how   24–25 *C* sware thatsor wele nor woo they
shold not leue other tyl   27 *W* Candebenet (*cf. p. 28, l. 1*)   27–28 *W* vi M
C v M   *F* cinq mile homes   32 *W* in M men   *C** thre thousand men   *F* trois
mile homes   32 with hym *not in C*

a passynge good man and a yonge, that he wold brynge four
11ʳ thousand good men of armys on horsebacke.

Than there swore kynge Lott, a passyng good knyght and
fadir unto sir Gawayne, that he wolde brynge fyve thousand
5 good men of armys on horsebak. Also the[re] swore kynge
Uryens that was sir Uwaynes fadir, of the londe of Goore,
and he wolde brynge six thousand men of armys on horsebak.
Also there swore kynge Idres of Cornuwaile that he wolde
brynge fyve thousand men of armys on horsebake. Also there
10 swore kynge Cradilmans to brynge fyve thousand men on
horsebacke. Also there swore kyng Angwysshauns of Irelonde to brynge fyve thousand men of armys on horsebak.
Also there swore kynge Nentres to brynge fyve thousand men
on horsebak. Also there swore kynge Carados to brynge fyve
15 thousand men of armys on horsebak. So hir hole oste was of
clene men of armys: on horsebacke was fully fyffty thousand,
and on foote ten thousand of good mennes bodyes.

Than they were sone redy and mounted uppon horsebacke, and sente forthe before the foreryders. For thes a
20 eleven kynges in hir wayes leyde a sege unto the castell of
Bedgrayne; and so they departed and drew towarde Arthure,
and leffte a fewe to byde at the sege, for the castell of Bedgrayne was an holde of kynge Arthurs and the men that
were within were kynge Arthurs men all.

(13) 25 So by Merlyons advice there were sente foreryders to
skymme the contrey; and they mette with the foreryders of
the Northe and made hem to telle which way the oste com.
And than they tolde kynge Arthure, and by kynge Ban and
Bors his counceile they lette brenne and destroy all the
30 contrey before them there they sholde ryde.

The Kynge of the Hondred Knyghtis that tyme mette
a wondir dreme two nyghtes before the batayle: that there
blew a grete wynde and blew downe hir castels and hir
townys, and aftir that com a watir and bare hit all away.
35 And all that herde of that swevyn seyde hit was a tokyn of
grete batayle. Than by counceile of Merlion, whan they wyst

which wey the an eleven kynges wolde ryde and lodge that
nyght, at mydnyght they sette uppon them as they were in
their pavilions. But the scowte-wacche by hir oste cryed:
'Lordis, to ⌐armes⌐! for here be oure enemyes at youre
honde!'   5

Than kynge Arthur and kynge Ban and Bors with hir   (14)
good and trusty knyghtes sette uppon them so fersely that
he made them overthrowe hir pavilions on hir hedis. But **11ᵛ**
the eleven kynges by manly prouesse of armys toke a fayre
champion, but there was slayne that morow tyde ten thou- 10
sand good mennes bodyes. And so they had before hem a
stronge passage; yet were there fyffty thousand of hardy
men. Than hit drew toward day.

'Now shall ye do by myne advice,' seyde Merlyon unto
the three kyngis, and seyde: 'I wolde kynge Ban and Bors 15
with hir felyship of ten thousand men were put in a woode
here besyde in an inbusshemente and kept them prevy, and
that they be leyde or the lyght of the day com, and that they
stire nat tyll that ye and youre knyghtes a fought with hem
longe. And whan hit ys daylyght, dresse youre batayle evyn 20
before them and the passage, that they may se all youre oste,
for than woll they be the more hardy whan they se you but
aboute twenty thousande, and cause hem to be the gladder
to suffir you and youre oste to com over the passage.'

All the three kynges and the hole barownes seyde how 25
Merlion devised passynge well, and so hit was done.

So on the morn whan aythir oste saw othir, they of the
Northe were well comforted. Than Ulphuns and Brastias
were delyvirde three thousand men of armys, and they sette
on them fersely in the passage, and slew on the ryght honde 30
and on the lyffte honde that hit was wondir to telle. But
whan the eleven kynges saw that there was so few a felyship
that dud such dedis of armys, they were ashamed and sette
on hem agayne fersely. And there was sir Ulphuns horse
slayne, but he dud mervelously on foote. But the duke 35

---

1 *C* the xj kynges   4 *W* to harneys *C** to armes *F* as armes   4 *C* your
enemyes   12 *S* passaye *C* were they   15 and seyde *not in C*   17 *C†* kepe
19 *O¹* [have] fought *W* and fought   25–27 *C* sayde that Merlyn said passyngly
wel and it was done anone as Merlyn had deuysed Soo   27–28 *C* other the
hoost of the north was well   28 *C* to Vlfyus   35 *C* slayne vnder hym
C merueyllously well on

Es⌐t⌐anse of Can⌐benet⌐ and kynge Clarivaunce of Northehumbirlonde were allwey grevously set on Ulphuns. Than
sir Brastias saw his felow yfared so withall, he smote the
duke with a spere, that horse and man felle downe. That
5 saw kyng Claryvauns, and returne[d] unto sir Brastias, and
eythir smote othir so that horse and man wente to the erthe.
And so they lay longe astoned, and theire horse knees braste
to the harde bone.

Than com sir Kay the Senesciall with six felowis with
10 hym and dud passynge well. So with that com the eleven
kyngis, and there was Gryfflette put to the erth horse and man,
and Lucas the Butler horse and man, kynge Brandegoris and
kynge Idres and kynge Angwyshaunce.

Than wexed the medlee passyng harde on both parties.
15 Whan sir Kay saw sir Grylflet on foote, he rode unto kynge
Nentres and smote hym downe, and ledde his horse unto
sir Gryfflette and horsed hym agayne. Also sir Kay with
12ʳ the same spere smote downe kynge Lotte and hurte hym
passynge sore. That saw the Kynge with the Hondred
20 Knyghtes and ran unto sir Kay and smote hym downe, and
toke hys horse and gaff hym kynge Lotte, whereof he seyde
gramercy. Whan sir Grylflet saw sir Kay and sir Lucas de
Butler on foote, he with a sherpe spere grete and square rode
to Pynnel, a good man of armys, and smote horse and man
25 downe, and than he toke hys horse and gaff hym unto sir Kay.

Than kynge Lotte saw kynge Nentres on foote, he ran
unto Meliot de la Roche and smote hym downe horse and
man, and gaff ⟨unto⟩ kynge Nentres the horse and horsed
hym agayne. Also the Kynge with the Hondred Knyghtes
30 saw kynge Idres on foote, he ran unto Gwyniarte de Bloy
and smote hym downe horse and man, and gaff kynge Idres
the horse and horsed hym agayne. Tha[n] kynge Lotte smote
downe Clarinaus de la Foreyste Saveage and gaff the horse
unto duke Estans. And so whan they had horsed the kyngis
35 agayne, they drew hem all eleven kynges togydir, and seyde

1 *C* Eustace of Cambenet   *W* Eskance of Candebenet   *F* Estams de Cambenit
(*cf. p. 31, line 10*)   2 *C* alweye greuous on Vlfyus   3 *C* felawe ferd so
5 *C* retorned   12 *O*¹ *C* man byʈ kynge   *F agrees with W*   18 *W* and hurte
repeated   23 *C* he tooke a sharp spere grete and square and rode   28 *W O*¹
hym to (*not in C**)   30 *C*ʈ Gwymyart   *F* Guynas   32 *W* That kynge   *C** &
kyng   34 *C* Eustace (*see note to l. 1*)

they wolde be revenged of the damage that they had takyn
that day.

The meanewhyle com in kyng Arthure with an egir coun-
tenans, and founde Ulphuns and Brastias on foote, in grete
perell of dethe, that were fowle defoyled undir the horse 5
feete. Than Arthure as a lyon ran unto kynge Cradilment
of North Walis and smote hym thorow the lyffte syde, that
horse and man felle downe. Than he toke the horse by the
reygne and led hym unto Ulphine and seyde,

'Have this horse, myne olde frende, for grete nede hast 10
thou of an horse.'

'Gramercy,' seyde Ulphuns.

Than kynge Arthure dud so mervaylesly in armys that
all men had wondir. Whan the Kyng with the Hondred
Knyghtes saw kynge Cradilmente on foote, he ran unto sir 15
Ector, sir Kayes fadir, that was well ihorsed and smote horse
and man downe, and gaff the horse unto the kynge and
horsed hym agayne. And whan kynge Arthure saw that
kynge ryde on sir Ectors horse he was wrothe, and with hys
swerde he smote the kynge on the helme, that a quarter of 20
the helme and shelde clave downe; and so the swerde carve
downe unto the horse necke, and so man and horse felle
downe to the grounde. Than sir Kay com unto kynge
Morganoure, senesciall with the Kynge of the Hondred
Knyghtes, and smote hym downe horse and man, and ledde 25
the horse unto hys fadir, sir Ector.

Than sir Ector ran unto a knyght that hyght Lardans and **12ᵛ**
smote horse and man downe, and lad the horse unto sir
Brastias, that grete nede had of an horse and was gretly
defoyled. Whan Brastias behelde Lucas the Butler that lay 30
lyke a dede man undir the horse feete—and ever sir Gryflet
dud mercyfully for to reskow hym, and there were allwayes
fourtene knyghtes upon sir Lucas—and than sir Brastias
smote one of them on the helme, that hit wente unto his tethe;
and he rode unto another and smote hym, that hys arme flow 35

---

3 *C* cam in syr Ector†   *F* le rois Artus   5–6 *C* vnder horsfeet   7–8 *C* that
the hors and the kynge fylle   13 *C* syre Arthur   16 *C* Ector that was wel
horsed syr kayes fader and smote   18–19 *C* sawe the kynge   21 *C* shelde fyll
doune   22 *C* and so the kyng & the hors   23–24 *C* syr Morganore (*cf. p. 33,*
l. 13)   27 that *not in C*   32 *C* dyd merueillously for   34 *C* to the teeth
35 *C* the arme

into the felde; than he wente to the thirde and smote hym on
the shulder, that sholdir and arme flow unto the felde. And
whan Gryfflet saw rescowis he smote a knyght on the templis,
that hede and helme wente of to the erthe; and Gryfflet
5 toke that horse and lad hym unto sir Lucas, and bade hym
mownte uppon that horse and revenge his hurtis—for sir
Brastias had slayne a knyght tofore—and horsed sir Lucas.

(15)　Than sir Lucas saw kynge Angwysschaunce that nygh⌐e⌐
had slayne Maris de la Roche; and Lucas ran to hym with
10 a sherpe spere that was grete, and he gaff hym suche a falle
that the horse felle downe to the erthe. Also Lucas founde
there on foote Bloyas de la Fla⌐un⌐dres and sir Gwynas,
two hardy knyghtes; and in that woodnes that Lucas was
in, he slew two bachelers and horsed them agayne. Than
15 wexed the batayle passynge harde one bothe partyes. But
kynge Arthur was glad that hys knyghtes were horsed
agayne. And than they fought togiders, that the noyse and
the sowne range by the watir and woode. Wherefore kynge
Ban and Bors made hem redy and dressed theire shyldis and
20 harneysse, and were so currageous that their enemyes shooke
and byverd for egirnesse.

All thys whyle sir Lucas, Gwynas, Bryaunte, and Bellias
of Flaundres helde stronge medlé agaynste six kynges, which
were kynge Lott, kynge Nentres, kynge Brandegoris, kynge
25 Idres, kyng Uriens and kynge Angwysshauns. So with the
helpe of sir Kay and of sir Gryfflet they helde thes six kyngis
harde, that unneth they had ony power to deffende them.
But whan kynge Arthure saw the batayle wolde nat be ended
by no maner, he fared woode as a lyon and stirred his horse
30 here and there on the ryght honde and on the lyffte honde,
that he stynted nat tylle he had slayne twenty knyghtes.
Also he wounded kynge Lotte sore on the shulder, and
made hym to leve that grownde, for sir Kay with sir Gryfflet
13ʳ dud with kynge Arthure grete dedis of armys there.
35 Than sir Ulphuns, Brastias and sir Ector encountirde

4 of *not in* C　　5 C took the hors of that knyght & lad　　7 C horsed Gry-
flet†　　8–9 W that nyght had　　C† that late hadde (*see note*)　　8–9 W
(*sidenote*): The dethe of Marys de la Roche　　9 C Morys　　10 C a short†
spere that was grete that he　　12 W Flawdres　　20 C that many knyghtes
shoke　　23–24 C that was kynge　　24 W kynge kynge Lott　　33 C kay &
gryflet　　34 W armys dud there　　C there grete dedes of armes

agaynste the duke Estans and kynge Cradilmante and kynge
Clarivauns of Northhumbirlonde and kynge Carados and
the Kynge with the Hondred Knyghtes. So thes kynges
encountird with thes knyghtes, that they made them to avoyde
the grounde. Than kynge Lotte made grete dole for his 5
damagis and his felowis, and seyde unto the kyngis,

'But if we woll do as I have devised, we all shall be slayne
and destroyed. Lette me have the Kynge with the Hondred
Knyghtes, and kynge Angwysshaunce, and kynge Idres,
and the duke of Can⌐benet⌐. And we fyve kyngis woll have 10
ten thousand men of armys with us, and we woll go on one
party whyle the six kynges holde the medlé with twelve
thousand. And whan we se that ye have foughtyn with hem
longe, than woll we com on freysshly; and ellis shall we
never macche them,' seyde kynge Lotte, 'but by thys 15
means.'

So they departed as they here devised, and thes six kyngis
made theire party stronge agaynste kyng Arthure and made
grete warre longe in the meanwhyle.

Than brake the bushemente of kynge Banne and Bors; 20
and Lionse and Phariaunce had that advaunte-garde, and
they two knyghtes mette with kynge Idres [and his felauship.
And there began a grete medelé of brekyng of speres and
smytyng of swerdys with sleying of men and horses, that
kynge Idres] was nere discomfited. That saw kynge An- 25
gwysshaunce, and put Lyonses and Phariaunce in poynte of
dethe, for the duke ⌐of Canbenet⌐ com on with a grete felyship. So thes two knyghtes were in grete daungere of their
lyves, that they were fayne to returne; but allweyes they
rescowed hemselff and hir felyship merveylously. Whan 30
kynge Bors saw tho knyghtes put on bak hit greved hym
sore. Than he com on so faste that his felyship semed as blak

---

1 *C*† Eustace (*F* Estams)   1–2 *C*† Cradelment & kyng Cradelmāt and kynge
Claryaunce   2–3 *C* Carados & ageynst the kyng with   3–4 *C* thes kny3tes
encountred with these kynges   6–7 *C* the x kynges but yf ye wil do as I
deuyse we shalle be slayn   10 *W* Candebenet   *C** Canbenec   *F* Cambenit
10–11 *C*† haue xv M men   *F* douze mile homes   11–12 *C* go on parte†
12–13 *C*† holde medle with XII M & we see   14 *C* com on fyersly   17 thes
not in C   19–20 *C* In the meane whyle brake   21 *C* Lyonses and Pharyaunce
had the aduant   22–25 *W* O¹ kynge Idres that was nere   25 *C* at discomfiture
That   25–26 *C* sawe Agwysaunce the kynge   27 *W* duke Candebenet
C duke of Canbenek   *F* duc de Cambenic   *C* on with all with a grete

as inde. Whan kynge Lotte had aspyed kynge Bors, he knew
hym well, and seyde,

'Jesu defende us from dethe and horryble maymes, for I
se well we be in grete perell of dethe; for I se yondir a kynge,
5 one of the moste worshipfullyst ⌈men, and the⌉ best knyghtes
of the worlde be inclyned unto his felyship.'

'What ys he?' seyde the Kynge with the Hu[n]dirde
Knyghtes.

'Hit ys,' he seyde, 'kynge Bors of Gaule. I mervayle,'
10 seyde he, 'how they com unto this contrey withoute wetynge
of us all.'

'Hit was by Merlions advice,' seyde a knyght.

'As for me,' seyde kynge Carados, 'I woll encountir with
kynge Bors, and ye woll rescow me whan myster ys.'

15 'Go on,' seyde they, 'for we woll all that we may.'

Than kynge Carados and hys oste rode on a soffte pace
tyll they com as nyghe kynge Bors as a bowe-draught. Than
13ᵛ eythir lette theire horsys renne as faste as they myght. And
Bleobris that was godson unto kynge Bors, he bare his chyeff
20 standard; that was a passyng good knyght.

'Now shall we se,' seyde kynge Bors, 'how thes northirne
Bretons can bere theire armys!'

So kynge Bors encountird with a knyght and smote hym
throwoute with a spere, that he felle dede unto the erthe;
25 and aftirwarde drew hys swerde and dud mervaylous dedis
of armys, that all partyes had grete wondir thereof. And his
knyght[es] fayled nat but dud hir parte. And kynge Carados
was smytten to the erthe. With that com the Kynge with the
Hondred Knyghtes and rescowed kynge Carados myghtyly
30 by force of armys, for he was a passynge good knyght and
(16) but a yonge man. Be than com into the felde kynge Ban as
ferse as a lyon, with bondis of grene and thereuppon golde.

'A ha,' seyde kynge Lott, 'we muste be discomfite, for
yondir I se the most valiante knyght of the worlde, and the
35 man of moste renowne, for such two brethirne as ys kynge
Ban and kynge Bors ar nat lyvynge. Wherefore we muste

2–3 *C* thenne he said O Ihesu   5 *W* and of the   *C* men & one of the (*see
note*)   9 *C* is said kyng Lot kyng   10 seyde he *not in C*   12 *C* said
the knyghte   13 *C* As for hym sayd   15 *C* they al we wil do all
18 eyther bataill lete   25 *C* after   30–31 *C* knyght of a kynge & but
35 *C* the most

nedis voyde or dye, and but if we avoyde manly and wysely
there ys but dethe.'

So whan thes two kyngis, Ban and Bors, com into the
batayle, they com in so fersely that the strokis re[d]ounded
agayne fro the woode and the watir. Wherefore kynge Lotte 5
wepte for pité and dole that he saw so many good knyghtes
take their ende. But thorow the grete force of kynge Ban
they made bothe the northirne batayles that were parted
hurteled togidirs for grete drede. And the three kynges and
their knyghtes slew on ever, that hit was pité to se and to 10
beholde the multitude of peple that fledde.

But kyng Lott and the Kynge with the Hundred Knyghtes
and kynge Morganoure gadred the peple togydir passynge
knyghtly, and dud grete proues of armys, and helde the
batayle all the day lyke harde. Whan the Kynge with the 15
Hundred Knyghtes behelde the grete damage that kynge
Ban [dyd] he threste unto hym with his horse and smote
hym an hyghe on the helme a grete stroke and stoned hym
sore. Than kynge Ban was wood wrothe with hym and
folowed on hym fersely. The othir saw that and caste up 20
hys shelde and spored hys horse forewarde, but the stroke
of kynge Ban downe felle and carve a cantell of the shelde,
and the swerde sloode downe by the hawbirke byhynde hys
backe and kut thorow the trappoure of stele and the horse
evyn in two pecis, that the swerde felle to the erth. Than the 25 **14ʳ**
Kynge of the Hundred Knyghtes voyded the horse lyghtly,
and with hys swerde he broched the horse of kynge Ban
thorow and thorow. With that kynge Ban voyded lyghtly
from the dede horse and smote at that othir so egirly on the
helme that he felle to the erthe. Also in that ire he felde 30
kynge Morganoure, and there was grete slawghtir of good
knyghtes and muche peple.

Be that tyme com into the prees kynge Arthure and
founde kynge Ban stondynge amonge the dede men and
dede horse, fyghtynge on foote as a wood lyon, that there 35

3 *C* whanne kynge Ban came   4 *C* he cam   4–5 *W* rebounded agayne   *C**
redounded ageyne   8 *C* were departed   10–11 *C* pyte on to behold that
multitude of the people   16–17 *C* kynge Ban dyd   19 wood *not in C*   22 *C*
felle downe and   25 *C*† the swerd felte the erth   *F* trebuche (*see note*)   29 *C*
hors and thenne kynge Ban smote at the other so egrely and smote hym on the
33 *C* by than come

com none nyghe hym as farre as he myght reche with hys swerde but he caught a grevous buffette; whereof kynge Arthure had grete pité. And kynge Arthure was so blody that by hys shylde there myght no man know hym, for all
5 was blode and brayne that stake on his swerde and on hys shylde. And as kynge Arthure loked besyde hym he sawe a knyght that was passyngely well horsed. And therewith kynge Arthure ran to hym and smote hym on the helme, that hys swerde wente unto his teeth, and the knyght sanke downe
10 to the erthe dede. And anone kynge Arthure toke hys horse by the rayne and ladde hym unto kynge Ban and seyde,

'Fayre brothir, have ye thys horse, for ye have grete myster thereof, and me repentys sore of youre grete damage.'

'Hit shall be sone revenged,' seyde kynge Ban, 'for I
15 truste in God myne hurte ys none suche but som of them may sore repente thys.'

'I woll welle,' seyde kynge Arthure, 'for I se youre dedys full actuall; nevertheles I myght nat com to you at that tyme.'

20 But whan kynge Ban was mounted on horsebak, than there began a new batayle whych was sore and harde, and passynge grete slaughtir. And so thorow grete force kyng Arthure, kynge Ban, and kynge Bors made hir knyghtes alyght to wythdraw hem to a lytyll wood, and so over a litill
25 ryvir; and there they rested hem, for on the nyght before they had no grete reste in the felde. And than the eleven kyngis put hem on an hepe all togydirs, as men adrad and oute of all comforte. But there was no man that myght passe them; they helde hem so harde togydirs bothe behynde
30 and before that kynge Arthure had mervayle of theire dedis of armys and was passynge wrothe.

'A, sir Arthure,' seyde kynge Ban and kynge Bors, 'blame
14ᵛ hem nat, for they do as good men ought to do. For be my fayth,' seyde kynge Ban, 'they ar the beste fyghtynge men
35 and knyghtes of moste prouesse that ever y saw other herde off speke. And tho eleven kyngis ar men of grete worship;

5-6 *C* braynes on his swerd And as Arthur loked by hym he sawe   10 *C*
tooke the hors   12 *C* haue this   15 *C* myn eure is not suche   18 *C* come
at yow   23-24 *C* knyghtes a litel† to with drawe   25-26 *C* nyght they myght
haue no rest   27 *C* kynges and knyghtes   28 that *not in C*   35-36 *C* or
herd speke of

and if they were longyng to you, there were no kynge undir
hevyn that had suche eleven kyngis nother off suche worship.'

'I may nat love hem,' seyde kynge Arthure, 'for they
wolde destroy me.'

'That know we well,' seyde kynge Ban and kynge Bors, 5
'for they ar your mortall enemyes, and that hathe bene
preved beforehonde. And thys day they have done their
parte, and that ys grete pité of their wylfulnes.'

Than all the eleven kynges drew hem togydir, and than
seyde Lott, 'Lordis, ye muste do othirwyse than ye do, othir 10
ellis the grete losses ys behynde: for ye may se what peple we
have loste and what good men we lese because we wayte allweyes on thes footemen; and ever in savyng of one of thes footemen we lese ten horsemen for hym. Therefore thys ys myne
advise: lette us putte oure footemen frome us, for hit ys nere 15
nyght. For thys noble kynge Arthure woll nat tarry on the
footemen, for they may save hemselff: the woode ys nerehonde. And whan we horsemen be togydirs, looke every of
you kyngis lat make such ordinaunce that none breke uppon
payne of deth. And who that seeth any man dresse hym to 20
fle lyghtly, that he be slayne; for hit ys bettir we sle a cowarde
than thorow a coward all we be slayned. How sey ye?' seyde
kynge Lotte. 'Answere me, all ye kynges!'

'Ye say well,' seyde kynge Nentres. So seyde the Kynge
with the Hondred Knyghtes; the same seyde kynge Carados 25
and kynge Uryens; so seyde kynge Idres and kynge Brandegoris; so dud kyng Cradilmasse and the duke of Can⌈benet;⌉
the same seyde kynge Claryaunce, and so dud kynge Angwysshaunce, and swore they wolde never fayle other for
lyff nothir for dethe, and whoso that fledde all they sholde 30
be slayne. Than they amended their harneyse and ryghted
their sheldis, and toke newe speris and sette hem on theire
thyghes, and stoode stylle as hit had be a plumpe of
woode.

Whan kynge Arthure and kynge Ban and Bors behelde 35 (17)
them and all hir knyghtes, they preysed them much for

2 *C* xj knyghtes and of   5 *C* that wote we   11 *C* losse   15 *W* for for hit
ys   16 *C* For the noble Arthur   17 *C*† hym self   18–19 *C* looke eueryche
of yow   22 *C* we to be slayne   24 *C* it is wel said quod kynge Nentres
26 *C* so dyd kynge Idres   27 *W* Candebenet. *Cf. p. 31, note 10*   28 so dud *not
in C*   29 *C* faille other neyther   30 *C* fledde but did as they dyd shold

their noble chere of chevalry, fo[r] the hardyeste fyghters that ever they herde other saw.

So furthwith there dressed ⟨twenty-one⟩ knyghtes, and seyde unto the three kynges they wolde breke their batayle.
5 And thes were their namys: Lyonses, Phariaunce, Ulphuns,
15ʳ Brastias, Ector, Kayus, Lucas de Butler, Gryfflet la Fyse de Deu, Marrys de la Roche, Gwynas de Bloy, Bryaunte de la Foreyste Saveage, Bellaus, Morians of the Castel Maydyns, Flaundreus of the Castel of Ladyes, Annecians that was
10 kynge Bors godson, a noble knyght, and Ladinas de la Rouse, Emerause, Caulas, Graciens le Castilion, Bloyse de la Case, and sir Colgrevaunce de Goore.

All thes knyghtes rode on before with sperys on theire thyghes and spurred their horses myghtyly. And the eleven
15 kyngis with parte of hir knyghtes rushed furthe as faste as they myght with hir sperys, and there they dud on bothe partyes merveylous dedes of armys. So there com into the thycke of the prees Arthure, Ban, and Bors, and slew downe-ryght on bothe hondis, that hir horses wente in blood up to
20 the fittlockys. But ever the eleven kyngis and the oste was ever in the visage of Arthure. Wherefore kynge Ban and Bors had grete mervayle consyderyng the grete slaughter that there was; but at the laste they were dryven abacke over a litill ryver. With that com Merlion on a grete blacke horse
25 and seyde unto kynge Arthure,

'Thou hast never done. Hast thou nat done inow? Of three score thousande thys day hast thou leffte on lyve but fyftene thousand! Therefore hit ys tyme to sey "Who!" for God ys wroth with the for thou woll never have done.
30 For yondir a eleven kynges at thys tyme woll nat be over-throwyn, but and thou tary on them ony lenger thy fortune woll turne and they shall encres. And therefore withdraw you unto youre lodgynge and reste you as sone as ye may, and rewarde youre good knyghtes with golde and with sylver, for
35 they have well deserved hit. There may no ryches be to dere

---

1 *W* fo the   3 *W* Oᴵ a fourty knyghtes   *C* there dressyd hem a xl noble knyghtes (xxj *mistaken for* a xl)   7 *C* mariet† de la roche   11 *C* Gracyens le castelyn one bloyse   14 *C** myghtely as the horses myȝte renne And the xj 15 *C* russched with their horses as fast   18 *W* thes prees *C* the prees 20 *C* and their hooste   28–29 *C* xv M and it is tyme to saye ho for god is wrothe with the that thow   30 a *not in C*

for them, for of so fewe men as ye have there was never men
dud more worshipfully in proues than ye have done to-day: for
ye have macched thys day with the beste fyghters of the worlde.'

'That ys trouthe,' seyde kynge Ban and Bors.

Than Merlyon bade hem, 'Withdraw where ye lyste, for 5
thys three yere I dare undirtake they shall nat dere you; and
by that tyme ye shall hyre newe tydyngis.' Than Merlion
seyde unto Arthure, 'These eleven kyngis have more on
hande than they are ware off, for the Sarezynes ar londed in
their contreies mo than fourty thousande, and brenne and 10
sle and have leyde syege to the castell Wandesborow, and
make grete destruction: therefore drede you nat thys [thre]
yere. Also, sir, all the goodis that be gotyn at this batayle
lette hit be serched, and whan ye have hit in your hondis **15ᵛ**
lette hit be geffyn frendly unto thes two kyngis, Ban and 15
Bors, that they may rewarde their knyghtes wythall: and that
shall cause straungers to be of bettir wyll to do you servyse
at nede. Also ye be able to rewarde youre owne knyghtes
at what tyme somever hit lykith you.'

'Ye sey well,' seyde Arthure, 'and as thou haste devised 20
so shall hit be done.'

Whan hit was delyverde to thes kynges, Ban and Bors,
they gaff the godis as frely to theire knyghtes as hit was
gevyn to them.

Than Merlion toke hys leve of kynge Arthure and of the 25
two kyngis, for to go se hys mayster Bloyse that dwelled in
Northhumbirlonde. And so he departed and com to hys
mayster that was passynge glad of hys commynge. And there
he tolde how Arthure and the two kynges had spedde at the
grete batayle, and how hyt was endyd, and tolde the namys 30
of every kynge and knyght of worship that was there. And
so Bloyse wrote the batayle worde by worde as Merlion tolde
hym, how hit began and by whom, and in lyke wyse how
hit was ended and who had the worst. And all the batayles
that were done in Arthurs dayes, Merlion dud hys mayster 35

1–2 *C* ther were neuer men dyd more of prowesse than they haue done   4–5 *C*
bors Also said Merlyn withdrawe yow where   7 *C* by than   10 *C* that
brenne   11 *C* att the castell   12 *F (Camb. f. 224ʳ)* trois anz ou plus   [thre]
not in Oᴵ   15 *C* gyuen frely vnto   18–19 *C* knyghtes of your owne goodes
whan someuer   20 *C* It is wel said qd Arthur   22 thes kynges *not in C*
23 *C* knyʒtes as frely as   26 *C* go and see   34 *C* the werre

Bloyse wryte them. Also he dud wryte all the batayles that every worthy knyght ded of Arthurs courte.

So aftir this Merlion departed frome his mayster and com to kynge Arthure that was in the castell of Bedgrayne, that was 5 one of the castels that stondith in the foreyste of Sherewood. And Merlion was so disgysed that kynge Arthure knewe hym nat, for he was all befurred in blacke shepis skynnes, and a grete payre of bootis, and a boowe and arowis, in a russet gowne, and brought wylde gyese in hys honde. And hit was on the 10 morne aftir Candilmasse day. But kynge Arthure knew hym nat.

'Sir,' seyde Merlion unto the kynge, 'woll ye geff me a gyffte?'

'Wherefore,' seyde kynge Arthure, 'sholde I gyff the a gyffte, chorle?'

15 'Sir,' seyd Merlion, 'ye were bettir to gyff me a gyffte that ys nat in youre honde than to lose grete rychesse. For here in the same place there the grete batayle was, ys grete tresoure hydde in the erthe.'

'Who tolde the so, chorle?'

20 'Sir, Merlyon tolde me so,' seyde he.

Than Ulphuns and Brastias knew hym well inowghe and smyled. 'Sir,' seyde thes two knyghtes, 'hit ys Merlion that so spekith unto you.'

Than kynge Arthure was gretly abaysshed and had 16ʳ 25 mervayle of Merlion, and so had kynge Ban and Bors. So they had grete disporte at hym.

Than in the meanewhyle there com a damesell that was an erlis doughter; hys name was Sanam and hir name was Lyonors, a passynge fayre damesell. And so she cam thidir 30 for to do omage as other lordis ded after that grete batayle. And kynge Arthure sette hys love gretly on hir, and so ded she uppon hym, and so the kynge had ado with hir and gate on hir a chylde. And hys name was Borre, that was aftir a good knyght and of the Table Rounde.

35 Than the[r] come worde that kynge Ryens of North Walis made grete warre on kynge Lodegreaunce of Camylarde, for the whiche kynge Arthure was wrothe, for he loved hym

---

1 *C* Bleyse do wryte Also he did do wryte   5 *C* stondyn   19 *C* chorle said Arthur   30 *C* after the   35 *W* Than the com   *C* thenne there cam 37 *C* whiche thyng† arthur

welle and hated kyng Royns, for allwayes he was agenst
hym.

(So by ordinauns of the three kynges ther were sente home
unto Benwyke [all th]⟨at⟩ wolde departe, for drede of kynge
Claudas. Thes knyghtes: Pharyaunce, Anthemes, Graciens 5
⌐and Lyonses of⌐ Payarne were the leders of them that sholde
kepe the two kynges londis.)

And than kynge Arthure, kynge Ban and kynge Bors (18)
departed with hir felyship, a twenty thousand, and cam
within seven dayes into the contrey of Camylarde; and there 10
rescowed kynge Lodegraunce, and slew there muche people
of kynge Ryons, unto the numbir of ten thousand, and putte
hem to flyght. And than had thes thre kynges grete chere
of kynge Lodegraunce, and ⟨he⟩ thanked them of theire grete
goodnes that they wolde revenge hym of his enemyes. 15

And there had Arthure the firste syght of queene Gwenyvere, the kyngis doughter of the londe of Camylarde, and
ever afftir he loved hir. And aftir they were wedded, as hit
tellith in the booke.

So breffly to make an ende, they took there leve to go into 20
hir owne contreyes, for kynge Claudas dud grete destruction
on their londis. Than seyde Arthure,

'I woll go with you.'

'Nay,' seyde the kyngis, 'ye shall nat at thys tyme, for
ye have much to do yet in thys londe. Therefore we woll 25
departe. With the grete goodis that we have gotyn in this
londe by youre gyfftis we shall wage good knyghtes and
withstonde the kynge Claudas hys malice, for, by the grace
of God, and we have nede, we woll sende to you for succour.
And ye have nede, sende for us, and we woll nat tarry, by 30
the feythe of oure bodyes.'

'Hit shall nat nede,' seyde Merlion, 'thes two kynges to
com agayne in the wey of warre; but I know well kynge

---

3 *C*† kynges that were   4 *W* Benwyke and wolde   *C** Benwyck all they
wolde   *F* (*Camb. f. 224ᵛ, col. 1*) tuz fors ceus seulment qui demorer i voudront
5 Thes knyghtes *not in C*   5–6 *W* Graciens lyonses and payarne   *C* Grasians
and lyonses payarne (*so in O¹*) with the   *F* Leonce de paerne   10 *C* within
VI dayes   12–13 *C* x M men and put hym to   14 *C* Lodegraunce that
thanked   16 queene *not in C**   17 of the londe *not in C*   18 And *not
in C*†   25, 26–27 *C* in these landes   26 *C* departe and with the   30 *C*
And yf ye   32 *C* not saide Merlyn nede that these

Arthure may nat be longe frome you. For within a yere or
16ᵛ two ye shall have grete nede, than shall he revenge you of
youre enemyes as ye have done on his. For thes eleven
kyngis shall dye all in one day by the grete myght and
5 prouesse of armys of two valyaunte knyghtes,'—as hit tellith
aftir. Hir namys [ben] Balyne le Saveage and Balan, hys
brothir, that were merveylous knyghtes as ony was tho
lyvynge.

Now turne we unto the eleven kynges that returned unto
10 a cité that hyght Surhaute, which cité was within kynge
Uriens londe; and there they refreysshed them as well as
they myght, and made lechys serche for their woundis and
sorowed gretly for the deth of hir people. So with that there
com a messyngere and tolde how there was comyn into theyre
15 londis people that were lawles, as well as Sarezynes a fourty
thousande, and have brente and slayne all the people that
they may com by withoute mercy, and have leyde sege unto
the castell Wandesborow.

'Alas!' seyde the eleven kyngis, 'here ys sorow uppon
20 sorow, and if we had nat warred agaynste Arthure as we
have done, he wolde sone a revenged us. And as for kynge
Lodegreaunce, he lovithe Arthure bettir than us; and as for
kynge Royens, he hath ynow ado with kynge Lodegreauns,
for he hath leyde sege unto hym.'

25 So they condescended togydir to kepe all the marchis of
Cornuwayle, of Walis, and of the Northe. So firste they put
kynge Idres in the cité of Nauntis in Bretayne with four
thousand men of armys to wacche bothe watir and the londe.
Also they ⌐put in the cyté of Wyndesan kynge Nauntres of
30 Garlott with four thousand knyghtes to watche both on water
and on lond. Also they⌐ had of othir men of warre mo than
eyght thousand for to fortefye all the fortresse in the marchys

2–3 *C* on youre   4 *C* in a day   6 *O¹* names Balyn   7–8 *C* that ben
merueillous good knyghtes as ben ony lyuyng   11 londe *not in C*   12 for
not in C   21 *C* soone reuenge vs   25 *O¹ C** they consentyd   *F (Camb. f. 227ᵛ,
col. 2)* si acordent a la fin qu'il garniront les marches de Galone et de Gorre et de
Cornewaille e devers Orquenie   28–31 *W* bothe water and the londe Also they
had of othir men   *C** bothe the water and the land Also they put in the cyte of
Wyndesan kynge Nauntres of garlott with four thousand knyghtes to watche
both on water and on lond Also they had   *F (Camb. f. 228ʳ, col. 1)* L'autre cité
qu'il envoient garnir aprés si out nom Windesan. A ceie ala le roi Nentres de
Garloth, si en mena avod lui trois mille (*homoeoteleuton in W*)

of Cornuwayle. Also they put mo kyngis in all the marchis
of Walis and Scotlonde with many good men of armys, and
so they kept hem togydirs the space of three yere and ever
alyed hem with myghty kynges and dukis. And unto them
felle kynge Royns of Northe Walis which was a myghty 5
kynge of men, and Nero that was a myghty man of men. And
all thys whyle they furnysshed and garnysshed hem of good
men of armys and vitayle and of all maner of ablemente that
pretendith to warre, to avenge hem for the batay[l]e of Bedgrayne, as hit tellith in the booke of adventures. 10

Than aftir the departynge of kynge Bans and Bors, kynge (19)
Arthure rode unto the cité of Carlyon. And thydir com unto
hym kynge Lottis wyff of Orkeney in maner of a message,
but she was sente thydir to aspye the courte of kynge Arthure,
and she com rychely beseyne with hir four sonnes, Gawayne, 15
Gaheris, Aggravayne and Gareth, with many other knyghtes 17ʳ
and ladyes, for she was a passynge fayre lady. Wherefore
the kynge caste grete love unto hir and desired to ly by her.
And so they were agreed, and [he] begate uppon hir sir Mordred. And she was syster on the modirs syde Igrayne unto 20
Arthure. So there she rested hir a monthe, and at the last she
departed.

Than the kynge dremed a mervaylous dreme whereof he
was sore adrad. (But all thys tyme kynge Arthure knew
nat [that] kynge Lottis wyff was his sister.) But thus was 25
the dreme of Arthure: hym thought there was com into
hys londe gryffens and serpentes, and hym thought they
brente and slowghe all the people in the londe; and than he
thought he fought with them and they dud hym grete harme
and wounded hym full sore, but at the laste he slew hem. 30

Whan the kynge waked, he was passynge hevy of hys
dreme; and so to putte hit oute of thought he made hym
redy with many knyghtes to ryde on huntynge. And as
sone as he was in the foreste, the kynge saw a grete harte
before hym. 35

1 *C* moo knyȝtes in   4 *C* dukes and lordes And   5–6 *C* myghty man of
men   9 *C* to the werre to auenge *W* batayne *C* bataille   10 *C* auentures folowynge   11 *C* and of kyng Bors   12 the cite of *not in C*
20–21 *C* his syster on the moder syde Igrayne So ther   19–22 *W* (*sidenote*)
A dreme of Arthure   25 [that] *not in O¹*   26–27 *C* in to this land
29 *C* passynge grete

'Thys harte woll I chace,' seyde kynge Arthure.

And so he spurred hys horse and rode aftir longe, and so be fyne force oftyn he was lyke to have smytten the herte. Wherefore as the kynge had chased the herte so longe that
5 hys horse lost his brethe and felle downe dede, than a yoman fette the kynge another horse.

So the kynge saw the herte unboced and hys horse dede, he sette hym downe by a fowntayne, and there he felle downe in grete thought. And as he sate so hym thought he herde
10 a noyse of howundis to the som of thirty, and with that the kynge saw com towarde hym the strongeste beste that ever he saw or herde of. So thys beste wente to the welle and dranke, and the noyse was in the bestes bealy ⌐lyke unto the questyng of thirty coupyl houndes, but alle the whyle the
15 beest dranke there was no noyse in the bestes bealy¬. And therewith the beeste departed with a grete noyse, whereof the kynge had grete mervayle. And so he was in a grete thought, and therewith he felle on slepe.

Ryght so there com a knyght on foote unto Arthure,
20 and seyde, 'Knyght full of thought and slepy, telle me if thou saw any stronge beeste passe thys way.'

'Such one saw I,' seyde kynge Arthure, 'that ys paste nye two myle. What wolde ye with that beeste?' seyde Arthure.

25 'Sir, I have folowed that beste longe and kylde myne horse, so wolde God I had another to folow my queste.'

Ryght so com one with the kyngis horse. And whan the
17ᵛ knyght saw the horse he prayde the kynge to gyff hym the horse, 'for I have folowed this queste thys twelve-monthe,
30 and othir I shall encheve hym othir blede of the beste bloode

2 *C* the horse　　3–4 *C* herte where as the kynge　　5 *C* hors had loste　　7 *C* the herte enbusshed and　　8–9 *C* fell in grete thoughtes　　11 *C* saw comyng 11 *C* the straungest　　*F* (*Huth Merlin, f.* 76*a*) estraingne de cors et de faiture. 12–15 *W* the noyse in the bestes bely and therewith　　*C** bely lyke unto the questyng of xxx coupyl houndes but alle the whyle the beest dranke there was no noyse in the bestes bely and therwith　　*F* (*loc. cit.*) elle a dedens son cors brakés (*Camb. f.* 230ᵛ, *col.* 2: faons) tout vis qui glatissent (*Camb.*: ausint com feroient brachet). . . . Et si tost comme elle ot commenchiet a boire, le (les ?) biestes qui dedens li estoient et glatissoient s'acoisent et se tinrent coiement. Quant elle ot beu et fu issue de la fontaine, si recommancierent a glatir autressi comme il faisoient devant　　21 *C* thow sawest a straunge best　　23 nye *not in C*　　*C* with the best　　25 *C* long tyme

in my body.' (Whos name was kynge Pellynor that tyme
folowed the questynge beste, and afftir hys dethe sir Palomydes folowed hit.)

'Sir knyght,' seyd the kynge, 'leve that queste and suffir (20)
me to have hit, and I woll folowe hit anothir twelve- 5
monthe.'

'A, foole!' seyde the kynge unto Arthure, 'hit ys in vayne
thy desire, for hit shall never be encheved but by me other
by my nexte kynne.'

And therewithe he sterte unto the kyngis horse and 10
mownted into the sadyl and seyde, 'Gramercy, for this horse
ys myne owne.'

'Well,' seyde the kynge, 'thou mayste take myne horse
by force, but and I myght preve hit I wolde weete whether
thou were bettir worthy to have hym or I.' 15

Whan the kynge herde hym sey so he seyde, 'Seke me
here whan thou wolte, and here nye thys welle thou shalte
fynde me,' ⌐and soo passed on his weye.

Thenne the kyng sat in a study⌐ and bade hys men fecche
another horse as faste as they myght. Ryght so com by hym 20
Merlyon lyke a chylde of fourtene yere of ayge and salewed
the kynge and asked hym whye he was so pensyff.

'I may well be pensiff,' seyde the kynge, 'for I have sene
the mervaylist syght that ever I saw.'

'That know I well,' seyde Merlyon, 'as welle as thyselff, 25
and of all thy thoughtes. But thou arte a foole to take
thought for hit that woll nat amende the. Also I know
what thou arte, and who was thy fadir, and of whom thou
were begotyn: for kynge Uther was thy fadir and begate
the on Igrayne.' 30

'That ys false!' seyde kynge Arthure. 'How sholdist
thou know hit? For thou arte nat so olde of yerys to know
my fadir.'

1–2 C† body Pellinore that tyme kynge folowed   7 C* said the Knyghte vnto
14–16 C preue the whether thow were better on horsbak or I wel said the knyght
seke me   18–20 C* and soo passyd on his weye thenne the kyng sat in a study
and bad his men fetche his hors as faste as euer they myghte   F (Huth Merlin, f.
77b) Atant s'em parti li chevaliers. . . . Illuec demoura li rois grant piece tant pensis
de cel aventure qu'il avoit le jour veues (sic; Camb. la nuite veus e le jour) que il ne
savoit preu consillier. Et en chou qu'il estoit si pensis etc.   25–26 know I well
. . . of all thy thoughtes *stands for the French* tu ne penses chose (Camb. 'a chose')
que je ne sache (Huth Merlin, f. 77c)   26 C art but a foole   27 C it wylle

'Yes,' seyde Merlyon, 'I know hit bettir than ye or ony man lyvynge.'

'I woll nat beleve the,' seyde Arthure, and was wrothe with the chylde.

5　So departed Merlyon, and com ayen in the lyknesse of an olde man of four score yere of ayge, whereof the kynge was passynge glad, for he semed to be ryght wyse. Than seyde the olde man,

'Why ar ye so sad?'

10　'I may well be sad,' seyde Arthure, 'for many thynges. For ryght now there was a chylde here, and tolde me many thynges that mesemythe he sholde nat knowe, for he was nat of ayge to know my fadir.'

'Yes,' seyde the olde man, 'the chylde tolde you trouthe,
15　and more he wolde a tolde you and [y]e wolde a suffirde hym, but ye have done a thynge late that God ys displesed with you, for ye have lyene by youre syster and on hir ye have

18ʳ　gotyn a childe that shall destroy you and all the knyghtes of youre realme.'

20　'What ar ye,' seyde Arthure, 'that telle me thys tydyngis?'

'Sir, I am Merlion, and I was he in the chyldis lycknes.'

'A,' seyde the kynge, 'ye ar a mervaylous man! But I
25　mervayle muche of thy wordis that I mou dye in batayle.'

'Mervayle nat,' seyde Merlion, 'for hit ys Goddis wylle that youre body sholde be punyss[h]ed for your fowle dedis. But I ought ever to be hevy,' seyde Merlion, 'for I shall dye a shamefull dethe, to be putte in the erthe quycke; and ye
30　shall dey a worshipfull dethe.'

And as they talked thus, com one with the kyngis horse, and so the kynge mownted on hys horse, and Merlion on anothir, and so rode unto Carlyon. And anone the kynge askyd Ector and Ulphuns how he was begotyn, and they tolde
35　hym how kynge Uther was hys fadir, and quene Igrayne hys modir.

7 *C* was ryght glad　　　10–11 wel be heuy said . . . thynges Also here was a
chyld and told　　15 *W* and he wolde　　25 *C* mote dye　　26–27 *C* wyll
youre body to be　　28 *C* but I may wel be sory said Merlyn　　31 *C*† talked
this　　35 *C* how *not in C*　　36–p. 45, l. 1　*C* moder thenne he sayd to Merlyn I wylle

'So Merlion tolde me. I woll that my modir be sente for, that I myght speke with hir. And if she sey so hirselff, than woll I beleve hit.'

So in all haste the quene was sente for, [and she came] and she brought with hir Morgan le Fay, hir doughter, that was 5 a fayre lady as ony myght be. And the kynge welcommed Igrayne in the beste maner. Ryght so com in Ulphuns and (21) seyde opynly, that the kynge and all myght hyre that were fested that day,

'Ye ar the falsyst lady of the wor[l]de, and the moste tray- 10 toures unto the kynges person.'

'Beware,' seyde kynge Arthure, 'what thou seyste: thou spekiste a grete worde.'

'Sir, I am well ware,' seyde Ulphuns, 'what I speke, and here ys my gloove to preve hit uppon ony man that woll 15 sey the contrary: that thys quene Igrayne ys the causer of youre grete damage and of youre grete warre, for and she wolde have uttirde hit in the lyff of Uther of the birth of you, and how ye were begotyn, than had ye never had the mortall warrys that ye have had. For the moste party of 20 your barownes of youre realme knewe never whos sonne ye were, ne of whom ye were begotyn; and she that bare you of hir body sholde have made hit knowyn opynly, in ex-cusynge of hir worship and youres, and in lyke [wyse] to all the realme. Wherefore I preve hir false to God and to 25 you and to all youre realme. And who woll sey the contrary, I woll preve hit on hys body.'

Than spake Igrayne and seyde, 'I am a woman and I may nat fyght; but rather than I sholde be dishonoured, there wolde som good man take my quarell. But,' thus she seyde, 30 'Merlion knowith well, and ye, sir Ulphuns, how kynge Uther com to me into the castell of Tyntagyl in the lyknes **18ᵛ** of my lorde that was dede three owres tofore, and there begate a chylde that nyght uppon me, and aftir the thirtenth day kynge Uther wedded me. And by his commaunde- 35 mente, whan the chylde was borne, hit was delyvirde unto Merlion and fostred by hym. And so I saw the childe never

4, 10 *Not emended in* O¹   5-6 *C* was a fayre a lady   7 *C* cam Vlfyus   18 *C*
Vther-pēdragon   19 *C* begoten ye had neuer had   *W* had ye neuer had   30 *C*
quarel More she   33-34 *C* † and therby gat a child   37 *C* and nourysshed by

aftir, nothir wote nat what ys hys name; for I knew hym never yette.'

Than Ulphuns seyde unto Merlion,

'Ye ar than more to blame than the queene.'

5 'Sir, well I wote I bare a chylde be my lorde kynge Uther, but I wote never where he ys becom.'

Than the kynge toke Merlion by the honde seying thys wordis:

'Ys this my modir?'

10 'Forsothe, sir, yee.'

And therewith com in sir Ector, and bare wytnes how he fostred hym by kynge Uthers commaundemente. And therewith kyng Arthure toke his modir, quene Igrayne, in hys armys and kyssed her, and eythir wepte uppon other. Than

15 the kynge lete make a feste that lasted eyght dayes.

So on a day there com into the courte a squyre on horse-backe ledynge a knyght tofore hym, wounded to the deth, and tolde how there was a knyght in the foreste that had rered up a pavylon by a welle, 'that hath slayne my mayster,

20 a good knyght: hys name was Myles. Wherefore I besech you that my maystir may be buryed, and that som knyght may revenge my maystirs dethe.'

Than the noyse was grete of that knyghtes dethe in the courte, and every man seyde hys advyce. Than com Gryfflet

25 that was but a squyre, and he was but yonge, of ⌈the ayge of the kyng Arthur⌉. So he besought the kynge for all hys servyse that he had done hym to gyff hym the Order of Knyghthoode.

(22) 'Thou arte but yonge and tendir of ayge,' seyd kynge

30 Arthure, 'for to take so hyghe an orde[r] uppon you.'

'Sir,' seyde Gryfflet, 'I beseche you to make me knyght.'

'Sir,' seyde Merlion, 'hit were pité to lose Gryfflet, for he woll be a passynge good man whan he ys of ayge, and he

2–5 C yet And there Vlfyus saide to the quene Merlyn is more to blame than ye wel I wote said the quene I bare   6 C wote not where   7–12 C* thenne Merlyn toke the kynge by the hand sayeng this is your moder and therwith syr Ector bare wytnes how he nourysshed hym   F (*Huth Merlin, f. 84c*) Lors prent Artu par le brach et li dist: 'Artu (*Camb.*: Amis) . . . la roine Ygerne est ta mere' 19 C and hath slayne   25–26 W of ayge so   F (*Camb. f. 238ʳ, col. 1*) estoit de l'aage le roi Artu   27 hym *not in* C   29 C arte full yong   30 C on the 32 C were grete pyte   33–p. 47, l. 1 C age abydynge with how the terme me† of

shall abyde with you the terme of hys lyff. And if he aventure
his body with yondir knyght at the fountayne, hit ys in grete
perell if ever he com agayne, for he ys one of the beste
knyghtes of the worlde and the strengyst man of armys.'

'Well,' seyde Arthure, 'at thyne owne desire thou shalt   5
be made knyght.'

⌐So at the desyre of Gryflet the kynge made hym knyght.⌐

'Now,' seyde Arthure unto Gryfflet, 'sith I have made the
knyght, thou muste gyff me a gyffte.'

'What ye woll,' seyde Gryfflet.   10

'Thou shalt promyse me by th[e] feyth of thy body, whan **19ʳ**
thou haste justed with that knyght at the fountayne, whether
hit falle ye be on horsebak othir on foote, that ryght so ye
shall com agayne unto me withoute makynge ony more
debate.'   15

'I woll promyse you,' seyde Gryfflet, 'as youre desire ys.'

Than toke Gryfflet hys horse in grete haste and dressed
hys shelde and toke a spere in hys honde, and so he rode
a grete walop tylle he com to the fountayne. And thereby he
saw a ryche pavilion, and thereby undir a cloth stood an   20
horse well sadeled and brydyled, and on a tre hynge a shelde
of dyvers coloures, and a grete spere thereby. Than Gryfflet
smote on the shylde with the butte of hys spere, that the
shylde felle downe.

With that the knyght com oute of the pavilion and seyde,   25
'Fayre knyght, why smote ye downe my shylde?'

'Sir, for I wolde juste with you,' seyde Gryfflet.

'Sir, hit ys bettir ye do nat,' seyde the kynge, 'for ye ar
but yonge and late made knyght, and youre myght ys nat
to myne.'   30

'As for that,' seyde Gryfflet, 'I woll jouste with you.'

'That ys me loth,' seyde the knyght, 'but sitthyn I muste
nedis, I woll dresse me thereto. Of whens be ye?' seyde the
knyght.

'Sir, I am of kynge Arthurs courte.'   35

So the two knyghtes ran togydir, that Gryfflettis spere all to-shevirde. And therewithall he smote Gryfflet thorow the shelde and the lyffte syde, and brake the spere, that the truncheon stake in hys body, and horse and man felle downe
5 to the erthe.

(23)   Whan the knyght saw hym ly so on the grounde he alyght and was passyng hevy, for he wente he had slayne hym. And than he unlaced hys helme and gate hym wynde; and so with the troncheon he sette hym on his horse and gate
10 hym wynde, and so betoke hym to God and seyde, 'He had a myghty herte!' And seyde, 'If he myght lyve, he wolde preve a passyng good knyght,' and so rode forthe sir Gryfflet unto the courte, whereof passyng grete dole was made for hym. But thorow good lechis he was heled and saved.

15   Ryght so com into the courte twelve knyghtes that were aged men, whiche com frome the Emperoure of Rome. And they asked of Arthure trwage for hys realme, othir ellis the Emperour wolde destroy hym and all hys londe.

'Well,' seyde kynge Arthure, 'ye ar messyngers: therefore
20 ye may sey what ye woll, othir ellis ye sholde dye therefore. But thys ys myne answere: I owghe the Emperour no trew-
19ᵛ age, nother none woll I yelde hym, but on a fayre fylde I shall yelde hym my trwage, that shall be with a sherpe spere othir ellis with a sherpe swerde. And that shall nat be longe,
25 be my fadirs soule Uther!'

And therewith the messyngers departed passyngly wrothe, and kyng Arthure as wrothe; for in an evyll tyme com they. But the kynge was passyngly wrothe for the hurte of sir Gryf-flet, and so he commaunded a prevy man of hys chambir that
30 or hit were day his beste horse and armoure 'and all that longith to my person be withoute the cité or to-morow day'. Ryght so he mette with his man and his horse, and so mownted up, and dressed his shelde and toke hys spere, and bade hys chambirlayne tary there tylle he com agayne.

35   And so Arthure rode a soffte pace tyll hit was day. And

4–6 *C* body that hors and knyghte fylle doune Capitulum XXIII Than the knyght   11 *C* hert and yf he   13 *C* court where grete   15–16 *C* & were aged men and they cam   17 *C* for this realme   18 all *not in C*   22 *C* will I hold hym   23 *C* shall yeue hym   25 *C* Vtherpendragon   27–28 *C* in euyl tyme cam they thenne for the kyng   30 *C* hit be day   31–32 *C* armour with all that longeth vnto his person   32 *C* Ryght so or to morow day he met

than was he ware of thre chorlys chasyng Merlion and wolde
have slayne hym. Than the kynge rode unto them and bade
hem: 'Fle, chorlis!' Than they fered sore whan they sawe
a knyght com, and fledde.

'A, Merlion!' seyde Arthure, 'here haddist thou be slayne 5
for all thy crafftis, had nat I bene.'

'Nay,' seyde Merlyon, 'nat so, for I cowde a saved myselffe and I had wolde. But thou arte more nere thy deth
than I am, for thou goste to thy dethe warde and God be
nat thy frende.'   10

So as they wente thus talkynge, they com to the fountayne
and the ryche pavilion there by hit. Than kynge Arthure
was ware where sate a knyght armed in a chayre.

'Sir knyght,' seyde Arthure, 'for what cause abydist thou
here, that there may no knyght ryde thys way but yf he juste 15
with the? I rede the to leve that custom.'

'Thys custom,' seyde the knyght, 'have I used and woll
use magré who seyth nay. And who that ys agreved with my
custum lette hym amende hit.'

'That shall I amende,' seyde Arthure.   20

'And I shall defende the,' seyde the knyght.

And anone he toke hys horse, and dressed hys shelde and
toke a grete spere in hys honde, and they come togydir so
harde that eythir smote other in mydde the shyldis, that all
to-shevird theire speris. Therewith anone Arthure pulled 25
oute his swerde.

'Nay, nat so,' seyde the knyght, 'hit ys bettir that we twayne
renne more togydirs with sherpe sperys.'

'I woll well,' seyde Arthure, 'and I had ony mo sperys
here.'   30

'I have inow,' seyde the knyght.

So there com a squyre and brought forthe two sperys,
and Arthure chose one and he another. So they spurred

---

3 *C* thenne were they aferd whan   4 com *not in C*   7–8 *C* coude saue
my self and I wold   9 *C* to the deth ward   16–17 *C* wyth the said the
kyng I rede the leue that custome said Arthur This customme   18 *C* & who is
19–20 *C* amende hit that wol I wil amende it said Arthur   21 *W Hand in margin
pointing to l. 21*   23 grete *not in C*   in hys honde *not in C*   23–25 *C*† they
met so hard either in others sheldes that al to sheuered their sperys   27 *C*
said the knyght it is fayrer sayd the kny3t that we   30 here *not in C*   32 *C*
brou3t ii (*S* in) good sperys

20^r theire horsis and come togydir with all theire myghtes, that eyther brake their sperys to their hondis. Than Arthure sette honde on his swerde.

'Nay,' seyde the knyght, 'ye shall do bettir. Ye ar a
5 passyng good juster as ever y mette withall, and onys for the hyghe Order of Knyghthode lette us jouste agayne.'

'I assente me,' seyde Arthure.

And anone there was brought forth two grete sperys, and anone every knyght gate a spere; and therewith they ran
10 togiders, that Arthures spere all to-shevirde. But this other knyght smote hym so harde in myddis the shelde that horse and man felle to the erthe. And therewith Arthure was egir, and pulde oute hys swerde, and seyde,

'I woll assay the, sir knyght, on foote, for I have loste
15 the honoure on horsebacke,' seyde the kynge.

'Sir, I woll be on horsebacke stylle to assay the.'

Than was Arthure wrothe and dressed his shelde towarde hym with his swerde drawyn. Whan the knyght saw that he alyght, for hym thought no worship to have a knyght
20 at such avayle, he to be on horsebacke and hys adversary on foote, and so he alyght and dressed his shelde unto Arthure. And there began a stronge batayle with many grete strokis, and so they hew with hir swerdis, that the cantels flowe unto the feldys, and muche bloode they bledde bothe, that all
25 the place thereas they fought was ovirbledde with bloode. And thus they fought longe and rested them. And than they went to the batayle agayne, and so hurteled togydirs lyke too rammes that aythir felle to the erthe. So at the laste they smote togyders, that bothe hir [swerdys] mette evyn
30 togyders. But kynge Arthurs swerde brake in two pecis, wherefore he was hevy.

Than seyde the knyght unto Arthure, 'Thou arte in my daungere, whethir me lyste to save the or sle the; and but thou yelde the to me as overcom and recreaunte, thou shalt
35 dey.'

'As for that,' seyde kynge Arthure, 'dethe ys wellcom to

5–6 *C* ones for the loue of the hyghe . . . Iuste ones ageyn　　11 *C* hyt hym . . . myddes of the shelde　　15–17 *C* horsbak I will be on horsebak said the knyght thenne was†　　20–21 *C* horsbak and he on foot　　23 they *not in C*†　　30 *C* But the swerd of the knyght smote kyng arthurs swerd in two pyeces　　34 to me *not in C*　　36–p. 51, l. 1 *C* as for deth† said kyng arthur welcome be it whan it

me whan hit commyth. But to yelde me unto the I woll
nat!'

And therewithall the kynge lepte unto kynge Pellynore,
and toke hym by the myddyll, and overthrew hym, and raced
of hys helme. So whan the knyght felte that, he was adradde, 5
for he was a passynge bygge man of myght. And so forthe-
with he wrothe Arthure undir hym and raced of hys helme,
and wolde have smytten off hys hede. And therewithall com (24)
Merlion and seyde,

'Knyght, holde thy honde, for and thou sle that knyght 10 **20ᵛ**
thou puttyst thys realme in the grettiste damage that evir
was realme: for thys knyght ys a man of more worshyp than
thou wotist off.'

'Why, what ys he?' seyde the knyght.

'For hit ys kynge Arthure,' seyde Merlyon.   15

Than wolde he have slayne hym for drede of hys wratthe,
and so he lyffte up hys swerde. And therewith Merlion caste
an inchauntemente on the knyght, that he felle to the erthe
in a grete slepe. Than Merlion toke up kynge Arthure and
rode forthe on the knyghtes horse.   20

'Alas!' seyde Arthure, 'what hast thou do, Merlion? Hast
thou slayne thys good knyght by thy craufftis? For there
lyvith nat so worshipffull a knyght as he was. For I had levir
than the stynte of my londe a yere that he were on lyve.'

'Care ye nat,' seyde Merlion, 'for he ys holer than ye: 25
he ys but on slepe and woll awake within thys owre. I
tolde you,' seyde Merlyon, 'what a knyght he was. Now
here had ye be slayne had I nat bene. Also there lyvith nat
a bygger knyght than he ys one; and afftir this he shall do
you goode servyse. And hys name ys kynge Pellinore, and 30
he shall have two sonnes that shall be passyng good men
as ony lyvynge: save one in thys worlde they shall have
no felowis of prouesse and of good lyvynge, and hir namys

1–3 *C** vnto the as recreaunt I had leuer deye than to be soo shamed And ther
with al   3 *C* vnto Pellinore   4 *C* and threwe hym doune and   6–7 *C*
myght and anone he broughte Arthur   14 *C* who is   15 seyde Merlyon
not in C   16–17 *C* wrathe and heue vp his   18 *C* to the knyght   21 *C*
thou done   26 *C* for he ys but   *C* within thre houres *No mention of time in*
F   27 Now *not in C*   29–30 *C* and he shal here after do yow ryght good
seruyse   32 as ony lyvynge *not in C*   in thys worlde *not in C*   33 *C*† or
prowesse

shall be Percyvall and sir Lamorake of Walis. And he shall
telle you the name of youre owne son begotyn of youre
syster, that shall be the destruccion of all thys realme.'

(25)   Ryght so the kynge and he departed and wente unto an
5 ermytage, and there was a good man and a grete leche. So
the ermyte serched the kynges woundis and gaff hym good
salves. And so the kyng was there three dayes, and than wer
his woundis well amended, that he myght ryde and goo;
and so departed. And as they rode, kynge Arthur seyde,
10 'I have no swerde.'

'No force,' seyde Merlyon, 'hereby ys a swerde that shall
be youre, and I may.'

So they rode tyll they com to a laake that was a fayre
watir and brode. And in the myddis Arthure was ware of
15 an arme clothed in whyght samyte, that helde a fayre swerde
in that honde.

'Lo,' seyde Merlion, 'yondir ys the swerde that I spoke
off.'

So with that they saw a damesell goynge uppon the laake.
20 ⌜'What damoysel is that?' said Arthur.

'That is the Lady of the Lake,'⌝ seyde Merlion. 'There
ys a grete roche, and therein ys as fayre a paleyce as ony on
erthe, and rychely besayne. And thys damesel woll come to
21ʳ you anone, and than speke ye fayre to hir, that she may gyff
25 you that swerde.'

So anone com this damesel to Arthure and salewed hym,
and he hir agayne.

'Damesell,' seyde Arthure, 'what swerde ys that yondir
that the arme holdith aboven the watir? I wolde hit were
30 myne, for I have no swerde.'

'Sir Arthure,' seyde the damesel, 'that swerde ys myne,
and if ye woll gyff me a gyffte whan I aske hit you, ye shall
have hit.'

1 *C* Persyual of walys & Lamerak   4–5 *C* went vn tyl an ermyte that was a
6 *C* serched all his woundys   13 *C* the whiche was a fayr   14 *C* myddes of
the lake Arthur   17 *C* that swerd   20–22 *C** what damoysel is that said
Arthur that is the lady of the lake said Merlyn And within that lake is a roche
22 *C†* a place as   *F* palais grans et miervilleus   24 *W* speke speke   *C* she
will gyue   28–29 *C* that that yonder the   31 *C* Syr Arthur kynge said
32–p. 53, l. 9 *W* (*sidenote*): Here ys a mencion of the Lady of the Laake whan she
asked Balyne le saveage his hede

'Be my feyth,' seyde Arthure, 'I woll gyff you what gyffte that ye woll aske.'

'Well,' seyde the damesell, 'go ye into yondir barge, and rowe yourselffe to the swerde, and take hit and the scawberde with you. And I woll aske my gyffte whan I se my tyme.' 5

So kynge Arthure and Merlion alyght and tyed their horsis unto two treys; and so they wente into the barge. And whan they com to the swerde that the honde hylde, than kynge Arthure toke hit up by the hondils and bare hit 10 with hym, and the arme and the honde wente undir the watir. And so he com unto the londe and rode forthe. And kynge Arthure saw a ryche pavilion.

'What signifieth yondir pavilion?'

'Sir, that ys the knyghtes pavilys that ye fought with 15 laste, sir Pellynore; but he ys oute. He ys nat at home, for he hath had ado with a knyght of youres that hyght Egglame, and they had foughtyn togyddyr; but at the laste Egglame fledde, and ellis he had bene dede, and he hath chaced hym evyn to Carlion. And we shall mete with hym anone in the 20 hygheway.'

'That ys well seyde,' seyde Arthure. 'Now have I a swerde I woll wage batayle with hym and be avenged on hym.'

'Sir,' seyde Merlion, 'nat so; for the knyght ys wery of fyghtynge and chasynge, that ye shall have no worship to 25 have ado with hym. Also he woll nat lyghtly be macched of one knyght lyvynge, and therefore hit ys my counceile: latte hym passe, for he shall do you good servyse in shorte tyme, and hys sonnes afftir hys dayes. Also ye shall se that day in shorte space that ye shall be ryght glad to gyff hym 30 youre syster to wedde for hys good servyse. Therefore have nat ado with hym whan ye se hym.'

'I woll do as ye avise me.'

Than kynge Arthure loked on the swerde and lyked hit passynge well. Than seyde Merlion,
35

2 that *not in C*   8–9 *C* the ship &   10–11 *C* handels & toke hit with hym
12 he *not in C*   15 *C* knyʒtes pauelion seid merlyn þ^t   16–17 *C* he is not
there he hath adoo   18 *C* & they haue fouʒten   *S* al the last   22–23 *C*
swerd now will I   24 *C* sir ye shal not so said   25 *C* so that   30 *C*
space ye shal   31–34 *C*† to wedde   When I see hym I wil doo as ye aduyse
me sayd Arthur Thenne   35 Than seyde Merlion *not in C*

'Whethir lyke ye better the swerde othir the scawberde?'

'I lyke bettir the swerde,' seyde Arthure.

'Ye ar the more unwyse, for the scawberde ys worth ten
21ᵛ of the swerde; for whyles ye have the scawberde uppon you
5 ye shall lose no blood, be ye never so sore wounded. Therefore kepe well the scawberde allweyes with you.'

So they rode unto Carlion; and by the wey they mette
with kynge Pellinore. But Merlion had done suche a crauffte
unto kynge Pellinore saw nat kynge Arthure, and so passed
10 by withoute ony wordis.

'I mervayle,' seyde Arthure, 'that the knyght wold nat
speke.'

'Sir, he saw you nat; for had he seyne you, ye had nat
lyghtly parted.'

15 So they com unto Carlion, wherof hys knyghtes were
passynge glad. And whan they herde of hys adventures,
they mervayled that he wolde jouppardé his person so alone.
But all men of worship seyde hit was myrry to be under such
a chyfftayne that wolde putte hys person in adventure as
20 other poure knyghtis ded.

(26)　　　So thys meanewhyle com a messyngere frome kynge Royns
of Northe Walis, and kynge he was of all Irelonde and of
Iles. And this was hys message, gretynge well kyng Arthure
on thys maner of wyse, sayng that kynge Royns had dis-
25 comfite and overcom eleven kyngis, and every of them dud
hym omage. And that was thus to sey they gaff theire beardes
clene flayne off, as much as was bearde; wherefore the
messyngere com for kynge Arthures berde. For kynge
Royns had purfilde a mantell with kynges berdis, and there
30 lacked one place of the mantell; wherefore he sente for hys
bearde, othir ellis he wolde entir into his londis and brenne
and sle, and nevir leve tylle he hathe the hede and the bearde
bothe.

'Well,' seyde Arthure, 'thou haste seyde thy message,
35 the whych ys the moste orgulus and lewdiste message that

---

1 *C* better sayd Merlyn　　　3 *C* are more vnwyse sayd Merlyn for　　　8–9 *C**
crafte that pellinore　　　13 *C* syr said Merlyn he　　　14 *C* departed
21 *For chapter number see p. 6*　　　23 *C* many Iles　　　24 *C* in this manere
wyse　　　25 *C* eueryche of　　　26 *C* that was this they gaf　　　27 *C* as
moche as ther was wher for　　　30 *W* he he sente　　　32 *C* haue the　　　33 bothe
not in C　　　35 *C* most vylaynous and

evir man had isente unto a kynge. Also thou mayste se
my bearde ys full yonge yet to make off a purphile. But telle
thou thy kynge thus, that I owghe hym [none homage]
ne none of myne elders; but or hit be longe to, he shall do
me omage on bothe his knees, other ellis he shall lese hys ₅
hede, by the fayth of my body! For thys ys the moste
shamefullyste message that ever y herde speke off. I have
aspyed thy kynge never yette mette with worshipfull man.
But telle hym I woll have hys hede withoute he do me
omage.' ₁₀

Than thys messyngere departed.

'Now ys there ony here that knowyth kynge Royns?'

Than answerde a knyght that hyght Naram: 'Sir, I know
the kynge well: he ys a passynge good man of hys body as
fewe bene lyvynge and a passynge proude man. And, sir, ₁₅
doute ye nat he woll make on you a myghty puyssaunce.'

'Well,' seyde Arthure, 'I shall ordayne for hym in shorte **22ʳ**
tyme.'

Than kynge Arthure lette sende for all the children that
were borne in May-day, begotyn of lordis and borne of ₂₀
ladyes; for Merlyon tolde kynge Arthure that he that sholde (27)
destroy hym and all the londe sholde be borne on May-day.
Wherefore he sente for hem all in payne of dethe, and so
there were founde many lordis sonnys and many knyghtes
sonnes, and all were sente unto the kynge. And so was ₂₅
Mordred sente by kynge Lottis wyff. And all were putte in
a shyppe to the se; and som were four wekis olde and som
lesse. And so by fortune the shyppe drove unto a castelle,
and was all to-ryven and destroyed the moste party, save
that Mordred was cast up, and a good man founde hym, ₃₀
and fostird hym tylle he was fourtene yere of age, and than
brought hym to the courte, as hit rehersith aftirward and
towarde the ende of the MORTE ARTHURE.

So, many lordys and barownes of thys realme were displeased for hir children were so loste; and many putte the ₃₅

---

1 *C* man herd sente   2 *C* make a pursyl of hit But   12 *C* ony here said
Arthur that   16 *C* make warre on yow with a myghty   19–20 *C* childrē
born on may day   22 and all the londe *not in C*   24–25 and many knyghtes
sonnes *not in C*   31 *C* and nourysshed hym tyl   *C* yere olde & thenne he
32–33 *W* aftirward and towarde and towarde the ende of the morte Arthure.
C afterward toward the ende of the deth of Arthur

wyght on Merlion more than o[n] Arthure. So what for
drede and for love, they helde their pece.

But whan the messynge com to the kynge Royns, than
was he woode oute of mesure, and purveyde hym for a grete
5 oste, as hit rehersith aftir in the BOOKE OF BALYNE LE SAVEAGE
that folowith nexte aftir: that was the adventure how Balyne
gate the swerde.

1 *W O*[1] than of Arthure   3 *C* the messager came   6–7 *C* next after
how by aduenture Balyn gat the swerd EXPLICIT LIBER PRIMUS INCIPIT LIBER
SECUNDUS *W* the swerde after *The last word belongs to the next sentence*: Afftir
the deth *etc. In the copy used by the scribe of W this was probably the end of a page,
and* after *was inserted as a catchword.*

II

BALYN LE SAUVAGE

OR

THE KNIGHT WITH THE TWO SWORDS

[Winchester MS., ff. 22ʳ–34ʳ;
Caxton, Book II]

CAXTON'S RUBRICS

Ch. 1. Of a damoysel whyche came gyrde wyth a swerde for to fynde a man of suche vertue to drawe it oute of the scabard.

„ 2. How Balen arayed lyke a poure knyght pulled out the swerde whyche afterward was cause of his deth.

„ 3. How the Lady of the Lake demaunded the knyghtes heed that had wonne the swerde, or the maydens hede.

„ 4. How Merlyn tolde th'adventure of this damoysel.

„ 5. How Balyn was pursyewed by syr Launceor, knyght of Irelonde, and how he justed and slewe hym.

„ 6. How a damoysel whiche was love to Launceor slewe hyrself for love, and how Balyn mette wyth his brother Balan.

„ 7. How a dwarfe reprevyd Balyn for the deth of Launceor, and how kyng Marke of Cornewayl founde them and maad a tombe over them.

„ 8. How Merlyn prophecyed that two the best knyghtes of the world shold fyght there, whyche were syr Launcelot and syr Trystram.

„ 9. How Balyn and his broder by the counceyl of Merlyn toke kyng Ryons and brought hym to kyng Arthur.

„ 10. How kyng Arthur had a bataylle ayenst Nero and kyng Loth of Orkeney, and how kyng Loth was deceyved by Merlyn, and how twelve kynges were slayne.

„ 11. Of the entyerement of twelve kynges and of the prophecye of Merlyn how Balyn should gyve the dolorous stroke.

„ 12. How a sorouful knyght cam tofore Arthur and how Balyn fet hym, and how that knyght was slayn by a knyght invysyble.

„ 13. How Balyn and the damoysel mette wyth a knyght whych was in lyke wyse slayn, and how the damoysel bledde for the custom of a castel.

„ 14. Ho⟨w⟩ Balyn mette wyth that knyght named Garlon at a feest and there he slewe hym to have his blood to hele therwith the sone of his hoost.

„ 15. How Balyn fought wyth kyng Pelham and how his swerde brake, and how he gate a spere werewyth he smote the dolorous stroke.

AFFTIR the deth of Uther regned Arthure, hys son, which
had grete warre in hys dayes for to gete all Inglonde
into hys honde; for there were many kyngis within the
realme of Inglonde and of Scotlonde, Walys and Cornuwayle.

So hit befelle on a tyme whan kynge Arthure was at
London, ther com a knyght and tolde the kynge tydyngis
how the kynge Royns of Northe Walis had rered a grete
numbir of peple and were entred in the londe and brente
and slew the kyngis trew lyege people.

'Iff thys be trew,' seyde Arthure, 'hit were grete shame
unto myne astate but that he were myghtyly withstonde.'

'Hit ys trouthe,' seyde the knyght, 'for I saw the oste
myselff.'

'Well,' seyde the kynge, 'I shall ordayne to wythstonde
hys malice.'

Than the kynge lette make a cry that all the lordis,
knyghtes and jantilmen of armys sholde draw unto the
castell called Camelot in tho dayes, and there the kynge
wolde lette make a counceile generall and a grete justis.
So whan the kynge was com thidir with all his baronage
and logged as they semed beste, also there was com ⌐a
damoisel⌐ the which was sente frome the grete Lady Lyle
of Avilion. And whan she com before kynge Arthure she
tolde fro whens she com, and how she was sente on message
unto hym for thys causis. Than she lette hir mantell falle
that was rychely furred, and than was she gurde with a noble
swerde, whereof the kynge had mervayle and seyde,

'Damesel, for what cause ar ye gurte with that swerde?
Hit besemyth you nought.'

'Now shall I telle you,' seyde the damesell. 'Thys swerde
that I am gurte withall doth me grete sorow and comber-
aunce, for I may nat be delyverde of thys swerde but by
a knyght, and he muste be a passynge good man of hys

5

10

15

20

22ᵛ

25

30

4–5 *C* Englonde and in walys Scotland and Cornewaille   15–17 I shall ordayne
. . . Than the kynge *not in C*†   18–19 *C* vnto a castel   19 *W* called Camelot
called in tho   22 also *not in C*   22–24 *W* com the which was sente frome
C* come a damoisel the whiche was sente on message from   *F* (*Huth Merlin, f. 99c*)
vint laiens une damoisiele riche et de grant biauté plainne, et est (*sic*) la dame
apielee la dame de l'isle Avalon (*see note*)   25 *C* from whome she

hondys and of hys dedis, and withoute velony other trechory
and withoute treson. And if I may fynde such a knyght
that hath all thes vertues he may draw oute thys swerde oute
of the sheethe. For I have bene at kynge Royns, for hit
5 was tolde me there were passyng good knyghtes; and he and
all his knyghtes hath assayde and none can spede.'

'Thys ys a grete mervayle,' seyde Arthure. 'If thys be
sothe I woll assay myselffe to draw oute the swerde, nat
presumynge myselff that I am the beste knyght; but I woll
10 begynne to draw youre swerde in gyvyng an insample to
all the barownes, that they shall assay everych one aftir othir
whan I have assayde.'

Than Arthure toke the swerde by the sheethe and gurdil
and pulled at hit egirly, but the swerde wolde nat oute.

15 'Sir,' seyd the damesell, 'ye nede nat for to pulle halffe
so sore, for he that shall pulle hit oute shall do hit with litill
myght.'

'Ye sey well,' seyde Arthure. ' Now assay ye all, my
barownes.'

20 'But beware ye be nat defoyled with shame, trechory,
nother gyle, for than hit woll nat avayle,' seyde the damesel,
'for he muste be a clene knyght withoute vylony and of
jantill strene of fadir syde and of modir syde.'

The moste parte of all the barownes of the Rounde Table
25 that were there at that tyme assayde all be rew, but there
myght none spede. Wherefore the damesel made grete
sorow oute of mesure and seyde,

'Alas! I wente in this courte had bene the beste knyghtes
of the worlde withoute trechory other treson.'

30 'Be my faythe,' seyde Arthure, 'here ar good knyghtes as
I deme as ony be in the worlde, but their grace ys nat to
23ʳ helpe you, wherefore I am sore displeased.'
(2)   Than hit befelle so that tyme there was a poore knyght
with kynge Arthure that had bene presonere with hym
35 half a yere for sleyng of a knyght which was cosyne unto
kynge Arthure. And the name of thys knyght was called
Balyne, and by good meanys of the barownes he was de-

6, 12 *C* assayed it   9 *C* presumynge vpon my self   *C* but that I   10 *C*
drawe at your   16 *C* so hard for   23–24 *C* syde Moost of all   29 *C* of
the worlde *not in C*   32 sore *not in C*   33 *C* felle hit so   35 *C* yere & more

lyverde oute of preson, for he was a good man named of
his body, and he was borne in Northehumbirlonde. And
so he wente pryvaly into the courte and saw thys adventure
whereoff hit reysed his herte, and wolde assayde as othir
knyghtes ded. But for he was poore and poorly arayde, 5
he put hymselff nat far in prees. But in hys herte he was
fully assured to do as well, if hys grace happed hym, as ony
knyght that there was. And as the damesell toke [her] leve
of Arthure and of all the barownes, so departynge, thys
knyght Balyn called unto her and seyde,   10

'Damesell, I pray you of youre curteysy suffir me as well
to assay as thes other lordis. Thoughe that I be pourely
arayed yet in my herte mesemyth I am fully assured as
som of thes other, and mesemyth in myne herte to spede
ryght welle.'   15

Thys damesell than behelde thys poure knyght and saw
he was a lyckly man; but for hys poure araymente she
thought he sholde nat be of no worship withoute vylony
or trechory. And than she seyde unto that knyght,

'Sir, hit nedith nat you to put me to no more payne, for 20
hit semyth nat you to spede thereas all thes othir knyghtes
have fayled.'

'A, fayre damesell,' seyde Balyn, 'worthynes and good
tacchis and also good dedis is nat only in araymente, but
manhode and worship [ys hyd] within a mannes person; and 25
many a worshipfull knyght ys nat knowyn unto all peple.
And therefore worship and hardynesse ys nat in araymente.'

'Be God,' seyde the damesell, 'ye sey soth. Therefore ye
shall assay to do what ye may.'

Than Balyn toke the swerde by the gurdyll and shethe and 30
drew hit oute easyly, and whan he loked on the swerde hit
pleased hym muche. Than had the kynge and all the barownes
grete mervayle that Balyne had done that aventure; many
knyghtes had grete despite at hym.

4 *C* assaye it as   8 *W* toke þer leue   *C** toke her leue   9–17 *W* (sidenote) Vertue and manhode ys hyed wythin the bodye   12 other *not in C*
12–13 *C* be so pourely clothed in my   16 *C* The damoysel beheld the poure
knyght   18 nat *not in C†*   20 *C* it nedith not to put me to more payn or
labour for   21–22 *C* there as other haue   24 *C* are not   25 *W* worship
within a mannes   *C** worship is hyd within mans (ys hyd *is confirmed by the*
sidenote to ll. 9–17 above   34 *C* despyte af Balen

'Sertes,' seyde the damesell, 'thys ys a passynge good knyght and the beste that ever y founde, and moste of worship withoute treson, trechory or felony. And many mervayles shall he do. Now, jantyll and curtayse knyght, geff me the swerde agayne.'

23ᵛ 5

'Nay,' seyde Balyne, 'for thys swerde woll I kepe but hit be takyn fro me with force.'

'Well,' seyde the damesell, 'ye ar nat wyse to kepe the swerde fro me, for ye shall sle with that swerde the beste frende that ye have and the man that ye moste love in the worlde, and that swerde shall be youre destruccion.'

10

'I shall take the aventure,' seyde Balyn, 'that God woll ordayne for me. But the swerde ye shall nat have at thys tyme, by the feythe of my body!'

'Ye shall repente hit within shorte tyme,' seyde the damesell, 'for I wolde have the swerde more for youre avauntage than for myne; for I am passynge hevy for youre sake, for and ye woll nat leve that swerde hit shall be **youre** destruccion, and that ys grete pité.'

15

So with that departed the damesell and grete sorow she made. And anone afftir Balyn sente for hys horse and armoure, and so wolde departe frome the courte, and toke his leve of kynge Arthure.

20

'Nay,' seyde the kynge, 'I suppose ye woll nat departe so lyghtly from thys felyship. I suppose that ye ar displesyd that I have shewed you unkyndnesse. But blame me the lesse, for I was mysseinfourmed ayenste you: but I wente ye had nat bene such a knyght as ye ar of worship and prouesse. And if ye woll abyde in thys courte amonge my felyship I shall so avaunce [you] as ye shall be pleased.'

25

30

'God thanke youre Hyghnesse,' seyde Balyne. 'Youre bounté may no man prayse halff unto the valew, butt at thys tyme I muste nedis departe, besechynge you allway of youre good grace.'

'Truly,' seyde the kynge, 'I am ryght wroth of youre

35

3 *C* or vylony   13 for *not in C*   16–17 *C* for your auaylle than   17–18 *C*† your sake For ye wil not byleue that swerd shal be   *F* (*Huth Merlin, f. 100d*) 'Et je vous di, fait elle, que se vous l'emportés qu'il vous en mal averra'   19–21 *C* pyte with that the damoysel departed makynge grete sorowe Anone after   30 *W* avaunce as ye shall   *C* auaunce yow as ye shalle   32 *C* bounte and hyhenes may   35 *C* for your

departynge. But I pray you, fayre knyght, that ye tarry nat
longe frome me, and ye shall be ryght wellcom unto me
and to my barownes, and I shall amende all mysse that I
have done agaynste you.'

'God thanke youre good grace,' seyde Balyn, and there-   5
with made hym redy to departe. Than the moste party of
the knyghtes of the Rounde Table seyde that Balyne dud
nat this adventure ⌐all⌐ on⌐l⌐y by myght but by wycche-
crauffte.

So the meanwhyle that thys knyght was makynge hym   10 (3)
redy to departe, there com into the courte the Lady of the
Laake, and she com on horsebacke rychely beseyne, and
salewed kynge Arthure and there asked hym a gyffte that
he promysed her whan she gaff hym the swerde.

'That ys sothe,' seyde Arthure, 'a gyffte I promysed you, 15 **24ʳ**
but I have forgotyn the name of my swerde that ye gaff me.'

'The name of hit,' seyde the lady, 'ys Excalibir, that ys
as muche to sey as Kutte Stele.'

'Ye sey well,' seyde the kynge. 'Aske what ye woll and
ye shall have hit and hit lye in my power to gyff hit.'   20

'Well,' seyde thys lady, 'than I aske the hede of thys
knyght that hath wonne the swerde, othir ellis the damesels
hede that brought hit. I take no force though I have both
theire hedis: for he slew my brothir, a good knyght and a
trew; and that jantillwoman was causer of my fadirs deth.'   25

'Truly,' seyde kynge Arthure, 'I may nat graunte you
nother of theire hedys with my worship; therefore aske what
ye woll els, and I shall fulfille youre desire.'

'I woll aske none other thynge,' seyde the lady.

So whan Balyn was redy to departe, he saw the Lady of   30
the Lake which by hir meanys had slayne hys modir; and
he had sought hir three yere before. And whan hit was
tolde hym how she had asked hys hede of kynge Arthure,
he wente to hir streyght and seyde,

2 frome me *not in C*   5 *C* thanke your grete lordship said   8 *W* ony by
myght   *C** al only by   *F* (*Le Roman de Balain* and *Camb.*): dient . . . qu'il savoit
d'enchantement et qu'il l'a fait plus par ceo que par la prouece de lui   *O*¹ only by
10 *W* þᵗ that that thys knyght   11–12 *C** a lady that hyght the lady of the
lake   21–22 *C* the knyght   26 you *not in C*   30–31 *W* saw the lady of
the lady of the lake   31 *C* slayne Balyns moder   32 before *not in C*
33 *C* hym that she   33–p. 66, l. 4 *W* (*sidenote*): The dethe of the Lady of the Lake

'Evyll be [y]e founde: ye wolde have myne hede, and therefore ye shall loose youres!'

And with hys swerde lyghtly he smote of hyr hede before
kynge Arthure.

5　'Alas, for shame!' seyde the kynge. 'Why have ye do
so? Ye have shamed me and all my courte, for thys lady
was a lady that I was much beholdynge to, and hyder she
com undir my sauffconduyghte. Therefore I shall never
forgyff you that trespasse.'

10　'Sir,' seyde Balyne, 'me forthynkith of youre displeasure,
for this same lady was the untrwyste lady lyvynge, and by
inchauntement and by sorcery she hath bene the destroyer
of many good knyghtes, and she was causer that my modir
was brente thorow hir falsehode and trechory.'

15　'For what cause soever ye had,' seyde Arthure, 'ye sholde
have forborne in my presence. Therefore thynke nat the
contrary: ye shall repente hit, for such anothir despite had
I nevir in my courte. Therefore withdraw you oute of my
courte in all the haste that ye may.'

20　Than Balyn toke up the hede of the lady and bare hit
with hym to hys ostry, and there mette with hys squyre that
was sory he had displeased kynge Arthure, and so they rode
forthe oute of towne.

'Now,' seyde Balyne, 'we muste departe; therefore take
25　thou thys hede and bere hit to my frendis and telle hem
how I have spedde, and telle hem in Northhumbirlonde how
24ᵛ　my moste foo ys dede. Also telle hem how I am oute of
preson, and what adventure befelle me at the getynge of
this swerde.'

30　'Alas!' seyde the squyre, 'ye ar gretly to blame for to
displease kynge Arthure.'

'As for that,' seyde Balyne, 'I woll hyghe me in all [the]
haste that I may [to] mete with kyng Royns and destroy
hym, othir ellis to dye therefore. And iff hit may happe me
35　to wynne hym, than woll kynge Arthure be my good frende.'

1 *W* be e founde　*C* be you† foûnde　　3 *W Hand in margin pointing to this line*
5–6 *C* done so　　7 *C* was be holden　　8, 24 therefore *not in C*　　16 *C* forborne her in　　23 *C* of the town　　26 *C* telle my frendys in　　32–33 *The
words in square brackets, supplied from C, also occur in W's second rendering of the
speech. See next page, note to lines 2–3*　　34 *S* or dye　　35–p. 67, l. 1 *C* my
good and gracious lord where

'Sir, [wher] shall I mete with you?' seyde his squyre.

'In kynge Arthurs courte,' seyde Balyne.

So his squyre and he departed at that tyme. Than kynge Arthure and all the courte made grete dole and had grete shame of the Lady of the Lake. Than the kynge buryed hir 5 rychely.

So at that tyme there was a knyght, the which was the (4) kynges son of Irelonde, and hys name was Launceor, the which was an orgulus knyght and accompted hymselff one of the beste of the courte. And he had grete despite at 10 Balyne for the enchevynge of the swerde, that ony sholde be accompted more hardy or more of prouesse, and he asked kynge Arthure licence to ryde afftir Balyne and to revenge the despite that he had done.

'Do youre beste,' seyde Arthur. 'I am ryght wrothe with 15 Balyne. I wolde he were quytte of the despite that he hath done unto me and my courte.'

Than thys Launceor wente to his ostré to make hym redy. So in the meanewhyle com Merlyon unto the courte of kynge Arthure, and anone was tolde hym the adventure of 20 the swerde and the deth of the Lady of the Lake.

'Now shall I sey you,' seyde Merlion; 'thys same damesell that here stondith, that brought the swerde unto youre courte, I shall telle you the cause of hir commynge. She ys the falsist damesell that lyveth—she shall nat sey nay! For 25 she hath a brothir, a passyng good knyght of proues and a full trew man, and thys damesell loved anothir knyght that hylde her as paramoure. And thys good knyght, her brothir, mette with the knyght that helde hir to paramoure, and slew hym by force of hys hondis. And whan thys false damesell 30 undirstoode this she wente to the lady Lyle of Avylion and besought hir of helpe to be revenged on hir owne brothir.

'And so thys lady Lyle of Avylion toke hir this swerde (5) **25ʳ**

2–3 *W* seyde Balyne I woll hyghe me in all the haste that I may to mete with kynge Royns So his *W repeats a line from Balyne's previous speech (see p. 66, ll. 32–33)* 4–5 *C* and had shame of the deth of the lady 13 *W* kynge kynge *C* Arthur yf he wold gyue hym leue to ryde 15–16 *C* wroth said† Balen I wold 20 *C* Arthur and there was told 24–25 *C* she was† the 25–26 *C*† lyueth say not so said they She hath a 28 *C* to peramour 31–32 *W O*¹ and toke hir hys swerde and besought (*contamination: cf. l. 33*) *F makes it plain that the damsel receives the sword from the Lady of Avalon*: et maintenant le chainst de l'espee que elle aporta en ceste court

that she brought with hir, and tolde there sholde no man
pulle hit oute of the sheethe but yf he be one of the beste
knyghtes of thys realme, and he sholde be hardy and full of
prouesse; and with that swerde he sholde sle hys brothir.
5 Thys was the cause, damesell, that ye com into thys courte.
I know hit as well as ye. God wolde ye had nat come here;
but ye com never in felyship of worshipfful folke for to do
good, but allwayes grete harme. And that knyght that hath
encheved the swerde shall be destroyed thorow the swerde;
10 for the which woll be grete damage, for there lyvith nat a
knyght of more prouesse than he ys. And he shall do unto
you, my lorde Arthure, grete honoure and kyndnesse; and
hit ys grete pité he shall nat endure but a whyle, for of his
strengthe and hardinesse I know hym nat lyvynge hys
15 macche.'

So thys knyght of Irelonde armed hym at all poyntes and
dressed his shylde on hys sholdir and mownted uppon
horsebacke and toke hys glayve in hys honde, and rode aftir
a grete pace as much as hys horse myght dryve. And within
20 a litill space on a mowntayne he had a syght of Balyne, and
with a lowde voice he cryde,

'Abyde, knyght! for ells ye shall abyde whethir ye woll
other no. And the shelde that ys tofore you shall nat helpe
you,' seyde thys Iryshe knyght, 'therefore com I affter you.'
25 'Peradventure,' seyde Balyne, 'ye had bene bettir to have
holde you at home. For many a man wenyth to put hys
enemy to a rebuke, and ofte hit fallith on hymselff. Oute
of what courte be ye com fro?' seyde Balyn.

'I am com frome the courte of kynge Arthure,' seyde the
30 knyght of Irelonde, 'that am com hydir to revenge the despite
ye dud thys day unto kynge Arthure and to his courte.'

4 C† slee her broder   F (*Huth Merlin, f. 104b*) Et si n'averra de ceste espee mie
seul mal a son frere, ains en mourront cil dui que je connois vraiement qui sont li
millor chevalier dou roiaume   5–8 *C* the cause that the damoysel came in to
this Courte I knowe it as wel as ye wolde god she had nat comen in to thys Courte
but she came neuer in felauship of worship to do good   9 *C* destroyed by
that suerd   14 hym *not in C*   16 *C* the knyght   18 *C* toke his spere
19 *C* myght goo and   22 ells *not in C*   22–23 *C* ye will or nyll and   23–24 *C*
helpe whan Balyn herd the noyse he tourned his hors fyersly and saide faire knyghte
what wille ye with me wille ye Iuste with me ye said the Irysshe   F (*Huth Merlin,
f. 105a*) *lends no support to this reading*   25 *C* it had been   27–28 *C* falleth
to hym self of   28 *C* ye sent fro

'Well,' seyde Balyne, 'I se well I must have ado with you,
that me forthynkith that I have greved kynge Arthure or
ony of hys courte. And youre quarell ys full symple,' seyde
Balyne, 'unto me; for the lady that ys dede dud to me grete
damage, and ellis I wolde have bene lothe as ony knyght that 5
lyvith for to sle a lady.'

'Make you redy,' seyde the knyght Launceor, 'and dresse
you unto me, for that one shall abyde in the fylde.'

Than they fewtred their spearis in their restis and com
togidirs as muche as their horsis myght dryve. And the 10 **25ᵛ**
Irysh knyght smote Balyn on the shylde that all wente to-
shyvers of hys spere. And Balyne smote hym agayne thorow
the shylde, and [the] hawbirk perysshed, and so bore hym
thorow the body and over the horse crowper; and anone
turned hys horse fersely and drew oute hys swerde, and 15
wyst nat that he had slayne hym.

Than he saw hym lye as a dede corse, he loked aboute (6)
hym and was ware of a damesel that com rydynge full faste
as the horse myght dryve, on a fayre palferey. And whan
she aspyed that Launceor was slayne she made sorow oute 20
of mesure and seyde,

'A! Balyne, two bodyes thou haste sla⟨in in⟩ one herte,
and two hertes in one body, and two soules thou hast loste.'

And therewith she toke the swerde frome hir love that lay
dede, and felle to the grounde in a swowghe. And whan she 25
arose she made grete dole oute of mesure, which sorow
greved Balyn passyngly sore. And he wente unto hir for to
have tane the swerde oute of hir honde; but she helde hit so
faste he myght nat take hit oute of hir honde but yf he sholde
have hurte hir. And suddeynly she sette the pomell to the 30
grounde, and rove hirselff thorowoute the body.

Whan Balyne aspyed hir dedis he was passynge hevy in
his herte and ashamed that so fayre a damesell had destroyed
hirselff for the love of hys dethe. 'Alas!' seyde Balyn, 'me
repentis sore the dethe of thys knyght for the love of thys 35
damesel, for there was muche tr[e]w love betwyxte hem.' And

2 *C* forthynketh for to greue kyng   9 *C* they toke their speres and   *W Hand
in margin opposite this line*   12 *C* Balyn hyt hym thorugh   13–14 *C* & so
percyd thurgh his body and the hors   *W* (*sidenote*) How Balyn slew Launceor
17–18 *C* loked by hym   18–19 *C* came ryde ful fast as the hors myghte ryde
on   22 *W* slayne one   *C* slayne and one (*see note*)   29 *C* hand onles he

so for sorow he myght no lenger beholde them, but turned
hys horse and loked towarde a fayre foreste.

And than was he ware by hys armys that there com rydyng
hys brothir Balan. And whan they were mette they put of
5 hyr helmys and kyssed togydirs and wepte for joy and pité.
Than Balan seyde,

'Brothir, I litill wende to have mette with you at thys
suddayne adventure, but I am ryght glad of youre delyveraunce of youre dolerous presonment: for a man tolde me in
10 the Castell of Four Stonys that ye were delyverde, and that
man had seyne you in the courte of kynge Arthure, and
therefore I com hydir into thys contrey, for here I supposed
to fynde you.'

And anone Balyne tolde hys brothir of hys adventure of
15 the swerde and the deth of the Lady of the Laake, and how
kynge Arthure was displeased with hym.

26ʳ   'Wherefore he sente thys knyght afftir me that lyethe here
dede. And the dethe of thys damesell grevith me sore.'

'So doth hit me,' seyde Balan, 'but ye must take the adven-
20 ture that God woll ordayne you.'

'Truly,' seyde Balyne, 'I am ryght hevy that my lorde
Arthure ys displeased with me, for he ys the moste wor-
shypfullist kynge that regnith now in erthe; and hys love
I woll gete othir ellis I woll putte my lyff in adventure. For
·25 kynge Ryons lyeth at the sege of the Castell Terrable, and
thydir woll we draw in all goodly haste to preve oure worship
and prouesse uppon hym.'

'I woll well,' seyde Balan, 'that ye so do; and I woll ryde
with you and put my body in adventure with you, as a brothir
30 ought to do.'

(7)   'Now go we hense,' seyde Balyne, 'and well we beth
mette.'

The meanewhyle as they talked there com a dwarff frome
the cité of Camelot on horsebacke as much as he myght,

---

1 *C* behold hym†   2 *C* a grete forest   *No adjective in F*   3–4 *C* by
the armes of his   7 Brothir *not in C*   8–9 *C* delyueraunce and of†   *F*
(*Huth Merlin, f. 105d*): par quel aventure estes vous delivrés de la dolereuse prison
ou vous estiés   13–14 *C* fynde you anon the knyʒt balyn   22–23 *C*
worshipful knyght that   25 *C* at a syege atte castel   26 goodly *not in*
C   28–30 *C* that we do & we wil helpe eche other as bretheren ouʒt to do CA VII
31–32 *C* wel be we met

and founde the dede bodyes; wherefore he made grete dole
and pulled hys heyre for sorowe and seyde,

'Which of two knyghtes have done this dede?'

'Whereby askist thou?' seyde Balan.

'For I wolde wete,' seyde the dwarff.   5

'Hit was I,' seyde Balyn, 'that slew this knyght in my de-
fendaunte; for hyder he com to chase me, and othir I muste
sle hym other he me. And this damesell slew hirself for his
love, which repentith me. And for hir sake I shall owghe all
women the bettir wylle and servyse all the dayes of my lyff.'   10

'Alas!' seyde the dwarff, 'thou hast done grete damage
unto thyselff. For thys knyght that ys here dede was one
of the moste valyauntis men that lyved. And truste well,
Balyne, the kynne of thys knyght woll chase you thorow the
worlde tylle they have slayne you.'   15

'As for that,' seyde Balyne, 'the⟨m⟩ I fere nat gretely; but
I am ryght hevy that I sholde displease my lorde, kynge
Arthure, for the deth of thys knyght.'

So as they talked togydirs there com a kynge of Cornuwayle rydyng, which hyght kyng Marke. And whan he saw   20
thes two bodyes dede, and undirstood howe they were dede,
⌐by⌐ the two knyghtes aboven-seyde, ⌐thenne⌐ made the
kynge grete sorow for the trew love that was betwyxte them,
and seyde, 'I woll nat departe tyll I have on thys erth made
a towmbe.' And there he pyght his pavylyons and sought all   25
the contrey to fynde a towmbe, and in a chirch they founde
one was fayre and ryche. And than the kyng lette putte
h[e]m bothe in the erthe, and leyde the tombe uppon them,   **26ᵛ**
and wrote the namys of hem bothe on the tombe, how 'here
lyeth Launceor, the kyngis son of Irelonde, that at hys owne   30
rekeyste was slayne by the hondis of Balyne', and how 'this

---

2 *C* pulled out his   3 *C* which of you kny3tes   4–5 *C* thou it said
balan . . . wete it said the dwarfe   10–11 *C* better loue Allas   16 *O*¹ the (*not
in C*)   17 *C* that I haue displeasyd   21–23 *W* dede the ii knyghtes
aboven seyde made to the kynge   *C** dede by the ii knyghtes aboue saide thenne
maade the kynge   *F (Huth Merlin, f. 106c)* quant il fu venus la ou le dui cors
gisoient a la terre et il en sot la verité ensi comme li dui frere li conterent, il dist
qu'il n'avoit onques mais oi parler de damoisiele qui si loiaument amast.   *W must
have overlooked* by *and added to* for the sense   25–26 *C* sought thurgh alle
the   27–p. 72, l. 6 *W (sidenote)*: how the lady Colume slew hirselfe for the deth of
Launceor   29 *W* hom bothe   *C* & put the tombe   31–p. 72, l. 2 *C* how
his lady colombe and peramoure slew her self with her louer's swerd for

lady Columbe and peramour to hym slew hirself with hys
swerde for dole and sorow.'

(8)　　　The meanewhyle as thys was adoynge, in com Merlion to
kynge Marke and saw all thys doynge.

5　　'Here shall be,' seyde Merlion, 'in this same place the
grettist bateyle betwyxte two [knyghtes] that ever was or
ever shall be, and the trewyst lovers; and yette none of hem
shall slee other.'

And there Merlion wrote hir namys uppon the tombe with
10　lettirs of golde, that shall feyght in that place: which namys
was Launcelot du Lake and Trystrams.

'Thou [art] a merveylous man,' seyde kynge Marke unto
Merlion, 'that spekist of such mervayles. Thou arte a boy-
steous man and an unlyckly, to telle of suche dedis. What ys
15　thy name?' seyde kynge Marke.

'At thys tyme,' seyde Merlion, 'I woll nat telle you. But
at that tyme sir Trystrams ys takyn with his soveraigne lady,
than shall ye here and know my name; and at that tyme ye
shall ⌜here⌝ tydynges that shall nat please you. A, Balyne!'
20　seyde Merlion, 'thou haste done thyselff grete hurte that
thou saved nat thys lady that slew herselff; for thou myghtyst
have saved hir and thou haddist wold.'

'By the fayth of my body,' seyde Balyne, 'I myght nat
save hir, for she slewe hirselff suddeynly.'

25　　'Me repentis hit,' seyde Merlion; 'because of the dethe
of that lady thou shalt stryke a stroke moste dolerous that ever
man stroke, excepte the stroke of oure Lorde Jesu Cryste. For
thou shalt hurte the trewyst knyght and the man of moste
worship that now lyvith; and thorow that stroke three kyng-
30　domys shall be brought into grete poverté, miseri and wrec-
chednesse twelve yere. And the knyght shall nat be hole
of that wounde many yerys.'

Than Merlion toke hys leve.

4–5 *C* mark seyng alle his doynge said　Here shalle be in　　　6 *W* two men
(*see note*)　*C* that was　　10 *C* that shold fyghte　　10–11 *C* whos names were
12 *W* Thou a　*C* thow art a　　16 you *not in C*　　19 *W* shall othir tydynges
*C** shal here tydynges　*F* (*Huth Merlin, f. 107a*) dont te dira on teuls nouvielles
de moi qui te desplairont　　19–20 *C* please yow Thenne said merlyn to balyn
thou　　20–21 *C* hurt by cause that thou sauest　　21–22 *C* her self that myght
haue saued her & thow woldest　　27 Jesu Cryste *not in C*　　30 *C* be in grete
34–p. 73, l. 2 *C* leue of balyn & balen said yf I wist it were soth that ye say I shold do
suche peryllous dede as that

'Nay,' seyde Balyn, 'nat so; for and I wyste thou seyde soth, I wolde do so perleous a dede that I wolde sle myself to make the a lyer.'

Therewith Merlion vanysshed away suddeynly, and than Balyn and his brother toke their leve of kynge Marke.   5

'But first,' seyde the kynge, 'telle me youre name.'

'Sir,' seyde Balan, 'ye may se he beryth two swerdis, and thereby ye may calle hym the Knyght with the Two Swerdis.'

And so departed kynge Marke unto Camelot to kynge 10
Arthure.

And Balyne toke the way to kynge Royns, and as they **27ʳ**
rode togydir they mette with Merlion disgysed so that they knew hym nought.

'But whotherward ryde ye?' seyde Merlion.   15

'We had litill ado to telle you,' seyde thes two knyghtes.

'But what ys thy name?' seyde Balyn.

'At thys tyme,' seyde Merlion, 'I woll nat telle.'

'Hit ys an evyll sygne,' seyde the knyghtes, 'that thou arte a trew man, that thou wolt nat telle thy name.'   20

'As for that,' seyde Merlion, 'be as hit be may. But I can telle you wherefore ye ryde thys way: for to mete with kynge Royns. But hit woll nat avayle you withoute ye have my counceyle.'

'A,' seyde Balyn, 'ye ar Merlion. We woll be ruled by 25
youre counceyle.'

'Com on,' seyde Merlion, 'and ye shall have grete worship. And loke that ye do knyghtly, for ye shall have nede.'

'As for that,' seyde Balyne, 'dred you nat, for we woll do what we may.'   30

Than there lodged Merlion and thes two knyghtes in (9)
a woode amonge the levis besydes the hyghway, and toke of the brydyls of their horsis and putte hem to grasse, and leyde hem downe to reste tyll hit was nyghe mydnyght. Than Merlion bade hem ryse and make hem redy: 'for here 35
commyth the kynge nyghehonde, that was stoolyn away

13 *C* desguysed but they   16–17 *C* we haue lytel to do saide the ij knyꝫtes to telle the but   18 *C* telle it the   19 *C* it is euyl sene   22 with *not in C*   28 *C* haue grete nede   31 *C* Thenne Merlyn lodged them in a 35–36 *C*† for the the kynge was nygh them that was *Direct speech in F (Huth Merlin, f. 108c–d)*

frome his oste with a three score horsis of hys beste knyghtes, and twenty of them rode tofore the lorde to warne the Lady de Vaunce that the kynge was commynge.' For that nyght kynge Royns sholde have lyen with hir.

5 'Which ys the kynge?' seyde Balyn.

'Abyde,' seyde Merlion, 'for here in a strete ⌈weye⌉ ye shall mete with hym.' And therewith he shewed Balyn and hys brothir the kynge.

And anone they mette with hym, and smote hym downe
10 and wounded hym freyshly, and layde hym to the growunde. And there they slewe on the ryght honde and on the lyffte honde mo than fourty of hys men; and the remanaunte fledde. Than wente they agayne unto kynge Royns and wolde have slayne hym, had he nat yelded hym unto hir
15 grace. Than seyde he thus:

'Knyghtes full of prouesse, sle me nat! For be my lyff ye may wynne, and by my dethe litill.'

'Ye say sothe,' seyde the knyghtes, and so leyde hym on an horse littur.

20 So with that Merlion vanysshed, and com to kynge Arthure aforehonde and tolde hym how hys moste enemy was takyn and discomfite.

'By whom?' seyde kynge Arthure.

'By two knyghtes,' seyde Merlion, 'that wolde fayne
27ᵛ 25 have youre lordship. And to-morow ye shall know what knyghtis they ar.'

So anone aftir com the Knyght with the Two Swerdis and hys brothir, and brought with them kynge Royns of Northe Waalis, and there delyverde hym to the porters, and
30 charged hem with hym. And so they two returned aghen in the dawnyng of the day.

Than kynge Arthure com to kynge Royns and seyde, 'Sir kynge, ye ar wellcom. By what adventure com ye hydir?'

---

2 the lord *not in* C   6 *C* in a streyte wey   F (*Huth Merlin, f. 109c*): et il venoient petit et petit, car li chemins par les tertres estoit estrois pour aler a la montaigne   8–9 *C* his broder where he rode anon balyn & his broder mette with the kyng & smote   10 *C* hym fyersly and   11–12 *C* lyfte hond and slewe moo   17–18 *C* dethe ye shalle wynne noo thynge Thenne sayd these two knyghtes ye say sothe & trouth and so leyd   20 *C* Merlyn was vanysshed 24–25 *C* wold please your lordship   28 *C* and balan his broder

'Sir,' seyde kynge Royns, 'I com hyder by an harde adventure.'

'Who wanne you?' seyde kynge Arthure.

'Sir,' seyde he, 'the Knyght with the Two Swerdis and hys brothir, which ar two mervayles knyghtes of prouesse.' 5

'I know hem nat,' seyde Arthure, 'but much am I be-holdynge unto them.'

'A, sir,' seyde Merlion, 'I shall telle you. Hit ys Balyn that encheved the swerde, and his brothir Balan, a good knyght: there lyvith nat a bettir of proues, nother of worthy- 10 nesse. And hit shall be the grettist dole of hym that ever y knew of knyght; for he shall nat longe endure.'

'Alas,' seyde kynge Arthure, 'that ys grete pité; for I am muche beholdynge unto hym, and I have evill deserved hit agayne for hys kyndnesse.' 15

'Nay, nay,' sede Merlion, 'he shall do much more for you, and that shall ye know in haste. But, sir, ar ye purveyde?' seyde Merlion. '[For to-morn] the oste of kynge Nero, kynge Royns brothir, woll sette on you or none with a grete oste. And therefore make you redy, for I woll departe 20 frome you.'

Than kynge Arthure made hys oste redy in ten batayles; (10) and Nero was redy in the fylde afore the Castell Terrable with a grete oste. And he had ten batayles with many mo peple than kynge Arthure had. Than Nero had the vawarde 25 with the moste party of the people. And Merlion com to kynge Lotte of the Ile of Orkeney and helde hym with a tale of the prophecy tylle Nero and his peple were destroyed. And there sir Kay the Senesciall dud passyngely well, that dayes of hys lyff the worship wente never frome hym, and 30 sir Hervis de Revel that dud merveylous dedys of armys that day with Arthur. And kynge Arthure slew that day twenty knyghtes and maymed fourty.

So at that tyme com in the Knyght with the Two Swerdis and his brothir, but they dud so mervaylously that the kynge 35

3-4 *C* said the kyng the knyght   10 *C* prowesse & of   14-15 *C* hit vnto hym for his   16 *C* nay said   18 *W* to morne for   *C** for to morne 26 *C* of his peple   27-28 *C* a tale of prophecye   29-30 *W* that dayes of hys lyff that the worship   *C** that the dayes of his lyf the worship   31-32 *C*† reuel did merueillous dedes with with kynge Arthur   35 *C* his broder Balan But they two did

and all the knyghtes mervayled of them. And all they that
behelde them seyde they were sente frome hevyn as angels
28ʳ other devilles frome helle. And kynge Arthure seyde hymself
they were the doughtyeste knyghtes that ever he sawe, for
5 they gaff such strokes that all men had wondir of hem.

So in the meanewhyle com one to kynge Lotte and tolde
hym whyle he tarryed there how Nero was destroyed and
slayne with all his oste.

'Alas,' seyde kynge Lotte, 'I am ashamed; for in my
10 defaute there ys [many a worshipful man slayne; for and
we had ben togyders there had ben] none oste undir hevyn
were able to have macched us. But thys faytoure with hys
prophecy hath mocked me.'

All that dud Merlion, for he knew well that ⌈and⌉ kynge
15 Lotte had bene with hys body at the first batayle, kynge
Arthure had be slayne and all hys peple distressed. And well
Merlion knew that one of the kynges sholde be dede that
day; and lothe was Merlion that ony of them bothe sholde
be slayne, but of the tweyne he had levir kyng Lotte of
20 Orkeney had be slayne than Arthure.

'What ys beste to do?' seyde kynge Lotte. 'Whether ys
me bettir to trete with kynge Arthur othir to fyght? For
the gretter party of oure people ar slayne and distressed.'

'Sir,' seyde a knyght, 'sette ye on Arthure, for they ar
25 wery and forfoughtyn, and we be freyssh.'

'As for me,' seyde kynge Lott, 'I wolde that every knyght
wolde do hys parte as I wolde do myne.'

Than they avaunced baners and smote togydirs and
brused hir sperys. And Arthurs knyghtes with the helpe
30 of the Knyght with Two Swerdys and hys brothir Balan
put kynge Lotte and hys oste to the warre. But allwayes
kynge Lotte hylde hym ever in the fore-fronte and dud
merveylous dedis of armys; for all his oste was borne up

---

4 *C* the best knyghtes   8–9 *C* al his peple Allas   9 *C* for by my   11–12 *C*
vnder the heuen that had ben abel for to haue matched with vs   14 *W* that
kynge   *C** that and kynge   *F* (*Huth Merlin, f. 117a*) 'Merlins m'a mort.
Se je eusse dés hui matin chevauchié a esfors, je eusse le roi desconfit.'   15 *C*
body there at   16 *C* peple destroyed   19–20 of Orkeney *not in C*   21 *C*
Now what   *C* kyng Lot of Orkeney   23 *C* slayne and destroyed   24 ye
not in C   28–29 *C* to gyders and al to sheuered their speres   32 ever *not*
in C   *C* formest front

by hys hondys, for he abode all knyghtes. Alas, he myght
nat endure, the whych was grete pité! So worthy a knyght
as he was one, that he sholde be overmacched, that of late
tyme before he had bene a knyght of kynge Arthurs, and
wedded the syster of hym. And for because that kynge 5
Arthure lay by hys wyff and gate on her sir Mordred, therefore kynge Lott helde ever agaynste Arthure.

So there was a knyght that was called the Knyght with
the Strange Beste, and at that tyme hys ryght name was
called Pellynore, which was a good man off prouesse as few 10
in tho dayes lyvynge. And he strake a myghty stroke at
kynge Lott as he fought with hys enemyes, and he fayled
of hys stroke and smote the horse necke, that he foundred
to the erthe with kyng Lott. And therewith anone kynge **28ᵛ**
Pellinor smote hym a grete stroke thorow the helme and 15
hede unto the browis.

Than all the oste of Orkeney fledde for the deth of kynge
Lotte, and there they were takyn and slayne, all the oste. But
kynge Pellynore bare the wyte of the dethe of kynge Lott,
wherefore sir Gawayne revenged the deth of hys fadir the ten 20
yere aftir he was made knyght, and slew kynge Pellynor hys
owne hondis. Also there was slayne at that batayle twelve
kynges on the syde of kynge Lott with Nero, and were buryed
in the chirch of Seynte Stevins in Camelot. And the remanent
of knyghtes and other were buryed in a grete roche.   25

So at the enterement com kyng Lottis wyff, Morgause, (11)
with hir four sonnes, Gawayne, Aggravayne, Gaheris, and
Gareth. Also there com thydir kyng Uryens, sir Uwaynes
fadir, and Morgan le Fay, his wyff, that was kynge Arthurs
syster. All thes com to the enterement. But of all the twelve 30
kyngis kynge Arthure lette make the tombe of kynge Lotte
passynge rychely, and made hys tombe by hymselff.

2–3 *C* pite that so worthy a knyyt as he was one shold be   4 *C* afore hadde
5–6 *C* the sister of kyng arthur & for kyng Arthur lay by kyng lots wyf the
whiche was arthurs syster & gat   7 ever *not in C*   9 *W* best⟨es⟩   *C**
beeste   *F (Huth Merlin, f. 118d)* li chevaliers a la diverse beste   10–11 as
few in tho dayes lyvynge *not in C*   11 *C* he smote a myghty   12 *C* with
all his   13–14 *C* he fylle to the grounde   14 *W* Hand in margin pointing
to this line.   18 *C* and there were slayn many moders sones But
19–20 *After* Lott *W repeats line 18*: and there were takyn and slayne all the hole oste
21 *C* Pellinore with his   23 *C* and all were   30 *C* alle these   32 *C* his
tombe by his owne

And than Arthure lette make twelve images of laton and cooper, and overgylte with golde in the sygne of the twelve kynges; and eche one of hem helde a tapir of wexe in hir honde that brente nyght and day. And kynge Arthure was 5 made in the sygne of a fygure stondynge aboven them with a swerde drawyn in hys honde, and all the twelve fygures had countenaunce lyke unto men that were overcom. All thys made Merlion by hys subtyle craufte.

And there he tolde the kynge how that whan he was dede 10 thes tapers sholde brenne no lenger, 'aftir the adventures of the Sankgreall that shall com amonge you and be encheved.' Also he tolde kynge Arthure how Balyn, the worshipfull knyght, shall gyff the dolerouse stroke, whereof shall falle grete vengeaunce.

15 'A, where ys Balyne, Balan, and Pellinore?'

'As for kynge Pellinore,' seyde Merlion, 'he woll mete with you soone. And as for Balyne, he woll nat be longe frome you. But the other brothir woll departe: ye shall se hym no more.'

20 'Be my fayth,' seyde Arthur, 'they ar two manly knyghtes, and namely that Balyne passith of proues off ony knyght that ever y founde, for much am I beholdynge unto hym. Wolde God he wolde abyde with me!'

'Sir,' seyde Merlion, 'loke ye kepe well the scawberd of 25 Excaleber, for ye shall lose no bloode whyle ye have the 29ʳ scawberde uppon you, thoughe ye have as many woundis uppon you as ye may have.'

So aftir for grete truste Arthure betoke the scawberde unto Morgan le Fay, hys sister. And she loved another knyght 30 bettir than hir husbande, kynge Uriens, othir Arthure. And she wolde have had Arthure hir brother slayne, and therefore she lete make anothir scawberd for Excaliber ⌜lyke it by

---

2 *C* ouer gylt hit with   1-8 *W* (*sidenote*): Here ys the dethe of kynge Lot and of the xii kyngis   2-3 *C* of xii   3-4 in hir honde *not in C*† *F* (*Huth Merlin, f. 119b*) chascuns tenoit en sa main un candeler   6 the *not in C*   9-11 *C* the kyng whā I am dede these tapers shalle brenne no lenger and soone after the aduentures of the Sangrayll shalle   15-16 *C* Pellinore saide kynge Arthur as for Pellinore   20-21 *C* two merueyllous knyghtes and namely Balyn   32-p. 78, l. 2 *W* scawberd for Excaliber And the *C** scauberd lyke it by enchauntement and gaf the scauberd Excalibur to her loue and the knyghtes   *F* (*Huth Merlin, f. 121b*) Lors bailla a son ami meismes tout en cel jour l'autre fuerre

enchauntement, and gaf the scawberd Excaliber to her lover[1].
And the knyghtes name was called Accolon, that aftir had
nere slayne kynge Arthure. But after thys Merlion tolde
unto kynge Arthure of the prophecy that there sholde be
a grete batayle besydes Salysbiry, and Mordred hys owne 5
sonne sholde be agaynste hym. Also he tolde hym that
Bagdemagus was his cosyne germayne, and unto kynge
Uryens.

So within a day or two kynge Arthure was somwhat syke, (12)
and he lette pycch hys pavilion in a medow, and there he 10
leyde hym downe on a paylet to slepe; but he myght have
no reste. Ryght so he herde a grete noyse of an horse, and
therewith the kynge loked oute at the porche dore of the
pavilion and saw a knyght commynge evyn by hym makynge
grete dole.   15

'Abyde, fayre sir,' seyde Arthure, 'and telle me wherefore
thou makyst this sorow.'

'Ye may litill amende me,' seyde the knyght, and so
passed forth to the Castell of Meliot.

And anone aftir that com Balyne. And whan he saw kyng 20
Arthur he alyght of hys horse and com to the kynge one
foote and salewed hym.

'Be my hede,' seyde Arthure, 'ye be wellcom. Sir, ryght
now com rydynge thys way a knyght makynge grete mone,
and for what cause I can nat telle. Wherefore I wolde 25
desire of you, of your curtesy and of your jantilnesse, to
fecche agayne that knyght othir by force othir by his good
wylle.'

'I shall do more for youre lordeship than that,' seyde
Balyne, 'othir ellis I woll greve hym.'   30

So Balyn rode more than a pace and founde the knyght
with a damesell undir a foreyste and seyde,

'Sir knyght, ye muste com with me unto kynge Arthure
for to telle hym of youre sorow.'

'That woll I nat,' seyde the knyght, 'for hit woll harme me 35
gretely and do you none avayle.'

7–8 *C* cosyn and germayn vnto kynge Vryence   13 dore *not in C*
20 *C* ther cam   29–31 *C* said balyn and so he   32 *C†* damoysel in a forest
F (*Huth Merlin, f. 124c*) au piet d'une montaigne   34 *W* for for to telle
35–36 *C* wylle scathe me gretely and now do

'Sir,' seyde Balyne, 'I pray you make you redy, for ye muste go with me othir ellis I muste fyght with you and brynge you by for⌐c⌐e. And that were me lothe to do.'

'Woll ye be my warraunte,' seyde the knyght, 'and I go
5 with you?'

'Yee,' seyde Balyne, 'othir ellis, by the fayth of my body,
29ᵛ I woll dye therefore.'

And so he made hym redy to go with Balyne and leffte the damesell stylle. And as they were evyn before Arthurs
10 pavilion, there com one invisible and smote the knyght that wente with Balyn thorowoute the body with a spere.

'Alas!' seyde the knyght, 'I am slayne undir youre con-duyte with a knyght called ⌐Garlon⌐. Therefore take my horse that is bettir than youres, and ryde to the damesell
15 and folow the queste that I was in as she woll lede you, and revenge my deth whan ye may.'

'That shall I do,' seyde Balyn, 'and that I make avow to God and knyghthode.'

And so he departed frome kynge Arthure with grete
20 sorow.

So kynge Arthure lette bury this knyght rychely, and made mencion [on] his tombe how here was slayne Berbeus and by whom the trechory was done of the knyght ⌐Garlon⌐. But ever the damesell bare the truncheon of the spere with
(13) 25 hir that sir Harleus le Berbeus was slayne withall.

So Balyne and the damesell rode into the foreyste and there mette with a knyght that had bene an-hontynge. And that knyght asked Balyn for what cause he made so grete sorow.

30 'Me lyste nat to telle,' seyde Balyne.

'Now,' seyde the knyght, 'and I were armed as ye be, I wolde fyght with you but iff ye tolde me.'

3 *W* by fore   *C* by force   *F* (*Huth Merlin, f. 124d*) 'Se vous ne retornés, fait li autres, vous me ferez faire une vilonnie, car je m'en prendrai a vous a bataille pleniere'
6 by the fayth of my body *not in C*†   10 *C* thys knyghte   13, 23 *W* Garlonde
*C** Garlon   *F* Garlan (*also* Gallan)   14–24 *W* (*sidenote*): Here Garlonde that went invisyble slew Harlews le Barbeus under the conduyt of Balyn   17 a *not in S*   18 God and *not in C*   19 *C* departed from thys knyghte†   *F* (*Huth Merlin, f. 125b*) Puis dist au roi: 'Sire, je m'en vois de chi, si vous commanc a Dieu'
22 *W* made mencion his tombe   *C** made a mensyon on his tombe   *C* Herlews le berbeus   23 of *not in C*†   25 le Berbeus *not in C*   26 *C* a forest   30 *C* telle yow   32 but iff ye tolde me *not in C*

'That sholde litell nede,' seyde Balyne, 'I am nat aferde to telle you,' and so tolde hym all the case how hit was.

'A,' seyde the knyght, 'ys thys all? Here I ensure you by the feyth of my body never to departe frome you whyle my lyff lastith.'

And so they wente to their ostré and armed hem and so rode forthe with Balyne. And as they com by an ermytage evyn by a chy[r]cheyerde, there com ⌜Garlon⌝ invisible and smote this knyght, Peryne de Mounte Belyarde, thorowoute the body with a glayve.

'Alas,' seyde the knyght, 'I am slayne by thys traytoure knyght that rydith invisible.'

'Alas,' seyde Balyne, 'thy ys nat the first despite that he hath done me.'

And there the ermyte and Balyne buryed the knyght undir a ryche stone and a tombe royall. And on the morne they founde letters of golde wretyn how that sir Gawayne shall revenge his fadirs dethe ⌜kynge Lot⌝ on kynge Pellynore.

And anone aftir this Balyne and the damesell rode forth tylle they com to a castell. And anone Balyne alyghte and wente in. And as sone as ⌜Balyne came⌝ with⌜in the castels yate⌝ the portecolys were lette downe at his backe, and there fell many men aboute the damesell and wolde have slayne hir. Whan Balyne saw that, he was sore greved for he myght nat helpe her. But than he wente up into a towre and lepte over the wallis into the dyche and hurte nat hymselff. And anone he pulled oute his swerde and wolde have foughtyn with them. And they all seyde nay, they wolde nat fyght with hym, for they dud nothynge but the olde custom of thys castell, and tolde hym that hir lady was syke and had leyne many yeres, and she myght nat be hole but yf she

5

10

15

20

30ʳ

25

30

2 *C* alle the cause   8–18 *W* (*sidenote*): Here Garlonde invisible slew Peryne de Mounte Beliard under the conduyght of Balyn   8 *See note to p. 80, l. 13*   8 *C* cam the knyght garlon   10 *C* with a spere†   *F*: ferus d'une glaive   9–11 *W* *Hand in margin pointing to these lines.*   18 *F* (*Huth Merlin, f. 129d*) vengera Gavains le roi Loth son pere   20–22 *W* alyght and wente in And as sone as they were with[in ?] the portecolys were lette downe   *C** alyghte and he and the damoysel wende to go into the castel and anone as balyn came within the castels yate the portecolys fylle downe   *F* (*Huth Merlin, f. 130c*) Et li chevailers aloit devant et la damoisiele aprés, loing l'un de l'autre. Et si tost comme il se fu mis el chastiel cil d'amont laissent avaler une porte couliche   25 *C* helpe the damoysel   *C* the toure   26 *C* hurte hym not   30 *C* hym how her

917.44   G

had bloode in a sylver dysshe full, of a clene mayde and a kynges doughter.

'And therefore the custom of thys castell ys that there shall no damesell passe thys way but she shall blede of hir
5 bloode a sylver dysshefull.'

'Well,' seyde Balyne, 'she shall blede as much as she may blede, but I woll nat lose the lyff of hir whyle my lyff lastith.'

And so Balyn made hir to bleede by hir good wylle, but
10 hir bloode holpe nat the lady. And so she and he rested there all that nyght and had good chere, and in the mornynge they passed on their wayes. And as hit tellith aftir in the SANKGREALL that sir Percivall his syster holpe that lady with hir blood, whereof she was dede.

(14) 15 Than they rode three or four dayes and nevir mette with adventure. And so by fortune they were lodged with a jantilman, ⌐that was a ryche man and well at ease⌐. And as they sate at souper Balyn herde one complayne grevously by hym in a chambir.

20 'What ys thys noyse?' seyde Balyn.

'For sothe,' seyde his oste, 'I woll telle you. I was but late at a justynge and there I justed with a knyght that ys brothir unto kynge Pellam, and twyse I smote hym downe. And than he promysed to quyte me on my beste frende.
25 And so he wounded thus my son that can nat be hole tylle I have of that knyghtes bloode. And he rydith all invisyble, but I know nat hys name.'

'A,' seyde Balyne, 'I know that knyghtes name, which ys ⌐Garlon⌐, and he hath slayne two knyghtes of myne in
30 the same maner. Therefore I had levir mete with that knyght than all the golde in thys realme, for the despyte he hath done me.'

'Well,' seyde hys oste, 'I shall telle you how. Kynge Pellam off Lystenoyse hath made do cry in all the contrey
35 a grete feste that shall be within thes twenty dayes, and no

---

1 *C* had a dysshe of syluer ful of blood of a clene   11 *C* had there ryght
good   16 *C* and by happe   17 *W O¹* jantelman. And as   *F* un vavasour
moult preudomme qui lour fist la plus biele chiere et la grignour feste qu'il pot
19 *C†* in a chayer   *F* (*Huth Merlin, f. 133b*) en une des chambres de laiens
25 thus *not in C*   26 *C* alwey Inuysyble   28–29 *C* knowe that knyght his
name is Garlon he hath   *F* Garlan   33 how *not in C*   34 *C* this countrey

knyght may com there but he brynge hys wyff with hym
othir hys paramoure. And that your enemy and myne ye 30ᵛ
shall se that day.'

'Than I promyse you,' seyde Balyn, 'parte of his bloode
to hele youre sonne withall.'   5

'Than we woll be forewarde to-morne,' seyde he.

So on the morne they rode all three towarde kynge Pellam,
and they had fyftene dayes journey or they com thydir. And
that same day began the grete feste. And so they alyght
and stabled their horsis and wente into the castell, but 10
Balynes oste myght ⌜not⌝ be lette in because he had no lady.
But Balyne was well receyved and brought unto a chambir
and unarmed hym. And there was brought hym robis to
his plesure, and wolde have had Balyn leve his swerde be-
hynde hym.   15

'Nay,' seyde Balyne, 'that woll I nat, for hit ys the custom
of my contrey a knyght allweyes to kepe hys wepyn with
hym. Other ells,' seyde he, 'I woll departe as I ⌜cam⌝.'

Than they gaff hym leve with his swerde, and so he wente
into the castell and was amonge knyghtes of worship and hys 20
lady afore hym. So aftir this Balyne asked a knyght and seyde,

'Ys there nat a knyght in thys courte which his name ys
⌜Garlon⌝?'

'Yes, sir, yondir he goth, the knyght with the blacke face,
for he ys the mervaylyste knyght that ys now lyvynge. And 25
he destroyeth many good knyghtes, for he goth invisible.'

'Well,' seyde Balyn, 'ys that he?' Than Balyn avised hym
longe, and thought: 'If I sle hym here, I shall nat ascape.
And if I leve hym now, peraventure I shall never mete with
hym agayne at such a stevyn, and muche harme he woll do 30
and he lyve.'

---

1 *C* but yf he   2 *C* & that knyȝte youre enemy   4 *C* I behote yow
6 *C* sayd his oost   11 *W* myght be   *C** myght not be   *F* (*Huth Merlin,*
f. 134c) li ost remest defors pour chou que il n'avoit avoec lui demoisele nule
11–12 *C* lady thenne Balyn   16 *C* that doo I not   17–18 *C** with hym and
that customme wylle I kepe or els I wyll   18 *W* as I am   *C* as I cam
F (*loc. cit.*): dist que . . . se il ne voloient souffrir a faire la coustume de son pais,
il s'en iroit avant la dont il estoit venus   19 *C* leue to were his swerd
20 *C* was sette amonge   21 *C* hym soone balyn   23–24 *C* Garlon
yonder he goth sayd a knyght he with the   *W* Garlonde   25–26 *C* lyuyng for he
27 *C* A wel   28 and thought *not in C†*   *F* (*Huth Merlin, f. 135a*) Lors
commenche li chevaliers a deus espees a penser, et quant il a grant pieche pensé *etc.*

And therewith thys ⌜Garlon⌝ aspyed that Balyn vysaged
hym, so he com and slapped hym on the face with the backe
of hys honde and seyde,

'Knyght, why beholdist thou me so? For shame, ete thy
5 mete and do that thou com fore.'

'Thou seyst soth,' seyde Balyne, 'thys ys nat the firste
spite that thou haste done me. And therefore I woll do that
I come fore.' And rose hym up fersely and clave his hede
to the sholdirs.

10 'Now geff me ⌜the⌝ troncheon,' seyde Balyn ⌜to his lady⌝,
'that he slew youre knyght with.'

And anone she gaff hit hym, for allwey she bare the
truncheoune with hir. And therewith Balan smote hym
thorow the body and seyde opynly,

31ʳ 15 'With that troncheon thou slewyste a good knyght, and
now hit stykith in thy body.' Than Balyn called unto hys oste
(15) and seyde, 'Now may we fecche blood inoughe to hele youre
son withall.'

So anone all the knyghtes rose frome the table for to sette
20 on Balyne. And kynge Pellam hymself arose up fersely and
seyde,

'Knyght, why hast thou slayne my brothir? Thou shalt
dey therefore or thou departe.'

'Well,' seyde Balyn, 'do hit youreselff.'

25 'Yes,' seyde kyng Pellam, 'there shall no man have ado
with the but I myselff, for the love of my brothir.'

Than kynge Pellam ⌜caught in his hand⌝ a grymme wepyn
and smote egirly at Balyn, but he put hys swerde betwyxte
hys hede and the stroke, and therewith hys swerde braste
30 in sundir. And whan Balyne was wepynles he ran into a
chambir for to seke a wepyn [and] fro chambir to chambir,

1 *W* Garlonde   1–2 *C* that this Balen behelde hym and thenne he came and
smote Balyn on the face   4 *C* therfor ete   7 *C* despyte   4–10 *W*
(*sidenote*): How Balyn slew Garlon the knyght that wente invisible   10–11 *W*
now geff me youre troncheon seyde Balyn that he slew youre knyght with   *C** gyue
me the truncheon sayd Balyn to his lady where with he slewe your knyght   *F* (*MS.
cit., f. 135c*) Lors redist a la damoisiele: 'Damoisiele, bailliés moi le tronchon de quoi
li chevaliers fu ferus.'   16–17 *C* vnto hym his hoost sayenge now may ye fetche
22 why *not in C*†   26 I *not in C*   27 *W* Pellam a grymme   *C** Pellam cauȝt
in his hand a grym   *F* (*Huth Merlin, f. 135d*) court a une grant perche de fust
qui estoit en mi la sale et le prent   28 *C* but balyn put   31 *C* seke somme
wepen and soo fro chamber

and no wepyn coude he fynde. And allwayes kyng Pellam
folowed afftir hym. And at the last he enterde into a chambir
⟨which⟩ was mervaylously dyght and ryche, and a bedde
arayed with cloth of golde, the rychiste that myght be, and
one lyyng therein. And thereby stoode a table of clene golde 5
⌜with four pelours of sylver that bare up the table⌝, and uppon
the table stoode a mervaylous spere strangely wrought.

So whan Balyn saw the spere he gate hit in hys honde and
turned to kynge Pellam and felde hym and smote hym
passyngly sore with that spere, that kynge Pellam [felle] 10
downe in a sowghe. And therewith the castell brake roffe and
wallis and felle downe to the erthe. And Balyn felle downe
and myght nat styrre hande nor foote, and for the moste
party of that castell was dede thorow the dolorouse stroke.

Ryght so lay kynge Pellam and Balyne three dayes. 15

Than Merlion com thydir, and toke up Balyn and gate (16)
hym a good horse, for hys was dede, and bade hym voyde
oute of that contrey.

'Sir, I wolde have my damesell,' seyde Balyne.

'Loo,' seyde Merlion, 'where she lyeth dede.' 20

And kynge Pellam lay so many yerys sore wounded, and
myght never be hole tylle that Galaad the Hawte Prynce heled
hym in the queste of the Sankgreall. For in that place was
parte of the bloode of oure Lorde Jesu Cryste, which Joseph
off Aramathy brought into thys londe. And there hymselff [lay] 25
in that ryche bedde. And that was the spere whych Longeus
smote oure Lorde with to the herte. And kynge Pellam was
nyghe of Joseph his kynne, and that was the moste worshipful- **31ᵛ**
list man on lyve in tho dayes, and grete pité hit was of hys hurte,
for thorow that stroke hit turned to grete dole, tray and tene. 30

Than departed Balyne frome Merlyon, 'for,' he seyde,
'nevir in thys worlde we parte nother meete no more.' So
he rode forthe thorow the fayre contreyes and citeys and

2 folowed *not in* C　　2–3 C chambyr that was merueillously wel dyȝte and rychely
4 C* that myght be thought　　6 F et seoit sor trois (*sic*) pilerez d'argent. *Not
emended in* O¹　　9 C and felde hym *not in* C　　11–12 C the castel roofe
and wallys brake and fylle to the erthe　　13–15 C† And so the moost parte of the
castel that was falle doune thorugh that dolorous stroke laye vpon Pellam and balyn
thre dayes　17–18 C hym ryde oute　　23–27 W (*sidenote*): here ys a pronostica-
cion of the Sank Greall　　24–26 C Ioseph of Armathe . . . hym self lay in that
26 C the same spere　　28–29 C worshipful man that lyued　　29 hit *not in* C
31–32 C Merlyn and sayd in this world we mete neuer nomore

founde the peple dede slayne on every syde, and all that evir
were on lyve cryed and seyde,

'A, Balyne! Thou hast done and caused grete vengeaunce
in thys contreyes! For the dolerous stroke thou gaff unto
5 kynge Pellam thes three contreyes ar destroyed. And doute
nat but the vengeaunce woll falle on the at the laste!'

But whan Balyn was past tho contreyes he was passynge
fayne, and so he rode eyght dayes or he mette with many
adventure. And at the last he com into a fayre foreyst in a
10 valey, and was ware of a towure. And there besyde he mette
with a grete horse tyed to a tree, and besyde there sate a fayre
knyght on the grounde and made grete mournynge, and he
was a lyckly man and a well made. Balyne seyde,

'God you save! Why be ye so hevy? Tell me, and I woll
15 amende hit, and I may, to my power.'

'Sir knyght,' he seyde, 'thou doste me grete gryeff, for I was
in ⌈mery⌉ thoughtes and now thou puttist me to more payne.'

Than Balyn went a litill frome hym and loked on hys
horse, than herde Balyne hym sey thus:

20 'A, fayre lady! Why have ye brokyn my promyse? For ye
promysed me to mete me here by noone. And I may curse
you that ever ye gaff me that swerde, for with thys swerde
I woll sle myselff,' and pulde hit out.

And therewith com Balyne and sterte unto hym and toke
25 hym by the honde.

'Lette go my hande,' seyde the knyght, 'or ellis I shall sle
the!'

'That shall nat nede,' seyde Balyn, 'for I shall promyse
you my helpe to gete you youre lady and ye woll telle me
30 where she ys.'

'What ys your name?' seyde the knyght.

'Sir, my name ys Balyne le Saveage.'

'A, sir, I know you well inowghe: ye ar the Knyght with

---

1 evir *not in C*   2 and seyde *not in C*   3 done and *not in C*
W grete vengeaunce   O¹ C* grete dommage   F *(Huth Merlin, f. 139a)* tu nous
as fait tant de mal que tous li mondes nel porroit amender   8 many *not in C*
10-11 C he sawe a grete horse of werre   16 C said he ageyne   17 W my
thoughtes   C* mery thoughtes   F *(Huth Merlin, f. 139d)* 'Vous m'avés mort, qui
mon penser m'avés tolut. Je ne cuic que g'i soie ja mais si doucement comme jou
i estoie orendroit'   20-21 C thow promysest   23 woll *not in C*   24 C therwith Balyn sterte   32 Sir *not in C*

the Two Swerdis, and the man of moste proues of youre
hondis lyvynge.'

'What ys your name?' seyde Balyne.

'My name ys Garnysh of the Mownte, a poore mannes
sonne, and be my proues and hardynes a deuke made me 5
knyght and gave me londis. Hys name ys duke Harmel,
and hys doughter ys [she that I love, and she me, as I demed.' *Caxton*

'Hou fer is she hens?' sayd Balyn.

'But eleven myle,' said the knyghte.

'Now ryde we hens,' sayde these two knyghtes. 10

So they rode more than a paas tyll that they cam to a fayr
castel wel wallyd and dyched.

'I wylle into the castel,' sayd Balen, 'and loke yf she be ther.'

Soo he wente in and serched fro chamber to chambir and
fond her bedde, but she was not there. Thenne Balen loked 15
into a fayr litil gardyn, and under a laurel tre he sawe her
lye upon a quylt of grene samyte, and a knyght in her armes
fast halsynge eyther other, and under their hedes grasse
and herbes. Whan Balen sawe her lye so with the fowlest
knyghte that ever he sawe, and she a fair lady, thenne Balyn 20
wente thurgh alle the chambers ageyne and told the knyghte
how he fond her as she had slepte fast, and so brought hym
in the place there she lay fast slepynge.

And whan Garnyssh beheld hir so lyeng, for pure sorou (17)
his mouth and nose brast oute on bledynge. And with his 25
swerd he smote of bothe their hedes, and thenne he maade
sorowe oute of mesure and sayd,

'O, Balyn! Moche sorow hast thow brought unto me, for
haddest thow not shewed me that syght I shold have passed
my sorow.' 30

'Forsoth,' said Balyn, 'I did it to this entent that it sholde
better thy courage, and that ye myght see and knowe her
falshede, and to cause yow to leve love of suche a lady. God
knoweth I dyd none other but as I wold ye dyd to me.'

'Allas,' said Garnysshe, 'now is my sorou doubel that I may 35
not endure, now have I slayne that I moost loved in al my lyf!'

And therwith sodenly he roofe hymself on his own swerd
unto the hyltys.

5 *C* But by my   *C* hath maade   7-p. 91, l. 16 *Lacuna in W* (*ff. 32–33*)
9 *O*¹ six myle

When Balen sawe that, he dressid hym thensward, lest folke wold say he had slayne them, and so he rode forth. And within thre dayes he cam by a crosse; and theron were letters of gold wryten that said: 'it is not for no knyght alone 5 to ryde toward this castel.' Thenne sawe he an old hore gentylman comyng toward hym that sayd,

'Balyn le Saveage, thow passyst thy bandes to come this waye, therfor torne ageyne and it will availle the,' and he vanysshed awey anone.

10 And soo he herd an horne blowe as it had ben the dethe of a best. 'That blast,' said Balyn, 'is blowen for me, for I am the pryse, and yet am I not dede.' Anone withal he sawe an honderd ladyes and many knyghtes that welcommed hym with fayr semblaunt and made hym passyng good chere 15 unto his syght, and ledde hym into the castel, and ther was daunsynge and mynstralsye and alle maner of joye. Thenne the chyef lady of the castel said,

'Knyghte with the Two Suerdys, ye must have adoo and juste with a knyght hereby that kepeth an iland, for ther may 20 no man passe this way but he must juste or he passe.'

'That is an unhappy custome,' said Balyn, 'that a knyght may not passe this wey but yf he juste.'

'Ye shalle not have adoo but with one knyghte,' sayd the lady.

25 'Wel,' sayd Balyn, 'syn I shalle, therto I am redy; but traveillynge men are ofte wery and their horses to, but though my hors be wery my hert is not wery. I wold be fayne ther my deth shold be.'

'Syr,' said a knyght to Balyn, 'methynketh your sheld is 30 not good; I wille lene yow a byggar, therof I pray yow.'

And so he tooke the sheld that was unknowen and lefte his owne, and so rode unto the iland and put hym and his hors in a grete boote. And whan he came on the other syde he met with a damoysel, and she said,

35 'O, knyght Balyn, why have ye lefte your owne sheld? Allas! ye have put yourself in grete daunger, for by your sheld ye shold have ben knowen. It is grete pyté of yow as ever was of knyght, for of thy prowesse and hardynes thou hast no felawe lyvynge.'

'Me repenteth,' said Balyn, 'that ever I cam within this countrey; but I maye not torne now ageyne for shame, and what aventure shalle falle to me, be it lyf or dethe, I wille take the adventure that shalle come to me.'

And thenne he loked on his armour and understood he 5 was wel armed, and therwith blessid hym and mounted upon his hors. Thenne afore hym he sawe come rydynge oute of (18) a castel a knyght, and his hors trapped all reed, and hymself in the same colour. Whan this knyghte in the reed beheld Balyn hym thought it shold be his broder Balen by cause of 10 his two swerdys, but by cause he knewe not his sheld he demed it was not he.

And so they aventryd theyr speres and came merveillously fast togyders, and they smote other in the sheldes, but theire speres and theire cours were soo bygge that it bare doune 15 hors and man, that they lay bothe in a swoun, but Balyn was brysed sore with the falle of his hors, for he was wery of travaille. And Balan was the fyrst that rose on foote and drewe his swerd and wente toward Balyn, and he aroos and wente ageynst hym; but Balan smote Balyn fyrste, and he put 20 up his shelde and smote hym thorow the shelde and tamyd his helme. Thenne Balyn smote hym ageyne with that unhappy swerd and wel-nyghe had fellyd his broder Balan, and so they fought ther togyders tyl theyr brethes faylled.

Thenne Balyn loked up to the castel and sawe the towres 25 stand ful of ladyes. Soo they went unto bataille ageyne and wounded everyche other dolefully, and thenne they brethed oftymes, and so wente unto bataille that alle the place thereas they fought was blood reed. And att that tyme ther was none of them bothe but they hadde eyther smyten other 30 seven grete woundes so that the lest of them myght have ben the dethe of the myghtyest gyaunt in this world.

Thenne they wente to batail ageyn so merveillously that doubte it was to here of that bataille for the grete blood shedynge; and their hawberkes unnailled, that naked they 35 were on every syde. Atte last Balan, the yonger broder, withdrewe hym a lytel and leid hym doune. Thenne said Balyn le Saveage,

'What knyghte arte thow? For or now I found never no knyght that matched me.'
40

'My name is,' said he, 'Balan, broder unto the good knyght Balyn.'

'Allas!' sayd Balyn, 'that ever I shold see this day,' and therwith he felle backward in a swoune.

5 Thenne Balan yede on al four feet and handes, and put of the helme of his broder, and myght not knowe hym by the vysage, it was so ful hewen and bledde; but whan he awoke he sayd,

'O, Balan, my broder! Thow hast slayne me and I the, 10 wherfore alle the wyde world shalle speke of us bothe.'

'Allas!' sayd Balan, 'that ever I sawe this day that thorow myshap I myght not knowe yow! For I aspyed wel your two swerdys, but bycause ye had another shild I demed ye had ben another knyght.'

15 'Allas!' saide Balyn, 'all that maade an unhappy knyght in the castel, for he caused me to leve myn owne shelde to our bothes destruction. And yf I myght lyve I wold destroye that castel for ylle customes.'

'That were wel done,' said Balan, 'for I had never grace 20 to departe fro hem syn that I cam hyther, for here it happed me to slee a knyght that kept this iland, and syn myght I never departe, and no more shold ye, broder, and ye myght have slayne me as ye have and escaped yourself with the lyf.'

Ryght so cam the lady of the toure with four knyghtes 25 and six ladyes and six yomen unto them, and there she herd how they made her mone eyther to other and sayd, 'We came bothe oute of one ⟨w⟩ombe, that is to say one moders bely, and so shalle we lye bothe in one pytte.' So Balan prayd the lady of her gentylnesse for his true servyse that 30 she wold burye them bothe in that same place there the bataille was done, and she graunted hem with wepynge it shold be done rychely in the best maner.

'Now wille ye sende for a preest, that we may receyve our sacrament and receyve the blessid body of oure Lord 35 Jesu Cryst?'

'Ye,' said the lady, 'it shalle be done;' and so she sente for a preest and gaf hem her ryghtes.

'Now,' sayd Balen, 'whan we are buryed in one tombe and the mensyon made over us how two bretheren slewe eche

27 *C* one tombe

other, there wille never good knyght nor good man see our
tombe but they wille pray for our soules,' and so alle the
ladyes and gentylwymen wepte for pyté.

Thenne anone Balan dyed, but Balyn dyed not tyl the
mydnyghte after. And so were they buryed bothe, and the 5
lady lete make a mensyon of Balan how he was ther slayne by
his broders handes, but she knewe not Balyns name.

In the morne cam Merlyn and lete wryte Balyns name (19)
on the tombe with letters of gold that 'here lyeth Balyn le
Saveage that was the knyght with the two swerdes and he 10
that smote the dolorous stroke.' Also Merlyn lete make
there a bedde, that ther shold never man lye therin but he
wente oute of his wytte. Yet Launcelot de Lake fordyd
that bed thorow his noblesse.

And anone after Balyn was dede Merlyn toke his swerd 15
and toke of the pomel and set on another pomel. So Merlyn]
bade a knyght that stood before hym to handyll the swerde, **34ʳ**
and he assayde hit and myght nat handyll hit. Than Merlion
lowghe.

'Why lawghe ye?' seyde the knyght. 20

'Thys ys the cause,' seyde Merlion: 'there shall never
man handyll thys swerde but the beste knyght of the worlde,
and that shall be sir Launcelot other ellis Galahad, hys sonne.
And Launcelot with [t]hys swerde shall sle the man in the
worlde that he lovith beste: that shall be sir Gawayne.' 25

And all thys he lette wryte in the pomell of the swerde.

Than Merlion lette make a brygge of iron and of steele
into that ilonde, and hit was but halff a foote brode: 'and
there shall never man passe that brygge nother have hardynesse to go over hit but yf he were a passynge good man 30
withoute trechery or vylany.' Also the scawberd off Balyns
swerde Merlion lefte hit on thys syde the ilonde, that Galaad
sholde fynde hit. Also Merlion lette make by hys suttelyté
that Balynes swerde was put into a marbil stone stondynge
upryght, as grete as a mylstone, and hoved allwayes above 35
the watir, and dud many yeres. And so by adventure hit

---

16 *End of the lacuna in W*   17 *C*† hym handeld that swerd   18 *C* assayed
and he myght   24 *O*¹ hys swerde   25 *C* loued best   30 hit *not in C*
30–31 *C* good man and a good knyght withoute   32 *S* this syde of the Iland
(*see note*)   35 *C* and the stone houed

swamme downe by the streme unto the cité of Camelot, that
ys in Englysh called Wynchester, and that same day Galahad
the Haute Prynce com with kynge Arthure, and so Galaad
brought with hym the scawberde and encheved the swerde
5 that was in the marble stone hovynge uppon the watir. And
on Whytsonday he enchevyd the swerde, as hit ys rehersed
in THE BOOKE OF THE SANKGREALL.

Sone aftir thys was done Merlion com to kynge Arthur
and tolde hym of the dolerous stroke that Balyn gaff kynge
10 Pellam, and how Balyn and Balan fought togydirs the merveyl[yste] batayle that evir was herde off, and how they were
buryed bothe in one tombe.

'Alas!' seyde kynge Arthure, 'thys ys the grettist pité that
ever I herde telle off of two knyghtes, for in thys worlde I
15 knewe never such two knyghtes.'

THUS ENDITH THE TALE OF BALYN AND BALAN, TWO
BRETHIRNE THAT WERE BORNE IN NORTHHUMBIRLONDE, THAT
WERE TWO PASSYNGE GOOD KNYGHTES AS EVER WERE IN THO
DAYES.

20　　　　　　　　　EXPLICIT.

---

5 *C* was there in　　　9 *C* to kyng　　　10–11 *W* merveylous　　　13–15 *C*
that ouer I herd telle of two knyʒtes for in the world I knowe not suche　　　17–19 *C*
bretheren born in northūberlãd good kniʒtes　　　20 *C* Sequitur iii liber　　　Explicit
not in C　　　Fol. 34ᵛ *blank in W*

III

TORRE AND PELLINOR

[Winchester MS., ff. 35^r–44^v;
Caxton, Book III]

CAXTON'S RUBRICS

Ch. 1. How kyng Arthur took a wyf and wedded Guenever, doughter to Leodegran, kyng of the londe of Camelerd, wyth whome he had the Rounde Table.

,, 2. How the knyghtes of the Rounde Table were ordeyned and theyr syeges blessyd by the Bysshop of Caunterburye.

,, 3. How a poure man ⟨came⟩ rydynge upon a lene mare and desyred of kyng Arthur to make his sone knyght.

,, 4. How syr Tor was knowen for sone of kyng Pellynore and how Gawayn was made knyght.

,, 5. How atte feste of the weddyng of kyng Arthur to Guenever a whyte herte came into the halle and thyrty couple houndes, and how a brachet pynched the herte whiche was taken awaye.

,, 6. How syr Gawayn rode for to fetche ageyn the herte and how two brethern fought eche ageynst other for the herte.

,, 7. How the herte was chaced into a castel and there slayn, and how Gauwayn slewe a lady.

,, 8. How four knyghtes faught ayenst sir Gawayn and Gaheryse, and how they were overcom and her lyves saved atte request of four ladyes.

,, 9. How syr Tor rode after the knyght wyth the brachet and of his adventure by the waye.

,, 10. How syr Tor fonde the brachet wyth a lady and how a knyght assayled hym for the sayd brachet.

,, 11. How syr Tor overcame the knyght and how he lost hys heed at the requeste of a lady.

,, 12. How kyng Pellenore rode after the lady and the knyght that ladde her awaye, and how a lady desyred helpe of hym, and how he faught wyth ii knyghtes for that lady, of whome he slewe that one at the fyrst stroke.

,, 13. How kyng Pellynore gate the lady and brought hyr to Camelot to the courte of kyng Arthur.

,, 14. How on the waye he herde two knyghtes as he laye by nyght in a valey, and of other adventures.

,, 15. How whan he was comen to Camelot he was sworne upon a book to telle the trouthe of his queste.

IN the begynnyng of Arthure, aftir he was chosyn kynge
by adventure and by grace, for the moste party of the
barowns knew nat he was Uther Pendragon son but as
Merlyon made hit opynly knowyn, but yet many kyngis
and lordis hylde hym grete werre for that cause. But well 5
Arthur overcom hem all: the moste party dayes of hys lyff
he was ruled by the counceile of Merlyon. So hit felle on
a tyme kyng Arthur seyde unto Merlion,

'My barownes woll let me have no reste but nedis I muste
take a wyff, and I wolde none take but by thy counceile and 10
advice.'

'Hit ys well done,' seyde Merlyon, 'that ye take a wyff,
for a man of youre bounté and nobles sholde not be withoute
a wyff. Now is there ony,' seyde Marlyon, 'that ye love more
than another?' 15

'Ye,' seyde kyng Arthure, 'I love Gwenyvere, the kynges
doughtir of Lodegrean, of the londe of Camelerde, the
whyche holdyth in his house the Table Rounde that ye tolde
me he had hit of my fadir Uther. And this damesell is the
moste valyaunte and fayryst that I know lyvyng, or yet that 20
ever I coude fynde.'

'Sertis,' seyde M[e]rlyon, 'as of her beauté and fayrenesse
she is one of the fayrest on lyve. But and ye loved hir not
so well as ye do, I scholde fynde you a damesell of beauté
and of goodnesse that sholde lyke you and please you, and 25
youre herte were nat sette. But thereas mannes herte is
sette he woll be loth to returne.'

'That is trouthe,' seyde kyng Arthur.

But M[e]rlyon warned the kyng covertly that Gwenyver
was nat holsom for hym to take to wyff. For he warned hym 30
that Launcelot scholde love hir, and sche hym agayne, and
so he turned his tale to the aventures of the Sankegreal.

Then Merlion desyred of the kyng for to have men with
hym that scholde enquere of Gwenyver, and so the kyng
gr[a]unted hym. And so Merlyon wente forthe unto 35
kyng Lodegrean of Camylerde, and tolde hym of the desire

---

3 *C* that he   5 *C* helde grete werre ayenst hym   6 *C* for the mooste party the
dayes   7 *C* ruled moche   10–11 *C* by thyne aduys   14 seyde Merlyon *not
in C*   22 *C* Syre sayd   26 *C* a mans herte   22, 29 *W* Marlyon

917.44   H

of the kyng that he wolde have unto his wyff Gwenyver, his
doughter.

'That is to me,' seyde kyng Lodegreauns, 'the beste tydynges that ever I herde, that so worthy a kyng of prouesse
5 and noblesse wol wedde my doug[h]ter. And as for my
35ᵛ londis, I wolde geff hit hym yf I wyste hyt myght please hym,
but he hath londis inow, he nedith none. But I shall sende
hym a gyffte that shall please hym muche more, for I shall
gyff hym the Table Rounde which Uther, hys fadir, gaff me.
10 And whan hit ys fullé complete there ys an hondred knyghtes
and fyfty. And as for an hondred good knyghtes, I have myselff, but I wante fyfty, for so many hathe be slayne in my
dayes.'

And so kyng Lodgreaunce delyverd hys doughtir Gweny-
15 ver unto Merlion, and the Table Rounde with the hondred
knyghtes; and so they rode freysshly with grete royalté,
what by watir and by londe, tyll that they com nyghe unto
(2) London. Whan kynge Arthure herde of the commynge of
quene Gwenyver and the hondred knyghtes with the Table
20 Rounde, than kynge Arthure made grete joy for hir commyng and that ryche presente, and seyde opynly,

'Thys fayre lady ys passyngly wellcome to me, for I have
loved hir longe, and therefore there ys nothynge so leeff to
me. And thes knyghtes with the Table Rownde pleasith me
25 more than ryght grete rychesse.'

And in all haste the kynge lete ordayne for the maryage
and the coronacion in the moste hono[r]ablyst wyse that
cowude be devised.

'Now, Merlion,' seyde kynge Arthure, 'go thou and aspye
30 me in all thys londe fyfty knyghtes which bene of moste
prouesse and worship.'

So within shorte tyme Merlion had founde such knyghtes
that sholde fulfylle twenty and eyght knyghtes, but no mo
wolde he fynde. Than the Bysshop of Caunturbiry was
35 [f]ette, and he blyssed the segis with grete royalté and
devocion, and there sette the eyght and twenty knyghtes in
her segis. And whan thys was done Merlion seyde,

6 *C* hym wyst I it myght   9 *C* Vtherpendragon gaue me   12 *C* but I fawte
C haue ben   19 quene *not in* *C**   27 *W* hononablyst   *C* honorable
33–34 *C* xx & xiii† knyghtes but no mo he coude fynde   35 *W* sette

'Fayre sirres, ye muste all aryse and com to kynge Arthure
for to do hym omage; he woll the better be in wylle to mayn-
teyne you.'

And so they arose and dud their omage. And whan they
were gone Merlion founde in every sege lettirs of golde that 5
tolde the knyghtes namys that had sitte[n] there, but two
segis were voyde. And so anone com in yonge Gawayne and
asked the kynge a gyffte.

'Aske,' seyde the kynge, 'and I shall graunte you.'

'Sir, I aske that ye shall make me knyght that same day 10
that ye shall wedde dame Gwenyver.'

'I woll do hit with a goode wylle,' seyde kynge Arthure,
'and do unto you all the worship that I may, for I muste be
reson ye ar my nevew, my sistirs son.'

Forthwithall there com a poore man into the courte and 15 (3)
brought with hym a fayre yonge man of eyghtene yere of **36ʳ**
ayge, rydynge uppon a lene mare. And the poore man asked
all men that he mette,

'Where shall I fynde kynge Arthure?'

'Yondir he ys,' seyde the knyghtes. 'Wolt tho[u] ony- 20
thynge with hym?'

'Ye,' seyde the poore man, 'therefore I cam hydir.' And
as sone as he com before the kynge he salewed hym and
seyde, 'Kynge Arthure, the floure of all kyngis, I beseche
Jesu save the! Sir, hit was tolde me that [at] thys tyme of 25
youre maryaige ye wolde gyff ony man the gyffte that he
wolde aske you excepte hit were unresonable.'

'That ys trouthe,' seyde the kynge, 'such cryes I lette
make, and that woll I holde, so hit appayre nat my realme
nor myne astate.' 30

'Ye sey well and graciously,' seyde the pore man. 'Sir, I
aske nothynge elis but that ye woll make my sonne knyght.'

'Hit ys a grete thynge thou askyst off me,' seyde the
kynge. 'What ys thy name?' seyde the kynge to the poore
man. 35

'Sir, my name ys Aryes the cowherde.'

---

2 *C* he will haue the better wil   6 *W* sitter   7 *C* syeges   9 *C*
graunte it yow   11 *C* faire Gweneuer   13 *first* I *repeated in W*   24 *C*
O kyng   *C* all knyghtes and kynges   25 *WO¹* as   27 *C* aske oute excepte
that were   32 *C* sone here a knyghte

'Whethir commith thys of the other ells of thy sonne?'
seyde the kynge.

'Nay, sir,' seyd Aryes, 'thys desyre commyth of my son
and nat off me. For I shall telle you, I have thirtene sonnes,
5 and all they woll falle to what laboure I putte them and woll
be ryght glad to do laboure; but thys chylde woll nat laboure
for nothynge that my wyff and I may do, but allwey he woll
be shotynge, or castynge dartes, and glad for to se batayles
and to beholde knyghtes. And allwayes day and nyght he
10 desyrith of me to be made knyght.'

'What ys thy name?' seyde the kynge unto the yonge man.

'Sir, my name ys Torre.'

Than the kynge behelde hym faste and saw he was pass-
yn[g]ly well vysaged and well made of hys yerys.

15 'Well,' seyde kynge Arthure unto Aryes the cowherde,
'go fecche all thy sonnes before me that I may see them.'

And so the pore man dud. And all were shapyn muche
lyke the poore man, but Torre was nat lyke hym nother in
shappe ne in countenaunce, for he was muche more than
20 ony of them.

'Now,' seyde kynge Arthur unto the cowherde, 'where ys
the swerde he shall [b]e made knyght withall?'

'Hyt ys here,' seyde Torre.

'Take hit oute of the shethe,' sayde the kynge, 'and requyre
25 me to make you knyght.'

Than Torre alyght of hys mare and pulled oute hys
36ᵛ swerde, knelynge and requyrynge the kynge to make hym
knyght, and that he made hym knyght of the Table Rounde.

'As for a knyght I woll make you,' and therewith smote
30 him in the necke with the swerde. 'Be ye a good knyght, and
so I pray to God ye may be, and if ye be of proues and worthynes ye shall be of the Table Rounde.'

'Now, Merlion,' seyde Arthure, 'whethir thys Torre shall
be a goode man?'

35 'Yee, hardely, sir, he ought to be a good man for he

---

7 *C* wyf or I   16 go *not in C*   18–19 *C* was not lyke none of hem al in shap-
22 *W* shall me made   27 *C* the kynge that he wold make   28 *C** knygh-
& that he myghte be a knyght of the   30 *C* swerd sayēg   31 *C* god so y-
may   33 *C** say whether (*S* wether)   34 *C* good knyghte or n-
35 hardely *not in C*

ys com of good kynrede as ony on lyve, and of kynges
bloode.'

'How so, sir?' seyd the kynge.

'I shall telle you,' seyde Merlion. 'Thys poore man
Aryes the cowherde ys nat his fadir, for he ys no sybbe to 5
hym; for kynge Pellynore ys hys fadir.'

'I suppose nat,' seyde the cowherde.

'Well, fecch thy wyff before me,' seyde Merlion, 'and
she shall nat sey nay.'

Anone the wyff was fette forth, which was a fayre hous- 10
wyff. And there she answerde Merlion full womanly, and
there she tolde the kynge and Merlion that whan she was
a mayde and wente to mylke hir kyne, 'there mette with me
a sterne knyght, and half be force he had my maydynhode.
And at that tyme he begate my sonne Torre, and he toke 15
awey fro me my grayhounde that I had that tyme with me,
and seyde he wolde kepe the grayhounde for my love.'

'A,' seyde the cowherde, 'I wente hit had nat be thus, but
I may beleve hit well, for he had never no tacchys of me.'

Sir Torre seyde unto Merlion,   20

'Dishonoure nat my modir.'

'Sir,' seyde Merlion, 'hit ys more for your worship than
hurte, for youre fadir ys a good knyght and a kynge, and
he may ryght well avaunce you and youre modir both, for
ye were begotyn or evir she was wedded.'   25

'That ys trouthe,' seyde the wyff.

'Hit ys the lesse gryff unto me,' seyde the cowherde.

So on the morne kynge Pellynor com to the courte of (4)
kyng Arthure. And he had grete joy of hym and tolde hym
of sir Torre, how he was hys sonne, and how he had made 30
hym knyght at the requeste of the cowherde. Whan kynge
Pellynor behelde sir Torre he plesed hym muche. So the
kynge made Gawayne knyght, but sir Torre was the firste
he made at that feste.

'What ys the cause,' seyde kynge Arthure, 'that there ys 35
two placis voyde in the segis?'

---

1 *C* comen of as good a man as ony is on lyue   5 *C* no thyng syb   7 *C*
I suppose nay   10 *C* was fet which   13 hir *not in C*†   *C* met with her
18 *C* I wende not thys but   29 *C* Arthur whiche had grete ioye of hym
and told hym

'Sir,' seyde Merlion, 'there shall no man sitte in tho placis but they that shall be moste of worship. But in the Sege
37ʳ Perelous there shall nevir man sitte but one, and yf there be ony so hardy to do hit he shall be destroyed, and he that shall
5 sitte therein shall have no felowe.' And therewith Merlyon toke kynge Pellinor by the honde, and in that one hande nexte the two segis, and the Sege Perelous, he seyde in opyn audiens, 'Thys [is] your place, for beste ar ye worthy to sitte thereinne of ony that here ys.'

10 And thereat had sir Gawayne grete envy and tolde Gaherys hys brothir,

'Yondir knyght ys putte to grete worship, whych grevith me sore, for he slewe oure fadir kynge Lott. Therefore I woll sle hym,' seyde Gawayne, 'with a swerde that was sette me
15 that ys passynge trencheaunte.'

'Ye shall nat so,' seyde Gaheris, 'at thys tyme, for as now I am but youre squyre, and whan I am made knyght I woll be avenged on hym; and therefore, brothir, hit ys beste to suffir tyll another tyme, that we may have hym oute of courte,
20 for and we dud so we shall trouble thys hyghe feste.'

'I woll well,' seyde Gawayne.

(5) Than was thys feste made redy, and the kynge was wedded at Camelot unto dame Gwenyvere in the chirche of Seynte Stephyns with grete solempnité. Than as every man was
25 sette as hys degré asked, Merlion wente to all the knyghtes of the Rounde Table and bade hem sitte stylle, 'that none of you remeve, for ye shall se a straunge and a mervailous adventure.'

Ryght so as they sate there com rennynge inne a whyght herte into the hall, and a whyght brachet nexte hym, and
30 thirty couple of blacke rennynge houndis com afftir with a grete cry. And the herte wente aboute the Rounde Table, and as he wente by the syde-bourdis the brachet ever boote hym by the buttocke and pulde outte a pece, wherethorow the herte lope a grete lepe and overthrew a knyght that sate at

---

2 *C* they that shall be of moost worship   that *not in S*   6 *C* and in the
(*see note*)   8 *Not emended in* O¹   9 *C* is here   10 *C* sat syr gawayne in
14 *C* sente me   16–17 *C* at this tyme For at this tyme I am   17 *C* but a
squyre   18–19 *C* ye suffre   20 *C* we shold   21 *C* said gauayn as ye
wylle   22 *C* the hyghe feeste   25 *C* set after his degree   26 *C* none of hem
32 *C* by other boordes   ever *not in C*   33 O¹ pulde on   34 *W* hand
in margin pointing to this line

the syde-bourde. And therewith the knyght arose and toke
up the brachet, and so wente forthe oute of the halle and toke
hys horse and rode hys way with the brachett.

Ryght so com in the lady on a whyght palferey and cryed
alowde unto kynge Arthure and seyd, 'Sir, suffir me nat to 5
have thys despite, for the brachet ys myne that the knyght
hath ladde away.'

'I may nat do therewith,' seyde the kynge.

So with thys there com a knyght rydyng all armed on 37ᵛ
a grete horse, and toke the lady away with forse wyth hym, 10
and ever she cryed and made grete dole. So whan she was
gone the kynge was gladde, for she made such a noyse.

'Nay,' seyde Merlion, 'ye may nat leve hit so, thys adventure, so lyghtly, for thes adventures muste be brought to an
ende, other ellis hit woll be disworshyp to you and to youre 15
feste.'

'I woll,' seyde the kynge, 'that all be done by your advice.'

Than he lette calle sir Gawayne, for he muste brynge
agayne the whyght herte.

'Also, sir, ye muste lette call sir Torre, for he muste brynge 20
agay[ne] the brachette and the knyght, other ellis sle hym.
Also lette calle kynge Pellynor, for he must brynge agayne
the lady and the knyght, other ellis sle hym, and thes three
knyghtes shall do mervayles adventures or they com agayne.'

Than were they called all three as hit ys rehersed afore 25
and every of them toke their charge and armed them surely.
But sir Gawayne had the firste requeste, and therefore we woll
begynne at hym, and so forthe to thes other.

HERE BEGYNNITH THE FYRST BATAYLE THAT EVER SIR GA-
WAYNE DED AFTER HE WAS MADE KNYGHT. 30

Syr Gawayne rode more than a pace and Gaheris, his (6)
brothir, rode with hym in the stede of a squyre to do hym
servyse. So as they rode they saw two knyghtes fyght on
horseback passynge sore. So sir Gawayne and hys brothir
rode betwyxte them and asked them for what cause they 35
foughte. So one of the knyghtes seyde,

---

1 *C* boord syde　　5 *C* to kyng　　*S* for the kyng　　and seyd *not in C*　　6 *C*
was myn　　6–7 *C* knyght lad　　13 hit so *not in C*　　14–15 *C* brought
agayne or els　　28 *C* and so forthe　　29–30 Here begynnith . . . was made
knyght *not in C*　　36 *C* so the one knyght ansuerd and sayd

'We fyght but for a symple mater, for we two be two brethirne and be begotyn of o[n]e man and of o[n]e woman.'

'Alas!' seyde sir Gawayne.

'Sir,' seyde the elther brother, 'there com a whyght herte
5 thys way thys same day and many houndis chaced hym, and
a whyght brachett was allwey nexte hym. And we undirstood
hit was an adventure made for the hyghe feste of Arthure.
And therefore I wolde have gone afftir to have wonne me
worship, and here my yonger brothir seyde he wolde go aftir
10 the harte for he was bygger knyght than I. And for thys
cause we felle at debate, and so we thought to preff which of
us was the bygger knyght.'

'Forsoth thys ys a symple cause,' seyde Gawayne, 'for
uncouth men ye sholde debate withall, and no brothir with
38ʳ 15 brothir. Therefore do be my counceyle: other ellis I woll
have ado with you bothe, other yelde you to me and that ye
go unto kynge Arthure and yelde you unto hys grace.'

'Sir knyght,' seyde the two brethirne, 'we are forfoughten
and much bloode have we loste thorow oure wylfulness, and
20 therefore we wolde be loth to have ado with you.'

'Than do as I woll have you do,' seyde sir Gawayne.

'We agré to fulfylle your wylle. But by whom shall we sey
that we be thydir sente?'

'Ye may sey, by the knyght that folowith the queste of
25 the herte. Now what ys youre name?' seyde Gawayne.

'Sir, my name ys Sorluse of the Foreyste,' seyde the elder.

'And my name ys,' seyde the yonger, 'Bryan of the Foreyste.'

And so they departed and wente to the kyngis courte, and
sir Gawayne folowed hys queste. And as he folowed the
30 herte by the cry of the howndis, evyn before hym there was
a grete ryver; and the herte swam over.

And as sir Gawayn wolde a folowed afftir there stood
a knyght on the othir syde and seyde, 'Sir knyght, com nat
over aftir thys harte but if thou wolt juste with me.'

1–2 *C* bretheren born & hegoten (*S* begoten) of one man & of one woman
3–4 *C* sir gauayn why do ye so syr said the eldar ther cam   5 same *not in C*
10 *C* better knyght   12 *C* better kny3t   13 Forsoth *not in C*   for *not in C*
15–16 *C* therfor but yf ye wil do by my coũceil I wil haue ado with yow that is ye
shal yelde   21 *C* haue yow said   22 *C* we will agree   25 *C* the herte
that was whyte   26 *C* Sorlouse   29 *C* Syr gauayne on his quest and as
gauayne   31 *C* ouer the other syde

'I woll nat fayle as for that,' seyde sir Gawayne, 'to folow
the queste that I am inne.'

And so made hys horse swymme over the watir. And anone
they gate their glayves, and ran togydirs fulle harde, but
Gawayne smote hym of hys horse and [turned hys horse and] 5
than he bade hym yelde hym.

'Nay,' seyde the knyght, 'nat so, for thoughe ye have the
better of me on horsebak, I pray the, valyaunte knyght, alyght
on foote and macche we togidir with oure swerdis.'

'What ys youre name?' seyde sir Gawayne.   10

'Sir, my name ys Alardyne of the Oute Iles.'

Than aythir dressed their shyldes and smote togydir,
but sir Gawayne smote hym so harde thorow the helme
that hit wente to the brayne and the knyght felle downe
dede.   15

'A,' seyde Gaherys, 'that was a myghty stroke of a yonge
knyght.'

Than sir Gawayne and Gaherys ⌐rode more than a paas (7)
after the whyte herte, and lete slyppe at the herte thre couple
of greyhoundes. And so they chace the herte into a castel, and 20
in the chyef place of the castel they slew the hert. Gawayne
and Gaherys⌐ folowed afftir. Ryght so there com a knyght
oute of a chambir with a swerde drawyn in hys honde and
slew two of the grayhoundes evyn in the syght of sir Gawayne,
and the remanente he chaced with hys swerde oute of the 25
castell. And whan he com agayne he seyde,

'A, my whyght herte, me repentis that thou arte dede, for **38ᵛ**
my soveraigne lady gaff the to me, and evyll have I kepte the,
and thy dethe shall be evyl bought and I lyve.'

And anone he wente into hys chambir and armyd hym, and 30

---

4 *C* gat theire speres†   *F* (*Huth Merlin, f. 160a*) glaive   5 *Not emended in O¹*
5–11 *W* (*sidenote*) How sir Gawayne slew Alerdyne knyght of the Iles   7 for
not in C   9 *C* a foote   11 Sir my name is *not in C*   *C* Alardyn of the Ilys
14 *C* braynes   18–22 *W* folowed afftir ryght so   *F* (*Huth Merlin, f. 161a*)
Et Gavains qui les (= les chiens) vint ataignant les commenche a crier et a huer
aprés le chierf . . . Tant a li cierf (*sic*) fui et li chien cachié et Gavains feri des
esperons entre lui et Gahariet, tant (*sic; not in Camb.*) qu'il issirent del bois par
deviers destre, et lors voient devant eus en une plaigne une forterece moult bien seant
. . . et li chiers qui trueve la porte ouverte se met dedens et s'adrece viers la sale et
entre laiens . . . Et . . . il orent tantost (*Camb.* verraiement) le chierf mort et occhis
O¹ *inserts* the whyte herte . . . slew the hert *between* afftir *and* Ryght   29 *C* dere
bought

com oute fersely. And there he mette with sir Gawayne and
he seyde,

'Why have ye slayne my howndys? ⌜For they dyd but
their kynde, and⌝ I wolde that ye had wrokyn youre angir
5 uppon me rather than uppon a dome beste.'

'Thou seyst trouth,' seyde the knyght. 'I have avenged
me on thy howndys, and so I woll on the or thou go.'

Than sir Gawayne alyght on foote and dressed hys shylde,
and stroke togydirs myghtyly and clave their shyldis and
10 stooned their helmys and brake their hawbirkes that their
blo[de] thirled downe to their feete. So at the last sir Gawayne
smote so harde that the knyght felle to the erthe, and than he
cryed mercy and yelded hym and besought hym as he was a
jantyll knyght to save hys lyff.

15 'Thou shalt dey,' seyd sir Gawayne, 'for sleynge of my
howndis.'

'I woll make amendys,' seyde the knyght, 'to my power.'

But sir Gawayne wolde no mercy have, but unlaced hys
helme to have strekyn of hys hede. Ryght so com hys lady
20 oute of a chambir and felle over hym, and so he smote of hir
hede by myssefortune.

'Alas,' seyde Gaherys, 'that ys fowle and shamefully done,
for that shame shall never frome you. Also ye sholde gyff
mercy unto them that aske mercy, for a knyght withoute
25 mercy ys withoute worship.'

So sir Gawayne was sore astoned of the deth of this fayre
lady, that he wyst nat what he dud, and seyde unto the
knyght,

'Aryse, I woll gyff the mercy.'

30 'Nay, nay,' seyd the knyght, 'I take no forse of thy mercy
now, for thou haste slayne with vilony my love and my lady
that I loved beste of all erthly t[h]ynge.'

'Me sore repentith hit,' seyde sir Gawayne, 'for I mente
the stroke unto the. But now thou shalt go unto kynge
35 Arthure and telle hym of thyne adventure and how thou

1-2 and he seyde *not in* C   3-4 C* houndes said syr gauayn for they dyd
but their kynde and leuer I had ye had wroken   F (*Huth Merlin, f.* 161c) il ont
fait chou que il durent (*so in Camb.*)   11 C blood ranne   13-14 C as he was
a knyghte and gentylman   21 C by misauenture   26 C was so stonyed
30 thy *not in* C   31 with vilony *not in* C   33-34 C for I thoughte to
stryke vnto the

arte overcom by the knyght that wente in the queste of the
whyght harte.'

'I take no force,' seyde the knyght, 'whether I lyve othir
dey.' But at the last, for feare of dethe, he swore to go unto
kynge Arthure, and he made hym to bere the one grehownde 5
before hym on hys horse and the other behynde hym.

'What ys youre name,' seyde sir Gawayne, 'or we departe?'

'My name ys,' seyde the knyght, 'Blamoure of the Maryse.'

And so he departed towarde Camelot. And sir Gawayne **39ᵣ**
wente unto the castell and made hym redy to lye there all 10 (8)
nyght and wolde have unarmed hym.

'What woll ye do?' seyde Gaherys. 'Woll ye unarme you
in thys contrey? Ye may thynke ye have many fooes in thys
contrey.'

He had no sunner seyde the worde but there com in four 15
knyghtes well armed and assayled sir Gawayne harde, and
seyde unto hym,

'Thou new made knyght, thou haste shamed thy knyghthode, for a knyght withoute mercy ys dishonoured. Also
thou haste slayne a fayre lady to thy grete shame unto the 20
worldys ende, and doute the nat thou shalt have grete nede
of mercy or thou departe frome us.'

And therewith one of hem smote sir Gawayne a grete
stroke, that nygh he felle to the erthe. And Gaherys smote
hym agayne sore. And so they were assayled on the one syde 25
and on the othir, that sir Gawayne and Gaherys were in jouparté
of their lyves. And one with a bowe, an archer, smote sir Gawayne thorow the arme, that hit greved hym wondirly sore.

And as they sholde have bene slayne, there com four fayre
ladyes and besought the knyghtes of grace for sir Gawayne. 30
And goodly at the requeste of thes ladyes they gaff sir Gawayne and Gaherys their lyves and made them to yelde
them as presoners. Than sir Gawayne and Gaherys made
grete dole.

'Alas,' seyde sir Gawayne, 'myn arme grevith me sore, 35
that I am lyke to be maymed,' and so made hys complaynte
pyteuously.

---

4 *C* but so for   6 *C* another   13–14 *C* many enemyes here they had
21 *C* doubte thow not thou   25 assayled *not in C*†   *F (Camb., f. 288ᵣ, col. 2)*
l'assaillent de toutes parz   36 that *not in C*

So erly on the morne there com to sir Gawayne one of the four ladyes that had herd hys complaynte, and seyd,

'Sir knyght, what chere?'

'Nat good.'

5   'Why so? Hit ys youre owne defaute,' seyde the lady, 'for ye have done passynge foule for the sleynge of thys lady, the whych woll be grete vylony unto you. But be ye nat of kynge Arthurs?' seyde the lady.

'Yes, truly,' seyde sir Gawayne.

10   'What ys youre name, Sir?' seyde [the] lady, 'for ye muste telle or ye passe.'

'Fayre lady, my name ys sir Gawayne, the kynges son Lotte of Orkeney, and my modir ys kynge Arthurs sister.'

'Than ar ye nevew unto the kynge,' seyde the lady.

39ᵛ 15   'Well,' seyde the lady, 'I shall so speke for you that ye shall have ⟨leve⟩ to go unto kynge Arthure for hys love.'

And so she departed and told the four knyghtes how the presonere was kynge Arthurs nevew, 'and hys name ys sir Gawayne, kynge Lottis son of Orkeney.' So they gaff hym leve
20   and toke hym the hartes hede with hym because hit was in the queste. And than they delyverde hym undir thys promyse, that he sholde bere the dede lady with hym on thys maner: the hede of her was hanged aboute hys necke, and the hole body of hir before hym on hys horse mane.

25   Ryght so he rode forthe unto Camelot. And anone as he was com Merlion dud make kynge Arthure that sir Gawayne was sworne to telle of hys adventure, and how he slew the lady, and how he wolde gyff no mercy unto the knyght, wherethorow the lady was slayne. Than the kynge and the
30   quene were gretely displeased with sir Gawayne for the sleynge of the lady, and there by ordynaunce of the queene there was sette a queste of ladyes uppon sir Gawayne, and they juged hym for ever whyle he lyved to be with all ladyes and to fyght for hir quarels; and ever that he sholde be
35   curteyse, and never to refuse mercy to hym that askith mercy.

2 *C* alle his   4 *C* not good said he   5 Why so *not in C*   6 *C* a passynge fowle dede in the   7–8 *C* of kynge Arthurs kyn   10 *W* seyde Sir lady   for *not in C*   12 Fayre lady *not in C*   15 Well seyde the lady *not in C* 15–16 *C* ye shall haue conduyte to go   19–20 *C* † and they gaf hym the hertes hede by cause   21 *C* delyuerd syr Gauayne   22–23 *C* in this maner   26–27 *C* merlyn desyred of kyng Arthur . . . shold be sworne   27 *C* auentures

Thus was sir Gawayne sworne uppon the four Evaungelystis
that he sholde never be ayenste lady ne jantillwoman but if
he fyght for a lady and hys adversary fyghtith for another.

AND THUS ENDITH THE ADVENTURE OF SIR GAWAYNE THAT
HE DUD AT THE MARIAGE OF ARTHURE.   5

Whan sir Torre was redy he mounted uppon horsebacke (9)
and rode afftir the knyght with the brachett. And so as he
rode he mette with a dwarff suddeynly, that smote hys horse
on the hede with a staff, that he reled bakwarde hys spere
lengthe.   10
  'Why dost thou so?' seyde sir Torre.
  'For thou shalt nat passe thys way but if thou juste withe
yondir knyghtes of the pavilions.'
  Than was sir Torre ware where were two pavilions, and
grete spery[s] stood oute, and two shildes hangynge on treys 15
by the pavilions.
  'I may nat tarry,' seyde sir Torre, 'for I am in a queste
that I muste nedys folow.'
  'Thou shalt nat passe thys wey,' seyde the dwarff, and **40ʳ**
therewithall he blew hys horne. Than there com one armed 20
on horsebacke and dressed hys shylde and com fast towarde
sir Torre. And than he dressed hym ayenste hem and so ran
togydirs, and sir Torre bare hym from hys horse, and anone
the knyght yelded hym to hys mercy.
  'But, sir, I have a felow in yondir pavilyon that woll have 25
ado with you anone.'
  'He shall be wellcom,' seyde sir Torre.
  Than was he ware of another knyght commynge with
grete rawndom, and eche of hem dressed to other, that
mervayle hit was to se. But the knyght smote sir Torre 30
a grete stroke in myddys the shylde, that his spere all to-
shyverde. And sir Torre smote hym thorow the shylde be-
nethe, that hit wente thorow the coste of the knyght; but
the stroke slew hym nat. And therewith sir Torre alyght
and smote hym on the helme a grete stroke, and therewith 35
the knyght yelded hym and besought hym of mercy.

3 *C* fought   *C* fouȝt   5 *C* Arthur Amen   6 *C* his horsbak
9 *C* he wente backward   19 thys wey *not in C*   23 *C* togyders
that Tor   31 *C* of the   32–33 *C** shelde by lowe of the sheld and it

'I woll well,' seyde sir Torre, 'but ye and youre felow muste go unto kynge Arthure and yelde you presoners unto hym.'

'By whom shall we sey we ar thydir sente?'

'Ye shall sey, by the knyght that wente in the queste of the
5 knyght with the brachette. Now, what be your two namys?' seyde sir Torre.

'My name ys,' seyde that one, 'sir Phelot of Langeduke.'

'And my name ys,' seyde the othir, 'sir Petipace of Wynchilsee.'

10 'Now go ye forthe,' seyde sir Torre, 'and God spede you and me.'

Than cam the dwarff and seyde unto sir Torre,

'I pray you gyff me my bone.'

'I woll well,' seyde sir Torre, 'aske and ye shall have.'

15 'I aske no more,' seyde the dwarff, 'but that ye woll suffir me to do you servyse, for I woll serve no more recreaunte knyghtes.'

'Well, take an horse,' seyde sir Torre, 'and ryde one with me.'

20 'For I wote,' seyde the dwarff, 'ye ryde afftir the knyght with the whight brachette, and I shall brynge you where he ys,' seyde the dwarff.

And so they rode thorowoute a foreste; and at the laste they were ware of two pavilions evyn by a pryory, ⌜with two
25 sheldes⌝, and that one shylde was enewed with whyght and that othir shylde was rede.

(10)   Therewith sir Torre alyght and toke the dwarff hys glayve, and so he com to the whyght pavilion. He saw three damesels lye in hyt on a paylette slepynge; and so he wente unto the
40ᵛ 30 tother pavylyon and founde a lady lyynge in hit slepynge, but therein was the whyght brachett that bayed at hym faste. And than sir Torre toke up the brachette and wente hys way and toke hit to the dwarffe.

---

5 *C* knyght that wente with   13 *C* gyue me a yefte   14 and ye shall have *not in C*   18 Well *not in C*   19–20 *C* me I wote ye ryde   24–25 *C** with two sheldes and the one shylde   *F (Huth Merlin, f. 169b)* A chascun des pavillons pendoit uns escus   29 *C* lye in it and one paylet†   30–p. 111, l. 3 *C** lyeng slepyng ther in But ther was the whyte brachet that bayed at her fast and therwith the lady yede oute of the pauelione & all her damoysels But anone as syr Tor aspyed the whyte brachet he took her by force and took her to the dwerf what wille ye so sayd the lady take my brachet

And with the noyse the lady com oute of the pavilion, and all hir damesels, and seyde,

'Woll ye take my brachette frome me?'

'Ye,' seyde sir Torre, 'this brachett have I sought frome kynge Arthures courte hydir.'

'Well,' seyde the lady, 'sir knyght, ye shall nat go farre with hir but that ye woll be mette with and greved.'

'I shall abyde what adventure that commyth by the grace of God,' and so mownted uppon hys horse and passed on hys way towarde Camelot.

But it was so nere nyght he myght nat passe but litill farther.

'Know ye any lodgyng here nye?' seyde sir Torre.

'I know none,' seyde the dwarff, 'but here besydys ys an ermytaige, and there ye muste take lodgynge as ye fynde.'

And within a whyle they com to the hermytage and toke such lodgynge as was there, and as grasse and otis and brede for their horsis. Sone hit was spedde, and full harde was their souper. But there they rested them all nyght tylle on the morne, and herde a masse devoutely and so toke their leve of the ermyte. And so sir Torre prayde the ermyte to pray for hym, and he seyde he wolde, and betoke hym to God. And so mownted uppon horsebacke and rode towardis Camelot a longe whyle.

So with that they herde a knyght calle lowde that com afftir them, and seyde,

'Knyght, abyde and yelde my brachette that thou toke frome my lady!'

Sir Torre returned agayne and behelde hym how he was a semely knyght and well horsed and armed at all poyntes. Than sir Torre dressed hys shylde and toke hys glayve in hys hondys. And so they com fersely on as freysshe men and droff both horse and man to the erthe. Anone they arose lyghtly and drew hir swerdis as egirly as lyons, and put their shyldis before them, and smote thorow their shyldys, that the cantels felle on bothe partyes. Also they tamed their helmys, that the hote bloode ran oute and the thycke

1 with the noyse *not in C*†   *F (loc. cit.)* Et la damoisele s'esveille erraument pour
la noise que cil faisoit   4 *W* shought   7 *C* mette and   12 here nye
not in C   15 *W* they com they com   15-16 *C* took lodgyng and was there gras
29 *C* and wel armed   30 *C* his spere in   31-32 *C* and the other cam fyersly
vpon hym and smote bothe hors & man to the erthe

mayles of their hawbirkes they carff and rooffe in sundir,
41ʳ that the hote bloode ran to the erthe. And bothe they had
many woundys and were passynge wery.

But sir Torre aspyed that the tothir knyght faynted, and
5 than he sewed faste uppon hym and doubled hys strokis
and stroke hym to the erthe on the one syde. Than sir Torre
bade hym yelde hym.

'That woll I nat,' seyde Abelleus, 'whyle lastith the lyff
and the soule in my body, onles that thou wolte geff me the
10 brachette.'

'That woll I nat,' seyde sir Torre, 'for hit was my queste
to brynge agayne the brachette, thee, other bothe.'

(11)   With that cam a damesell rydynge on a palferey as faste as
she myght dryve, and cryed with lowde voice unto sir Torre.
15 'What woll ye with me?' seyde sir Torre.

'I beseche the,' seyde the damesell, 'for kynge Arthurs
love, gyff me a gyffte, I requyre the, jantyll knyght, as thou
arte a jantillman.'

'Now,' seyde sir Torre, 'aske a gyffte and I woll gyff hit
20 you.'

'Grauntemercy,' seyde the damesell. 'Now I aske the hede
of thys false knyght Abelleus, for he ys the moste outera-
geous knyght that lyvith, and the grettist murtherer.'

'I am lothe,' seyde sir Torre, 'of that gyffte I have gyvyn
25 you; but lette hym make amendys in that he hathe trespasced
agayne you.'

'Now,' seyde the damesell, 'I may nat, for he slew myne
owne brothir before myne yghen that was a bettir knyght
than he, and he had had grace; and I kneled halfe an owre
30 before hym in the myre fo[r] to sauff my brothirs lyff that
had done hym no damage, but fought with hym by adventure
of armys, and so for all that I coude do he strake of hys hede.
Wherefore I requyre the, as thou arte a trew knyght, to gyff
me my gyffte, othir ellis I shall shame the in all the courte of
35 kynge Arthure; for he ys the falsyste knyght lyvynge, and
a grete destroyer of men, and namely of good knyghtes.'

6 *C* and garte hym go to   8–9 *C* whyle my lyf lasteth and the soule is within
my body   11 *C* not doo   26 *C* vnto yow   27 *W* I may nat I may nat
C he may not†   *F* (*Huth Merlin, f. 171d*) Ja Dieus n'ait merchi de m'arme se je
en ai merchi   36 of men and namely *not in C*

So whan Abellyus herde thys he was more aferde and
yelded hym and asked mercy.

'I may nat now,' seyde sir Torre, 'but I sholde be founde
false of my promyse, for erewhyle whan I wolde have tane
you to mercy ye wolde none aske, but iff ye had the brachett 5
agayne that was my queste.'

And therewith he toke off hys helme, and therewith he
arose and fledde, and sir Torre afftir hym, and smote of hys **41ᵛ**
hede quyte.

'Now, sir,' seyde the damesell, 'hyt ys nere nyght. I pray 10
you come and lodge with me hereby at my place.'

'I woll well,' seyde sir Torre, 'for my horse and I have
fared evyll syn we departed frome Camelot.'

And so he rode with her, and had passynge good chere
with hir. And she had a passyng fayre olde knyght unto 15
hir husbande that made hym good chere and well easyd both
hys horse and hym. And on the morne [he] herde hys masse
and brake hys faste, and toke hys leve of the knyght and of
the lady that besought hym to telle hys name.

'Truly,' he seyde, 'my name ys sir Torre, that was late 20
made knyght, and thys was the firste queste of armys that
ever y ded, to brynge agayne that thys knyght Abelleus toke
away frome kynge Arthurs courte.'

'Now, fayre knyght,' seyde the lorde and the lady, 'and
ye come here in oure marchys, se here youre poore lodgynge, 25
and hit shall be allwayes at youre commaundemente.'

So sir Torre departed and com to Camelot on the third
day by noone. And the kynge and the quene and all the
courte was passynge fayne of hys commynge, and made
grete joy that he was com agayne, for he wente frome the 30
courte with litill succour but as kynge Pellynor, hys fadir,
gaff hym an olde courser, and kynge Arthur gaff hym armour
and swerde; othir ellis had he none other succour, but rode
so forthe hymself alone. And than the kynge and the quene
by Merlions advice made hym swere to telle of hys adven- 35
tures, and so he tolde and made prevys of hys dedys as hit ys

4 *C* for whyle I   11 *C* here at my place it is here fast by   12 *C* his
hors and he had   13 *C* syn they departed   17 *C* hors and he   24 *C*
O fayr knyght said the lady and her husband   25 *C* marches come and see
oure poure

before reherced, wherefore the kynge and the quene made grete joy.

'Nay, nay,' seyde Merlion, 'thys ys but japis that he hath do, for he shall preve a noble knyght of proues as few lyvynge, 5 and jantyl and curteyse and of good tacchys, and passyng trew of hys promyse, and never shall he outerage.'

Wherethorow Merlions wordis kynge Arthure gaff an erledom of londis that felle unto hym. AND HERE ENDITH THE QUESTE OF SIR TORRE, KYNGE PELLYNORS SONNE.

42ʳ (12) 10 Than kynge Pellynore armed hym and mownted uppon hys horse, and rode more than a pace after the lady that the knyght lad away. And as he rode in a foreyste he saw in a valey a damesell sitte by a well and a wounded knyght in her armys, and kynge Pellynor salewed hir. And whan she was 15 ware of hym, she cryed on lowde and seyde, 'Helpe me, knyght, for Jesuys sake!' But kynge Pellynore wolde nat tarry, he was so egir in hys queste; and ever she cryed an hondred tymes aftir helpe. Whan she saw he wolde nat abyde, she prayde unto God to sende hym as much nede of 20 helpe as she had, and that he myght feele hit or he deyed. So, as the booke tellith, the knyght there dyed that was wounded, wherefore for pure sorow the lady slew hirselff with hys swerde.

As kynge Pellynore rode in that valey he mette with a 25 poore man, a laborer, ⟨and⟩ seyde,

'Sawyst thou ony knyght rydynge thys way ledyng a lady?'

'Ye, sir,' seyde the man. 'I saw that knyght and the lady that made grete dole. And yondir beneth in a valey there shall ye se two pavilions, and one of the knyghtes of the 30 pavilions chalenged that lady of that knyght, and seyde she was hys cosyne nere, wherefore he shold lede hir no farther. And so they waged batayle in that quarell; that one seyde he wolde have hir by force, and that other seyde he wold have the rule of her, for he was hir kynnesman and wolde lede hir 35 to hir kynne.' So for thys quarell he leffte hem fyghtynge.

1–2 *S* made hym grete   3–4 *C** these ben but Iapes to that he shalle doo
4 *C* as good as ony is lyuyng   6 he *not in C*   7 *C* gaf hym an
15 *C* ouer lowde helpe   16 *C* for crystes sake kynge Pellinore & he wold not
25–26 *C* labourer Sawest thow not saide Pellinore a knyghte rydynge and ledyng
W a laborer which (⁊ *misread as* þᵗ *which in a later copy was changed to* which)
34 *C* by cause he was

'And if ye woll ryde a pace ye shall fynde them fyghtynge, and the lady was leffte with two squyers in the pavelons.'

'God thanke the,' seyde kynge Pellynor.

Than he rode a walop tylle he had a syght of the two pavilons, and the two knyghtys fyghtynge. And anone he rode unto the pavilons and saw the lady how she was there, for she was hys queste, and seyde, 5

'Fayre lady, ye muste go with me unto the courte of kynge Arthure.'

'Sir knyght,' seyde the two squyres, 'yondir ar two knyghtes that fyght for thys lady. Go ye thyder and departe them, and be ye agreed with them, and than may ye have hir at youre plesure.' 10

'Ye sey well,' seyde kynge Pellynor.

And anone he rode betwixte hem and departed them, and asked them their causis why they fought. 15

'Sir knyght,' seyde that one, 'I shall telle you. Thys lady ys my kynneswoman nye, my awntis doughtir, and whan I herde hir complayne that she was with hym magré hir hede, I waged batayle to fyght with hym.' 20

'Sir knyght,' seyde thys othir whos name was Outelake of Wentelonde, 'and thys lady I gate be my prouesse of hondis and armys thys day at Arthurs courte.'

'That ys nat trew,' seyde kynge Pellynor, 'for ye com in suddeynly thereas we were at the hyghe feste and toke awey thys lady or ony man myght make hym redy, and therefore hit was my queste to brynge her agayne and you bothe, othir ellis that one of us to leve in the fylde. Therefore thys lady shall go with me, othir I shall dye therefore, for so have I promysed kynge Arthur. And therefore fyght ye no more, for none of you shall have parte of hir at thys tyme. And if ye lyst for to fyght for hir with me, I woll defende hir.' 25 30

'Well,' seyde the knyghtes, 'make you redy, and we shall assayle you with all oure power.' 35

And as kynge Pellynor wolde have put hys horse frome

6-7 *C* the lady that was his quest   10 *C* squyres that were with her yonder
23 hondis and *not in C*   24 *C* that is vntruly said said   28 *C* to abyde in the
29-30 *C* dye for it for I haue promysed hit kynge   31 *C* haue no parte
32-33 *C* her fyȝte with me and I wille defende her

hym, sir Outelake roff hys horse thorow with a swerde, and seyde,

'Now art thou afoote as well as we ar.'

Whan kynge Pellynore aspyed that hys horse was ⌈slayne⌉,
5 lyghtly he lepe frome hys horse, and pulled oute hys swerde, and put hys shyld afore hym and seyde,

'Knyght, kepe the well, for thou shalt have a buffette for the sleynge of my horse.'

So kynge Pellynor gaff hym such a stroke uppon the helme
10 that he clave the hede downe to the chyne, and felle downe
(13) to the erthe dede. Than he turned hym to the other knyght that was sore wounded. But whan he saw that buffette he wolde nat fyght, but kneled downe and seyde,

'Take my cosyn, thys lady, with you, as ys youre queste,
15 and I require you, as ye be a trew knyght, put hir to no shame nother vylony.'

'What?' seyde kynge Pellynore, 'woll ye nat fyght for hir?'

'No,' seyde the knyght, 'I woll nat fyght with such a knyght of proues as ye be.'

20 'Well,' seyde kynge Pellynore, 'I promyse you she shall have no vyllany by me, as I am trew knyght.'

'But now me wantis an horse,' seyde kynge Pellynor, 'but I woll have Outelakis horse.'

'Sir, ye shall nat nede,' seyde the knyght, 'for I shall gyff
25 you such an horse as shall please you, so that ye woll lodge with me, for hit ys nere nyght.'

'I woll well,' seyde kynge Pellynore, 'abyde with you all nyght.'

43ʳ And there he had with hym ryght good chere and fared
30 of the beste with passyng good wyne, and had myry reste that nyght.

And on the morne he harde masse and dyned. And so was brought hym a fayre bay courser, and kynge Pellynors sadyll sette uppon hym.

35 'Now, what shall I calle you,' seyde the knyght, 'inasmuch as ye have my cousyn at youre desyre of youre queste?'

1 C† them syr   4 *W* horse was   *C* hors was slayne   F (*Huth Merlin*, f. 175a) li uns laisse aler l'espee et fiert le cheval en costé seniestre, si l'ochist et li chevaus chiet mors   7 *C* kepe wel thy heede for   12 *C* sawe the others buffet   14 *C* yow at youre request   20 *C* Pellenore ye say wel   22 *C* me lacketh

'Sir, I shalle telle you: my name ys kynge Pellynor, kynge
of the Ilis, and knyght of the Table Rounde.'

'Now am I glad,' seyde the knyght, 'that such a noble
man sholde have the rule of my cousyn.'

'Now, what ys youre name?' seyde kynge Pellynor. 'I 5
pray you telle me.'

'Sir, my name ys sir Meliot de Logurs, and thys lady, my
cosyn, hir name ys called Nenyve. And thys knyght that
was in the other pavilion was my sworne brother, a passynge
good knyght, and hys name ys Bryan of the Ilis, and he ys 10
full lothe to do ony wronge or to fyght with ony man but if
he be sore sought on.'

'Hit ys mervayle,' seyde kynge Pellynor, 'he wolde nat
have ado with me.'

'Sir, he woll nat have ado with no man but if hit be at hys 15
requeste.'

'I pray you brynge hym to the courte one of thes dayes,'
seyde kynge Pellynor.

'Sir, we woll com togydirs.'

'Ye shall be wellcom,' seyde kynge Pellynore, 'to the 20
courte of kynge Arthure, and ye shall be gretely alowed for
youre commynge.'

And so he departed with the lady and brought her to
Camelot.

But so as they rode in a valey, hit was full of stonys, and 25
there the ladyes horse stumbled and threw her downe, and
hir arme was sore brused, that nerehonde she swooned for
payne.

'Alas!' seyde the lady, 'myn arme ys oute of lythe, wherethorow I muste nedys reste me.' 30

'Ye shall well,' seyde kynge Pellynor.

And so he alyght undir a tre where was fayre grasse, and
he put hys horse thereto, and so rested hem undir the tree
and slepte tylle hit was ny nyght. And when he awoke he
wolde have rydden forthe, but the lady seyde, 35

1–2 *C* Pellenore of the ⸿ 8 *C* cosyn hyght Nymue   9 *C* is my   11 *C* ful
loth to do wronge and ful lothe to fyghte with   12 *C** sought on so that for
shame he may not leue it   13 *C* Pellinore that he wille not   17 I pray you
not in C   21 *C* and gretely allowed   26–27 *C* that her arme   27 *C*
brysed and nere she   32 *C* a fayr tree   33 *C* so leyd hym   35 *C*
ryden Sir said the lady

'Ye may as well ryde backwarde as forewarde, hit ys so durke.'

So they abode stylle and made there theire lodgynge. Than kynge Pellynor put of hys armoure. Tha[n] so a litill tofore
5 mydnyght they herde the trottynge of an horse. 'Be ye stylle,'
43ᵛ seyde kynge Pellynor, 'for we shall hyre of som adventure.'
(14)   And therewith he armed hym. So ryght evyn before hym there mette two knyghtes, that one com frowarde Camelot, and that othir com from the Northe, and eyther salewed
10 other and asked:

'What tydynges at Camelot?' seyde that one knyght.

'Be my hede,' ⌜seyde the other⌝, 'there have I bene and aspied the courte of kynge Arthure, and there ys such a felyshyp that they may never be brokyn, and well-nyghe all
15 the world holdith with Arthure, for there ys the floure of chevalry. And now for thys cause am I rydyng into the Northe: to telle oure chyfftaynes of the felyship that ys with-holdyn with kynge Arthure.'

'As for that,' seyde the othir knyght, 'I have brought
20 a remedy with me that ys the grettist poysen that ever ye herde speke off. And to Camelot woll I with hit, for we have a frende ryght nyghe the kynge, well cheryshed, that shall poysen kynge Arthur, for so hath he promysed oure chyfftaynes, and receyved grete gyfftis for to do hit.'

25   'Beware,' seyde the othir knyght, 'of Merlion, for he knowith all thynges by the devylles craffte.'

'As for that, woll I nat lett,' seyde the knyght; and so they departed in sondir.

And anone aftir that kynge Pellynor made hym redy, and
30 hys lady, and rode towarde Camelot. And as they com by the welle thereas the wounded knyght was and the lady, there he founde the knyght and the lady etyn with lyons othir with wylde bestis, all save the hede, wherefore he made grete sorow and wepte passynge sore, and seyde,

35   'Alas! hir lyff myght I have saved, but I was ferse in my queste that I wolde nat abyde.'

4 *W* that so a litill   *C** thēne a lytel   10 and asked *not in C*   11–12 *W* seyde that one knyght Be my hede there   *C** sayd the one by my hede saide the other ther   *F* (*Huth Merlin, f. 176b*) 'Ques nouvieles aportés vous?' 'Je n'aporch, fait il, nules nouvieles qui me plaisent'   27 *C* therfore wille I not lete it
30 *S* lady rode   35–36 *C* so fyers in my quest therfore I

'Wherefore make ye such doole?' seyde the lady.

'I wote nat,' seyde kynge Pellinore, 'but my herte rwyth sore of the deth of hir that lyeth yondir, for she was a passyng fayre lady, and a yonge.'

'Now, woll [ye] do by myne advise? Take the knyght and 5 lette hym be buryed in an ermytage, and than take the ladyes hede and bere hit with you unto kynge Arthure.' So kynge Pellynor toke thys dede knyght on hys shyld and brought hym to the ermytage, and charged the heremyte with the corse, that servyse sholde be done for the soule. 10

'And take ye hys harneyse for youre payne.'

'Hit shall be done,' seyde the hermyte, 'as I woll answere to God.'

And therewith they departed and com thereas the lady (15) 44ʳ lay with a fayre yalow here. That greved kynge Pellynore 15 passynge sore whan he loked on hit, for much hys herte caste unto that vysage. And so by noone they come unto Camelot, and the kynge and the quene was passyng fayne of hys commynge to the courte. And there he was made to swere uppon the four Evangelistes to telle the trouthe of hys 20 queste frome the one ende to that other.

'A, kynge Pellynor,' seyde quene Gwenyver, 'ye were gretly to blame that ye saved nat thys ladyes lyff.'

'Madam,' seyde kynge Pellynore, 'ye were gretely to blame and ye wolde nat save youre owne lyff and ye myght. 25 But, salf youre displesure, I was so furyous in my queste that I wolde nat abyde, and that repentis me and shall do dayes of my lyff.'

'Truly ye ought sore to repente hit,' seyde Merlion, 'for that lady was youre owne doughtir, begotyn of the lady of 30 the Rule, and that knyght that was dede was hir love and sholde have wedded hir, and he was a ryght good knyght of a yonge man, and wolde a proved a good man. An[d] to this courte was he commynge, and hys name was sir Myles of the Laundis, and a knyght com behynde hym and slew 35 hym with a spere, and hys name was Lorayne le Saveage,

2 *C* herte morneth   3 that lyeth yondir *not in C*   5 *C* aduys said the lady
8 *C* on his sholders   *F* devant soi   14 *C** the hede of the lady   16–17 *C*
he cast his herte on the vysage   21 ende *not in C*†   26 *C* sauf your pleasir
27 do *not in C*   30 *C* begotyn on the

a false knyght and a cowherde. And she for grete sorow and dole slew hirselff with his swerde, and hyr name was Alyne. And because ye wolde nat abyde and helpe hir, ye shall se youre best frende fayle you whan ye be in the grettist dis-
5 tresse that ever ye were othir shall be. And that penaunce God hath ordayned you for that dede, that he that ye sholde truste moste on of ony man on lyve, he shall leve you there ye shall be slayne.'

'Me forthynkith hit,' seyde kynge Pellynor, 'that thus
10 shall me betyde, but God may well fordo desteny.'

Thus whan the queste was done of the whyght herte the whych folowed sir Gawayne, and the queste of the brachet whych folowed sir Torre, kynge Pellynors son, and the queste of the lady that the knyghte toke away, whych at
15 that tyme folowed kynge Pellynor, than the kynge stab-
44ᵛ lysshed all the knyghtes and gaff them rychesse and londys; and charged them never to do outerage nothir morthir, and allwayes to fle treson, and to gyff mercy unto hym that askith mercy, uppon payne of forfiture [of their] worship
20 and lordship of kynge Arthure for evirmore; and allwayes to do ladyes, damesels, and jantilwomen and wydowes [socour:] strengthe hem in hir ryghtes, and never to enforce them, uppon payne of dethe. Also, that no man take no batayles in a wrongefull quarell for no love ne for no worldis goodis.
25 So unto thys were all knyghtis sworne of the Table Rounde, both olde and younge, and every yere so were the[y] sworne at the hyghe feste of Pentecoste.

EXPLICIT THE WEDDYNG OF KYNG ARTHUR.

7 *C* most truste to   9 hit *not in C*   9–10 *C* that this shalle   10 *C*
fordoo wel   12–13 *C* brachet folowed of syr Tor Pellenors sone   14–15 *C*
awey the whiche kynge Pellinre† at that tyme folowed Thenne   16 *C** all his
knyghtes and gaf them that were of londes not ryche he gaf them londes   17 *C*
doo outragyousyte   18 *C* treason Also by no meane to be cruel but to gyue mercy
19 *W* othir worship   21–23 *C* gentylwymmen socour* vpon payne of dethe (and
wydowes . . . enforce them *omitted†*)   24 *C* for no lawe ne for noo worldes

IV

THE DEATH OF MERLIN

AND

THE WAR WITH THE FIVE KINGS

[Winchester MS., ff. 45ʳ–49ʳ;
Caxton, Book IV, chs. 1–5]

CAXTON'S RUBRICS

† S Badgemagus

SO aftir thes questis of syr Gawayne, syr Tor and kynge
Pellynore, than hit befelle that Merlyon felle in dotage
on the damesell that kynge Pellynore brought to courte;
and she was one of the damesels of the Lady of the Laake,
that hyght Nenyve. But Merlion wolde nat lette her have 5
no reste, but allwayes he wolde be wyth her. And ever she
made Merlion good chere tylle sche had lerned of hym all
maner of thynges that sche desyred; and he was assoted
uppon hir, that he myght nat be from hir.

So on a tyme he tolde to kynge Arthure that he scholde 10
nat endure longe, but for all his craftes he scholde be putte
into the erthe quyk. And so he tolde the kyng many thyngis
that scholde befalle, but allwayes he warned the kyng to
kepe well his swerde and the scawberde, ⌜for he told hym
how the swerde and the scawberde⌝ scholde be stolyn by a 15
woman frome hym that he moste trusted. Also he tolde
kyng Arthure that he scholde mysse hym:

'And yett had ye levir than all youre londis have me agayne.'

'A,' sayde the kyng, 'syn ye knowe of youre evil adventure, purvey for hit, and putt hit away by youre crauftes, 20
that mysseadventure.'

'Nay,' seyde Merlion, 'hit woll not be.'

He departed frome the kyng, and within a whyle the
damesell of the Lake departed, and Merlyon went with her
evermore wheresomever she yeode. And oftyntymes Merlion 25
wolde have had hir prevayly away by his subtyle crauftes.
Than she made hym to swere that he sholde never do none
inchauntemente uppon hir if he wolde have his wil, and so
he swore. Than she and Merlyon wente over the see unto
the londe of Benwyke thereas kyng Ban was kyng, that had 30
grete warre ayenste kyng Claudas.

And there Merlion spake with kyng Bayans wyff, a fayre
lady and a good; hir name was Elayne. And there he saw
yonge Launcelot. And there the queene made grete sorowe

2 *C* it felle   3 *S* to the Courte   4 *C*† damoysels of the lake   5 O¹ *C* Ny-
neue   nat *not in C*   8 *C* maner thynge   11 *C* dure long   14–15 *C** scaubard
for he told hym how the swerd and the scaubard shold   *F* (*Huth Merlin, f. 188b*)
sa boine espee od tout le fuerre   18 *C* to haue   19 evil *not in C*   25 *C* she
wente   32 *C* Bans

for the mortal werre that kyng Claudas made on hir lord
[and on hir lond]is.

45ᵛ   'Take none hevynesse,' seyde Merlyon, 'for this same
chylde yonge Launcelot shall within this twenty yere revenge
5   you on kyng Claudas, that all Crystendom shall speke of hit;
and this same chylde shall be the moste man of worship of
the worlde. And his fyrst name ys Galahad, that know I
well,' seyde Merlyon, 'and syn ye have confermed hym
Launcelot.'

10   'That is trouth,' seyde the quene, 'his name was fyrst
Galahad. A, Merlyon,' seyde the quene, 'shall I lyve to se
my son suche a man of prouesse?'

'Yee, hardely, lady, on my perelle ye shall se hit, and lyve
many wyntirs aftir.'

15   Than sone aftir the lady and Merlyon departed. And by
weyes he shewed hir many wondyrs, and so come into
Cornuayle. And allwayes he lay aboute to have hir maydynhode, and she was ever passynge wery of hym and wolde
have bene delyverde of hym, for she was aferde of hym for
20   cause he was a devyls son, and she cowde not be skyfte of
hym by no meane. And so one a tyme Merlyon ded shew
hir in a roche whereas was a grete wondir and wrought
by enchauntement that went undir a grete stone. So by hir
subtyle worchyng she made Merlyon to go undir that stone
25   to latte hir wete of the mervayles there, but she wrought so
there for hym that he come never oute for all the craufte he
coude do, and so she departed and leffte Merlyon.

(2)   And as kyng Arthure rode to Camelot and helde there
a grete feste with myrth and joy, and sone aftir he returned
30   unto Cardolle. And there come unto Arthure newe tydynges
that the kyng of Denmarke and the kyng of Irelonde, that
was his brothir, and the kyng of the Vale and the kynge
of Sorleyse and the kyng of the Ile of Longtaynse, all these
fyve kynges with a grete oste was entirde into the londis of
35   kyng Arthure and brent and slewe and distroyed clene byfore
hem bothe the citeis and castels, that hit was pité to here.

1–2 *W* hir lordis   *C** her lord and on her landes   *O*¹ hir londis   4 yonge
Launcelot *not in C*†   13 hardely *not in C*   15–16 *C* by the waye
17 *C* Merlyn lay about the lady to   18 *C* fayne wold   20–21 *C* beskyfte
hym   *W* of of   34 *C* the lãd   35 and distroyed *not in C*

'Alas!' seyde Arthure, 'yet had I never reste one monethe **46ʳ**
syne I was kyng crowned of this londe. Now shall I never
reste tylle I mete with tho kyngis in a fayre felde, that I
make myne avow; for my trwe lyege peple shall not be
destroyed in my defaughte. Therefore go with me who so 5
woll, and abyde who that wyll.'

Than kyng Arthure lette wryte unto kyng Pellynor and
prayde hym in all haste to make hym redy 'with suche peple
as we myght lyghtlyeste arere,' and to hyghe hym aftir in
haste. Than all the barownes were wrothe prevayly that the 10
kynge wolde departe so suddaynly; but the kynge by no
meane wolde abyde, but made wrytyng unto them that were
nat ther and bade hyghe them aftir hym suche as were nat at
that tyme at that courte. Than the kynge come to quene
Gwenyver and seyde unto her, 15

'Madame, make you redy, for ye shall go with me, for I
may nat longe mysse you. Ye shall cause me to be the more
hardy, what adventure so befalle me; yette woll I nat wyghte
my lady to be in no joupardye.'

'Sir,' she seyde, 'I am at youre commaundemente, and shall 20
be redy at all tymes.'

So on the morne the kyng and the quene departed with
suche felyship as they had and come into the North, into a
forerste besyde Humbir, and there lodged hem. So whan this
worde come unto the fyve kynges abovynseyde that Arthure 25
was besyde Humbir in a foreste, so there was a knyght, brothir
unto one of the fyve kynges, that gaff hem suche counseyle:

'Ye knowe well that sir Arthur hath the floure of chevalry
of the worlde with hym, and hit preved by the grete batayle
he did with the eleven kynges. And therefore hyghe ye unto 30
hym nyght and day tyll that we be nyghe hym, for the lenger
he taryeth the bygger he is, and we ever the weyker. And he **46ᵛ**
is so corageous of hymself that he is com to the felde with
lytyll peple, and therefore lette us sette uppon hym or day,
and we shall sle downe of his knyghtes that none shall helpe 35
other of them.'

5 Therefore *not in C*   9 *C* rere   14 *C* in the Courte   15–16 *C* sayd lady
make   18 *C* me I wille   21 *C** redy what tyme so ye be redy   24–25 *C* the
word & tydynge came   27 *C* this counceille   29 *C* as it is   35–36 *C*
knyghtes ther shal none escape

(3)   Soo unto this counseyle these five kynges assented, and
so they passed forth with hir oste thorow North Walys and
come uppon Arthure be nyght and sette uppon his oste as
the kynge and his knyghtes were in theire pavylyons. So
5 kynge Arthure was unarmed and leyde hym to reste with
his quene Gwenyvere.

'Sir,' seyde sir Kayyus, hit is nat beste we be unarmed.'

'We shall have no nede,' seyde sir Gawayne and sir Gryflet
that lay in a lytyll pavylyon by the kynge.

10   So with that they harde a grete noyse and many cryed
'Treson!'

'Alas!' seyde Arthure, 'we be betrayed! Unto armys,
felowys!' than he cryed.

So they were armed anone at all poyntes. Than come
15 there a wounded knyght unto the kynge and seyde,

'Sir, save youreself and my lady the quene, for oure oste is
destroyed, and slayne is much of oure people.'

So anone the kynge and the quene and the three knyghtes
toke hir horses and rode toward Humbir to passe over hit,
20 and the water was so rowghe that they were aferde to passe
over hit.

'Now may ye chose,' seyde kynge Arthure, 'whethir ye
woll abyde and take the adventure on this syde, for and ye
be takyn they wol sle you.'

25   'Yet were me lever to dey in this watir than to falle in youre
enemyes handis,' seyde the quene, 'and there to be slayne.'

And as they stode talkyng sir Kayus saw the fyve kynges
47ʳ commynge on horsebak by hemself alone, wyth hir sperys
in hir hondis, evyn towarde hem.

30   'Lo,' seyde sir Kayus, 'yondir be tho fyve kynges. Lette
us go to them and macche hem.'

'That were foly,' seyde sir Gawayne, 'for we ar but four,
and they be fyve.'

'That is trouth,' seyde sir Gryfflette.

35   'No force,' seyd sir Kayus. 'I woll undirtake for two of
the beste of hem, and than may ye three undirtake for all the
othir three.'

And therewithall sir Kay lette his horse renne as faste as he myght to encountir with one of them, and strake one of the kynges thorow the shelde and also the body a fadom, that the kynge felle to the erthe starke dede. That sawe sir Gawayne and ran unto anothir kyng so harde that he smote 5 hym downe and thorow the body with a spere, that he felle to the erthe dede. Anone sir Arthure ran to anothir and smote hym thorow the body with a spere, that he fell to the erthe dede. Than sir Gryfflet ran to the fourth kynge and gaff hym suche a falle that his necke brake in sondir. Than sir Kay 10 ran unto the fyfth kynge and smote hym so harde on the helme that the stroke clave the helme and hede to the erthe.

'That was well stryken,' seyde kynge Arthur, 'and worship-fully haste thou holde thy promyse; therefore I shall honoure the whyle that I lyve.'   15

And therewithall they sette the quene in a barge into Humbir. But allwayes quene Gwinyvere praysed sir Kay for his dedis and seyde,

'What lady that ye love and she love you nat agayne, she were gretly to blame. And amonge all ladyes,' seyde the 20 quene, 'I shall bere your noble fame, for ye spake a grete worde and fulfylled hit worshipfully.'

And therewith the quene departed. Than the kynge and the three knyghtes rode into the forer[s]te, for there they supposed to here of them that were ascapid, and there founde 25   **47ᵛ** the moste party of his peple, and tolde hem how the fyve kynges were dede.

'And therefore lette us holde us togedyrs tyll hit be day, and whan hir oste have aspyed that their chyfteynes be slayne they woll make such dole that they shall nat helpe hemself.'   30

And ryght as the kynge seyde, so hit was, for whan they founde the fyve kynges dede they made such dole that they felle downe of there horsis. And therewithall com in kyng Arthure but with a fewe peple and slewe on the ryght honde

2–3 *C* myghte and strake one of them thorow   6 downe and *not in C*   6–7 with a spere that he felle to the erthe dede *not in C*   7–10 *W* Oᴵ dede Than sir Gryfflet . . . brake in sondir. Anone sir Arthure . . . erthe dede. Than   *C** And ther with all kyng Arthur . . . erthe dede Thenne' syr Gryflet . . . brake   10 in sondir *not in C*   12 *C* and the hede   20 all *not in C*   24 *W* forerte   26 *W* the moste party of the fyve kynges (the moste party *is repeated from previous line*)   26 *C* hem all how   30 *C* shalle not mowe helpe   33 *C* fell fro their   in *not in C*

and the lyffte honde, that well nye there ascaped no man,
but all were slayne to the numbir of thirty thousand. And
whan the batayle was all ended the kynge kneled downe and
thanked God mekely. And than he sente for the quene.
5 And anone she was com and made grete joy of the over-
commynge of that batayle.

(4)   Therewithall come one to kynge Arthure and tolde hym
that kynge Pellynore was within three myle with a grete oste.
And [so he] seyde, 'Go unto hym and let hym undirstonde
10 how we have spedde.' So within a whyle kyng Pellynore com
with a grete oste and salewed the peple and the kynge, and
there was grete joy on every syde. Than the kynge let serch
how many peple he had slayne, and there was founde but
lytyll paste two hondred men slayne and eyght knyghtes of
15 the Table Rounde in their pavylyons. Than the kynge lat
rere and devyse, in the same place thereas the batayle was
done and made, a fayre abbay, and endewed hit with grete
lyvelode, and let calle hit the Abbay of La Beale Adventure.

But whan som of them come into there contrayes thereas
20 the fyve kynges were kynges, and tolde hem how they were
slayne, there was made grete dole. And all the kynge Arthurs
enemyes, as the kynge of North Walis and the kynges of the
48ʳ Northe, knewe of this batayle; they were passynge hevy.
And so the kynge retourned unto Camelot in haste. And
25 whan he was com to Camelot he called kyng Pellynore unto
hym and seyde,

'Ye undirstonde well that we have loste eyght knyghtes
of the beste of the Table Rounde, and by youre advyse we
must chose eyght knyghtes of the beste we may fynde in this
30 courte.'

'Sir,' seyde Pellynore, 'I shall counsayle you aftir my
conceyte the beste wyse. There ar in youre courte full noble
knyghtes bothe of olde and yonge. And be myne advyse ye
shall chose half of the olde and half of the yonge.'

35   'Whych be the olde?' seyde kynge Arthure.

'Sir, mesemyth kynge Uryence that hath wedded youre

---

5 *C* and soone she   13 *C* how moche people ther was slayne   17 and made
not in C   23 *C* wyste of   25 *W* Camelot and he   28–29 *C* we wille chese vii
ageyne of the   32 wyse *not in C*   36 *C* Syre said kynge Pellinore mesemeth
that kynge

sistir Morgan le Fay, and the Kynge of the Lake, and sir
Hervyse de Revell, a noble knyght, and sir Galagars the
fourthe.'

'This is well devysed,' seyde Arthure, 'and ryght so shall
hit be. Now, whyche ar the four yonge knyghtes?'   5

'Sir, the fyrste is sir Gawayne, youre nevew, that is as
good a knyght of his tyme as is ony in this londe. And the
secunde as mesemyth beste is sir Gryfflette le Fyse de Du,
that is a good knyght and full desyrous in armys, and who
may se hym lyve, he shall preve a good knyght. And the   10
thirde as mesemyth ys well worthy to be one of the Table
Rounde, sir Kay the Senesciall, for many tymes he hath
done full worshipfully. And now at youre laste batayle he
dud full honorably for to undirtake to sle two kynges.'

'Be my hede,' seyde Arthure, 'ye sey soth. He is beste   15
worthy to be a knyght of [the] Rounde Table of ony that is
rehersed yet and he had done no more prouesse his lyve
dayes.'

'Now,' seyde kynge Pellynore, 'chose you of two knyghtes   (5)
that I shall reherce whyche is most worthy, of sir Bagdemagus   20
and sir Tor, my son; but for because he is my son I may nat
prayse hym, but ellys and he were nat my son I durste say   48ᵛ
that of his age there is nat in this londe a better knyght than
he is, nother of bettir condycions, and loth to do ony wronge
and loth to take ony wronge.'   25

'Be my hede,' seyde Arthure, 'he is a passyng good knight
as ony ye spake of this day. That wote I well,' seyde the
kynge, 'for I have sene hym proved; but he seyth but lytil,
but he doth much more, for I know none in all this courte,
and he were as well borne on his modir syde as he is on   30
youre syde, that is lyke hym of prouesse and of myght.
And therefore I woll have hym at this tyme and leve sir
Bagdemagus tyll anothir tyme.'

So whan they were chosyn by the assent of the barouns, so
were there founden in hir seges every knyghtes name that   35
here ar reherced. And so were they sette in hir seges, whereof

5 *C* kny3tes said Arthur   6 *C* Syre said Pellinore the   8 *C* † fyse the dene
F (*Huth Merlin, f. 195b*) li fiex Dou (*var.* Do)   11 worthy *not in C*   15 ye
sey soth *not in C*   16–17 *C* ye haue reherced and   19–20 *C* Pellenore I shalle putte
to yow two knyghtes and ye shalle chese whiche is moost worthy that is Syr Bagdemagus   28 *C* seyth lytyll   34 *C* of alle the

sir Bagdemagus was wondirly wrothe that sir Tor was
avaunced afore hym. And therefore soddeynly he departed
frome the courte and toke his squyre with hym and rode
longe in a foreste tyll they come to a crosse, and there he
5 alyght and seyde his prayers devoutely. The meanewhyle
his squyre founde wretyn uppon the crosse that Bagdemagus
sholde never retourne unto the courte agayne tyll he had
wonne a knyght of the Table Rounde body for body.

'Loo,' seyde his squyer, 'here I fynde wrytyng of you;
10 therefore I rede you, returne agayne to the courte.'

'That shall I never,' seyde Bagdemagus, 'tyll men speke
of me ryght grete worship, and that I be worthy to be a
kn[y]ght of the Rounde Table.'

And so he rode forth, and there by the way he founde a
15 braunche of holy herbe that was the signe of the Sancgreall,
and no knyght founde no suche tokyns but he were a good
49ʳ lyver and a man of prouesse.

So as sir Bagdemagus rode to se many adventures, so hit
happed hym to come to the roche thereas the Lady of the
20 Lake had put Merlyon undir the stone, and there he herde
hym make a grete dole; wherefore sir Bagdemagus wolde
have holpyn hym, and wente unto the grete stone, and hit was
so hevy that an hondred men myght nat lyffte hit up. Whan
Merlyon wyste that he was there, he bade hym leve his
25 laboure, for all was in vayne: for he myght never be holpyn
but by her that put hym there. And so Bagdemagus departed
and dud many adventures and preved aftir a full good knyght,
and come ayen to the courte and was made knyght of the
Rounde Table. So on the morne there befelle new tydyngis
30 and many othir adventures.

1 *W* Bagdemagus tyll anothir tyme   *A repetition of p. 131, line 33*   4 he
not in C   8 *C* a knyȝtes body of the round table   9 *C* lo syr
11 *S* Bagdemagus by men   16 *C* founde suche   17 and a man of
prouesse *not in C*   22–23 *C*† he was so heuy   24 hym *not in C*   26 *W* hir her
30 many *not in C*

V

ARTHUR AND ACCOLON

[Winchester MS., ff. 49ʳ–58ʳ;
Caxton, Book IV, chs. 6–15]

CAXTON'S RUBRICS

T HAN hit befelle that Arthure and many of his knyghtes **49ʳ** (6) rode on huntynge into a grete foreste. And hit happed kynge Arthure and kynge Uryence and sir Accalon of Gawle folowed a grete harte; for they three were well horsed, and so they chaced so faste that within a whyle they three were 5 more than ten myle from her felyshep. And at the laste they chaced so sore that they slewe hir horsis undirnethe them; and the horses were so fre that they felle downe dede. Than were all three on foote and ever they saw the harte before them passynge wery and inboced. 10

'What shall we do?' seyde kynge Arthure, 'we ar harde bestadde.'

'Lette us go on foote,' seyde kynge Uryence, 'tyll we may mete with somme lodgyng.'

Than were they ware of the harte that lay on a grete watir 15 banke, and a brachette bytyng on his throte; and mo othir houndis come aftir. Than kynge Arthure blewe the pryce **49ᵛ** and dyght the harte. Than the kynge loked aboute the worlde and sawe before hym in a grete water a lytyll shippe all apparayled with sylke downe to the watir. And the shippe 20 cam ryght unto them and landed on the sandis. Than Arthure wente to the banke and loked in and saw none erthely creature therein.

'Sirs,' seyde the kynge, 'com thens and let us se what is in this shippe.' 25

So at the laste they wente into the shippe all three, and founde hit rychely behanged with cloth of sylke. So by that tyme hit was durke nyght, there suddeynly was about them an hondred torchis sette uppon all the shyppe-bordis, and hit gaff grete lyght. And therewithall there come twelve fayre 30 damesels and salued kynge Arthure on hir kneis, and called hym be his name and seyde he was ryght wellcom, and suche chere as they had he sholde have of the beste. Than the kynge thanked hem fayre. Therewythall they ledde the kynge and his felawys into a fayre chambir, and there was 35

---

6 more *not in C F* (*Huth Merlin, f. 197c*) ot plus alé de dis liues englesques   8 and the horses were so fre that they felle downe dede *not in C* (*see note*)   10 *C* and enbusshed   26 at the laste *not in C*   *C* wente in al   29 *C* the sydes of the shyp bordes   30 *C* cam out   35 *C* his two felawes

a clothe leyde rychely beseyne of all that longed to a table,
and there were they served of all wynes and metys that they
coude thynke of. But of that the kynge had grete mervayle,
for he never fared bettir in his lyff as for one souper.

5   And so whan they had souped at her leyser kyng Arthure
was lad into a chambir, a rycher besene chambir sawe he
never none; and so was kynge Uryence se[r]ved and lad
into such anothir chambir; and sir Accolon was lad into the
thirde chambir passyng rychely and well besayne. And so
10   were they leyde in their beddis easly, and anone they felle
on slepe and slepte merveylously sore all the nyght.

And on the morne kynge Uryence was in Camelot abedde
in his wyves armys, Morgan le Fay. And whan he woke he
50ᵣ had grete mervayle how he com there, for on the evyn before
15   he was two dayes jurney frome Camelot. And whan kyng
Arthure awoke he founde hymself in a durke preson, heryng
aboute hym many complayntes of wofull knyghtes.

(7)   'What ar ye that so complayne?' seyde kyng Arthure.

'We bene here twenty knyghtes presoners, and som of us
20   hath layne here eyght yere, and som more and somme lesse.'

'For what cause?' seyde Arthure.

'We shall tell you,' seyde the knyghtes.

'This lorde of this castell his name is sir Damas, and he is
the falsyst knyght that lyvyth, and full of treson, and a very
25   cowarde as [ony] lyvyth. And he hath a yonger brothir,
a good knyght of prouesse, and his name is sir Oughtlake.
And this traytoure Damas, the elder brother, woll geff hym
no parte of his londis but as sir Outlake kepyth thorow
prouesse of his hondis. And so he kepith frome hym a full
30   fayre maner and a rych, and therein sir Outlake dwellyth
worshypfully and is well beloved with all peple. And this
sir Damas oure mayster is a[s] evyll beloved, for he is withoute
mercy, and he is a cowarde, and grete warre hath bene
betwyxte them. But Outlake hath ever the bettir, and ever
35   he proferyth sir Damas to fyght for the lyvelode, body for
body, but he woll nat of hit, other ellys to fynde a knyght
to fyght for hym. Unto that sir Damas hath grauntid to

---

3 *C*† thynke of that the kynge   19 *C* prysoners sayd they   20 *C* seuen yer
28 *C* noo parte of his lyuelode but   31 *C* biloued of al peple   34 *C* them
bothe   36 *C* wylle not doo other

fynde a knyght, but he is so evyll beloved and hated that
there is no knyght woll fyght for hym. And whan Damas
saw this, that there was never a knyght wolde fyght for hym,
he hath dayly layne a wayte wyth many a knyght with hym
and takyn all the knyghtes in this contray to se and aspye 5
hir aventures: he hath takyn hem by force and brought hem
to his preson. And so toke he us severally, as we rode on oure 50ᵛ
adventures, and many good knyghtes hath deyde in this
preson for hunger, to the numbir of eyghtene knyghtes. And
yf ony of us all that here is or hath bene wolde have foughtyn 10
with his brother Outlake he wolde have delyverde us; but
for because this Damas ys so false and so full of treson we
wolde never fyght for hym to dye for hit, and we be so megir
for hungir that unnethe we may stonde on oure fete.'

'God delyver you for His grete mercy!' 15

Anone withall come a damesel unto Arthure and asked
hym, 'What chere?'

'I can nat say,' seyde Arthure.

'Sir,' seyde she, 'and ye woll fyght for my lorde ye shall
be delyverde oute of preson, and ellys ye ascape never with 20
the lyff.'

'Now,' seyde Arthure, 'that is harde. Yet had I lever
fyght with a knyght than to dey in preson. Wyth this,' seyde
Arthure, 'I may be delyverde and all thes presoners, I woll
do the batayle.' 25

'Yes,' seyde the damesell.

'Than I am redy,' seyde Arthure, 'and I had horse and
armoure.'

'Ye shall lak none,' seyde the damesell.

'Mesemethe, damesell, I shold have sene you in the courte 30
of Arthure.'

'Nay,' seyde the damesell, 'I cam never there. I am the
lordis doughter of this castell.'

Yet was she false, for she was one of the damesels of
Morgan le Fay. Anone she wente unto sir Damas and tolde 35
hym how he wolde do batayle for hym, and so he sente for
Arthure. And whan he com he was well coloured and well

2 *C* there nys neuer a knyght   4 *C* many knyghtes   7 *C* seueratly
13-14 *C* soo lene for   15 *C* his mercy sayd Arthur   18 *C* sayd he   20 with
not in C   22-23 *C* leuer to fyghte

made of his lymmes, that all knyghtes that sawe hym seyde
hit were pité that suche a knyght sholde dey in preson. So
sir Damas and he were agreed that he sholde fyght for hym
uppon this covenaunte, that all the othir knyghtes sholde be
5 delyverde. And unto that was sir Damas sworne unto Arthur
and also he to do the batayle to the uttermoste. And with
51ʳ that all the twenty knyghtes were brought oute of the durke
preson into the halle and delyverde, and so they all abode to
se the batayle.

(8) 10 Now turne we unto Accalon of Gaule, that whan he awoke
he founde hymself by a depe welles syde within half a foote,
in grete perell of deth. And there com oute of that fountayne
a pype of sylver, and oute of that pype ran water all on hyghe
in a stone of marbil. Whan sir Accolon sawe this he blyssed
15 hym and seyde, 'Jesu, save my lorde kynge Arthure and
kynge Uryence, for thes damysels in this shippe hath betrayed us. They were fendis and no women. And if I may
ascape this mysadventure I shall distroye them, all that I
may fynde of thes false damysels that faryth thus with theire
20 inchauntementes.'

And ryght with that there com a dwarf with a grete
mowthe and a flatte nose, and salewed sir Accalon and tolde
hym how he cam fromme quene Morgan le Fay.

'And she gretys yow well and byddyth you be of stronge
25 herte, for ye shall fyght to-morne wyth a knyght at the houre
of pryme. And therefore she hath sent the Excalebir, Arthurs
swerde, and the scawberde, and she byddyth you as ye love
her that ye do that batayle to the uttirmoste withoute ony
mercy, lyke as ye promysed hir whan ye spoke laste togedir in
30 prevyté. And what damesell that bryngyth her the kynges
hede whyche ye shall fyght withall, she woll make hir a
quene.'

'Now I undirstonde you,' seyde Accalon. 'I shall holde
that I have promysed her, now I have the swerde. Sir, whan
35 sawe ye my lady Morgan le Fay?'

'Ryght late,' seyde the dwarff.

6 he *not in* C†   8 *W* Oⁱ delyvered hem   11 *W* with with in   17 *C* were
deuyls and   18–19 *C* destroye all where I may fynde these   19–20 *C* that
vsen enchaũtementys   22–23 *C* and said how   26 *C* sente yow here Excalibur
28 *C* doo the batail   *S omits* the   29 *C* had promysed   laste *not in* C
30–31 the knyghtes hede   33 *C* yow wel sayd

Than Accalon toke hym in his armys and sayde, 'Re-commaunde me unto my lady the quene and telle hir all shall be done that I promysed hir, and ellis I woll dye for hit. Now I suppose,' seyde Accalon, 'she hath made all this crauftis and enchauntemente for this batayle.'   5 **51ᵛ**

'Sir, ye may well beleve hit,' seyde the dwarff.

Ryght so there come a knyght and a lady wyth six squyers, and salewed Accalon and prayde hym to aryse and com and reste hym at his maner. And so Accalon mounted uppon a voyde horse and wente with the [knyght] 10 unto a fayre maner by a pryory, and there he had passyng good chere.

Than sir Damas sente unto his brothir Outelake and bade make hym redy be to-morne at the houre of pryme, and to be in the felde to fyght with a good knyght; for he had 15 founden a knyght that was redy to do batayle at all poyntis. Whan this worde come to sir Outlake he was passyng hevy, for he was woundid a lytyll tofore thorow bothe his thyghes with a glayve, and he made grete dole; but as he was wounded he wolde a takyn the batayle an honde.   20

So hit happed at that tyme, by the meanys of Morgan le Fay, Accalon was with sir Oughtlake lodged. And whan he harde of that batayle and how Oughtlake was wounded he seyde that he wolde fyght for hym because that Morgan le Fay had sent hym Excaliber and the shethe for to fyght with 25 the knyght on the morne. This was the cause sir Accalon toke the batayle uppon hym. Than sir Outelake was passyng glad and thanked sir Accolon with all his herte that he wolde do so muche for hym. And therewithall sir Outlake sente unto his brother sir Damas that he hadde a knyght redy that 30 sholde fyght with hym in the felde be the houre of pryme. So on the morne sir Arthure was armed and well horsed, and asked sir Damas,

'Whan shall we to the felde?'

'Sir,' seyde sir Damas, 'ye shall hyre masse.'   35

And so Arthur herde a masse, and whan masse was done

---

2 *C* my lady Quene   6 Sir *not in C*   8 *C* for to aryse   10 *W* the kyng *C** the knyghte   16 *C* a good knyght   19 *C* with a speret   *F d'une glaive par mi la cuisse*   27 *C* bataille on hand thenne   29–30 *W* sente unto   *C** sente word vnto   30–31 *C* knyȝte þᵗ for hym shold be redy in the

52ʳ there com a squyre ⌈on a grete hors⌉ and asked sir Damas
if his knyght were redy, 'for oure k[n]yght is redy in the felde.'
Than sir Arthure mounted uppon horsebak. And there were
all the knyghtes and comons of that contray, and so by all
5   their advyces there was chosyn twelve good men of the
contrey for to wayte uppon the two knyghtes.

And ryght as Arthure was on horsebak, there com a
damesel fromme Morgan le Fay and brought unto sir
Arthure a swerde lyke unto Excaliber and the scawberde,
10 and seyde unto Arthure, 'She sendis here youre swerde for
grete love.' And he thanke hir and wente hit had bene so;
but she was falce, for the swerde and the scawberde was
counterfete and brutyll and false.

(9)   Than they dressed hem on two partyes of the felde and
15 lette their horses ren so faste that aythir smote other in the
myddis of the shelde, and their sperys helde, that bothe horse
and man wente to the erthe, and than they stert up bothe and
pulde oute their swerdis.

The meanewhyle that they were thus at the batayle com
20 the Damesel of the Lake into the felde that put Merlyon
undir the stone. And she com thidir for the love of kynge
Arthur, for she knew how Morgan le Fay had ordayned for
Arthur shold have bene slayne that day, and therefore she
come to save his lyff.

25   And so they went egerly to the batayle and gaff many
grete strokes. But allwayes Arthurs swerde bote nat lyke
Accalons swerde, and for the moste party every stroke that
Accalon gaff he wounded sir Arthure sore, that hit was
mervayle he stood, and allwayes his blood felle frome hym
30 faste. Whan Arthure behelde the grounde so sore bebledde
he was dismayde. And than he demed treson, that his
swerde was chonged, for his swerde bote nat steele as hit
52ᵛ was wonte to do. Therefore he dred hym sore to be dede, for
ever hym semyd that the swerde in Accalons honde was
35 Excaliber, for at every stroke that Accalon stroke he drewe
bloode on Arthure.

---

1 *W* a squyre and and asked   *C** a squyer on a grete hors & asked   *F* (*Huth
Merlin, f. 208a*) sour un grant ronchin   5 their *not in C*   10 *C* Morgan
le fey sendeth   14 *C* on bothe partyes   16 *C* shelde with their speres hede†
22–23 *C* had soo ordeyned that kynge Arthur shold   32 *C* boote not styl†

'Now, knyght,' seyde Accolon unto Arthure, 'kepe the well frome me!'

But Arthure answered not agayne, but gaff hym such a buffette on the helme that he made hym to stowpe nyghe fallyng to the erthe. Than sir Accalon wythdrewe hym a 5 lytyll, and com on wyth Excaliber on heyght, and smote sir Arthure suche a buffette that he fylle ny to the erthe. Than were they bothe wrothe oute of mesure and gaff many sore strokis.

But allwayes sir Arthure loste so muche bloode that hit 10 was mervayle he stoode on his feete, but he was so full of knyghthode that he endured the payne. And sir Accolon loste nat a dele of blood; therefore he waxte passynge lyght, and sir Arthure was passynge fyeble and [wente] veryly to have dyed, but for all that he made countenaunce as he 15 myght welle endure and helde Accolon as shorte as he myght. But Accolon was so bolde because of Excalyber that he wexed passyng hardy. But all men that behelde hem seyde they sawe nevir knyght fyght so well as Arthur ded, conciderynge the bloode that he had bled; but all that peple 20 were sory that thes two brethirne wolde nat accorde.

So allwayes they fought togedir as fers knyghtes, and at the laste kynge Arthure withdrew hym a lytyll for to reste hym, and sir Accolon callyd hym to batayle and seyde, 'Hit is no tyme for me to suffir the to reste,' and therewith he 25 come fersly uppon Arthure. But Arthur therewith was wroth for the bloode that he had loste, and smote Accolon on hyghe uppon the helme so myghtyly that he made hym **53ᴿ** nyghe falle to the erthe; and therewith Arthurs swerde braste at the crosse and felle on the grasse amonge the 30 bloode, and the pomell and the sure handyls he helde in his honde. Whan kynge Arthure saw that, he was in grete feare to dye, but allwayes he helde up his shelde and loste no grounde nother batyd no chere.

Than sir Accolon began with wordis of treson and seyde, 35 (10) 'Knyght, thou art overcom and mayste nat endure, and

8 oute of mesure *not in C*   *C* gaf eche other   12 *C* that knyghtly he endured   14 *W* and veryly   *C** and wende veryly   15–16 *C* as though he myght endure   20–21 *C†* he bled Soo was all the peple sory for hym but the two bretheren   22–23 at the last *not in C*   29 *C* to falle   32 *C* handes   36 *S* maxste not

also thou art wepynles, and loste thou haste much of thy bloode, and I am full loth to sle the. Therefore yelde the to me recreaunte.'

'Nay,' seyde sir Arthur, 'I may nat so, for I promysed by
5 the feythe of my body to do this batayle to the uttermuste whyle my lyff lastith, and therefore I had levir to dye with honour than to lyve with shame. And if hit were possible for me to dye an hondred tymes, I had levir to dye so oufte than yelde me to the. For though I lak wepon, yett shall I
10 lak no worshippe, and if thou sle me wepynles that shall be thy shame.'

'Welle,' seyde Accolon, 'as for that shame I woll nat spare. Now kepe the fro me, for thou art but a dede man!' And therewith Accolon gaff hym such a stroke that he fell nyghe
15 to the erthe, and wolde have had Arthure to have cryed hym mercy. But sir Arthure preced unto Accolon with his shelde and gaff hym wyth the pomell in his honde suche a buffette that he reled three strydes abake.

Whan the Damesell of the Lake behelde Arthure, how
20 full of prouesse his body was, and the false treson that was wrought for hym to have had hym slayne, she had grete peté that so good a knyght and such a man of worship sholde so be destroyed. And at the nexte stroke sir Accolon
53ᵛ stroke at hym suche a stroke that by the damesels inchaunte-
25 mente the swerde Excaliber fell oute of Accalons honde to the erthe, and therewithall sir Arthure lyghtly lepe to hit and gate hit in his honde, and forthwithall he knew hit that hit was his swerde Excalyber.

'A,' seyde Arthure, 'thou haste bene frome me all to longe
30 and muche damage hast thou done me!'

And therewith he aspyed the scawberde by his syde, and suddaynly he sterte to hym and pulled the scawberte frome hym and threw hit frome hym as fer as he myght throw hit.

'A, sir knyght,' seyde kynge Arthur, 'this day haste thou
35 done me grete damage wyth this swerde. Now ar ye com unto youre deth, for I shall nat warraunte you but ye shall

---

3 *C* as recreaunt   4 *C* haue promysed   6 *C* whyle me lasteth the lyf
9 *C* wepen I shalle   12 *C* for the shame   18 *C* that he went   24 *C*
stroke hym   24–25 *W* inchauntemente that the swerde   *C** enchauntement
the swerd   27 *C* knewe that   29 *C* & sayd thow   31 *C* hangyng by

be as well rewarded with this swerde or ever we departe as
ye have rewarded me, for muche payne have ye made me
to endure and much bloode have y loste.'

And therewith sir Arthure raced on hym with all his myght
and pulde hym to the erthe, and than raced of his helme and 5
gaff hym suche a buffette on his hede that the bloode com
oute at his erys, nose, and mowthe.

'Now woll I sle the!' seyde Arthure.

'Sle me ye may well,' seyde sir Accolon, 'and hit please
you, for ye ar the beste knyght that ever I founde, and I se 10
well that God is with you. But for I promysed,' seyde
Accolon, 'to do this batayle to the uttirmyst and never to
be recreaunte while I leved, therefore shall I never yelde me
with my mowthe, but God do with my body what He woll.'

Than sir Arthure remembirde hym and thought he 15
scholde have sene this knyght.

'Now telle me,' seyde Arthure, 'or I woll sle the, of what
contrey ye be and of what courte.'

'Sir knyght,' seyde sir Accolon, 'I am of the ryall courte
of kyng Arthure, and my name is Accolon of Gaule.'   20

Than was Arthure more dismayde than he was tofore- 54ʳ
honde, for than he remembirde hym of his sister Morgan
le Fay and of the enchauntement of the shippe.

'A, sir k[n]yght, I pray you [telle me] who gaff you this
swerde and by whom ye had hit.'   25 (11)

Than sir Accolon bethought hym and seyde, 'Wo worthe
this swerde! for by hit I have gotyn my dethe.'

'Hit may well be,' seyde the kynge.

'Now, sir,' seyde Accolon, 'I woll tell you: this swerde
hath bene in my kepynge the moste party of this twelve- 30
monthe, and Morgan le Fay, kyng Uryence wyff, sente hit
me yestirday by a dwarfe to the entente to sle kynge Arthure,
hir brothir; for ye shall undirstonde that kynge Arthur ys
the man in the worlde that she hatyth moste, because he is
moste of worship and of prouesse of ony of hir bloode. 35
Also she lovyth me oute of mesure as paramour, and I hir
agayne. And if she myght bryng hit aboute to sle Arthure

---

3 *W* ye loste   4, 5 *C* russhed   6 *C* the hede   19 ryall *not in C*
24 *C* knyght sayd he I   32 *C* this entente that I shold slee   32-33 entente
. . . undirstonde *repeated in C*

by hir crauftis, she wolde sle hir husbonde kynge Uryence
lyghtly. And than had she devysed to have me kynge in
this londe and so to reigne, and she to be my quene. But that
is now done,' seyde Accolon, 'for I am sure of my deth.'

5   'Well,' seyde kyng Arthure, 'I fele by you ye wolde have
bene kynge of this londe, yett hit had be grete damage to
have destroyed your lorde,' seyde Arthur.

    'Hit is trouthe,' seyde Accolon, 'but now I have tolde
you the trouthe, wherefore I pray you tell me of whens ye
10 ar and of what courte.'

    'A, Accolon,' seyde kynge Arthure, 'now y let the wete that
I am kynge Arthure that thou haste done grete damage t[o].'

    Whan Accolon herd that he cryed on-lowde, 'Fayre swete
lorde, have mercy on me, for I knew you nat.'

15   'A, sir Accolon,' seyde kynge Arthur, 'mercy thou shalt
have because I fele be thy wordis at this tyme thou knewest
54ᵛ me nat, but I fele by thy wordis that thou haste agreed to the
deth of my persone, and therefore thou art a traytoure; but
I wyte the the less for my sistir Morgan le Fay by hir false
20 crauftis made the to agré to hir fals lustes. But I [shall] be
sore avenged uppon hir, that all Crystendom shall speke of
hit. God knowyth I have honoured hir and worshipped hir
more than all my kyn, and more have I trusted hir than my
wyff and all my kyn aftir.'

25   Than kynge Arthure called the kepers of the felde and seyde,
    'Sirres, commyth hyder, for here ar we two knyghtes that
have foughtyn unto grete damage unto us bothe, and lykly
eche of us to have slayne other, and had ony of us knowyn
othir, here had bene no batayle nothir no stroke stryken.'

30   Than all alowde cryed Accolon unto all the knyghtes and
men that were [there,] and seyde,

    'A, lordis! This knyght that I have foughten withall is
the moste man of prouesse and of worship in the worlde, for

---

2 *C* she me deuysed to be kyng   6 yett *not in C*†   12 *C* Arthur to
whome thou haste done grete dommage   *W* te   16–17 *C* knowest not my
persone But I vnderstand wel by   20 *C* agree and consente   21 *C* her and I
lyue that   23–24 *C* myn owne wyf   27–28 *C** lyke echone of vs to haue slayne
other yf it had happed soo And   29 *W* had had bene   31 *C** were thēne there
gadred to gyder and sayd to them in this manere   32 *C* this noble knyghte
32–33 *C** with all the whiche me sore repenteth is the moste man of prowesse of
manhode and of worship

hit is hymself kynge Arthure, oure al[ther] lyege lorde, and
with myssehappe and mysseadventure have I done this batayle with the lorde and kynge that I am withholdyn withall.'

Than all the peple felle downe on her knees and cryed (12)
kynge Arthure mercy.

'Mercy shall ye have,' seyde Arthure. 'Here may ye se
what soddeyn adventures befallys ouftyn of arraunte
knyghtes, how that I have foughtyn with a knyght of myne
owne unto my grete damage and his bothe. But, syrs, because I am sore hurte and he bothe, and I had grete nede of 10
a lytyll reste, ye shall undirstonde this shall be the opynyon
betwyxte you two brethirne:

'As to the, sir Damas, for whom I have bene champyon
and wonne the felde of this knyght, yett woll I juge. Because 55ʳ
ye, sir Damas, ar called an [o]rgulus knyght and full of 15
vylony, and nat worth of prouesse of youre dedis, therefore
woll I that ye geff unto youre brother all the hole maner
with the apportenaunce undir this fourme, that sir Outelake
holde the maner of you and yerely to gyff you a palfrey to
ryde uppon, for that woll becom you bettir to ryde on than 20
uppon a courser. Also I charge the, sir Damas, uppon
payne of deth, that thou never distresse no knyghtes araunte
that ryde on their adventure, and also that thou restore thyse
twenty knyghtes that thou haste kepte longe presoners of
all theire harmys that they be contente for. And ony of 25
them com to my courte and complayne on the, be my hede,
thou shalt dye therefore!

'Also, sir Oughtlake, as to you, because ye ar named a
good knyght and full of prouesse and trew and jantyll in all
youre dedis, this shall be youre charge I woll gyff you: that in 30
all goodly hast ye com unto me and my courte, and ye shall
be a knyght of myne, and if youre dedis be thereaftir I shall so
proferre you by the grace of God that ye shall in shorte
tyme be in ease as for to lyve as worshipfully as youre brother
Damas.' 35

'God thonke youre largenesse of youre grete goodnesse
and of youre bounté! I shall be frome hens forewarde in all

1 *W* oure all   3 *C* am holden   7 soddeyn *not in C*   11 this shall
be *not in C†*   15 *W* ergulus   25 *C* and yf ony   26 *C* of the
34 *C* ease for   36 grete *not in C*

tymes at your commaundement. For, [sir,' said] sir Oughtlake, 'as God wolde, I was hurte but late with an adventures
knyght thorow bothe the thyghes, and ellys had I done this
batayle with you.'

5 'God wolde,' seyde sir Arthure, 'hit had bene so, for than
had nat I bene hurte as I am. I shall tell you the cause why:
for I had nat bene hurte as I am, had nat bene myne owne
55ᵛ swerde that was stolyn frome me by treson; and this batayle
was ordeyned aforehonde to have slayne me, and so hit was
10 broughte to the purpose by false treson and by enchauntment.'

'Alas,' seyde sir Outlake, 'that is grete pité that ever so
noble a man as ye ar of your dedis and prouesse, that ony
man or woman myght fynde in their hertis to worche ony
treson aghenst you.'

15 'I shall rewarde them,' seyde Arthure. ' Now telle me,'
seyde Arthure, 'how far am I frome Camelot?'

'Sir, ye ar two dayes jurney.'

'I wolde be at som place of worship,' seyde sir Arthur, 'that
I myght reste me.'

20 'Sir,' seyde Outlake, 'hereby is a ryche abbey of youre
elders foundacion, of nunnys, but three myle hens.'

So the kynge toke his leve of all the peple and mounted
uppon horsebak and sir Accolon with hym. And whan they
were com to the abbey he lete fecch lechis and serchid his
25 woundis and sir Accolons bothe. But sir Accolon deyed
within four dayes, for he had bled so much blood that he
myght nat lyve, but kynge Arthure was well recoverde. So
whan Accolon was dede he lette sende hym in an horse-bere
with six knyghtes unto Camelot, and bade 'bere hym unto
30 my systir, Morgan le Fay, and sey that I sende her hym to a
present. And telle hir I have my swerde Excalyber and the
scawberde.' So they departed with the body.

(13) The meanewhyle Morgan le Fay had wente kynge
Arthure had bene dede. So on a day she aspyed kynge
35 Uryence lay on slepe on his bedde, than she callyd unto hir
a mayden of her counseyle and sayde,

2 *C*† wold as I   3 *C** thyes that greued me sore & els   10 *C* by fals
enchauntement   15 *C** Arthur in short tyme by the grace of god Now
17–18 *C* iourney ther fro I wold fayn be at   29 *C* and said bere   35 *C* lay
in his bedde slepynge

'Go fecche me my lordes swerde, for I saw never bettir
tyme to sle hym than now.'

'A, madame,' seyde the damesell, 'and ye sle my lorde ye
can never ascape.'

'Care the not,' sayde Morgan, 'for now I se my tyme is 5 **56ʳ**
beste to do hit, and therefore hyghe the faste and fecche me
the swerde.'

Than this damesell departed and founde sir Uwayne
slepyng uppon a bedde in anothir chambir. So she wente
unt[o] sir Uwayne and awaked hym and bade hym 'aryse and 10
awayte on my lady youre modir, for she woll sle the kynge
youre fadir slepynge on his bedde, for I go to fecch his
swerde.'

'Well,' seyde sir Uwayne, 'go on your way and lette me
dele.'   15

Anone the damesell brought the quene the swerde with
quakyng hondis. And lyghtly she toke the swerde and
pullyd hit oute, and wente boldely unto the beddis syde and
awayted how and where she myght sle hym beste. And as
she hevyd up the swerde to smyte, sir Uwayne lepte unto 20
his modir and caught hir by the honde and seyde,

'A, fende, what wolt thou do? And thou were nat my
modir, with this swerde I sholde smyte of thyne hede! A,'
seyde sir Uwayne, 'men seyde that Merlyon was begotyn of
a fende, but I may say an erthely fende bare me.'   25

'A, fayre son Uwayne, have mercy uppon me! I was
tempted with a fende, wherefore I cry the mercy. I woll nevermore do so. And save my worship and discover me nat!'

'On this covenaunte,' seyde sir Uwayne, 'I woll forgyff
you: so ye woll never be aboute to do such dedis.'   30

'Nay, son, and that I make you assuraunce.'

Then come tydynges unto Morgan le Fay that Accolon (14)
was dede and his body brought unto the chirche, and how
kyng Arthure had his swerde ayen. But whan quene Morgan
wyste that Accolon was dede, she was so sorowfull that nye 35
hir herte to-braste, but bycause she wolde nat hit were **56ᵛ**

5 *C* tyme in the whiche it is   8 and *not in C*   10 *W* unte   16 *C*
brought Morgan the   17 she *not in C*   20 *C* she lyfte vp   24–25 *C* of
a deuylle   25 *C* erthely deuylle   27 *C* with a deuylle   29 *C* forgyue it
31 *C* sone said she   35–36 *C* nere hir

knowyn oute, she kepte hir countenaunce and made no
sembelaunte of dole. But welle sche wyste, and she abode
tylle hir brother Arthure come thydir, there sholde no golde
go for hir lyff. Than she wente unto the quene Gwenyvere
5 and askid hir leve to ryde into hir contrey.

'Ye may abyde,' seyde the quene, 'tyll youre brother the
kynge com home.'

'I may nat, madame,' seyde Morgan le Fay, 'for I have
such hasty tydynges.'

10 'Well,' seyde the quene, 'ye may departe whan ye woll.'

So erely on the morne, or hit was day, she toke hir horse
and rode all that day and moste party of the nyght, and on the
morne by none she com to the same abbey of nonnys whereas
lay kynge Arthure, and she wyste ⟨welle⟩ that he was there.
15 And anone she asked where he was, and they answerde and
seyde how he was leyde hym on his bedde to slepe, 'for he
had but lytyll reste this three nyghtes.'

'Well,' seyde she, 'I charge that none of you awake hym
tyll I do.'

20 And than she alyght of hir horse and thought for to
stele away Excaliber, his swerde. And she wente streyte
unto his chambir, and no man durste disobey hir commaundement. And there she found Arthur aslepe on his bedde,
and Excalyber in his ryght honde naked. Whan she sawe
25 that, she was passyng hevy that she myght nat com by the
swer[d]e withoute she had awaked hym, and than she wyste
welle she had bene dede. So she toke the scawberde and
went hir way to horsebak. When the kynge awoke and
myssed his scawberde, he was wroth, and so he asked who
57ʳ 30 had bene there, and they seyde his sister, quene Morgan le
Fay, had bene there and had put the scawberde undir hir
mantell and is gone.

'Alas,' seyde Arthure, 'falsly have ye wacched me.'

'Sir,' seyde they all, 'we durst nat disobey your sistyrs
35 commaundemente.'

'A,' seyde the kynge, 'lette fecch me the beste horse that

1 *C* oute ward   *C*† countece naun &   2 *C* of sorowe but   8 madame
not in C   9 *C** tydynges that I maye not tary   14–15 *C* & she knowyng
he was there she asked   *W* wyste nat that (*see note*)   15–16 and seyde *not in C*
16 *C* he had leyd   17 *C* had had   28 *C** on horsbak   30–31 le Fay *not
in C*   32 *C* was gone   36–p. 151, l. 1 *C* fetche the best hors maye

may be founde, and bydde sir Outlake arme hym in all hast
and take anothir good horse and ryde with me.'

So anone the kynge and sir Outlake were well armyd and
rode aftir this lady. And so they com be a crosse and founde
a cowherde, and they asked the pore man if there cam ony 5
lady late rydynge that way.

'Sir,' seyde this pore man, 'ryght late com a lady rydynge
this way with a fourty horses, ⌐and to yonder forest she rode.⌐'

And so they folowed faste, and within a whyle Arthur had
a syght of Morgan le Fay. Than he chaced as faste as he 10
myght. Whan she aspyed hym folowynge her, she rode a
grete pace thorow the foreste tyll she com to a playn. And
when she sawe she myght nat ascape she rode unto a lake
thereby and seyde, 'Whatsoever com of me, my brothir shall
nat have this scawberde!' And than she lete throwe the 15
scawberde in the deppyst of the watir. So hit sanke, for hit
was hevy of golde and precious stonys.

Than she rode into a valey where many grete stonys were,
and whan she sawe she muste be overtake, she shope hirself,
horse and man, by enchauntemente unto grete marbyll 20
stonys. And anone withall come kynge Arthure and sir Outlake whereas the kynge myght know his sistir and her men
and one knyght frome another.

'A,' seyde the kynge, 'here may ye se the vengeaunce of
God! And now am I sory this mysaventure is befalle.' 25

And than he loked for the scawberde, but hit wold nat be
founde; so he turned to the abbey there she come fro. So
whan Arthure was gone they turned all their lyknesse as she 57ᵛ
and they were before, and seyde,

'Sirs, now may we go where we wyll.' 30

Than seyde Morgan le Fay, 'Saw ye of Arthure, my (15)
brother?'

'Yee,' seyde hir men, 'and that ye sholde have founde, and
we myght a stered of one stede; for by his amyvestyall
countenaunce [he] wolde have caused us to have fledde.' 35

'I beleve you,' seyde the quene.

6 late *not in* S   8–9 *C** (*see note*) with a xl horses and to yonder forest she rode
Thenne they spored theire horses and folowed   12 *C* gretter paas   20–21 *C* a
grete marbyl stone†   22 *W* myght nat (*see note*)   27 *C* retorned   28 *C*
she torned all in the   31 le Fay *not in C*   33 *C** her knyghtes ryght wel and
34 *W* we me myght   *C* armyuestal (*see note*)   36 *C* said Morgan

So anone after as she rode she mette a knyght ledynge another knyght on horsebake before hym, bounde hande and foote, blyndefelde, to have drowned hym in a fowntayne. Whan she sawe this knyght so bounde she asked,

5 'What woll ye do with that knyght?'

'Lady,' seyde he, 'I woll drowne hym.'

'For what cause?' she asked.

'For I founde hym with my wyff, and she shall have the same deth anone.'

10 'That were pyté,' seyde Morgan le Fay. 'Now, what sey ye, knyght? Is hit trouthe that he seyth of you?'

'Nay, truly, madame, he seyth nat ryght on me.'

'Of whens be ye,' seyde the quene, 'and of what contrey?'

'I am of the courte of kynge Arthure, and my name is
15 Manessen, cosyn unto Accolon of Gaule.'

'Ye sey well, and for the love of hym ye shall be delyverde, and ye shal have youre adversary in the same case that ye were in.'

So this Manessen was loused, and the other kn[y]ght
20 bounde. And anone Manessen unarmed hym and armede hymself in his harneyse, and so mounted on horsebak and the knyght afore hym, and so threw hym in the fountayne and so drowned hym. And than he rode unto Morgan ayen and asked if she wolde onythyng unto Arthure.

25 'Telle hym,' seyde she, 'that I rescewed the nat for the love of hym, but for the love of Accolon, and tell hym I feare hym nat whyle I can make me and myne in lyknesse of stonys,
58ʳ and lette hym wete I can do much more whan I se my tyme.'

And so she departed into the contrey of Gore, and there
30 was she rychely receyved, and made hir castels and townys strong, for allwey she drad muche kyng Arthure.

2 *C* on his hors   4 *C* asked hym   11–12 *C** of yow she said to the knyght that shold be drowned nay truly   16 *C* wel said she and   17–18 *C* caas ye be in   25 seyde she *not in C*   27 *C* me and them that ben with me in   28 much (*C* moche) *not in S*   31 *C* passynge stronge

VI

GAWAIN, YWAIN, AND MARHALT

[*Winchester MS.*, ff. 58^r–70^v;
Caxton, Book IV, chs. 16–29]

CAXTON'S RUBRICS

* *C* Marhans

WHAN the kynge had well rested hym at the abbey he
rode unto Camelot and founde his quene and his
barownes ryght glad of his commyng. And whan they
herde of his stronge adventures, as hit is before rehersed,
they all had mervayle of the falsehede of Morgan le Fay. 5
Many knyghtes wysshed hir brente. Than come Manessen
to courte and told the kynge of his adventure.

'Well,' seyde the kyng, 'she is a kynde sister! I shall so be
avengid on hir and I lyve that all crystendom shall speke of
hit.'   10

So on the morne there cam a damesell on message frome
Morgan le Fay to the kynge, and she brought with hir the
rycheste mantell that ever was sene in the courte, for hit
was sette all full of precious stonys as one myght stonde
by another, and therein were the rycheste stonys that ever 15
the kynge saw. And the damesell seyde,

'Your sister sendyth you this mantell and desyryth that
ye sholde take this gyfte of hir, and what thynge she hath
offended she woll amende hit at your owne plesure.'

When the kyng behelde this mantell hit pleased hym much. 20
He seyde but lytyll. With that come the Damesell of the
Lake unto the kynge and seyde,   (16)

'Sir, I muste speke with you in prevyté.'

'Sey, on,' seyde the kynge, 'what ye woll.'

'Sir,' seyde this damesell, 'putt nat uppon you this mantell 25
tylle ye have sene more, and in no wyse lat hit nat com on
you nother on no knyght of youres tyll ye commaunde the
brynger thereof to putt hit uppon hir.'

'Well,' seyde the kynge, 'hit shall be as you counseyle me.'

And than he seyde unto the damesell that com frome his 30
sister, 'Damesell, this mantell that ye have brought me, I
woll se hit uppon you.'

'Sir,' she seyde, 'hit woll nat beseme me to were a kynges
garmente.'

'Be my hede,' seyde Arthure, 'ye shall were hit or hit 35
com on my bak other on ony mannys bak that here is.'

And so the kynge made to putt hit uppon hir. And

4 hit *not in* C   11 on message *not in* C   14 C as ful   18 C* in what
29 C be done as ye   36 C mans that

forthwithall she fell downe deede and never spoke worde
after, and brente to colys. Than was the kynge wondirly
wroth more than he was toforehande, and seyde unto
kynge Uryence,

5   'My sistir, your wyff, is allway aboute to betray me, and
welle I wote other ye or my nevewe, your son, is accounseyle
with hir to have me distroyed. But as for you,' seyde the
kynge unto kynge Uryence, 'I deme nat gretly that ye be of
counseyle, for Accolon confessed to me his owne mowthe
10 that she wolde have distroyed you as well as me; therefore
y holde you excused. But as for your son sir Uwayne, I holde
hym suspecte. Therefore I charge you, putt hym oute of my
courte.' So sir Uwayne was discharged.

And whan sir Gawayne wyste that, he made hym redy
15 to go with hym, 'for whoso banyshyth my cosyn jarmayne
shall banyshe me.' So they too departed and rode into a
grete foreste, and so they com unto an abbey of monkys,
and there were well logged. Butt whan the kynge wyste
that sir Gawayne was departed frome the courte, there was
20 made grete sorowe amonge all the astatis.

'Now,' seyde Gaherys, Gawaynes brother, 'we have loste
two good knyghtes for the love of one.'

So on the morne they herde the masses in the abbey and
so rode forth tyll they com to the grete foreste. Than was
59ʳ 25 sir Gawayne ware in a valey by a turrette twelve fayre
damesels and two knyghtes armed on grete horses, and the
damesels wente to and fro by a tre. And than was sir
Gawayne ware how there hynge a whyght shelde on that
tre, and ever as the damesels com by hit they spette uppon
(17) 30 hit and som threwe myre uppon the shelde. Than sir Gawayne and sir Uwayne wente and salewed them, and asked
why they dud that dispyte to the shelde.

'Sir,' seyde the damesels, 'we shall telle you. There is a
knyght in this contrey that owyth this whyght shelde, and
35 he is a passyng good man of his hondis, but he hatyth all
ladyes and jantylwomen, and therefore we do all this dyspyte
to that shelde.'

'I shall sey you,' seyde sir Gawayne, 'hit besemyth evyll

---

a good knyght to dispyse all ladyes and jantyllwomen; and
peraventure thoughe he hate you he hath som cause, and
peraventure he lovyth in som other placis ladyes and jantyllwomen and y⟨s⟩ belovyd agayne, and he be suche a man of
prouesse as ye speke of. Now, what is his name?'   5

'Sir,' they seyde, 'his name is sir Marhaus, the kynges son
of Irelonde.'

'I knowe hym well,' seyde sir Uwayne, 'he is a passynge
good knyght as ony on lyve, for I sawe hym onys preved
at a justys where many knyghtes were gadird, and that tyme   10
there myght no man withstonde hym.'

'A,' sayde sir Gawayne, 'damesels, methynke ye ar to
blame, for hit is to suppose he that hyng that shelde there
he woll nat be longe therefro, and than may tho knyghtes
macche hym on horsebak. And that is more youre worshyp   15
than thus to do, for I woll abyde no lenger to se a knyghtes
shelde so dishonoured.'

And therewith sir Gawayne and sir Uwayne departed a
lytyll fro them. And than ware they ware where sir Marhaus
com rydynge on a grete horse streyte toward hem. And   20 **59ᵛ**
whan the twelve damesels sawe sir Marhaus they fledde to
the turret as they were wylde, that som of hem felle by the
way. Than that one of the knyghtes of the towre dressed
his shylde and seyde on hyghe, 'Sir Marhaus, defende the!'
And so they ran togedyrs that the knyght brake his spere on   25
sir Marhaus, but Marhaus smote hym so harde that he brake
his necke and his horse bak. That sawe the other knyght of
the turret and dressed hym to Marhaus, that so egerly they
mette that this knyght of the turret was smyte doune, horse
and man, dede.   30

And than sir Marhaus rode unto his shylde and sawe how   (18, 19)
hit was defoyled, and sayde, 'Of this dispyte of parte I am
avenged. But yet for hir love that gaff me this whyght
shelde I shall were the and hange myne where that was.'
And so he honged hit aboute his necke. Than he rode   35
streyte unto sir Gawayne and to sir Uwayne and asked them

2 cause *not in* C†   3 *W* and &   4 *W* ye   C† to be loued   9 *C* ony
is on   16 to do *not in* C   28–29 *C* they mette so egrely to gyders   30 *C*
stark dede   32–33 *C* despyte I am a parte auengyd But for   34 *C** where
thow was

what they dud there. They answerde hym and seyde they
come frome kynge Arthurs courte for to se aventures.

'Welle,' seyde sir Marhaus, 'here am I redy, an adventures
knyght that woll fulfylle any adventure that ye woll desyre.'
5 And so departyd frome hem to fecche his raunge.

'Late hym go,' seyde sir Uwayne unto sir Gawayne, 'for
he is a passynge good knyght os ony lyvynge. I wolde not
be my wylle that ony of us were macched with hym.'

'Nay,' seyde sir Gawayne, 'nat so! Hit were shame to us
10 and he were nat assayed, were he never so good a knyght.'

'Welle,' seyde sir Uwayne, 'I wolle assay hym before you,
for I am weyker than ye, and yff he smyte me downe than
may ye revenge me.'

So thes two knyghtes come togedir with grete raundom,
60ʳ 15 that sir Uwayne smote sir Marhaus, that his spere braste
in pecis on the shelde. And sir Marhaus smote hym so
sore that horse and man he bare to the erthe, and hurte
sir Uwayne on the lefte syde. Than sir Marhaus turned his
horse and rode thidir as he com fro and made hym redy
20 with his spere. Whan sir Gawayne saw that, he dressed his
shelde, and than they feautirde their sperys, and they com
togedyrs with all the myght of their horses, that eyther
knyght smote other so harde in myddis the sheldis. But sir
Gawaynes spere brake, but sir Marhaus speare helde, and
25 therewith sir Gawayne and his horse russhed downe to the
erthe.

And lyghtly sir Gawayne wan on his feete and pulde oute
his swerde and dressed hym toward sir Marhaus on foote.
And sir Marhaus saw that he pulde oute his swerde, and
30 began to com to sir Gawayne on horsebak.

'Sir knyght,' seyde sir Gawayne, 'alyght on foote, or ellis
I woll sle thyne horse.'

'Gramercy,' sayde sir Marhaus, 'of your jentylnesse! Ye
teche me curtesy, for hit is nat commendable one knyght
35 to be on horsebak and the other on foote.'

And therewith sir Marhaus sette his spere agayne a tre,

---

1 *C* hym that they   7 *C* ony is lyuynge   19–20 *C* rode toward
Gawayne with his spere   21 *C* they auentryd their   23 *C* of theyr sheldes
27 *C* Gawayne rose   29 *C** that and pulled   34–35 *C* not for one knyȝt
to be on foote and the other on horsbak

and alyght and tyed his horse to a tre, and dressed his shelde,
and eyther com unto other egirly and smote togedyrs with hir
swerdys, that hir sheldis flew in cantellys, and they bresed
their helmys and hawbirkes and woundid eyther other.

But sir Gawayne, fro hit was nine of the clok, wexed ever 5
strenger and strenger, for by than hit cam to the howre of
noone he had three tymes his myght encresed. And all this
aspyed sir Marhaus and had grete wondir how his myght
encreced. And so they wounded eyther other passyng sore.
So whan hit was ⌐past noone, and whan it drew⌐ toward 10
evynsonge, sir Gawayns strength fyebled and woxe passyng
faynte, that unnethe he myght dure no lenger, and sir Marhaus was than bygger and bygger.

'Sir knyght,' seyde sir Marhaus, 'I have welle felt that 60ᵛ
ye ar a passynge goode knyght and a mervaylous man of 15
myght as ever I felte ony whyle hit lastyth, and oure quarellys
ar nat grete, and therefore hit were pyté to do you hurte, for
I fele ye ar passynge fyeble.'

'A,' seyde sir Gawayne, 'jantyll knyght, ye say the worde
that I sholde sey.' 20

And therewith they toke of her helmys and eyther kyssed
other and there they swore togedyrs eythir to love other as
brethirne. And sir Marhaus prayde sir Gawayne to lodge
with hym that nyght. And so they toke their horsis and
rode towarde sir Marhaus maner. 25

And as they rode by the way, 'Sir knyght,' seyde sir
Gawayne, 'I have mervayle of you, so valyaunte a man as ye
be of prouesse, that ye love no ladyes and damesels.'

'Sir,' seyde sir Marhaus, 'they name me wrongfully, for
hit be the damesels of the turret that so name me and other 30
suche as they be. Now shall I telle you for what cause I
hate them: for they be sorsseres and inchaunters many of
them, and be a knyght never so good of his body and as
full of prouesse as a man may be, they woll make hym a
starke cowerde to have the bettir of hym. And this is the 35
pryncipall cause that I hate them. And all good ladyes

5 *C* it passed ix   6 by *not in C*   7 *C* noone & thryes his myghte was
encreaced   10–11 F (*MS. B.N. fr. 112, f. 19c*) Et quant ce vint aprés nonne
25 *C* syr Marhaus hous   27–28 *C* merueylle that so valyaunt a man as ye be loue
no ladyes ne damoysels   29–30 *C** wrongfully tho that gyue me that name but
wel I wote it ben the damoyseles   33 as *not in C*

917.44   M

and jantyllwomen, I owghe them my servyse as a knyght
ought to do.'

For, as the booke rehersyth in Freynsch, there was this
many knyghtes that overmacched sir Gawayne for all his
5 thryse double myghte that he had: sir Launcelot de Lake,
sir Trystrams, sir Bors de Gaynes, sir Percivale, sir Pelleas,
sir Marhaus; thes six knyghtes had the bettir of sir Gawayne.

Than within a lytyll whyle they come to sir Marhaus
place [which] was in a lytyll pryory, and there they alyght,
10 and ladyes and damesels unarmed them and hastely loked
to their hurtes, for they were all three hurte. And so they
61ʳ had good lodgyng with sir Marhaus and good chere, for
whan he wyste that they were kynge Arthurs syster-sonnes
he made them all the chere that lay in his power. And so
15 they sojourned there a sevennyght and were well eased of
their woundis, and at the laste departed.

'Nay,' sayde sir Marhaus, 'we woll nat departe so lyghtly,
for I woll brynge you thorow the foreste.'

So they rode forth all three. And sir Marhaus toke with
20 hym his grettyste spere. And so they rode thorow the foreste,
and rode day be day well-nye a seven dayes or they founde
ony aventure. So at the laste they com into a grete foreste
that was named the contrey and foreste of Arroy, and the
contrey is of stronge adventures.

25 'In this contrey,' seyde Marhaus, 'cam nevir knyght syn
hit was crystynde but he founde strange adventures.'

And so they rode and cam into a depe valey full of stonys,
and thereby they sawe a fayre streme of watir. Aboven
thereby was the hede of the streme, a fayre fountayne, and
30 three damesels syttynge thereby. And than they rode to
them and ayther salewed othir. And the eldyst had a garlonde
of golde aboute her hede, and she was three score wyntir of
age or more, and hir heyre was whyght undir the garlonde.
The secunde damselle was of thirty wyntir of age, wyth a
35 cerclet of golde aboute her hede. The thirde damesel was but
fiftene yere of age, and a garlonde of floures aboute hir hede.
Whan thes knyghtes had so beholde them they asked hem
the cause why they sate at the fountayne.

3–4 *C* ther were many   4–5 *C* alle the thryes myght   12 *C* had all thre good
17 *C*† Now   19–20 So they rode ... the foreste *not in C*†   24 is *not in C*†

'We be here,' seyde the damesels, 'for this cause: if we may se ony of arraunte knyghtes to teche hem unto stronge aventures. And ye be three knyghtes adventures and we be three damesels, and therefore eche one of you muste chose one of us; and whan ye have done so, we woll lede you unto 5 three hyghewayes, and there eche of you shall chose a way and his damesell with hym. And this day twelve moneth ye 61ᵛ muste mete here agayne, and God sende you the lyves, and thereto ye muste plyght your trouth.'

'This is well seyde,' seyde sir Marhaus. 'Now shall 10 (20) everyche of us chose a damesell.'

'I shall tell you,' seyde sir Uwayne, 'I am yongyst and waykest of you bothe, therefore lette me have the eldyst damesell, for she hath sene much and can beste helpe me whan I have nede, for I have moste nede of helpe of you 15 bothe.'

'Now,' seyde sir Marhaus, 'I woll have the damesell of thirty wyntir age, for she fallyth beste to me.'

'Well,' seyde sir Gawayne, 'I thanke you, for ye have leffte me the yongyst and the fayryste, and hir is me moste levyste.' 20

Than every damesell toke hir knyght by the reygne of his brydyll and brought hem to the three wayes, and there was made promesse to mete at the fountayne that day twelve monthe and they were lyvynge. And so they kyssed and departed, and every k[n]yght sette his lady behynde hym. 25 And sir Uwayne toke the way that lay weste, and sir Marhaus toke the way that lay sowthe, and sir Gawayne toke the way that lay northe.

Now woll we begyn at sir Gawayne that helde that way tyll that he com to a fayre maner where dwelled an olde 30 knyght and a good householder. And there sir Gawayne asked the knyght if he knewe of any aventures.

'I shall shewe you to-morne,' seyde the knyght, 'mervelos adventures.'

So on the morne they rode all in same to the foreste of 35 aventures tyll they com to a launde, and thereby they founde

2 of *not in C*	3 *C* knyghtes that seken auentures	8 *C* your lyues
13 *C* therfor I wyl haue	20 *C* and she is moost leuest to me	22–23 *C* was their othe made to	32 *C* knew ony auentures in that countrey	33–35 *C*†
yow somme to morne sayd the old knyghte and that merueyllous Soo	35 all
in same *not in C*

a crosse. And as they stood and hoved, there cam by them the fayreste knyght and the semelyest man that ever they sawe, but he made the grettyst dole that ever man made. And than he was ware of sir Gawayne and salewed hym, and prayde to God to sende hym muche worshyp.

'As for that,' seyde sir Gawayne, 'gramercy. Also I pray to God sende you honoure and worshyp.'

'A,' sayde the knyght, 'I may lay that on syde, for sorow and shame commyth unto me after worshyppe.'

And therewyth he passed unto that one syde of the lawnde, and on that other syde saw sir Gawayne ten knyghtes that hoved and made hem redy with hir sheldis and with hir sperys agaynste that one knyght that cam by sir Gawayne. Than this one knyght feautred a grete spere, and one of the ten knyghtes encountird with hym. But this wofull knyght smote hym so harde that he felle over his horse tayle. So this dolorous knyght served them all, that at the leste way he smote downe horse and man, and all he ded with one spere. And so whan they were all ten on foote they wente to the one knyght, and he stoode stone-stylle and suffyrde hem to pulle hym downe of his horse, and bounde hym honde and foote, and tyed hym undir the horse bely, and so led hym with hem.

'A, Jesu,' seyde sir Gawayne, 'this is a dolefull syght to se the yondir knyght so to be entreted. And hit semyth by the knyght that he sufferyth hem to bynde hym so, for he makyth no resistence.'

'No,' seyde [his] hoste, 'that is trouth, for, and he wolde, they all were to weyke for hym.'

'Sir,' seyde the damesell unto sir Gawayne, 'mesemyth hit were your worshyp to helpe that dolerouse knyght, for methynkes he is one of the beste knyghtes that ever I sawe.'

'I wolde do for hym,' seyde sir Gawayne, 'but hit semyth he wolde have no helpe.'

'No,' seyde the damesel, 'methynkes ye have no lyste to helpe hym.'

Thus as they talked they sawe a knyght on the other

3 sawe makynge the grettest   5 *C* god that he send   11 *C*† & knyȝtes
12 *C* houed stylle and make   14 *C* auentryd a   29 *C*† weyke soo to doo hym
34–35 *C* helpe thenne sayd   35 *C* luste

syde of the launde all armed save the hede. And on the **62ᵛ**
other syde there com a dwarff on horsebak all armed save
the hede, with a grete mowthe and a shorte nose. And whan
the dwarff com nyghe he seyde, 'Where is this lady sholde
mete us here?' And therewithall she com forth oute of the ₅
woode. And than they began to stryve for the lady, for the
knyght seyde he wolde have hir [and the dwerf said he wold
have her].

'Woll we do welle?' seyde the dwarff. 'Yondir is a knyght
at the crosse. Lette hit be putt uppon hym, and as he demeth ₁₀
hit, so shall hit be.'

'I woll well,' seyde the knyght.

And so they wente all three unto sir Gawayne and tolde
hym wherefore they stroof.

'Well, sirres, woll ye putt the mater in myne honde?' ₁₅
'Ye, sir,' they seyde bothe.

'Now, damesell,' seyde sir Gawayne, 'ye shall stonde
betwyxte them bothe, and whethir ye lyste bettir to go to
he shall have you.'

And whan she was sette betwene hem bothe she lefte ₂₀
the knyght and went to the dwarff. And than the dwarff
toke hir up and wente his way syngyng, and the knyght
wente his way with grete mournyng.

Than com there two knyghtes all armed and cryed on hyght,
'Sir Gawayne, knyght of the courte of kynge Arthure! ₂₅
Make the redy in haste and juste with me!'

So they ran togedirs, that eyther felle downe. And than
on foote they drew there swerdis and dud full actually. The
meanewhyle the other knyght went to the damesell and asked
hir why she abode with that knyght, and seyde, ₃₀
'If ye wolde abyde with me I wolde be your faythefull
knyght.'

'And with you woll I be,' seyde the damesell, 'for I may
nat fynde in my herte to be with hym, for ryght now here
was one knyght that scomfyted ten knyghtes, and at the ₃₅
laste he was cowardly ledde away. And therefore let us two
go whyle they fyght.'

63ʳ

7–8 *Not emended in* O¹   10 *C* lete vs put it bothe vpon   15 *C* syrs said he
16 *C* ye they   25 of the courte *not in C*   26 *C* in al hast   30–31 *C*
knyghte and yf   33 *C* for with syr Gawayn I   34 ryght *not in C*

And sir Gawayne fought with that othir knyght longe, but at the laste they accorded bothe. And than the knyght prayde sir Gawayne to lodge with hym that nyght. So as sir Gawayne wente with this knyght he seyde,

5 'What knyght is he in this contrey that smote downe the ten knyghtes? For whan he had done so manfully he suffirde hem to bynde hym hande and foote, and so led hym away.'

'A,' sayde the knyght, 'that is the beste knyght I trow in the worlde and the moste man of prouesse. And hit is the 10 grettyst pyté of hym as of ony knyght lyvynge, for he hath be served so as he was this tyme more than ten tymes. And his name hyght sir Pelleas; and he lovyth a grete lady in this contrey, and hir name is Ettarde. And so whan he loved hir there was cryed in this contrey a grete justis three dayes, 15 and all this knyghtes of this contrey were there and jantyll-women. And who that preved hym the beste knyght sholde have a passyng good ⌈swerd⌉ and a cerclet of golde, and that cerclet the knyght sholde geff hit to the fayryste lady that was at that justis.

20 'And this knyght sir Pelleas was far the beste of ony that was there, and there were fyve hondred knyghtes, but there was nevir man that ever sir Pelleas met but he stroke hym downe other ellys frome his horse, and every day of three dayes he strake downe twenty knyghtes. And therefore they 25 gaff hym the pryce. And furthewithall he wente thereas the lady Ettarde was and gaff her the cerclet and seyde opynly she was the fayreste lady that there was, and that wolde he preve uppon ony knyght that wolde sey nay.

(22) 'And so he chose hir for his soveraygne lady, and never to 30 love other but her. But she was so prowde that she had 63ᵛ scorne of hym and seyde she wolde never love hym thoughe he wolde dye for hir; wherefore all ladyes and jantyllwomen had scorne of hir that she was so prowde, for there were fayrer than she, and there was none that was there but and

---

4 *C* he asked hym   9–10 hit is the grettyst pyté of hym as of any knyght lyvynge, for *not in C*† (*homoeoarcheion*)   *F* (*MS. B.N. fr. 112, f. 24a*) c'est la greigneur douleur qui soit en ce païs et le chevalier que je plus plaings   11 *C* was ēne more than   17 swerd *not in W*   *F* (*MS. B.N. fr. 112, f. 24a*) le tournoie-ment estoit assemblés en tel maniere que celle qui provee y seroit a plus belle pour loier de sa beauté emporteroit un cercle d'or qui estoit mis dessus ung glaive   20 of ony *not in C*

sir Pelleas wolde have profyrde hem love they wolde have
shewed hym the same for his noble prouesse. And so this
knyght promysed Ettarde to folow hir into this contray and
nevir to leve her tyll she loved hym, and thus he is here the
moste party nyghe her and logged by a pryory.   5

'And every weke she sendis knyghtes to fyght with hym,
and whan he hath putt hem to the worse, than woll he suffir
hem wylfully to take hym presonere because he wolde have
a syght of this lady. And allwayes she doth hym grete
dispyte, for somtyme she makyth hir knyghtes to tye hym   10
to his horse tayle, and somtyme bynde hym undir the horse
bealy. Thus in the moste shamfyllyste wyse that she can
thynke he is brought to hir, and all she doth hit for to cawse
hym to leve this contrey and to leve his lovynge. But all this
cannat make hym to leve, for, and he wolde a fought on   15
foote, he myght have had the bettir of the ten knyghtes as
well on foote as on horsebak.'

'Alas,' sayde sir Gawayne, 'hit is grete pyté of hym, and
aftir this nyght I woll seke hym to-morow in this foreste to
do hym all the helpe I can.'   20

So on the morow sir Gawayne toke his leve of his oste,
sir Carados, and rode into the foreste. And at the laste he
mette with sir Pelleas makynge grete mone oute of mesure;
so eche of hem salewed other, and asked hym why he made
such sorow.   25

And as hit above rehersyth sir Pelleas tolde sir Gawayne:
'But allwayes I suffir her knyghtes to fare so with me as ye   64ʳ
sawe yestirday, in truste at the laste to wynne hir love; for
she knoweth well all hir knyghtes sholde nat lyghtly wynne
me and me lyste to fyght with them to the uttirmoste. Where-   30
fore and I loved hir nat so sore I had lever dye an hondred
tymes, and I myght dye so ofte, rathir than I wolde suffir that
dispyte, but I truste she woll have pyté uppon me at the laste;
for love causyth many a good knyght to suffir to have his
entente, but alas, I am infortunate!'   35

And therewith he made so grete dole that unnethe he
myght holde hym on his horse bak.

'Now,' sayde sir Gawayne, 'leve your mournynge, and

I shall promyse you by the feyth of my body to do all that
lyeth in my powere to gete you the love of your lady, and
thereto I woll plyghte you my trouthe.'

　　'A,' seyd sir Pelleas, 'of what courte ar ye?'

5　　'Sir, I am of the courte of kynge Arthure, and his sistir
son, and kynge Lotte of Orkeney was my fadir, and my
name is sir Gawayne.'

　　'And my name is sir Pelleas, born in the Iles, and of many
iles I am lorde. And never loved I lady nother damesel tyll
10　nowe. And, sir knyght, syn ye ar so nye cosyn unto kyng
Arthure and ar a kynges son, therefore betray me nat, but
help me, for I may nevir com by hir but by some good
knyght. For she is in a stronge castell here faste by, within
this four myle, and over all this contrey she is lady off.

15　　'And so I may never com to hir presence but as I suffir hir
knyghtes to take me, and but if I ded so that I myght have
a syght of hir, I had bene dede longe ar this tyme. And yet
fayre worde had I never none of hir. But whan I am brought
tofore hir she rebukyth me in the fowlyst maner; and than
20　they take me my horse and harneyse and puttyth me oute of
the yatis, and she woll nat suffir me to ete nother drynke.
And allwayes I offir me to be her presoner, but that woll she
64ᵛ　nat suffir me; for I wolde desire no more, what paynes that
ever I had, so that I myght have a syght of hir dayly.'

25　　'Well,' seyde sir Gawayne, 'all this shall I amende, and
ye woll do as I shall devyse. I woll have your armoure, and
so woll I ryde unto hir castell and tell hir that I have slayne
you, and so shall I come within hir to cause hir to cheryshe
me. And than shall I do my trew parte, that ye shall nat
30　fayle to have the love of hir.'

(23)　　And there, whan sir Gawayne plyght his trouthe unto sir
Pelleas to be trew and feythfull unto hym, so eche one
plyght their trouthe to other, and so they chonged horse and
harneyse. And sir Gawayne departed and com to the castel
35　where stood hir pavylyons withoute the gate. And as sone
as Ettarde had aspyed sir Gawayne she fledde in toward

4–5 *C** are ye telle me I praye yow my good frend And thenne syr gawayne sayd
I am　　8 *C* And thenne he sayd my　　10 *C* now in an vnhappy tyme and
11 ar *not in C*　　18 none *not in C*　　20 me *not in C*　　26 *C* your hors and your
armour　　31 *C* there with syr　　35 *C* stoode the pauelions of this lady withoute

the castell. But sir Gawayne spake on hyght and bade hir
abyde, for he was nat sir Pelleas.

'I am another knyght that have slayne sir Pelleas.'

'Than do of your helme,' seyde the lady Ettarde, 'that I
may se your vysage.'   5

So whan she saw that hit was nat sir Pelleas she made hym
alyght and lad hym into hir castell, and asked hym feythfully
whethir he had slayne sir Pelleas, and he seyde yee. Than he
tolde hir his name was sir Gawayne, of the courte of kynge
Arthure and his sistyrs son, and how he had slayne sir Pelleas. 10

'Truly, 'seyde she, 'that is grete pyté for he was a passynge
good knyght of his body. But of all men on lyve I hated hym
moste, for I coude never be quytte of hym. And for ye have
slayne hym I shall be your woman and to do onythynge that
may please you.'   15

So she made sir Gawayne good chere. Than sir Gawayne
sayde that he loved a lady and by no meane she wolde love
hym.

'Sche is to blame,' seyde Ettarde, 'and she woll nat love
you, for ye that be so well-borne a man and suche a man of 20
prouesse, there is no lady in this worlde to good for you.'   65^r

'Woll ye,' seyde sir Gawayne, 'promyse me to do what
that ye may do be the fayth of your body to gete me the love
of my lady?'

'Yee, sir, and that I promyse you be my fayth.'   25

'Now,' seyde sir Gawayne, 'hit is yourself that I love so
well; therefore holde your promyse.'

'I may nat chese,' seyde the lady Ettarde, 'but if I sholde
be forsworne.'

And so she graunted hym to fulfylle all his desyre.   30

So it was in the monthe of May that she and sir Gawayne
wente oute of the castell and sowped in a pavylyon, and there
was made a bedde, and there sir Gawayne and Ettarde wente
to bedde togedyrs. And in another pavylyon she leyde hir
damesels, and in the thirde pavylyon she leyde parte of 35
hir knyghtes, for than she had no drede of sir Pelleas. And

---

8 *C* sayd her ye   10 and how he had slayne sir Pelleas *not in C*†   15 *C*
myghte   22–23 *C* doo alle that   25 *C* ye syre sayd she and that I
promyse yow by the feythe of my body   27 *C* therfore I praye yow hold
31 *C* was thenne in   33 *C* the lady Ettard

there sir Gawayne lay with hir in the pavylyon two dayes
and two nyghtes.

And on the thirde day on the morne erly sir Pelleas armed
hym, for he hadde never slepte syn [sir Gawayne departed
5 from hym, for] sir Gawayne promysed hym by the feythe of
his body to com to hym unto his pavylyon by the pryory
within the space of a day and a nyght. Than sir Pelleas
mounted uppon horsebak and com to the pavylyons that
stood withoute the castell, and founde in the fyrste pavylyon
10 three knyghtes in three beddis, and three squyres lyggynge
at their feete. Than wente he to the secunde pavylyon and
founde four jantyllwomen lyggyng in four beddis. And than
he yode to the thirde pavylyon and founde sir Gawayne
lyggyng in the bed with his lady Ettarde and aythir clyppynge
15 other in armys. And whan he sawe that, his hert well-nyghe
braste for sorow, and sayde, 'Alas, that ever a knyght sholde
be founde so false!'

And than he toke his horse and myght nat abyde no lenger
for pure sorow, and whan he had ryden nyghe half a myle he
65ᵛ 20 turned agayne and thought for to sle hem bothe. And whan
he saw hem lye so bothe slepynge faste that unnethe he myght
holde hym on horsebak for sorow, and seyde thus to hymself:
'Though this knyght be never so false, I woll never sle hym
slepynge, for I woll never dystroy the hyghe Ordir of Knyght-
25 hode,' and therewith he departed agayne. And or he had
rydden half a myle he returned agayne and thought than to
sle hem bothe, makynge the grettyst sorow that ever man
made. And whan he come to the pavylyons he tyed his horse
to a tre and pulled oute his swerde naked in his honde and
30 wente to them thereas they lay. And yet he thought shame
to sle hem, and leyde the naked swerde overthawrte bothe
their throtis, and so toke his horse and rode his way. And
whan sir Pelleas com to his pavylyons he tolde his knyghtes
and his squyers how he had spedde, and seyde thus unto
35 them:

'For youre good and true servyse ye have done me I shall
gyff you all my goodes, for I woll go unto my bedde and

---

5 *Not emended in O*¹   *C* had promysed   21 *C* hem bothe soo lye   that
not in *C*·   30–31 *C*· thought it were shame to slee them slepynge   32 *C*
waye   *S* awaye

never aryse tyll I be dede. And whan that I am dede, I
charge you that ye take the herte oute of my body and bere
hit her betwyxte two sylver dysshes and telle her how I sawe
hir lye wyth that false knyght sir Gawayne.'

Ryght so sir Pelleas unarmed hymself and wente unto his 5
bedde makyng merveylous dole and sorow.

Than sir Gawayne and Ettarde awoke of her slepe and
founde the naked swerd overthawrte their throtis. Than she
knew hit was the swerde of sir Pelleas.

'Alas!' she seyde, 'Sir Gawayne, ye have betrayde sir 10
Pelleas and me, ⌐for you told me you had slayne hym, and
now I know well it is not so: he is on lyve⌐. But had he bene
so uncurteyse unto you as ye have bene to hym, ye had bene
a dede knyght. But ye have dissayved me, that all ladyes
and damesels may beware be you and me.' And therewith 15
sir Gawayne made hym redy and wente into the foreste.   66ʳ

So hit happed the Damesell of the Lake, Nynyve, mette
with a knyght of sir Pelleas that wente on his foote in this
foreste makynge grete doole, and she askede hym the cause;
and so the wofull knyght tolde her all how his mayster and 20
lorde was betrayed thorow a knyght and a lady, and how he
woll never aryse oute of his bedde tyll he be dede.

'Brynge me to hym,' seyde she anone, 'and y woll waraunte
his lyfe. He shall nat dye for love, and she that hath caused
hym so to love she shall be in as evylle plyte as he is or hit 25
be longe to, for hit is no joy of suche a proude lady that woll
nat have no mercy of suche a valyaunte knyght.'

Anone that knyght broute hir unto hym, and whan she sye
hym lye on his bedde she thought she sawe never so lykly a
knyght. And therewith she threw an enchauntemente uppon 30
hym, and he fell on slepe. And than she rode unto the lady
Ettarde and charged that no man scholde awake hym tyll she
come agayne. So within two owres she brought the lady
Ettarde thidir, and bothe the ladyes founde hym on slepe.

1 *C* I am dede   9 *C* knewe wel   9–12 *C** syr Pelleas swerd Allas sayd
she to sir Gawayne ye haue bitrayed me and syr Pelleas bothe for ye told me ye
had slayne hym and now I knowe wel it is not soo he is on lyue And yf syre Pelleas
had ben   *F* (*MS. B.N. fr. 112, f. 27c*) vous me faisiés entendant que vous aviez
Pellias occis, mez non avez   14 *C** deceyued me and bytrayd me falsly that
17 *C* happed thenne that the   20 all *not in C*   31 *C* And ther whyle she
32 *C* charged no man to awake

'Loo,' seyde the Damesell of the Lake, 'ye oughte to be
ashamed for to murther suche a knyght,' and therewith she
threw such an inchauntemente uppon hir that she loved hym
so sore that well-nyghe she was nere oute of hir mynde.

5 'A, Lorde Jesu,' seyde this lady Ettarde, 'how is hit
befallyn unto me that I love now that I have hatyd moste of
ony man on lyve?'

'That is the ryghteuouse jugemente of God,' seyde the
damesell.

10 And than anone sir Pelleas awaked and loked uppon
Ettarde, and wha[n] he saw hir he knew her, and than he
hated hir more than ony woman on lyve, and seyde,

66ᵛ 'Away, traytoures, and com never in my syght!'

And whan she herde hym sey so she wepte and made grete
15 sorow oute of mynde.

(24) 'Sir knyght Pelleas,' seyde the Damesel of the Lake, 'take
your horse and com forthwith oute of this contrey, and ye
shall love a lady that woll love you.'

'I woll well,' seyde sir Pelleas, 'for this lady Ettarde hath
20 done me grete dispyte and shame;' and there he tolde hir
the begynnyng and endyng, and how he had never purposed
to have rysen agayne tyll he had bene dede. 'And now suche
grace God hath sente me that I hate hir as much as I have
loved hir.'

25 'Thanke me therefore,' seyde the Lady of the Lake.

Anone sir Pelleas armed hym and toke his horse and
commaunded his men to brynge aftir his pavylyons and his
stuffe where the Lady of the Lake wolde assyngne them. So
this lady Ettarde dyed for sorow, and the Damesel of the
30 Lake rejoysed sir Pelleas, and loved togedyrs duryng their
lyfe.

(25) Now turne we unto sir Marhaute that rode with the
damesel of thirty wynter of ayge southwarde. And so they
come into a depe foreste, and by fortune they were nyghted
35 and rode longe in a depe way, and at the laste they com unto
a courtlage and there they asked herborow. But the man

---

4 so *not in* C†   nere *not in* C   6 C now hym that   8 C ryght wys
Iugement   15 C of mesure   22 agayne *not in* C   23–24 C as euer I
loued   25 C me sayde the damoysel of the   28 them *not in* C   31 C
lyf dayes

of the courtlage wolde nat logge them for no tretyse that
they coulde trete, but this much the good man seyde: 'And
ye woll take the adventure of youre herbourage, I shall bryng
you there ye may be herbourde.'

'What aventure is that [that] I shall have for my herborow?'   5
seyde sir Marhaute.

'Ye shall wete whan ye com there,' seyde the good man.

'Sir, what aventure so hit be, I pray the to brynge me
thidir, for I am wery, my damesel and my horse both.'

So the good man wente uppon his gate before hym in   10
a lane, and within an houre he brought hym untyll a fayre
castell. And than the pore man called the porter, and anone   67ʳ
he was lette into the castell. And so he tolde the lorde how
he had brought hym a knyght arraunte and a damesell
wolde be lodged with hym. 'Lette hym in,' seyde the lorde,   15
'for hit may happen he shall repente that they toke theire
herborow here.' So sir Marhaute was let in with a torche-
lyght, and there was a grete syght of goodly men that wel-
comed hym; and than his horse was lad into a stable, and he
and the damesel were brought into the halle, and there   20
stoode a myghty duke and many goodly men aboute hym.
Than this duke asked hym what he hyght, and fro whens he
com, and with whom he dwelte.

'Sir,' he seyde, 'I am a knyght of kynge Arthurs and knyght
of the Table Rounde, and my name is sir Marhaute, and   25
borne I was in Irelonde.'

'That me repentes,' seyde the duke, 'for I love nat thy
lorde nother none of thy felowys of the Table Rounde. And
therefore ease thyself this nyght as well as thou mayste, for
as to-morne I and my six sonnes shall macch with you.'   30

'Is there no remedy,' seyde sir Marhaute, 'but that I must
have ado with you and your six sunnes at onys?'

'No,' seyde the duke, 'for this cause. I made myne avowe,
for sir Gawayne slew my sevynth sonne in a recountre,
therefore I made myne avow that there sholde never knyght   35

3 *C* youre lodgyng   4 *C* ye shalle be lodged   5 *O*¹ that I   *C* my
lodgynge   8–9 *C* be bryng me thyder I pray the sayd syr Marhaus for
9 both *not in C*   10–11 *C*† wente and opened the gate and within (*see note*)
16–17 *C* their lodgyng   18 *C* was a goodely syghte   22 *C* this lord asked
27 *C* And thenne sayd the duke to hym that me sore repenteth the cause is this for
34 *C*† seuen sonnes

of kynge Arthurs courte lodge with me or com thereas I
myght have ado with hym but I wolde revenge me of my
sonnes deth.'

'What is your name?' sayde sir Marhaute, 'I requyre you
5 telle me, and hit please you.'

'Wete thou well I am the duke of Southe Marchis.'

'A!' seyde sir Marhaute, 'I have herde seyde that ye
have been longe tyme a grete foo unto my lorde Arthure
and unto his knyghtes.'

10 'That shall ye fele to-morne,' seyde the duke, 'and ye
leve so longe.'

67ᵛ   'Shall I have ado with you?' seyde sir Marhaute.

'Ye,' seyde the duke, 'thereof shalt thou not chose. And
therefore let take hym to his chambir and lette hym have all
15 that tyll hym longis.' So sir Marhaute departed and was led
unto his chambir, and his damesel was led in tyll hir chambir.

And on the morne the duke sente unto sir Marhaute and
bade hym make hym redy. And so sir Marhaute arose and
armed hym. And than there was a masse songe afore hym,
20 and brake his faste, and so mounted on horsebak in the
courte of the castell there they sholde do batayle. So there
was the deuke all ready on horsebak and clene armed, and
his six sonnys by hym, and everyche had a spere in his honde.
And so they encountirde whereas the deuke and his [two]
25 sonnys brake her sperys uppon hym, but sir Marhaute hylde
up his spere and touched none of hem.

(26)   Than come the four sonnes by couple, and two of them
brake their sperys, and so dud the other two. And all this
whyle sir Marhaute towched hem nat. Than sir Marhaute
30 ran to the deuke and smote hym downe with his speare, that
horse and man felle to the erthe, and so he served his sonnes.
Than sir Marhaute alyght downe and bade the deuke yelde
hym, other he wolde sle hym. Than som of his sonnes
recovirde and wolde have sette uppon sir Marhaute. Than
35 sir Marhaute seyde, 'Sir deuke, cese thy sonnys, and ellys
I woll do the uttirmust to you all.' Than the deuke sye he

2-3 *C* wold haue a reuengyng of my   7 *C* herd saye   10-11 and ye
leve so longe *not in C†*   14-15 *C* therfore take yow to your chambre and ye shalle
haue all that to yow longeth   16 *C* to a chamber   *C* vnto her   21 *W* of of
24 two *not in O¹*   30 downe *not in C*   35 *C* sayd to the duke sease

myght nat ascape the deth, he cryed to his sonnes and
charged them to yelde them to sir Marhaute, and than they
kneled alle adowne and putt the pomels of their swerdis to
the knyght, and so he receyvid them; and than they hove up
their fadir on his feete. And so by their comunal assent ₅
promysed to sir Marhaute never to be fooys unto kynge Arthure, and thereuppon at Whytsonday next aftir to com, he
and his sonnes, and there to putt them in the kynges grace.
Then sir Marhaute departed.   **68ʳ**

And within two dayes sir Marhautes damesel brought ₁₀
hym whereas was a grete turnemente that the lady Vawse
had cryed, and who that dud beste sholde have a ryche
cerclet of golde worth a thousand besauntis. And there sir
Marhaute dud so nobely that he was renomed, and had
smeten doune forty knyghtes, and so the cerclet of golde was ₁₅
rewarded hym. Than he departed thens with grete honoure.

And so within sevennyght his damesel brought hym to
an erlys place. His name was the erle Fergus that aftir was
sir Trystrams knyght, and this erle was but a yonge man
and late com to his londis, and there was a gyaunte faste ₂₀
by hym that hyght Taulurd, and he had another brother in
Cornuayle that hyght Taulas that sir Trystram slewe whan
he was oute of his mynde. So this erle made his complaynte
unto sir Marhaute that there was a gyaunte by hym that
destroyed all his londis and how he durste nowhere ryde ₂₅
nother go for hym.

'Sir,' seyde he, 'whether usyth he to fyght on horsebak
othir on foote?'

'Nay,' seyde the erle, 'there may no horse bere hym.'

'Well,' seyde sir Marhaute, 'than woll I fyght with hym ₃₀
on foote.'

So on the morne sir Marhaute prayde the erle that one
of his men myght brynge hym where the gyaunte was,
and so one brought hym where he syghe hym sytte undir
a tre of hooly, and many clubbis of ironne and gysernes ₃₅
aboute hym. So this knyght dressed hym to the gyaunte

---

4 *W* and & so   4–5 *C* they halp vp their fader and soo   7 next *not*
in C   8 there to *not in C*   15 *C* somtyme† doune   16 *C* fro them
with grete worship   27 *C* sayd the knyghte   34 *C* and so he was for
he saw

and put his shylde before hym, and the gyaunte toke an ironne club in his honde, and at the fyrste stroke he clave syr Marhautis shelde. And there he was in grete perell, for the gyaunte was a sly fyghter. But at the laste sir
5 Marhaute smote of his ryght arme aboven the elbow. Than the gyaunte fledde and the knyght afftir hym, and so he
68ᵛ drove hym into a watir; but the gyaunte was so hyghe that he myght nat wade aftir hym. And than sir Marhaute made the erle Fergus man to fecche hym stonys, and with
10 that stonys the knyght gave the gyaunte many sore strokis tylle at the laste he made hym falle downe in the watir, and so was he there dede.

Than sir Marhalte wente into the gyauntes castell, and there he delyverde four-and-twenty knyghtes oute of the
15 gyauntes preson and twelve ladyes; and there he had grete rychesse oute of numbir, that dayes of his lyff he was nevir poore man. Than he returned to the erle Fergus, the whyche thanked hym gretly and wolde have yevyn hym half his londys, but he wolde none take. So sir Marhaute dwellid
20 with the erle nye half a yere, for he was sore brused with the gyaunte. So at the laste he toke his leve, and as he rode by the way with his damysel he mette with sir Gawayne and wyth sir Uwayne.

So by adventure he mette with four knyghtes of Arthurs
25 courte: the fyrst was sir Sagramour le Desyrus, sir Ozanna le Cure Hardy, sir Dodynas le Saveage, and sir Felotte of Lystynoyse; and there sir Marhaute with one spere smote downe these four knyghtes and hurte them sore. And so departed to mete at his day.

(27) 30 Now turne we unto sir Uwayne that rode westwarde with his damesell of three score wyntir of ayge. And there was a turnemente nyghe the marche of Walys, and at that turnemente sir Uwayne smote doune thirty knyghtes. Therefore was gyffyn hym the pryce, and that was a jarfaucon
35 and a whyght stede trapped with cloth of golde. So than sir Uwayne ded many strange adventures by the meanys of

---

1 gyant putting his   3 C* shelde in ii pyeces   4 C a wyly fyghter
10 CO¹ tho stonys   C sore knockes   14–15 C xxiiii ladyes and twelue knyȝtes
oute of the gyants pryson   16 C withoute nombre   26 le cure hardy *not in* C
C syre felot   29 C day afore sette   31–32 C and she broughte hym there
as was a turnement   34 C gerfaukon

the olde damesel, and so she brought [hym] to a lady that was **69ʳ**
called the Lady of the Roch, the whyche was curtayse.

So there was in that contrey two knyghtes that were
brethirne, and they were called two perelous knyghtes: that
one hyght sir Edwarde of the Rede Castell, and that other 5
sir Hew of the Rede Castell, and these two brethirne had
disheryted the Lady of the Roche of a baronnery of londis by
their extorsion. And as this knyghte was lodged with this lady,
she made hir complaynte to hym of thes two knyghtes.

'Madam,' seyde sir Uwayne, 'they ar to blame, for they 10
do ayenste the hyghe Order of Knyghthode and the oth
that they made. And if hit lyke you I woll speke with hem,
because I am a knyght of kyng Arthurs, and to entrete them
with fayrenesse; and if they woll nat, I shall do batayle with
them for Goddis sake and in the defence of your ryght.' 15

'Gramercy,' seyde the lady, 'and thereas I may nat acquyte
you, God shall.'

So on the morne the two knyghtes were sente fore, that
they sholde speke with the Lady of the Roche, and wete
you well they fayled nat, for they com with an hondred 20
horses. But whan this lady sawe them in suche maner so
bygge she wolde nat suffir sir Uwayne to go oute to them
uppon no sureté ne of fayre langage, but she made hym to
speke with them over a toure. But fynally thes two brethirne
wolde nat be entreted, and answerde that they wolde kepe 25
that they had.

'Well,' seyde syr Uwayne, 'than woll I fyght with one
of you and preve that ye do this lady wronge.'

'That woll we nat,' seyde they, 'for and we do batayle we
two woll fyght bothe at onys with one knyght. And therefore, 30
yf ye lyste to fyght so, we woll be redy at what oure ye woll
assygne, and yf ye wynne us in batayle, she to have hir londis **69ᵛ**
agayne.'

'Ye say well,' seyde sir Uwayne. 'Therefore make you redy,
and that ye be here to-morne in the defence of this ladyes 35
ryght.'

---

2 *C* moche curtoys   3 *C* there were in the countrey   13 *C* and I
wylle entrete   15 for Goddis sake *not in C*   19 *C* shold come thyder to speke
21 *C* this maner   23 *C* ne for no fayr   30 *C* fyght with one knyȝt at ones
31 *C* yf ye wille fyghte   32 *C* bataille the lady shal haue

(28)   So was there sykernesse made on bothe partyes, that no treson sholde be wrought. And so thes knyghtes departed and made them redy.

And that nyght sir Uwayne had grete chere, and on the
5 morne he arose erly and harde masse and brake his faste, and so rode into the playne withoute the gatis where hoved the two brethirne abydyng hym. So they ran togedyrs passynge sore, that sir Edwarde and sir Hew brake their sperys uppon sir Uwayne, and sir Uwayne smote sir Edwarde, that he
10 felle over his horse and yette his spere braste nat. And than he spurred his horse and com uppon sir Hew and overthrew hym. But they sone recoverde and dressed their shyldes and drew oute their swerdes, and bade sir Uwayne alyght and do his batayle to the utteraunce.

15   Than sir Uwayne devoyded his horse delyverly and put his shylde before hym and drew his swerde, and so they threste togedyrs and eythir gave other grate strokis. And there thes two brethirne wounded sir Uwayne passyng grevously, that the Lady of the Roche wente he sholde have
20 deyed. And thus they fought togedyrs fyve oures as men outraged of reson, and at the laste sir Uwayne smote sir Edwarde uppon the helme suche a stroke that his swerde kerved unto his canellbone; and than sir Hew abated his corrage, but sir Uwayne presed faste to have slayne hym.
25 That saw sir Hew and kneled adowne and yelded hym to sir Uwayne, and he of his jantylnesse resceyved his swerde and toke hym by the honde, and wente into the castell togedirs.

Than this Lady of the Roche was passyng glad, and sir
30 Hew made grete sorow for his brothirs deth. But this lady
70^r was restored ayen of all hir londis, and sir Hew was commaunded to be at the courte of kynge Arthure at the next feste of Pentecoste. So sir Uwayne dwelled with this lady nyghe halfe a yere, for hit was longe or he myght be hole
35 of his grete hurtis. And so, whan hit drew nyghe the termeday that sir Gawayne, sir Marhaute and sir Uwayne made

2 *C* wrought on neyther partye soo thenne the knyghtes   7 *C* they rode†
13 oute *not in C*   14 *C* to the vttermest   15 *C* hors sodenly   16–17 *C* they
dressyd   17 *C* suche strokes†   20–21 *C* men raged oute of   *W* men outraged
of of   25 *C* Hue he kneled   29–30 *C* and the other broder made
30 dethe thenne the lady   31 ayen *not in C*   36—p. 179, l. 1 *C* Vwayne shold mete

to mete at the crosseway, than every knyght drew hym
thydir to holde his promyse that they made. And sir Marhalte and sir Uwayne brought their damesels with hem, but
sir Gawayne had loste his damesel.

Ryght so at the twelve-monthis ende they mette all three 5 (29)
knyghtes at the fountayne and theire damesels, but the
damesell that sir Gawayne had coude sey but lytyll worshyp
of hym. So they departed frome the damesels and rode
thorowe a grete foreste, and there they mette with a messyngere that com from kynge Arthurs courte that had 10
sought hem well-nyghe a twelve-monthe thorowoute all
Ingelonde, Walis, and Scotlonde, and charged yf ever he
myght fynde sir Gawayne and sir Uwayne to haste hem
unto the courte agayne. And than were they all glad, and
so they prayde sir Marhaute to ryde with hem to the kynges 15
courte.

And so within twelve dayes they come to Camelot, and
the kynge was passyng glad of their commyng, and so was
all the courte. Than the kynge made hem to swere uppon
a booke to telle hym all their adventures that had befalle 20
them that twelve-monthe before, and so they ded. And
there was sir Marhaute well knowyn, for there were knyghtes
that he had macched aforetyme, and he was named one of
the best knyghtes lyvyng.

So agayne the feste of Pentecoste cam the Damesell of 25
the Laake and brought with hir sir Pelleas, and at the
hyghe feste there was grete joustys. Of all knyghtes that
were at that justis sir Pelleas had the pryce and syr Marhaute
was named next. But sir Pelleas was so stronge that there **70ᵛ**
myght but few knyghtes stonde hym a buffette with a 30
spere. And at the next feste sir Pelleas and sir Marhalt
were made knyghtes of the Rounde Table; for there were
two segis voyde, for two knyghtes were slayne that twelve-
monthe.

And grete joy had kynge Arthure of sir Pelleas and of 35
sir Marhalte, but Pelleas loved never after sir Gawayne but as

---

2 *C* had made   4 *C* damoysel as it is afore reherced   10-11 *C* kynge
Arthur that had sought (had *not in S*)   13 *C* to brynge hem   21 before
not in C   22 *W* Marhaute was well   27 *C* grete Iustynge of knyghtes
and of al knyghtes that   30 *C* sytte hym   32 *C* table roũd

he spared hym for the love of the kynge; but oftyntymes
at justis and at turnementes sir Pelleas quytte sir Gawayne,
for so hit rehersyth in the booke of Frensh.

So sir Trystrams many dayes aftir fought with sir Mar-
5 haute in an ilande. And there they dud a grete batayle, but
the laste sir Trystrams slew hym. So sir Trystrams was so
wounded that unnethe he myght recover, and lay at a nunrye
half a yere.

And sir Pelleas was a worshypfull knyght, and was one of
10 the four that encheved the Sankgreal. And the Damesel of
the Laake made by her meanes that never he had ado with
sir Launcelot de Laake, for where sir Launcelot was at ony
justis or at ony turnemente she wolde not suffir hym to be
there that day but yf hit were on the syde of sir Launcelot.

15 HERE ENDYTH THIS TALE, AS THE FREYNSHE BOOKE SEYTH,
FRO THE MARYAGE OF KYNGE UTHER UNTO KYNG ARTHURE
THAT REGNED AFTIR HYM AND DED MANY BATAYLES.

AND THIS BOOKE ENDYTH WHEREAS SIR LAUNCELOT AND
SIR TRYSTRAMS COM TO COURTE. WHO THAT WOLL MAKE ONY
20 MORE LETTE HYM SEKE OTHER BOOKIS OF KYNGE ARTHURE OR
OF SIR LAUNCELOT OR SIR TRYSTRAMS; FOR THIS WAS DRAWYN
BY A KNYGHT PRESONER, SIR THOMAS MALLEORRÉ, THAT GOD
SENDE HYM GOOD RECOVER. AMEN.

25 EXPLICIT.

---

1 *C* of kyng arthur   6 *C** at the last   13 to *not in C*   14–25 *C*
launcelot Explicit liber quartus   *The colophon (from* Here endyth *to* Amen) *is not
in C†*   24 *W* Amen &c.

THE TALE

OF THE

NOBLE KING ARTHUR

THAT WAS EMPEROR HIMSELF
THROUGH DIGNITY OF
HIS HANDS

[*Winchester MS., ff. 71^r–96^r*
Caxton, Book V]

CAXTON'S RUBRICS

1. How twelve aged Ambassaytours of Rome came to kyng Arthur to demaunde truage for Brytayne.

2. How the kynges and lordes promysed to kyng Arthur ayde and helpe ageynst the Romayns.

3. How kyng Arthur helde a parlement at Yorke and how he ordeyned how the royame shold be governed in his abscence.

4. How kyng Arthur beyng shypped and lyeng in his caban had a mervayllous dreme, and of th'exposycion therof.

5. How a man of the contreye tolde to hym of a mervayllous geaunte, and how he faught and conquerd hym.

6. How kyng Arthur sente syr Gawayn and other to Lucius and how they were assayled and escaped wyth worshyp.

7. How Lucius sente certeyn espyes in a busshement for to have taken hys knyghtes beyng prysonners, and how they were letted.

8. How a senatour tolde to Lucius of their dyscomfyture, and also of the grete batayl betwene Arthur and Lucius.

9. How Arthur after he had achyeved the batayl ayenst the Romayns entred into Almayn and so into Ytalye.

10. Of a bataylle doon by Gauwayn ayenst a Sarasyn whiche after was yelden and became Crysten.

11. How the Sarasyns came oute of a wode for to rescowe theyr beestys, and of a grete bataylle.

12. How syr Gauwayn retorned to kyng Arthur wyth his prysoners. And how the kyng wanne a cyté, and how he was crowned Emperour.

The text in small type is a reprint of Caxton's Book V. Caxton's chapter-numbers are given in round brackets in the margin. Asterisks denote Caxton's variant readings supported by earlier texts.

In the critical text, based here as elsewhere on the Winchester MS., the following symbols are used: ` ´ *for alliterating lines;* ⌐ ¬ *for readings supplied by Caxton and attested by at least one of the earlier texts;* [ ] *for emendations based on Caxton; and* ⟨ ⟩ *for all other emendations. Rejected readings are given in footnotes.*

The line-numbers in square brackets refer to the unique surviving copy of the alliterative Morte Arthure *(MA).*

HYT BEFELLE whan kyng Arthur had wedded quene Gwenyvere and fulfylled the Rounde Table, and so aftir his mervelous knyghtis and he had venquyshed the moste party of his enemyes, than sone aftir com sir Launcelot de Lake unto the courte, and sir Trystrams come that tyme 5 also, and than ⌜kyng Arthur helde a ryal feeste and Table Rounde⌝.

So hit befelle that the Emperour Lucius, ⌜Procurour of [78] the publyke wele of Rome⌝, sente unto Arthure messyngers commaundynge hym to pay his trewage that his auncettryes 10 have payde before hym. Whan kynge Arthure wyste what they mente he loked up with his gray yghen and angred at the messyngers passyng sore. Than were this messyngers aferde and knelyd stylle and durste nat aryse, they were so aferde of his grymme countenaunce. Than one of the 15 knyghtes messyngers spake alowde and seyde, [124]

'Crowned kynge, myssedo no messyngers, for we be com at his commaundemente, as servytures sholde.'

Than spake the Conquerrour, 'Thou recrayedest coward

C WHanne kyng Arthur had after longe werre rested and held a (1) Ryal feeste and table rounde* (*MA* 74: thus on ryall araye he helde his rounde table) with his alyes of kynges prynces and noble knyghtes all of the round table there cam in to his halle he syttynge in his throne Ryal xij aūcyen men berynge eche of them a braunche of 5 Olyue in token that they cam as Embassatours* (*Geoffrey* 247 'ecce duodecim viri maturae aetatis, reverendi vultus, ramos olivae in signum legationis in dextris ferentes'; *Wace* 115–16 'Es vous douse homes blans, quenus, Bien atornés et bien vestus . . . Douse estoient, et douse rains D'olive portent en lor mains'; *Huth Merlin* 180 'Es vous par 10 laiens entrer douze hommes qui tout estoient vestu de blanc samit. Et estoient tout li honme viel et anchiien et tout blanc de kenissure(s), et portoit chascuns en sa main un rain d'olive par senefiance') and messa- gers fro the Emperour Lucyus whiche was called at that tyme Dicta- tour or procurour of the publyke wele of Rome* (*W* Emperour of 15 Roome Lucius; *Geoffrey* 247 reipublicae procurator), whiche sayde messagers after their entryng & comyng in to the presence of kynge Arthur dyd to hym theyr obeyssaūce in makyng to hym reuerence said to hym in this wyse The hyghe & myghty Emperour Lucyus sendeth

8 *W* Emperour of Roome Lucius

knyghte, why feryst thou my countenaunce? There be in
this halle, and they were sore aggreved, thou durste nat
for a deukedom of londis loke in their facis.'

[136] 'Sir,' seyde one of the senatoures, 'so Cryste me helpe,
5 I was so aferde whan I loked in thy face that myne herte
wolde nat serve for to sey my message. But sytthen hit is
[86] my wylle for to sey myne erande, the gretis welle Lucius,
the Emperour of Roome, and commaundis the uppon
payne that woll falle to sende hym the trewage of this realme
10 that thy fadir Uther Pendragon payde, other ellys he woll
bereve the all thy realmys that thou weldyst, ⌈and thou as
rebelle, not knowynge hym as thy soverayne, withholdest
and reteynest, contrary to the statutes and decrees maade
[115] by the noble and worthy Julius Cezar, conquerour of this
15 realme⌉.'

[140] 'Thow seyste well,' seyde Arthure, 'but for all thy brym
wordys I woll nat be to over-hasty, and therfore thou and
71ᵛ thy felowys shall abyde here seven dayes; and shall calle
unto me my counceyle of my moste trusty knyghtes and
20 deukes and regeaunte kynges and erlys and barowns and
of my moste wyse doctours, and whan we have takyn oure
avysement ye shall have your answere playnly, suche as I
shall abyde by.'

⌈Than somme of the yonge knyghtes, heryng this their

to the kyng of Bretayne gretyng cōmaūdyng the to knouleche hym
for thy lord and to sende hym the truage due of this Royamme vnto
thempyre whiche thy fader and other to fore thy precessours haue paid
as is of record And *thou as rebelle not knowynge hym as thy soue-
5 *rayne withholdest and reteynest contrary to the statutes and decrees
*maade by the noble and worthy Iulius Cezar conquerour of this
Royame (*MA* 103–15 Why thow arte rebelle to Rome and rentez
them wythholdez . . . That Iulius Cesar wan) and fyrst Emperour of
Rome And yf thou refuse his demaunde and commaundement knowe
10 thou for certayne that he shal make stronge werre ageynst the thy
Royames & londes and shall chastyse the and thy subgettys that it shal
be ensample (*S* ensamble) perpetuel vnto alle kynges and prynces for
to denye their truage vnto that noble empyre whiche domyneth vpon
the vnyuersal world Thenne whan they had shewed theffecte of their
15 message the kyng commaunded them to withdrawe them And said he
shold take auyce of counceylle and gyue to them an ansuere Thenne
*somme of the yonge knyghtes heryng this their message wold haue

message, wold have ronne on them to have slayne them,
sayenge that it was a rebuke to alle the knyghtes there beyng
present to suffre them to saye so to the kynge. And anone
the kynge commaunded that none of them upon payne of
dethe to myssaye them ne doo them ony harme.[1]   5

Than the noble kyng commaunded sir Clegis to loke that [155]
thes men be seteled and served with the beste, that there
be no deyntés spared uppon them, that nother chylde nor
horse faught nothynge, 'for they ar full royall peple. And
thoughe they have greved me and my courte, yet we muste 10
remembir on oure worshyp.' So they were led into chambyrs
and served as rychely of deyntés that myght be gotyn. So
the Romaynes had therof grete mervayle.

Than the kynge unto counsayle called his noble ⌐lordes [243]
and⌐ knyghtes, and within a towre there they assembled, the 15
moste party of the knyghtes of the Rounde Table. Than the
kynge commaunded hem of theire beste counceyle.

'Sir,' seyde sir Cador of Cornuayle, 'as for me, I am nat [427]
hevy of this message, for we have be many dayes rested
now. The lettyrs of Lucius the Emperoure lykis me well, 20
for now shall we have warre and worshyp.'

*ronne on them to haue slayne them sayenge that it was a rebuke to
*alle the knyghtes there beyng present to suffre them to saye so to the
*kynge And anone the kynge commaunded that none of them vpon
payne of dethe to myssaye them ne doo them ony harme (*Vulgate
Merlin* 425 'Si dient et jurent qu'il deshoneureront les messages qui les 5
lettres avoient aportees. Si lor eusent fait assés de honte et de laidure
se li rois Artus ne fust qui lor dist moult doucement: "Biaus signeur,
laisés les!" '; *Wace* 119–20 'Que cil seront deshonoré Qui le message
ont aporté, Et lors ont mult as messagiers Dit ramprones et reproviers
Mais li rois se leva em piés, Si lor cria: "Taisiés, taisiés!" ') and com- 10
maūded a knyghte to brynge them to their lodgynge and see that they
haue alle that is necessary and requysyte for them with the best chere
and that noo deyntee be spared For the Romayns ben grete lordes and
though theyr message please me not ne my court yet I must remembre
myn honour After this the kyng lete calle alle his lordes* and knyghtes 15
(*MA* 244 lordes) of the round table to counceyl vpon this mater and
desyred them to saye theire aduys thenne syr Cador of Cornewaile
spacke fyrste and sayd Syre this message lyketh me wel for we haue
many days rested vs and haue ben ydle and now I hope ye shalle make
sharp warre on the Romayns where I doubte not we shal gete honour 20

[259]   'Be Cryste, I leve welle,' seyde the kyng, 'sir Cador, this
message lykis the. But yet they may nat be so answerde,
for their spyteuous speche grevyth so my herte. That truage
to Roome woll I never pay. Therefore counceyle me, my
5 knyghtes, for Crystes love of Hevyn. For this muche have
I founde in the cronycles of this londe, that ` sir Belyne and
sir Bryne, of my bloode elders' that borne were in Bretayne,
and they hath ocupyed the empyreship eyght score wyntyrs;
and aftir ` Constantyne, oure kynnesman, conquerd hit,' and
72ʳ 10 ` dame Elyneys son, of Ingelonde, was Emperour of Roome';
and he ` recoverde the Crosse that Cryste dyed uppon.'
And thus was the Empyre kepte be my kynde elders, and
thus have we evydence inowghe to the empyre of holé
Rome.'

[288] 15   Than answerde kynge Angwysshaunce unto Arthure: 'Sir,
thou oughte to be aboven all othir Crysten kynges for of
knyghthode and of noble counceyle that is allway in the.
And Scotlonde had never scathe syne ye were crowned
kynge, and ` whan the Romaynes raynede uppon us they
20 raunsomed oure elders' and raffte us of oure lyves. ` There-
fore I make myne avow unto mylde Mary' and unto Jesu
Cryste that I shall be avenged uppon the Romayns, and to
farther thy fyght I shall brynge the ferce men of armys, fully
twenty thousand of tyred men. I shall yeff hem my wages

I byleue wel sayd Arthur that this mater pleaseth the wel but these
ansuers may not be ansuerd for (*S* sor) the demaunde greueth me sor
For truly I wyl neuer paye truage to Rome wherfore I pray yow to
counceylle me I haue vnderstande that Bellinus* and Brenius* (*Geoffrey*
5 250 Belinus, Brennius) kynges of (*S* os) Bretayne haue had thempyre
in their handes many dayes And also Constantyn the sone of Heleyne
whiche is an open euydence that we owe noo trybute to Rome but of
ryght we that ben descended of them haue ryght to clayme the tytle of
thempyre
(2) 10   Thenne ansuerd kynge Anguysshe of Scotland Syr ye oughte of
ryght to be aboue al other kynges for vnto yow is none lyke ne pareylle
in Crystendome of knyȝthode ne of dygnyte & I counceylle you neuer
to obeye the Romayns for whan they regned on vs they destressyd oure
elders and putte this land to grete extorcions & taylles wherfore I
15 make here myn auowe to auenge me on them and for to strengthe
youre quarel I shall furnysshe xx M good men of warre and wage
them on my costes whiche shal awayte on yow with my self whan it

for to go and warre on the Romaynes and to dystroy hem,
and all shall be within two ayges to go where the lykes.'

Than the kyng of Lytyll Brytayne sayde unto kynge [304]
Arthure, 'Sir answere thes alyauntes and gyff them their
answere, and I shall somen my peple, and thirty thousand 5
men shall ye have at my costis and wages.'

'Ye sey well,' seyde the kynge Arthure.

Than spake a myghty deuke that was lorde of Weste
Walys: 'Sir, I make myne avowe to God to be revenged on [320]
the Romaynes, and to have the vawarde, and there to 10
`vynquysshe with vyctory the vyscounte of Roome.´ For
onys` as I paste on pylgrymage all by the Poynte Tremble´,
than the vyscounte was in Tu⟨s⟩kayne, and toke up my
knyghtys and raunsomed them unresonablé. And than `I
complayned me to the Potestate the Pope hymself´, but 15
I had nothynge ellys but plesaunte wordys; other reson at
Roome myght I none have, and so I yode my way sore **72ᵛ**
rebuked. And therefore to be avenged I woll arere of my
wyghteste Walshemen, and of myne owne fre wagis brynge
you thirty thousand.' 20

Than sir Ewayne and his son Ider that were nere cosyns [337]
unto the Conquerrour, yet were they cosyns bothe twayne,
and `they helde Irelonde and Argayle and all the Oute
Iles:´ 'Sir,' seyde they unto kynge Arthure, 'here we make
oure avowes untoo Cryste manly to ryde into Lumbardy 25
and so unto Melayne wallys, and so over the Poynte Tremble
`into the vale of Vyterbe, and there to vytayle my knyghtes;´
and for to be avenged on the Romayns we shall bryng the
thirty thousand of good mennys bodyes.'

Than leepe in yong`sir Launcelot de Laake with a lyght 30 [368]
herte´ and seyde unto kynge Arthure, 'Thoughe my londis

shal please yow and the kyng of lytel Bretayne graunted hym to the
same xxx M wherfor kynge Arthur thanked them And thenne
euery man agreed to make warre and to ayde after their power that is
to wete the lorde of westwalis promysed to brynge xxx M men And
syr Vwayne syre Ider his sone with their cosyns promysed to brynge 5
xxx M thenne syre launcelot with alle other promysed in lyke wyse
euery man a grete multytude And whan kynge Arthur vnderstood
theire courages and good wylles he thanked them hertely and after

13 *W* Tulkayne

marche nyghe thyne enemyes, yet shall I make myne avow
aftir my power that of good men of armys aftir my bloode
thus many I shall brynge with me: twenty thousand helmys
in haubirkes attyred that shall never fayle you whyles oure
5 lyves lastyth.'

[382]   Than lowghe sir Bawdwyn of Bretayne and carpys to the
kynge: 'I make myne avow unto the vernacle noble for to
brynge with me ten thousand good mennys bodyes that
shall never fayle whyle there lyvis lastyth.'

[395] 10   'Now I thanke you,' seyde the kynge, 'with all my trew
herte. I suppose by the ende be done and dalte the Romaynes
had bene bettir to have leffte their proude message.'

[415]   So whan the sevennyghte was atte an end the Senatours
besought the kynge to have an answere.

15   'Hit is well,' seyde the kynge. 'Now sey ye to youre
Emperour that I shall in all haste me redy make with my
73ʳ keene knyghtes, and ʾby the rever of Rome holde my Rounde
Table.ʾ And I woll brynge with me the beste peple of fyftene
realmys, and with hem ryde on the mountaynes in the
20 maynelondis, ʾand myne doune the wallys of Myllayne the
proude,ʾ ʾand syth ryde unto Roome with my royallyst
knyghtes.ʾ Now ye have youre answere, hygh you that ye
were hense, andʾfrome this place to the porte there ye shall
passe over;ʾ and I shall gyff you seven dayes to passe unto
25 Sandwyche.

[449]   "Now spede you, I counceyle you, and spare nat youre
horsis,ʾʾand loke ye go by Watlynge strete and no way ellys,ʾ
and where nyght fallys on you, loke ye there abyde, be hit

lete calle thembassatours to here theire ansuere And in presence of
alle his lordes and knyghtes* (*MA* 417 The kyng in his concell) he
sayd to them in thys wyse I wylle that ye retorne vnto your lord and
procurour of the comyn wele for the Romayns and saye ye to hym
5 Of his demaunde and commaundement I sette nothyng And that
I knowe of no truage ne trybute that I owe to hym ne to none erthely
prynce Crysten ne hethen but I pretende to haue and occupye the
soueraynte of thempyre wherin I am entytled by the ryght of my
predecessours somtyme kynges of this lond and saye to hym that I am
10 delybered and fully concluded to goo wyth myn armye with strengthe
and power vnto Rome by the grace of god to take possession in thempyre and subdue them that ben rebelle wherfore I commaunde hym

felle other towne, I take no kepe; for hit longyth nat to
none alyauntis for to ryde on nyghtes. And may ony be
founde a spere-lengthe oute of the way and that ye be in
the watir by the sevennyghtes ende, there shall no golde
undir God pay for youre raunsom.'   5

'Sir,' seyde this senatoures, 'this is an harde conduyte. [467]
We beseche you that we may passe saufly.'

`'Care ye nat,' seyde the kynge, 'youre conduyte is able.'´

Thus they passed fro Carleyle unto Sandwyche-warde [479]
that hadde but seven dayes for to passe thorow the londe, and 10
so sir Cador brought hem on her wayes. But the senatours
spared for no horse, but hyred hem hakeneyes frome towne
to towne, and `by the sonne was sette at the seven dayes
ende´ they come unto Sandwyche; so blythe were they never.
And so the same nyght they toke the watir and passed into 15 [493]
Flaundres, ⌜Almayn⌝, and aftir that over the grete mountayne
that hyght Godarde, and so aftir thorow Lumbardy and
thorow Tuskayne, and sone aftir they come to the Emperour
Lucius, and there they shewed hym the lettyrs of kynge **73ᵛ**
Arthure, and how he was the gastfullyst man that ever they 20
on loked. Whan the Emperour Lucius hadde redde the [507]
lettyrs and undirstoode them welle of theire credence, he
fared as a man were rased of his wytte:

'I wente that Arthure wold have obeyed you and served
you ⌜hymself⌝ unto your honde, for so he besemed, other 25
ony kynge crystynde, for to obey ony senatour that is sente
fro my persone.'

and alle them of Rome that incontynent they make to me their
homage & (*S* or) to knouleche me for their Emperour and gouernour
vpon payne that shalle ensiewe   And thenne he commaunded his
tresorer to gyue to them grete and large yeftes and to paye alle theyr
dispencys and assygned syre Cador to conueye them oute of the land   5
and soo they took theire leue and departed and tooke theyr shyppynge
at Sandwyche and passed forthe by flaundrys Almayn* (*MA* 496 Till
Akyn in Almayn) the montayns and all ytalye vntyl they cam vnto
Lucius And after the reuerence made they made relacyon of their
answer lyke as ye to fore haue herd   whan themperour Lucyus had 10
wel vnderstonde theyre credence he was sore meued as he had ben al
araged & sayd I had supposed that Arthur wold haue obeyed to my
commaundement and haue serued yow hym self* (*MA* 514 hafe

[515]   `'Sir,' sayde the senatours, 'lette be suche wordis,' for
that we have ascaped on lyve we may thonke God ever; for
we wolde nat passe ayen to do that message for all your
brode londis. And therfore, sirres, truste to our sawys, ye
5 shall fynde hym your uttir enemye; and seke ye hym and
ye lyste, for into this londis woll he com, and that shall ye
fynde within this half-yere, for he thynkys to be Emperour
hymself. For he seyth ye have ocupyed the Empyre with
grete wronge, for all his trew auncettryes sauff his fadir
10 Uther were Emperoures of Rome.

[532]   'And of all the soveraynes that we sawe ever he is the
royallyst kynge that lyvyth on erthe, for we sawe on Newerys
day at his Rounde Table nine kyngis, and the fayryst felyship
of knyghtes ar with hym that durys on lyve, and thereto of
15 wysedome and of fayre speeche and all royalté and rychesse
they fayle of none. Therefore, sir, be my counsayle, rere up
your lyege peple and sende kynges and dewkes to loke unto
your marchis, and that `the mountaynes of Almayne be
myghtyly kepte.'

[554] 20   'Be Estir,' seyde the Emperour, 'I caste me for to passe
Almayne and so furth into Fraunce and there bereve hym
his londis. I shall brynge with me many gyauntys of Geene,
that one of them shall be worth an hondred of knyghtes,

seruede þe hym seluen) as hym wel bysemed or ony other kyng to doo
O syre sayd one of the senatours late be suche vayn wordes for we
late yow wete that I and my felawes were ful sore aferd to beholde
his countenaunce I fere me ye haue made a rodde for your self for
5 he entendeth to be lord of this empyre whiche sore is to be doubted
yf he com for he is al another mā than ye wene and holdeth the most
noble courte of the world alle other kynges ne prynces maye not
compare vnto his noble mayntene On newe yeres daye we sawe hym
in his estate whiche was the ryallest that euer we sawe for he was
10 serued at his table with ix kynges and the noblest felauship of other
prynces lordes and knyghtes that ben in the world and euery knyghte
approued and lyke a lord and holdeth table roūd And in his persone
the moost manly man that lyueth and is lyke to conquere alle the
world for vnto his courage it is to lytel wherfore I aduyse yow to kepe
15 wel youre marches and straytes in the montayns For certaynly he is
a lord to be doubted Wel sayd Lucius bifore Eester I suppose to passe
the moūtayns and soo forth in to fraunce and there byreue hym his
londes with Ianeweyes and other myghty warryours of Tuskane and

and perleous passage shall be surely kepte with my good
knyghtes.'

Than the Emperour sente furth his messyngers of wyse [570] **74¹**
olde knyghtes unto a contrey callyd `Ambage, and Arrage,
and unto Alysundir,´ to Ynde, to Ermony that the rever 5
of Eufrate rennys by, `and to Assy, Aufryke, and Europe
the large,´ `and to Ertayne, and Elamye, to the Oute Yles,´
to Arrabé, to Egypte, to Damaske, and to Damyake, and to
noble deukis and erlys. Also the kynge of Capydos, and
the kyng of Tars, and of Turké, `and of Pounce, and of 10
Pampoyle, and oute of Preter Johanes londe,´ also the
sowdon of Surre. And frome Nero unto Nazareth, and frome
Garese to Galely, there come Sarysyns and becom sudgettis
unto Rome. So they come glydyng in galyes. Also ther
come the kynge of Cypres, and `the Grekis were gadirde 15
and goodly arayed´ with the kynge of Macidony, and `of
Calabe and of Catelonde bothe kynges and deukes,´ and the
kynge of Portyngale with many thousande Spaynardis.

Thus all thes kynges and dukys and admyrallys noblys [609]
assembled with syxtene kynges at onys, and so they com 20
unto Rome with grete multytude of peple. Whan the
Emperour undirstood their comynge he made redy all his
noble Romaynes and all men of warre betwyxte hym and
Flaundyrs. Also he had gotyn with hym `fyffty gyauntys
that were engendirde with fendis,´ and all tho he lete ordeyne 25
for to awayte on his persone and for to breke the batayle of

lombardye And I shall sende for them all that ben subgettys and alyed
to thēpyre of Rome to come to myn ayde and forthwith sente old wyse
knyghtes vnto these countrayes folowynge fyrste to ambage and arrage
to Alysaundrye to ynde to hermonye where as the ryuer of Eufrates
renneth in to Asye to Auffryke and Europe the large to ertayne and 5
Elamye to Arabye Egypte and to damaske to damyete and Cayer to
Capadoce to tarce Turkye pounce and pampoylle to Surrye and gallacye
And alle these were subgette to Rome and many moo as Grece Cypres
Macydone Calabre Cateland portyngale with many thousandes of
spaynardys Thus alle these kynges dukes and admyrals assembled 10
aboute Rome with xvj kynges attones with grete multytude of peple
whan themperour vnderstood their comyng he made redy his Romayns
and alle the peple bytwene hym & Flaundres Also he hadde goten wyth
hym fyfty Geaunts whiche had ben engendred of fendys And they

the frunte of Arthurs knyghtes, but they were so muche
of their bodyes that horsys myght nat bere them. And
thus the Emperour with all hys horryble peple drew to
passe Almayne to dystroy Arthures londys that he wan
5 thorow warre of his noble knyghtes.

[623]   And so Lucius`com unto Cullayne, and thereby a castelle
besegys,´ and wanne hit within a whyle, and feffyd hit with
Saresyns. And thus Lucius within a whyle destryed many
74ᵛ fayre contrayes that Arthure had wonne before of the myghty
10 kynge Claudas. So this Lucius dispercled abrode his oste
syxty myle large, and commaunde hem to mete with hym
in Normandy, in the contray of Constantyne, 'and at Barflete there ye me abyde, for the douchery of Bretayne I shall
thorowly dystroy hit.'

[625] 15   Now leve we sir Lucius and speke we of kyng Arthure
that commaunded all that were undir his obeysaunce, aftir
the utas of Seynte Hyllary that all shulde be assembled for
to holde a parlement at Yorke, within the wallys. And there
they concluded shortly to arest all the shyppes of this londe,
20 and within fyftene dayes to be redy at Sandwych.

'Now, sirrys,' seyde Arthure,`'I purpose me to passe many
perelles wayes´ and to ocupye the Empyre that myne elders
afore have claymed. Therefore I pray you, counseyle me
that may be beste and most worshyp.'

25   The kynges and knyghtes gadirde hem unto counsayle

were ordeyned to garde his persone and to breke the frounte of the
batayle of kynge Arthur And thus departed fro Rome and came
doune the montayns for to destroye the londes that Arthur had conquerd and cam vnto Coleyne and byseged a Castel there by and wanne
5 it soone and stuffed hit with two honderd sarasyns or Infydeles and
after destroyed many fayr countrees whiche Arthur had wonne of
kyng Claudas And thus Lucius cam with alle his hoost whiche were
disperplyd lx myle in brede and commaunded them to mete with
hym in Burgoyne for he purposed to destroye the Royame of lytyl
10 Bretayne.

(3)   Now leue we of Lucius the emperour and speke we of kynge
Arthur that commaunded alle them of his retenue to be redy atte vtas
of hyllary for to holde a parlement at yorke And at that parlement was
concluded to areste alle the nauye of the lond and to be redy within xv
15 dayes at sandwyche and there he shewed to his armye how he purposed
to conquere thempyre whiche he ought to haue of ryght And there

and were condecended for to make two chyfftaynes, that
was sir Baudwen of Bretayne, an auncient and an honorable
knyght, for to counceyle and comforte; sir Cadore son of
Cornuayle, that was at the tyme called sir Constantyne, that
aftir was kynge aftir Arthurs dayes. And there in the 5
presence of all the lordis the kynge res[yn]ed all the rule
unto thes two lordis and quene Gwenyvere.

And sir Trystrams at that tyme beleft with kynge Marke
of Cornuayle for the love of La Beale Isode, wherefore sir
Launcelot was passyng wrothe.   10

Than quene Gwenyver made grete sorow that the kynge [715]
and all the lordys sholde so be departed, and there she fell
doune on a swone, and hir ladyes bare hir to her chambir.
Than the kynge commaunded hem to God and belefte the
quene in sir Constantynes and sir Baudewens hondis, and 15 75ʳ
all Inglonde holy to rule as themselfe demed beste. And whan
the kynge was an horsebak he seyde in herynge of all the
lordis,

'If that I dye in this jurney, here I make the, sir Constantyne, my trew ayre, for thou arte nexte of my kyn save sir 20
Cadore, thy fadir, and therefore, if that I dey, I woll that ye
be crowned kynge.'

Ryght so he sought and his knyghtes towarde Sande- [720]
wyche where he founde before hym many galyard knyghtes,
for there were the moste party of all the Rounde Table redy 25
on tho bankes for to sayle whan the kynge lyked. Than in

he ordeyned two gouernours of this (*S* his) Royame that is to say Syre
Bawdewyn of Bretayne for to counceille to the best and syr Constantyn
sone to syre Cador of Cornewaylle whiche after the dethe of Arthur was
kyng of this Royamme And in the presence of all his lordes he resyned
the rule of the royame and Gweneuer his quene to them wherfore syre 5
launcelot was wrothe for he lefte syre Trystram with kynge marke
for the loue of beal Isoulde Thenne the quene Gweneuer made grete
sorowe for the departynge of her lord and other and swouned in
suche wyse that the ladyes bare her in to her chambre Thus the kyng
with his grete armye departed leuyng the queene and Royamme in 10
the gouernaunce of syre Bawduyn and Constantyn And whan he was
on his hors he sayd with an hyhe voys yf I dye in this iourney I wyl
that syre Constantyn be myn heyer and kyng crowned of this royame

6 *WO*¹ resceyved

all haste that myght be they shypped their horsis and harneyse
and all maner of ordynaunce that fallyth for the werre, and
tentys and pavylyons many were trussed, and so they shotte
frome the bankes many grete caryckes and many shyppes of
5 forestage with coggis and galeyes and spynnesse full noble
with galeyes and galyottys, rowing with many ores. And thus
`they strekyn forth into the stremys many sadde hunderthes.´

[756]   HERE FOLOWYTH THE DREME OF KYNGE ARTHURE.

As the kynge was in his cog and lay in his caban, he felle
10 in a slumberyng and `dremed how a dredfull dragon dud
drenche muche of his peple´ and com fleyng one wynge
oute of the weste partyes. And his hede, hym semed, was
enamyled with asure, and his shuldyrs shone as the golde,
and his wombe was lyke mayles of a merveylous hew, and
15 his tayle was fulle of tatyrs, and `his feete were florysshed
as hit were fyne sable.´ And his clawys were lyke clene
golde, ⌐and⌐ `an hydeouse flame of fyre there flowe oute of
his mowth,´ lyke as the londe and the watir had flawmed
all on fyre.

[774] 20   Than hym semed there com oute of the Oryent a grymly
75ᵛ beare, all blak, in a clowde, and his pawys were as byg as a
poste. He was all to-rongeled with lugerande lokys, and he
was the fowlyst beste that ever ony man sye. He romed and
rored so rudely that merveyle hit were to telle.

[786] 25   `Than the dredfull dragon dressyd hym ayenste hym´
and come in the wynde lyke a faucon, and freyshely strykis
as next of my blood And after departed and entred in to the see atte
Sandwyche with alle his armye with a greete multitude of shyppes
galeyes Cogges and dromoundes sayllynge on the see.

(4)   And as the kyng laye in his caban in the shyp he fyll in a slomerynge
5 and dremed a merueyllous dreme hym semed that a dredeful dragon
dyd drowne moche of his people and he cam fleynge oute of the west
and his hede was enameled with asure and his sholders shone as gold
his bely lyke maylles of a merueyllous hewe his taylle ful of tatters
his feet ful of fyne sable & his clawes lyke fyne gold And* (*W* with;
10 *MA* 772 and) an hydous flamme of fyre flewe oute of his mouthe
lyke as the londe and water had flammed all of fyre After hym semed
there came oute of thoryent a grymly bore al blak in a clowde and his
pawes as bygge as a post he was rugged lokynge roughly he was the
foulest beest that euer man sawe he rored and romed soo hydously
15 that it were merueill to here Thenne the dredeful dragon auaunced

the beare. And agayne the gresly beare kuttis with his grysly
tuskes, that his breste and his bray⟨l⟩e was bloodé, and
⌈the reed blood⌉ rayled all over the see. Than the worme
wyndis away and fleis uppon hyght and com downe with
such a sowghe, and towched the beare on the rydge that   5
'fro the toppe to the tayle was ten foote large'. And so he
rentyth the beare and brennys hym up clene that all felle
on pouder, both the fleysh and the bonys, and so hit flotered
abrode on the sea.

Anone the kynge waked ⌈and was sore abasshed⌉ of his   10 [806]
dreme, and in all haste he sente for a philozopher and
charged hym to telle what sygnyfyed his dreme.

'Sir,' seyde the phylozopher, 'the dragon thou dremyste   [814]
of betokyns thyne owne persone that thus here sayles with
thy syker knyghtes; and the coloure of his wyngys is thy   15
kyngdomes that thou haste with thy knyghtes wonne. And
his tayle that was all to-tatered sygnyfyed your noble
knyghtes of the Rounde Table. And the beare that the
dragon slowe above in the clowdis ˋbetokyns som tyraunte
that turmentis thy peple,' other thou art lyke to fyght with   20
som gyaunt boldely in batayle be thyself alone. Therefore
ˋof this dredfull dreme drede the but a lytyll,' and ˋcare
nat now, sir conquerroure, but comfort⌈h⌉ thyself.''

hym and cam in the wynde lyke a fawcon gyuynge grete strokes on
the bore and the bore hytte hym ageyne with his grysly tuskes that
his brest was al blody and that the hote blood* made alle the see reed*
of his blood (*W* and hit rayled; *MA* 795 Rynnande on reede blode
as rayne of the heuen). Thenne the dragon flewe awey al on an hey3te   5
and came doune with suche a swough and smote the bore on the rydge
whiche was x foote large fro the hede to the taylle and smote the
bore all to powdre bothe flesshe and bonys that it flytteryd (*S* flutteryd)
al abrode on the see And therwith the kynge awoke anone and was
sore abasshed* (*MA* 806 wery foretrauaillede) of this dreme And   10
sente anone for a wyse philosopher commaundynge to telle hym the
sygnyfycacion of his dreme Syre sayd the philosopher the dragon that
thow dremedest of betokeneth thyn owne persone that sayllest here
& the colours of his wynges ben thy Royames that thow haste wonne
And his taylle whiche is al to tatterd sygnefyeth the noble knyghtes   15
of the round table And the bore that the dragon slough comyng fro

2 *W* brayre (*cf. MA* 793)   3 *W* and hit rayled   23 *W* comforte

[834]   Than within a whyle they had a syght of the bankys of
Normandy, and at the same tyde the kynge aryved at Bar-
fflete and founde there redy many of his grete lordis, as he
76 had commaunded at Crystemasse before hymselfe.

5   And than come there an husbandeman oute of the contrey
and talkyth unto the kyng wondourfull wordys and sayde,
'Sir, here is ⌐besyde¬ a ⌐grete¬ gyaunte of Gene that tur-
mentyth thy peple; mo than fyve hundred and many mo
of oure chyldren, ˋthat hath bene his sustynaunce all this
10 seven wynters.ˊ Yet is the sotte never cesid, but in the
contrey of Constantyne he hath kylled ⌐and destroyed¬ all
oure knave chyldren, and this nyght he hath cleyghte the
duches of Bretayne ˋas she rode by a ryver with her ryche
knyghtes,ˊ and ledde hir unto yondir mounte to ly by hir
15 whyle hir lyff lastyth.

[856]   ˋ'Many folkys folowed hym, mo than fyve hundirdˊ
barounes and bachelers and knyghtes full noble, but ever
she sh[r]yked wondirly lowde, that the sorow of the lady

the clowdes betokeneth some tyraunt that tormenteth the people or
else thow arte lyke to fyghte with somme Geaunt thy self beynge
horryble and abhomynable whoos pere ye sawe neuer in your dayes
wherfore of this dredeful dreme doubte the no thynge but as a Con-
5 querour come forth* (*W* comforte; *MA* 830 comforth) thy self
Thenne after this soone they had syghte of londe and saylled tyl they
arryued atte Barflete in Flaundres and whanne they were there he
fond many of his grete lordes redy as they had ben commaunded to
awayte vpon hym
(5) 10 Thenne came to hym an husbond man of the countrey and told
hym how there was in the countre of Constantyn besyde* Bretayne
a grete* (*W* here is a foule gyaunte of Gene; *MA* 842 Here es a
teraunt besyde that tourmentez thi pople, A grett geaunte of Geen)
gyaunt whiche hadde slayne murthered and deuoured moche people
15 of the countreye and had ben susteyned seuen yere with the children
of the comyns of that land in soo moche that alle the children ben alle
slayne and destroyed* (*MA* 850 clenly dystroyede) and now late he
hath taken the duchesse of Bretayne as she rode (*S* rode by) with her
meyne and hath ledde her to his lodgynge whiche is in a montayne
20 for to rauysshe and lye by her to her lyues ende and many people
folowed her moo than v C but alle they myghte not rescowe her but
they lefte her shrykyng* and cryenge lamentably wherfore I suppose

4–5 *W* hymselfe etc Than   7 *W* a foule gyaunte

cover shall we never. She was thy cousyns wyff, sir Howell
the Hende, a man that we calle nyghe of thy bloode. Now,
ʻas thou arte oure ryghtwos kynge, rewe on this ladyʼ and
on thy lyege peple, and revenge us as a noble conquerroure
sholde.ʼ

'Alas,' seyde kynge Arthure, 'this is a grete myscheffe!
I had levir than all the realmys I welde unto my crowne that
ʻI had bene before that freyke a furlonge wayʼ for to have
rescowed that lady, and I wolde have done my payne.
Now, felow,' seyde Arthure, 'woldist thow ken me where
that carle dwellys? I trowe I shall trete with hym or I far
passe.'

'Sir Conquerrour,' seyde the good man, 'beholde yondir
two fyrys, for there shalte thou fynde that carle beyonde the
colde strendys, and tresoure oute of numbir there mayste
thou sykerly fynde, more tresoure, as I suppose, than is in
all Fraunce aftir.'

The kynge seyde, 'Good man, pees! and carpe to me no
more. ʻThy soth sawys have greved sore my herte.ʼ Than
he turnys towarde his tentys and carpys but lytyll.

Than the kynge ⌈called to hym⌉ sir Kay in counceyle,
and to sir Bedwere the bolde thus seyde he: 'Loke that ye
two aftir evynsonge be surely armed, and your beste horsis,
for I woll ryde on pylgrymage prevayly, and none but we

that he hath slayn her in fulfyllynge his fowle lust of lechery She
was wyf vnto thy Cosyn syre Howel whome we calle ful nyhe of thy
blood Now as thow a ryghtful kynge haue pyte on this lady and
reuenge vs al as thow arte a noble conquerour Alas sayd kynge
Arthur this is a grete meschyef I had leuer than the best Royame that
I haue that I hadde ben a forlonge way to fore hym for to haue
rescowed that lady Now felawe sayd kynge Arthur canst thou brynge
me there as thys gyaunt haunteth ye syre sayd the good man loo yonder
where as thow seest tho two grete fyres there shalt thou fynde hym
and more tresour than I suppose is in al Fraunce whanne the kynge
hadde vnderstanden this pyteous caas he retorned in to his tente
Thenne he callyed* to hym syre kaye (*W* seyde unto sir Kay; *MA* 892
He calles sir Cayous) and syre Bedewere & commaunded them
secretely to make redy hors and harneis for hym self and them tweyne
For after euensonge he wold ryde on pylgremage with them two only

21 *W* the kynge seyde unto sir Kay

three. And whan my lordis is served we woll ryde`to Seynte
Mychaels Mounte where mervayles ar shewed.'

[900]   Anone sir Arthure wente to his wardrop and caste on
his armoure, bothe his gesseraunte and his basnet with his
5 brode shylde. And so he buskys hym tyll his stede that on
the bente hoved. Than he stertes uppon loffte and hentys
the brydyll, and stirres hym stoutly, and sone he fyndis
his knyghtes two full clenly arayed. And than they trotted
on stylly togedir over a blythe contray full of many myrry
10 byrdis, and whan they com to the forlonde Arthure and they
alyght on hir foote. ⌐And the kynge commaunded them to
tarye there.⌐

'Now fastenys,' seyde Arthure, 'oure horsis that none
nyghe other,`for I woll seche this seynte be myself alone´
15 and speke wyth this maystir-man that kepys this mountayne.'
[941]   Than the kynge yode up to the creste of the cragge, and
than he comforted hymself with the colde wynde; and than
he yode forth by two welle-stremys, and there`he fyndys two
fyres flamand full hyghe.´ And at that one fyre he founde
20 a carefull wydow wryngande hir handys, syttande on a grave
that was new marked. Than Arthure salued hir and she
hym agayne, and asked hir why she sate sorowyng.
[957]   'Alas,' she seyde, `carefull knyght! Thou carpys over
lowde!´ Yon is a werlow woll destroy us bothe. I holde the
25 unhappy. What doste thou on this mountayne? Thoughe
77ʳ here were suche fyffty, ye were to feyble for to macche hym

vnto saynt Mychels mounte And thenne anone he maad hym redy
and armed hym* (*MA* 902) at alle poyntes and tooke his hors and his
shield And soo they thre departed thens and rode* (*MA* 920 they
roode) forthe as faste as euer they myȝt tyl that they cam to the forlond
5 of that mount And there they alyghted and the kynge commaunded
them to tarye there* (*MA* 935–6 comandyde his knyghtez For to
byde) for he wold hym self goo vp in to that mounte And soo he
ascended vp in to that hylle tyl he came to a grete fyre and there he
fonde a careful wydowe wryngynge her handes and makyng grete
10 sorowe syttynge by a graue newe made And thenne kynge Arthur
salewed her and demaunded of her wherfore she made suche lamentacion to whome she ansuerd and sayd Syre knyghte speke softe for
yonder is a deuyll yf he here the speke he wylle come and destroye
the I hold the vnhappy what dost thow here in this mountayne For
15 yf ye were suche fyfty as ye be ye were not able to make resystence

all at onys. Whereto berys thou armoure? Hit may the lytyll
avayle, for he nedys none other wepyn but his bare fyste.
Here is a douches dede, the fayryst that lyved; ˎhe hath
murthered that mylde withoute ony mercy;ˊ he forced hir
by fylth of hymself, and so aftir slytte hir unto the navyll.'   5
                                                                [986]

'Dame,' seyde the kynge, 'I com fro the ⌜noble⌝ Conquerrour, sir Arthure, for to trete with the tirraunte for his
lyege peple.'

'Fy on suche tretyse,' she seyde than, 'for he settys   [993]
nought by the kynge nother by no man ellys. But and thou   10
have brought Arthurs wyff, dame Gwenyvere, he woll be
more blyther of hir than thou haddyste geffyn hym halfen-
dele Fraunce. And but yf thou have brought hir, prese hym
nat to nyghe. Loke what he hath done unto fyftene kynges:
he hath made hym a coote full of precious stonys, and the   15
bordoures thereof is the berdis ⟨of⟩ fyftene kynges, and they
were of the grettyst blood that dured on erthe. Othir
farme had he none of fyftene realmys. This presente was
sente hym to this laste Crystemasse, they sente hym in
faythe for savyng of their peple. And for Arthurs wyffe he   20
lodgys hym here, for he hath more tresoure ˎthan ever had
Arthure or ony of his elders.ˊ And now thou shalt fynde
hym at souper with syx knave chyldirne, and there he hath
made ˎpykyll and powder with many precious wynes,ˊ and

ageynst this deuyl here lyeth a duchesse deede the whiche was the
fayrest of alle the world wyf to syre Howel duc of Bretayne he hath
murthred her in forcynge her and hath slytte her vnto the nauyl
Dame sayd the kynge I come (*S* came) fro the noble* Conqueroure
(*MA* 987 þe conquerour curtaise and gentill) kynge Arthur for to   5
treate with that tyraunt for his lyege peple Fy on suche treatys sayd
she he setteth not by the kynge ne by no man els But and yf thou
haue broughte Arthurs wyf dame Gweneuer he shalle be gladder than
thow haddest gyuen to hym half fraunce Beware approche hym not to
nygh for he hath vaynquysshed xv kynges and hath maade hym a cote   10
ful of precious stones enbrowdred with theyre berdes whiche they sente
hym to haue his loue for sauacion of theyr peple at this laste Crystemasse And yf thow wylt speke with hym at yonder grete fyre at souper
wel sayd Arthur I wyll accomplysshe my message for al your ferdful
wordes and wente forth by the creast of that hylle and sawe where he   15
satte atte souper gnawynge on a lymme of a man bekynge his brode
lymmes by the fyre and bercheles and thre fayr damoysels tornynge

three fayre maydens that turnys the broche that bydis to go
to his bed, for they three shall be dede within four oures
`or the fylth is fulfylled that his fleyshe askys".

'Well,' seyde Arthure, 'I woll fulfylle my message for
5 alle your grym wordis.'

[1041]   `'Than fare thou to yondir fyre that flamys so hyghe,´
and there thou shalt fynde hym sykerly for sothe.'

Than he paste forth to the creste of the hylle `and syghe
where he sate at his soupere alone´ gnawyng on a lymme of
10 a large man, and there `he beekys his brode lendys by the
77ᵛ bryght fyre´ and brekelys hym s⟨e⟩mys. And three damesels
turned three brochis, and thereon was twelve chyldir but late
borne, and they were broched in maner lyke birdis. Whan
the kynge behylde that syght his herte was nyghe bledyng
15 for sorow. Than he haylesed hym with angirfull wordys:

[1059]   'Now He that all weldys geff the sorow, theeff, there thou
syttes! `For thou art the fowlyste freyke that ever was
fourmed,´ and fendly thou fedyst the, the devill have thy
soule! And `by what cause, thou carle, hast thou kylled
20 thes Crysten chyldern?´ `Thou haste made many martyrs
by mourtheryng of this londis.´ Therefore thou shalt have
thy mede thorow Mychael that owyth this mounte. And
also, why haste thou slayne this fayre douches? Therefore
dresse the, doggys son, `for thou shalt dye this day thorow
25 the dynte of my hondis."

[1074]   `Than the gloton gloored and grevid full foule.´ He had
teeth lyke a grayhounde, he was the foulyst wyghte that
ever man sye, and there was never suche one fourmed on
erthe, for there was never devil in helle more horryblyer
30 made: for he was `fro the hede to the foote fyve fadom longe´
and large. And therewith sturdely he sterte uppon his leggis
and `caughte a clubbe in his honde all of clene iron.´

thre broches wheron were broched twelue yonge children late borne
lyke yonge byrdes Whanne kynge Arthur beheld that pyteous syȝte
he had grete compassion on them so that his hert bledde for sorowe and
hayled hym sayeng in this wyse he that alle the world weldeth gyue
5 the shorte lyf & shameful dethe And the deuyl haue thy soule why
hast thow murthred these yonge Innocent children and murthred this
duchesse Therfore aryse and dresse the thow gloton For this day shall
thou dye of my hand Thenne the gloton anone starte vp and tooke a

'Than he swappis at the kynge with that kyd wepyn.' 'He cruysshed downe with the club the coronal doune' to the colde erthe. The kynge coverede hym with his shylde and rechis a boxe evyn infourmede in the myddis of his forehede, that the slypped blade unto the brayne rechis. Yet he shappis at sir Arthure, but the kynge shuntys a lytyll and rechis hym a dynte hyghe uppon the haunche, and there he swappis his genytrottys in sondir.

Than he rored and brayed and yet angurly he strykes, [1124] and fayled of sir Arthure and the erthe hittis, that he kutte into the swarffe a large swerde-length and more. Than the kynge sterte up unto hym and raught hym a buffette and **78r** kut his baly in sundir, that oute wente the gore, that 'the grasse and the grounde all foule was begone.'

'Than he kaste away the clubbe and caughte the kynge' 15 [1132] in his armys and handeled the kynge so harde that he crusshed his rybbes. Than the balefull maydyns wronge hir hondis and kneled on the grounde and to Cryste called ⌐for helpe and comforte of Arthur⌐. With that the warlow wrath Arthure undir, and so they waltyrde and tumbylde 20 over the craggis and busshys, and eythir cleyght other full faste in their armys. And other whyles Arthure was aboven and other whyle undir, and so ⌐weltryng and walowynge they rolled doune the hylle, and⌐ they never leffte tyll they fylle thereas the floode marked. But ever in the walterynge 25 Arthure ⌐smyttes and⌐ hittis hym with a shorte dagger up to the hyltys, and in his fallynge there braste of the gyauntes rybbys three evyn at onys.

grete clubbe in his hand and smote at the kynge that his coronal fylle to the erthe and the kynge hytte hym ageyn that he carf his bely* (*MA* 1122 Ewyn into [þe] inmette the gyaunt he hyttez) and cutte of his genytours that his guttes & his entraylles fylle doune to the ground thenne the gyaunt threwe awey his clubbe and caught the kynge in his 5 armes that he crusshyd his rybbes Thenne the thre maydens knelyd doune and callyd to Cryst for helpe and comforte of Arthur* (*MA* 1138 Criste comforthe ȝone knyghte and kepe hym fro sorowe And latte neuer ȝone fende fell hym o lyfe) And thenne Arthur weltred and wrong that he was other whyle vnder and another tyme aboue 10 And so weltryng and walowynge they rolled doune the hylle* (*MA* 1142 Welters and walowes ouer within þase [wilde] buskez) tyl they came to the see marke and euer as they soo weltred Arthur smote*

[1152]   And by fortune they felle thereas the two knyghtes aboode
with theire horsis. Whan sir Kay saw the kynge and the
gyaunte so icelyght togyder,

       'Alas,' sayd sir Kay, 'we ar forfete for ever! Yondir is our
5 lorde overfallen with a fende.'

       'Hit is nat so,' seyde the kynge, 'but helpe me, sir Kay,
for this corseynte have I clegged oute of the yondir clowys.'

       'In fayth,' seyde sir Bedwere, 'this is a foule carle,' `and
caughte the corseynte oute of the kynges armys´ and there
10 he seyde, 'I have mykyll wondir, and Mychael be of suche a
makyng, that ever God wolde suffir hym to abyde in hevyn.
`And if seyntis be suche that servys Jesu,´ I woll never seke
for none, be the fayth of my body!'

[1170]   The kynge than lough at Bedwers wordis and seyde,
15   'This seynte have I sought nyghe unto my grete daunger.
But stryke of his hede and sette hit on a trouncheoune of a
speare, and geff hit to thy servaunte that is swyffte-horsed,
and bere hit unto sir Howell that is in harde bondis, and
bydde hym be mery, for his enemy is destroyed. And aftir
78ᵛ 20 in Barflete lette brace hit on a barbycan, that all the comyns
of this contrey may hit beholde.

[1184]   'And than ye two go up ⌜to the montayn⌝ and fecche me
my shelde, my swerde, and the boystouse clubbe of iron,
and yf ye lyste ony tresoure, take what ye lyst, for there may
25 ye fynde tresoure oute of numbir. So I have the curtyll
⌜and the clubbe⌝, I kepe no more. For this was a freysh
[1174] gyaunte and mykyll of strength, for I mette nat with suche

(*MA* 1148–9 smyttez and hittez) hym with his daggar and it fortuned
they came to the place where as the two knyghtes were and kept
Arthurs hors thenne when they sawe the kynge fast in the gyaunts
armes they came and losed hym And thenne the kynge commaunded
5 syr kaye to smyte of the gyaunts hede and to sette it vpon a truncheon
of a spere and bere it to syre howel and telle hym that his enemy was
slayne and after late this hede be bounden to a barbycan that alle the
peple may see and behold hit and go ye two up to the montayn* (*MA*
1185) and fetche me my sheld my suerd and the clubbe of yron And
10 as for the tresour take ye it for ye shalle fynde there good oute of
nombre So I haue the kertyl and the clubbe* (*MA* 1191 Haue I the
kyrtyll and þe clubb) I desyre no more This was the fyerst gyaunt
that euer I mette with sauf one in the mount of Arabe whiche I

one this fyftene wyntir sauff onys in the mounte of Arrabé
I mette with suche another, but this was ferser; that had I
nere founden, had nat my fortune be good.'

Than the knyghtes fecched the clubbe and the coote and [1192]
all the remenaunte, and toke with hem what tresoure that 5
hem lyked. Than the kynge and they sterte uppon their
horsys, and so they rode fro thens thereas they come fro.

And anone the clamoure was howge aboute all the contrey, [1198]
and than they wente with one voyse tofore the kynge and
thanked God and hym that their enemy was destroyed. 10

'All thanke ye God,' seyde Arthure, 'and no man ellys.
Looke that the gooddys be skyffted, that none playne of
his parte.'

Than he commaunded his cosyn, sir Howell, to make a
kyrke on that same cragge in the worshyppe of Seynte 15
Mychael.

On the morne frome Barflete remevyth the kynge with [1222]
all his grete batayle proudly arayed, and so they shooke over
the stremys into a fayre champayne, and thereby doune in
a valey they pyght up hir tentys. And evyn at the mete- 20 [1231]
whyle come two messyngers, that one was the marchall of
Fraunce, that seyde to the kynge how the Emperour was
⌜entryd⌝ into Fraunce, 'and hath destroyed much of oure
marchis, and is com into Burgayne, and many borowys hath
destroyed, and hath made grete slaughtir of your noble 25
people. And where that he rydyth all he destroyes. And now 79ʳ
he is comyn into Dowse Fraunce, and there he brennys all

ouercame but this was gretter and fyerser Thenne the knyghtes fette
the clubbe and the kyrtyl and some of the tresour they took to them
self and retorned ageyne to the host And anone this was knowen
thurgh alle the countrey wher for the peple came and thanked the
kynge And he sayd ageyne yeue the thanke to god and departe the 5
goodes among yow And after that kynge Arthur sayd and commaunded
his Cosyn howel that he shold ordeyne for a chirche to be bylded on
the same hylle in the worship of saynte Mychel And on the morne the
kynge remeuyd with his grete bataylle and came in to Champayne and
in a valeye and there they pyght their tentys and the kynge beynge set 10
at his dyner ther cam in two messagers of whome that one was Marchal
of frauce and sayd to the kyng that themperour was entryd* (*W* was

22–23 *W* was com into

clene. Now all the ⟨dowseperys⟩, bothe deukys and other, and the peerys of Parys towne, ar fledde downe into the Lowe Contrey towarde Roone, and but yf thou helpe them the sunner they muste yelde hem all at onys, bothe the bodyes and townys. They can none othir succour, but nedys they muste yelde them in haste.'

[1263]　　Than ⟨the kynge byddis sir Borce: 'Now bowske the blythe⟨ and sir Lyonel and sir Bedwere, loke that ye fare with sir Gawayne, my nevew, with you, and take as many good knyghtes, and looke that ye ryde streyte unto sir Lucius and sey I bydde hym in haste to remeve oute of my londys. And yf he woll nat, so bydde hym dresse his batayle and lette us redresse oure ryghtes with oure handis, and that is more worshyppe than thus to overryde maysterlesse men.'

[1279] 15　　Than anone in all haste they dressed hem to horsebak, thes noble knyghtes, and whan they com to the grene wood they sawe before hem many prowde pavylyons of sylke of dyverse coloures that were sette in a medow besyde a ryver, and the Emperoures pavylyon was in the myddys with an egle displayed on loffte. Than thorow the wood oure knyghtes roode tylle that they com unto the Emperoures tente. But behynde them they leffte stuff of men of armys in a boyshemente; and there he leffte in the boyshemente sir Lyonel and sir Bedwere. Sir Gawayne and sir Borce wente with the message.

com; *MA* 1239 es entirde) in to fraunce and had destroyed a grete parte and was in Burgoyn and had destroyed and made grete slaughter of peple & brente townes and borowes wherfor yf thou come not hastely they must yelde vp their bodyes and goodes

(6) 5　　Thenne the kynge dyd doo calle syre Gawayne syre Borce syr Lyonel and syre Bedewere and commaunded them to goo strayte to syre Lucius and saye ye to hym that hastely he remeue oute of my land And yf he wil not bydde hym make hym redy to bataylle and not distresse the poure peple* (*MA* 1276 raunsone the pople) Thenne anone these noble knyghtes dressyd them to horsbak And whanne they came to the grene wood they sawe many pauelions sette in a medowe of sylke of dyuerse colours besyde a ryuer And themperours pauelione was in the myddle with an egle displayed aboue To the which tente our knyghtes rode toward and ordeyned syr Gawayn and syre Bors to doo the message And lefte in a busshement syre

1 *W* Dowse leperys

So they rode worthyly into the Emperoures tente and [1301]
spoke bothe at onys with hawté wordys: ˋ'Now geff the
sorow, sir Emperour, and all thy sowdyars the aboute.'
For why ocupyest thou with wronge the empyreship of
Roome? That is kynge Arthures herytage be kynde of his 5
noble elders: there lakked none but Uther, his fadir. Therefore the kynge commaundyth the to ryde oute of his londys,
other ellys to fyght for all and knyghtly hit wynne.'   **79ᵛ**

'Ye sey well,' seyde the Emperour, 'as youre lorde hath [1326]
you commaunded. But ⌜saye to⌝ your lorde I sende hym 10
gretynge, but I have no joy of youre renckys thus to rebuke
me and my lordys. But sey youre lorde I woll ryde downe
by Sayne and wynne all that thereto longes, and aftir ryde
unto Roone and wynne hit up clene.'

'Hit besemys the ylle,' seyde sir Gawayne, 'that ony such 15 [1342]
an elffe sholde bragge suche wordys, for I had levir than all
Fraunce to fyghte ayenste the.'

'Other I,' seyde sir Borce, 'than to welde all Bretayne other
Burgayne the noble.'

Than a knyght that hyght sir Gayus that was cosyn unto 20 [1347]
the Emperour, he seyde thes wordys: ⌜'Loo! how⌝ thes
Englyshe Bretouns be braggars of kynde, for ye may see
how ˋthey boste and bragge as they durste bete all the
worlde.'

ˋThan grevid sir Gawayne at his grete wordys', and ˋwith 25
his bowerly bronde that bryght semed' he stroke of the hede
of sir Gayus the knyght.

Lyonel and syre Bedwere And thenne syre Gawayn and syr Borce
dyd their message and commaunded Lucius in Arthurs name to auoyde
his lond or shortly to adresse hym to bataylle To whome Lucius
ansuerde* and sayd (*MA* 1326 The emperour ansuerde) ye shalle
retorne to your lord and saye* ye to (*W* But telle; *MA* 1330 But say 5
to) hym that I shall subdue hym and alle his londes Thenne syre
Gawayn was wrothe and sayde I hadde leuer than alle Fraunce fyghte
ageynste the and so hadde I saide syr Borce leuer than alle Bretayne
or burgoyne Thenne a knyght named syre Gaynus nyghe cosyn
to the Emperour sayde loo how* (*MA* 1349 loo how he brawles 10
hym) these Bretons ben ful of pryde and boost and they bragge as
though they bare vp alle the world Thenne syre Gawayne was sore
greued with these wordes and pulled oute his swerd and smote of his

10 *W* But tell your   26–27 *W* (*sidenote*) The deth of sir Gayus

[1355]   And so they turned their horsis and rode over watyrs and woodys into they com ny the busshemente there sir Lyonell and sir Bedwere were hovyng stylle. Than the Romaynes folowed faste on horsebak and ˋon foote over a fayre cham-
5 peyne unto a fayre wood.ˊ

Than turnys hym sir Borce wyth a freyshe wylle and sawe a gay knyght ⌜come fast on⌝, all florysshed in golde, that bare downe of Arthures knyghtes wondirfull many. Than sir Borce aspyed hym, he kaste in feautir a spere and gyrdis hym
10 thorowoute the body, that his guttys fylle oute and the knyght ⌜fylle doune⌝ to the grounde that gresly gronyd.

[1374]   Than preced in a bolde barowne all in purpull arayed. He threste into the prece of kyng Arthures knyghtes and frusshed downe many good knyghtes, and he was called
80r 15 Calleborne, the strengyste of Pavynes Londis. And sir Borce turned hym to and ˋbare hym thorow the brode shylde and the brode of his bresteˊ, that he felle to the erthe as dede as a stone.

[1382]   Than sir Feldenake the myghty that was a praysed man
20 of armys, ˋhe gurde to sir Gawayne for greff of sir Gayusˊ and his other felowys, and sir Gawayne was ware and drew Galantyne, his swerde, and hyt hym such a buffette that he cleved hym to the breste, and than he caughte his courser and wente to his ferys.

[1391] 25   Than a rych man of Rome, one of the senatours, called

hede And therwith torned theyr horses and rode ouer waters and thurgh woodes tyl they came to theyre busshement where as syr Lyonel and syr Bedeuer were houyng The romayns folowed fast after on horsbak and on foote ouer a chāpayn vnto a wood thenne syre Boors
5 torned his hors and sawe a knyghte come fast on* (*MA* 1367 folowes faste on owre folke) whome he smote thurgh the body with a spere that he fylle dede doune* (*MA* 1372 at þe grounde lyggez) to the erthe thenne cam Callyburne one of the strengest of pauye and smote doun many of Arthurs knyghtes And whan syr Bors
10 sawe hym do soo moche harme he adressyd toward hym & smote hym thurȝ the brest that he fylle doune dede to the erthe Thenne syr Feldenak thought to reuenge the dethe of gaynus vpon syre Gawayn but syre gawayn was ware therof and smote hym on the hede whiche stroke stynted not tyl it came to his breste And thenne he retorned

22–24 *W* (*sidenote*) The deth of sir Feldenak

to his felowys and bade hem returne, 'for yondir ar shrewed
messengers and bolde boosters. If we folow them ony farther the harme shall be owrys.' And so the Romaynes returned lyghtly to theire tentys and tolde the Emperour how
they had spedde, and how the marchall of Rome was slayne, 5
and mo than fyve thousand in the felde dede.

But yet ore they wente and departe, ʻoure bushemente [1407]
brake on bothe sydysʻ of the Romaynes, and there the bolde
Bedwer and sir Lyonel bare downe the Romaynes on every
syde. There oure noble knyghtes of mery Ingelonde bere 10
hem thorow the helmys and bryght sheldis and slew hem
downe, and there the hole roughte returned unto the Emperour and tolde hym at one worde his men were destroyed,
ten thousand, by batayle of tyred knyghtes, 'for they ar the
brymmyst men that evir we saw in felde.' 15

But allwayes sir Borce and sir Gawayne freyshly folowed [1426]
on the Romaynes evyn unto the Emperoures tentes. Than
oute ran the Romaynes on every syde, bothe on horse
and on foote, to many oute of numbir. But sir Borce and
sir Berelʻwere formeste in the frunte and freyshly faughtʻ as 20
ever dud ony knyghtes. But sir Gawayne was on the ryght
honde and dud what he myght, but there were so many hym
agaynste he myght nat helpe there his ferys, but was fayne
to turne on his horse othir his lyffe muste he lese. Sir Borce **80ᵛ**
and sir Berell, the good barounnes, fought as two boorys 25
that myght no farther passe. But at the laste, thoughe
they loth were, they were yolden and takyn and saved their
lyves, yet the stale stoode a lytyll on fer with sir Gawayne
that made sorow oute of mesure for thes two lordys.

But than cam in a freysh knyght clenly arayed, sir Idres, 30 [1439]
sir Uwaynes son, a noble man of armys. He brought fyve
hondred good men in haubirkes attyred, and whan he wyste

and came to his felawes in the busshement And there was a recountre
for the busshement brake on the Romayns and slewe and hewe doune
the Romayns and forced the Romayns to flee and retorne whome the
noble knyghtes chaced vnto theyr tentes Thenne the Romayns gadred
more peple and also foote men cam on and ther was a newe bataille 5
and soo moche peple that syr Bors and syr Berel were taken but whan
syre gawayn sawe that he tooke with hym syre Idrus the good knyght
and sayd he wold neuer see kynge Arthur but yf be (*S* he) rescued

sir Borce and sir Berel were cesed of werre, 'Alas,' he sayde,
'this is to muche shame and overmuche losse! For with
kynge Arthure, and he know that thes two knyghtes bene
thus loste, he woll never mery be tyll this be revenged.'

5 'A, fayre knyght,' sayde sir Gawayne, 'thou moste nedis
be a good man, for so is thy fadir. I knowe full well thy
modir. In Ingelonde was thou borne. Alas, thes Romaynes
this day have chaced us as wylde harys, and they have oure
noble chyfften takyn in the felde. There was never a bettir
10 knyght that strode uppon a steede. Loo `where they lede
oure lordys over yondir brode launde.´ I make myne avowe,'
seyde sir Gawayne, 'I shall never se my lorde Arthure but
yf I reskew hem that so lyghtly ar ledde us fro.'

'That is knyghtly spokyn,' seyde sir Idres, and pulde up
15 her brydyls and halowed over that champayne. There was
russhynge of sperys and swappyng of swerdis, and sir Gawayne with Galantyne, his swerde, dud many wondyrs.
Than he threste thorow the prece unto hym that lad
sir Bors, and bare hym thorow up to the hyltys, and lade
20 away sir Bors strayte unto his ferys. Than sir Idrus the
yonge, sir Uwaynes son, he threste unto a knyght that
had sir Berell, that the brayne and the blode clevid on his
swerde.

[1476]   There was a proude senatoure preced aftir sir Gawayne,
25 and gaff hym a grete buffet. That sawe sir Idres and aftir
rydyth, and had slayne the senatour but that he yelded hym
81ʳ in haste. Yet he was loth to be yoldyn but that he nedys
muste, and with that sir Idrus ledde hym oute of the prees
unto sir Lyonel and unto sir Lovel, Idrus brothir, and com-
30 maunded hem to kepe hym on payne of theire hedis.

Than there began a passynge harde stoure, for the
Romaynes ever wexed ever bygger. Whan sir Gawayne that
aspyed he sente forth a knyght unto kyng Arthure. 'And

them and pulled out galatyn his good swerd and folowed them that
ledde tho ij knyghtes awaye and he smote hym that lad syre Bors and
took syr Bors fro hym and delyuerd hym to his felawes And syre
Idrus in lyke wyse rescowed syr Berel thenne beganne the bataill to be
5 grete that our knyʒtes were in grete Ieopardy wherfore syre Gawayn
sente to kyng Arthur for socour and that he hye hym for I am sore
wounded and that our prysoners may paye good oute of nombre. And

telle hym what sorow we endure, and how we have takyn
the chefe chaunceler of Rome. And Petur is presoner, a [1543]
senatoure full noble, and odir proude pryncis, we knowe
nat theire namys. And pray hym, as he is oure lorde, to
rescowe us betyme, for oure presoners may pay rychesse 5
oute of numbir; and telle hym that I am wounded wondirly
sore.'

Whan the messyngers com to the kyng and tolde hym [1559]
thes wordys`the kynge thanked Cryste clappyng his hondys.'
'And for thy trew sawys, and I may lyve many wyntyrs, 10
there was never no knyght better rewardid. But there is no
golde undir God that shall save their lyvys, I make myne
avow to God, and sir Gawayne be in ony perell of deth; for
I had levir that the Emperour and all his chyff lordis were
sunkyn into helle than ony lorde of the Rounde Table were 15
byttyrly wounded.'

So forth the presoners were brought before Arthure, and
he commaunded hem into kepyng of the conestablys warde,
surely to be kepte as noble presoners. So within a whyle
com in the foreryders, that is for to say sir Bors, sir Bedwere, 20
sir Lyonell, and sir Gawayne that was sore wounded, with
all hir noble felyshyp. They loste no man of worshyppe. So
anone the kyng lete rensake sir Gawayne anone in his syght
and sayde,

'Fayre cosyn, me ruys of thy hurtys! And yf I wyste hit 25
myght glad thy hert othir fare the bettir with hit, I sholde
presente the with hir hedys thorow whom thou art thus
rebuked.'

'That were lytyll avayle,' sayde sir Gawayne, 'for theire
hedys had they lorne, and I had wolde myself, and hit were 30
shame to sle knyghtes whan they be yolden.'

81ᵛ

the messager came to the kyng and told hym his message And anon
the kynge dyd doo assemble his armye but anone or he departed the
prysoners were comen and syre gawayn and his felawes gate the felde
and put the Romayns to flyght and after retorned and came with their
felauship in suche wyse that no man of worship was loste of them sauf 5
that syr Gawayn was sore hurte Thenne the kynge dyd do ransake
his woundes and comforted hym And thus was the begynnynge of the
fyrst iourney of the brytons and Romayns and ther were slayne of the
Romayns moo than ten thousand and grete ioye and myrthe was made

Than was there joy and game amonge the knyghtes of
Rounde Table, and spoke of the grete prouesse `that the
messyngers ded that day thorow dedys of armys.´

[1601]   So on the morne whan hit was day the kyng callyd unto
5 hym sir Cador of Cornuayle, `and sir Clarrus of Clereounte,
a clene man of armys,´ and sir Cloudres, sir Clegis, two
olde noble knyghtes, and sir Bors, sir Berell, noble good
men of armys, and also sir Bryan de les Ylyes, and sir Bedwere
the bolde, and also he called sir Launcelot in heryng of all
10 peple, and seyde,

'I pray the, sir, as thow lovys me, take hede to thes other
knyghtes and boldely lede thes presoners unto Paryse towne
there for to be kepte surely as they me love woll have, and
yf ony rescowe befalle, moste I affye the in me, as Jesu me
15 helpe.'

Than sir Launcelot and sir Cador with thes other knyghtes
attyred oute of their felyshyp ten thousand be tale of bolde
men arayed of the beste of their company, and then they
unfolde baners and let hem be displayed.

[1621] 20   Now turne we to the Emperour of Rome that wyste by
a spye whethir this presoners sholde wende. He callyd unto
hym sir Edolf and sir Edwarde, two myghty kynges, and
`sir Sextore of Lybye, and senatours many,´ and the kynge
of Surré, and the senatoure of Rome Sawtre. All thes turned
25 towarde Troyes with many proved knyghtes to betrappe the
kynges sondismen that were charged with the presoners.

Thus ar oure knyghtes passed towarde Paryse. A busshemente lay before them of sixty thousand men of armys.

'Now, lordis,' seyde sir Launcelot, 'I pray you, herkyns me
30 a whyle. I drede that in this woodys be leyde afore us many

that nyghte in the hoost of kynge Arthur And on the morne he sente
alle the prysoners in to parys vnder the garde of syre launcelot with
many knyghtes & of syr Cador

(7)   Now torne we to the Emperour of Rome whiche aspyed that these
5 prysoners shold be sente to Parys and anone he sente to leye in a
busshement certayne knyghtes and prynces with syxty thousand men
for to rescowe his knyghtes and lordes that were prysoners And so
on the morne as Launcelot and syre Cador chyuetayns and gouernours
of all them that conueyed the prysoners as they sholde passe thurgh
10 a wode syr Laūcelot sente certayne knyghtes tespye yf ony were in

of oure enemyes. Therefore be myne advyse sende we three good knyghtes.'

'I assente me,' seyde sir Cador, and all they seyde the same, and were aggreed that sir Claryon and sir Clement the noble that they sholde dyscover the woodys, bothe the dalys and 5 the downys. So forth rode thes three knyghtes and aspyed 82ʳ in the woodis men of armys rydyng on sterne horsys. Than [1649] sir Clegys cryed on lowde, 'Is there ony knyght, kyng, other cayser, that dare for his lordis love that he servyth recountir with a knyght of the Rounde Table? ˋBe he kyng other 10 knyght, here is his recounter redy.'˃

ˋAn erle hym answeryd angirly agayne˃ and seyde, 'Thy [1661] lorde wennys with his knyghtes to wynne all the worlde! I trow your currage shall be aswaged in shorte tyme.'

'Fye on the, ˋcowarde!' seyde sir Clegis, 'as a cowarde 15 [1671] thou spekyste,˃ for, by Jesu, myne armys ar knowyn thorowoute all Inglonde and Bretayne, and I am com of olde barounes of auncetry noble, and sir Clegis is my name, a knyght of the Table Rounde. And frome Troy Brute brought myne elders.' 20

'Thou besemeste well,' seyde the kyng, 'to be one of the good be thy bryght browys, but for all that thou canst conjeoure other sey, there shall none that is here medyll with the this tyme.'

Than sir Clegis returned fro the ryche kyng and rode 25 [1706] streyghte to sir Launcelot and unto sir Cador and tolde hem what he had seyne in the woodis of the fayryste syght of men of armys to the numbir of sixty thousand.

'And therefore, lordynges, fyght you behovys, ˋother ellys shunte for shame, chose whether ye lykys.'˃ 30

'Nay, be my fayth,' sayde sir Launcelot, 'to turne is no [1718] tyme, for here is all olde knyghtes of grete worshyp that were never shamed. And as for me and my cousyns of my bloode, we ar but late made knyghtes, yett wolde we be loth to lese the worshyp that oure eldyrs have deservyd.' 35

the woodes to lette them And whanne the said knyghtes cam in to the wood anone they aspyed and sawe the grete enbusshement and retorned and told syr Laūcelot that ther lay in a wayte for them thre score thousand Romayns And thenne syr Launcelot with suche knyghtes as he hadde and men of warre to the nombre of x M put 5

'Ye sey well,' seyde sir Cador and all these knyghtes;
'of youre knyghtly wordis comfortis us all. And I suppose
here is none woll be glad to returne, and as for me,' seyde
sir Cador, 'I had lever dye this day than onys to turne my
5 bak.'

'Ye sey well,' seyde sir Borce, 'lette us set on hem freyshly,
82ᵛ and the worshyp shall be oures, and cause oure kyng to
honoure us for ever and to gyff us lordshyppis and landys
for oure noble dedys. And he that faynes hym to fyght,
10 the devyl have his bonys! And who save ony knyghtes for
lycoure of goodys tylle all be done and know who shall have
the bettir, he doth nat knyghtly, so Jesu me helpe!'

Than anone sir Launcelot and sir Cador, tho two myghty
dukis, dubbed knyghtys worshyp to wynne. Joneke was the
15 fyrste, a juster full noble; sir Hectimer and sir Alyduke,
bothe of Inglonde borne; and sir Hamerel and sir Hardolf,
full hardy men of armys'; also sir Harry and sir Harygall
that good men were bothe.

'Now, felowys,' seyde sir Launcelot and sir Cador the
[1744] 20 kene, 'com hydir, sir Bedwere and sir Berel, take with you
`sir Raynolde and sir Edwarde that ar sir Roulondis
chyldir,´ and loke that ye take kepe to thes noble presoners.
What chaunce so us betyde, save them and yourself. This
commaundement we geff you as ye woll answere to oure
25 soverayne lorde, and for ony stowre that ever ye se us
bestadde `stondys in your stale and sterte ye no ferther.´
And yf hit befalle that ye se oure charge is to muche, than
recover yourself unto som kydde castell, and than ryde you
faste unto oure kynge and pray hym of soccour, as he is
30 oure kynde lorde.'

[1753]   And than they fruyshed forth all at onys, `of the bourelyest
knyghtes that ever brake brede,´ `with mo than fyve hondred
at the formyst frunte,´ and caste their spears in feawter all
at onys, and save trumpettes there was no noyse ellys. Than
35 the Romaynes oste remeved a lytyll, and the lorde that was
kynge of Lybye, that lad all the formyste route, he keste

them in araye and met wyth them and foughte with them manly
and slewe and dretenchid many of the Romayns and slewe many
knyghtes & admyrals of the party of the Romayns and sarasyns ther
was slayne the kynge of lylye and thre grete lordes Aladuke herawde

his spere in feautyr and bare his course evyn to sir Berel,
and strake hym thorow the gorge, that he and his horse felle
to the grounde, and so he was brought oute of his lyff.

'Alas,' sayde sir Cadore, 'now carefull is myne herte that
now lyeth dede my cosyn that I beste loved.'   5

He alyght off his horse and toke hym in his armys and **83ʳ**
'there commaunded knyghtes to kepe well the corse.' Than
the kynge craked grete wordys on lowde and seyde,   [1781]

'One of yon prowde knyghtes is leyde full lowe.'

'Yondir kyng,' seyde sir Cador, 'carpis grete wordis.'   10
But and I may lyve or this dayes ende 'I shall countir with
yondir kynge, so Cryste me helpe!''

'Sir,' seyde sir Launcelot, 'meve you nat to sore, but take
your spear in your honde and we shall you not fayle.'

Than sir Cador, sir Launcelot, and sir Bors, the good   15 [1790]
men of armys, thes three feawtyrd their sperys and threste
into the myddys and ran thorowoute the grete oste twyse
other three tymes, and whan their sperys were brokyn 'they
swange oute their swerdis and slowe of noble men' of armys
mo than an hondred, and than they rode ayen to their ferys. 20
Than alowde the kynge of Lybye cryed unto sir Cador,

'Well have ye revenged the deth of your knyght, for I have
loste for one knyght an hondred by seven score.'

And therewith the batayle began to joyne, and grete [1809]
slaughter there was on the Sarysens party, but thorow the 25
noble prouesse of kyng Arthurs knyghtes ten were takyn
and lad forth as presoners. That greved sore sir Launcelot,
sir Cador, and sir Bors the brym. The kynge of Lybye behelde their dedis and sterte on a sterne horse and umbely-
closed oure knyghtes and drove downe to the grounde 30
many a good man, for there was sir Aladuke slayne, and
also sir Ascamour sore wounded, and 'sir Herawde and
sir Heryngale hewyn to pecis,' and sir Lovell was takyn,
and sir Lyonell also, and nere had sir Clegis, sir Cleremonde
had nat bene, with the knyghthode of sir Launcelot: tho 35
newe made knyghtes had be slayne everych one.

and heryngdale but syr Launcelot fought soo nobly that no man myght
endure a stroke of his hande but where he came he shewed his prowesse

2–4 *W* (*sidenote*) The deth of Sir Berel   32–36 *W* (*sidenote*) The deth of
iii. knyghtes Sir Aladuke Sir Herawde & Sir Heryngale

[1830]　　Than sir Cador rode unto the kyng of Lybye with a
swerde well stelyd and smote hym an hyghe uppon the
hede, that the brayne folowed. 'Now haste thow,' seyde
sir Cador, 'corne-boote agaynewarde, and the devyll have
5　thy bonys that ever thou were borne!' Than the sowdan of
Surré was wood wroth, for the deth of that kynge grevid
83ᵛ　hym at his herte, and recomforted his peple and sette sore
on oure knyghtes.

Than sir Launcelot and sir Bors encountyrs with hym sone,
10　and within a whyle, as tellyth the romaynes, they had slayne
[1864]　of the Sarazens mo than fyve thousand. And sir Kay the kene
had takyn a captayne, and Edwarde had takyn two erlys,
and the sawdon of Surré yeldid hym up unto sir Launcelot,
and the senatur of Sautre yeldid hym unto sir Cador.

[1872] 15　Whan the Romaynes and the Sarezens aspyed how the
game yode they fledde with all hir myght to hyde there
hedis. Than oure knyghtes folowed with a freysshe fare
and slew downe of the Sarezens ⌐on every syde⌐.

And sir Launcelot ded so grete dedys of armys that day
20　that sir Cador and all the Romaynes had mervayle of his
myght, for there was nother kynge, cayser, nother knyght
that day myght stonde hym ony buffette. Therefore was he
honoured dayes of his lyff, for never ere or that day was he
proved so well, for he and sir Bors and sir Lyonel was but
25　late afore at an hyghe feste made all three knyghtes.

And thus were the Romaynes and the Sarezens slayne
adowne clene, save a fewe were recovirde thereby into a
[1882]　lytyll castell. And than the noble renckys of the Rounde
Table, thereas the felde was, toke up hir good bodyes of the
30　noble knyghtes and garte sende them unto kyng Arthure
into the erthe to be caste. So they all rode unto Paryse
and beleffte the presoners there with the pure proveste,

and myght for he slewe doune ryght on euery syde And the Romayns
and sarasyns fledde from hym as the sheep fro the wulf or fro the
lyon and putt them alle that abode alyue to flyght And so longe they
fou3te that tydynges came to kynge Arthur And anone he graythed
5　hym and came to the bataille and sawe his knyghtes how they had
vaynquysshed the bataylle he enbraced them knyght by kny3te in

4–5 *W* (*sidenote*) The deth of the kyng of lybye　　18 *W* Sarezens and folowed
with a freysshe fare (*see note*)

and than they were delyverde into sure sauffgarde. Than
every knyght toke a spere and dranke of the colde
wyne, and than fersely in a brayde returned unto the
kynge.

Whan the kynge his knyghtes sawe he was than mer- 5
velously rejoyced and cleyght knyght be knyght in his armys
and sayde, 'All the worshyp in the worlde ye welde! Be
my fayth, there was never kyng sauff myselff that welded
evir such knyghtes.'

'Sir,' seyde sir Cador, 'there was none of us that fayled 84ʳ [1892]
othir, but of the knyghthode of sir Launcelot hit were
mervayle to telle. And of his bolde cosyns ar proved full
noble knyghtes, but of wyse wytte and of grete strengthe
of his ayge sir Launcelot hath no felowe.'

Whan the kynge herde sir Cador sey such wordys he 15
seyde, 'Hym besemys for to do such dedis.' And sir Cadore
tolde Arthure whyche of the good knyghtis were slayne:
'the kynge of Lybye, and he slew the fyrste knyght on oure [1900]
syde, that was sir Berell; and sir Aladuke was another, a
noble man of armys, and sir Maurel and sir Mores that 20
were two brethyrn, with sir Manaduke and sir Mandyff,
two good knyghtes.'

Than the kynge ⌜wepte and⌝ with a keuerchoff wyped his [1920]
iyen and sayde, 'Youre corrage and youre hardynesse nere-
hande had you destroyed, for and ye had turned agayne ye 25
had loste no worshyp, for I calle hit but foly to abyde whan
knyghtes bene overmacched.'

'Not so,' sayde sir Launcelot, 'the shame sholde ever have
bene oures.'

his armes and said ye be worthy to welde all your honour and worship
there was neuer kynge sauf my self that had so noble knyghtes Syre
sayd Cador there was none of vs failled other but of the prowesse and
manhode of syre Launcelot were more than wonder to telle and also
of his cosyns whiche dyd that daye many noble feates of werre And 5
also syre Cador tolde who of his knyghtes were slayne as syr beriel
& other syr Morys and syr Maurel two good knyghtes thenne the
kynge wepte* (*MA* 1920 the worthy kynge wrythes and wepede with
his eygh[e]ne) and dryed his eyen with a keuerchyef & sayd your
courage had nere hand destroyed yow For though ye had retorned 10
ageyne ye had lost no worship For I calle hit foly knyghtes to abyde

'That is trouthe,' seyde sir Clegis and sir Bors, 'for knyghtes ons shamed recoverys hit never.'

Now leve sir Arthure and his noble knyghtes and speke we of a senatoure that ascaped fro the batayle. Whan he
5 com to Lucius the Emperour of Rome he seyde,

'Sir, withdraw the! What doste thou here in this marchis
[1954] and to overren poore peple? Thou shalt wynne nothyng ellys, and if thou dele with kynge Arthure and his doughty knyghtes thou wynnys naught ellys but grete strokys oute
10 of mesure. For this day one of Arthurs knyghtes was worth in batayle an hondred of oures.'

'Fye on the,' seyde Lucyus, 'for cowardly thou spekyste! Yf my harmys me greve, thy wordys greveth me muche more.' Than he called to hym his counceyle, men of noble
15 bloode. So by all theire advyse he sent forth a knyght that
84ᵛ [1971] hyght sir Leomye. He dressed his peple and hyghe hym he bade, and take hym of the beste men of armys many sad hundrethis, 'and go before, and we woll follow aftir'.

[1973]   But the kynge of their commynge was prevely warned,
20 and than into Sessoyne he dressid his peple and forstalled the Romaynes from the kyd castels and the walled townes. And there ʼsir Vyllers the valyaunte made his avow evyn byfore the kyngeʼ to take other to sle the vycounte of Rome, or ellys to dye therefore.

25   Than the kynge commaunded sir Cadore to take hede to the rerewarde: 'And take renkys of the Rounde Table whan they be ouermatched Nay sayd Launcelot and the other For ones shamed maye neuer be recouerd

(8)   Now leue we kynge Arthur and his noble knyghtes whiche had wonne the felde and had brought theyre prysoners to parys and speke
5 we of a senatour whiche escaped fro the bataille and came to Lucius themperour & sayd to hym Syre emperour I aduyse the for to withdrawe the what dost thow here thow shalt wynne noo thynge in these marches but grete strokes oute of al mesure For this day one of Arthurs knyghtes was worth in the batayll an hondred of ours Fy on the sayd Lucius
10 thow spekest cowardly for thy wordes greue me more than alle the losse that I had this day and anone he sende forth a kynge whiche hyghte syr leomye with a grete armye and badde hym hye hym fast to fore and he wold folowe hastely after kynge Arthur was warned pryuely & sente his peple to Sessoyne and toke vp the townes & castels
15 fro the Romayns Thenne the kyng commaunded syr Cador to take

that the beste lykes, sauff sir Launcelot and sir Bors, with
many mo othir. Sir Kay, sir Clegis shall be there als, and
sir Marroke, sir Marhaulte shall be with me in fere, and all
thes with mo other shall awayte uppon my persone.'

Thus kynge Arthure dispercled all his oste, in dyverse par-   5
tyes that they sholde nat ascape, but to fyght them behovys.

Whan the Emperour was entyrd into the vale of Sessoyne   [2006]
he myght se where kyng Arthure hoved in batayle with
baners displayed. On every syde was he besette, that he
myght nat ascape but other to fyght other to yelde hym,   10
there was none other boote.

'Now I se well,' seyde sir Lucyus, 'yondir traytour hath
betrayed me.'

Than he redressis his knyghtes on dyverse partyes, and
sette up a dragon with eglys many one enewed with sabyl,   15
and than he lete blow up with trumpettes and with
tabours, that all the vale dyndled. And than he lete crye on
lowde, that all men myght here: 'Syrs, ye know well that the   [2033]
honoure and worshyp hath ever folowyd the Romaynes. And
this day let hit nevir be loste for the defaughte of herte, for I   20
se well by yondyr ordynaunce this day shall dye much peple.
And therefore do doughtly this day, and the felde is   85ᵉ
ourys.'

Than anone the Welshe kyng was so nygh that he herde   [2044]

the rereward & to take with hym certayne knyghtes of the round table
and syre Launcelot syre Bors syr kay syre Marrok with syre Marhaus
shalle awayte on our persone Thus the kynge Arthur disperplyd his
hoost in dyuerse partyes to thende that his enemyes sold not escape
whanne the Emperour was entyrd in to the vale of Sessoyne he myghte   5
see where kynge Arthur was enbatailled and his baner dysplayed and
he was bysette round aboute with his enemyes that nedes he must
fyghte or yelde hym for he myght not flee But sayd openly vnto the
Romayns syrs I admoneste you that this day ye fyghte and acquyte
yow as men and remembre how Rome domyneth and is chyef and   10
hede ouer alle the erthe* (*MA* 2035 that regnede in erthe) and vynuer-
sal world and suffre not these bretons thys day to abyde ageynste vs &
ther with he dyd commaunde hys trōpettes to blowe the blody sownes in
suche wyse that the ground trembled and dyndled Thenne the batails
approuched and shoue and showted on bothe sydes and grete strokes   15

18 *W* lowde with trumpettes and with tabours that all the vale dyned and than (*see
note*)

sir Lucyus. Than he dressed hym to the vycounte his avow
for to holde. His armys were full clene and therein was a
dolefull dragon, and into the vawarde he p⟨r⟩ykys hym with
styff spere in honde, and there he mette wyth ˋthe valyaunte
5 Vyllers hymself that was vycounte of Rome,´ and there he
smote hym thorow the shorte rybbys with a speare, that the
bloode braste oute on every syde, and so fylle to the erthe
[2066] and never spake mo wordys aftir. Than the noble sir Uwayne
boldely approched and gyrde thorowoute the Emperoures
10 batayle where was the thyckest prece, and slew a grete lorde
by the Emperours standard, and than flow to the baner and
strake hit thorowoute with his bryght swerde, and so takyth
hit fro hem and rydyth with hit away unto his felyship.

[2073]   Than sir Launcelot lepe forth with his stede evyn streyght
15 unto sir Lucyus, and in his wey he smote thorow a kynge
that stoode althirnexte hym, and his name was Jacounde,
a Sarezen full noble. And than he russhed forth unto
sir Lucyus and smote hym on the helme with his swerde,
that he felle to the erthe; and syth he rode thryse over
20 hym on a rowe, and so toke the baner of Rome and rode
with hit away unto Arthure hymself. And all seyde that
hit sawe there was never knyght dud more worshyp in his
dayes.

[2085]   Than dressed hym sir Bors unto a sterne knyght and
25 smote hym on the umbrell, that his necke braste. Than he
joyned his horse untyll a sterne gyaunte, and smote hym
thorow bothe sydys, and yet he slewe in his way turnyng
two other knyghtes.

[2095]   Be than the bowemen of Inglonde and of Bretayne began
85ᵛ 30 to shote, and these othir, Romaynes and Sarezens, shotte
with dartis and with crosse-bowys. There began a stronge
batayle on every syde and muche slaughter on the Romaynes
party, and the Douchemen with quarels dud muche harme,
for they were with the Romaynes with hir bowys of horne.
35 And the grete gyauntes of Gene kylled downe many knyghtes,

were smyten on bothe sydes many men ouerthrowen hurte & slayn and
grete valyaunces prowesses and appertyces of werre were that day
shewed whiche were ouer long to recounte the noble feates of euery
man For they shold conteyne an hole volume But in especyal kynge
5 Arthur rode in the bataille exhortynge his knyghtes to doo wel and hym

with clubbys of steele crusshed oute hir braynes. Also they
sqwatte oute the braynes of many coursers.

Whan Arthure had aspyed the gyauntes workes he cryed [2119]
on lowde that knyghtes myght here and seyde, 'Fayre
lordys, loke youre name be nat loste! Lese nat youre wor- 5
shyp for yondir bare-legged knavys, and ye shall se what I
shall do as for my trew parte.' He toke there oute Excalyber
`and gurdys towarde Galapas that grevid hym moste.` `He
kut hym of by the kneis clenly there in sondir:` 'Now art
thou of a syse,' seyde the kynge, 'lyke unto oure ferys,' and 10
than he strake of his hede swyftely.

Than come in sir Cadore and sir Kay, sir Gawayne and
good sir Launcelot, sir Bors, sir Lyonel, and sir Ector de
Marys, and sir Ascamore the good knyght that never fayled
his lorde, sir Pelleas and sir Marhault that were proved 15
men of armys. All thes grymly knyghtes sette uppon the
gyauntys, and `by the dyntys were dalte and the dome yoldyn`
they had felled hem starke dede of fyffty all to the bare erthe.

So forth they wente wyth the kynge, tho knyghtes of the [2135]
Rounde Table. Was never kyng nother knyghtes dud 20
bettir syn God made the worlde. They leyde on with longe
swerdys and swapped thorow braynes. Shyldys nother no
shene armys myght hem nat withstonde tyll they leyde on
the erthe ten thousand at onys. Than the Romaynes reled
a lytyl, for they were somwhat rebuked, but kyng Arthure 25
with his pryce knyghtes preced sore aftir. **86**^r

Than sir Kay, sir Clegis and sir Bedwere the ryche en- [2157]
countyrs with them by a clyffsyde, and there they three by
good meanys slowe in that chace mo than fyve hondred.
And also sir Kay roode unto a kyng of Ethyopé and bare 30
hym thorow, and as he turned hym agayne towarde his
ferys a tyrraunte strake hym betwyxte the breste and the

---

self dyd as nobly with his handes as was possyble a man to doo he drewe
oute Excalibur his swerd and awayted euer where as the romayns were
thyckest and moost greued his peple and anone he adressyd hym on that
parte and hewe and slewe doune ry3t and rescued his peple and he slewe
a grete gyaunt named galapas whiche was a man of an huge quantyte 5
and heyghte he shorted hym and smote of bothe his legges by the knees
sayenge Now arte thow better* (*MA* 2128 handsomere in hye) of
a syse to dele with than thou were and after smote of his hede there syre

bowellys, and as he was hurte yet he turned hym agayne
and smote the todir on the hede, that to the breste hit raughte,
and seyde, 'Thoughe I dey of thy dente, thy praysyng shall
be lytyll.'

5 Whan sir Clegys and sir Bedwere saw that sir Kay was hurt
they fared with the Romaynes as grayhoundis doth with
[2185] harys. And than they returned ayen unto noble kynge Arthure and tolde hym how they had spedde.

'Sir kyng,' sayde sir Kay, 'I have served the longe. Now
10 bryng me unto som beryellys for my fadyrs sake, and commaunde me to dame Gwenyvere, thy goodly quene, and grete
well `my worshypfull wyff that wratthed me never,´ and byd
hir for my love to worche for my soule.'

Than wepte kynge Arthure for routhe at his herte and
15 seyde, 'Thou shalt lyve for ever, my herte thynkes.' And
therewith the kynge hymself pulled oute the truncheoune of
the speare and made lechis to seche hym sykerly, and founde
nother lyvir nor lungys nother bowelles that were attamed.
And than the kyng putte hym in hys owne tente with syker
20 knyghtes and sayde, 'I shall revenge thy hurte and I may
aryght rede.'

[2204] Than the kynge in this malyncoly metys with a kynge,
and with Excalyber he smote his bak in sundir. Than in
that haste he metys with anothir, and gurde hym in the
25 waste thorow bothe sydes. Thus he russhed here and there
`thorow the thyckyst prees more than thirty tymes.´

[2218] Than sir Launcelot, sir Gawayne and sir Lovelys son
gerde oute one that one hande where Lucyus the Emperoure
86ᵛ hymself in a launde stoode. Anone as sir Lucyus sawe sir
30 Gawayne he sayde all on hyght, 'Thou art welcom iwys, for
thou sekyst aftir sorow. Here thou shalt be sone overmacched!' Sir Launcelot was wroth at hys grymme wordys
and gurde to hym with his swerde aboven uppon hys bryght
helme, that the raylyng bloode felle doune to his feete.

[2226] 35 And sir Gawayne wyth his longe swerde leyde on faste,
that three amerallys deyde thorow the dynte of his hondis.
And so Lovel fayled nat in the pres; he slew a kynge and

gawayn foughte nobly and slewe thre admyrales in that bataill And

36–p. 223, l. 2 *W (sidenote)* How sir Gawayne slew iii. admyrayllys in batayle

a deuke that knyghtes were noble. Than the Romaynes [2234]
releved. Whan they sye hir lorde so hampred they chaced and
choppedde doune many of oure knyghtes good, and in that
rebukyng they bare the bolde Bedwere to the colde erthe,
and wyth a ranke swerde he was merveylously wounded. Yet 5
sir Launcelot and sir Lovel rescowed hym blyve.

With that come in kynge Arthure with the knyghtes of [2242]
the Table Rounde and rescowed the ryche men that never
were lyke to ascape at that tyme, for oftetymes thorow envy
grete hardynesse is shewed that hath bene the deth of many 10
kyd knyghtes; for thoughe they speke fayre many one unto
other, yet whan they be in batayle eyther wolde beste be
praysed.

Anone as kynge Arthure had a syght of the Emperour [2244]
Lucyus, for kynge nother for captayne he taryed no lenger. 15
And eythir with her swerdys swapped at othir. So sir Lucyus with his swerde hit Arthure overthwarte the nose and
gaff hym a wounde nyghe unto the tunge. Sir Arthure was
wroth and gaff hym another with all the myght that in his
arme was leved, that frome the creste of his helme unto the 20
bare pappys hit wente adoune, and so ended the Emperour. [2255]
Than the kynge mette with sir Cadore, his kene cousyn, [2261]
and prayde hym, 'Kylle doune clene for love of sir Kay, my
foster-brother, and for the love of sir Bedwer that longe hath 87ʳ

so dyd alle the knyghtes of the round table Thus the bataill bitwene
kynge Arthur and Lucius themperour endured longe Lucius had on
his syde many sarasyns whiche were slayn and thus the bataille was grete
and oftsydes that one party was at a fordele and anone at an afterdele
whiche endured so longe tyl at the last kyng Arthur aspyed where 5
Lucius themperour fought and dyd wonder with his owne handes
And anon he rode to hym And eyther smote other fyersly and atte last
Lucyus smote Arthur thwart the vysage and gaf hym a large wound
And whanne kyng Arthur felte hym self hurte anon he smote hym
ageyne with Excalibur that it clefte his hede fro the somette of his hede 10
and stynted not tyl it cam to his breste And thenne themperour fylle
doune dede and there ended his lyf And whan it was knowen that
themperour was slayne anone alle the Romayns with all their hoost
put them to flyght and kynge Arthur with alle his knyghtes folowed
the chaas and slewe doune ryght alle them that they myghte atteyne 15

20–21 *W* (*sidenote*) How kyng Arthure slew the Emperour of rome sir lucyus

me served. Therefore save none for golde nothir for sylver:
for they that woll accompany them with Sarezens, the man
that wolde save them were lytyll to prayse. And therefore
sle doune and save nother hethyn nothir Crystyn.'

5 `Than sir Cadore, sir Clegis, ⟨they⟩ caughte to her
swerdys´, and sir Launcelot, sir Bors, sir Lyonel, sir Ector
de Marys, they whyrled thorow many men of armys. And
sir Gawayne, sir Gaherys, sir Lovell and sir Florens, his brothir that was gotyn of sir Braundyles systir uppon a moun-
10 tayne, all thes knyghtes russhed forth in a frunte with many
mo knyghtes of the Rounde Table that here be not rehersid.
They hurled over hyllys, valeyes, and clowys, and slow
downe on every honde wondirfull many, `that thousandis
in an hepe lay thrumbelyng togedir.´

15 But for all that the Romaynes and the Sarezens cowde do
other speke to y⟨e⟩lde themself there was none saved, but
all yode to the swerde. For evir kynge Arthure rode in the
thyckeste of the pres and raumped downe lyke a lyon many
senatours noble. He wolde nat abyde uppon no poure man
20 for no maner of thyng, and `ever he slow slyly and slypped
to another´ tylle all were slayne to the numbir of a hondred
thousand, and yet many a thousande ascaped thorow prevy
frendys.

[2278] And than relevys the kynge with his noble knyghtes and
25 rensaked over all the feldis for his bolde barouns. And tho
that were dede were buryed as their bloode asked, and they
that myght be saved there was no salve spared nother no
deyntés to dere that myght be gotyn for golde other sylver.
And thus he let save many knyghtes that wente never to
30 recover, but for sir Kayes recovir and of sir Bedwers the
ryche was never man undir God so glad as hymself was.

And thus was the vyctory gyuen to kynge Arthur & the tryumphe and
there were slayne on the party of Lucius moo than an honderd thousand
And after kyng Arthur dyd doo ransake the dede bodyes and dyd doo
burye them that were slayne of his retenue euery man accordynge to
5 the state & degree that he was of And them that were hurte he lete
the surgyens doo serche their hurtes and woundes and commaunded
to spare no salues ne medecynes tyl they were hole Thenne the kyng
rode strayte to the place where themperour lucius lay dede and with

6 *W* sir Bors sir Lyonel sir Bors sir Ector   16 *W* yolde

Than the kynge rode streyte thereas the Emperoure lay, 87ᵛ [2290]
and garte lyffte hym up lordely with barounes full bolde,
and the sawdon of Surré and of Ethyopé the kyng, and of
Egypte and of Inde two knyghtes full noble, wyth seventene
other kynges were takyn up als, and also syxty senatours 5
of Roome that were honoured full noble men, and all the
elders. The kynge let bawme all thes with many good
gummys and setthen lette lappe hem in syxtyfolde of sendell
large, and than lete lappe hem in lede that for chauffynge
other chongyng they sholde never savoure, and sytthen lete 10
close them in chestys full clenly arayed, and their baners
abovyn on their bodyes, and their shyldys turned upwarde,
that eviry man myght knowe of what contray they were.

So on the morne they founde in the heth three senatours [2306]
of Rome. Whan they were brought to the kynge he seyde 15
thes wordis:

'Now to save your lyvys I take no force grete, with that ye
woll meve on my message unto grete Rome and presente
thes corses unto the proude Potestate and aftir [shewe] hym
my lettyrs and my hole entente. And telle hem in haste they 20
shall se me, and I trow they woll beware how they bourde
with me and my knyghtes.'

Than the Emperour hymself was dressed in a charyot, [2338]
and every two knyghtys in a charyot cewed aftir other, and
the senatours com aftir by cowplys in a corde. 25

'Now sey ye to the Potestate and all the lordys aftir that I

hym he fond slayne the Sowdan of Surrey the kynge of Egypte and of
Ethyope which were two noble kynges with xvij other kynges of
dyuerse regyons and also syxty senatours of Rome al noble men whome
the kynge dyd do bawme and gomme with many good gommes aroma-
tyk and after dyd do cere them in syxty fold of cered clothe of Sendale 5
and leyd them in chestys of leed by cause they shold not chauffe ne
sauoure and vpon alle these bodyes their sheldes with theire armes and
baners were sette to thende they shold be knowen of what countrey
they were and after he fonde thre Senatours whiche were on lyue to
whome he sayd for to saue your lyues I wylle that ye take these dede 10
bodyes and carye them with yow vnto grete Rome and presente them
to the potestate on my behalue shewynge hym my letters and telle
them that I in my persone shal hastely be atte Rome And I suppose the
Romayns shalle beware how they shal demaunde ony trybute of me
And I commaunde yow to saye whan ye shal come to Rome to the 15

Q

sende hem the trybet that I owe to Rome, for this is the trew
trybet that I and myne elders have loste this ten score
wyntyrs. And sey hem as mesemes I have sent hem the
hole somme, and yf they thynke hit nat inowe, I shall amend
5 hit whan that I com. ⌐And ferthermore I charge you to saye
to them never to demaunde trybute ne taxe of me ne of
my londes¬, for suche tresoure muste they take as happyns
us here.'

88ʳ   So on the morne thes senatours rayked unto Rome, and
10 within eyghtene dayes they come to the Potestate and tolde
[2358] hym how they hadde brought ˋthe taxe and the trewage
of ten score wynters´ ˋbothe of Ingelonde, Irelonde, and of
all the Est londys.´ 'For kyng Arthure commaundys you
nother trybet nother taxe ye never none aske uppon payne
15 of youre hedys, but yf youre tytil be the trewer than ever
ought ony of your elders. And for these causys ˋwe have
foughtyn in Fraunce, and there us is foule happed,´ for all
is chopped to the deth bothe the bettir and the worse. Therefore I rede you store you wyth stuff, for war is at honde.
20 ˋFor in the moneth of May this myscheff befelle´ ˋin the
contrey of Constantyne by the clere stremys,´ and there he

potestate and all the counceylle and Senate that I sende to them these
dede bodyes for the trybute that they haue demaunded And yf they be
not content with these I shal paye more at my comynge for other
trybute owe I none ne none other wylle I paye And me thynketh this
5 suffyseth for Bretayne Irlond and al Almayne with germanye And
ferthermore* I charge yow to saye to them that I commaunde them
*vpon payne of theyre hedes neuer to demaunde trybute ne taxe of
me ne of my bondes (S londes) (*MA* 2348–50 Bott byde them
neuere be so bolde, whylls my blode regnes, Efte for to brawlle þem
10 for my brode landez, Ne to aske trybut ne taxe be nakyn tytle, Bot
syche tresoure as this, whilles my tym lastez) Thenne with this charge
and commaundement the thre Senatours afore sayd departed with alle
the sayd dede bodyes leynge the body of Lucius in a carre* (*MA* 2355
Bekende them the caryage) couerd with tharmes of the Empyre al
15 alone And after alwey two bodyes of kynges in a charyot and thenne
the bodyes of the Senatours after them and soo wente toward Rome and
shewed theyr legacyon & message to the potestate and Senate recount-
yng the bataylle done in Fraunce and how the feld was lost and moche
people & Innumerable slayne wherfore they aduysed them in no wyse
20 to meue no more warre ageynste that noble conqueroure Arthur For

hyred us with his knyghtes and heled them that were hurte
that same day and to bery them that were slayne.'

Now turne we to Arthure with his noble knyghtes that [2386]
entryth streyghte into Lushburne and so thorowe Flaundirs
and than to Lorayne. He laughte up all the lordshyppys, and 5
sytthen he drew hym into Almayne and unto Lumbardy the
ryche, and `setee lawys in that londe that dured longe aftir.´
`And so into Tuskayne, and there the tirrauntys destroyed,´
`and there were captaynes full kene that kepte Arthurs com-
yng,´ and at streyte passages slew muche of his peple, and 10
there they vytayled and garnysshed many good townys.

But there was a cité kepte sure defence agaynste Arthure [2416]
and his knyghtes, and therewith angred Arthure and seyde
all on hyght, 'I woll wynne this towne other ellys many a
doughty shall dye!' And than the kynge approched to the 15
wallis withoute shelde sauff his bare harneys.

`'Sir,' seyde sir Florence, 'foly thou workeste´ for to nyghe
so naked this perleouse cité.'

'And thow be aferde,' seyde kyng Arthure, 'I rede the faste
fle, `for they wynne no worshyp of me but to waste their 20
toolys;´ for there `shall never harlot have happe, by the helpe 88ᵛ
of oure Lord´, `to kylle a crowned kynge that with creyme is
anoynted.'´

Than the noble knyghtes of the Rounde Table approched [2448-64]
unto the cité and their horsis levys. They hurled on a 25
frunte streyght unto the barbycans, and there they slewe
downe all that before them stondys, and in that bray the
brydge they wanne; and had nat the garnyson bene, they had
wonne within the yatys and the cité wonne thorow wyght- [2472]
nesse of hondys. And than oure noble knyghtes withdrew 30
them a lytyll and wente unto the kynge and prayde hym to

his myght and prowesse is most to be doubted seen the noble kynges
and grete multytude of knyghtes of the round table to whome none
erthely prynce may compare

Now torne we vnto kynge Arthur and his noble knyghtes whiche (9)
after the grete bataylle acheued ageynste the Romayns entryd in to 5
Lorayne braban and Flaundres and sythen retorned in to hault Almayn
and so ouer the mōtayns in to lombardye and after in to Tuskane
wherein was a Cyte whiche in no wyse wold yelde them self ne obeye
wherfore kynge Arthur biseged it and lay longe aboute hit and gaf

†

take his ⟨herborgage⟩. ˋAnd than he pyght his pavylyons of palle, and plantys all aboute´ the sege, and there he lette sett up suddeynly many engynes.

[2483] Than the kynge called unto hym sir Florens and seyde
5 these wordys: 'My folk ys wexen feble for wantynge of vytayle, and ˋhereby be forestes full fayre, and thereas oure foomen many.´ And I am sure they have grete store of bestes. And thyder shall thou go to forrey that forestes, and with the shall go sir Gawayne, ˋand sir Wysharde with
10 sir Walchere, two worshypfull knyghtes,´ ˋwith all the wyseste men of the Weste marchis.´ ˋAlso sir Cleremount and sir Clegis that were comly in armys,´ ˋand the captayne of Cardyff that is a knyght full good.´ Now go ye and warne all this felyshep that hit be done as I commaunde.'

15 So ˋwith that forth yode sir Florens, and his felyshyp was
[2503] sone redy,´ and so they rode thorow holtys and hethis, thorow foreste and over hyllys. And than they com into a lowe medow that was full of swete floures, and there thes noble knyghtes bayted her ⌐horses⌐.

[2510] 20 And in the grekynge of the day sir Gawayne hente his hors wondyrs for to seke. ˋThan was he ware of a man armed walkynge a paase by a woodis ease´ by a revers syde, and his shelde braced on his sholdir, and he on a stronge horse

many assaultes to the Cyte And they within deffended them valyauntly Thenne on a tyme the kynge called syr florence a knyght and sayd to hym they lacked vytaylle and not ferre from hens ben grete forestes and woodes wherin ben many of myn enemyes with moche bestyayl I
5 wyl that thou make the redy and goo thyder in foreyeng and take with the syr Gawayn my neuew Syre wysshard syre Clegys Syre Cleremond and the Captayn of Cardef with other & brynge with yow alle the beestes that ye there can gete And anone these knyghtes made them redy and rode ouer holtys & hyllys thurgh forestes and woodes* (*MA*
10 2503-4 Thorowe hopes and hymland, hillys and oþer, Holtis and hare-woddes) tyl they cam in to a fayr medow ful of fayre floures and grasse And there they rested them & theyr horses* (*W* her stedis; *MA* 2509 þeire horses) alle that nyghte And in the spryngynge of the day in the next morne syre Gawayn took his hors and stale away*
15 (*MA* 2513 weendes owtt) from his felauship to seke some aduentures And anon he was ware of a man armed walkynge his hors easyly by

1 *W* take his baronage (*MA* 2475 hyes to þe harbergage)   19 *W* her stedis

rydys withoute man wyth hym save a boy alone that bare **89ʳ**
a grymme speare. The knyght bare in his shelde ╵of golde
glystrand three gryffons in sabyll╵ and charbuckkle, the
cheff of sylver. Whan sir Gawayne was ware of that gay
knyght, than he gryped a grete spere and rode streyght ₅
towarde hym on a stronge horse for to mete with that sterne
knyght where that he hoved. Whan sir Gawayne com hym
nyghe, in Englyshe he asked hym what he was. And that
other knyght answerde in his langage of Tuskayne and
sayde,   ₁₀
  ╵'Whother pryckyst thou, pylloure, that profers the so [2533]
large?╵ Thou ⌜getest⌝ no pray, prove whan the lykys, for
╵my presoner thou shalt be for all thy proude lokys.╵' 'Thou
spekyste proudly,' seyde sir Gawayne, 'but I counseyle the
for all thy grymme wordis that ╵thou gryppe to the thy gere ₁₅
or [gretter] grame falle.╵'
  Than hir launcis ⌜and speres⌝ they handylde by crauff
of armys, and com on spedyly with full syker dyntes, and
there ╵they shotte thorow shyldys and mayles, and thorow
there shene shuldyrs╵ they were thorowborne the brede ₂₀
of an hande. ╵Than were they so wroth that away wolde
they never╵, but rathly russhed oute their swerdys ╵and
hyttys on their helmys with hatefull dyntys,╵ ╵and stabbis
at hir stomakys with swerdys well steled.╵ ╵So freysshly

a wodes syde and his sheld laced to his sholdre syttynge on a stronge
courser withoute ony man sauyng (*S* sauyng to) a page berynge a
myghty spere The knyght bare in his sheld thre gryffons of gold in
sable charbuncle the chyef of syluer whan syre Gawayn aspyed this
gay knyght he fewtryd his spere and rode strayt to hym and demaūded ₅
of hym from whens that he was that other ansuerd and sayd he was of
Tuscane and demaunded of syre gawayn what profryst thow proude
knyghte the so boldly here getest* (*MA* pykes) thou no praye thou
mayst proue whā thou wylt for thou shalt be my prysoner or thou departe Thenne sayd gawayn thou auauntest the gretely and spekest ₁₀
proude wordes I coūceylle the for alle thy boost that thou make the
redy and take thy gere to the to fore gretter* (*W* or more) grame falle
to the
  Thenne they took theyr speres* (*MA* 2541–2 Than þeire launces (10)
they lachen, thes lordlyche byernes, Laggen with longe speres) and ₁₅
ranne eche at other with alle the myghte they had and smote eche other
thurgh their sheldes in to theyr sholders wherfore anone they pulled

tho fre men fyghtes on the grounde´, `whyle the flamynge
fyre flowe oute of hir helmys.´

[2557]   Than sir Gawayne was grevid wondirly sore and swynges
his ⌐good⌐ swerde Galantyne, and grymly he strykys, and
5 clevys the knyghtes shylde in sundir. And thorowoute the
thycke haubirke made of sure mayles, and the rubyes that
were ryche, he russhed hem in sundir, that men myght
beholde the lyvir and longes. `Than groned the knyght for
his grymme woundis and gyrdis to sir Gawayne´ and
10 awkewarde hym strykes, and brastyth the rerebrace and
the vawmbrace bothe, and kut thorow a vayne, that Gawayne
89ᵛ sore greved, for `so worched his wounde that his wytte
chonged,´ and therewithall his armure was all blody berenne.

[2574]   Than that knyght talked to sir Gawayne and `bade hym
15 bynde up his wounde, 'or thy ble chonge,´ `for thou all
bebledis this horse and thy bryght wedys,´ `for all the
barbers of Bretayne shall nat thy blood staunche.´ For
who that is hurte with this blaade bleed shall he ever'.

[2579]   `'Be God,' sayde sir Gawayne, 'hit grevys me but lytyll,´
20 yet shalt thou nat feare me for all thy grete wordis. `Thow
trowyste with thy talkynge to tame my herte´, but yet thou
betydys tene or thou parte hense but thou telle me in haste
who may stanche my bledynge.'

'That may I do, and I woll, so thou wolt succour me

oute their swerdes and smote grete strokes that the fyre sprange oute
of their helmes Thenne syre gawayne was al abasshed and with
galatyn his good swerd* (*W* his swerde Galantyne; *MA* 2558 Galuthe
his gude swerde) he smote thurgh shelde and thycke hauberke made of
5 thyck maylles and al to russhed and brake the precious stones and made
hym a large wounde that men myghte see* (*MA* 2561 men myghte see)
bothe lyuer and long Thenne groned that knyght and adressyd hym
to syre Gawayn & with an awke stroke gaf hym a grete wound and
kytte a vayne whiche greued gawayn sore and he bledde sore Thenne
10 the knyghte sayd to syre Gawayn bynde thy wounde or thy blee chaunge
for thou bybledest al thy hors and thy fayre armes For alle the Barbours
of Bretayne shal not conne staunche thy blood For who someuer is
hurte with this blade he shalle neuer be staunched of bledynge Thenne
ansuerd gawayn hit greueth me but lytyl thy grete wordes shalle not
15 feare me ne lasse my courage but thow shalt suffre tene and sorow or
we departe but telle me in hast who maye staunche my bledynge That

4 *O¹* Galantyne, his good swerde

that I myght be fayre crystynde and becom meke for my
mysdedis. Now mercy I Jesu beseche, and I shall becom
Crysten and in God stedfastly beleve, `and thou mayste for
thy manhode have mede to thy soule.'

`'I graunte,' seyde sir Gawayne, 'so God me helpe' to 5 [2589]
fullfyll all thy desyre; thou haste gretly hit deservyd. So
thou say me the soth, `what thou sought here thus sengly
thyself alone,' and what lorde or legeaunte thou art undir.'

'Sir,' he seyde, 'I hyght Priamus, and a prynce is my fadir, [2595]
and `he hath bene rebell unto Rome and overredyn muche of 10
hir londis.' And my fadir is com of Alysaundirs bloode
that was overleder of kynges, and of Ector also was he com
by the ryght lyne; and many mo were of my kynrede, bothe
Judas Macabeus and deuke Josue. And ayre I am alther-
nexte of `Alysaundir and of Aufryke and of all the Oute 15
Iles.' `Yet woll I beleve on thy Lorde that thou belevyst
on,' and take the for thy labour tresour inow. `For I was
so hauté in my herte I helde no man my pere,' so was I
sente into this werre by the assente of my fadir with seven
score knyghtes, and now I have encountred with one hath 20
geevyn [me of] fyghtyng my fylle. Therefore, sir knyght, **90ᵉ**
for thy kynges sake telle me thy name.'

'Sir,' seyde sir Gawayne, 'I am no knyght, but I have be [2620]
brought up in the wardrope with the noble kyng Arthure

may I doo sayd the knyght yf I wylle And so wyll I yf thou wylt
socoure and ayde me that I maye be crystned and byleue on god And
therof I requyre the of thy manhode and it shalle be grete meryte for
thy soule I graunte said Gawayne so god helpe me taccomplysshe alle
thy desyre But fyrst telle me what thou soughtest here thus allone and 5
of what londe and legeaunce thou arte of Syre he sayd my name is
Pryamus and a grete prynce is my fader and he hath ben rebelle vnto
Rome and ouer ryden many of theyr londes My fader is lyneally
descended of Alysaunder and of hector by ryght lynge And duke Iosue
and Machabeus were of oure lygnage I am ryght enherytour of 10
Alysaunder and auffryke and alle the oute yles yet wyl I byleue on thy
lord that thow byleuest on And for thy laboure I shalle yeue the tresour
ynough I was soo elate and hauteyn in my hert that I thought no man
my pere ne to me semblable I was sente in to this werre with seuen score
knyghtes and now I haue encountred with the whiche hast gyuen to 15
me of *fyghtyng my fylle wherfore syr knyghte I pray the to tell me
what thow arte I am no knyght sayd gawayn I haue ben brought vp

wyntyrs and dayes for to take hede to his armoure and all his
other wedis and to poynte all the paltokkys that longe to
hymself `and to dresse doublettis for deukys and erlys.´
`And at Yole he made me yoman and gaff me good gyfftys,´
5 more than `an hondred pounde and horse and harneyse
rych.´ And yf I have happe ⟨to⟩ my hele to serve my lyege
lorde I shall be well holpyn in haste.´

[2632] 'A,' sayde sir Priamus, `'and his knavys be so kene, his
knyghtes ar passynge good.´ Now for thy Kynges love of
10 Hevyn and for thy kyngys love, whether thou be knave
other knyght, telle thou me thy name.'

'Be God,' seyde sir Gawayne, 'now woll I telle the soth.
[2638] ⌜My name is syre Gawayn.⌝ `I am knowyn in his courte
and kyd in his chambir´ `and rolled with the rychest of the
15 Rounde Table,´ and I am a deuke dubbed wyth his owne
hondis. `Therefore grucche nat, good sir, if me this grace is
behappened:´ hit is the goodnesse of God that lente me
this strength.'

[2646] 'Now am I bettir pleased,' sayde sir Pryamus, 'than thou
20 haddest gyff me the Provynce ⌜and⌝ Perysie the ryche, for I
had levir have be toryn with four wylde horse than ony
yoman had suche a loose wonne of me, other els ony page
other prycker sholde wynne of me the pryce in this felde

in the garderobe with the noble kynge Arthur many yeres for to take
hede to his armour and his other araye and to poynte his paltockes that
longen to hym self At yole last he made me yoman and gaf to me hors
and harneys and an honderd pound in money And yf fortune be my
5 frend I doubte not but to be wel auaunced and holpen by my lyege lord
A sayd Pryamus yf his knauys be so kene and fyers his knyȝtes ben passynge good Now for the kynges loue of heuen whether thou be a knaue
or a knyghte telle thou me thy name By god sayd syre Gawayn Now
wyl I saye the sothe my name is syre gawayn* (*MA* 2638 My name es
10 sir Gawayne) and knowen I am in his courte and in his chambre and
one of the knyghtes of the round table he dubbed me a duke with his
owne (*S* with owne) hand Therfore grutche not yf this grace is to me
fortuned hit is the goodnesse of god that lente to me my strengthe Now
am I better pleasyd sayd Pryamus than thou haddest gyuen to me al
15 the prouynce and* (*MA* 2647 Thane I of Provynce warre prynce and
of Paresche ryche) parys the ryche I had leuer to haue ben torn with

6 *W* happe my hele (*MA* 2630 happe to my hele)   20 *W* provynce of Perysie
the the

gotyn. But now I warne the, sir knyght of the Rounde
Table, here is by the deuke of Lorayne with his knyghtes,
and `the doughtyeste of Dolphyne landys with many Hyghe
Duchemen,´ and many lordis of Lumbardy, and the garneson
of Godarde, `and men of Westewalle, worshypfull kynges;´ 5
and `of Syssoyne and of Southlonde Sarezyns many num-
birde,´ and there named ar in rollys sixty thousand of syker
men of armys.

'Therefore `but thou hyghe the fro this heth, hit woll [2660]
harme us both,´ and sore be we hurte never lyke to recover. 10 **90ᵛ**
But `take thou hede ⟨to the⟩ haynxman that he no horne
blow,´ for and he do, than loke that he be hewyn on pecis:
for here hovys at thy honde a hondred of good knyghtes´
that ar of my retynew and to awayte uppon my persone.
For and thou be raught with that rought, raunsom nother 15
rede golde´ woll they none aske.'

Than sir Gawayne rode over a water for to gyde hymself, [2668]
and that worshypfull knyght hym folowed sore wounded.
And so they rode tylle they com to their ferys that were
baytand hir horsys in a low medow `where lay many lordys 20
lenyng on there shyldys´, `with lawghyng and japyng and
many lowde wordys.´ Anone as sir Wycharde was ware of
sir Gawayne and aspyed that he was hurte `he wente towarde
hym wepyng and wryngyng his hondys.´

Than sir Gawayne tolde hym `how he had macched with 25 [2686]

wylde horses than ony varlet had wonne suche loos or ony page or
pryker shold haue had prys on me But now syre knyghte I warne the
that here by is a duke of Lorayne with his armye and the noblest men
of Dolphyne and lordes of lombardye with the garneson of godard and
sarasyns of Southland ynombred lx M of good men of armes wherfore 5
but yf we hye vs hens it wylle harme vs bothe for we ben sore hurte
neuer lyke to recouer but take hede to my page that he no horne blowe
For yf he doo ther ben houynge fast by an C knyȝtes awaytynge on my
persone and yf they take the ther shall no raunson of gold ne syluer
acquyte the Thenne syre gawayne rode ouer a water for to saue hym 10
And the knyghte folowed hym and soo rode forthe tyle they came to
his felawes whiche were in the medowe where they had ben al the
nyghte* (*MA* 2675 And some was sleghte one slepe with slaughte of
þe pople) Anone as syre wychard was ware of syre gawayn and sawe
that he was hurte he ranne to hym soroufully wepynge and demaunded 15
of hym who had soo hurte hym and gawayn told how he had foughten

that myghty man of strengthe.⸗ 'Therefore greve yow nat,
good sir, for thoughe my shylde be now thirled and my
sholdir shorne, yett ⸌thys knyght sir Pryamus hath many
perelouse woundys.⸗ But he hath salvys, he seyth, that woll
5 hele us bothe. But here is new note in honde nere than ye
wene, fore by an houre aftir none I trow hit woll noy us all.'

[2692]   Than sir Pryamus and sir Gawayne alyght bothe and lette
hir horsys bayte in the fayre medow. ⸌Than they lette
brayde of hir basnettys and hir brode shyldys.⸗ Than eythir
10 bled so muche that every man had wondir ⸌they myght sitte
in their sadyls or stonde uppon erthe.⸗

[2704]   'Now fecche me,' seyde sir Pryamus, 'my vyall that hangys
by the gurdyll of my haynxman, for ⸌hit is full of the floure
of the four good watyrs⸗ that passis from Paradyse, ⸌th⟨at⟩
15 mykyll fruyte in fallys that at one day fede shall us all.⸗
Putt that watir in oure fleysh where the syde is tamed, and
we shall be hole within four houres.'

91ʳ   Than they lette clense their woundys with colde whyght
wyne, and than they lete anoynte them with bawme over
20 and over, and holer men than they were within an houres
[2713] space was never lyvyng syn God the worlde made. So whan
they were clensed and hole ⸌they broched barellys and
brought them the wyne⸗ ⸌wyth brede and brawne and many
ryche byrdys.⸗ And whan they had etyn, ⸢than with a
25 trompet they alle assembled to counceylle, and⸣ sir Gawayne
seyde, 'Lordynges, go to armys!' And whan they were
armed and assembled togedyrs, ⸌with a clere claryon callys
them togedir⸗ to counceyle, and sir Gawayne of the case hem
tellys.

with that man and eche of them hadde hurte other and how he had
salues to hele them but I can telle yow other tydynges that soone we
shal haue adoo with many enemyes Thenne syre pryamus and syre
gawayn alyghted and lete theire horses grase in the medowe and
5 vnarmed them And thenne the blood ranne fresshly fro theyre woundes
And pryamus toke fro his page a vyolle ful of the four waters that came
oute of paradys and with certayne baume enoynted theyr woundes and
wesshe them with that water* (*MA* 2711 with clere watire) & within
an houre after they were both as hole as euer they were And thenne
10 with a trompet were they alle assembled to counceylle* (*MA* 2718–19
With a clayroune clere, thire knyghtez togedyre, callys to concell)

'Now tell us, sir Pryamus, all the hole purpose of yondir pryce knyghtes.'

'Sirs,' seyde sir Pryamus, 'for to rescow me they have made a vowe, other ellys `manfully on this molde to be marred all at onys.´ `This was the pure purpose, whan I 5 passed thens´ `at hir perellys, to preff me uppon payne of their lyvys.´

`'Now, good men,' seyde sir Gawayne, 'grype up your [2725] hertes,´ `and yf we g⟨et⟩tles go ⟨thus⟩ away hit woll greffe oure kynge.´ And sir Florens in this fyght shall here abyde 10 for to kepe the stale as a knyght noble, `for he was chosyn and charged in chambir with the kynge´ `chyfften of this chekke and cheyff of us all.´ `And whethir he woll fyght other fle we shall folow aftir;´ for as for me, `for all yondir folkys faare forsake hem shall I never.´ 15

`'A, fadir!' seyde Florens, 'full fayre now ye speke,´ `for [2735] I am but a fauntekyn to fraysted men of armys,´ and yf I ony foly do the faughte muste be youres. Therefore lese nat youre worshyp. My wytt is but symple, and ye ar oure allther governoure; therefore worke as ye lykys.' 20

'Now, fayre lordys,' seyde sir Pryamus, 'cese youre wordys, I warne you betyme; for ye shall fynde in yondir woodys many perellus knyghtes. They woll putte furth beystys to bayte you oute of numbir, and ye ar fraykis in this fryth nat paste seven hondred, `and that is feythfully to 25 fewe to fyght with so many,´ `for harlottys and haynxmen wol helpe us but a lytyll,´ `for they woll hyde them in haste 91ᵛ for all their hyghe wordys.´

And there pryamus told vnto them what lordes and knyghtes had sworne to rescowe hym and that without faill they shold be assailled with many thousandes wherfor he counceilled them to withdrawe them Thenne syre gawayn sayd it were grete shame to them to auoyde withoute ony strokes Wherfore I aduyse to take oure armes and to 5 make vs redy to mete with these sarasyns and mysbyleuyng men and wyth the helpe of god we shal ouerthrowe them and haue a fayre day on them And syre Florens shall abyde styll in thys felde to kepe the stale as a noble knyghte and we shal not forsake yonder felawes Now sayd Pryamus (*S* Pyramus) seasse your wordes for I warne yow ye shal 10 fynde in yonder woodes many peryllous knyghtes they wylle put forthe

p. 234, l. 14 *WO*¹ the   9 *W* gyltles (*MA* 2727 gettlesse) go this

'Ye sey well,' seyde sir Gawayne, 'so God me helpe!'
'Now, fayre sonne,' sayde sir Gawayne unto Florens, 'woll
ye take youre felyshyp of the beste provyd men to the numbir
of a hondred knyghtes and ˋprestly prove yourself and yondir
5 pray wynne?ˊ

'I assent me with good hert,' seyde Florence.

[2755]   ˋThan sir Florens called unto hym sir Florydas with
fyve score knyghtesˊ, ˋand forth they flynged a faste tro⟨tt⟩eˊ
and the folke of the bestes dryvys. Than folowed aftir
10 sir Florens with noble men of armys fully seven hondred,
and one ˋsir Feraunte of Spayne before on a fayre stedeˊ
ˋthat was fostred in Farmagos: the fende was his fadir.ˊ ˋHe
flyttys towarde sir Florens and sayde, 'Whother flyest thou,ˊ
false knyght?' Than ˋsir Florens was fayne, and in feautyr
15 castis his spereˊ, ˋand rydys towarde the rought and restys
no lengerˊ, and full but in the forehede he hyttys sir Feraunte
[2772]   and brake his necke-bone. Than Feraunte ˋhis cosyn had
grete care and cryed full lowde:ˊ 'Thou haste slayne a knyght
and kynge anoynted that or this tyme founde never frayke
20 that myght abyde hym a buffette. Therefore ye shall dey,
there shall none of you ascape!'

'Fye on the,' seyde Florydas, 'thou eregned wrecche!'

And therewith to hym he flyngis with a swerde, that ˋall
the fleysshe of his flanke he flappys in sundir,ˊ that all the
25 fylth of the freyke and many of his guttys fylle to the erthe.

[2784]   ˋThan lyghtly rydis a raynke for to rescowe that barowneˊ
that was borne in the Rodis, and rebell unto Cryste. ˋHe
preced in proudly and aftir his pray wyndys.ˊ But ˋthe
raynke Rycharde of the Rounde Tableˊ ˋon a rede stede rode

beestes to calle yow on they be out of nombre and ye are not past
vij C whiche ben ouer fewe to fyght with soo many Neuertheless sayd
syr gawayn we shal ones encountre them and see what they can do and
the beste shalle haue the vyctory

(11) 5   Thenne syre Florence callyd to hym syre florydas with an honderd
knyghtes and droofe forth the herde of bestes Thenne folowed hym
vij honderd men of armes and syr Feraunt of spayne on a fayr stede
came spryngynge oute of the woodes and came to syre Florence and
axyd hym why he fledde Thenne syre Florence took his spere and rode
10 ageynste hym and smote hym in the forhede and brake his necke bone

8 *W* trolle (*MA* 2257 trotte)   16–18 *W* (*sidenote*) How Sir fflorens slew Sir fferaunte

hym agaynste´ and threste hym thorow the shylde evyn to
the herte. `Than he rored full rudely, but rose he never-
more.´

`Than alle his feerys mo than fyve hondred´ `felle uppon [2796]
sir Florence and on his fyve score knyghtes.´ `Than sir Flo- 5 **92ʳ**
rens and sir Florydas in feautir bothe castys´ their spearys,
and `they felled fyve at the frunte at the fyrste entré,´ and
sore they assayled our folke and brake browys and brestys
and felde many adowne. `Whan sir Pryamus, the pryse [2811]
knyght, perceyved their gamys´ he yode to sir Gawyne and 10
thes wordys seyde:

'Thy pryse men ar sore begone and put undir, for they ar
oversette with Sarazens mo than five hondred. Now wolde
thou suffir me for the love of thy God with a small parte of
thy men to succoure hem betyme?' 15

`'Sir, grucch ye nat,' seyde sir Gawayne, 'the gre is there [2819]
owne,´ `for they mowe have gyfftys full grete igraunted of
my lorde.´ Therefore lette them fyght whylys hem lystes,
the freysh knyghtes; for som of hem `fought nat their fylle
of all this fyve wyntyr.´ Therefore `I woll nat styrre wyth 20
my stale half my steede length´ `but yf they be stadde wyth
more stuff than I se hem agaynste.'´

So by that tyme was sir Gawayne ware by the woodys [2825]
syde men commynge woodly with all maner of wepon, for
there rode `the erle of Ethelwolde havyng on eyther half´ 25
many hole thousandys; `and the deuke of Douchemen
dressys hym aftir´ and passis with Pryamus knyghtes.

Thenne all thother were meued and thought to auenge the dethe of
syr Feraunt and smote in emonge them and there was grete fyghte and
many slayne and leyd doune to grounde and syr Florence with his
C knyghtes alwey kepte the stale and foughte manly Thenne whan
Pryamus the good knyght perceyued the grede fyght he went to syre 5
Gawayn and badde hym that he shold goo and socoure his felauship
whiche were sore bystad with their enemyes Syr greue yow not sayd
syre Gawayn For theyr gree shall be theirs I shall not ones meue my
hors to them ward but yf I see mo than ther ben For they ben stronge
ynough to matche them & with that he sawe an erle called syre Ethel- 10
wold and the duk of duchemen cam lepyng out of a wood with many
thousādes & pryamus knyȝtes & cam strayte vn to the bataylle thēne sir

27 *W* hym hym aftir

[2851] Than Gawayne, the good knyght, he chered his knyghtes and sayde,

      ˋ'Greve you nat, good men, for yondir grete syght,ˊ and
ˋbe nat abaysshed of yondir boyes in hir bryghte weedis,ˊ
5 ˋfor and we feyght in fayth the felde is ourys!'ˊ

      Than they haled up their brydyls and began walop, and
by that they com nygh by a londys length they jowked
[2875] downe with her hedys many jantyll knyghtes. A more
jolyar joustynge was never sene on erthe. ˋThan the ryche
10 men of the Rounde Table ran thorow the thykkesteˊ with
hir stronge sperys, that many a raynke for that prouesse ran
into the grevys, and durste ˋno knavys but knyghtes kene
92ᵛ of herteˊ fyght more in this felde, but fledde.

      ˋ'Be God,' seyde sir Gawayne, 'this gladys my herteˊˋthat
15 yondir gadlynges be gone, for they made a grete numbir.ˊ
ˋNow ar they fewer in the felde whan they were fyrst num-
byrdˊ by twenty thousand, in feyth, for all their grete boste.'

[2889]   Than Jubeaunce of Geane, a myghty gyaunte, he feautred
his speare to sir Garrarde, a good knyght of Walys. He
20 smote the Waylshe knyght evyn to the herte. Than our
knyghtes myghtyly meddeled wyth hir myddylwarde. But
anone at all assemble many Saresyns were destroyed, ˋfor
[2916] the soveraynes of Sessoyne were salved for ever.ˊ By that
tyme ˋsir Pryamus, the good prynce, in the presence of
25 lordysˊ royall to his penowne he rode and lyghtly hit hentys,
ˋand rode with the royall rought of the Rounde Table,ˊ and
streyte all his retynew folowed hym aftyr oute of the woode.
They folowed as shepe oute of a folde, and streyte they yode
to the felde and stood by their kynge lorde. ˋAnd sytthyn
30 they sente to the deuke thes same wordis:ˊ

gawayn comforted his knyghtes and bad them not to be abasshed for al
shall be ours thēne they began to wallope & mette with their enemyes
ther were mē slayn & ouerthrowen on euery syde Thenne threstyd
in amonge them the knyghtes of the table round and smote doune to
5 the erthe alle them that wythstode them in soo moche that they made
them to recuyelle & flee By god sayd syre Gawayn this gladeth my
herte for now ben they lasse in nombre by xx M Thenne entryd in to
the bataylle Iubaunce a geaunt and fought and slewe doune ryght and
distressyd many of our knyghtes emonge whome was slayne syre Ghe-
10 rard a knyght of walys Thenne oure knyghtes toke herte to them✱

''Sir, we have bene thy sowdyars all this seven wynter', [2925]
and now we forsake the for the love of oure lyege lorde
Arthure, 'for we may with oure worshype wende where us
lykys,' for garneson nother golde have we none resceyved.'

'Fye on you, the devyll have your bonys! For suche 5
sowdyars I sette but a lytyll.'

Than the deuke dressys his Dowchmen streyte unto sir [2940]
Gawayne and to sir Pryamus. So they two gryped their
spearys, and at the gaynyste in he gurdys, wyth hir noble
myghtes. And there sir Pryamus 'metyth with the marquesse 10
of Moyseslonde' and smytyth hym thorow.

'Than Chastelayne, a chylde of kyng Arthurs chambir,'
'he was a warde of sir Gawaynes of the Weste marchis,'
'he chasis to sir Cheldrake that was a chyfteyne noble',
and with his spere he smote thorow Cheldrake, and so 15 **93ᵉ**
'that chek that chylde cheved by chaunce of armys.' But
than they chaced that chylde, that he nowhere myght ascape,
for one with a swerde the halse of the chylde he smote in
too. Whan sir Gawayne hit sawe he wepte wyth all his herte
and inwardly he brente for sorow. 20

But anone Gotelake, a good man of armys, 'for Chastelayne the chylde he chongyd his mode,' 'that the wete
watir wente doune his chykys.' Than sir Gawayne dressis [2971]
hym and to a deuke rydys, and sir Dolphyn the deuke droff
harde agaynste hym. But sir Gawayne hym dressyth with 25
a grete spere, that the grounden hede droff to his herte.
Yette he gate hit oute and ran to another one, sir Hardolf,
an hardy man of armys, and slyly in he lette hit slyppe
thorow, and sodeynly he fallyth to the erthe. Yet he slow
in the slade of men of armys mo than syxty with his hondys. 30
Than was sir Gawayne ware of the man that slew Chaste- [2979]

(*MA* 2903 Rade furth full ernestly) and slewe many sarasyns And
thenne came in syr Priamus with his penon and rode with the knyghtes
of the round table and fought so manfully that many of their enemyes
lost theyr lyues And ther syr Pryamus slewe the Marquys of Moyses
land and syre gawayn with his felawes so quytte hem that they had the 5
feld but in that stoure was syr Chestelayne a chyld and ward of syre
Gawayne slayne wherfor was moche sorou made and his deth wes soone

layne his chylde, and `swyfftly with his swerde he smyttyth
hym thorow.´

  `'Now and thou haddyst ascaped withoutyn scathe, the
scorne had bene oures!'´

5   And aftir sir Gawayne dressis hym unto the route and
russhyth on helmys, and rode streyte to the rerewarde and
so his way holdyth, and sir Pryamus hym allthernexte,
gydynge hym his wayes. And there `they hurtleyth and
hewyth downe hethyn knyghtes many,´ and sir Florence on
10 the other syde dud what he myght. `There the lordys of
Lorayne and of Lumbardy both´ were takyn and lad away
with oure noble knyghtes. `For suche a chek oure lordys
cheved by chaunce of that were´ that they were so avaunced,
for hit avayled hem ever.

[3001] 15   Whan sir Florence and sir Gawayne had the felde wonne,
than they sente before fyve score of knyghtes, `and her
prayes and hir presoners passyth hem aftir.´ And sir Gawayne in a streyte passage he hovyth tyll all the prayes
were paste that streyte patthe that so sore he dredith. So
20 they rode tyll they the cité sawe, and `sothly the same day
93ᵛ with asawte hit was gotyn.´

[3013]   Than sir Florence and sir Gawayne harborowed surely
their peple, and `sytthen turnys to a tente and tellyth the
kynge´ `all the tale truly, that day how they travayled´ and
25 how his ferse men fare welle all.

  'And fele of thy foomen ar brought oute of lyff, and many
worshypfull presoners ar yolden into oure handys. `But
Chastelayne, thy chylde, is chopped of the hede,´ yette slewe
he a cheff knyghte his owne hondys this day.'

30 'Now thanked be God,' sayde the noble kynge, 'but I mervayle muche of that bourely knyght that stondyth by the, for
hym semys to be a straungere, for presonere is he none lyke.'

auengyd Thus was the bataille ended and many lordes of lombardye
and sarasyns left dede in the feld Thenne syre florence and syre
Gawayne herberowed surely theyr peple and token grete plente of
bestyal of gold & syluer and grete tresour and rychesse and retorned
5 vnto kyng Arthur whiche lay styl at the syege And whanne they came
to the kynge they presented theyr prysoners and recounted theyre
aduentures and how they had vaynquysshed theyre enemyes

(12)   Now thanked be god sayd the noble kynge Arthur But what maner

'Sir,' seyde sir Gawayne, 'this is a good man of armys:
he macched me sore this day in the mournyng, and had nat
his helpe bene ⟨dethe⟩ had I founden. And now is he yolden
unto God and to me, sir kyng, for to becom Crysten and on
good beleve. And whan he is crystynde and in the fayth 5
belevys, there lyvyth nat a bettir knyght nor a nobler of
his hondis.'

Than the kynge in haste crystynde hym fayre and lette
conferme hym Priamus, as he was afore, and lyghtly lete
dubbe hym a deuke with his hondys, and made hym knyght 10
of the Table Rounde.

And anone the kynge lette cry asawte unto the towne, [3032]
and there was rerynge of laddyrs and brekynge of wallys.
`The payne that the peple had was pyté to se!´ `Than the [3044]
duches hir dressed with damesels ryche,´ `and the countes 15
of Clarysyn with hir clere maydyns,´ `they kneled in their
kyrtyls there the kynge hovyth´ `and besought hym of
socoure for the sake of oure Lorde:´

'And sey us som good worde and cetyl thy peple`or the
cité suddeynly be with asawte wonne,´ for than shall dye 20
many a soule that grevid the never.'

The kynge ⌜avalyd and⌝ lyffte up his vyser with a knyghtly [3054]
countenaunce, and kneled to hir myldely with full meke
wordes and seyde,

                                                        94ʳ

man is he that standeth by hym self hym semed no prysoner Syre sayd
Gawayne this is a good man of armes he hath matched me but he is
yolden vnto god and to me for to bycome Crysten had not he haue be
we sholde neuer haue rotorned wherfore I pray yow that he may be
baptysed sor (*sic*; *S* for) ther lyueth not a nobler man ne better knyght 5
of his handes thenne the kyng lete hym anon be crystned and dyd doo
calle hym his fyrste name Pryamus and made hym a duke and knyghte
of the table round And thenne anon the kynge lete do crye assaulte to
the cyte and there was rerynge of laddres brekyng of wallys and the
dyche fylled that men with lytel payne myȝt entre in to the cyte thēne 10
cam out a duchesse & Clarysyn the countesse with many ladyes &
damoysels and knelyng bifore kynge Arthur requyred hym for the loue
of god to receyue the cyte & not to take it by assaulte for thenne sholde
many gyltles be slayne thēne the kyng aualyd* (*W* of Walys; *MA* 3054
He weres his vesere) his vyser with a meke & noble coūtenaūce & 15

3 *W* bene þᵗ (*see note*)   22 *W* kynge of Walys

ʻ"Shall none myssedo you, madam, that to me longis,ʼ
ʻfor I graunte the chartyrs and to thy cheff maydyns,ʼ ʻunto
thy chyldern and to thy chyff men in chambirʼ that to the
longis. ʻBut thy deuke is in daunger, my drede ys the lesse.ʼ
5 But ye shall have lyvelode to leve by as to thyne astate fallys.ʼ

[3062] ʻThan Arthure sendyth on eche syde wyth sertayne
lordisʼ ʻfor to cese of their sawte, for the cité was yolden,
and therewith the deukeis eldyst sonne com with the keyes
and kneled downe unto the kynge and besought hym of his
10 grace. ʻAnd there he cesed the sawte by assente of his
lordisʼ, ʻand the deuke was dressed to Dover with the
kynges dere knyghtesʼ ʻfor to dwelle in daunger and dole
dayes of his lyff.ʼ ʻThan the kynge with his crowne on his
hede recoverde the citéʼ and the castell, ʻand the captaynes
15 and connestablys knew hym for lorde,ʼ and there ʻhe delyverde and dalte byfore dyverse lordisʼ a dowré for the
deuches and hir chyldryn. Than he made wardens to welde
all that londis.

[3092] And so ʻin Lorayne and Lumbardy he lodged as a lorde
20 in his owne,ʼ ʻand sette lawys in the londis as hym beste
lyked.ʼ ʻAnd than at Lammas he yode, unto Lusarne he
sought,ʼ ʻand lay at his leyser with lykynges inowe.ʼ ʻThan
he mevys over the mountaynes and doth many mervayles,ʼ
ʻand so goth in by Godarte that Gareth sonne wynnys.ʼ
25 ʻThan he lokys into Lumbardy and on lowde spekyth:ʼ
ʻ"In yondir lykynge londis as lorde woll I dwelle."ʼ

[3112] Sir Florence and sir Floridas that day passed with fyve
hondred good men of armys unto the cité of Virvyn. They
sought at the gaynyste and ʻleyde there a buysshement as

said madame ther shal none of my subgettys mysdoo you ne your
maydens ne to none that to yow longen but the duke shal abyde my
Iugement thenne anone the kyng commaunded to leue the assault
& anon the dukes oldest sone brought out the keyes & knelyng delyuerd
5 them to the kyng & bysouȝt hym of grace & the kyng seased the toun
by assent of his lordes & toke the duc & sent hym to douer there for to
abyde prysoner terme of his lyf & assigned certayn rentes for the dower
of the duchesse & for her children Thenne he made lordes to rule tho
londes & lawes as a lord ought to do in his owne countrey & after he took
10 his iourney toward Rome & sent sir Florys & syr florydas to fore with
v C men of armes & they cam to the cyte of vrbyne & leid there a

hem beste lykys.' So there ⌐yssued⌐ oute of that cité many
hundretthis and skyrmysshed wyth oure foreryders as hem
beste semed. `Than broke oute oure buysshemente and
the brydge wynnys,' and so rode unto their borowys with 4
baners up dysplayed. There fledde much folke oute of 94ᵛ [3068]
numbir `for ferde of sir Florence and his fers knyghtes.'
Than `they busked up a baner abovyn the gatis,' and `of sir
Florence in fayth so fayne were they never.'

The kynge than hovyth on an hylle and lokyth to the [3074]
wallys and sayde, `'I se be yondir sygne the cité is wonne.' 10
Than he lete make a cry thorow all the oste that `uppon
payne of lyff and lymme and also lesynge of his goodys' that
no lyegeman that longyth to his oste sholde lye be no maydens
ne ladyes nother no burgessis wyff that to the cité longis.
So whan this conquerrour com into the cité he passed into 15 [3128]
the castell, and there he lendis and `comfortis the carefull
men with many knyghtly wordis,' and made there a captayne
a knyght of his owne contrey, and the commo⟨n⟩s accorded
theretyll.

Whan the soveraygnes of Myllayne herde that the cité 20 [3134]
was wonne they sente unto kynge Arthure `grete sommys
of sylver, syxty horsys well charged,' and besought hym
as soverayne to have ruthe of the peple, and seyde they
wolde be sudgectes untyll hym for ever `and yelde hym
servyse and sewte surely for hir londys,' `bothe for Pleas- 25
aunce ⌐and Pavye⌐ and Petresaynte and for the Porte
Trembyll,' and `so mekly to gyff ⌐yerly⌐ for Myllayne a

busshement there as them semed most best for them & rode to fore the
toune where anon yssued* (*W* com; *MA* 3116 ischewis) out moche
peple & scarmusshed with the fore rydars thēne brake out the busshement & wan the brydge & after the toun & set vpon the wallis the
kynges baner thēne cam the kynge vpon an hille & sawe the Cyte 5
& his baner on the wallys by whiche he knewe that the Cyte was
wonne & anone he sente & commaunded that none of his lyege men
shold defoule ne lygge by no lady wyf ne maide & whan he cam in
to the cyte he passid to the castel and comforted them that were in
sorou & ordeyned ther a captayn a knyȝt of his own coūtrey & whan 10
they of Melane herd that thylk cyte was wōne they sent to kyng Arthur
grete sōmes of money* (*MA* 3136 golde) & besouȝt hym as their lord

1 *W* ther com

myllyon of golde,´ and ʾmake homage unto Arthure all hir
lyff tymes.´ ʾThan the kynge by his counceyle a conduyte
hem sendys´ so to com in and know hym for lorde.

[3150] ʾThan into Tuskayne he turned whan he tyme semed,´
5 and ʾthere he wynnys towrys and townys full hyghe,´ and
ʾall he wasted in his warrys there he away ryddys.´ ʾThan he
spedys towarde Spolute with his spedfull knyghtys,´ ʾand so
unto Vyterbe he vytayled his knyghtes,´ ʾand to the vale
of Vysecounte he devysed there to lygge´ ʾin that vertuouse
10 vale amonge vynys full.´ ʾAnd there he suggeournys, that
95ʳ soveraigne, with solace at his harte,´ for to wete whether the
senatours wolde hym of succour beseke.

[3176] ʾBut sone after, on a Saturday, sought unto kynge Arthure´
all the senatoures that were on lyve and of the cunnyngst
15 cardynallis that dwelled in the courte, and ʾprayde hym of
pece and profird hym full large;´ and besought hym as a
soverayne ʾmoste governoure undir God for to gyff them
lycence´ for syx wekys large, that they myght be assembled
all, and than in the cité of Syon that is Rome callyd ʾto
20 crowne hym there kyndly, with crysemed hondys,´ with
septure, forsothe, as an Emperoure sholde.

'I assente me,' seyde the kynge, 'as ye have devysed, and
[3213] comly be Crystmas to be crowned, hereafter to reigne in
my asstate and to kepe my Rounde Table ʾwith the rentys

to haue pyte of them promysyng to be his subgettys for euer & yelde
to hym homage & fealte for the lādes of plesaūce & pauye* (*MA* 3141
and for Pavy) petersaynt & the port of tremble & to gyue hym yerly*
(*MA* 3144 ilke a ȝere) a melyon of gold al his lyf tyme thēne he rydeth
5 in to Tuskane & wynneth tounes & castels & wasted al in his way that
to hym wil not obeye & so to spolute & viterbe & fro thens he rode in
to the vale of vycecoūte emong the vynes And fro thens he sente to
the senatours to wete whether they wold knowe hym for theyr lord
But soone after on a saterday came vnto kynge Arthur alle the senatours
10 that were left on lyue and the noblest Cardynals that thenne dwellyd
in Rome And prayd hym of pees and profered hym ful large And
bysought hym as gouernour to gyue lycence for vj wekes for to assemble
alle the Romayns And thenne to crowne hym Emperour with creme
as it bylongeth to so hyhe astate I assente sayd the kynge lyke as
15 ye haue deuysed and at crystemas there to be crowned and to holde
my round table with my knyghtes as me lyketh And thenne the
senatours maade redy for his Intronysacyon And at the day appoynted

of Rome to rule as me lykys;' and than, as I am avysed, to gete me over the salte see with good men of armys to deme for His deth that for us all on the roode dyed.' [3217]

Whan the senatours had this answere, unto Rome they turned and made rydy for his corownemente in the moste 5 noble wyse. And at the day assigned, as the romaynes me tellys, he was crowned Emperour by the Poopys hondis, with all the royalté in the worlde to welde for ever. There they suggeourned that seson tyll aftir the tyme, and stabelysshed all the londys frome Rome unto Fraunce, and gaff 10 londis and rentys unto knyghtes that had hem well deserved. There was none that playned on his parte, ryche nothir poore. Than he commaunded sir Launcelot and sir Bors to take kepe unto their fadyrs landys that kynge Ban and kynge Bors welded and her fadyrs: 15

'Loke that ye take seynge in all your brode londis, and cause youre lyege men to know you as for their kynde lorde, and suffir never your soveraynté to be alledged with your 95ᵛ subjectes, nother the soveraygne of your persone and londys. Also the myghty kynge Claudas I gyff you for to parte 20 betwyxte you evyn, for to mayntene your kynrede, that be noble knyghtes, so that ye and they to the Rounde Table make your repeyre.'

Sir Launcelot and sir Bors de Gaynys thanked the kynge fayre and sayde their hertes and servyse sholde ever be his 25 owne.

'Where art thou, Priamus? Thy fee is yet behynde. Here I make the and gyff the deukedom of Lorayne for ever unto the and thyne ayres; and whan we com into Ingelonde, for to purvey the of horse-mete, a fifty thousand quarterly, for 30 to mayntene thy servauntes. So thou leve not my felyship, this gyffte ys thyne owne.'

The knyght thankys the kynge with a kynde wylle and sayde, 'As longe as I lyve my servys is your owne.'

as the Romaunce telleth he came in to Rome and was crouned emperour by the popes hand with all the ryalte that coude be made And sudgerned there a tyme and establysshed all his londes from Rome in to Fraunce and gaf londes and royammes vnto his seruauntes and knyghtes to eueryche after his desert in suche wyse that none complayned ryche 5 ne poure & he gafe to syre Pryamus the duchye of Lorayne and he

Thus the kynge gaff many londys. There was none that wolde aske that myghte playne of his parte, for of rychesse and welth they had all at her wylle. Than the knyghtes and lordis that to the kynge longis called a counsayle uppon a
5 fayre morne and sayde,

'Sir kynge, we beseche the for to here us all. We are undir youre lordship well stuffid, blyssed be God, of many thynges; and also we have wyffis weddid. We woll beseche youre good grace to reles us to sporte us with oure wyffis, for, worshyp
10 be Cryste, this journey is well overcom.'

'Ye say well,' seyde the kynge, 'for inowghe is as good as a feste, for to attemte God overmuche I holde hit not wyse-dom. And therefore make you all redy and turne we into Ingelonde.'

15 Than there was trussynge of harneyse with caryage full
96ʳ noble. And the kynge toke his leve of the holy fadir the Pope and patryarkys and cardynalys and senatoures full ryche, and leffte good governaunce in that noble cité and all the contrays of Rome for to warde and to kepe on payne
20 of deth, that in no wyse his commaundement be brokyn. Thus he passyth thorow the contreyes of all partyes.

And so kyng Arthure passed over the see unto Sandwyche haven. Whan quene Gwenyvere herde of his commynge she mette with hym at London, and so dud all other quenys
25 and noble ladyes. For there was never a solempner metyng

thanked hym and sayd he wold serue hym the dayes of his lyf and after made dukes and erles and made euery man ryche Thenne after this alle his knyghtes and lordes assembled them afore hym and sayd blessyd be god your warre is fynysshed and your conquest acheued in soo moche
5 that we knowe none soo grete ne myghty that dar make warre ageynst yow wherfore we byseche you to retorne homeward and gyue vs lycence to goo home to oure wyues fro whome we haue ben longe and to reste vs for your Iourney is fynysshed with honour & worship (*S* woship) Thenne sayd the kyng ye saye trouthe and for to tempte god
10 it is no wysedome And therfore make you redy and retorne we in to Englond Thenne there was trussyng of harneis and bagage and grete caryage And after lycence gyuen he retorned and commaunded that noo man in payne of dethe shold not robbe ne take vytaylle ne other thynge by the way but that he shold paye therfore And thus he came
15 ouer the see and londed at sandwyche ageynste whome Quene Gwene-uer his wyf came and mette hym and he was nobly receyued of alle his

in one cité togedyrs, for all maner of rychesse they brought
with hem at the full.

HERE ENDYTH THE TALE OF THE NOBLE KYNGE ARTHURE
THAT WAS EMPEROURE HYMSELF THOROW DYGNYTÉ OF HIS
HONDYS.   5

AND HERE FOLOWYTH AFFTYR MANY NOBLE TALYS OF SIR
LAUNCELOT DE LAKE.

EXPLYCIT THE NOBLE TALE BETWYXT
KYNGE ARTHURE AND LUCIUS THE EMPEROUR OF ROME.

comyns in euery cyte and burgh and grete yeftes presented to hym at
his home comyng to welcome hym with Thus endeth the fyfthe booke
of the conqueste that kynge Arthur hadde ageynste Lucius the Emperoure of Rome and here foloweth the syxth book whiche is of syr
Launcelot du lake

THE NOBLE TALE

OF

SIR LAUNCELOT DU LAKE

[*Winchester MS., ff. 96^r–113^r;*
Caxton, Book VI]

CAXTON'S RUBRICS

SONE aftir that kynge Arthure was com from Rome into
Ingelonde, than all the knyghtys of the Rounde Table
resorted unto the kynge and made many joustys and turnementes. And some there were that were but knyghtes
encresed in armys and worshyp that passed all other of her ⁵
felowys in prouesse and noble dedys, and that was well
proved on many.

But in especiall hit was prevyd on sir Launcelot de Lake,
for in all turnementes, justys, and dedys of armys, both for
lyff and deth, he passed all other knyghtes, and at no tyme ¹⁰
was he ovircom but yf hit were by treson other inchaunte- 96ᵛ
ment. So this sir Launcelot encresed so mervaylously in
worship and honoure; therefore he is the fyrste knyght that
the Frey[n]sh booke makyth me[n]cion of aftir kynge
Arthure com frome Rome. Wherefore quene Gwenyvere ¹⁵
had hym in grete favoure aboven all other knyghtis, and so
he loved the quene agayne aboven all other ladyes dayes
of his lyff, and for hir he dud many dedys of armys and
saved her from the fyre thorow his noble chevalry.

Thus sir Launcelot rested hym longe with play and game; ²⁰
and than he thought hymself to preve in straunge adventures,
and bade his nevew, sir Lyonell, for to make hym redy, 'for
we muste go seke adventures'. So they mounted on their
horses, armed at all ryghtes, and rode into a depe foreste and
so into a playne. ²⁵

So the wedir was hote aboute noone, and sir Launcelot
had grete luste to slepe. Than sir Lyonell aspyed a grete
appyll-tre that stoode by an hedge, and seyde, 'Sir, yondir
is a fayre shadow, there may we reste us and oure horsys.'

'Hit is trouthe,' seyde sir Launcelot, 'for this seven yere ³⁰
I was not so slepy as I am nowe.'

So there they alyted and tyed there horsys unto sondry
treis, and sir Launcelot layde hym downe undir this appyll-
tre, and his helmet undir his hede. And sir Lyonell

5 *C** which encreased   *C* that they passed   9 *C* turnementys and Iustes
11 *C* he was neuer ouercome   14 *C* frensshe   16–17 *C* and in certayne he
17–18 *C*† ladyes damoysels of   21 *C* preue hym self   23 *C* we two wylle seke
25 *C* a depe playne   28 *C* said broder yonder   29 *C* vs on †oure   30 *C*
is wel saide faire broder said   *C* viij yere   34 *C* helme he layd vnder

waked whyles he sl[e]pte. So sir Launcelot slepte passyng faste.

And in the meanewhyle com there three knyghtes rydynge, as faste fleynge as they myght ryde, and there folowed hem
5 three but one knyght. And whan sir Lyonell hym sawe, he thought he sawe never so grete a knyght nother so well-farynge a man and well appareyld unto all ryghtes. So within a whyle this stronge knyght had overtakyn one of the three knyghtes, and there he smote hym to the colde erth, that he
10 lay stylle; and than he rode unto the secunde knyght and smote hym so that man and horse felle downe. And so
97ʳ streyte unto the thirde knyght, and smote hym behynde his horse ars a spere-lengthe; and than he alyght downe and rayned his horse on the brydyll and bounde all three knyghtes
15 faste with the raynes of theire owne brydelys.

Whan sir Lyonell had sene hym do thus, he thought to assay hym and made hym redy, and pryvaly he toke his horse and thought nat for to awake sir Launcelot, and so mounted uppon his hors and overtoke the strong knyght. He bade hym
20 turne, and so he turned and smote sir Lyonell so harde that hors and man he bare to the erth. And so he alyght downe and bounde hym faste and threw hym overthwarte his owne horse as he had served the other three, and so rode with hem tyll he com to his owne castell. Than he unarmed them and bete
25 them with thornys all naked, and aftir put them in depe preson where were many mo knyghtes that made grete dole.

(2)   So whan sir Ector de Marys wyste that sir Launcelot was paste oute of the courte to seke adventures, he was wroth with hymsel[f] and made hym redy to seke sir Launcelot.
30 And as he had redyn longe in a grete foreste, he mette with a man was lyke a foster.

'Fayre felow,' seyde sir Ector, 'doste thou know this contrey or ony adventures that bene nyghe here honde?'

1 *C* launcelot was a slepe   5–6 *C* hym thought   8–9 *C* of these knyghtes
12 *C** knyghte he rode and   13–14 *S* doune arayned   16 *C* sawe hym
17 *C* redy & stylly and pryuely   18–20 *C* And whan he was mounted vpon
his hors he ouertoke this strong kynght & bad hym torne and the other smote
22–24 *C* hors and soo he serued hem al foure & rode with hem awey to his owne
castel   And whan he came there he garte vnarme them   26 *C* grete doloure
29 *C* hym self   *W* hym selt   32–33 *C** Ector knowest thou in thys countrey
ony aduentures that ben here nyghe hand

'Sir,' seyde the foster, 'this contrey know I well. And
hereby within this myle is a stronge maner and well dyked,
and by that maner on the lyffte honde there is a fayre fourde
for horse to drynke off, and over that fourde there growys
a fayre tre. And thereon hongyth many fayre shyldys that 5
welded somtyme good knyghtes, and at the bo[le] of the tre
hongys a basyn of couper and latyne. And stryke uppon that
basyn with the butte of thy spere three tymes, and sone aftir
thou shalt hyre new tydynges; and ellys haste thou the fayreste
[grace] that ever had knyghte this many yeres that passed 10
thorow this foreste.'

'Gramercy,' seyde sir Ector and departed. And com unto
this tre and sawe many fayre shyldys, and amonge them all   **97ᵛ**
he sawe hys brothirs shylde, sir Lyonell, and many mo that
he knew that were of his felowys of the Rounde Table, 15
the whyche greved his herte, and promysed to revenge his
brother. Than anone sir Ector bete on the basyn as he were
woode, and than he gaff his horse drynke at the fourde. And
there com a knyghte behynde hym and bade hym com oute
of the water and make hym redy. Sir Ector turned hym 20
shortly, and in feawtir caste his spere and smote the other
knyght a grete buffette, that his horse turned twyse abowte.

'That was well done,' seyde the stronge knyght, 'and
knyghtly thou haste strykyn me.'

And therewith he russhed his horse on sir Ector and caught 25
hym undir his ryght arme and bare hym clene oute of the
sadyll, and so rode with hym away into his castell and threw
hym downe in myddyll of the floure. [The name of this
knyghte was sir Tarquyn.] Than this seyde T⌐ar⌐quyn seyde
unto sir Ector,   30

'For thou hast done this day more unto me than ony knyght
dud this twelve yere, now woll I graunte the thy lyff, so
thou wolt be sworne to be my trew presoner.'

---

4 *C* horses   6 *W* body of the tre   *C* atte hoole of the tree (*see note*)   9–10 *W*
fayreste knyght   9–10 *C** fayrest grace that many a yere had euer knyght that
passed   13 all *not in C*   15 *C* were his felawes   23 *C* This was   25–26 *C*
cley3te hym   27 *C* in to his owne halle &   *F* (*MS. Add. 10293, f. 281b*) en sa
tour   28–29 *Not emended in* O¹   29–30 *C* than he said vnto   *W* Traquyn
C Turquyne   *F* Terriquan (*see note*)   33 trew *not in C*†   *C* my prysoner all
thy lyf dayes   *F* (*ibid., f. 281b–c*) ne vous metrai jou ja en prison se vous me
volés fianchier que vous de chaiens n'isterés mie sans congié

'Nay,' sayde sir Ector, 'that woll I never promyse the
but that I woll do myne advauntage.'

'That me repentis,' seyde sir Tᵀarᵀquyn. Than he gan
unarme hym and bete hym with thornys all naked, and
5 sytthyn put hym downe into a depe dongeon, and there he
knewe many of his felowys.

But whan sir Ector saw sir Lyonell, than made he grete
sorow.

'Alas, brother!' seyde sir Ector, 'how may this be, and
10 where is my brothir sir Launcelot?'

'Fayre brother, I leffte hym on slepe, whan that I frome
hym yode, undir an appil-tre, and what is becom of hym I
can nat telle you.'

'Alas,' seyde the presoneres, 'but yf sir Launcelot helpe us
15 we shall never be delyverde, for we know now no knyght
98ʳ that is able to macch with oure maystir Tarquyne.'

(3)   Now leve we thes knyghtes presoners, and speke we of
sir Launcelot de Lake that lyeth undir the appil-tre slepynge.
Aboute the none so there com by hym four queenys of
20 a grete astate; and for the hete sholde nat nyghe hem, there
rode four knyghtes aboute hem and bare a cloth of grene
sylke on four sperys betwyxte hem and the sonne. And the
quenys rode on four whyghte mulys.

Thus as they rode they herde a grete horse besyde them
25 grymly nyghe. Than they loked and were ware of a slepynge
knyght lay all armed undir an appil-tre. And anone as they
loked on his face they knew well hit was sir Launcelot, and
began to stryve for that knyght, and every of hem seyde they
wolde have hym to hir love.

30   'We shall nat stryve,' seyde Morgan le Fay, that was kyng
Arthurs sister. 'I shall put an inchauntement uppon hym
that he shall nat awake of all this seven owres, and than I woll
lede hym away unto my castell. And whan he is surely
within my holde, I shall take the inchauntement frome hym,
35 and than lette hym chose whych of us he woll have unto
peramour.'

3 *W* Traquyn   3–4 *C* he garte to vnarme   9 how may this be and *not in C*
14 *C* the knyghtes yf *not in C*†   15 *C* we may neuer   16 with *not in C*   19 *C*
euen aboute   24–25 *C* herde by them a grete hors grymly neye thenne were they
ware   26–27 *C* these quenes loked   27 well *not in C*   28 *C* euerychone sady
32 *C* awake in syxe owres

So this enchauntemente was caste uppon sir Launcelot, and than they leyde hym uppon his shylde and bare hym so on horsebak betwyxte two knyghtes, and brought hym unto the Castell Charyot; and there they leyde hym in a chambir colde, and at nyght they sente unto hym a fayre dameselle with his souper redy idyght. Be that the en- chauntement was paste.

And whan she com she salewed hym and asked hym what chere.

'I can not sey, fayre damesel,' seyde sir Launcelot, 'for I wote not how I com into this castell but hit be by in- chauntemente.'

'Sir,' seyde she, 'ye muste make good chere; and yf ye be suche a knyght as is seyde ye be, I shall telle you more to-morn be pryme of the day.'

'Gramercy, fayre damesel,' seyde sir Launcelot, 'of your good wylle.'

And so she departed, and there he laye all that nyght withoute ony comforte. And on the morne erly com thes four quenys passyngly well besene, and all they byddynge hym good morne, and he them agayne.

'Sir knyght,' the four quenys seyde, 'thou muste undir- stonde thou art oure presonere, and we know the well that thou art sir Launcelot du Lake, kynge Banis sonne. And because that we undirstonde youre worthynesse, that thou art the noblest knyght lyvyng, and also we know well there can no lady have thy love but one, and that is quene Gweny- vere, and now thou shalt hir love lose for ever, and she thyne. For hit behovyth the now to chose one of us four, for I am quene Morgan le Fay, quene of the londe of Gore, and here is the quene of North Galys, and the quene of Estlonde, and the quene of the Oute Iles. Now chose one of us, whyche that thou wolte have to thy peramour, other ellys to dye in this preson.'

'This is an harde case,' seyde sir Launcelot, 'that other I muste dye other to chose one of you. Yet had I lever dye

---

11–12 *C* by an enchauntement   14 *C* as it is   17 *C* wyl I requyre yow
19 *C* withoute comforte of ony body   23 *C* we here knowe   25 *C* by cause
we   26 *C* And as we   28–29 *C* thow shalt lose her for euer and she the
and therfore the behoueth now   33–34 *C* peramour for thou mayst not chese or
els in thys pryson to dye

in this preson with worshyp than to have one of you to my
peramoure, magré myne hede. And therefore ye be answeryd: I woll none of you, for ye be false enchaunters.
And as for my lady, dame Gwenyvere, were I at my lyberté
as I was, I wolde prove hit on youres that she is the treweste
lady unto hir lorde lyvynge.'

'Well,' seyde the quenys, 'ys this your answere, that ye
woll refuse us?'

'Ye, on my lyff,' seyde sir Launcelot, 'refused ye bene
of me.'

99^r So they departed and leffte hym there alone that made
grete sorow.

(4) So aftir that noone com the damesel unto hym with his
dyner and asked hym what chere.

'Truly, damesel,' seyde sir Launcelot, 'never so ylle.'

'Sir,' she seyde, 'that me repentis, but and ye woll be
ruled by me I shall helpe you oute of this dystresse, and ye
shall have no shame nor velony, so that ye wol⟨d⟩ [hold] my
promyse.'

'Fayre damesel, I graunte you; but sore I am of thes
quenys crauftis aferde, for they have destroyed many a good
knyght.'

'Sir,' seyde she, 'that is soth, and for the renowne and
bounté that they here of you they woll have your love.
And, sir, they sey youre name is sir Launcelot du Lake, the
floure of knyghtes, and they be passyng wroth with you
that ye have refused hem. But, sir, and ye wolde promyse
me to helpe my fadir on Tewysday nexte commynge, that
hath made a turnemente betwyxt hym and the kynge of
North Galys—for the laste Tewysday past my fadir loste
the felde thorow three knyghtes of Arthurs courte—and yf
ye woll be there on Tewysday next commynge and helpe
my fadir, and to-morne be pryme by the grace of God I shall
delyver you clene.'

'Now, fayre damesell,' seyde sir Launcelot, 'telle me your
fadyrs name, and than shall I gyff you an answere.'

---

3 *C** enchauntresses　　5 *C** on you or on yours　　13 *C* Ryght so at the noone
15 *C** fayre damoysel sayd syre Launcelot in my lyf dayes neuer　　18 *W*
woll my　*C** hold me a (*see note*)　　20 *C* wil graunte　　21 *C* quenes sorceresses
aferd　　24 *C* they wold haue　　25 *C* they sayne　　31 yf *not in C*　　33 *C*
fader to morne or pryme　　35 *C* me what is your

'Sir knyght,' she seyde, 'my fadyrs name is kynge Bagdemagus, that was foule rebuked at the laste turnemente.'

'I knowe your fadir well,' seyde sir Launcelot, 'for a
noble kyng and a good knyght, and by the fayth of my
body, your fadir shall have my servyse, and you bothe at 5
that [day].'

'Sir,' she seyde, 'gramercy, and to-morne loke ye be redy
betymys, and I shall delyver you and take you your armoure,
your horse, shelde and spere. And hereby wythin this ten
myle is an abbey of whyght monkys, and there I pray you 10 **99ᵛ**
to abyde me, and thydir shall I brynge my fadir unto you.'

'And all this shall be done,' seyde sir Launcelot, 'as I am
trew knyght.'

And so she departed and come on the morne erly and
founde hym redy. Than she brought hym oute of twelve 15
lockys, and toke hym his armour and his owne horse; and
lyghtly he sadyld hym and toke his spere in his honde, and
so rode forth, and sayde,

'Damesell, I shall not fayle, by the grace of God.'

And so he rode into a grete foreste all that day, and never 20
coude fynde no hygheway. And so the nyght fell on hym,
and than was he ware in a slade of a pavylyon of rede sendele.
'Be my feyth,' seyde sir Launcelot, 'in that pavylyon woll
I lodge all this nyght.' And so he there alyght downe, and
tyed his horse to the pavylyon, and there he unarmed hym. 25
And there he founde a bed, and layde hym therein, and felle
on slepe sadly.

Than within an owre there com that knyght that ought (5)
the pavylyon. He wente that his lemman had layne in that
bed, and so he leyde hym adowne by sir Launcelot and 30
toke hym in his armys and began to kysse hym. And whan
sir Launcelot felte a rough berde kyssyng hym he sterte
oute of the bedde lyghtly, and the othir knyght after hym.
And eythir of hem gate their swerdys in their hondis, and
oute at the pavylyon dore wente the knyght of the pavylyon, 35

1 *C* fader is   5–6 *C*** body ye shalle haue my body redy to doo your fader and
you seruyse at that   *End of line in W*   7 *C* awayte ye   8 *C*** shal be she that
shal   10–11 *C* you that ye me abyde and   16 *C* & brouȝt hym vnto his
armour & whan he was clene armed she brought hym vntyl his owne hors   17 *C*
toke a grete spere   19 *C* fayre damoysel I shal not faile you   28–29 *C*
knyghte to whome the pauelione ought And he   30 *C* doune besyde syr

and sir Launcelot folowed hym. And there by a lytyll slad sir Launcelot wounded hym sore nyghe unto the deth. And than he yelded hym to sir Launcelot, and so he graunted hym, so that he wolde telle hym why he com into the bed.

5 'Sir,' sayde the knyghte, 'the pavylyon is myne owne. And as this nyght I had assigned my lady to have slepte with hir, and now I am lykly to dye of this wounde.'

'That me repentyth,' seyde sir Launcelot, 'of youre hurte, but I was adrad of treson, for I was late begyled. And
10 therefore com on your way into youre pavylyon, and take youre reste, and as I suppose I shall staunche your bloode.'

100ʳ And so they wente bothe into the pavylyon, and anone sir Launcelot staunched his bloode. Therewithall com the knyghtes lady that was a passynge fayre lady. And whan
15 [she] aspyed that her lorde Belleus was sore wounded she cryed oute on sir Launcelot and made grete dole oute of mesure.

'Pease, my lady and my love,' seyde sir Belleus, 'for this knyght is a good man and a knyght of aventures.' And there he tolde hir all the case how he was wounded. 'And whan
20 that I yelded me unto hym he laffte me goodly, and hath staunched my bloode.'

'Sir,' seyde the lady, 'I require the, telle me what knyght thou art, and what is youre name.'

'Fayre lady,' he sayde, 'my name is sir Launcelot du
25 Lake.'

'So me thought ever be youre speche,' seyde the lady, 'for I have sene you oftyn or this, and I know you bettir than ye wene. But now wolde ye promyse me of youre curtesye, for the harmys that ye have done to me and to my lorde,
30 sir Belleus, that whan ye com unto kyng Arthurs court for to cause hym to be made knyght of the Rounde Table? For he is a passyng good man of armys and a myghty lorde of londys of many oute iles.'

'Fayre lady,' sayde sir Launcelot, 'latte hym com unto
35 the courte the next hyghe feste, and loke ye com with hym, and I shall do my power; and he preve hym doughty of his hondis he shall have his desyre.'

So within a whyle the nyght passed and the day shone.
Than sir Launcelot armed hym and toke his horse, and so
he was taughte to the abbey.

And as sone as he come thydir the doughter of kyng (6)
Bagdemagus herde a grete horse trotte on the pa[vy]mente, 5
and she than arose and yode to [a] wyndowe, and there she
sawe sir Launcelot. And anone she made men faste to take
his horse frome hym, and lette lede hym into a stable; and
hymself [was ledde] unto a chambir and unarmed hym.
And this lady sente hym a longe gowne, and com hirself 10
and made hym good chere; and she seyde he was the knyght
in the worlde that was moste welcom unto hir.

100ᵛ

Than in all haste she sente for hir fadir Bagdemagus that
was within twelve myle of that abbey, and afore evyn he
come with a fayre felyshyp of knyghtes with hym. And 15
whan the kynge was alyght of his horse he yode streyte
unto sir Launcelotte his chambir, and there he founde his
doughtir. And than the kynge toke hym in his armys and
eythir made other good chere.

Than sir Launcelot made his complaynte unto the kynge, 20
how he was betrayed; and how he was brother unto sir
Lyonell, whyche was departed frome hym he wyste not
where, and how his doughter had delyverde hym oute of
preson. 'Therefore, whyle that I lyve, I shall do hir servyse
and all hir kynrede.' 25

'Than am I sure of your helpe,' seyde the kyng, 'on
Tewysday next commyng?'

'Yee, sir,' seyde sir Launcelot, 'I shall nat fayle you, for
so have I promysed my lady youre doughter. But, sir, what
knyghtes be tho of my lorde kyng Arthurs that were with 30
the kyng of North Galys?'

'Sir, hit was sir Madore de la Porte and sir Mordred and
sir Gahalantyne that all forfared my knyghtes, for agaynste
hem three I nother none of myne myght bere no strenghthe.'

1 *C* whyle as they thus talked the nyghte   2–3 *C** and they taught hym to the
Abbaye and thyder he rode within the pace of two owrys   4 *C* And soone as
syre launcelott came withyn the Abbeye yarde the   5 *C* hors goo on   6 *W* to
dwyndowe   9 *C* in to a fayre chamber   11 *C* And thēne she made launcelot
passyng good   18 *C* enbraced syr Launcelot in hys   21–22 *C* how his broder
syre lyonel was   22 *C* nyst   24 that *not in C*   31–32 *C* Northgalys and
the kyng said it   34 *C* I nor my knyghtes

'Sir,' seyde sir Launcelot, 'as I here sey that the turnement shall be here within this three myle of this abbay. But, sir, ye shall sende unto me three knyghtes of youres suche as ye truste, and loke that the three knyghtes have all whyght sheldis and no picture on their shyldis, and ye shall sende me another of the same sewte; and we four wyll oute of a lytyll wood in myddys of bothe partyes com, and we shall falle on the frunte of oure enemys and greve hem that we may. And thus shall I not be knowyn what maner a knyght I am.'

So they toke their reste that nyght. And this was on the Sonday, and so the kynge departed and sente unto sir Launcelot three knyghtes with four whyght shyldys. And on the Tewysday they lodged hem in a lytyll leved wood besyde thereas the turnemente sholde be. And there were scaffoldys and ⌐holes¬, that lordys and ladyes myght beholde and gyff the pryse.

Than com into the fylde the kynge of North Galys with nyne score helmys, and than the three knyghtis of kyng Arthurs stood by themself. Than com into the felde kynge Bagdemagus with four score helmys; and than they featured their sperys and come togydyrs with a grete daysshe. And there was slayne of knyghtes at the fyrste recountir twelve knyghtes of kynge Bagdemagus parté, and syx of the kynge of North Galys syde and party; and kynge Bagdemagus his party were ferre sette asyde and bak.

(7)   Wyth that com in sir Launcelot, and he threste in with his spere in the thyckyst of the pres; and there he smote downe with one spere fyve knyghtes, and of four of them he brake their backys. And in that thrange he smote downe the kynge of North Galys, and brake his thygh in that falle. All this doynge of sir Launcelot saw the three knyghtes of Arthurs, and seyde, 'Yondir is a shrewde geste, therefore have here ons at hym.' So they encountred, and sir Launce-

---

2 But sir *not in C*   5–6 *C* sheldes & I also & no paynture on the sheldes & we four will come out   7 com *not in C*   8 *C* falle in   9 *C* maner a *not in C*
16 *W* and towrys that   *C** and holes that   F (*MS. Add. 10293, f. 284a*) firent li doy roy drechier loges en mi les prés ou il avoit fenestres as dames et as damoiseles (*see note*)   17 *C* to gyue   19 *C* eyght score   21 *C* score of helmys
25 syde and *not in C*   26 asyde and *not in C*   33 and seyde *not in C*   *C** gest sayd syre Madore de la port therfore

lot bare hym downe horse and man so that his sholdir wente
oute of joynte.

'Now hit befallyth me,' seyde sir Mordred, 'to stirre me,
for sir Mador hath a sore falle.' And than sir Launcelot
was ware of hym, and gate a spere in his honde and mette 5
with hym. And sir Mordred brake his spere uppon hym;
and sir Launcelot gaff hym suche a buffette that the arson
of the sadill brake, and so he drove over the horse tayle, that
his helme smote into the erthe a foote and more, that nyghe
his nek was broke, and there he lay longe in a swowe.   10

Than com in sir Gahalantyne with a grete spere, and sir
Launcelot agaynste hym in all that they myght dryve, that
bothe hir sperys to-braste evyn to their hondys; and than
they flange oute with her swerdes and gaff many sore strokys. **101ᵛ**
Than was sir Launcelot wroth oute of mesure, and than he 15
smote sir Gahalantyne on the helme, that his nose, erys and
mowthe braste oute on bloode; and therewith his hede hynge
low, and with that his horse ran away with hym, and he felle
downe to the erthe.

Anone therewithall sir Launcelot gate a speare in his 20
honde, and or ever that speare brake he bare downe to the
erthe syxtene knyghtes, som horse and man and som the
man and nat the horse; and there was none that he hitte
surely but that he bare none armys that day. And than he
gate a spere and smote downe twelve knyghtes, and the 25
moste party of hem never throoff aftir. And than the knyghtes
of the kyng of North Galys party wolde jouste no more,
and there the gre was gevyn to kyng Bagdemagus.

So eythir party departed unto his owne, and sir Launcelot
rode forth with kynge Bagdemagus unto his castel. And 30
there he had passynge good chere bothe with the kyng
and with his doughter, and they profyrde hym grete yefftes.
And on the morne he toke his leve and tolde the kynge
that he wolde seke his brothir sir Lyonell that wente frome

2 *C* oute of lyth   3–4 *C* befalleth it to me to Iuste sayd Mordred for   4 And
than *not in C*   5 *C* a grete spere   6 with *not in C*   *C* a spere   8 *C* he
flewe ouer   9 *C* butte in to   12 *C** hym with al theyre strength that they
my3t dryue   14 *C* many a grym stroke   16–17 *C* nose braste out on blood
and eerys and mouthe bothe and ther with   20 *C* a greete spere   21 *C* that
grete spere   23–24 *C* none but that he hyt surely he bare   25 *C* another grete
spere   29 *C* his owne place   34 *C* wold goo and seke

hym whan he slepte. So he toke his horse and betaughte
hem all to God, and there he seyde unto the kynges doughter,

'Yf that ye have nede ony tyme of my servyse, I pray you
let me have knowlecche, and I shall nat fayle you, as I am
5 trewe knyght.'

And so sir Launcelot departed, and by adventure he com
into the same foreste there he was takynge his slepe before;
and in the myddys of an hygheway he mette a damesel
rydynge on a whyght palfray, and there eythir salewed
10 other.

'Fayre damesel,' seyde sir Launcelot, 'know y[e] in this
contrey ony adventures nere hande?'

'Sir knyght,' seyde the damesel, 'here ar adventures
nyghe, and thou durste preve hem.'

15 'Why sholde I not preve?' seyde sir Launcelot. 'For for
that cause com I hydir.'

'Welle,' seyde she, 'thou semyst well to be a good knyght,
102ʳ and yf thou dare mete with a good knyght I shall brynge
the where is the beste knyght and the myghtyeste that ever
20 thou founde, so thou wolte telle me thy name and what
knyght thou art.'

'Damesell, as for to telle you my name, I take no grete
force. Truly, my name is sir Launcelot du Lake.'

'Sir, thou besemys well; here is adventures fast by that
25 fallyth for the. For hereby dwellyth a knyght that woll nat
be overmacched for no man I know but ye do overmacche
hym. And his name is sir Tarquyn. And, as I undirstonde,
he hath in his preson of Arthurs courte good knyghtes
three score and four that he hath wonne with his owne
30 hondys. But whan ye have done that journey, ye shall
promyse me, as ye ar a trew knyght, for to go and helpe me
and other damesels that ar dystressed dayly with a false
knyght.'

'All youre entente, damesell, and desyre I woll fulfylle,
35 so ye woll brynge me unto this knyght.'

'Now, fayre knyght, com on youre way.'

1 *C* whan that he   3 that *not in C*   7–8 *C* was take slepyng† And   11 *W*
know you   *C* * knowe ye   12 nere hande *not in C*   13–14 *C* aduentures nere
hand and thou   15 *C* not preue aduentures   15–16 *C* launcelot for that
20 *C* telle me what is thy   24–25 *C* here ben aduentures by that fallen   26 do
not in C   31 *C* go with me and to helpe

And so she brought hym unto the fourde and the tre
where hynge the basyn. So sir Launcelot lette his horse
drynke, and sytthen he bete on the basyn with the butte of
his spere tylle the bottum felle oute. And longe dud he so,
but he sye no man. Than he rode endlonge the gatys of 5
that maner nyghe halfe an howre.

And than was he ware of a grete knyght that droffe an
horse afore hym, and overthwarte the horse lay an armed
knyght bounden. And ever as they com nere and nere sir
Launcelot thought he sholde know hym. Than was he ware 10
that hit was sir Gaherys, Gawaynes brothir, a knyght of
the Table Rounde.

'Now, fayre damesell,' seyde sir Launcelot, 'I se yondir
a knyght faste ibounden that is a felow of myne, and brother
he is unto sir Gawayne. And at the fyrste begynnynge I 15
promyse you, by the leve of God, for to rescowe that
knyght. But yf his maystir sytte the bettir in his sadyl, I shall **102ᵛ**
delyver all the presoners that he hath oute of daungere,
for I am sure he hath two bretherne of myne presoners with
hym.'   20

But by that tyme that eythir had sene other they gryped
theyre sperys unto them.

'Now, fayre knyght,' seyde sir Launcelot, 'put that
wounded knyghte of that horse and lette hym reste a whyle,
and lette us too preve oure strengthis. For, as hit is enfourmed 25
me, thou doyste and haste done me grete despyte, and shame
unto knyghtes of the Rounde Table. And therefore now
defende the!'

'And thou be of [the] Rounde Table,' seyde Terquyn,
'I de[fy] the and all thy felyshyp!'   30

'That is overmuche seyde,' sir Launcelot seyde, 'of the
at thys tyme.'

And than they put there sperys in their restys and come (8)
togedyrs with hir horsis as faste as they myght ren; and
aythir smote other in myddys of their shyldis, that both 35
their horsys backys braste undir them, and the knyghtes

---

4 *C* spere so hard with al his my3t tyl   4–5 *C* he dyd so but he sawe noo thynge
10 *C* Thenne sir launcelot was ware   13–14 *C* yonder cometh a   17 *C*
sytte better in the sadel   21 But *not in C*   25 *C* us two   26 *C* done grete
30 *W* I desyre the   31–33 *C* sayd sayd syre launcelot Capitulum VIII And
thēne

were bothe astoned. And as sone as they myght they avoyded
their horsys and toke their shyldys before them and drew
oute their swerdys and com togydir egirly; and eyther gaff
other many stronge strokys, for there myght nothir shyldis
5 nother harneyse holde their strokes.

And so within a whyle they had bothe many grymme
woundys and bledde passyng grevously. Thus they fared
two owres and more, trasyng and rasyng eyther othir where
they myght hitte ony bare place. Than at the laste they were
10 brethles bothe, and stode lenyng on her swerdys.

'Now, felow,' seyde sir Terquyne, 'holde thy honde a
whyle, and telle me that I shall aske of the.'

'Sey on,' seyde sir Launcelot.

Than sir Terquyn seyde, 'Thou art the byggyst man that
15 ever I mette withall, and the beste-brethed, and as lyke one
knyght that I hate abovyn all other knyghtes. So be hit
103ʳ that thou be not he, I woll lyghtly acorde with the, and for
thy love I woll delyver all the presoners that I have, that is
three score and four, so thou wolde telle me thy name. And
20 thou and I woll be felowys togedyrs and never to fayle the
whyle that I lyve.'

'Ye sey well,' seyde sir Launcelot, 'but sytthyn hit is so
that I have thy frendeshyppe and may have, what knyght is
that that thou hatyste abovyn all thynge?'

25 'Feythfully,' seyde sir Terquyn, 'his name is sir Launcelot
de Lake, for he slowe my brothir sir Carados at the Dolerous
Towre, that was one of the beste knyghtes on lyve; and
therefore hym I excepte of alle knyghtes, for may I hym onys
mete, the tone shall make an ende, I make myne avow. And
30 for sir Launcelottis sake I have slayne an hondred good
knyghtes, and as many I have maymed all uttirly, that they
myght never aftir helpe themself, and many have dyed in
preson. And yette have I three score and four, and all [shal]
be delyverde, so thou wolte telle me thy name, so be hit that
35 thou be nat sir Launcelot.'

1–2 *C* myghte auoyde theyre horses they took　　　　6–7 *C* bothe grymly woundes
8 *C* or mo　　　12 *C* what I shal aske the　　　　13 seyde sir Launcelot *not in C*†
15–16 *C* and lyke on knyȝt　　　　19 *C* thou wylt　　　　20 *C* and I we wyl be
22 *C* it is wel sayd sayd　　　23 *C* I may haue thy frendship what　　　24 *C* al other
26 *C* du lake　　　28–29 *C* I ones mete with hym the one of vs shal make an ende
of other I

'Now se I well,' seyde sir Launcelot, 'that suche a man
I myght be, I myght have pease; and suche a man I myght[e
be] that there sholde be mortall warre betwyxte us. And
now, sir knyght, at thy requeste I woll that thou wete and
know that I am sir Launcelot du Lake, kynge Bannys son 5
of Benwyke, and verry knyght of the Table Rounde. And
now I defyghe the, and do thy beste!'

'A!' seyde sir Tarquyne, 'thou arte to me moste welcom
of ony knyght, for we shall never departe tylle the tone of
us be dede.'   10

Than they hurteled togedyrs as two wylde bullys,
russhynge and laysshyng with hir shyldis and swerdys, that
somtyme they felle bothe on their nosys. Thus they foughte
stylle two owres and more and never wolde have reste, and
sir Tarquyne gaff sir Launcelot many woundys, that all   15
the grounde thereas they faughte was all besparcled with **103ᵛ**
bloode.

Than at the laste sir Terquyne wexed faynte and gaff (9)
somwhat abakke, and bare his shylde low for wery. That
aspyed sir Launcelot, and lepte uppon hym fersly and gate 20
hym by the bavoure of hys helmette and plucked hym
downe on his kneis, and anone he raced of his helme and
smote his necke in sundir. And whan sir Launcelot had done
this he yode unto the damesell and seyde,

'Damesell, I am redy to go with you where ye woll have 25
me, but I have no horse.'

'Fayre sir,' seyde this wounded knyght, 'take my horse,
and than lette me go into this maner and delyver all thes
presoners.' So he toke sir Gaheris horse and prayde hym
nat to be greved.   30

'Nay, fayre lorde, I woll that ye have hym at your commaundemente, for ye have bothe saved me and my horse.
And this day I sey ye ar the beste knyght in the worlde,

---

3 *C* warre mortal   7 *P* doo   *Wh* doe   8 *C* Turquyne launcelot thou
8–9 *C* welcome that euer was knyghte   13 *C* ouer theyr   16 *P* besperkled
Wh bespeckled   19 *P* shelde   *Wh* sheld   19 *C* for werynesse   23–25 *W*
(*sidenote*): The deth of Terquyn by sir Launcelot   27–28 *C* sayd she take this
wounded knyghtes hors and sende hym in to this manoyr and commaunde hym to
delyuer all the   29–32 *C* Soo syr launcelot wente vnto Gaheryes and praid hym
not to be agreued for to leue hym his hors Nay fayr lord said Gaheryes I wyll that
ye take my hors atte your owne commaundement   33 *P* world   *Wh* worlde

for ye have slayne this day in my syght the myghtyeste man and the beste knyght excepte you that ever I sawe. But, fayre sir,' seyde sir Gaherys, 'I pray you telle me your name.'

5 'Sir, my name is sir Launcelot du Lake that ought to helpe you of ryght for kynge Arthurs sake, and in especiall for my lorde sir Gawayne his sake, youre owne brother. And whan that ye com within yondir maner, I am sure ye shall fynde there many knyghtes of the Rounde Table; for I have sene many of their shyldys that I know hongys on 10 yondir tre. There is sir Kayes shylde, ⌐and sir Brandeles shylde⌐, and sir Galyhuddys shylde, and sir Bryan de Lystenoyse his shylde, and sir Alydukis shylde, with many mo that I am nat now avysed of, and sir Marhaus, and also my too brethirne shyldis, sir Ector de Marys and sir Lyonell. 15 Wherefore I pray you grete them all frome me and sey that I bydde them to take suche stuff there as they fynde, that in ony wyse my too brethirne go unto the courte and abyde me there tylle that I com, for by the feste of Pentecoste I caste me to be there; for as at thys tyme I muste ryde with this
104ʳ 20 damesel for to save my promyse.'

And so they departed frome Gaherys; and Gaherys yode into the maner, and there he founde a yoman porter kepyng many keyes. Than sir Gaherys threw the porter unto the grounde and toke the keyes frome hym; and hastely he 25 opynde the preson dore, and there he lette all the presoners oute, and every man lowsed other of their bondys. And whan they sawe sir Gaherys, all they thanked hym, for they wente that he had slayne sir Terquyne because that he was wounded.

30 'Not so, syrs,' seyde sir Gaherys, 'hit was sir Launcelot that slew hym worshypfully with his owne hondys, and he gretys you all well and prayeth you to haste you to the courte. And as unto you, sir Lyonell and sir Ector de Marys,

1 *P* myghtyest   *Wh* myghtest   2–3 *P* sawe & fayr syre   *Wh* sawe & fore syre
6 *C* gawayns sake your owne dere broder   7 *P* manoyr   *Wh* manayr
9 hongys *not in C*   10–11 *C** shelde & sir braundeles sheld and syr Marhaus sheld and syre Galyndes shelde   *F mentions Brandelis among the prisoners delivered by Kay (MS. Add. 10293, f. 322b)*   13 and sir Marhaus *not in C*   17 too *not in C*   21 *C* and soo he   22 *P* manoir   *Wh* manore   22–23 *C* kepyng ther many keyes Anone with al syre   25–26 *C* lete oute all the prysoners   28 that he had slayne sir Terquyne because *not in C†*   30 *P* was   *Wh* wos   31 *C** handes I sawe it with myn owne eyen and he   33 you *not in C*

he prayeth you to abyde hym at the courte of kynge
Arthure.'

'That shall we nat do,' seyde his bretherne. 'We woll
fynde hym and we may lyve.'

'So shall I,' seyde sir Kay, 'fynde hym or I com to the 5
courte, as I am trew knyght.'

Than they sought the house thereas the armour was,
and than they armed them; and every knyght founde hys
owne horse and all that longed unto hym. So forthwith
there com a foster with four horsys lade with fatte venyson. 10
And anone sir Kay seyde, 'Here is good mete for us for one
meale, for we had not many a day no good repaste.' And so
that venyson was rosted, sodde, and bakyn; and so aftir
souper som abode there all nyght. But sir Lyonell and
sir Ector de Marys and sir Kay rode aftir sir Launcelot to 15
fynde hym yf they myght.

Now turne we to sir Launcelot that rode with the damesel (10)
in a fayre hygheway.

'Sir,' seyde the damesell, 'here by this way hauntys a
knyght that dystressis all ladyes and jantylwomen, and at 20
the leste he robbyth them other lyeth by hem.'

'What?' seyde sir Launcelot, 'is he a theff and a knyght?
And a ravyssher of women? He doth shame unto the Order
of Knyghthode, and contrary unto his oth. Hit is pyté
that he lyvyth! But, fayre damesel, ye shall ryde on before 25 **104ᵛ**
youreself, and I woll kepe myself in coverte; and yf that he
trowble yow other dystresse you I shall be your rescowe
and lerne hym to be ruled as a knyght.'

So thys mayde rode on by the way a souffte amblynge
pace, and within a whyle com oute a knyght on horseba[k] 30
owte of the woode and his page with hym. And there he
put the damesell frome hir horse, and than she cryed. With
that com sir Launcelot as faste as he myght tyll he com to
the knyght, sayng,

'A, false knyght and traytoure unto knyghthode, who dud 35
lerne the to distresse ladyes, damesels and jantyllwomen!'

1–2 of kynge Arthure *not in C*   3 *P* sayd   *Wh* says   5 *C* come at   6 *P*
true   *Wh* trne   7 *C* Thenne alle tho knyghtes sought   9 *P* that   *Wh* thet
9–10 *C* hym And whan this was done ther   10 *Wh* soster   13 *C* baken and
soden   14 *C* al that nyghte   30 *W* horsbat   35 *C* O thou fals
36 damesels *not in C*

Whan the knyght sy sir Launcelot thus rebukynge hym
he answerde nat, but drew his swerde and rode unto sir
Launcelot. And sir Launcelot threw his spere frome hym
and drew his swerde, and strake hym suche a buffette on
5 the helmette that he claffe his hede and necke unto the
throte.

'Now haste thou thy paymente that longe thou haste
deserved!'

'That is trouth,' seyde the damesell, 'for lyke as Terquyn
10 wacched to dystresse good knyghtes, so dud this knyght
attende to destroy and dystresse ladyes, damesels and jantyllwomen; and his name was sir Perys de Foreste Savage.'

'Now, damesell,' seyde sir Launcelot 'woll ye ony more
servyse of me?'

15 'Nay, sir,' she seyde, 'at thys tyme, but Allmyghty Jesu
preserve you wheresomever ye ryde or goo, for the curteyst
knyght thou arte, and mekyste unto all ladyes and jantylwomen that now lyvyth. But one thyng, sir knyght, methynkes ye lak, ye that ar a knyght wyveles, that ye woll nat
20 love som mayden other jantylwoman. For I cowde never
here sey that ever ye loved ony of no maner of degré, and
that is grete pyté. But hit is noysed that ye love quene
Gwenyvere, and that she hath ordeyned by enchauntemente
that ye shall never love none other but hir, nother none
25 other damesell ne lady shall rejoyce you; where[fore] there
105ʳ be many in this londe, of hyghe astate and lowe, that make
grete sorow.'

'Fayre damesell,' seyde sir Launcelot, 'I may nat warne
peple to speke of me what hit pleasyth hem. But for to
30 be a weddyd man, I thynke hit nat, for than I muste couche
with hir and leve armys and turnamentis, batellys and adventures. And as for to sey to take my pleasaunce with
peramours, that woll I refuse: in prencipall for drede of
God, for knyghtes that bene adventures sholde nat be
35 advoutrers nothir lecherous, for than they be nat happy
nother fortunate unto the werrys; for other they shall be
overcom with a sympler knyght than they be hemself,

---

4 *C* drewe oute   4–10 *W* (*sidenote*): Here sir Launcelot slew Perys de Forest
Saveage   10 *C* to destroye knyghtes   16 *S* perserue   21 *C* maner degree
25–26 there be *not in C*   34–35 *C*† ben aduenturous or lecherous shal not be happy

other ellys they shall sle by unhappe and hir cursednesse
bettir men than they be hemself. And so who that usyth
peramours shall be unhappy, and all thynge unhappy that
is aboute them.'

And so sir Launcelot and she departed. And than he rode 5
in a depe foreste two dayes and more, and hadde strayte
lodgynge. So on the thirde day he rode on a longe brydge,
and there sterte uppon hym suddeynly a passyng foule
carle. And he smote his horse on the nose, that he turned
aboute, and asked hym why he rode over that brydge with- 10
oute lycence.

'Why sholde I nat ryde this way?' seyde sir Launcelotte,
'I may not ryde besyde.'

'Thou shalt not chose,' seyde the carle, and laysshed at
hym with a grete club shodde with iron. 15

Than sir Launcelot drew his swerde and put the stroke
abacke, and clave his hede unto the pappys.

And at the ende of the brydge was a fayre vyllage, and all
peple, men and women, cryed on sir Launcelot and sayde,
'Sir knyght, a worse dede duddyst thou never for thyself, 20
for thou haste slayne the cheyff porter of oure castell.'
Sir Launcelot lete hem sey what they wolde, and streyte he
rode into the castelle.

And whan he come into the castell he alyght and tyed his
horse to a rynge on the walle. And there he sawe a fayre 25
grene courte, and thydir he dressid hym, for there hym **105ᵛ**
thought was a fayre place to feyght in. So he loked aboute
hym and sye muche peple in dorys and in wyndowys that
sayde, 'Fayre knyghte, thou arte unhappy to com here!'

Anone withall there com uppon hym two grete gyauntis 30 (11)
well armed all save there hedy[s], with two horryble clubbys
in their hondys. Sir Launcelot put his shylde before hym
and put the stroke away of that one gyaunte, and with hys
swerde he clave his hede in sundir. Whan his felowe sawe
that, he ran away as he were woode, and sir Launcelot aftir 35
hym with all his myght, and smote hym on the shuldir and
clave hym to the navyll.

---

3 *C* is vnhappy   11 *C* his lycence   18–19 *C* al the people   20 Sir knyght
not in C   22–23 *C* he wente in to   28 hym *not in C*   29 to com here *not*
in C†   35 *C* wood for fere of the horryble strokes and laūcelot

Than sir Launcelot wente into the halle, and there com afore hym three score of ladyes and damesels, and all kneled unto hym and thanked God and hym of his delyveraunce.

'For,' they seyde, 'the moste party of us have bene here
5 this seven yere [theire] presoners, and we have worched all maner of sylke workys for oure mete, and we are all grete jentylwomen borne. And blyssed be the tyme, knyght, that ever thou were borne, for thou haste done the moste worshyp that ever ded knyght in this worlde; that woll we beare
10 recorde. And we all pray you to telle us your name, that we may telle oure frendis who delyverde us oute of preson.'

'Fayre damesellys,' he seyde, 'my name is sir Launcelot du Laake.'

'A, sir,' seyde they all, 'well mayste thou be he, for ellys
15 save yourself, as we demed, there myght never knyght have the bettir of thes two jyauntis; for many fayre knyghtes have assayed, and here have ended. And many tymes have we here wysshed aftir you, and thes two gyauntes dredde never knyght but you.'

20 'Now may ye sey,' seyde sir Launcelot, 'unto your frendys, and grete them all fro me; and yf that I com in ony of your
106ʳ marchys, shew me such chere as ye have cause. And what tresoure that there is in this castel I yeff hit you for a rewarde for your grevaunces. And the lorde that is the ownere of this
25 castel, I wolde he ressayved hit as is his ryght.'

'Fayre sir,' they seyde, 'the name of this castell is called Tyntagyll, and a deuke ought hit somtyme that had wedded fayre Igrayne, and so aftir that she was wedded to Uther Pendragon, and he gate on hir Arthure.'

30 'Well,' seyde sir Launcelot, 'I undirstonde to whom this castel longith.'

And so he departed frome them and betaught hem unto God, and than he mounted uppon his horse and rode into many stronge countreyes and thorow many watyrs and
35 valeyes, and evyll was he lodged. And at the laste by fortune hym happynd ayenste nyght to come to a fayre courtelage, and therein he founde an olde jantylwoman that lodged

---

1-4 *W* (*sidenote*): Here sir Launcelot slew two Gyauntes in the castel of Tyntagil
3 *C* their delyueraunce 　5 *Not emended in* O¹ 　17 *C* assayed hit and 　20-21 *C**
frendes how & who hath delyuerd you and grete 　*W* gretes 　26 called *not in* C
28-29 *C* & after wedded her Vtherpendragon 　34 *C* straunge & wyld countreyes

hym with goode wyll; and there he had good chere for hym
and his horse. And whan tyme was his oste brought hym
into a garret over the gate to his bedde. There sir Launcelot
unarmed hym and set his harneyse by hym and wente to
bedde, and anone he felle on slepe.   5

So aftir there com one on horsebak and knokked at the
gate in grete haste. Whan sir Launcelot herde this he arose
up and loked oute at the wyndowe, and sygh by the moone-
lyght three knyghtes com rydyng aftir that one man, and all
three laysshynge on hym at onys with swerdys; and that one   10
knyght turned on hem knyghtly agayne and defended hym.

'Truly,' seyde sir Launcelot, 'yondir one knyght shall I
helpe, for hit were shame for me to se three knyghtes on one,
and yf [he] be there slayne I am partener of his deth.'

And therewith he toke his harneys and wente oute at   15
a wyndowe by a shete downe to the four knyghtes. And
than sir Launcelot seyde on hyght,

'Turne you, knyghtis, unto me, and leve this feyghtyng
with that knyght!'

And than they three leffte sir Kay and turned unto sir   20
Launcelot, and assayled hym on every honde. Than sir Kay
dressid hym to have holpen sir Launcelot.   **106ᵛ**

'Nay, sir,' sayde he, 'I woll none of your helpe. Therefore,
as ye woll have my helpe, lette me alone with hem.'

Sir Kay for the plesure of that knyght suffyrd hym for to   25
do his wylle and so stoode on syde. Than anone within seven
strokys sir Launcelot had strykyn hem to the erthe. And
than they all three cryed,

'Sir knyght, we yelde us unto you as a man of myght
makeles.'   30

'As to that, I woll nat take youre yeldyng unto me, but
so that ye woll yelde you unto thys knyght; and on that
covenaunte I woll save youre lyvys, and ellys nat.'

'Fayre knyght, that were us loth, for as for that knyght,
we chaced hym hydir, and had overcom hym, had nat ye   35

---

3 *C* a fayre garet   6 *C* So soone after   10 *C* lasshed   18 *C* your fyghtyng
20 *C* alle thre   21 *C** and there beganne grete bat, aylle for they alyghte al thre
and strake many grete strokes at syr launcelot and assaylled *Homoeoteleuton in W?*
21 *C* euery syde   26–27 *C* vi strokes   31 *C* that said sir laūcelot I will
32 *C* vnto syr kay the Seneschal   34 *C* knyghte sayd they that were we lothe
to doo (we *not in* S) For as for syr kay

bene. Therefore to yelde us unto hym hit were no reson.'

'Well, as to that, avyse you well, for ye may chose whether ye woll dye other lyve. For and ye be yolden hit shall be unto sir Kay.'

5 'Now, fayre knyght,' they seyde, 'in savyng of oure lyvys, we woll do as thou commaundys us.'

'Than shall ye,' seyde sir Launcelot, 'on Whytsonday nexte commynge go unto the courte of kynge Arthure, and there shall ye yelde you unto quene Gwenyvere and putte 10 you all three in hir grace and mercy, and say that sir Kay sente you thydir to be her presoners.'

'Sir,' they seyde, 'hit shall be done, by the feyth of oure bodyes, and we be men lyvyng.'

And there they sware every knyght uppon his swerde, and 15 so sir Launcelot suffyrd hem to departe. And than sir Launcelot cnocked at the gate with the pomell of his swerde; and with that come his oste, and in they entyrd, he and sir Kay.

'Sir,' seyde his oste, 'I wente ye had bene in your bed.'

'So I was, but I arose and lepe oute at my wyndow for 20 to helpe an olde felowe of myne.'

So whan they come nye the lyght sir Kay knew well hit was sir Launcelot, and therewith he kneled downe and
107ʳ thanked hym of all his kyndenesse, that he had holpyn hym twyse frome the deth.

25 'Sir,' he seyde, 'I have nothyng done but that me ought for to do. And ye ar welcom, and here shall ye repose you and take your reste.'

Whan sir Kay was unarmed he asked aftir mete. Anone there was mete fette for hym and he ete strongly. And whan 30 he had sowped they wente to their beddys and were lodged togydyrs in one bed.

So on the morne sir Launcelot arose erly and leffte sir Kay slepyng. And sir Launcelot toke sir Kayes armoure and his shylde and armed hym; and so he wente to the stable and 35 sadylde his horse, and toke his leve of his oste and departed. Than sone aftir arose sir Kay and myssid sir Launcelot, and than he aspyed that he had his armoure and his horse.

2 *C* that said laūcelot   5 *C* Fayre knyght thenne they   13 men *not in C*†
13–15 *W* (*sidenote*): Here sir Launcelot bete iii knyghtes and rescowed sir Kay
17 *C* sir kay and he   19 *C* I was sayd sire launcelot But   29 *C* mete fette
hym   34–35 *C* and toke his hors and toke his leue

'Now, be my fayth, I know welle that he woll greve som
of the courte of kyng Arthure, for on hym knyghtes woll
be bolde and deme that hit is I, and that woll begyle them.
And bycause of his armoure and shylde I am sure I shall
ryde in pease.'   5

And than sone sir Kay departed and thanked his oste.

Now turne we unto sir Launcelot that had ryddyn longe (12)
in a grete foreste. And at the laste he com unto a low countrey
full of fayre ryvers and fayre meedys; and before hym he
sawe a longe brydge, and three pavylyons stood thereon, of 10
sylke and sendell of dyverse hew. And withoute the pavylyons hynge three whyght shyldys on trouncheouns of sperys,
and grete longe sperys stood upryght by the pavylyons, and
at every pavylyon dore stoode three freysh knyghtes.

And so sir Launcelot passed by hem and spake no worde. 15
But whan he was paste the three knyghtes knew hym and
seyde hit was the proude sir Kay:

'He wenyth no knyght so good as he, and the contrary is
oftyn proved. Be my fayth,' seyde one of the knyghtes, his
name was sir Gawtere, 'I woll ryde aftir hym and assay hym 20
for all his pryde; and ye may beholde how that I spede.'

So sir Gawtere armed hym and hynge his shylde uppon
his sholdir, and mounted uppon a grete horse, and gate his **107ᵛ**
speare in his honde, and wallopte aftir sir Launcelot. And
whan he come nyghe hym he cryed, 'Abyde, thou proude 25
knyght, sir Kay! for thou shalt nat passe all quyte.' So sir
Launcelot turned hym, and eythir feautyrd their sperys and
com togedyrs with all their myghtes. And sir Gawters speare
brake, but sir Launcelot smote hym downe horse and man.

And whan he was at the erthe his brethyrn seyde,   30

'Yondir knyght is nat sir Kay, for he is far bygger than he.'

'I dare ley my hede,' seyde sir Gylmere, 'yondir knyght
hath slayne sir Kay and hath takyn hys horse and harneyse.'

'Whether hit be so other no,' seyde sir Raynolde, 'lette
us mounte on oure horsys and rescow oure brothir, sir 35

1 *C* my seythe†   6 *C* soone after departed sir kay &   9 *C* Ryuers and
medowes   14 *C* fresshe squyers   16–17 *C*† knyghtes sayden hym that hit
was   19 *C* oftyme   22 *C* Soo this knyght syre Gaunter   26 all *not in C*
30 *C* whan syr gaunter was   *C* sayd echone to other   31 *C* byggar
S bygger   34–35 *C* Raynold the thyrd broder lete vs now goo mounte vpon our
35–p. 276, l. 1 *C* our broder sir Gaunter vpon payne

Gawtere. For payne of deth, we all shall have worke inow to macche that knyght; for ever mesemyth by his persone hit is sir Launcelot other sir Trystrams other sir Pelleas, the good knyght.

5 Than anone they toke their horsys and overtoke sir Launcelot. And sir Gylmere put forth his speare and ran to sir Launcelot, and sir Launcelot smote hym downe, that he lay in a sowghe.

'Sir knyght,' seyde sir Raynolde, 'thou arte a stronge man, 10 and as I suppose thou haste slayne my two bretherne, for the whyche rysyth my herte sore agaynste the. And yf I myght wyth my worshyppe I wolde not have ado with the, but nedys I muste take suche parte as they do. And therefore, knyght, kepe thyselfe!'

15 And so they hurtylde togydyrs with all their myghtes and all to-shevird bothe there spearys, and than they drew hir swerdys and laysshed togydir egirly. Anone there[with]all arose sir Gawtere and come unto his brother sir Gyllymere, and bade hym aryse, 'and helpe we oure brothir, sir Raynolde, 20 that yondir merveylously macchyth yondir good knyght.' Therewithall they hurteled unto sir Launcelot. And whan he sawe them com he smote a sore stroke unto sir Raynolde, 108ʳ that he felle of his horse to the grounde, and than he caste to the othir two bretherne, and at two strokys he strake hem 25 downe to the erthe. Wyth that sir Raynolde gan up sterte with his hede all blody and com streyte unto sir Launcelot.

'Now let be,' seyde sir Launcelot, 'I was not far frome the whan thou were made knyght, sir Raynolde, and also I know thou arte a good knyght, and lothe I were to sle the.' 30 'Gramercy,' seyde sir Raynolde, 'of your goodnesse, and I dare say as for me and my bretherne, [we] woll nat be loth to yelde us unto you, with that we know youre name; for welle we know ye ar not sir Kay.'

'As for that, be as be may. For ye shal yelde you unto 35 dame Gwenyvere, and loke that ye be there on Whytsonday and yelde you unto hir as presoners, and sey that sir Kay

---

1 *C* vpon payne   13 suche *not in C*   14 *C* knyghte as he sayd kepe   21 *C** they lepte on theyr horses & hurtled   24 *C* he stroke to   25 *C* beganne to starte vp   30 *C* raynold as for your   32 *C* knewe youre (*S* your)   34 *C* be it as it be   35 *C** be with her on

sente you unto hir.' Than they swore hit sholde be done,
and [so] passed forth sir Launcelot, and ecchone of the
bretherne halpe other as well as they myght.

So sir Launcelotte rode into a depe foreste, and there by (13)
hym in a slade he sey four knyghtes hovynge undir an oke,　5
and they were of Arthurs courte: one was sir Sagramour le
Desyrus, and sir Ector de Marys, and sir Gawayne, and sir
Uwayne. And anone as these four knyghtes had aspyed sir
Launcelot they wende by his armys that hit had bene sir Kay.

'Now, be my fayth,' sayde sir Sagramoure, 'I woll preve　10
sir Kayes myght,' and gate his spere in his honde and com
towarde sir Launcelot.

Than sir Launcelot was ware of his commyng and knew hym
well, and featured his speare agaynste hym and smote sir Sagramoure so sore that horse and man wente bothe to the erthe.　　15

'Lo, my felowys,' seyde sir Ector, 'yondir may ye se
what a buffette he hath gyffen! Methynkyth that knyght is
muche bygger than ever was sir Kay. Now shall ye se what
I may do to hym.'

So sir Ector gate his spere in his honde and walopte　20
towarde sir Launcelot, and sir Launcelot smote hym evyn
thorow the shylde and his sholdir, that man and horse wente　**108ᵛ**
to the erthe, and ever his spere helde.

'Be my fayth,' sayde sir Uwayne, 'yondir is a stronge
knyght, and I am sure he hath slayne Kay. And I se be his　25
grete strengthe hit woll be harde to macche hym.'

And therewithall sir Uwayne gate his speare and rode
towarde sir Launcelot. And sir Launcelot knew hym well
and lette hi⟨s⟩ horse renne on the playne and gaff hym suche
a buffette that he was astooned, and longe he wyste nat　30
where he was.

'Now se I welle,' seyde sir Gawayne, 'I muste encountir
with that knyght,' and dressed his shylde and gate a good
speare in his honde and lete renne at sir Launcelot with all
his myght; and eyther knyght smote other in myddys of　35
the shylde. But sir Gawaynes spere braste, and sir Launcelot

5 hym *not in* C　　　13 of his commyng *not in* C　　　15 C man felle bothe
16 C sayd he†　　　17 gyffen Methynkyth *not in* C　　　21 evyn *not in* C　　　22 his
not in C　　　27 C spere in his hand and　　　29 W hir horse　　C and soo he mette
hym on　　33 C knyȝt Thenne he dressid he† his　　34–35 C and syre launcelot
knewe hym wel and thenne they lete renne theyr horses with all theyr myghtes and

charged so sore uppon hym that his horse reversed up-so-
downe, and muche sorow had sir Gawayne to avoyde his
horse. And so sir Launcelot passed on a pace and smyled
and seyde, 'God gyff hym joy that this spere made, for
5 there cam never a bettir in my honde.'

Than the four knyghtes wente echone to other and comforted each other and seyde,

'What sey ye by this geste,' seyde sir Gawayne, 'that with
one spere hath felde us all four?'

10 'We commaunde hym to the devyll,' they seyde all, 'for
he is a man of grete myght.'

'Ye may say hit well,' seyde sir Gawayne, 'that he [is] a
man of myght, for I dare ley my hede hit is sir Launcelot:
I know hym well by his rydyng.'

15 'Latte hym go,' seyde sir Uwayne, 'for whan we com to
the courte we shall wete.'

Than had they much sorow to gete their horsis agayne.

(14) Now leve we there and speke we of sir Launcelot that
rode a grete whyle in a depe foreste. And as he rode he
20 sawe a blak brachette sekyng in maner as hit had bene in
the feaute of an hurte dere. And therewith he rode aftir
109ʳ the brachette and he saw lye on the grounde a large feaute
of bloode. And than sir Launcelot rode faster, and ever the
brachette loked behynde hir, and so she wente thorow a
25 grete marys, and ever sir Launcelot folowed.

And than was he ware of an olde maner, and thydir ran
the brachette and so over a brydge. So sir Launcelot rode
over that brydge that was olde and feble, and whan he com
in the myddys of a grete halle there he seye lye dede a knyght
30 that was a semely man, and that brachette lycked his woundis.
And therewithall com oute a lady wepyng and wryngyng
hir hondys, and sayde,

'Knyght, to muche sorow hast thou brought me.'

'Why sey ye so?' seyde sir Launcelot. 'I dede never this
35 knyght no harme, for hydir by the feaute of blood this
brachet brought me. And therefore, fayre lady, be nat

7 and seyde *not in C*   8 with *not in C*   8–12 *W* (*sidenote*): Here sir Launcelot
with one spere smote downe sir Sagramour sir Ector sir Uwayne and sir Gawayne
12 *C* may wel saye it   14 *C* knowe it by   15 *C* sayd syre Gawayn†
18 *C* speke of   19 *C* forest where he   23 *C* rode after And   27 *C*
the brydge   32–33 *C* And thenne she sayd O knyghte

dyspleased with me, for I am full sore agreved for your grevaunce.'

'Truly, sir,' she seyde, 'I trowe hit be nat ye that hath slayne my husbonde, for he that dud that dede is sore wounded and is never lykly to be hole, that shall I ensure 5 hym.'

'What was youre husbondes name?' seyde sir Launcelot.

'Sir, his name was called sir Gylberd the Bastarde, one of the beste knyghtys of the worlde, and he that hath slayne hym I know nat his name.'   10

'Now God sende you bettir comforte,' seyde sir Launcelot.

And so he departed and wente into the foreste agayne, and there he mette with a damesell the whyche knew hym well. And she seyde on lowde,

'Well be ye founde, my lorde. And now I requyre you 15 of your knyghthode helpe my brother that is sore wounded and never styntyth bledyng; for this day he fought with sir Gylberte the Bastarde and slew hym in playne batayle, and there was my brother sore wounded. And there is a lady, a sorseres, that dwellyth in a castel here bysyde, and this 20 day she tolde me my brothers woundys sholde never be hole **109ᵛ** tyll I coude fynde a knyght wolde go into the Chapel Perelus, and there he sholde fynde a swerde and a blody cloth that the woundid knyght was lapped in; and a pece of that cloth and that swerde sholde hele my brother, with that 25 his woundis were serched with the swerde and the cloth.'

'This is a mervelouse thyng,' seyde sir Launcelot, 'but what is your brothirs name?'

'Sir,' she seyde, 'sir Melyot de Logyrs.'

'That me repentys,' seyde sir Launcelotte, 'for he is a 30 felow of the Table Rounde, and to his helpe I woll do my power.'

Than she sayde, 'Sir, folow ye evyn this hygheway, and hit woll brynge you to the Chapel Perelus, and here I shall abyde tyll God sende you agayne. And yf you spede nat 35 I know no knyght lyvynge that may encheve that adventure.'

---

1 *C* of your   5 *C* to recouer that   8 *C* Syre sayd she   22 *C* knyght wold
S knyght that wold   25 *C* broders woundes so that   29 *C* she sayd his
name was syre   33 *C* Thenne syre said she folowe euen   35–36 *C* and but
you spede I

(15)   Ryght so sir Launcelot departed, and whan he com to the Chapell Perelus he alyght downe and tyed his horse unto a lytyll gate. And as sone as he was within the chyrche-yerde he sawe on the frunte of the chapel many fayre ryche
5 shyldis turned up-so-downe, and many of tho shyldis sir Launcelot had sene knyghtes bere byforehande. With that he sawe by hym there stonde a thirty grete knyghtes, more by a yerde than any man that ever he had sene, and all they grenned and gnasted at sir Launcelot. And whan he sawe
10 their countenaunce he dredde hym sore, and so put his shylde before hym and toke his swerde in his honde redy unto batayle.

And they all were armed all in blak harneyse, redy with her shyldis and her swerdis redy drawyn. And as sir
15 Launcelot wolde have gone thorow them they skaterd on every syde of hym and gaff hym the way, and therewith he wexed bolde and entyrde into the chapel. And there he sawe no lyght but a dymme lampe brennyng, and than was he ware of a corpus hylled with a clothe of sylke. Than
20 sir Launcelot stouped doune and kutte a pese away of that cloth, and than hit fared undir hym as the grounde had
110ʳ quaked a lytyll; therewithall he feared.

And than he sawe a fayre swerde lye by the dede knyght, and that he gate in his honde and hyed hym oute of the
25 chapell. Anone as ever he was in the chapell-yerde all the knyghtes spake to hym with grymly voyces and seyde,

'Knyght, sir Launcelot, lay that swerde frome the or thou shalt dye!'

'Whether that I lyve other dye,' seyde sir Launcelot, 'with
30 no wordys grete gete ye hit agayne. Therefore fyght for hit and ye lyst.'

Than ryght so he passed thorowoute them. And byyonde the chapell-yarde there mette hym a fayre damesell and seyde,
35 'Sir Launcelot, leve that swerde behynde the, other thou wolt dye for hit.'

'I leve hit not,' seyde sir Launcelot, 'for no thretyng.'

---

9 *C* grened   *S* greued   11 *C* swerd redy in   14 *C* swerdes drawen
17 *C* al bold   21 *C* the erthe had   26 *C* a grymly voys   30 *C* noo
grete word   37 *C* no treatys

'No,' seyde she, 'and thou dyddyste leve that swerde
quene Gwenyvere sholde thou never se.'

'Than were I a foole and I wolde leve this swerde.'

'Now, jantyll knyghte,' seyde the damesell, 'I requyre the
to kysse me but onys.'   5

'Nay,' seyde sir Launcelot, 'that God me forbede.'

'Well, sir,' seyde she, 'and thou haddyst kyssed me thy
lyff dayes had be done. And now, alas,' she seyde, 'I have
loste all my laboure, for I ordeyned this chapell for thy sake
and for sir Gawayne. And onys I had hym within me, and   10
at that tyme he fought with this knyght that lyeth dede in
yondir chapell, sir Gylberte the Bastarde, and at that tyme
he smote the lyffte honde of sir Gylberte. And, sir Launcelot,
now I telle the: I have loved the this seven yere, [but] there
may no woman have thy love but quene Gwenyver; and   15
sytthen I myght nat rejoyse the nother thy body on lyve,
I had kepte no more joy in this worlde but to have thy body
dede. Than wolde I have bawmed hit and sered hit, and so to
have kepte hit my lyve dayes; and dayly I sholde have
clypped the and kyssed the, dispyte of quene Gwenyvere.'   20

'Ye sey well,' seyde sir Launcelot, 'Jesu preserve me frome
your subtyle crauftys!'

And therewithall he toke his horse and so departed frome
hir. And as the booke seyth, whan sir Launcelot was departed
she toke suche sorow that she deyde within a fourtenyte; and   25
hir name was called Hallewes the Sorseres, lady of the castell   **110ᵛ**
Nygurmous. And anone sir Launcelot mette with the dame-
sel, sir Melyottis systir, and whan she sawe hym she clapped
hir hondys and wepte for joy. And than they rode into a
castell thereby where lay sir Melyot, and anone as sir Launce-   30
lot sye hym he knew hym, but he was passyng paale as the
erthe for bledynge. Whan sir Melyot saw sir Launcelot he
kneled uppon his kneis and cryed on hyghte:

'A, lorde, sir Launcelot, helpe me anone!'

Than sir Launcelot lepe unto hym and towched his   35
woundys with sir Gylbardys swerde, and than he wyped his

---

1 *C* dydest louet that   10 *C* had syr Gawayne within   11 *C* that knyght
that lyeth there dede   13 *C* of of sir Gylbert the bastard   16 *C* I
maye not reioyce the to haue thy body   20 *C** in despyte of Quene   25 *C*
a fourten nyghte   26 *C* was Hellawes   33 *C* on hyghe   34 *C* helpe
me Anone syre

woundys with a parte of the bloody cloth that sir Gylbarde was wrapped in; and anone an holer man in his lyff was he never.

And than there was grete joy betwene hem, and they made
5 sir Launcelot all the chere that they myghte. And so on the morne sir Launcelot toke his leve and bade sir Melyot hyghe hym 'to the courte of my lorde Arthure, for hit drawyth nyghe to the feste of Pentecoste. And there, by the grace of God, ye shall fynde me.' And therewith they departed.

(16) 10 And so sir Launcelot rode thorow many stronge contrayes, over mores and valeis, tyll by fortune he com to a fayre castell. And as he paste beyonde the castell hym thought he herde bellys rynge, and than he was ware of a faucon com over his hede fleyng towarde an hyghe elme, and longe
15 lunes aboute her feete. And she flowe unto the elme to take hir perche, the lunes overcast aboute a bowghe; and whan she wolde have tane hir flyght she hynge by the leggis faste. And sir Launcelot syghe how ⟨s⟩he hynge, and behelde the fayre faucon perygot; and he was sory for hir. The
20 meanewhyle cam a lady oute of a castell and cryed on hyghe:

'A, Launcelot, Launcelot! as thow arte floure of all knyghtes, helpe me to gete me my hauke; for and my hauke be loste my lorde wolde destroy me, for I kepte the hauke and
25 she slypped fro me. And yf my lorde my husbande wete hit,
111ʳ he is so hasty that he wyll sle me.'

'What is your lordis name?' seyde sir Launcelot.

'Sir,' she seyde, 'his name is sir Phelot, a knyght that longyth unto the kynge of North Galys.'

30 'Welle, fayre lady, syn that ye know my name and requyre me of knyghthode to helpe, I woll do what I may to gete youre hauke; and yet God knowyth I am an evyll clymber, and the tre is passynge hyghe, and fewe bowys to helpe me withall.'

And therewith sir Launcelot alyght and tyed his horse to
35 the same tre, and prayde the lady to onarme hym. And so whan he was unarmed he put of all his clothis unto his shurte and his breche, and with myght and grete force he clambe

---

5–9 *W* (*sidenote*): Here sir Launcelot heled sir Melyot de Logyrs with sir Gylberde the Basterdis swerde   11 *C* ouer marys   13 *C* herde the bellys   31 *C* helpe yow   37 grete *not in C*   *C* clamme

up to the faucon and tyed the lunes to a grete rotyn boysh, and threwe the hauke downe with the buysh.

And anone the lady gate the hauke in hir honde; and therewithall com oute sir Phelot oute of the grevys suddeynly, that was hir husbonde, all armed and with his naked swerde in his honde, and sayde,

'A knyght, sir Launcelot, now I have founde the as I wolde,' he stondyng at the boole of the tre to sle hym.

'A, lady!' seyde sir Launcelot, 'why have ye betrayed me?'

'She hath done,' seyde sir Phelot, 'but as I commaunded hir, and therefore there is none othir boote but thyne oure is com that thou muste dye.'

'That were shame unto the,' seyde sir Launcelot, 'thou an armed knyght to sle a nakyd man by treson.'

'Thou gettyste none other grace,' seyde sir Phelot, 'and therefore helpe thyself and thou can.'

'Truly,' seyde sir Launcelot, 'that shall be thy shame; but syn thou wolt do none other, take myne harneys with the and hange my swerde there uppon a bowghe that I may gete hit, and than do thy beste [to] sle me and thou can.'

'Nay,' seyde sir Phelot, 'for I know the bettir than thou wenyste. Therefore thou gettyst no wepyn and I may kepe the therefro.'

'Alas,' seyde sir Launcelot, 'that ever a knyght sholde dey wepynles!'

And therewith he wayted above hym and undir hym, and over hym above his hede he sawe a rowgh spyke, a bygge **111ᵛ** bowghe leveles. And therewith he brake hit of by the body, and than he com lowar, and awayted how his owne horse stoode, and suddenyly he lepe on the farther syde of his horse froward the knyght. And than sir Phelot laysshed at hym egerly to have slayne hym, but sir Launcelot put away the stroke with the rowgh spyke, and therewith toke hym on the hede, that downe he felle in a sowghe to the grounde.

2 *C* doune and it with alle   8 *C* wold and stode at the bole   17, 21–22 *C* thou canst   20 there *not in C*   23 *C* Nay nay   24–25 *C* kepe you   29 *C†* ouer his hede he sawe a rownsepyke   32–33 *C* of the hors   34 *C* egerly wenynge to   35 *C* rounsepyk   35–36 *C** ther with he smote hym on the one syde of the hede that he felle doune in

So than sir Launcelot toke his swerde oute of his honde and
strake his necke in two pecys.

'Alas!' than cryed that lady, 'why haste thou slayne my
husbonde?'

5 'I am nat causer,' seyde sir Launcelot, 'but with falshede
ye wolde have had me slayne with treson, and now hit is
fallyn on you bothe.'

And than she sowned as though she wolde dey. And
therewith sir Launcelot gate all his armoure as well as he
10 myght and put hit uppon hym for drede of more resseite,
for he dredde hym that the knyghtes castell was so nyghe
hym; and as sone as he myght he toke his horse and departed, and thanked God that he had escaped that harde
adventure.

(17) 15 So sir Launcelot rode many wylde wayes thorowoute
morys and mares, and as he rode in a valay, he sey a knyght
chasyng a lady with a naked swerde to have slayne hir.
And by fortune, as this knyght sholde have slayne thys lady,
she cryed on sir Launcelot and prayde hym to rescowe her.

20 Whan sir Launcelot sye that myschyff, he toke his horse
and rode betwene hem, sayynge,

'Knyght, fye for shame, why wolte thou sle this lady?
Shame unto the and all knyghtes!'

'What haste thou to do betwyxte me and my wyff? I
25 woll sle her magré thyne hede.'

'That shall ye nat,' sayde sir Launcelot, 'for rather we
woll have ado togydyrs.'

'Sir Launcelot,' seyde the knyght, 'thou doste nat thy
parte, for thys lady hath betrayed me.'

30 'Hit is not so,' seyde the lady, 'truly, he seyth wronge on
me. And for bycause I love [and] cherysshe my cousyn
112ʳ jarmayne, he is jolowse betwyxte me and hym; and as I
mutte answere to God there was never sene betwyxte us
none suche thynges. But, sir,' seyde the lady, 'as thou arte
35 called the worshypfullyest knyght of the worlde, I requyre

2–3 *C* neck fro the body Thenne cryed the lady Allas why   5 *C* for with
6 *C* had slayne me†   10 *C* more resorte†   11, 12 hym *not in C*   13 harde
not in C   16 morys and *not in C*   *C*† mares and many wylde wayes   23 *C*
Thou dost shame   24 *C* wyf sayd the knyght I   32 *W* jarmayne and he
32–33 *C* hym and me And as I shalle   33–34 *C* three† was neuer synne be-
twyxe vs But

the of trewe knyghthode, kepe me and save me, for whatsomever he sey he woll sle me, for he is withoute mercy.'

'Have ye no doute: hit shalle nat lye in his power.'

'Sir,' seyde the knyght, 'in your syght I woll be ruled as
ye woll have me.'   5

And so sir Launcelot rode on the one syde and she on the
other syde. And he had nat redyn but a whyle but the knyght
bade sir Launcelot turne hym and loke behynde hym, and
seyde, 'Sir, yondir com men of armys aftir [us] rydynge.'
And so sir Launcelot turned hym and thought no treson;   10
and therewith was the knyght and the lady on one syde, and
suddeynly he swapped of the ladyes hede. And whan sir
Launcelot had aspyed hym what he had done, he seyde and
so called hym: 'Traytoure, thou haste shamed me for evir!'
And suddeynly sir Launcelot alyght of his horse and pulde   15
oute his swerde to sle hym. And therewithall he felle to the
erthe and gryped sir Launcelot by the thyghes and cryed
mercy.

'Fye on the,' seyde sir Launcelot, 'thou shamefull knyght!
Thou mayste have no mercy: therefore aryse and fyghte   20
with me!'

'Nay,' sayde the knyght, 'I woll never aryse tylle ye
graunte me mercy.'

'Now woll I proffyr the fayre: I woll unarme me unto my
shyrte [and I woll have nothyng upon me but my sherte]   25
and my swerde in my honde, and yf thou can sle me, quyte
be thou for ever.'

'Nay, sir, that woll I never.'

'Well,' seyde sir Launcelot, 'take this lady and the hede,
and bere [it] uppon the; and here shalt thou swere uppon   30
my swerde to bere hit allwayes uppon thy bak and never to
reste tyll thou com to my lady, quene Gwenyver.'

'Sir, that woll I do, by the feyth of my bo[d]y.'

'Now what is youre name?'

'Sir, my name is sir Pedy[v]ere.'   35

'In a shamefull oure were thou borne,' seyde sir Launcelot. **112ᵛ**

3 *C* doubte sayd launcelot it shal   9 *W* aftir hym rydynge   *C** after vs
rydynge   12 *C* of his ladyes   14 so *not in C*   16 *C*† hrs swerd   16 *C*
fell flat to   24 *C* fayr said launcelot   25 *C* I wyll   26 *C*† and my hand
28 *C* sir said Pedyuere that   32 my lady *not in C*   33 *W* my boby
34 *C* Now said launcelot telle me what is   35 *W* Pedynere   *C* Pedyuere

So sir Pedyvere departed with the lady dede and the
hede togydir, and founde the quene with kynge Arthure at
Wynchestir; and there he tolde all the trouthe.

'Sir knyght,' seyde the quene, 'this is an horryble dede
5 and a shamefull, and a grete rebuke unto sir Launcelot, but
natwythstondyng his worshyp is knowyn in many dyverse
contreis. But this shall I gyff you in penaunce: make ye
as good skyffte as ye can, ye shall bere this lady with you
on horsebak unto the Pope of Rome, and of hym resseyve
10 youre penaunce for your foule dedis. And ye shall nevir
reste one nyght thereas ye do another, and ye go to ony
bedde the dede body shall lye with you.'

This oth he there made and so departed. And as hit
tellyth in the Frenshe booke, whan he com unto Rome the
15 Pope there bade hym go agayne unto quene Gwenyver, and
in Rome was his lady buryed by the Popys commaundement. And after thys knyght sir Pedyvere fell to grete
goodnesse and was an holy man and an hermyte.

(18)   Now turne we unto sir Launcelot du Lake that com home
20 two dayes before the feste of Pentecoste, and the kynge
and all the courte were passyng fayne. And whan Gawayne,
sir Uwayne, sir Sagramoure, and sir Ector de Mares sye
sir Launcelot in Kayes armour, than they wyste well that hit
was he that smote hem downe all wyth one spere. Than there
25 was lawghyng and smylyng amonge them, and ever now and
now com all the knyghtes home that were presoners with
sir Terquyn, and they all honoured sir Launcelot.

Whan sir Gaherys herde h[e]m speke he sayde, 'I sawe
all the batayle from the begynnynge to the endynge,' and
30 there he tolde kynge Arthure all how hit was and how sir
113ʳ Terquyn was the strongest knyght that ever he saw excep[t]e
sir Launcelot; and there were many knyghtes bare hym
recorde, three score. Than sir Kay tolde the kynge how sir
Launcelot rescowed hym whan he sholde have bene slayne,
35 and how 'he made the three knyghtes yelde hem to me and
nat to hym'. And there they were all three and bare recorde.

---

1 *C* the dede lady   2 togydir *not in C*   6 *C†* not knowen   6–11 *W* (*sidenote*): Here sir Launcelot made sir Pedyvere bere the dede body of the lady to quene
Gwenyvere   17 knyght *not in C*   21 *C* fayne of his comynge   26–27 *C*
that sir Turquyn hadde prysoners and   27 *C* honoured and worshypped syre
28 *W* hym   33 *C* nyghe thre   34 *C* had rescowed   36 three *not in C*

'And by Jesu,' seyde sir Kay, 'sir Launcelot toke my
harneyse and leffte me his, and I rode in Goddys pece and
no man wolde have ado with me.'

Anone therewith com three knyghtes that fought with
sir Launcelot at the longe brydge; and there they yelded 5
them unto sir Kay, and sir Kay forsoke them and seyde he
fought never with hem. 'But I shall ease your hertes,' seyde
sir Kay, 'yondir is sir Launcelot that overcam you.' Whan
they wyste that, they were glad. And than sir Melyot de
Logrys come home and tolde hym and the kynge how 10
sir Launcelot had saved hym frome the deth, and all his
dedys was knowyn: how the quenys sorserers four had hym
in preson, and how he was delyverde by the kynge Bagdemagus doughter.

Also there was tolde all the grete armys that sir Launcelot 15
dud betwyxte the two kynges, that ys for to say the kynge
of North Galys and kyng Bagdemagus: all the trouth sir Gahalantyne dud telle, and sir Mador de la Porte, and sir Mordred, for they were at the same turnement. Than com
in the lady that knew sir Launcelot whan that he wounded 20
sir Belleus at the pavylyon; and there at the requeste of
sir Launcelot sir Belleus was made knyght of the Rounde
Table.

And so at that tyme sir Launcelot had the grettyste name
of ony knyght of the worlde, and moste he was honoured of 25
hyghe and lowe.

EXPLICIT A NOBLE TALE OF SIR LAUNCELOT DU LAKE.

1 *C* Kay by cause syr   2 *C* his I rode in good peece   10 hym and *not in C*
12 *C* how foure quenes sorceresses had   15 *C** alle the (*not in S*) grete dedes
of armes   27 *C* Explicit the noble tale of syr Launcelot du lake whiche is the vi
book Here foloweth the tale of syr Gareth of Orkeney that was called Beaumayns
by syr kay and is the seuenth book

THE TALE

OF

SIR GARETH OF ORKNEY

THAT WAS CALLED
BEWMAYNES

———

[Winchester MS., ff. 113ᵛ–148ʳ;
Caxton, Book VII]

CAXTON'S RUBRICS

IN Arthurs dayes, whan he helde the Rounde Table moste   **113ᵛ** (1)
plenoure, hit fortuned the kynge commaunded that the
hyghe feste of Pentecoste sholde be holden at a cité and a 5
castell, in tho dayes that was called Kynke Kenadonne,
uppon the sondys that marched nyghe Walys. So evir the
kynge had a custom that at the feste of Pentecoste in especiall
afore other festys in the yere, he wolde nat go that day to
mete unto that he had herde other sawe of a grete mervayle. 10
And for that custom all maner of strange adventures com
byfore Arthure, as at that feste before all other festes.

And so sir Gawayne, a lytyll tofore the none of the day of
Pentecoste, aspyed at a wyndowe three men uppon horsebak
and a dwarfe uppon foote. And so the three men alyght, and 15
the dwarff kepte their horsis, and one of the men was hyghar
than the tothir tweyne by a foote and an half. Than sir
Gawayne wente unto the kyng and sayde,

'Sir, go to your mete, for here at hande commyth strange
adventures.' 20

So the kynge wente unto his mete with many other
kynges, and there were all the knyghtes of the Rounde
Table, onles that ony were presoners other slayne at re-
countyrs. Than at the hyghe feste evermore they sholde
be fulfylled the hole numbir of an hondred and fyffty, for 25
than was the Rounde Table fully complysshed.

Ryght so com into the halle two men well besayne and
rychely, and uppon their sholdyrs there lened the goodlyest
yonge man and the fayreste that ever they all sawe. And he
was large and longe and brode in the shuldyrs, well-vysaged, 30
and the largyste and the fayreste handis that ever man sye.
But he fared as he myght nat go nothir bere hymself but
yf he lened uppon their shuldyrs. Anone as the kynge saw
hym there was made peas and rome, and ryght so they yode
with hym unto the hyghe deyse withoute seyynge of ony 35

3 *C* Whan Arthur held his round   4 *C* fortuned that he commaunded   16 *C*
the thre men   21 *C* So Arthur   23 *C* table only tho that were   31 *C**
handed   33 *C* Anone as Arthur

wordys. Than this yonge muche man pullyd hym abak and
easyly [stretched] streyghte upryght, seynge,

'The moste noble kynge, kynge Arthure! God you blysse
114ͬ and all your fayre felyshyp, and in especiall the felyshyp of
5 the Table Rounde. And for this cause I come hydir, to pray
you and requyre you to gyff me three gyftys. And they shall
nat be unresenablé asked but that ye may worshypfully
graunte hem me, and to you no grete hurte nother losse.
And the fyrste do[n]e and gyffte I woll aske now, and the
10 tothir two gyfftes I woll aske this day twelve-monthe, where-
someover ye holde your hyghe feste.'

'Now aske ye,' seyde kyng Arthure, 'and ye shall have
your askynge.'

'Now, sir, this is my petycion at this feste, that ye woll
15 geff me mete and drynke suffyciauntly for this twelve-monthe,
and at that day I woll aske myne other two gyfftys.'

'My fayre son,' seyde kyng Arthure, 'aske bettyr, I
counseyle the, for this is but a symple askyng; for myne
herte gyvyth me to the gretly, that thou arte com of men of
20 worshyp, and gretly my conceyte fayleth me but thou shalt
preve a man of ryght grete worshyp.'

'Sir,' he seyde, 'thereof be as be may, for I have asked
that I woll aske at this tyme.'

'Well,' seyde the kynge, 'ye shall have mete and drynke
25 inowe, I nevir forbade hit my frynde nother my foo. But
what is thy name, I wolde wete?'

'Sir, I can nat tell you.'

'That is mervayle,' seyde the kynge, 'that thou knowyste
nat thy name, and thou arte one of the goodlyest yonge men
30 that ever I saw.'

Than the kyng betoke hym to sir Kay the Styewarde, and
charged hym that he had of all maner of metys and drynkes
of the beste, and also that he had all maner of fyndynge as
though he were a lordys sonne.

35 'That shall lytyll nede,' seyde sir Kay, 'to do suche coste
uppon hym, for I undirtake he is a vylayne borne, and

1 *C* moche yong man   2–3 *C* vp streyghte sayeng kynge Arthur (*not emended
in O¹*)   7–8 *C** worshipfully and honorably   9 *W* dome   14 *C* for thy
feest   23 at this tyme *not in C†*   25 *C* neuer deffended p̃ none nother my
27 *C* you sayd he   29–30 *C†* arte the goodlyest yong man one that   32 *C*
he shold gyue hym of al   36 *C* dare vndertake

never woll make man, for and he had be com of jantyllmen,
he wolde have axed horse and armour, but as he is, so he
askyth. And sythen he hath no name, I shall gyff hym a
name whyche shall be called Beawmaynes, that is to say
Fayre Handys. And into the kychyn I shall brynge hym, 5
and there he shall have fatte browes every day that he shall **114ᵛ**
be as fatte at the twelve-monthe ende as a porke hog.'

Ryght so the two men departed and lefte hym with sir Kay
that scorned and mocked hym. Thereat was sir Gawayne (2)
wroth. And in especiall sir Launcelot bade sir Kay leve 10
his mockyng, 'for I dare ley my hede he shall preve a man
of grete worshyp.'

'Lette be,' seyde sir Kay, 'hit may not be by reson, for
as he is, so he hath asked.'

'Yett beware,' seyde sir Launcelot, 'so ye gaff the good 15
knyght Brunor, sir Dynadans brothir, a name, and ye called
hym La Cote Male Tayle, and that turned you to anger
aftirwarde.'

'As for that,' seyde sir Kay, 'this shall never preve none
suche, for sir Brunor desyred ever worshyp, and this 20
desyryth ever mete and drynke and brotthe. Uppon payne
of my lyff, he was fosterde up in som abbey, and howsomever
hit was, they fayled mete and drynke, and so hydir he is
com for his sustynaunce.'

And so sir Kay bade gete hym a place and sytte downe to 25
mete. So Bewmaynes wente to the halle dore and sette hym
downe amonge boyes and laddys, and there he ete sadly. And
than sir Launcelot aftir mete bade hym com to his chambir,
and there he sholde have mete and drynke inowe, and so ded
sir Gawayne; but he refused them all, for he wolde do none 30
other but as sir Kay commaunded hym, for no profyr. But as
towchyng sir Gawayne, he had reson to proffer hym lodgyng,
mete, and drynke, for that proffer com of his bloode, for he
was nere kyn to hym than he wyste off; but that sir Launcelot
ded was of his grete jantylnesse and curtesy. 35

So thus he was putt into the kychyn and lay nyghtly as
the kychen boyes dede. And so he endured all that twelve-

---

1 *C* had com   2 *C* axed of you   *C* suche as   4 to say *not in C*
8 *C* belefte hym to syr   13 *C* by no reason   15 Yett *not in C*   21 *C* desyreth
breed and drynke   34 *C* wyst But that as syre   37 *C* the boyes of the kechen

monthe and never dyspleased man nother chylde, but allwayes he was meke and mylde. But ever whan he saw ony
justyng of knyghtes, that wolde he se and he myght. And
ever sir Launcelot wolde gyff hym golde to spende and
115ʳ 5 clothis, and so ded sir Gawayne. And where there were ony
mastryes doynge, thereat wolde he be, and there myght none
caste barre nother stone to hym by two yardys. Than wolde
sir Kay sey, 'How lykyth you my boy of the kychyn?'

So this paste on tyll the feste of Whytsontyde, and at that
10 tyme the kynge hylde hit at Carlyon, in the moste royallyst
wyse that myght be, lyke as he dud yerely. But the kyng
wolde no mete ete uppon Whytsonday untyll he harde of
som adventures.

Than com there a squyre unto the kynge and seyde, 'Sir,
15 ye may go to your mete, for here commyth a damesell with
som strange adventures.' Than was the kyng glad and sette
hym doune. Ryght so there cam a damesell unto the halle
and salewed the kyng and prayde hym of succoure.

'For whom?' seyde the kynge. 'What is the adventure?'
20 'Sir,' she seyde, 'I have a lady of grete worshyp to my
sustir, and she is beseged with a tirraunte, that she may nat
oute of hir castell. And bycause here ar called the noblyst
knyghtes of the worlde, I com to you for succoure.'

'What is youre lady called, and where dwellyth she? And
25 who is he and what is his name that hath beseged her?'

'Sir kynge,' she seyde, 'as for my ladyes name that shall
nat ye know for me as at thys tyme, but I lette you wete she
is a lady off grete worshyp and of grete londys; and as for
that tyrraunte that besegyth her and destroyeth hir londys,
30 he is kallyd the Rede Kn[y]ght of the Rede Laundys.'

'I know hym nat,' seyde the kyng.

'Sir,' seyde sir Gawayne, 'I know hym well, for he is one
of the perelest knyghtes of the worlde. Men sey that he
hath seven mennys strengthe, and from hym I ascapyd
35 onys full harde with my lyff.'

'Fayre damesell,' seyde [the] kynge, 'there bene knyghtes
here that wolde do hir power for to rescowe your lady, but

---

6 *C* maystryes done   12–13 *C* herd some aduentures   20–21 *C* worship
and renomme and she   21 *C* tyraunte so that she   23 *C* you to praye
you of socour   24 *C* What heteth your lady and   37 that *not in C*

bycause ye woll not telle hir name nother where she
dwellyth, therfore none of my knyghtes that here be nowe
shall go with you be my wylle.'

'Than muste I seke forther,' seyde the damesell.

So with thes wordys com Beawmaynes before the kyng 5 (3) **115**ᵛ
whyle the damesell was there, and thus he sayde:

'Sir kyng, God tha[n]ke you, I have bene this twelve-
monthe in your kychyn and have had my full systynaunce.
And now I woll aske my other two gyfftys that bene behynde.'

'Aske on now, uppon my perell,' seyde the kynge.   10

'Sir, this shall be my fyrste gyffte of the two gyfftis: that
ye woll graunte me to have this adventure of this damesell,
for hit belongyth unto me.'

'Thou shalt have it,' seyde the kynge, 'I graunte hit the.'

'Than, sir, this is that other gyffte that ye shall graunte 15
me: that sir Launcelot du Lake shall make me knyght, for
of hym I woll be made knyght and ellys of none. And whan
I am paste I pray you lette hym ryde aftir me and make me
knyght whan I requyre hym.'

'All thys shall be done,' seyde the kynge.   20

'Fy on the,' seyde the damesell, 'shall I have none but one
that is your kychyn knave?' Than she wexed angry and
anone she toke hir horse.

And with that there com one to Bewmaynes and tolde
hym his horse and armour was com for hym, and a dwarff 25
had brought hym all thyng that neded hym in the rycheste
wyse. Thereat the courte had muche mervayle from whens
com all that gere. So whan he was armed there was none
but fewe so goodly a man as he was.

And ryght so he cam into the halle and toke his leve of 30
kyng Arthure and sir Gawayne and of sir Launcelot, and
prayde hym to hyghe aftyr hym. And so he departed and
rode after the damesell, but there wente many aftir to beholde (4)
how well he was horsed and trapped in cloth of golde, but

---

4 *C*† must I speke further   5 *C* came before the kynge Beaumayns   9 *C*
my two yeftes   10 *C*† Aske vpon   11 *C* my two gyftes fyrst that
15–16 that ye shall graunt me *not in C*†   16 *C* that ye shal bydde Launcelot
du lake to make   22–23 *C* kechyn page thenne was she wrothe and toke her
hors and departed   25–26 *C* and there was the dwarf come with all thyng
27 *C* maner therat al the court   30 *C* ryght soo as   32 *C* prayed
that he wolde hyhe

he had neyther speare nother shylde. Than sir Kay seyde all opynly in the hall,

'I woll ryde aftir my boy of the kychyn to wete whether he woll know me for his bettir.'

116�r 5 'Yet,' seyde sir Launcelot and sir Gawayne, 'abyde at home.'

So sir Kay made hym redy and toke his horse and his speare and rode aftir hym. And ryght as Beawmaynes over-toke the damesell, ryght so com sir Kay and seyde,

10 'Beawmaynes! What, sir, know ye nat me?'

Than he turned his horse and knew hit was sir Kay that had done all the dyspyte to hym, as ye have herde before. Than seyde Beawmaynes,

'Yee, I know you well for an unjantyll knyght of the courte, 15 and therefore beware of me!'

Therewith sir Kay put his spere in the reest and ran streyght uppon hym, and Beawmaynes com as faste uppon hym with his swer[d]e [in his hand, and soo he putte awey his spere with his swerde,] and with a foyne threste hym 20 thorow the syde, that sir Kay felle downe as he had bene dede. Than Beawmaynes alyght down and toke sir Kayes shylde and his speare and sterte uppon his owne horse and rode his way.

All that saw sir Launcelot and so dud the damesell. And 25 than he bade his dwarff sterte uppon sir Kayes horse, and so he ded. By that sir Launcelot was com, and anone he profyrde sir Launcelot to juste, and ayther made hem redy and com togydir so fersly that eyther bare other downe to the erthe and sore were they brused. Than sir Launcelot 30 arose and halpe hym frome his horse, and than Beawmaynes threw his shylde frome hym and profyrd to fyght wyth sir Launcelot on foote.

So they russhed togydyrs lyke two borys, trasyng and traversyng and foynyng the mountenaunce of an houre. 35 And sir Launcelot felte hym so bygge that he mervayled

---

1 *C* shelde nor spere   1-2 *C* al open   3 *C* boye in the   12 *C* hym alle the despyte as   13-14 *C* Ye sayd beumayns I knowe yow   18-19 *C** his swerd in his hand and soo he putte awey his spere with his swerd and with (*homoeoteleuton in W*)   21 *C* dede & he alyght   25-28 *W* (*sidenote*): Here Beawmaynes had all moste slayne sir Kay   33-34 *C* tracynge rasynge and foynynge to the mountenaunce

of his strengthe, for he fought more lyker a gyaunte
than a knyght, and his fyghtyng was so passyng durable
and passyng perelous. For sir Launcelot had so much
ado with hym that he dred hymself to be shamed, and
seyde,   5

'Beawmaynes, feyght nat so sore! Your quarell and myne
is nat grete but we may sone leve of.'

'Truly that is trouth,' seyde Beawmaynes, 'but hit doth me **116ᵛ**
good to fele your myght. And yet, my lorde, I shewed nat
the utteraunce.'   10

'In Goddys name,' seyde sir Launcelot, 'for I promyse (5)
you be the fayth of my body I had as muche to do as I myght
have to save myself fro you unshamed, and therefore have
ye no dought of none erthely knyght.'

'Hope ye so that I may ony whyle stonde a preved   15
knyght?'

'Do as ye have done to me,' seyde sir Launcelot, 'and I
shall be your warraunte.'

'Than I pray you,' seyde Beawmaynes, 'geff me the Order
of Knyghthod.'   20

'Sir, than muste ye tell me your name of ryght, and of
what kyn ye be borne.'

'Sir, so that ye woll nat dyscover me, I shall tell you my
name.'

'Nay, sir,' seyde sir Launcelotte, 'and that I promyse you 25
by the feyth of my body, untyll hit be opynly knowyn.'

Than he seyde, 'My name is Garethe, and brothir unto
sir Gawayne of fadir syde and modir syde.'

'A, sir, I am more gladder of you than I was, for evir me
thought ye sholde be of grete bloode, and that ye cam nat   30
to the courte nother for mete nother drynke.'

Than sir Launcelot gaff hym the Order of Knyghthode;
and than sir Gareth prayde hym for to departe, and so he to
folow the lady. So sir Launcelot departed frome hym and
come to sir Kay, and made hym to be borne home uppon his 35
shylde; and so he was heled harde with the lyff. And all men

---

2 so passyng *not in C*   7 *C* not so grete but we may leue of   16–17 *C*
knyghte sayde Beaumayns ye sayd Launcelot doo as ye haue done and I   21 *C*
name seyd launcelot and   23–24 *C* shal sayd Beaumayns   28–29 *C* fader and
moder A syr said Lanncelot   33–34 *C* departe and lete hym goo Soo syre

scorned sir Kay, and in especiall sir Gawayne. And sir Launcelot seyde that hit was nat his parte to rebuke no yonge man: 'For full lytyll knowe ye of what byrthe he is com of, and for what cause he com to the courte.'

5   And so we leve of sir Kay and turne we unto Beawmaynes. Whan that he had overtakyn the damesell, anone she seyde, 'What doste thou here? Thou stynkyst all of the kychyn, thy clothis bene bawdy of the grece and talow. What **117ʳ** wenyste thou?' seyde the lady, 'that I woll alow the for 10 yondir knyght that thou kylde? Nay, truly, for thou slewyst hym unhappyly and cowardly. Therefore turne agayne, thou bawdy kychyn knave! I know the well, for sir Kay named the Beawmaynes. What art thou but a luske, and a turner of brochis, and a ladyll-waysher?'

15   'Damesell,' seyde sir Beawmaynes, 'sey to me what ye woll, yet woll nat I go fro you whatsomever ye sey, for I have undirtake to kynge Arthure for to encheve your adventure, and so shall I fynyssh hit to the ende, other ellys I shall dye therefore.'

20   'Fye on the, kychyn knave! Wolt thou fynyssh myne adventure? Thou shalt anone be mette withall, that thou woldyst nat for all the broth that ever thou souped onys to loke hym in the face.'

'As for that, I shall assay,' seyde Beawmaynes.

25   So ryght thus as they rode in the wood there com a man fleyng all that ever he myght.

'Whother wolt thou?' seyde Beawmaynes.

'A, lorde,' he seyde, 'helpe me, for hereby in a slade is six theffis that have takyn my lorde and bounde hym sore, 30 and I am aferde lest that they woll sle hym.'

'Brynge me thydir,' seyde Beawmaynes.

And so they rode togydirs unto they com thereas was the knyght bounden; and streyte he rode unto them and strake one to the deth, and than another, and at the thirde stroke 35 he slew the thirde, and than the other three fledde. And he

---

3 *C* ful lytel knewe he† of what byrth he is comen and   5 *C* leue sir
8–9 *C** talowe that thou gaynest in kyng Arthurs kechyn wenest thou sayd she that I alowe the   9 *W* alow the the   10 *C* kyllest   12 *C* kechyn page
15–16 *C* ye wylle I wylle not goo   22 *C* soupest   24 As for that *not in C*
28–29 *C* are syxe   29–30 *C* hym soo I am   33 *C* and thenne he rode
35 *C* thyrdde theef

rode aftir them and overtoke them, and than they three
turned agayne and assayled sir Beawmaynes harde, but at
the laste he slew them and returned and unbounde the
knyght. And the knyght thanked hym and prayde hym to
ryde with hym to his castell there a lytyll besyde, and he 5
sholde worshypfully rewarde hym for his good dedis.

'Sir,' seyde Beawmaynes, 'I woll no rewarde have. Sir,
this day I was made knyght of noble sir Launcelot, and therefore I woll no rewarde have but God rewarde me. And also
I must folowe thys damesell.' 10

So whan he com nyghe to hir she bade hym ryde uttir, **117ᵛ**
'for thou smellyst all of the kychyn. What wenyst thou?
That I have joy of the for all this dede? For that thou haste
done is but myssehappe, but thou shalt se sone a syght that
shall make the to turne agayne, and that lyghtly.' 15

Than the same knyght rode aftir the damesell and prayde
hir to lodge with hym all that nyght. And because hit was
nere nyght the damesell rode with hym to his castell and there
they had grete chere. And at souper the knyght sette sir Beawmaynes afore the damesell. 20

'Fy, fy,' than seyde she, 'sir knyght, ye ar uncurtayse to
sette a kychyn page afore me. Hym semyth bettir to styke
a swyne than to sytte afore a damesell of hyghe parage.'

Than the knyght was ashamed at hir wordys, and toke
hym up and sette hym at a sydebourde and sate hymself 25
before hym. So all that nyght they had good chere and
myrry reste. And on the morne the damesell toke hir leve (6)
and thanked the knyght, and so departed and rode on hir way
untyll they come to a grete foreste. And there was a grete
ryver and but one passage, and there were redy two knyghtes 30
on the farther syde to lette the passage.

'What sey[st th]ou?' seyde the damesell. 'Woll ye macche
yondir two knyghtis other ellys turne agayne?'

'Nay,' seyde sir Bewmaynes, 'I woll nat turne ayen, and
they were six mo!' 35

And therewithall he russhed unto the watir, and in

---

1 *C* thenne tho thre theues   11 *C* ryde fro her   12 *C* kechyn Wenest thou
13 *C* this dede that   14 *C* nys but myshappen the   sone *not in C*
16 *C** knyght whiche was rescowed of the theues   27 *C* the damoisel & he took
their leue   31-32 *C** lette them the passage what saist thou   *W* what sey you

myddys of the watir eythir brake her sperys uppon other to
their hondys. And than they drewe their swerdis and smote
egirly at othir. And at the laste sir Beawmaynes smote the
othir uppon the helme, that his hede stoned, and therewithall
5 he felle downe in the watir and there was he drowned. And
than he spored his horse uppon the londe, and therewithall
the tother knyght felle uppon hym [and] brake his spere.
And so they drew hir swerdys and fought longe togydyrs,
but at the laste sir Beawmaynes clevid his helme and his
10 hede downe to the shuldyrs. And so he rode unto the
118ʳ damesell and bade hir ryde furth on hir way.

'Alas,' she seyde, 'that ever suche a kychyn payge sholde
have the fortune to destroy such two knyghtes. Yet thou
wenyste thou haste done doughtyly? That is nat so; for the
15 fyrste knyght his horse stumbled and there he was drowned
in the watir, and never hit was be thy force nother be thy
myghte. And the laste knyght, by myshappe thou camyste
behynde hym, and by myssefortune thou slewyst hym.'

'Damesell,' seyde Beawmaynes, 'ye may sey what ye
20 woll, but whomsomever I have ado withall, I truste to God
to serve hym or I and he departe, and therefore I recke nat
what ye sey, so that I may wynne your lady.'

'Fy, fy, foule kychyn knave! Thou shalt se knyghtes that
shall abate thy boste.'

25 'Fayre damesell, gyff me goodly langgage, and than my
care is paste, for what knyghtes somever they be, I care nat,
ne I doute hem nought.'

'Also,' seyde she, 'I sey hit for thyne avayle, for yett
mayste thou turne ayen with thy worshyp; for and thou
30 folow [me] thou arte but slayne, for I se all that evir thou doste
is by mysseadventure and nat by preues of thy hondys.'

'Well, damesell, ye may sey what ye woll, but wheresomever ye go I woll folow you.'

So this Beawmaynes rode with that lady tyll evynsonge,
35 and ever she chydde hym and wolde nat reste. So at the
laste they com to a blak launde, and there was a blak

6–7 *C* londe where the other　　　7–10 *W* (*sidenote*): Here sir Bewmaynes slew two
knyghtes at a passage　　12 suche *not in C*　　　13 *C* that fortune　　*C** suche
two douȝty knyghtes thou　　　18 *C* and myshappely thou slewe hym
21 I and *not in C†*　　　30 *Not emended in O¹*　　　31 *C* is but by　　　34 *C*
euensong tyme　　　35–36 *C* reste And they cam

hauthorne, and thereon hynge a baner, and on the other syde
there hynge a blak shylde, and by hit stoode a blak speare,
grete and longe, and a grete blak horse covered wyth sylk,
and a blak stone faste by. Also there sate a knyght all armed (7)
in blak harneyse, and his name was called the Knyght of 5
the Blak Laundis.

This damesell, whan she sawe that knyght, she bade hym
fle downe that valey, for his hors was nat sadeled.

'Gramercy,' seyde Beawmaynes, 'for allway ye wolde have
me a cowarde.'   10 **118ᵛ**

So whan the Blak Knyght saw hir he seyde, 'Damesell,
have ye brought this knyght frome the courte of kynge Arthure to be your champyon?'

'Nay, fayre knyght, this is but a kychyn knave that was
fedde in kyng Arthurs kychyn for almys.'   15

Than sayde the knyght, 'Why commyth he in such aray?
For hit is shame that he beryth you company.'

'Sir, I can not be delyverde of hym, for with me he rydyth
magré my hede. God wolde,' seyde she, 'that ye wolde
putte hym from me, other to sle hym and ye may, for he is 20
an unhappy knave, and unhappyly he hath done this day
thorow myssehappe; for I saw hym sle two knyghtes at the
passage of the watir, and other dedis he ded beforne ryght
mervaylouse and thorow unhappynesse.'

'That mervayles me,' seyde the Blak Knyght, 'that ony 25
man of worshyp woll have ado with hym.'

'Sir, they knewe hym nat,' seyde the damesell, 'and for
bycause he rydyth with me they wene that he be som man
of worshyp borne.'

'That may be,' seyde the Blak Knyght; 'howbehit as ye 30
say that he is no man of worshyp borne, he is a full lykly
persone, and full lyke to be a stronge man. But this muche
shall I graunte you,' seyde the knyght, 'I shall put hym
downe on foote, and his horse and harneyse he shall leve with
me, for hit were shame to me to do hym ony more harme.'   35

Whan sir Beawmaynes harde hym sey thus, he seyde,

---

4 *C*† sat knyghte   5 *C* was þe   10–11 *C* coward with that the blak knyghte
whanne she came nyghe hym spak & sayd   12 frome the courte *not in C*
15–16 *C* almesse Why   23 *C* besorne†   31 borne *not in C*   32 *C* thus
moche   34 *C* vpon one† foote

'Sir knyght, thou arte full large of my horse and harneyse!
I lat the wete hit coste the nought, and whether thou lyke
well othir evyll, this launde woll I passe magré thyne hede,
and horse ne harneyse gettyst thou none of myne but yf
5 thou wynne hem with thy hondys. Therefore lat se what
thou canste do.'

'Seyste thou that?' seyde the Blak Knyght. 'Now yelde thy
lady fro the! For hit besemed never a kychyn knave to ryde
with such a lady.'

10 'Thou lyest!' seyde Beawmaynes. 'I am a jantyllman
119ᴿ borne, and of more hyghe lynage than thou, and that woll
I preve on thy body!'

Than in grete wretth they departed their horsis and com
togydyrs as hit had bene thundir, and the Blak Knyghtes
15 speare brake, and Beawmaynes threste hym thorow bothe
sydis. And therewith his speare brake and the truncheon
was left stylle in his syde. But nevirtheles the Blak Knyght
drew his swerde and smote many egir strokys of grete myght,
and hurte Bewmaynes full sore. But at the laste the Blak
20 Knyght, within an owre and an half, he felle downe of his
horse in a sowne and there dyed.

And than sir Bewmaynes sy hym so well horsed and
armed, than he alyght downe and armed hym in his armour,
and so toke his horse and rode aftir the damesell. Whan
25 she sawe hym com she seyde,

'Away, kychyn knave, oute of the wynde, for the smelle
of thy bawdy clothis grevyth me! Alas!' she seyde, 'that
ever such a knave sholde by myssehappe sle so good a
knyght as thou hast done! But all is thyne unhappynesse.
30 But hereby is one that shall pay the all thy paymente, and
therefore yett I rede the flee.'

'Hit may happyn me,' seyde Bewmaynes, 'to be betyn
other slayne, but I warne you, fayre damesell, I woll nat
fle away nothir leve your company for all that ye can sey;
35 for ever ye sey that they woll sle me othir bete me, but howsomever hit happenyth I ascape and they lye on the grounde.

2–3 *C* whether hit lyketh the or not this   4 *W* of of myne   8 *C* kechyn
page   13 *C* with theyr   22–23 *W* (*sidenote*): The deth of the blak knyght
slayne by the handis of Bewmaynes   25 *C** come nyghe   29 *C* alle thys is
30 that *not in C*   31 *C* I counceylle the   35 *C* wil kylle me

And therefore hit were as good for you to holde you stylle
thus all day rebukyng me, for away wyll I nat tyll I se the
uttermuste of this journay, other ellys I woll be slayne othir
thorowly betyn. Therefore ryde on your way, for folow you
I woll, whatsomever happyn me.'   5

Thus as they rode togydyrs they sawe a knyght comme (8)
dryvande by them, all in grene, bothe his horse and his
harneyse. And whan he com nye the damesell he asked hir,
'Is that my brothir the Blak Knyght that ye have
brought with you?'   10
'Nay, nay,' she seyde, 'this unhappy kychyn knave hath
slayne thy brothir thorow unhappynes.'   **119ᵛ**
'Alas!' seyde the Grene Knyght, '[that] is grete pyté that
so noble a knyght as he was sholde so unhappyly be slayne,
and namely of a knavis honde, as ye say that he is. A,   15
traytoure!' seyde the Grene Knyght, 'thou shalt dye for
sleyng of my brothir! He was a full noble knyght, and his
name was sir Perarde.'
'I defye the,' seyde sir Bewmaynes, 'for I lette the wete,
I slew hym knyghtly and nat shamfully.'   20

Therewythall the Grene Knyght rode unto an horne that
was grene, and hit hynge uppon a thorne. And there he
blew three dedly motis, and anone there cam two damesels
and armed hym lyghtly. And than he toke a grete horse,
and a grene shylde, and a grene spere; and than they ran   25
togydyrs with all their myghtes and brake their sperys unto
their hondis.

And than they drewe their swerdys and gaff many sad
strokys, and eyther of them wounded other full ylle, and at
the laste at an ovirtwarte stroke sir Bewmaynes with his   30
horse strake the Grene Knyghtes horse uppon the syde, that
he felle to the erthe. And than the Grene Knyght voyded
his horse delyverly and dressed hym on foote. That sawe
Bewmaynes, and therewithall he alyght and they russhed
togydyrs lyke two myghty kempys a longe whyle, and sore   35
they bledde bothe. Wyth that come the damesell and seyde,
'My lorde the Grene Knyght, why for shame stonde ye so
longe fyghtynge with that kychyn knave? Alas! hit is shame

---

4 *C* truly beten   5 me *not in C*   30 *C* at an ouerthwart† Beaumayns
32-33 *C* auoyded his hors lightly

that evir ye were made knyght to se suche a lad to macche
you as the wede growyth over the corne.'

Therewith the Grene Knyght was ashamed, and therewithall he gaff a grete stroke of myght and clave his shylde
5 thorow. Whan Beawmaynes saw his shylde clovyn asundir
he was a lytyll ashamed of that stroke and of hir langage.

And than he gaff hym suche a buffette uppon the helme
that he felle on his kneis, and so suddeynly Bewmaynes
pulde hym on the grounde grovelynge. And than the Grene
120ʳ 10 Knyght cryed hym mercy and yelded hym unto Bewmaynes
and prayde hym nat to sle hym.

'All is in vayne,' seyde Bewmaynes, 'for thou shalt dye
but yf this damesell that cam with me pray me to save thy
lyff,' and therewithall he unlaced his helme lyke as he
15 wolde sle hym.

'Fye uppon the, false kychyn payge! I woll never pray
the to save his lyff, for I woll nat be so muche in thy daunger.'

'Than shall he dye,' seyde Beawmaynes.

'Nat so hardy, thou bawdy knave!' seyde the damesell,
20 'that thou sle hym.'

'Alas!' seyde the Grene Knyght, 'suffir me nat to dye for
a fayre worde spekyng. Fayre knyght,' seyde the Grene
Knyght, 'save my lyfe and I woll forgyff the the deth of
my brothir, and for ever to becom thy man, and thirty
25 knyghtes that hold of me for ever shall do you servyse.'

'In the devyls name,' seyde the damesell, 'that suche a
bawdy kychyn knave sholde have thirty knyghtes servyse
and thyne!'

'Sir knyght,' seyde Bewmaynes, 'all this avaylyth the
30 nought but yf my damesel speke to me for thy lyff,' and
therewithall he made a semblaunte to sle hym.

'Lat be,' seyde the dameselle, 'thou bawdy kychyn knave!
Sle hym nat, for and thou do thou shalt repente hit.'

'Damesell,' seyde Bewmaynes, 'your charge is to me a
35 plesure, and at youre commaundemente his lyff shall be
saved, and ellis nat.' Than he said, 'Sir knyght with the

1–2 *C* matche suche a knyghte as the wede ouer grewe the   17 *C* will neuer be
22 *C* word may saue me   27–28 *C* the and thyrtty knyghtes seruyse
29–32 *W* (*sidenote*): Here sir B. overcome the Grene Knyght   30 *C* with me
32 kychyn *not in C*

grene armys, I releyse the quyte at this damesels requeste,
for I woll nat make hir wroth, for I woll fulfylle all that she
chargyth me.'

And than the Grene Knyght kneled downe and dud hym
homage with his swerde. Than sayde the damesell,   5

'Me repentis of this Grene Knyghtes damage, and of your
brothirs deth, the Blak Knyght, for of your helpe I had grete
mystir; for I drede me sore to passe this foreste.'

'Nay, drede you nat,' seyde the Grene Knyght, 'for ye
all shall lodge with me this nyght, and to-morne I shall helpe   10
you thorow this forest.'

Soo they toke their horsys and rode to his maner that was   **120ᵛ**
faste by. And ever this damesell rebuked Bewmaynes and   (9)
wolde nat suffir hym to sitte at hir table, but as the Grene
Knyght toke hym and sate with hym at a syde table.   15

'Damesell, mervayle me thynkyth,' seyde the Grene
Knyght, 'why ye rebuke this noble knyghte as ye do, for
I warne you he is a full noble man, and I knowe no
knyght that is able to macche hym. Therefore ye do grete
wronge so to rebuke hym, for he shall do you ryght goode   20
servyse. For whatsomever he makyth hymself he shall
preve at the ende that he is com of full noble blood and of
kynges lynage.'

'Fy, fy!' seyde the damesell, 'hit is shame for you to sey
hym suche worshyp.'   25

'Truly,' seyde the Grene Knyght, 'hit were shame to me
to sey hym ony dysworshyp, for he hath previd hymself a
bettir knyght than I am; and many is the noble knyght that
I have mette withall in my dayes, and never or this tyme
founde I no knyght his macche.'   30

And so that nyght they yoode unto reste, and all nyght
the Grene Knyght commaundede thirty knyghtes prevyly
to wacche Bewmaynes for to kepe hym from all treson.

[And so on the morn] they all arose and herde their

2 *C* wrothe I wille fulfylle   6 *C* me repenteth grene knyghte of your dommage
10 all *not in C*   13 *C* fast there besyde   *C* euer she rebuked   15–16 *C* sat
hym at a syde table Merueylle   17 *C* knyght to the damoysel   18 *C* you
damoysel he is a full noble knyght   19 that *not in C*   20 so *not in C*   21 *C*
yet† shall   24–25 *C* saye of hym   27 *C* sey of hym   28–30 *C* I am yet
haue I mett with many knyghtes in my dayes and neuer or this tyme haue I fond no
knyght his matche

masse and brake their faste. And than they toke their
horsis and rode their way, and the Grene Knyght conveyed
hem thorow the foreste. Than the Grene Knyght seyde,

'My lorde, sir Bewmaynes, my body and this thirty
5 knyghtes shall be allway at your somouns, bothe erly and
late at your callynge, and whothir that ever ye woll sende us.'

'Ye sey well,' seyde sir Bewmaynes. 'Whan that I calle
uppon you ye muste yelde you unto kynge Arthure, and all
your knyghtes, if that I so commaunde you.'

10 'We shall be redy at all tymes,' seyde the Grene Knyght.

'Fy, fy uppon the, in the devyls name!' seyde the damesell, 'that ever [o]ny good knyght sholde be obedyent unto
a kychyn knave!'

So than departed the Grene Knyght and the damesell,
121ʳ 15 and than she seyde unto Bewmaynes,

'Why folowyste thou me, kychyn knave? Caste away thy
shylde and thy spere and fle away. Yett I counseyle the betyme, or thou shalt sey ryght sone "Alas!" For and thou
were as wyght as sir Launcelot, sir Tristrams or the good
20 knyght sir Lamerok, thou shalt not passe a pace here that is
called the Pace Perelus.'

'Damesell,' seyde Bewmaynes, 'who is aferde let hym fle,
for hit were shame to turne agayne syth I have ryddyn so
longe with you.'

25 'Well,' seyde she, 'ye shall sone, whether ye woll or woll
not.'

(10) So within a whyle they saw a whyght towre as ony snowe,
well macchecolde all aboute and double-dyked, and over
the towre gate there hynge a fyffty shyldis of dyvers coloures.
30 And undir that towre there was a fayre medow, and therein
was many knyghtes and squyres to beholde, scaffoldis and
pavylons; for there, uppon the morne, sholde be a grete
turnemente.

And the lorde of the towre was within his castell, and
35 loked oute at a wyndow and saw a damesell, a dwarff, and
a knyght armed at all poyntis.

4–5 *C* Beaumanys I & these thyrty knyghtes   7 *C* it is wel said   9–10 *C* yf
that ye so commaunde vs We   12 *W* eny   16 *C* kechyn boy   18–20 *C**
for were thou as wyȝte as euer was wade or Laūcelot Trystram or the good knyghte
syr lamaryk (*see note*)   27 *C* a toure as whyte ony

'So God me helpe,' seyde the lorde, 'with that knyght woll I juste, for I see that he is a knyght arraunte.'

And so he armed hym and horsed hym hastely. Whan he was on horsebak with his shylde and his spere, hit was all rede, bothe his horse and his harneyse and all that to hym belonged. And whan that he com nyghe hym he wente hit had be his brother the Blak Knyght, and than lowde he cryed and seyde,

'Brothir, what do ye here in this marchis?'

'Nay, nay,' seyde the damesell, 'hit is nat he, for this is but a kychyn knave that was brought up for almys in kynge Arthurs courte.'

'Neverthelesse,' seyde the Rede Knyght, 'I woll speke with hym or he departe.'

'A,' seyde this damesell, 'this knave hathe slayne your brother, and sir Kay named hym Bewmaynes; and this horse and this harneyse was thy brothirs, the Blak Knyght. **121ᵛ** Also I sawe thy brothir the Grene Knyght overcom of his hondys. But now may ye be revenged on hym, for I may nevir be quyte of hym.'

Wyth this every knyght departed in sundir and cam togydir all that they myght dryve. And aythir of their horsis felle to the erthe. Than they avoyde theire horsis and put their shyldis before hem and drew their swerdys, and eythir gaff other sad strokys now here now there, trasyng, traversyng, and foynyng, rasyng and hurlyng lyke two borys, the space of two owrys. Than she cryde on hyght to the Rede Knyght:

'Alas, thou noble Rede Knyght! Thynke what worshyp hath evermore folowed the! Lette never a kychyn knave endure the so longe as he doth!'

Than the Rede Knyght wexed wroth and doubled his strokes and hurte Bewmaynes wondirly sore, that the bloode ran downe to the grounde, that hit was wondir to see that stronge batayle. Yet at the laste Bewmaynes strake hym to the erthe. And as he wolde have slayne the Rede Knyght, he cryed,

6 *C* longeth   8 and seyde *not in C*   9 here *not in C*   15 *C* hath kylled
21 *C** eyther knyghtes   22 *C* to gyder with alle their myght and   25–26 *C*
rasyng tracyng foynynge and   30 evermore *not in C*

'Mercy, noble knyght, sle me nat, and I shall yelde me
to the wyth fyffty knyghtes with me that be at my commaundemente, and forgyff the all the dispyte that thou
haste done to me, and the deth of my brothir the Blak
5 Knyght, and the wynnyng of my brothir the Grene Knyght.'

'All this avaylyth nat,' seyde Beawmaynes, 'but if my
damesell pray me to save thy lyff.' And therewith he made
semblaunte to stryke of his hede.

'Let be, thou Bewmaynes, and sle hym nat, for he is a
10 noble knyght, and nat so hardy uppon thyne hede but that
thou save hym.'

Than Bewmaynes bade the Rede Knyght to stonde up,
'and thanke this damesell now of thy lyff.' Than the Rede
Knyght prayde hym to se his castell and to repose them all
15 that nyght. So the damesell graunte hym, and there they
122ʳ had good chere. But allwayes this damesell seyde many foule
wordys unto Bewmaynes, whereof the Rede Knyght had
grete mervayle. And all that nyght the Rede Knyght made
three score knyghtes to wacche Bewmaynes, that he sholde
20 have no shame nother vylony.

And uppon the morne they herde masse and dyned, and
the Rede Knyght com before Bewmaynes wyth his three
score knyghtes, and there he profyrd hym his omage and
feawté at all tymes, he and his knyghtes to do hym servyse.
25 'I thanke you,' seyde Bewmaynes, 'but this ye shall
graunte me: whan I calle uppon you, to com before my
lorde, kynge Arthure, and yelde you unto hym to be his
knyghtes.'

'Sir,' seyde the Rede Knyght, 'I woll be redy and all my
30 felyship at youre somouns.'

So sir Bewmaynes departed and the damesell, and ever
she rode chydyng hym in the fowleste maner wyse that she
cowde.

(11) 'Damesell,' seyde Bewmaynes, 'ye ar uncurteyse so to
35 rebuke me as ye do, for mesemyth I have done you good
servyse, and ever ye thretyn me I shall be betyn wyth

---

1 *C* mercy sayeng Noble   5 and the wynnyng of my brothir the Grene
Knyght *not in C†*   12–14 *W* (*sidenote*): Here sir Bewmaynes overcom the Rede
Knyght   12 to *not in C*   14–15 *C* and to be there al nyghte   15–16 *C*
thenne graunted hym and there they had mery chere   29 all *not in C*
32–33 wyse that she cowde *not in C*

knyghtes that we mete, but ever for all your boste they all
lye in the duste or in the myre. And therefore y pray you,
rebuke me no more, and whan ye se me betyn or yoldyn as
recreaunte, than may you bydde me go from you shamfully,
but erste, I let you wete, I woll nat departe from you; for 5
than I were worse than a foole and I wolde departe from you
all the whyle that I wynne worshyp.'

'Well,' seyde she, 'ryght sone shall mete the a knyght
that shall pay the all thy wagys, for he is the moste man of
worshyp of the worlde excepte kyng Arthure.' 10

'I woll well,' seyde Bewmaynes, 'the more he is of worshyp the more shall be my worshyp to have ado with
hym.'

Than anone they were ware where was afore them a cyté
rych and fayre, and betwyxte them and the cité, a myle and 15
more, there was a fayre medow that semed new mowyn, **122ᵛ**
and therein was many pavylons fayre to beholde.

'Lo,' seyde the damesell, 'yondir is a lorde that owyth
yondir cité, and his custom is, whan the wedir is fayre, to
lye in this medow, to juste and to turnay. And ever there 20
is aboute hym fyve hondred knyghtes and jantyllmen of
armys, and there is all maner of gamys that ony jantyllmen
can devyse.'

'That goodly lorde,' seyde Bewmaynes, 'wolde I fayne se.'

'Thou shalt se hym tyme inowe,' seyde the damesell. 25
And so as she rode nere she aspyed the pavelon where the
lorde was.

'Lo!' seyde she, 'syeste thou yondir pavylyon that is all
of the coloure of inde?' And all maner of thyng that there
is aboute, men and women and horsis, trapped shyldis and 30
sperys, was all of the coloure of inde. 'And his name is
sir Parsaunte of Inde, the moste lordlyest knyght that ever
thou lokyd on.'

'Hit may well be,' seyde sir Bewmaynes, 'but be he never
so stoute a knyght, in this felde I shall abyde tyll that I se 35
hym undir his shylde.'

'A, foole!' seyde she, 'thou were bettir to flee betymes.'

1–2 *C* they lye   *W* all all lye   5 *C* but fyrste   5–6 *C* for I were
8–9 *C* soone there shall mete a knyght shal paye   15–16 *C* a myle and an (*S* a)
half there   26–27 *C* where he was   33 *C* lokest on   37 *C* better flee

'Why ?' seyde Bewmaynes. 'And he be suche a knyght as ye make hym he woll nat sette uppon me with all his men, for and there com no more but one at onys I shall hym nat fayle whylys my lyff may laste.'

5 'Fy, fy!' seyde the damesell, 'that evir suche a stynkyng kychyn knave sholde blowe suche a boste!'

'Damesell,' he seyde, 'ye ar to blame so to rebuke me, for I had lever do fyve batayles than so to be rebuked. Lat hym com and than lat hym doo his worste.'

10 'Sir,' she seyde, 'I mervayle what thou art and of what kyn thou arte com; for boldely thou spekyst and boldely thou haste done, that have I sene. Therefore, I pray the,
123ʳ save thyself and thou may, for thyne horse and thou have had grete travayle, and I drede that we dwelle ovirlonge
15 frome the seege; for hit is hens but seven myle, and all perelous passage[s] we are paste sauff all only this passage, and here I drede me sore last ye shall cacche som hurte. Therefore I wolde ye were hens, that ye were nat brused nothir hurte with this stronge knyght. But I lat you wete
20 this sir Persaunte of Inde is nothyng of myght nor strength unto the knyght that lyeth at the seege aboute my lady.'

'As for that,' seyde Bewmaynes, 'be as be may, for sytthen I am com so nye this knyght I woll preve his myght or I departe frome hym, and ellis I shall be shamed and I now
25 withdrawe fro hym. And therefore, damesell, have ye no doute: by the grace of God, I shall so dele with this knyght that within two owrys after none I shall delyver hym, and than shall we com to the seege be daylyght.'

'A, Jesu! mervayle have I,' seyde the damesell, 'what
30 maner a man ye be, for hit may never be other but that ye be com of jantyll bloode, for so fowle and so shamfully dud never woman revyle a knyght as I have done you, and ever curteysly ye have suffyrde me, and that com never but of jantyll bloode.'

35 'Damesell,' seyde Bewmaynes, 'a knyght may lytyll do that may nat suffir a jantyllwoman, for whatsomever ye

2-3 *C** men or with his v *C* knyghtes For   4 *C* lyf lasteth   11 *C* for
not in C   13 *C* thou mayst   18 *C* wolde haue ye   21 *C* leid the
22 *C* be it as it be   25 *C* withdrawe me   29 *C* O Ihesu   30 *C* neuer
ben otherwyse   31 *C* a noble blood   32 *C** woman rule   36 *C* a damoisel
for

seyde unto me I toke none hede to your wordys, for the more
ye seyde the more ye angred me, and my wretthe I wrekid
uppon them that I had ado withall. [And therefore all] the
mysseyyng that ye mysseyde me in my batayle furthered me
much and caused me to thynke to shewe and preve myselffe 5
at the ende what I was, for peraventure, thoughe hit lyst me
to be fedde in kynge Arthures courte, I myght have had mete
in other placis, but I ded hit for to preve my frendys, and that **123ᵛ**
shall be knowyn another day whether that I be a jantyllman
borne or none; for I latte yow wete, fayre damesell, I have 10
done you jantyllmannys servyse, and peraventure bettir
servyse yet woll I do or I departe frome you.'

'Alas!' she seyde, 'fayre Bewmaynes, forgyff me all that
I have mysseseyde or done ayenste you.'

'With all my wyll,' seyde he, 'I forgeff hit you, for ye dud 15
nothyng but as ye sholde do, for all youre evyll wordys
pleased me. Damesell,' seyde Bewmaynes, 'syn hit lykyth
you to sey thus fayre unto me, wote ye well hit gladdyth
myne herte gretly, and now mesemyth there is no knyght
lyvyng but I am able inow for hym.' 20

Wyth this sir Persaunte of Inde had aspyed them as (12)
they hoved in the fylde, and knyghtly he sente unto them
whether he cam in warre or in pece.

'Sey to thy lorde I take no force but whether as hym
lyste.' 25

So the messyngere wente ayen unto sir Persaunte and
tolde hym all his answere.

'Well, than I woll have ado with hym to the utteraunce!'
and so he purveyede hym and rode ayenste hym.

Whan Bewmaynes sawe hym he made hym redy, and 30
[there they] mette with all theire myghtes togedir as faste as
their horse myght ren, and braste their spearys eythir in
three pecis, and their horsis [rassed so togyders that bothe
their horsis] felle downe to the erthe. And delyverly they
avayded their horsis and put their shyldis before them and 35
drew their swerdys and gaff many grete strokys, that som-

3 *Not emended in* O¹   5 much *not in* C   6–7 C† though I had mete in kyng
Arthurs kechyn yet I myȝt haue had mete ynouȝ   8 C but alle that I dyd it
for to preue & assaye my   10 for *not in* C   15 C alle my herte   24 C lord
said beaumayns   24–25 C lyst hym self   32 C euer theyr horses myght renne
33–34 *Not emended in* O¹   34–35 C felle dede to the erthe & lyȝtly they auoyded

tyme they hurled so togydir that they felle grovelyng on the grounde.

Thus they fought two owrys and more, that there shyldes and hawbirkes were all forhewyn, and in many placis [were they] wounded. So at the laste sir Bewmaynes smote hym thorow the coste of the body, and than he retrayed hym here and there and knyghtly maynteyned his batayle longe tyme.

And at the laste, though hym loth were, Beawmaynes smote sir Persaunte abovyn uppon the helme, that he felle grovelynge to the erthe, and than he lepte uppon hym overthwarte and unlaced his helme to have slayne hym. Than sir Persaunte yelded hym and asked hym mercy. Wyth that com the damesell and prayde hym to save his lyff.

'I woll well,' he seyde, 'for hit were pyté this noble knyght sholde dye.'

'Gramercy,' seyde sir Persaunte, 'for now I wote well hit was ye that slew my brother, the Blak Knyght, at the Blak Thorne. He was a full noble knyght! His name was sir Perarde. Also, I am sure that ye ar he that wan myne other brother, the Grene Knyght: his name is sir Pertholepe. Also ye wan my brother the Rede Knyght, sir Perymones. And now, sir, ye have wonne me. This shall I do for to please you: ye shall have homage and feawté of me and of an hondred knyghtes to be allwayes at your commaundemente, to go and ryde where ye woll commaunde us.'

And so they wente unto sir Persauntes pavylyon and dranke wyne and ete spycis. And afterwarde sir Persaunte made hym to reste uppon a bedde untyll supper tyme, and aftir souper to bedde ayen. So whan sir Bewmaynes was a-bedde—sir Persaunte had a doughter, a fayre lady of eyghtene yere of ayge—and there he called hir unto hym and charged hir and commaunded hir uppon his blyssyng to go unto the knyghtis bed:

'And lye downe by his syde and make hym no strange chere but good chere, and take hym in your armys and kysse hym and loke that this be done, I charge you, as ye woll have my love and my good wylle.'

4–5 *C* in many stedys they were wounded　　　13 hym *not in C*　　　14 he seyde *not in C*　　　16–19 *W* (*sidenote*): Here sir Bewmaynes overcom sir Persaunte of Inde　16 *C* Persaunt gentyl knyȝt & damoysel For certeynly now　　　22 *C* now syn ye haue wonne these† this　　　23–24 *C* & an C　　　30 *C*† had a lady a faire douȝter　34 *C* thyne armes　　　36 *P* my boue　　*R* my loue

So sir Persauntis doughter dud as hir fadir bade hir, and
so she yode unto sir Bewmaynes bed and pryvyly she dis-
poyled hir and leyde hir downe by hym. And than he awooke
and sawe her and asked her what she was.

'Sir,' she seyde, 'I am sir Persauntis doughter that by the 5
commaundemente of my fadir I am com hydir.'

'Be ye a pusell or a wyff?'

'Sir,' she seyde, 'I am a clene maydyn.'

'God deffende me,' seyde he, 'than that ever I sholde
defoyle you to do sir Persaunte suche a shame! Therefore 10
I pray you, fayre damesell, aryse oute of this bedde, other **124ᵛ**
ellys I woll.'

'Sir,' she seyde, 'I com nat hydir by myne owne wyll, but
as I was commaunded.'

'Alas!' seyde sir Bewmaynes, 'I were a shamefull knyght 15
and I wolde do youre fadir ony disworshyp.'

But so he kyste her, and so she departed and com unto
sir Persaunte hir fadir and tolde hym all how she had sped.

'Truly,' seyde sir Persaunte, 'whatsomever he be he is com
of full noble bloode.'   20

And so we leve hem there tyll on the morne.

And so on the morne the damesell and sir Bewmaynes (13)
herde masse and brake there faste and so toke their leve.

'Fayre damesell,' seyde sir Persaunte, 'whothirwarde ar
ye away ledynge this knyght?'   25

'Sir,' she seyde, 'this knyght is goynge to the Castell
Daungerous thereas my systir is beseged.'

'Aha,' seyde sir Persaunte, 'that is the Knyghte of the
Rede Launde whyche is the moste perelyste knyght that
I know now lyvynge and a man that is wythouten mercy, 30
and men sey that he hath seven mennes strength. God save
you, sir Bewmaynes, frome that knyght, for he doth grete
wronge to that lady, and that is grete pyté, for she is one of
the fayreste ladyes of the worlde, and mesemyth that your
damesell is hir sister. Ys nat your name Lyonet?'   35

'Sir, so I hyght, and my lady my sister hyght dame Lyones.'

2 *C* she wente vnto   7 *C* Be ye a mayde or a wyf   9 me *not in C*   *C* he
that I   11 I pray you *not in C†*   13 *C* not to you by   17 *C* and so he
20 *C* of a noble   25 *C* way ledyng   26-28 *C†* to the sege that besyegeth
my syster in the castle Dangerus A a   32 *C* you said he to Beaumayns
35-36 *C* Lynet said he ye sir said she and my lady my susters name is dame

'Now shall I tell you,' seyde sir Persaunte, 'this Rede
Knyght of the Rede Laundys hath layne longe at that seege,
well-nye this two yerys, and many tymes he myght have had
hir and he had wolde, but he prolongyth the tyme to this
5 entente, for to have sir Launcelot du Lake to do batayle
with hym, or with sir Trystrams, othir sir Lamerok de
Galys, other sir Gawayne, and this is his taryynge so longe
at the sege. Now, my lorde,' seyde sir Persaunt of Inde, 'be
ye stronge and of good herte, for ye shall have ado with a
10 good knyght.'

'Let me dele,' seyde sir Bewmaynes.

125ʳ 'Sir,' seyde this damesell Lyonet, 'I requyre you that ye
woll make this jauntyllman knyght or evir he fyght with the
Red Knyght.'

15 'I woll, with all myne herte,' seyde sir Persaunte, 'and
hit please hym to take the Order of Knyghthode of so
symple a man as I am.'

'Sir,' seyde Bewmaynes, 'I thanke you for [your good will,
for] I am bettir spedde, for sertay[n]ly the noble knyghte
20 sir Launcelot made me knyght.'

'A,' seyde sir Persaunte, 'of a more renomed man myght
ye nat be made knyghte of, for of all knyghtes he may be
called cheff of knyghthode, and so all the worlde seythe that
betwyxte three knyghtes is departed clerely knyghthode,
25 that is sir Launcelot du Lake, sir Trystrams de Lyones and
sir Lamerok de Galys. Thes bere now the renowne, yet there
be many other noble knyghtis, as sir Palomydes the Saresyn
and sir Saphir, his brothir, also sir Bleobrys and sir Blamour
de Ganys, his brothir; also sir Bors de Ganys, and sir Ector de
30 Marys, and sir Percivale de Galys. Thes and many mo bene
noble knyghtes, but there be none that bere the name but thes
three abovyn seyde. Therefore God spede you well,' seyde
sir Persaunte, 'for and ye may macche that Rede Knyght
ye shall be called the fourth of the worlde.'

35 'Sir,' seyde Bewmaynes, 'I wolde fayne be of good fame
and of knyghthode. And I latte you wete, I am com of

8–12 *C*† Now my lord syre Persaunt of ynde saide the damoysel Lynet I requyre you
18–19 *Not emended in O¹*   22 of *not in C*   26 renommee there   27 noble
not in C   28 *C* Saseret†   31–32 *C* none þᵗ passe þᵉ iij aboue said   36 *C* I cam
of (*S* I am of)

good men, for I dare say my fadir was a nobleman. And so
that ye woll kepe hit in cloce and this damesell, I woll tell
you of what kynne I am com of.'

'We woll nat discover you,' seyde they bothe, 'tylle ye   5
commaunde us, by the fayth we owe to Jesu.'

'Truly,' than sayde he, 'my name is sir Gareth of Orkenay,
and kynge Lott was my fadir, and my modir is kyng Arthurs
sister, hir name is dame Morgawse. And sir Gawayne ys
my brothir, and sir Aggravayne and sir Gaherys, and I am   **125ᵛ**
yongeste of hem all. And yette wote nat kynge Arthure   10
nother sir Gawayne what I am.'

So the booke seyth that the lady that was beseged had   (14)
worde of hir sisteris comyng by the dwarff, and a knyght
with hir, and how he had passed all the perelus passages.

'What maner a man is he?' seyde the lady.   15

'He is a noble knyght, truly, madam,' seyde the dwarff, 'and
but a yonge man, but he is as lykly a man as ever ye saw ony.'

'What is he, and of what kynne,' seyde the lady, 'is he
com, and of whom was he made knyght?'

'Madam,' seyde the dwarff, 'he was kynges son of Orkeney, 20
but his name I woll nat tell you as at this tyme; but wete
you well, of sir Launcelot was he made knyght, for of none
other wolde he be made knyght, and sir Kay named hym
Bewmaynes.'

'How ascaped he,' seyde the lady, 'frome the brethyrn of   25
sir Persaunte?'

'Madam,' he seyde, 'as a noble knyght sholde. First he
slew two bretherne at a passage of a watir.'

'A!' seyde she, 'they were two good knyghtes, but they
were murtherers. That one hyght sir Gararde le Breuse and 30
that other hyght sir Arnolde le Bruse.'

'Than, madam, he recountird at the Blak Knyght and
slew hym in playne batayle, and so he toke his hors and his
armoure and fought with the Grene Knyght and wanne
hym in playne batayle. And in lyke wyse he served the   35
Rede Knyght, and aftir in the same wyse he served the Blew
Knyght and wanne hym in playne batayle.'

3-4 *C* I am We   5 *C* owe vnto god   18-19 *C* is he sayd the damoysel and
of what kynne is he comen   20 *C* he is the kynges   31 *C** other knyght
hyght   32 *C* recountred with the

'Than,' sayde the lady, 'he hath overcom sir Persaunte of
Inde that is one of the noblest knyghtes of the worlde?'

'Trewly, madam,' seyde the dwarff, 'he hath wonne all the
four bretherne and slayne the Blak Knyght, and yet he dud
5 more tofore: he overthrew sir Kay and leffte hym nye dede
126ʳ uppon the grounde. Also he dud a grete batayle wyth sir
Launcelot, and there they departed on evyn hondis. And
than sir Launcelot made hym knyght.'

'Dwarff,' seyde the lady, 'I am gladde of thys tydynges.
10 Therefore go thou unto an hermytage of myne hereby and
bere with the of my wyne in too flagons of sylver—they ar
of two galons—and also two caste of brede, with the fatte
venyson ibake and deynté foules; and a cuppe of golde
here I delyver the that is ryche of precious stonys. And bere
15 all this to myne hermytage and putt hit in the hermytis
hondis.

'And sytthyn go thou to my sistir and grete her welle,
and commaunde me unto that jantyll knyght, and pray hym
to ete and drynke and make hym stronge, and say hym I
20 thanke hym of his curtesy and goodnesse that he wolde take
uppon hym suche labur for me that never ded hym bounté
nother curtesy. Also pray hym that he be of good herte
and corrage hymself, for he shall mete with a full noble
knyght, but he is nother of curtesy, bounté, nother jantyl-
25 nesse; for he attendyth unto nothyng but to murther, and
that is the cause I can nat prayse hym nother love hym.'

So this dwarff departed and com to sir Persaunt where he
founde the damesell Lynet and sir Bewmaynes, and there he
tolde hem all as ye have herde. And than they toke their
30 leve, but sir Persaunte toke an amblynge hakeney and conveyed them on their wayes and than betoke he them unto
God.

And so within a lytyll whyle they com to the hermytage,
and there they dranke the wyne and ete the venyson and the
35 foulys bakyn. And so whan they had repasted them well
the dwarff retourned ayen with his vessell unto the castell.

---

2 that is *not in* C   2–3 C world & þᵉ dwarf said he hath   10 C in an
10–11 C here by and there shalt thow bere   14 C ryche and precyous and
19 C say ye   23 hymself *not in* C   31–32 C belefte hem to god   36 C†
castel ageyne

And there mette wyth hym the Rede Knyght of the Rede
Laundys and asked hym from whens he com and where
he had ben.

'Sir,' seyde the dwarff, 'I have bene with my ladyes sistir
of the castell, and she hath bene at kynge Arthurs courte 5
and brought a knyght with her.'

'Than I acompte her travayle but lorne, for though she had **126ᵛ**
brought with hir sir Launcelot, sir Trystrams, sir Lameroke,
othir sir Gawayne, I wolde thynke myselfe good inowe for
them all.'   10

'Hit may well be,' seyde the dwarff, 'but this knyght hathe
passed all the perelouse passages and slayne the Blak Knyghte
and other two mo, and wonne the Grene Knyght, the Rede
Knyght, and the Blew Knyght.'

'Than is he one of thes four that I have before rehersyd?' 15

'He is none of thes,' seyde the dwarff, 'but he is a kynges
son.'

'What is his name?' seyde the Rede Knyght of the Rede
Laundis.

'That woll I nat tell you, but sir Kay on scorne named 20
hym Bewmaynes.'

'I care nat,' seyde the knyght, 'whatsomevir he be, for
I shall sone delyver hym, and yf I overmacche hym he shall
have a shamfull deth as many othir have had.'

'That were pyté,' seyde the dwarff, 'and hit is pyté that 25
ye make suche shamfull warre uppon noble knyghtes.'

Now leve we the knyght and the dwarff and speke we of (15)
Bewmaynes that all nyght lay in the hermytage. And uppon
the morne he and the damesell Lynet harde their masse
and brake their faste, and than they toke their horsis and 30
rode thorowoute a fayre foreste. And than they com to a
playne and saw where was many pavylons and tentys and
a fayre castell, and there was muche smoke and grete noyse.

And whan they com nere the sege sir Bewmaynes aspyed
on grete trees, as he rode, how there hynge full goodly armed 35
knyghtes by the necke, and their shyldis about their neckys
with their swerdis and gylte sporys uppon their helys. And

7 *C* loste For   20 *C* telle you seyd the dwarf but   22 *C* what knyghte soo
euer   23 *C*† & yf I euer matche hym   25 *C* it is merueill that   32 *C*
where were

so there hynge nyghe a fourty knyghtes shamfully with full
ryche armys. Than sir Bewmaynes abated his countenaunce
and seyde, 'What menyth this?'

    'Fayre sir,' seyde the damesell, 'abate nat youre chere for
5 all this syght, for ye muste corrage youreself, other ellys ye
127ʳ bene all shente. For all these knyghtes com hydir to this
sege to rescow my sistir dame Lyones, and whan the Rede
Knyght of the Rede Launde had overcom hem he put them
to this shamefull deth withoute mercy and pyté. And in the
10 same wyse he woll serve you but yf ye quyte you the bettir.'

    'Now Jesu defende me,' seyde sir Bewmaynes, 'frome
suche vylans deth and shondeshyp of harmys, for rathir
than I sholde so be faryn withall I woll rather be slayne in
playne batayle.'

15   'So were ye bettir,' seyde the damesell, 'for trust nat, in
hym is no curtesy, but all goth to the deth other shamfull
mourther. And that is pyté,' seyde the damesell, 'for he is
a full lykly man and a noble knyght of proues, and a lorde
of grete londis and of grete possessions.'

20   'Truly,' seyde sir Bewmaynes, 'he may be well a good
knyght, but he usyth shamefull customys, and hit is mervayle that he enduryth so longe, that none of the noble
knyghtes of my lorde Arthurs have nat dalte with hym.'

    And than they rode unto the dykes and sawe them
25 double-dyked wyth full warly wallys, [and there were lodged
many grete lordes nyghe the wallys,] and there was grete
noyse of mynstralsy. And the see bete uppon that one syde
of the wallys where were many shyppis and marynars noyse
with hale and how.

30   And also there was faste by a sygamoure tre, and thereon
hynge an horne, the grettyst that ever they sye, of an
olyvauntes bone, and this Knyght of the Rede Launde hath
honged hit up there to this entente, that yf there com ony
arraunte knyghte he muste blowe that horne and than woll
35 he make hym redy and com to hym to do batayle.

    'But, sir, pray you,' seyde the damesell, 'blow ye nat the

12 *C** suche a vylanous   *C* shenship of armes   13 *C* wolde rather be slayn
manly in   17 seyde the damesell *not in C*   18 *C** man wel made of body
and a ful noble   19 *C* and possessions   27 *C* betyd   33 to this
entente *not in C*   36 *C* I pray you

horne tyll hit be hygh none, for now hit is aboute pryme,
and now encresyth his myght, that as men say he hath seven
mennys strength.'

'A! fy for shame, fayre damesell! Sey ye nevir so more
to me, for and he were as good a knyght as ever was ony   5 127ᵛ
I shall never fayle hym in his moste myght, for other I wylle
wynne worshyp worshypfully othir dye knyghtly in the
felde.'

And therewith he spored his horse streyte to the sygamoure tre and so blew the horne egirly that all the seege   10
and the castell range thereoff. And than there lepe oute
many knyghtes oute of their tentys and pavylyons, and they
within the castell loked ovir the wallys and oute at wyndowis.

Than the Rede Knyght of the Rede Laundis armed hym
hastely and too barouns sette on his sporys on his helys, and 15
all was blood-rede: his armour, spere, and shylde. And an
erle buckled his helme on his hede, and than they brought
hym a rede spere and a rede stede. And so he rode into a
lytyll vale undir the castell, that all that were in the castell
and at the sege myght beholde the batayle.   20

'Sir,' seyde the damesell Lynet unto sir Bewmaynes, 'loke   (16)
ye be glad and lyght, for yondir is your dedley enemy, and
at yondir wyndow is my lady, my sistir dame Lyones.'

'Where?' seyde Bewmaynes.

'Yondir,' seyde the damesell, and poynted with her fyngir. 25

'That is trouth,' seyde Bewmaynes, 'she besemyth afarre
the fayryst lady that ever I lokyd uppon, and truly,' he seyde,
'I aske no better quarell than now for to do batayle, for truly
she shall be my lady and for hir woll I fyght.'

And ever he loked up to the wyndow with glad coun-   30
tenaunce, and this lady dame Lyones made curtesy to
hym downe to the erth, holdynge up bothe her hondys.
Wyth that the Rede Knyghte calle unto Bewmaynes and
seyde,

'Sir knyght, leve thy beholdyng and loke on me, I coun- 35
sayle the, for I warne the well, she is my lady, and for hir
I have done many stronge batayles.'

---

2 *C* encreaced   5 ony *not in C*   12 many *not in C*   32 *C* erthe with
holdynge vp bothe their† handes   33–35 *C* knyghte of the reed laundes called
to Beaumayns leue syr knyghte thy lokynge and behold me

128ʳ 'Geff thou so have done,' seyde Bewmaynes, 'mesemyth hit was but waste laboure, for she lovyth none of thy felyshyp, and thou to love that lovyth nat the is but grete foly. For and I undirstoode that she were nat ryght glad of my
5 commynge I wolde be avysed or I dud batayle for hir; but I undirstonde by the segynge of this castell she may forbere thy felyshyp. And therefore wete thou well, thou Rede Knyght, I love hir and woll rescow hir, othir ellys to dye therefore.'
10 'Sayst thou that?' seyde the Rede Knyght. 'Mesemyth thou oughtyste of reson to beware by yondir knyghtes that thou sawyste hange on yondir treis.'

'Fy for shame!' seyde Bewmaynes, 'that ever thou sholdyst sey so or do so evyll, for in that thou shamest thyself
15 and all knyghthode, and thou mayste be sure there woll no lady love the that knowyth the and thy wykked customs. And now thou wenyste that the syght of tho honged knyghtes shulde feare me? Nay, truly, nat so! That shamefull syght cawsyth me to have courrage and hardynesse ayenst th[e]
20 muche more than I wolde have agaynste the and thou were a well-ruled knyght.'

'Make the redy,' seyde the Rede Knyght, 'and talke no more with me.'

Than they putt their sperys in the reste and com togedyrs
25 with all the myght that they had bothe, and aythir smote other in the myddys of their shyldis, that the paytrels, sursynglys and crowpers braste, and felle to the erthe bothe, and the raynys of their brydyls in there hondys. And so they lay a grete whyle sore astoned, that all that were in the
30 castell and in the sege wente their neckys had bene broste.

Than many a straunger and othir seyde that the straunge knyght was a bygge man and a noble jouster, 'for or now we sawe never no knyght macche the Rede Knyght of the Rede Laundys.' Thus they seyde bothe within and with-
35 oute.

128ᵛ Than lyghtly and delyverly they avoyded their horsis and

4 ryght *not in* C   8 C knyghte of the reed laundes   9 therefore *not in* C
14 C saye or   15 all *not in* C   16 the and *not in* C†   19 W ayenst thou
20 muche *not in* C   22–23 C no lenger   24 C* Thenne syre Beaumayns badde
the damoysel goo from hym and thenne they putte   30 C ben broken   34 C
within the castel and   36 and delyverly *not in* C

putt their shyldis afore them and drew theire swerdys and
ran togydyrs lyke two fers lyons, and eythir gaff othir suche
two buffettys uppon their helmys that they reled bakwarde
bothe two stredys. And than they recoverde bothe and hew
grete pecis of othyrs harneyse and their shyldys, that a grete 5
parte felle in the fyldes.

And than thus they fought tyll hit was paste none, and (17)
never wolde stynte tyll at the laste they lacked wynde bothe,
and than they stoode waggyng, stagerynge, pantynge,
blowynge, and bledyng, that all that behelde them for the 10
moste party wepte for pyté. So whan they had rested them
a whyle they yode to batayle agayne, trasyng, traversynge,
foynynge, and rasynge as two borys. And at som tyme they
toke their bere as hit had bene two rammys and horled
togydyrs, that somtyme they felle grovelynge to the erthe; 15
and at som tyme they were so amated that aythir toke others
swerde in the stede of his owne.

And thus they endured tyll evynsonge, that there was
none that behelde them myght know whethir was lyke to
wynne the batayle. And theire armoure was so forhewyn 20
that men myght se their naked sydys, and in other placis
they were naked; but ever the nakyd placis they dud defende.
And the Rede Knyghte was a wyly knyght in fyghtyng, and
that taught Bewmaynes to be wyse, but he abought hit full
sore or he did aspye his fyghtynge. 25

And thus by assente of them both they graunted aythir
othir to reste, and so they sette hem downe uppon two
mollehyllys there besydys the fyghtynge place, and eythir
of them unlaced othir helmys and toke the colde wynde, for
aythir of their pagis was faste by them to com whan they 30
called them to unlace their harneyse and to sette hem on
agayne at there commaundemente. And than sir Bew- **129ʳ**
maynes, whan his helme was off, he loked up to the wyndowe,
and there he sawe the fayre lady dame Lyones, and she
made hym suche countenaunce that his herte waxed lyght 35
and joly. And therewith he bade the Rede Knyght of the

5 *C* of theire harneis   9 *C* scateryng pontyng   12–13 *C* tracyng
racyng foynyng as two bores   14 *C* toke their renne   16 *C* so amased†
18 *C* euensong tyme   20 *C* fer hewen   23–24 *C* knyght of werre
and his wyly fyghtyng taughte syr Beaumayns   29 *C* vnlaced his helme
31 them *not in C*   32–33 *C* thenne whan syr Beaumayns helme was of

Rede Laundes make hym redy, 'and lette us do oure batayle to the utteraunce.'

'I woll well,' seyde the knyght. And than they laced on their helmys, and avoyded their pagys, and yede togydyrs
5 and fought freysshly. But the Rede Knyght of the Rede Laundys wayted hym at an overthwarte and smote hym with[in the honde,] that his swerde felle oute of his honde. And yette he gaff hym another buffette uppon the helme, that he felle grovellynge to the erthe, and the Rede Knyghte
10 felle over hym for to holde hym downe.

Than cryed the maydyn Lynet on hyght and seyde,

'A, sir Bewmaynes! Where is thy corrayge becom? Alas! my lady my sister beholdyth the, and she shrekys and wepys so that hit makyth myne herte hevy.'

15 Whan sir Bewmaynes herde hir sey so, he abrayded up with a grete myght, and gate hym uppon hys feete, and lyghtly he lepe to his swerde and gryped hit in his honde and dowbled his pace unto the Rede Knyght, and there they fought a new batayle togydir.

20 But sir Bewmaynes than doubled his strokys and smote so thycke that his swerde felle oute of his honde. And than he smote hym on the helme, that he felle to the erthe, and sir Bewmaynes felle uppon hym and unlaced his helme to have slayne hym. And than he yelded hym and asked
25 mercy and seyde with a lowde voyce,

'A, noble knyght! I yelde me to thy mercy!'

Than sir Bewmaynes bethought hym on his knyghtes that he had made to be honged shamfully, and than he seyde,

'I may nat with my worship to save thy lyff for the shame-
30 full de[the]s that thou haste caused many full good knyghtes to dye.'

129ᵛ 'Syr,' seyde the Rede Knyght, 'holde youre hande and ye shall knowe the causis why I putte hem to so shameful a deth.'

'Sey on!' seyde sir Bewmaynes.

---

1 *C* doo the bataille   3-4 *C* lc ed vp their helmes and their pages auoyded & they stepte to gyders   6 *C* & at an ouerthwart   7 *C* within the hand (*see note*)   11-12 *C* on hyghe O syr   13-14 *C* she sobbeth and wepeth that maketh   15 *C* abrayed   17 *C* he lepte   21 *C* that he smote the swerd oute   23-26 *W* (*sidenote*): Here sir Bewmaynes overcom the Rede Knyght of the Rede Laundys   27 *C* vpon the knyghtes   30 *W* dedys   32 *C* knyghte of the reed laundes

'Sir, I loved onys a lady fayre, and she had hir bretherne slayne, and she tolde me hit was sir Launcelot du Lake othir ellys sir Gawayne. And she prayed me as I loved hir hertely that I wolde make hir a promyse by the faythe of my knyght-hode for to laboure in armys dayly untyll that I had mette 5 with one of them, and all that I myght overcom I sholde put them to vylans deth. And so I ensured her to do all the vylany unto Arthurs knyghtes, and that I sholde take vengeaunce uppon all these knyghtes. And, sir, now I woll telle the that every day my strengthe encresyth tylle none 10 untyll I have seven mennys strength.'

Than cam there many erlys and barowns and noble (18) knyghtes and prayde that knyght to save his lyff, 'and take hym to your presoner.' And all they felle uppon their kneis and prayde hym of mercy that he wolde save his lyff. 15

'And, sir,' they all seyde, 'hit were fayrer of hym to take omage and feauté and lat hym holde his londys of you than for to sle hym, for by his deth ye shall have none advauntage, and his myssededys that he done may not be undone. And therefore make ye amendys for all partyes, and we all woll 20 becom youre men and do you omage and feauté.'

'Fayre lordys,' seyde Bewmaynes, 'wete you well I am full loth to sle this knyght, neverthelesse he hath done passynge ylle and shamefully. But insomuche all that he dud was at a ladyes requeste I blame hym the lesse, and so 25 for your sake I woll relece hym, that he shall have his lyff uppon this covenaunte: that he go into this castell and yelde hym to the lady, and yf she woll forgyff and quyte hym I woll well, with this he make hir amendys of all the trespasse that he hath done ayenst hir and hir landys. And also, whan 30 that is done, that he goo unto the courte of kyng Arthur and that he aske sir Launcelot mercy and sir Gawayne for **130ʳ** the evyll wylle he hath had ayenst them.'

'Sir,' seyde the Rede Knyght, 'all this woll I do as ye com-maunde me, and syker assuraunce and borowys ye shall have.' 35

1 *C* a lady a faire damoisel   2 *C* and she said hit   5 *C* vnto I mette
7 *C** vnto a vylaynous dethe and this is the cause that I haue putte alle these knyghtes to dethe and soo (*homoeoteleuton in W?*)   8 *C* kynge Arthurs   10–11 *C* none and al this tyme haue I   15 *C* and that   18 for *not in C*   20 *C* therfor he shal make amendys to al   27 *C* goo within the castel   28 *C* hym there to
31 *C* ye goo   32 *C* ye aske   33 *C* wil ye haue   35 me *not in C*

So whan the assurauns was made he made his omage and
feauté, and all the erlys and barouns with hym.

And than the maydyn Lynet com to sir Bewmaynes and
unarmed hym and serched his woundis and staunched the
5 blood, and in lyke wyse she dud to the Rede Knyght of the
Rede Laundis. And there they suggeourned ten dayes in
there tentys. And ever the Rede Knyght made all his lordis
and servauntys to do all the plesure unto sir Bewmaynes
that they myght do.

10 And so within a whyle the Rede Knyghte yode unto the
castell and putt hym in her grace, and so she resseyved hym
uppon suffyciaunte sureté so that all her hertys were well
restored of all that she coude complayne. And than he
departed unto the courte of kynge Arthure, and there
15 opynly the Rede Knyght putt hymself in the mercy of sir
Launcelot and of sir Gawayne; and there he tolde opynly
how he was overcom and by whom, and also he tolde all
the batayles frome the begynnyng to the endynge.

'Jesu mercy!' seyde kynge Arthure and sir Gawayne,
20 'we mervayle muche of what bloode he is com, for he is a
noble knyght.'

'Have ye no mervayle,' seyde sir Launcelot, 'for ye shall
ryght well know that he is com of full noble bloode, and as
for hys myght and hardynesse, there bene but full few now
25 lyvynge that is so myghty as he is, and of so noble prouesse.'

'Hit semyth by you,' seyde kynge Arthure, 'that ye know
his name and frome whens he com.'

'I suppose I do so,' seyde sir Launcelot, 'or ellys I wolde
not have yeffyn hym the hyghe Order of Knyghthode, but
30 he gaff me suche charge at that tyme that I woll never
130ᵛ discover hym untyll he requyre me, or ellis hit be knowyn
opynly by som other.'

(19)   Now turne we unto sir Bewmaynes that desyred [of] dame
Lynet that he myght se hir lady.

35   'Sir,' she seyde, 'I wolde ye saw hir fayne.'

Than sir Bewmaynes all armed toke his horse and his

4–5 *C* stynted his blood   7 ever *not in C*   all *not in C*   8–9 *C* pleasyre that
they myghte vnto syre Beaumayns   12 that *not in C*   23 *C* wel wete
24 full *not in C*   25 *C* so noble of   27 *C** come and of what blood he is
29 *C* thordre   30 *C* I shold neuer   31 *C* requyred   34 *C** her syster
his lady   35 *C* wold fayne ye sawe her   36 *C* armed hym and toke

spere and rode streyte unto the castell, and whan he com
to the gate he founde there men armed, and pulled up the
drawbrygge and drew the portcolyse.

Than he mervayled why they wolde nat suffir hym to
entir, and than he loked up to a wyndow and there he sawe 5
fayre dame Lyones that seyde on hyght,

'Go thy way, sir Bewmaynes, for as yet thou shalt nat
have holy my love unto the tyme that thou be called one of
the numbir of the worthy knyghtes. And therefore go and
laboure in worshyp this twelve-monthe, and than ye shall 10
hyre newe tydyngis.'

'Alas! fayre lady,' seyde sir Bewmaynes, 'I have nat
deserved that ye sholde shew me this straungenesse. And
I hadde wente I sholde have had ryght good chere with
you, and unto my power I have deserved thanke. And well 15
I am sure I have bought your love with parte of the beste
bloode within my body.'

'Fayre curteyse knyghte,' seyde dame Lyonesse, 'be nat
displeased, nother be nat overhasty, for wete you well youre
grete travayle nother your good love shall nat be loste, for 20
I consyder your grete laboure and your hardynesse, your
bounté and your goodnesse as me ought to do. And therefore go on your way and loke that ye be of good comforte,
for all shall be for your worshyp and for the best; and, pardé,
a twelve-monthe woll sone be done. And trust me, fayre 25
knyght, I shall be trewe to you and never betray you, but
to my deth I shall love you and none other.'

And therewithall she turned frome the wyndowe, and sir
Bewmaynes rode awaywarde from the castell makynge grete
dole. And so he rode now here, now there, he wyste nat 30
whother, tyll hit was durke nyght. And than hit happened **131ʳ**
hym to com to a pore mannys house, and there he was her-
borowde all that nyght. But sir Bewmaynes had no reste, but
walowed and wrythed for the love of the lady of that castell.

And so uppon the morne he toke his horse and rode 35
untyll undyrn, and than he com to a brode watir, [and thereby

2 *C* many men   3 *C* the porte cloose   6 *C* the fair Lyones   *C* on hyghe
19 *C* nor ouer hasty   20 *C* nor good   21–22 *C* trauaill & labour your
bounte   26 *C* neuer te bitraye you   30–31 *C* rode here and there & wyste
not ne where he rode tyl   34 *C* the castel   36–p. 328, l. 1 *Not emended in* O¹

was a grete lodge.] And there he alyght to slepe and leyde
his hede uppon hys shylde and betoke his horse to the
dwarff and commaunded the dwarff to wacche all nyght.

Now turne we to the lady of the same castell that thought
5　muche uppon Bewmaynes. And than she called unto hir sir
Gryngamoure, hir brother, and prayde hym in all maner, as he
loved hir hertely, that he wolde ryde afftir sir Bewmaynes:

'And ever have ye wayte uppon hym tyll ye may fynde
hym slepyng, for I am sure in his hevynesse he woll alyght
10　adowne in som place and lay hym downe to slepe. And
therefore have ye youre wayte uppon hym in prevy maner,
and take his dwarff and com your way wyth hym as faste
as ye may[e or sir Bewmaynes awake:] for my sistir Lynet
tellyth me that he can telle of what kynrede he is com of.
15　And in the meanewhyle I and my sistir woll ryde untyll your
castell to wayte whan ye brynge with you the dwarff, and
than woll I have hym in examynacion myself, for tyll that
I know what is his ryght name and of what kynrede he is
commyn shall I never be myrry at my herte.'

20　'Sistir,' seyde sir Gryngamour, 'all this shall be done aftir
your entente.'

And so he rode all that other day and the nyght tyll he
had lodged hym. And whan he sawe sir Bewmaynes faste
on slepe he com stylly stalkyng behynde the dwarff and
25　plucked hym faste undir his arme and so rode his way with
hym untyll his owne castell. And this sir Gryngamoure was
all in blak, his armour and his horse and all that tyll hym
131ᵛ　longyth. But ever as he rode with the dwarff towarde the
castell he cryed untyll his lorde and prayde hym of helpe.
30　And therewyth awoke sir Beawmaynes, and up he lepte
lyghtly and sawe where the blak knyght rode his way wyth
the dwarff, and so he rode oute of his syght.

(20)　　Than sir Bewmaynes put on his helme and buckeled on

11–12 *C* hym and in the preuyest manere ye can take　13 *Not emended in O*[1]
14 *C** come and what is his ryghte name　17 *C* thenne whan ye haue
broughte hym vnto your Castel I wyll haue　*C†* my self vnto the tyme that
22–23 *C** tylle that he fond syre Beaumayns lyenge by a water and his hede vpon
his shelde for to slepe And thenne whanne he　25–26 *C* he rode aweye with
hym as faste as euer he myghte vnto　26–27 *C* Gryngamours armes were all
black and that to hym　29 *S* for helpe　31 *C* the Gryngamor† rode
W way way　32 *C* so syr Gryngamor rode　33–p. 329, l. 1 *C* buckeled his

his shylde and toke his horse and rode afftir hym all that
ever he myght, thorow mores and fellys and grete sloughis,
that many tymes his horse and he plunged over their hedys
in depe myres, for he knewe nat the way but toke the gayneste
way in that woodenesse, that many tymes he was lyke to 5
peryshe. And at the laste hym happened to com to a fayre
grene way, and there he mette with a poore man of the
contray and asked hym whether he mette nat with a knyght
uppon a blak horse and all blak harneyse, and a lytyll dwarff
syttynge behynde hym with hevy chere.   10

'Sir,' seyde the poore man, 'here by me com sir Gryngamoure the knyght with suche a dwarff, and therefore I rede
you nat to folow hym, for he is one of the perelyst knyghtes
of the worlde, and his castell is here nerehonde but two
myle. Therefore we avyse you, ryde nat aftir sir Grynga- 15
mour but yf ye owe hym good wylle.'

So leve we sir Bewmaynes rydyng toward the castell, and
speke we of sir Gryngamoure and the dwarff. Anone as
the dwarff was com to the castell dame Lyonesse and dame
Lynet, hir systir, asked the dwarff where was his mastir 20
borne and of what lynage was he com. 'And but yf thou telle
me,' seyde dame Lyonesse, 'thou shalt never ascape this
castell but ever here to be presonere.'

'As for that,' seyde the dwarff, 'I feare nat gretly to telle
his name and of what kynne he is commyn of. Wete you well, 25
he is a kynges son and a quenys, and his fadir hyght kynge
Lot of Orkeney, and his modir is sistir to kyng Arthure, and **132ʳ**
he is brother to sir Gawayne, and his name is sir Gareth of
Orkenay. And now I have tolde you his ryght name, I pray
you, fayre lady, lat me go to my lorde agayne, for he woll 30
never oute of this contrey tyll he have me agayne; and
yf he be angry he woll do harme or that he be stynted, and
worche you wrake in this contrey.'

'As for that, be as be may.'

'Nay,' seyde sir Gryngamoure, 'as for that thretynge, we 35
woll go to dynere.'

2–3 *C* marys and feldes and grete dales that   8 *C** countreye whom he salewed &
12 *C** dwerf mornyng as ye saye &   14 *C* here nyhe hande   25 *C* is come
Wete   26–27 and a quenys and his fadir hyght kynge Lot of Orkeney *not in C*†
28 *C* broder to the good knyghte of† syre   32 *C* doo moche harme   34–36 *C*
for that thretyng sayd syr Gryngamore be it as it be may We will (*see note*)

And so they wayshed and wente to mete and made hem mery and well at ease. Bycause the lady Lyonesse of the Castell Perelus was there, they made the gretter joy.

'Truly, madam,' seyde Lynet unto hir sistir, 'well may
5 he be a kyngys son, for he hath many good tacchis: for he is curtyese and mylde, and the most sufferynge man that ever I mette withall. For I dare sey there was never jantyllwoman revyled man in so foule a maner a[s] I have rebuked hym. And at all tymes he gaff me goodly and meke answers agayne.'

10 And as they sate thus talkynge there cam sir Gareth in at the gate with hys swerde drawyn in his honde and cryed alowde that all the castell myght hyre:

'Thou traytour knyght, sir Gryngamoure! delyver me my dwarff agayne, or by the fayth that I owghe to God and to the
15 hygh Ordir of Knyghthode I shall do the all the harme that may lye in my power!'

Than sir Gryngamour loked oute at a wyndow and seyde,

'Sir Gareth of Orkenay, leve thy bostyng wordys, for thou gettyst nat thy dwarff agayne.'

20 'Than, cowarde knyght,' seyde Gareth, 'brynge hym with the, and com and do batayle with me, and wynne hym and take hym.'

'So woll I do,' seyde sir Gryngamoure, 'and me lyste, but for all thy grete wordys thou gettyst hym nat.'

132ᵛ 25 'A, fayre lady,' seyde dame Lynet, 'I wolde he hadde his dwarff agayne, for I wolde he were nat wroth: for now he hath tolde me all my desyre, I kepe no more of the dwarff. And also, brother, he hath done muche for me and delyverde me from the Rede Knyght of the Rede Laundis. And
30 therefore, brother, I owe hym my servyse afore all knyghtes lyvynge, and wete you well that I love hym byfore all othyr knyghtes lyvynge, and full fayne I wolde speke with hym. But in no wyse I wolde nat that he wyste what I were but as I were anothir strange lady.'

35 'Well, sistir,' seyde sir Gryngamour, 'sythen that I know no[w] your wyll I woll obey me now unto hym.' And so

---

3 Perelus *not in C*   5 *C* tatches on hym for   8 *C* reulyd man   11 *C**
with an angry countenaunce and his swerd   12 *C* here hit sayeng   14–15
C† owe to the ordre   15–17 *C* harme that I can Thenne   20 *C** Thou
coward   25 *C** fayr broder said dame Lyones I wold   31–32 *C* before al
other and   33 nat *not in C*   34 *C* that I   35 sistir *not in C*   36 me *not in C*

therewith he wente downe and seyde, 'Sir Gareth, I cry you
mercy, and all that I have myssedone I woll amende hit at
your wylle. And therefore I pray you that ye wolde alyght
and take suche chere as I can make you in this castell.'

'Shall I have my dwarff?' seyde sir Gareth.			5

'Yee, sir, and all the plesure that I can make you, for as
sone as your dwarff tolde me what ye were and of what
kynde ye ar com and what noble dedys ye have done in
this marchis, than I repented me of my dedys.'

Than sir Gareth alyght, and there com his dwarff and toke 10
his horse.

'A, my felow!' seyde sir Gareth, 'I have had muche
adventures for thy sake!'

And so sir Gryngamoure toke hym by the honde and ledde
hym into the halle where his owne wyff was. And than com 15 (21)
forth dame Lyones arayde lyke a prynces, and there she
made hym passyng good chere and he hir agayne, and they
had goodly langage and lovely countenaunce.

And sir Gareth thought many tymes: 'Jesu, wolde that
the lady of this Castell Perelus were so fayre as she is!' And 20
there was all maner of gamys and playes, of daunsyng and
syngynge, and evermore sir Gareth behelde that lady. And
the more he loked on her, the more he brenned in love, that
he passed hymself farre in his reson. And forth towardys
nyght they yode unto souper, and sir Gareth myght nat 25
ete, for his love was so hoote that he wyst nat were he was.

And thes lokys aspyed sir Gryngamour, and than aftir **133ʳ**
souper he called his sistir dame Lyonesse untyll a chambir
and sayde,

'Fayre sistir, I have well aspyed your countenaunce 30
betwyxte you and this knyght, and I woll, sistir, that ye
wete he is a full noble knyght, and yf ye can make hym to
abyde here I woll do hym all the plesure that I can, for
and ye were bettir than ye ar, ye were well bewared uppon
hym.'												35

'Fayre brother,' seyde dame Lyonesse, 'I undirstond

1 *C* doun vnto syr Gareth aud (*S* and) said syr I   6 *C* the pleasaunce that   9 me
not in C   12 *C* had many   15 *Wrong chapter-number in C:* xxii *instead of*
xxi   18 *C* countenaunce to gyder   20–21 *C* she was there   22–24 *C*
And euer the more syre Gareth bihelde that lady the more he loued her and so he
brenned in loue that he was past hym self in his reason   27 *C* at after

well that the knyght is a good knyght and com he is oute
of a noble house. Natwithstondyng I woll assay hym bettir,
howbehit I am moste beholde to hym of ony erthely man,
for he hath had grete labour for my love and passed many
5 dangerous passagis.'

Ryght so sir Gryngamour wente unto sir Gareth and
seyde, 'Sir, make ye good chere, for ye shall have none
other cause, for this lady my sistir is youres at all tymes,
hir worshyp saved, for wete you well she lovyth you as well
10 as ye do hir and better, yf bettir may be.'

'And I wyste that,' seyde sir Gareth, 'there lyved nat a
gladder man than I wolde be.'

'Uppon my worshyp,' seyde sir Gryngamoure, 'truste
unto my promyse. And as longe as hit lykyth you ye shall
15 suggeourne with me, and this lady shall be wyth us dayly and
nyghtly to make you all the chere that she can.'

'I woll well,' seyde sir Gareth, 'for I have promysed to
be nyghe this contray this twelve-monthe, and well I am
sure kynge Arthure and other noble knyghtes woll fynde
20 me where that I am wythin this twelve-monthe, for I shall
be sought and founden yf that I be on lyve.'

And than sir Gareth wente unto the lady dame Lyonesse
and kyssed hir many tymes, and eythir made grete joy of
other, and there she promysed hym hir love, sertaynly to
25 love hym and none other dayes of hir lyff. Than this lady
dame Lyonesse by the assent of hir brother tolde sir Gareth
all the trouthe what she was, and how she was the same lady
that he dud batayle fore, and how she was lady of the Castell
133^v Perelus. And there she tolde hym how she caused hir
(22) 30 brother to take away his dwarff, 'for this cause: to know the
sertayne, what was your name and of what kyn ye were
com.' And than she lette fette before hym hir systir Lynet
that had ryddyn with hym many a wylsom way. Than was
syr Gareth more gladder than he was tofore.

35 And than they trouthe-plyghte other to love and never to
fayle whyle their lyff lastyth. And so they brente bothe in
hoote love that they were acorded to abate their lustys

1–2 *C* is good & come he is of   3 *C* beholdyng   22 *C* than the noble knyghte
syre   22–23 *C** Lyones whiche he thēne moche loued & kyst   31 *C* certaynte
32 *C* fetche   32–33 *C* hym Lynet the damoysel that   37 hoote *not in C*

secretly. And there dame Lyonesse counceyled sir Gareth to slepe in none other place but in the halle, and there she promysed hym to com to his bed a lytyll afore mydnyght.

This counceyle was nat so prevyly kepte but hit was undirstonde, for they were but yonge bothe and tendir of ayge and had nat used suche craufftis toforne. Wherefore the damesell Lyonett was a lytyll dysplesed; and she thought hir sister dame Lyonesse was a lytyll overhasty that she myght nat abyde hir tyme of maryage, and for savyng of hir worshyp she thought to abate their hoote lustis. And she lete ordeyne by hir subtyle craufftes that they had nat theire intentys neythir with othir as in her delytes untyll they were maryed.

And so hit paste on. At aftir souper was made a clene avoydaunce, that every lorde and lady sholde go unto his reste. But sir Gareth seyde playnly he wolde go no farther than the halle, for in suche placis, he seyde, was conveny-aunte for an arraunte knyght to take his reste in. And so there was ordayned grete cowchis and thereon fethir beddis, and there he leyde hym downe to slepe. And within a whyle came dame Lyonesse wrapped in a mantell furred with ermyne, and leyde hir downe by the sydys of sir Gareth. And there-withall he began to clyppe hir and to kysse hir.

And therewithall he loked before hym and sawe an armed knyght with many lyghtes aboute hym, and this knyght had a longe gysarne in his honde and made a grymme counte-naunce to smyte hym. Whan sir Gareth sawe hym com in that wyse he lepte oute of his bedde and gate in his hande a swerde and lepte towarde that knyght. And whan the knyght sawe sir Gareth com so fersly uppon hym he smote hym with a foyne thorow the thycke of the thygh, that the wounde was a shafftemonde brode and had cutte a-too many vaynes and synewys. And therewithall sir Gareth smote hym uppon the helme suche a buffette that he felle grovel-yng, and than he lepe over hym and unlaced his helme and smote off his hede from the body. And than he bled so faste

6 *C* vsed none suche   9 *C* sauyng their   20 he *not in C*   22 *C* besydes syr
23 to clyppe hir and *not in C*†   24–25 *C*† hym and there he apperceuyued and sawe
come an armed knyght with many lyghtes aboute hym and sawe come an armed
knyӡt with many lyghtes about hym   29 *C* his swerd and lepte strayte toward

that he myght not stonde, but so he leyde hym downe uppon his bedde and there he sowned and lay as he had bene
dede.

Than dame Lyonesse cryed alowde that sir Gryngamoure
5 harde hit and com downe; and whan he sawe sir Gareth so
shamefully wounded he was sore dyspleased and seyde,

'I am shamed that this noble knyght is thus dishonoured.
Si⟨sti⟩r,' seyde sir Gryngamour, 'how may this be that this
noble knyght is thus wounded?'

10 'Brothir,' she seyde, 'I can nat telle you, for hit was nat
done by me nother by myne assente, for he is my lorde and
I am his, and he muste be myne husbonde. Therefore,
brothir, I woll that ye wete I shame nat to be with hym nor
to do hym all the plesure that I can.'

15 'Sistir,' seyde Gryngamour, 'and I woll that ye wete hit
and Gareth bothe that hit was never done by me, nother
be myne assente this unhappy dede was never done.'

And there they staunched his bledyng as well as they
myght, and grete sorow made sir Gryngamour and dame
20 Lyonesse. And forthwithall com dame Lyonett and toke
up the hede in the syght of them all, and anoynted hit with
an oyntemente thereas hit was smyttyn off, and in the same
wyse [s]he ded to the othir parte thereas the hede stake.
And then she sette hit togydirs, and hit stake as faste as
25 ever hit ded. And the knyght arose lyghtly up and the
damesell Lyonett put hym in hir chambir.

All this saw sir Gryngamour and dame Lyonesse, and
134ᵛ so ded sir Gareth, and well he aspyed that hit was dame
Lyonett that rode with hym thorow the perelouse passages.

30 'A, well, damesell!' seyde sir Gareth, 'I wente ye wolde
nat have done as ye have done.'

'My lorde sir Gareth,' seyde Lyonett, 'all that I have
done I woll avowe hit, and all shall be for your worshyp
and us all.'

35 And so within a whyle sir Gareth was nyghe hole and

4-5 *C* that her broder syr Gryngamor herd and   7 *C*† thus honoured
8 *Not emended in* O¹   8-9 *C* that ye be here and thys noble knyghte wounded
13 *C* shame me   17 *C* assente that this vnhappy dede was done   20,
28-29 *C* Dame Lynet   26 *C* Lynet   30 *C* I wende wold†   32 *C* My
lord Gareth said Lynet   33-34 *C* auowe and alle that I haue done shal be for
youre honoure and worship and to vs alle

waxed lyght and jocunde, and sange and daunced. Tha[n]
agayne sir Gareth and dame Lyonesse were so hoote in
brennynge love that they made their covenauntes at the
tenth nyght aftir, that she sholde com to his bedde. And
because he was wounded afore, he leyde his armour and his 5
swerde nygh his beddis syde.

And ryght as she promysed she com. And she was nat (23)
so sone in his bedde but she aspyed an armed knyght
commynge towarde the bed, and anone she warned sir
Gareth. And lyghtly thorow the good helpe of dame 10
Lyonesse he was armed, and they hurled togydyrs with
grete ire and malyce all aboute the halle. And there was
grete lyght as hit had be the numbir of twenty torchis bothe
byfore and behynde. So sir Gareth strayned hym so that his
olde wounde braste ayen on-bledynge. But he was hote 15
and corragyous and toke no kepe, but with his grete forse
he strake downe the knyght and avoyded hys helme and
strake of his hede.

Than he hew the hede uppon an hondred pecis, and whan
he had done so he toke up all tho pecis and threw them oute 20
at a wyndow into the dychis of the castell. And by this done
he was so faynte that unnethis he myght stonde for bledynge,
and by than he was allmoste unarmed he felle in a dedly
sowne in the floure.

Than dame Lyonesse cryed, that sir Gryngamoure herde 25
her, and when he com and founde sir Gareth in that plyght
he made grete sorow. And there he awaked sir Gareth and
gaff hym a drynke that releved hym wondirly well. But the **135ͬ**
sorow that dame Lyonesse made there may no tunge telle,
for she so fared with hirself as she wolde have dyed. 30

Ryght so come this damesell Lyonett before hem all, and
she had fette all the gobbettis of the hede that sir Gareth had
throwe oute at the wyndow, and there she anoynted hit as she
dud tofore, and put them to the body in the syght of hem all.

'Well, damesell Lyonett,' seyde sir Gareth, 'I have nat 35
deserved all this dyspyte that ye do unto me.'

1–2 *C* sange daunced and gamed and he and dame Lyones   1 *W* That   9 *C*
bedde there with alle she   14 *C* soo that† syr   19 *C* in an   25 *C* soo
that   26 her *not in C*   32 *O*¹ sette   *S* goblets   *C* gobbets   33–35 *C* enoynted
hem* as she had done to fore & set them to gyder ageyn wel damoisel Lynet

'Sir knyght,' she seyde, 'I have nothynge done but I woll avow hit, and all that I have done shall be to your worshyp and to us all.'

Than was sir Gareth staunched of his bledynge, but the
5 lechis seyde there was no man that bare the lyff sholde heale hym thorowly of his wounde but yf they heled them that caused the stroke by enchauntemente.

So leve we sir Gareth there wyth sir Gryngamour and his sisters, and turne we unto kyng Arthure that at the nexte feste
10 of Pentecoste [helde his feste.] There cam the Grene Knyght and fyfty knyghtes with hym, and yeldyd them all unto kynge Arthure. Than there com the Rede Knyghte, his brother, and yelded them to kynge Arthure wyth three score knyghtes with them. Also there com the Blew Knyght, his brother, and yelded
15 hem to kyng Arthure. And the Grene Knyghtes name was sir Partholype, and the Rede Knyghtes name was sir Perymones, and the Blew Knyghtes name was sir Persaunte of Inde.

Thes three bretherne tolde kynge Arthure how they were overcom by a knyght that a damesell had with hir, and she
20 called hym sir Bewmaynes.

'Jesu!' seyde the kynge, 'I mervayle what knyght he is and of what lynage he is com. Here he was with me a twelve-monthe and poorely and shamefully he was fostred. And sir Kay i[n] scorne named hym Bewmaynes.'

25 So ryght as the kynge stode so talkyng with thes three
135ᵛ bretherne there com sir Launcelot du Lake and tolde the kynge that there was com a goodly lorde with fyve hondred knyghtys with hym. Than the kynge was at Carlyon, for there was the feste holde, and thidir com to hym this lorde
30 and salewed the kynge with goodly maner.

'What wolde ye?' seyde kynge Arthure, 'and what is your erande?'

'Sir,' he seyde, 'I am called the Rede Knyght of the Rede

1–2 *C* do but I will auowe And   6 *W* hym thorowly of of   *C* hym thorou oute of   10 *C** Pentecost helde his feest and there   10–11 *C* knyght with fyfty knyghtes and   12–13 *C** reed knyghte his broder and yelded hym   13 *C* Arthur and   13–14 *C* with hym   14–15 *C** blewe knyghte broder to them with an hondred knyghtes & yelded hem   19 she *not in C*   27–28 *C* with vi C knyghtes   28–29 *C* kynge wente oute of† Carlyon for there was the feest and there came   31 *C* wylle ye   33–p. 337, l. 1 *C* my name† (*S* naname) is the reed knyghte of the reed laundes but my name is

Laundis, but my name is sir Ironsyde; and, sir, wete you
well, hydir I am sente unto you frome a knyght that is called
sir Bewmaynes, for he wanne me in playne batayle hande
for hande, and so ded never knyght but he that ever had the
bettir of me this twenty wyntir. And I am commaunded 5
to yelde me to you at your wyll.'

'Ye ar welcom,' seyde the kynge, 'for ye have bene longe
a grete foo of owres to me and to my courte, and now, I
truste to God, I shall so entrete you that ye shall be my
frende.'   10

'Sir, bothe I and thes fyve hondred knyghtes shall allwayes be at your sommons to do you suche servyse as may
lye in oure powers.'

'Gramercy,' seyde kynge Arthure, 'I am muche beholdyng
unto that knyght that hath so put his body in devoure to 15
worshyp me and my courte. And as to the, sir Ironsyde,
that is called the Rede Knyght of the Rede Laundys, thou
arte called a perelouse knyght, and yf thou wolte holde of
me I shall worshyp the and make the knyght of the Table
Rounde, but than thou muste be no man-murtherer.'   20

'Sir, as to that, I have made my promyse unto sir Bewmaynes nevermore to use such customs, for all the shamefull
customs that I used I ded hit at the requeste of a lady that
I loved. And therefore I muste goo unto sir Launcelot and
unto sir Gawayne and aske them forgyffnesse of the evyll 25
wyll I had unto them; for all tho that I put to deth was all
only for the love of sir Launcelot and of sir Gawayne.'

'They bene here,' seyde the kynge, 'before the. Now
may ye sey to them what ye woll.'   **136ʳ**

And than he kneled downe unto sir Launcelot and to 30
sir Gawayne and prayde them of forgeffnesse of his en-
myté that he had ayenste them. Than goodly they seyde all at (24)
onys,

'God forgyff you and we do. And we pray you that ye woll
telle us where we may fynde sir Bewmaynes.'   35

'Fayre lorde,' sayde sir Ironsyde, 'I can nat telle you, for

2 *C* of a knyght   4 *C* neuer no knyght   5 *C* xxx wynter the whiche commaunded   8 of owres *not in C*   12 suche *not in C*   14 *C* Ihesu mercy said
15 *C* put soo *C* deuoyre   20 *C* no more a murtherer   21 *C* I haue promysed
26 tho *not in C*   28 *C* here now said   32 *C* that euer he   34 we *not in C*†

hit is full harde to fynde hym: for such yonge knyghtes as he
is, whan they be in their adventures, bene never abydyng
in no place.'

But to sey the worshyp that the Rede Knyght of the Rede
5 Laundys and sir Persaunte and his br[other] seyde by hym,
hit was mervayle to hyre.

'Well, my fayre lordys,' seyde kynge Arthure, 'wete you
well I shall do you honour for the love of sir Bewmaynes,
and as sone as ever I may mete with hym I shall make you
10 all uppon a day knyghtes of the Table Rounde. And as
to the, sir Persaunte of Inde, thou hast bene ever called a
full noble knyght, and so hath evermore thy three bretherne
bene called. But I mervayle,' seyde the kynge, 'that I here
nat of the Blak Knyght, your brother. He was a full noble
15 knyght.'

'Sir,' seyde Pertolype the Grene Knyght, 'sir Bewmaynes
slew hym in a recountir with hys spere. His name was sir
Perarde.'

'That was grete pyté,' seyde the kynge, and so seyde
20 many knyghtes, for thes four brethyrne were full well
knowyn in kynge Arthures courte for noble knyghtes, for
long tyme they had holdyn werre ayenst the knyghtes of
the Rownde Table.

Than Partolype the Grene Knyght tolde the kyng that
25 at a passage of the watir of Mortayse there encountird sir
Bewmaynes with too bretherne that ever for the moste
party kepte that passage, and they were two dedly knyghtes.
And there he slew the eldyst brother in the watir and
136ᵛ smote hym uppon the hede suche a buffette that he felle
30 downe in the watir and there was he drowned. And his
name was sir Garrarde le Brewse. And aftir he slew the
other brother uppon the londe: hys name was sir Arnolde
le Brewse.

(25, 26)   So than the kynge [and they] wente to mete and were
35 served in the beste maner. And as they sate at the mete
there com in the quene of Orkenay with ladyes and knyghtes

1–2 *C* he is one   5 *W* bretherne (*not emended in O¹*)   5–6 *C* * his broder said of
Beaumayns it was   9 may *not in C*   10 *C* vpon one day   11 *P* of Inde
R o Inde   12–13 *C* soo haue euer ben thy thre bretheren called   24–25 *C*
Thenne sayd Pertolepe the grene knyghte to the kynge atte a   30 *C* he was
34 *C* Capitulum XXVI (XXV *omitted*)

a grete numbir. And than sir Gawayne, sir Aggravayne, and sir Gaherys arose and wente to hir modir and salewed hir uppon their kneis and asked hir blyssynge, for of twelve yere before they had not sene hir. Than she spake uppon hyght to hir brother kynge Arthure: 5

'Where have ye done my yonge son, sir Gareth? For he was here amongyst you a twelve-monthe, and ye made a kychyn knave of hym, the whyche is shame to you all. Alas! Where have ye done myn owne dere son that was my joy and blysse?'   10

'A, dere modir,' seyde sir Gawayne, 'I knew hym nat.'

'Nothir I,' seyde the kynge, 'that now me repentys, but, thanked be God, he is previd a worshypfull knyght as ony that is now lyvyng of his yerys, and I shall nevir be glad tyll that I may fynde [hym].'   15

'A, brothir!' seyde the quene, 'ye dud yourself grete shame whan ye amongyst you kepte my son in the kychyn and fedde hym lyke an hogge.'

'Fayre sistir,' seyde kynge Arthure, 'ye shall ryght well wete that I knew hym nat, nother no more dud sir Gawayne,   20 nothir his bretherne. But sytthe hit is so,' seyde the kynge, 'that he thus is gone frome us all, we muste shape a remedy to fynde hym. Also, sistir, mesemyth ye myght have done me to wete of his commynge, and than, if I had nat done well to hym, ye myght have blamed me. For whan he com   25 to this courte he cam lenynge uppon too mennys sholdyrs as though he myght nat have gone. And than he asked me **137**[r] three gyfftys; and one he asked that same day, and that was that I wolde gyff hym mete inowghe that twelve-monthe. And the other two gyfftys he asked that day twelve-monthe,   30 and that was that he myght have the adventure of the damesel Lyonett; and the thirde, that sir Launcelot sholde make hym knyght whan he desyred hym. And so I graunted hym all [his] desyre. And many in this courte mervayled that he desyred his sustynaunce for a twelve-   35

---

2 modir *not in C*   3–4 *C* in xv yere they   4–5 *C* spak on hyghe ❡ 6 For *not in C*   9 owne *not in C*   11 *C* O dere   12 *C* Nor I   16 *C** quene vnto kyng Arthur and vnto syr Gawayne and to alle her sones ye dyd   18 *C* a poure hog   20–21 *C* not nor nomore ... nor   21 *S* it *C* hit   22 *C* is thus   28 *C* the same day that   30 *C* day a twelue moneth   32 *C* Lynet *C* thyrd was that   34 *W* all my desyre *C** alle his desyre

monthe, and thereby we demed many of us that he was nat
com oute of a noble house.'

'Sir,' seyde the quene of Orkenay unto kynge Arthure her
brother, 'wete you well that I sente hym unto you ryght
5 well armed and horsed and worshypfully besene of his body,
and golde and sylver plenté to spende.'

'Hit may be so,' seyde the kyng, 'but thereof sawe we
none, save that same day that he departed frome us knyghtes
tolde me that there com a dwarff hyder suddeynely and
10 brought hym armour and a good horse full well and rychely
beseyne. And thereat all we had mervayle, frome whens
that rychesse com. Than we demed all that he was com of
men of worshyp.'

'Brother,' seyde the quene, 'all that ye sey we beleve hit,
15 for ever sytthen he was growyn he was [mervaylously
wytted, and ever he was] feythfull and trew of his promyse.
But I mervayle,' seyde she, 'that sir Kay dud mok and scorne
hym and gaff hym to name Bewmaynes; yet sir Kay,' seyde
the quene, 'named hym more ryghteously than he wende,
20 for I dare sey he is as fayre an handid man ⌈and wel disposed⌉,
and he be on lyve, as ony lyvynge.'

'Sistir,' seyde Arthure, 'lat this langage now be stylle, and
by the grace of God he shall be founde and he be within this
seven realmys. And lette all this passe and be myrry, for
25 he is preved to [be] a man of worshyp, and that is my joy.'

(27)   Than seyde sir Gawayne and his bretherne unto kynge
Arthure,

137ᵛ   'Sir, and ye woll gyff us leve we woll go seke oure brother.'

'Nay,' sayde sir Launcelot, 'that shall not nede.' And so
30 seyde sir Bawdwyn of Brytaygne. 'For as by oure advyse,
the kynge shall sende unto dame Lyonesse a messyngere
and pray hir that she wolle come to the courte in all haste that
she may. And doute ye nat she woll com, and than she may
gyff you the beste counceyle where ye shall fynde sir Gareth.'

---

5 of *not in* S   7 so *not in* C   11 C we al   12 C came that we   14–15 C
I byleue for   15–16 C* he was merueillously wytted and euer he was feythful
(*homoeoteleuton in* W; *see note*)   17–18 C mocke hym and scorne hym and gaf hym
that name   20–21 C* I dare saye and he be on lyue he is as fair an handed man
and wel disposed as ony is lyuynge (*see note*)   22 P Syre† said Arthur lete (R†
Arthurle te)   25 WO¹ to a man   29 C shalle ye not   31 W lyonesse
for as by our avyse a messyngere   34 C fynde hym

'This is well seyde of you,' seyde the kynge.

So than goodly lettyrs were made, and the messyngere
sente forth, that nyght and day wente tyll he com to the
Castell Perelous. And than the lady, dame Lyonesse, was
sente fore thereas she was with sir Gryngamour, hir brother,   5
and sir Gareth. And whan she undirstoode this messyngere
she bade hym ryde on his way unto kynge Arthure, and she
wolde com aftir in all the moste goodly haste.

Than she com unto sir Gryngamour and to sir Gareth,
and tolde hem all how kyng Arthure hadde sente for hir.   10

'That is because of me,' seyde sir Gareth.

'Now avyse ye me,' seyde dame Lyonesse, 'what I shall
sey, and in what maner I shall rule me.'

'My lady and my love,' seyde sir Gareth, 'I pray you in
no wyse be ye aknowyn where I am. But well I wote my   15
modir is there and all my bretherne, and they woll take
uppon hem to seke me: I woll that they do. But this, madam,
I woll ye sey and avyse the kynge whan he questyons with
you of me: than may ye sey this is your avyse, that and hit
lyke his good grace, ye woll do make a cry ayenst the   20
Assumpcion of Oure Lady, that what knyght that prevyth
hym beste, he shall welde you and all your lande. And yf
so be that he be a wedded man that wynnes the degré, he
shall have a coronall of golde sette with stonys of vertu
to the valew of a thousand pound, and a whyght jarfawcon.'   25

So dame Lyonesse departed. And to com off and to breff
this tale, whan she com to kynge Arthure she was nobly
resseyved, and there she was sore questyonde of the kynge
and of the quene of Orkeney. And she answerde where   **138ʳ**
sir Gareth was she coude not tell, but this muche she seyde   30
unto kynge Arthure:

'Sir, by your avyse I woll let cry a turnemente that shall
be done before my castell at the Assumpcion of Oure Lady;

6 *C* this message   8 the moste *not in C*   9–10 *C* Thenne whan she came to
syr Gryngamor and to sir Gareth she told   12 *C* what shalle I   17 *C** I wote
wel that   18 *C* wold ye sayd and aduysed the kynge whan he questyoned
20–21 *C* ayenst the feest of thassumpcion   21 *C* knyghte there preueth
23–24 *C* a wedded man that his wyf† shall the degre and a coronal of gold besette with
stones (*see note*)   26 *C* Lyones   26–27 *C*† departed and came to   27 *C*
where she was   30 *C* thus moche   31 kynge *not in C*   32 by your avyse
not in C

and the cry shall be this, that you, my lorde Arthure, shall
be there and your knyghtes, and I woll purvey that my
knyghtes shall be ayenste youres; and than I am sure I shall
hyre of sir Gareth.'

5   'This is well avysed,' seyde kynge Arthure.

And so she departed; and the kynge and she made grete
provysion to the turnemente.

Whan dame Lyonesse was com to the Ile of Avylyon—
that was the same ile thereas hir brother, sir Gryngamour,
10 dwelled—than she tolde hem all how she had done, and
what promyse she had made to kynge Arthure.

'Alas!' seyde sir Gareth, 'I have bene so sore wounded
with unhappynesse sitthyn I cam into this castell that I shall
nat be able to do at that turnemente lyke a knyght; for I was
15 never thorowly hole syn I was hurte.'

'Be ye of good chere,' seyde the damesell Lyonett, 'for
I undirtake within this fyftene dayes to make you as hole
and as lusty as ever ye were.'

And than she leyde an oynemente and salve to hym as
20 hit pleased hir, that he was never so freyshe nother so lusty
as he was tho.

Than seyde the damesell Lyonett, 'Sende you unto sir Persaunte of Inde, and assumpne hym that he be redy there
with hole assomons of knyghtes, lyke as he made his promyse.
25 Also that ye sende unto Ironsyde that is knyght of the Rede
Laundys, and charge hym that he be there with you wyth
his hole somme of knyghtes; and than shall ye be able to
macche wyth kynge Arthure and his knyghtes.'

So this was done and all knyghtes were sente fore unto
30 the Castell Perelous. Than the Rede Knyght answerde and
sayde unto dame Lyonesse and to sir Gareth,

'Ye shall undirstonde that I have bene at the courte of
kynge Arthure, and sir Persaunte of Inde and his brotherne,
138ᵛ and there we have done oure omage as ye comaunded us.
35 Also,' seyde sir [Ironsyde], 'I have takyn upon me with

3 *C* ye shall   12 *C* ben   *S* been   sore *not in C*   17 as *not in C*   19 *C* &
a salue   20–22 pleasyd to her that he was neuer so fressh nor soo lusty Thenne
22–25 *C* Persaunt of ynde and assomone hym and his knyghtes to be here with you
as they haue promysed Also   25–26 *C* syr Ironsyde that is the reed knyghte of
the reed laundys   26 *C* be redy with you   31–32 *C* Gareth Madame & my
lord syr Gareth ye shal   35 *W* Also seyde sir Gareth   *C* Also syr Ironsyde* sayd

sir Persaunte of Inde and his bretherne to holde party
agaynste my lorde sir Launcelot and the knyghtes of that
courte, and this have I done for the love of my lady, dame
Lyonesse, and you, my lorde sir Gareth.'

'Ye have well done,' seyde sir Gareth, 'but wete ye well, 5
we shall be full sore macched with the moste nobleste
knyghtes of the worlde: therefore we muste purvey us of
good knyghtes where we may gete hem.'

'Ye sey well,' seyde sir Persaunte, 'and worshypfully.'

And so the cry was made in Ingelonde, Walys, Scot- 10
londe, Irelonde, and Cornuayle, and in all the Oute Iles, and
in Bretayne and many contrayes, that at oure Lady Day, the
Assumpsion next folowynge, [men] sholde com to the Castell
Perelus besyde the Ile of Avylon, and there all knyghtes,
whan they com there, sholde chose whethir them lyste to be 15
on the tone party with the knyghtes of the Castell, other to
be with kyng Arthur on the tothir party. And two monthis
was to the day that the turnamente sholde be.

And so many good knyghtys that were at hir large helde
hem for the moste party all this tyme ayenste kynge Arthure 20
and the knyghtes of the Rounde Table: and so they cam
in the syde of [them of the] castell. And sir Epynogrys was
the fyrste, and he was the kynges son of Northumbirlonde;
and sir Palamydes the Saresyn was another, and sir Safere
and sir Segwarydes, hys bretherne—but they bothe were 25
crystynde—and sir Malegryne, and sir Bryan de les Iles, a
noble knyght, and sir Grummor and Grummorson, two noble
knyghtes of Scotland, and sir Carados of the Dolowres
Towre, a noble knyght, and sir Terquyne his brother, and
sir Arnolde and sir Gauter, two bretherne, good knyghtes of 30
Cornuayle.

Also there com sir Trystrams de Lyones, and with **139ʳ**
hym sir Dynas the Senesciall, and sir Saduk. But this

6 *C* moost noble   8 *W* may may gete   9 *C* That is wel said said Persaunt
10–11 *C* England walis and scotland Ireland Cornewaille   12 *C* in many   *C* at
the feest of our lady   13 *C* next comyng men* shold   14 *C* Auylyon
14–17 *C* there al the knyghtes that ther came shold haue the choyse whether them
lyst to be on the one party with the knyghtes of the castel or on the other party with
kynge Arthur and   19 *C* & so ther cam many   *C* large and helde   20 all
this tyme *not in C*   21 and so they *not in C*   22 *O¹* syde of the (*see note*)
25 *C* his broder   26 *C* Malegryne another and   27–28 *C†* Grummore
grummursun a good knyghte of Scotland   33 Dynadas† the seneschal

sir Trystrams was nat at that tyme knyght of the Rounde
Table; but he was at that tyme one of the beste knyghtes
of the worlde. And so all thes noble knyghtes accompanyed
hem with the lady of the Castell, and with the Rede Knyght
5 of the Rede Laundys. But as for sir Gareth, he wolde nat
take uppon hym but as othir meane knyghtis.

(28)   Than turne we to kynge Arthure that brought wyth hym
sir Gawayne, Aggravayne, Gaherys, his brethern; and than
his nevewys, as sir Uwayne le Blaunche Maynes, and sir
10 Agglovale, sir Tor, sir Percivale de Galys, sir Lamerok de
Galys. Than com sir Launcelot du Lake with his bretherne,
nevewys, and cosyns, as sir Lyonell, sir Ector de Marys,
sir Bors de Gaynys, and sir Bleobrys de Gaynes, sir Blamour
de Gaynys and sir Galyhodyn, sir Galyhud, and many mo
15 of sir Launcelottys kynne; and sir Dynadan, sir La Cote
Male Tayle, his brother, a knyght good, and sir Sagramoure
le Desyrus, sir Dodynas le Saveage; and all the moste party
of the Rounde Table.

Also there cam with kynge Arthure thes kynges: the
20 kyng of Irelonde, kynge Angwysauns, and the kynge of
Scotlonde, kynge Carados, and kynge Uryens of the londe
of Gore, and kynge Bagdemagus and his son sir Mellyagauns, and sir Galahalte, the noble prynce,—all thes prynces
and erlys, barowns and noble knyghtes, as sir Braundyles,
25 sir Uwayne les Avoutres, and sir Kay, sir Bedyvere, sir
Melyot de Logres, sir Petypace of Wynchilsé, sir Gotlake—
all thes com with kynge Arthure and mo that be nat here
rehersid.

Now leve we of thes knyghtes and kynges, and lette us
30 speke of the grete aray that was made within the castell and
aboute the castell; for this lady, dame Ly[o]nesse, ordayned
139ᵛ grete aray uppon hir party for hir noble knyghtys, for all
maner of lodgynge and vytayle that cam by londe and by

2 at that tyme *not in C*   6 *C* hym more but   7–8 *C* And thenne ther cam
with kynge Arthur sir Gawayn   9 as *not in C*   10 *C* and syre Lamorrak
13–14 and sir Bleobrys de Gaynes, sir Blamour de Gaynys *not in C*†   15 *C*
Launcelots blood   16 *C* a good knyghte   16–17 *C* Sagramore a good knyght
And al   19 *C* these knyghtes†   22–23 *C* Melyaganus†   23 *C* Gala-
hault   23–24 *C* these kynges prynces and Erles Barons and other noble
26 *C* Petypase of wynkelsee   *C* Godelake   27–28 *C* that can not ben
reherced   29 *C* kynges and knyghtes   31 *C* aboute the castel for bothe partyes
the lady Dame Lyones   *W* Lynesse

watir, that there lacked nothynge for hir party, nother for
the othir party, but there was plenté to be had for golde and
sylver for kynge Arthure and all his knyghtes. And than
there cam the herbygeours frome kynge Arthure for to
herborow hym and his kyngys, deukis, erlys, barons, [and] 5
knyghtes.

Than sir Gareth prayde dame Lyonesse and the Rede
Knyght of the Rede Laundys, and sir Persaunte and his
bretherne, and sir Gryngamour, that in no wyse there sholde
none of them telle his name, and make no more of hym than 10
of the leste knyght that there was: 'for,' he seyde, 'I woll
nat be knowyn of neythir more ne lesse, nothir at the begynnynge nother at the endyng.'

Than dame Lyones seyde unto sir Gareth, 'Sir, I wolde
leve with you a rynge of myne; but I wolde pray you, as ye 15
love me hertely, lette me have hit agayne whan the turnemente
is done: for that rynge encresyth my beawté muche more
than hit is of myself. And the vertu of my rynge is this:
that that is grene woll turne to rede, and that that is rede
woll turne in lyknesse to grene, and that that is blewe woll 20
turne to whyghte, and that that is whyght woll [turne] in
lyknesse to blew; and so hit woll do of all maner of couloures;
also who that beryth this rynge shall lose no bloode. And
for grete love I woll gyff you this rynge.'

'Gramercy,' seyde sir Gareth, 'myne owne lady. For this 25
rynge is passynge mete for me; for hit woll turne all maner
of lyknesse that I am in, and that shall cause me that I shall
nat be knowyn.'

Than sir Gryngamour gaff sir Gareth a bay coursor that
was a passynge good horse. Also he gaff hym good armour 30
and sure, and a noble swerde that somtyme sir Gringamours
fadir wan uppon an hethyn tyrraunte. And so thus every
knyght made hym redy to that turnemente.

And kynge Arthure was commyn two dayes tofore the **140^r**
Assumpcion of Oure Lady; and there was all maner of 35

---

2 *C* other but there   3 all *not in C*   8–9 *C* and his broder   10 *C* telle
not   14–15 *C* I wylle lene you a rynge but   18 *C* of hym†self   18 this
not in C   19–22 *C* it will torne to reed and that is reede it wil torne in lykenes
to grene And that is blewe it wil torne to (*S* in) lykenes of whyte and that is whyte
it wil torne in lykenes to blewe   23 *C* bereth my rynge   26 *C* hit   *S* it
35–p. 346, l. 1 *C* al maner of Royalte of al mynstralsye

royalté, of all maner of mynstralsy that myght be founde.
Also there cam quene Gwenyvere and the quene of Orkeney,
sir Garethis mother.

And uppon the Assumpcion day, whan masse and matyns
5 was done, there was herodys with trumpettis commaunded
to blow to the felde. And so there com oute sir Epynogrys,
the kynges son of Northumbirlonde, frome the castell; and
there encountyrde with hym sir Sagramoure le Desyrous,
and eythir of them brake there sperys to theire handis. And
10 than com in sir Palomydes oute of the castell; and there
encountyrd with hym sir Gawayne, and eythir of them
smote other so harde that bothe good knyghtes and their
horsis felle to the erthe. And than the knyghtes of eythir
party rescowed other.

15 Than cam in sir Safer and sir Segwarydes, bretherne to
Palamydes; and there encountyrd sir Aggravayne with sir
Safer, and sir Gaherys encountyrd with sir Segwarydes. So
sir Safer smote downe sir Aggravayne. And sir Malegryne,
a knyght of the castell, encountyrd with sir Uwayne le
20 Blaunche Maynes, and smote downe sir Malegryne, that
he had allmoste broke his necke.

(29)   Than sir Bryan de les Iles, and Grummor and Grummorson, knyghtes of the castell, encountyrde with sir Agglovale,
and sir Tor smote them of the castell downe.

25   Than com in sir Carados of the Dolowres Towre, and sir
Terquyne, knyghtes of the castell; and there encountyrd
with hem sir Percivale de Galys, and sir Lamerok, his
brother; and there [encountryd sir Percivale with sir Carados,
and eyther brake their speres unto their handes, and than
30 sir Terquyne with sir Lamerok, and eyther] smote downe
othir, hors and man, to the erthe; and eythir partyes rescowed
other and horsed them agayne.

---

5 *C* were done   12 *C* the good   13 *C* thenne knyghtes   14 *C* rescowed
their knyghtes   18–20 *C** doune Agrauayne syr Gawayns broder and sir Segwarydes syr Saferys broder And sir Malgryne And there syr Vwayne gaf syr
Malgryn a falle that   22–23 *C†* Grummore grummorssum   23 encountyrde *not
in C†*   24 *C** and syre Tor smote doun syr Gromere Gromorson† to the erth
W and smote   27–31 *C* syr Persyuale de galys & syr Launcelot† de galys that
were two bretheren And there encountred syr Percyuale with syre Caradus and
eyther brake their speres vnto their handes & thenne syr Turquyn with syre Lamerak
and eyther of hem smote doune others hors and allet to the   *W* there they smote
31 *W* eche othir (*see note*)

And sir Arnolde and sir Gawter, knyghtes of the castell, encountird wyth sir Brandyles and sir Kay; and thes four knyghtes encountyrde myghtely, and brake their sperys to theyre handis.

Than com in sir Trystrams, sir Saduk, and sir Dynas, knyghtes of the castell; and there encountyrd with sir Trys- **140ᵛ** trams sir Bedyvere, and sir Bedyvere was smyttyn to the erthe bothe horse and man. And sir Sadoke encountyrde wyth sir Petypace, and there sir Sadoke was overthrowyn. And there sir Uwayne les Avoutres smote downe sir Dynas the Senesciall.

Than com in sir Persaunte of Inde, a knyght of the castell; and there encountyrde with hym sir Launcelot du Lake, and there he smote sir Persaunte, horse and man, to the erthe. Than com in sir Pertolype frome the castell; and there encountyrde with hym sir Lyonell, and there sir Pertolype, the Grene Knyght, smote downe sir Lyonell, brothir to sir Launcelot.

And all this was marked wyth noble herrodis, who bare hym beste, and their namys.

And than com into the felde sir Perimones, the Grene Knyght, sir Persauntis brothir, that was a knyght of the castell; and he encountyrde wyth sir Ector de Marys, and aythir of hem smote other so harde that hir sperys and horsys and they felle to the erthe.

And than com in the Rede Knyght of the Rede Laundis and sir Gareth, frome the castell; and there encountyrde with hem sir Bors de Gaynys and sir Bleobrys. And there the Rede Knyght and sir Bors smote other so harde that hir sperys braste and their horsys felle grovelynge to the erthe. Than sir Blamour brake another spere uppon sir Gareth; but of that stroke sir Blamour felle to the erthe.

That sawe sir Galyhuddyn, and bade sir Gareth kepe hym; and sir Gareth smote hym anone to the erthe. Than sir Galyhud gate a spere to avenge his brother; and in the same wyse sir Gareth served hym. And in the same maner sir Gareth served sir Dynadan and his brother, sir La Kote

Male Tayle, and sir Sagramoure le Desyrus, and sir Donyas le Saveage: all these knyghtes he bare hem downe with one speare.

141ʳ　Whan kynge Anguyshauns of Irelonde sawe sir Gareth fare so, he mervayled what knyght he was; for at one tyme he semed grene, and another tyme at his gayne-commynge hym semed blewe. And thus at every course that he rode too and fro he chonged whyght to rede and blak, that there myght neyther kynge nother knyght have no redy cognys-shauns of hym.

Than kynge Anguyshaunce, the kynge of Irelonde, encountyrde with sir Gareth, and there sir Gareth smote hym frome his horse, sadyll and all. And than com in kynge Carados of Scotlonde, and sir Gareth smote hym downe horse and man; and in the same wyse he served kynge Uryens of the londe of Gore. And than come in sir Bagdemagus, and sir Gareth smote hym downe horse and man to the erthe; and kynge Bagdemagus son, sir Mellyagauns, brake a spere uppon sir Gareth myghtyly and knyghtly.

And than sir Galahalte the noble prynce cryed on hyght: 'Knyght with the many coloures, well haste thou justed! Now make the redy, that I may juste with the!'

Sir Gareth herde hym, and gate a grete spere, and so they encountyrde togydir, and there the prynce brake his spere; but sir Gareth smote hym uppon the buff syde of the helme, that he reled here and there, and had falle downe had nat his men recoverde hym.

'So God me helpe,' seyde kynge Arthure, 'that same knyght with the many coloures is a good knyght.' Where-fore the kynge called unto hym sir Launcelot and prayde hym to encountir with that knyght.

'Sir,' seyde sir Launcelot, 'I may well fynde in myne herte for to forbere hym as at this tyme, for he hath had travayle inowe this day. And whan a good knyght doth so well uppon som day, hit is no good knyghtes parte to lette hym of his

1 *C* Sagramor desirus　　2 *C* All these he bare doun　　4 *C* Aguysaûce† (*F* Anguins)　　5–6 *C* what he myght be þᵗ one tyme semed　　6–7 *C* ageyne comynge he semed blewe　　8–10 *C* chaunged his colour so that ther myghte neyther kynge nor knyghte haue redy conguyssaunce (*S* congnyssaunce) of hym　　11 *C* syr Anguyssaunce　　13 in *not in C*　　18 *C* Melyganus† (*F* Meleagans)　　23 *C* he gat　　25 *C* the lyfte syde　　26 *C* he had falle

worshyp, and namely whan he seyth a good knyghte hath
done so grete labur. For peraventure,' seyde sir Launcelot,
'his quarell is here this day, and peraventure he is beste
beloved with this lady of all that bene here: for I se well he   **141ᵛ**
paynyth hym and enforsyth hym to do grete dedys. And   5
therefore,' seyde sir Launcelot, 'as for me, this day he shall
have the honour: thoughe hit lay in my power to put hym
frome hit, yet wolde I nat.'

Than whan this was done there was drawynge of swerdys,   (30)
and than there began a sore turnemente. And there dud   10
sir Lameroke mervaylus dedys of armys; and bytwyxte sir
Lameroke and sir Ironsyde, that was the Rede Knyght of
the Rede Laundys, there was a stronge batayle. And sir
Palomydes and sir Bleobrys, betwyxte them was full grete
batayle. And sir Gawayne and sir Trystrams mett; and there   15
sir Gawayne had the worse, for he pulled sir Gawayne frome
his horse, and there he was longe uppon foote and defouled.

Than com in sir Launcelot, and he smote sir Terquyn,
and he hym. And than cam therein sir Carados, his brother,
and bothe at onys they assayled hym, and he as the moste   20
noblyst knyght of the worlde worshypfully fought with
hem bothe and helde them hote, that all men wondred of
the nobles of sir Launcelot.

And than com in sir Gareth, and knew that hit was sir Launcelot that fought with tho perelous knyghtes, and parted   25
them in sundir; and no stroke wolde he smyte sir Launcelot.
That aspyed sir Launcelot and demed hit sholde be the good
knyght sir Gareth.

And than sir Gareth rode here and there and smote on
the ryght honde and on the lyffte honde, that all folkys   30
myght well aspye where that he rode. And by fortune he
mette with his brother, sir Gawayne; and there he put hym
to the wors, for he put of his helme. And so he served fyve
or six knyghtes of the Rounde Table, that all men seyde he
put hym in moste payne and beste he dud his dever.   35

1 good *not in C*   8 *C* it I wold not   13–15 *C* & betwix syre Palamides &
Bleoberys there was a strong batail   19 therein *not in C*   22 and helde them
hote *not in C*†   25–26 *C** with tho peryllous knyghtes And thenne syr
Gareth came with his good hors and hurtled hem in sonder   26 *C* smyte to syr
Launcelot   30 *C* alle the folke   32–33 *C* put syr Gawayne to   35 *C*
in the most   *C* his deuoyr

For whan sir Trystrams behylde hym how he fyrste justed and aftir fought so welle with a swerde, than he rode **142ʳ** unto sir Ironsyde and to sir Persaunte of Inde, and asked hem be their fayth what maner a knyght yondir knyght is 5 that semyth in so many dyvers coloures.

'Truly mesemyth,' seyde sir Trystrams, 'that he puttyth hymself in grete payne, for he never sesyth.'

'Wote nat ye what he is?' seyde Ironsyde.

'No,' seyde sir Trystrams.

10 'Than shall ye knowe that this is he that lovyth the lady of the castell, and she hym agayne. And this is he that wanne me whan I beseged the lady of this castell; and this is he that wanne sir Persaunte of Inde and his three brethirne.'

'What is his name?' seyde sir Trystrams, 'and of what 15 bloode is he com?'

'Sir, he was called in the courte of kynge Arthure Bewmaynes, but his ryght name is sir Gareth of Orkeney, brother unto sir Gawayne.'

'By my hede,' seyde sir Trystrams, 'he is a good knyght 20 and a bygge man of armys: and yf he be yonge, he shall preve a full noble knyght.'

'Sir, he is but a chylde,' he seyde, 'and of sir Launcelot he was made knyght.'

'Therefore is he muche the bettir,' seyde sir Trystrams.

25 And than sir Trystrams, sir Ironsyde, and sir Persaunte and his bretherne rode togydyrs for to helpe sir Gareth. And than there was many sadde strokis, and than sir Gareth rode oute on the tone syde to amende his helme.

Than seyde his dwarff, 'Take me your rynge, that ye lose 30 hit nat whyle that ye drynke.' And so whan he had drunkyn he gate on hys helme, and egirly toke his horse and rode into the felde, and leffte his rynge with his dwarff: for the dwarf was glad the rynge was frome hym, for than he wyste well he sholde be knowyn.

35 And whan sir Gareth was in the felde, all folkys sawe hym well and playnly that he was in yealow colowres. And

4 *C* knyghte is yonder knyght   7 *W* hymselfe   11 *C* she gym† (*S* hym)
12 *C* wannne (*S* wanne)   is *not in C*†   15–16 *C* come he was   19 *C*† kniȝt
knyght   22 Sir *not in C*   *C* child they all saide   24 *C* mykel the better
26 *C* his broder   27 *C* there were gyuen many strong strokes   32 *C* and
the dwerf   35 *C* And thenne whan

there he raced of helmys and pulled downe knyghtes, that
kynge Arthure had mervayle what knyght he was. For the
kynge sawe by his horse that hit was the same knyght, 'but **142ᵛ**
byfore he was in so many coloures, and now he is but in one (31)
coloure, and that is yolowe.' 5

'Now goo,' seyde kynge Arthure unto dyvers herowdys,
and bede hem, 'Ryde aboute hym, and aspye yf ye can se what
maner of knyght he is; for I have spered of many knyghtes
this day that is uppon his party, and all sey that they knowe
hym nought.' 10

But at the laste an herrowde rode nyghe sir Gareth as he
coude, and there he sawe wryten aboute his helme in golde,
seyynge: 'This helme is sir Garethis of Orkeney.' Than
the heroude cryed as he were woode, and many herowdys
with hym: 15

'This is sir Gareth of Orkenay in the yealow armys!'

Thereby all the kynges and knyghtes of kynge Arthurs
party behelde and awayted; and than they presed all knyghtes
to beholde hym, and ever the herrowdys cryed and seyde:
'This is sir Gareth, kynge Lottys son of Orkeney!' 20

And whan sir Gareth aspyed that he was discoverde, than
he dowbled his strokys and smote downe there sir Sagramoure and his brother sir Gawayne.

'A, brother,' seyde sir Gawayne, 'I wente ye wolde have
smyttyn me.' 25

So whan he herde hym sey so, he thrange here and there,
and so with grete payne he gate oute of the pres, and there
he mette with his dwarff.

'A, boy!' seyde sir Gareth, 'thou haste begyled me fowle
this day of my rynge. Geff hit me faste, that I may hyde my 30
body withall!' And so he toke hit hym; and than they all
wyst [not] where he was becom.

And sir Gawayne had in maner aspyed where sir Gareth

3 *C* by his here†   5 *C* colour that is yelowe   7 bede hem *not in C*   yf ye
can se *not in C*   8 of *not in C*   *C* knyght *S* knyghte   9 *C* that ben vpon
10–11 *C* hym not And so an heroude   13 seyynge *not in C*   17–18 *C* that†
by all kynges and knyghtes of Arthurs beheld hym & awayted   18 knyghtes
not in C   19 and seyde *not in C*   20 *C* gareth of Orkeney kyng Lots sone
22 there *not in C*   24 *C* O broder   24–26 *C* ye wolde not haue stryken me so
whan (*see note*)   29 *C* O boye   30 *C* day that thou kepte my rynge Gyue
it me anone ageyn that   32 *W* wyste

rode, and than he rode aftir with all his myght. That aspyed
sir Gareth and rode wyghtly into the [foreste]. For all that
sir Gawayne coude do, he wyste nat where he was becom.

And whan sir Gareth wyste that sir Gawayne was paste,
5 he asked the dwarff of beste counsayle.

'Sir,' seyde the dwarff, 'mesemyth hit were beste, now
that ye ar ascaped frome spyynge, that ye sende my lady,
143ʳ dame Lyones of the castell, hir rynge.'

'Hit is well avysed,' seyde sir Gareth. 'Now have hit
10 here and bere hit her, and sey that I recommaunde me unto
hir good grace; and sey hir I woll com whan I may, and
pray hir to be trewe and faythfull to me as I woll be to
hir.'

'Sir,' seyde the dwarff, 'hit shall be done as ye com-
15 maunde me.'

And so he rode his way and dud his erande unto the lady.
Than seyde she, 'Where is my knyght, sir Gareth?'

'Madam, he bade me sey that he wolde nat be longe frome
you.'

20 And so lyghtly the dwarff com agayne unto sir Gareth
that wolde full fayne have had a lodgynge, for he had nede
to be reposed.

And than fell there a thundir and a rayne, as hevyn and
erthe sholde go togydir. And sir Gareth was nat a lytyll
25 wery, for of all that day he had but lytyll reste, nother his
horse nor he. So thus sir Gareth rode longe in that foreste
untyll nyght cam; and ever hit lyghtend and thundirde as
hit had bene wylde. At the laste by fortune he cam to a cas-
(32) tell, and there he herde the waytis uppon the wallys. Than
30 sir Gareth rode unto the barbycan of the castell, and prayed
the porter fayre to lette hym into the castell. The porter
answerde ungoodly agayne and sayde,

'Thou gettyste no lodgynge here.'

'Fayre sir, sey not so, for I am a knyght of kynge Arthurs;
35 and pray the lorde and the lady of this castell to gyff me
herborow for the love of kynge Arthour.'

2-3 *W* the castel (*not emended in O¹*)   *C* rode lyghtely in to the forest* (*cf. l. 26*)
that syr Gawayn wist not where   8 of the castell *not in C*   10 *C* to her
11-12 *C* and I pray   15 me *not in C*   18 *C* Madam said the dwerf he
26 *C* thist syr Gareth rode soo longe   27 *C* the nyghte   28 *C* ben woode
35 *C* lord or the

Than the porter wente unto the douches and tolde hir how there was a knyght of kynge Arthures wolde have herborow.

'Latte hym in,' seyde the douches, 'for I woll see that knyght. And for kynge Arthurs love he shall nat be her- 5
borowles.'

Than she yode up into a towre over the gate with tourchis ilyght. Whan sir Gareth saw that lyght he cryed on hyghe:

'Whethir thou be lorde or lady, gyaunte other champyon, I take no forse, so that I may have herborow as for this 10
nyght: and yf hit be so that I muste nedis fyght, spare me nat to-morne whan I have rested me; for bothe I and myne **143ᵛ**
horse be wery.'

'Sir knyght,' seyde the lady, 'ye speke knyghtly and boldely; but wete you well the lorde of this castell lovyth nat 15
kynge Arthure nother none of hys courte, for my lorde hath ever bene ayenste hym. And therefore thow were bettir nat to com within his castell; for and thou com in this nyght, thou muste com undir this fourme, that wheresomever thou mete hym, by fylde other by strete, thou muste yelde the to 20
hym as presonere.'

'Madam,' seyde sir Gareth, 'what is your lorde and what is his name?'

'Sir, my lordys name is the deuke de la Rouse.'

'Well, madam,' seyde sir Gareth, 'I shal promyse you in 25
what place I mete youre lorde I shall yelde me unto hym and to his good grace, with that I undirstonde that he woll do me no shame. And yf I undirstonde that he woll, I woll relece myself and I can with my spere and my swerde.'

'Ye say well,' seyde the deuches.   30

Than she lette the drawbrygge downe; and so he rode into the halle and there he alyght, and the horse was ladde into the stable. And in the halle he unarmed hym and seyde,

'Madam, I woll nat oute of this halle this nyght. And whan hit is daylyght, lat se who woll have ado with me; than 35
he shall fynde me redy.'

---

5 *C* Arthurs sake   7–8 *C* with greete torche lyght   8 *C* that torche lyght
10 as for *not in C*   13 *C* ben wery   14 *C* thou spekest   15 *C* wete thou
19 *C* in vnder suche fourme   20 *C** mete my lord by sty3 or by strete   28 *C*
no harme   *C* I wil I (*S* I wil)   32 *C* his hors   35 than *not in C*

917.44   A a

Than was he sette unto souper and had many good dysshis. Than sir Gareth lyste well to ete, and full knyghtly he ete his mete and egirly. Also there was many a fayre lady by hym, and som seyd they nevir sawe a goodlyer man 5 nothir so well of etynge. Than they made hym passynge good chere; and shortly, whan he had souped, his bedde was made there, and so he rested hym all nyght. And in the morne he herde masse and brake hys faste, and toke his leve at the douches and at them all, and thanked hir goodly of 10 hir lodgyng and of hir good chere. And than she asked hym his name.

'Truly, madam,' he seyde, 'my name is sir Gareth of **144ʳ** Orkeney, and som men call me Bewmaynes.'

Than knew she well hit was the same knyght that faught 15 for dame Lyonesse.

So sir Gareth departed and rode up unto a mountayne, and there mette hym a knyght, his name was sir Bendaleyne. And he seyde to sir Gareth,

'Thou shalt nat passe this way, for other thou shalt juste 20 with me othir ellys be my presonere.'

'Than woll I juste,' seyde sir Gareth.

And so they lette their horsis ren, and there sir Gareth smote hym thorowoute the body, and sir Bendelayne rode forth to his castell there besyde, and there dyed. So sir 25 Gareth wolde have rested hym fayne. So hit happed hym to com to sir Bendalaynes castell. Than his knyghtys and servauntys aspyed that hit was he that had slayne there lorde. Than they armed twenty good men and com oute and assayled sir Gareth. And so he had no spere, but his swerde, 30 and so he put his shylde afore hym, and there they brake ten sperys uppon hym. And they assayled hym passyngly sore, but ever sir Gareth defended hym as a knyght.

(33)　　So whan they sawe they myght nat overcom hym they rode frome hym, and toke their counceyle to sle his horse. 35 And so they cam in uppon sir Gareth, and so with hir sperys they slewe his horse, and than they assayled hym harde.

2 full *not in* C　　10 *C* of his good　　10–12 *C* asked gym† his name Madame
he saide truly my　　18 he *not in* C　　25–26 *C* rested hym and he cam rydynge
to Bendalaynis　　30 so he *not in* C　　30–31 *C* brake their sperys　　31 *C*
assailled hem†　　35 hir *not in* C

But whan he was on foote there was none that he raught
but he gaff hym such a buffette that he dud never recover.
So he slew hem by one and one tyll they were but four; and
there they fledde. And sir Gareth toke a good horse that
was one of theires and rode his way. Than he rode a grete 5
pace tyll that he cam to a castell, and there he herde muche
mournyng of ladyes and jantyllwomen. So at the laste there
cam by hym a payge. Than he asked of hym,

'What noyse is this that I hyre within this castell?'

'Sir knyght,' seyde the payge, 'here be within this castell 10
thirty ladyes, and all they be wydowys. For here is a knyght **144ᵛ**
that waytyth dayly uppon this castell, and he is callyd the
Browne Knyght wythoute Pyté, and he is the perelust
knyght that now lyvyth. And therefore, sir,' seyde the
payge, 'I rede you fle.' 15

'Nay,' seyde sir Gareth, 'I woll nat fle, though thou be
aferde of hym.'

Than the payge saw where cam the Browne Knyght, and
sayde,

'Lo yondir he commyth!' 20

'Lat me dele with hym,' seyde sir Gareth. And whan aythir
of othir had a syghte, they let theire horsis ren, and the Browne
Knyght brake his spere, and sir Gareth smote hym thorow
the body, that he overthrewe [hym] to the grounde sterke
dede. So sir Gareth rode into the castell and prayde the 25
ladyes that he myght repose hym.

'Alas!' seyde the ladyes, 'ye may nat be lodged here.'

'Yes, hardely, make hym good chere,' seyde the payge,
'for this knyght hath slayne your enemy.'

Than they all made hym good chere as lay in theire power. 30
But wete you well they made hym good chere, for they
myght none other do, for they were but poore. And so on
the morne he wente to masse and there he sawe the thirty
ladyes knele and lay grovelynge uppon dyverse toumbis,
makynge grete dole and sorow. Than sir Gareth knew well 35
that in tho tombis lay their lordys.

7 at the laste *not in C*   8–9 *C* page what noyse is this said syr gareth that
12 *C* and his name is   18–20 *C* knyghte loo said the page yonder   23 *C* thorou
oute   24 *Not emended in* O¹   28 Yes, hardely *not in C*   28–30 *W*
(*sidenote*): How sir Gareth slew the Browne Knyght   28 *P omits sig. p iiii*
32 *C* otherwyse doo   36 *C* the tombes

'Fayre ladyes,' seyde sir Gareth, 'ye muste at the next feste be at the courte of kynge Arthure, and sey that I, sir Gareth, sente you thydir.'

'Sir, we shall do your commaundemente,' seyde the ladyes.

5 So he departed; and by fortune he cam to a mountayne, and there he founde a goodly knyght that bade hym 'Abyde, sir knyght, and juste with me!'

'What ar ye?' seyde sir Gareth.

'My name is,' he seyde, 'called deuke de la Rowse.'

10 'A, sir, ye ar the same knyght that I lodged onys within your castell, and there I made promyse unto youre lady that I sholde yelde me to you.'

'A,' seyde the deuke, 'arte thou that proude knyght that profyrde to fyght with my knyghtes? Therefore make the 15 redy, for I woll have ado wyth you.'

So they let their horsis renne, and there sir Gareth smote the deuke downe frome his horse: but the deuke lyghtly 145ʳ avoyded his horse and dressed his shylde and drew his swerde, and bade sir Gareth alyght and fyght with hym.

20 So he dud alyght, and they dud grete batayle togedyrs more than an houre, and eythir hurte other full sore. But at the laste sir Gareth gate the deuke to the erthe, and wolde have slayne hym; and than he yelded hym.

'Than muste ye go,' seyde sir Gareth, 'unto kynge 25 Arthure, my lorde, at the next hyghe feste, and sey that I, sir Gareth, sente you thydir.'

'We shall do this,' seyde the deuke, 'and I woll do you omage and feauté wyth an hondredsom of knyghtes with me, and all the dayes of my lyff to do you servyse where ye 30 woll commaunde me.'

(34) So the deuke departed, and sir Gareth stoode there alone. And as he stoode he sey an armed knyght on horsebak commynge towarde hym. Than sir Gareth mownted uppon horsebak, and so withoute ony wordis they ran togedir as

2 *C* feeste of Pentecost   3–4 *C* thyder we shal doo this said the ladyes   5 *C* monntayne (*S* mountayne)   9 *C* is said he the duke   14 *C* proferest
21 But *not in C*   23 *C* yelded hym to hym   24–25 *C* syr Arthur   26–27 *C* sir Gareth of Orkeney sente you vnto hym hit shal be done said the duke   28 *C* an
C knyȝtes   31–32 *C* alone and there he sawe   32 on horsebak *not in C*
33–p. 357, l. 1 *C** Gareth toke the dukes shelde and mounted vpon horsbak and soo withoute bydyng they ranne to gyder as it had ben the thonder

thundir. And there that knyght hurte sir Gareth undir the
syde with his spere, and than they alyght and drewe there
swerdys and gaff grete strokys, that the bloode trayled downe
to the grounde; and so they fought two owres. So at the laste
there com the damesell Lyonette that som men calle the dame- 5
sell Savyage. And she com rydynge uppon an ambelynge
mule, and there she cryed all on hygh:

'Sir Gawayne! leve thy fyghtynge with thy brothir, sir
Gareth!'

And whan he herde hir sey so, he threwe away his shylde 10
and his swerde, and ran to sir Gareth and toke hym in his
armys, and sytthen kneled downe and asked hym mercy.

'What ar ye,' seyde sir Gareth, 'that ryght now were so
stronge and so myghty, and now so sodeynly is yelde to me?'

'A, sir Gareth, I am your brother, sir Gawayne, that for 15
youre sake have had grete laboure and travayle.'

Than sir Gareth unlaced hys helme, and kneled downe
to hym and asked hym mercy. Than they arose bothe, and
braced eythir othir in there armys, and wepte a grete whyle
or they myght speke; and eythir of them gaff other the pryse 20
of the batayle, and there were many kynde wordys betwene
them.

'Alas! my fayre brother,' seyde sir Gawayne, 'I ought of **145ᵛ**
ryght to worshyp you, and ye were nat my brother, for ye
have worshipte kynge Arthure and all his courte, for ye 25
have sente mo worshypfull knyghtes this twelve-monthe
than fyve the beste of the Rounde Table hath done excepte
sir Launcelot.'

Than cam the lady Savyaige, that was the lady Lyonet that
rode with sir Gareth so long; and there she dud staunche 30
sir Gareths woundis and sir Gawaynes.

'Now what woll ye do?' seyde the damesell Saveaige.
'Mesemyth hit were beste that kynge Arthure had wetynge
of you bothe: for your horsis ar so brused that they may not
beare.'   35

'Now, fayre damesell,' seyde sir Gawayne, 'I pray you

3 downe *not in C*   5 *C* ther   *S* there   8 *C* syr Gawayne syr Gawayne
14–15 *C* sodenly yelde you to me O Gareth   16–17 *C* grete sorou and labour
Thenne   18–19 *C* rose both and enbraced   23–24 *C* gawayn perde I owe of
ryghte   26 *C* sente me† to   27 *C* than syxe the best   29, 32 *C* the
damoysel saueage   33 *C* me semeth that it were wel do þᵗ Arthur

ryde unto my lorde, myne unkle kynge Arthure, and tell
hym what adventure is betydde me here; and I suppose he
woll nat tary longe.'

Than she toke hir mule and lyghtly she rode to kynge
5 Arthure, that was but two myle thens. And whan she had
tolde hir tydynges to the kynge, the kynge bade, 'Gete me
a palefrey!' And whan he was on horsebak he bade the
lordys and ladyes com aftir and they wolde; and there was
sadelyng and brydelyng of quenys and prynces horsis, and
10 well was he that sonneste myght be redy.

So whan the kynge cam there, he saw sir Gawayne and
sir Gareth sitt uppon a lytyll hyllys syde. Than the kynge
avoyded his horse, and whan he cam nye to sir Gareth he
wolde a spokyn and myght nat, and therewyth he sanke
15 downe in a sowghe for gladnesse.

And so they sterte unto theire uncle and requyred hym
of his good grace to be of good comforte. Wete you well
the kynge made grete joy! And many a peteuous complaynte
he made to sir Gareth, and ever he wepte as he had bene
20 a chylde.

So with this com his modir, the quene of Orkeney, dame
Morgawse, and whan she saw sir Gareth redyly in the
vysage she myght nat wepe, but sodeynly felle downe in
146ʳ a sowne and lay there a grete whyle lyke as she had bene
25 dede. And than sir Gareth recomforted hir in suche wyse
that she recovirde and made good chere.

Than the kynge commaunded that all maner of knyghtes
that were undir his obeysaunce sholde make their lodgynge
ryght there, for the love of his two nevewys. And so hit
30 was done, and all maner of purveya[n]s purveyde, that there
lacked nothynge that myght be gotyn for golde nother
sylver, nothir of wylde nor tame.

And than by the meanys of the damesell Saveaige sir Gawayne and sir Gareth were heled of their woundys; and

---

2 *C* aduenture is to me betyd here   4 *C* lyghtly she came to   6–7 *C* told
hym tydynges the kynge bad gete hym a palfroy   7 *C* was vpon his bak he
badde   8 *C* after who that wold   9–10 *C* quenes horses and prynces horses
& well was hym that soonest   11 *C* there as they were he sawe   13 to *not*
in C   14 *C* wold haue spoken but he myghte not   20–21 *C* chyld With that
25 *C* recomforted his moder   30 *C** of purueaunce *WO*¹ purveyars
31–33 *C* goten of tame nor wylde for gold or syluer And

there they suggeourned eyght dayes. Than seyde kynge Arthure unto the damesell Saveaige,

'I mervayle that youre sistyr, dame Lyonesse, comyth
nat hydir to me; and in especiall that she commyth nat to
vysyte hir knyght, my nevewe, sir Gareth, that hath had so 5
muche travayle for hir love.'

'My lorde,' seyde the damesell Lyonette, 'ye muste of
your good grace holde hir excused, for she knowyth nat that
my lorde sir Gareth is here.'

'Go ye than for hir,' seyde kynge Arthure, 'that we may 10
be apoynted what is beste to done accordynge to the plesure
of my nevewe.'

'Sir,' seyde the damesell, 'hit shall be do.'

And so she rode unto hir sistir, and as lyghtly as she myght
make hir redy she cam on the morne with hir brother, sir 15
Gryngamour, and with hir fourty knyghtes. And so whan
she was com she had all the chere that myght be done bothe
of the kynge and of many other knyghtes and also quenys.
And amonge all thes ladyes she was named the fayryst and (35)
pyereles. Than whan sir Gareth mette with hir, there was 20
many a goodly loke and goodly wordys, that all men of worshyp had joy to beholde them.

Than cam kynge Arthure and many othir kynges, and
dame Gwenyvere and quene Morgawse, his modir; and
there the kynge asked his nevew, sir Gareth, whether he 25
wolde have this lady as peramour, other ellys to have hir to
his wyff.

'My lorde, wete you well that I love hir abovyn all ladyes
lyvynge.'   **146ᵛ**

'Now, fayre lady,' sayde kynge Arthure, 'what sey ye?'   30

'My moste noble kynge,' seyde dame Lyonesse, 'wete
you well that my lorde, sir Gareth, ys to me more lever to
have and welde as my husbonde than ony kyng other prynce
that is crystyned; and if I may nat have hym, I promyse
you I woll never have none. For, my lorde Arthure,' seyde 35
dame Lyonesse, 'wete you well he is my fyrste love, and he

4 *C* not here to   10 ye *not in C*   15 *C* made her redy & she   18 *R*
many other kynges and quenys   *P* many other (kynges and quenes *omitted*)
20 *C*† Gawayn sawe her   24–25 *C* Gweneuer & the quene of Orkeney
And there   26 *C* peramour or to haue her   31 *My not in C*

shall be the laste; and yf ye woll suffir hym to have his wyll
and fre choyse, I dare say he woll have me.'

'That is trouthe,' seyde sir Gareth, 'and I have nat you
and welde you as my wyff, there shall never lady nother
5 jantyllwoman rejoyse me.'

'What, nevewe?' seyde the kynge. 'Is the wynde in that
dore? For wete you well I wolde nat for the stynte [of] my
crowne to be causer to withdraw your hertys. And wete you
well ye can nat love so well but I shall rather encrece hyt
10 than discrece hit; and also ye shall have my love and my
lordeshyp in the uttirmuste wyse that may lye in my power.'
And in the same wyse seyde sir Garethys modir.

So anone there was made a provision for the day of
maryaige, and by the kynges advyse hit was provyded that hit
15 sholde be at Mychaelmasse folowyng, at Kyng Kenadowne,
by the seesyde; for there is a plenteuouse contrey. And so
hit was cryed in all the placis thorow the realme. And than
sir Gareth sente his somons to all tho knyghtes and ladyes
that he had wonne in batayle tofore, that they sholde be at
20 his day of maryage at Kyng Kenadowne, by the seeseyde.

And than dame Lyonesse and the damesell Lyonet wyth
sir Gryngamour rode to their castell, and a goodly and a
ryche rynge she gaff to sir Gareth, and he gaff hir another.
And kynge Arthure gaff hir a ryche bye of golde, and so she
147ʳ 25 departed. And kynge Arthure and his felyshyp rode towarde
Kyng Kenadowne; and sir Gareth brought his lady on the
way, and so cam to the kynge agayne, and rode wyth hym.
Lorde, the grete chere that sir Launcelot made of sir Gareth
and he of hym! For there was no knyght that sir Gareth
30 loved so well as he dud sir Launcelot; and ever for the moste
party he wolde ever be in sir Launcelottis company.

For evir aftir sir Gareth had aspyed sir Gawaynes condu-
cions, he wythdrewe hymself fro his brother sir Gawaynes
felyship, for he was evir vengeable, and where he hated
35 he wolde be avenged with murther: and that hated sir
Gareth.

4 *C* weld not you   9 *C*† you con not   10 *C*† dystresse hit   13 *C* thenne
there was   15, 26 *C* kynkenadon   16 *C* is a (a *not in S*) plentyful   20 *C*
kynkenadon by the sandes   24 *C* ryche bee   29 *C* there was neuer no
31 *C* he wolde be   32 *C* for after   34 evir *not in C*

So hit drew faste to Mychaelmas, that hydir cam the lady (36)
dame Lyonesse, the lady of the Castell Perelus, and hir
sister, the damesell Lyonet, with sir Gryngamour, her
brother, with hem; for he had the conduyte of thes ladyes.
And there they were lodged at the devyse of kynge Arthure. 5

And uppon Myghelmas day the bysshop of Caunturbyry
made the weddyng betwene sir Gareth and dame Lyonesse
with grete solempnyté. And kynge Arthure made sir Gaherys to wedde the damesell Saveage, dame Lyonet. And
sir Aggravayne kynge Arthure made to wedde dame Lyones- 10
seis neese, a fayre lady; hir name was dame Lawrell.

And so whan this solempnyté was done, than com in the
Grene Knyght, sir Pertolope, with thirty knyghtes; and there
he dud omage and feauté to sir Gareth, and all thes knyghtes
to holde of hym for evermore. Also sir Pertolope seyde,   15
'I pray you that at this feste I may be your chambirlayne.'
'With good wyll,' seyde sir Gareth, 'syth hit lyke you to
take so symple an offyce.'

Than com in the Rede Knyght wyth three score knyghtes
with hym, and dud to sir Gareth omage and feauté, and all 20
tho knyghtes to holde of hym for evermore. And than sir
Perimones prayde sir Gareth to graunte hym to be his chyeff
butler at the hygh feste.   147ᵛ
'I woll well,' seyde sir Gareth, 'that ye have this offyce and
hit were bettir.'   25

Than com in sir Persaunte of Inde wyth an hondred
knyghtes with hym, and there he dud omage and feauté,
and all his knyghtes sholde do hym servyse and holde their
londis of hym for evir. And there he prayde sir Gareth to
make hym his sewear cheyff at that hyghe feste.   30
'I woll well,' seyde sir Gareth, 'that ye have hit and hit
were bettir.'

Than com in the deuke de la Rouse with an hondred
knyghtes with hym; and there he dud omage and feauté
to sir Gareth, and so to holde there londis of hym for ever- 35

1–2 *C* and thyder came dame Lyones   1–3 *W* (*sidenote*): The weddynge of
sir Gareth and of sir Aggravayne his brothir   9–11 *C* saueage that was dame
Lynet and kyng Arthur made syr Agrauayne to wedde dame Lyones nees   11 *C*
Laurel   12 *C* solemnacion   17 *C* a good   *C* it lyketh   18 *C* on† offyce
21–22 *C* this syr Perymonyes   23 *C* that hyghe   30–31 *C* at the feest I will (*S*
wil)   33 *C* dukde† la rowse   35–p. 362, l. 1 *C* for euer And

more. And he requyred sir Gareth that he myght serve hym of the wyne that day of the hyghe feste.

'I woll well,' seyde sir Gareth, 'and hit were bettir.'

Than cam the Rede Knyght of the Rede Laundis that
5 hyght sir Ironsyde, and he brought with hym three hondred knyghtes; and there he dud omage and feauté, and all tho knyghtes to holde their londys of hym for ever. And than he asked of sir Gareth to be his kerver.

'I woll well,' seyde sir Gareth, 'and hit please you.'

10 Than com into the courte thirty ladyes, and all they semed wydows; and tho ladyes brought with hem many fayre jantyllwomen, and all they kneled downe at onys unto kynge Arthure and unto sir Gareth; and there all tho ladyes tolde the kynge how that sir Gareth had delyverde them fro the
15 Dolorous Towre, and slew the Browne Knyght withoute Pyté: 'and therefore all we and oure ayres for evermore woll do omage unto sir Gareth of Orkeney.'

So than the kynges, quenys, pryncis, erlys, barouns, and many bolde knyghtes wente to mete; and well may ye wete
20 that there was all maner of plenté and all maner revels and game, with all maner of mynstralsy that was used tho dayes. Also there was grete justys three dayes, but the kynge wolde nat suffir sir Gareth to juste, because of his new bryde; for, as the Freynsh boke seyth, that dame Lyonesse desyred
148ʳ 25 of the kynge that none that were wedded sholde juste at that feste.

So the fyrste day there justed sir Lameroke de Gelys, for he [o]verthrewe thirty knyghtes and dud passyng mervelus dedis of armys. And than kynge Arthure made sir Per-
30 saunte and his bretherne knyghtes o[f] the Rounde Table to their lyvys ende, and gaff hem grete landys.

Also the secunde day there justed sir Trystrams beste, and he overthrew fourty knyghtes, and dud there mervelus dedis of armys. And there kynge Arthure made sir Ironsyde,
35 that was the Rede Knyght of the Rede Laundys, a knyght of the Table Rounde to his lyvis ende, and gaff hym grete landis.

2 *C* day at that feest   4 *C* came in   11 *C* tho thyrtty ladyes   14 had
not in C   18 *C* prynces & erlys   20–21 *C* there were al maner (*S* manere) of
mete plentyuously alle manere rules† and games with al manere of mynstralsy
28 *W* euerthrewe   *C* passyng merueillously   30 *W* ot the rounde   *C* of the
round

Than the thirde day there justed sir Launcelot, and he
overthrew fyfty knyghtes and dud many dedis of armys,
that all men wondird. And there kynge Arthure made the
deuke de la Rowse a knyght of the Table Rounde to his
lyvys ende, and gaff hym grete londis to spende.   5

But whan this justis was done, sir Lameroke and sir
Trystrams departed suddeynly and wolde nat be knowyn;
for the whych kyng Arthure and all the courte was sore
dysplesid.

And so they helde the courte fourty dayes with grete 10
solempnyté. And thus sir Gareth of Orkeney was a noble
knyght, that wedded dame Lyonesse of the Castell Parelus.
And also sir Gaheris wedded her sistir, dame Lyonette, that
was called the damesell Saveaige. And sir Aggravayne
wedded dame Lawrell, a fayre lady wyth grete and myghty 15
londys, wyth grete ryches igyffyn wyth them, that ryally
they myght lyve tyll theire lyvis ende.

AND I PRAY YOU ALL THAT REDYTH THIS TALE TO PRAY
FOR HYM THAT THIS WROTE, THAT GOD SENDE HYM GOOD
DELYVERAUNCE SONE AND HASTELY. AMEN.   20

HERE ENDYTH THE TALE OF SIR GARETH OF ORKENEY.

1 *C* launcelot du lake   2 *C* many merueyllous dedes   3 *C* wondred on hym
8 *C* were sore   11–12 *C* And this syr Gareth was a noble knyghte and a wel
rulyd and fayr langaged Thus endeth this tale of syr Gareth of Orkeney that
wedded   15 *C* and grete   16 *C* gaf with them kyng Arthur that ryally
17–21 *C* ende Here foloweth the viii book the which is the first book of sir Tristram
de Lyones & who was his fader & his moder & hou he was borne and fosteryd And
how he was made knyghte

THE BOOK

OF

SIR TRISTRAM DE LYONES

[*Winchester MS., ff. 148ᵛ–346ᵛ; Caxton, Books VIII–XII*]

I

ISODE THE FAIR

[*Winchester MS., ff. 148ᵛ–181ᵛ;*
Caxton, Book VIII, chs. 1–37]

CAXTON'S RUBRICS

1. How syr Trystram de Lyones was borne and how his moder deyed at his byrthe, wherfore she named hym Tristram.

2. How the stepmoder of syr Trystram had ordeyned poyson for to have poysened syr Trystram.

3. How syr Trystram was sente into Fraunce and had one to governe hym named Governayle, and how he lernyd to harpe, hawke, and hunte.

4. How syr Marhaus came out of Irelonde for to aske trewage of Cornewayle, or ellys he wold fyght therfor.*

5. How Trystram enterprysed the bataylle to fyght for the trewage of Cornwayl and how he was made knyght.

6. How syr Trystram arryved into the ilond for to furnysshe the bataylle with syr Marhaus.

7. Hoow syr Tristram faught ayenst syr Marhaus and achyeved his batayl, and how syr Marhaus fledde to his shyppe.

8. How syr Marhaus after that he was arryved in Irelonde dyed of the stroke that syr Trystram had gyven to hym, and how Trystram was hurte.

9. How syr Trystram was put to the kepyng of La Bele Ysoude fyrst to be helyd of hys wounde.

10. How syr Trystram wanne the degree at a tournoyment in Irelonde, and there made Palomydes to bere no harnoys in a yere.

11. How the quene espyed that syr Tristram had slayn hir broder syr Marhaus by his swerde and in what jeopardye he was.

12. How syr Trystram departed fro the kyng and La Bele Isoude out of Irelonde for to come into Cornewayl.

13. How syr Trystram and kyng Marke hurted eche other for the love† of a knyghtes wyf.

14. How syr Trystram laye wyth the lady, and how her husbond faught wyth syr Trystram.

15. How syr Bleoberis demaunded the fayrest lady in kyng Marks court, whom he toke awaye, and how he was foughten with.

16. How syr Trystram faught wyth two knyghtes of the Rounde Table.

17. How syr Tristram‡ faught with syr Bleoberis for a lady, and how the lady was put to choyse to whome she wold goo.

* S therefor   † C lone   S loue   ‡ C Tristcum

18. How the lady forsoke syr Tristram and abode with syr Bleoberis, and how she desyred to goo to hyr husbond.

19. How kyng Mark sent syr Trystram for La Beale Isoude toward Irelond, and how by fortune he arryved into Englond.

20. How kyng Anguysshe of Irelonde was somoned to come to kyng Arthurs courte for treason.

21. How syr Trystram rescowed a chylde fro a knyght, and how Governayle tolde hym* of kyng Anguysshe.

22. How syr Trystram faught for syr Anguysshe and overcame hys adversarye, and how his adversarye wold never yelde hym.

23. How syr Blamor desyred Trystram to slee hym, and how syr Tristram spared hym, and how they took appoyntement.

24. How syr Tristram demaunded La Bele Isoude for kynge Mark, and how syr Trystram and Isoude dronken the love drynke.

25. How syr Tristram and Isoude were in pryson, and how he faughte for hir beauté and smote of another ladyes hede.

26. How syr Trystram faught wyth syr Breunor and atte laste smote of his hede.

27. How syr Galahad faught wyth syr Tristram, and how syr Tristram yelded hym and promysed to felaushyp with Lancelot.

28. How syr Launcelot mette with syr Carados beryng awaye sir Gawayn, and of the rescows of syr Gawayn.

29. Of the weddyng of kyng Marke to La Beale Isoude, and of Brangwayn, hyr mayde, and of Palamydes.

30. How Palamydes demaunded quene Isoude, and how Lambegus rode after to rescowe hyr, and of th' escape of Isoude.

31. How syr Trystram rode after Palamydes and how he fonde hym and faught wyth hym, and by the moyne of Isoude the batayl seced.

32. How syr Trystram brought quene Isoude home, and of the debate of kyng Marke and syr Trystram.

33. How syr Lamerok justed wyth thirty knyghtes, and syr Tristram atte requeste of kyng Mark smote his hors doun.

34. How syr Lamerok sente an horne to kyng Marke in despyte of syr Trystram, and how syr Trystram was dryven into a chapel.

35. How syr Tristram was holpen by his men, and of quene Isoude which was put in a lazarcote†, and how Tristram was hurt.

36. How syr Trystram served in warre the kyng Howel of Brytayn and slewe hys adversarye in the felde.

37. How syr Suppynabyles tolde syr Trystram how he was deffamed in the courte of kyng Arthur.

* C bym   S hym   † S in lazaroote

THERE was a kynge that hyght Melyodas, and he was 5 (1)
lorde of the contrey of Lyones. And this Melyodas
was a lykly knyght as ony was that tyme lyvyng. And by
fortune he wedded kynge Markis sister of Cornuayle, and she
was called Elyzabeth, that was called bothe good and fayre.

And at that tyme kynge Arthure regned, and he was hole 10
kynge of Ingelonde, Walys, Scotlonde, and of many othir
realmys. Howbehit there were many kynges that were
lordys of many contreyes, but all they helde their londys of
kynge Arthure; for in Walys were two kynges, and in the
Northe were many kynges, and in Cornuayle and in the 15
Weste were two kynges; also in Irelonde were two or three
kynges, and all were undir the obeysaunce of kynge Arthure;
so was the kynge of Fraunce and the kyng of Bretayne, and
all the lordshyppis unto Roome.

So whan this kynge Melyodas had bene with his wyff, 20
wythin a whyle she wexed grete with chylde. And she was
a full meke lady, and well she loved hir lorde and he hir
agayne, so there was grete joy betwyxte hem.

So there was a lady in that contrey that had loved kynge
Melyodas longe, and by no meane she never cowde gete 25
his love. Therefore she let ordayne uppon a day as kynge
Melyodas rode an-huntynge, for he was a grete chacer of
dere, and there be enchauntemente she made hym chace an
harte by hymself alone tyll that he com to an olde castell,
and there anone he was takyn presoner by the lady that 30
loved hym.

Whan Elyzabeth, kynge Melyodas his wyff, myssed hir **149ʳ**
lorde she was nyghe oute of hir wytte, and also, as grete with
chylde as she was, she toke a jantylwoman with hir and ran
into the fereste suddeynly to seke hir lorde. And whan she 35

---

5 *C* Hit was   6 *C* lord and kynge of   27–28 of dere *not in C*†   31 *C* hym
loued   32 his wyff *not in C*†   33 *C* lord and she   35 suddeynly *not in C*

was farre in the foreste she myght no farther, but ryght
there she gan to travayle faste of hir chylde, and she had
many grymly throwys, but hir jantyllwoman halpe hir all
that she myght.

5   And so by myracle of Oure Lady of Hevyn she was
delyverde with grete paynes, but she had takyn suche colde
for the defaute of helpe that the depe draughtys of deth toke
hir, that nedys she muste dye and departe oute of thys
worlde; there was none othir boote. Whan this quene
10 Elyzabeth saw that she myght nat ascape she made grete
dole and seyde unto hir jantylwoman,

'Whan ye se my lorde, kynge Melyodas, recommaunde
me unto hym and tell hym what paynes I endure here for
his love, and how I muste dye here for his sake for defawte
15 of good helpe, and lat hym wete that I am full sory to departe
oute of this worlde fro hym. Therefore pray hym to be
frende to my soule. Now lat me se my lytyll chylde for whom
I have had all this sorrow.'

And whan she sye hym she seyde thus: 'A, my lytyll son,
20 thou haste murtherd thy modir! And therefore I suppose
thou that arte a murtherer so yonge, thow arte full lykly to
be a manly man in thyne ayge; and bycause I shall dye of the
byrth of the, I charge my jantyllwoman that she pray my
lorde, the kynge Melyodas, that whan he is crystened let
25 calle hym Trystrams, that is as muche to say as a sorowfull
byrth.'

And therewith the quene gaff up the goste and dyed. Than
the jantyllwoman leyde hir undir an umbir of a grete tre, and
than she lapped the chylde as well as she myght fro colde.

30   Ryght so there cam the barowns of kynge Melyodas
folowyng aftir the quene. And whan they sye that she was
dede and undirstode none othir but that the kynge was de-
(2) **149ᵛ** stroyed, than sertayne of them wolde have slayne the chylde
bycause they wolde have bene lordys of that contrey of
35 Lyonesse. But than, thorow the fayre speche of the jantyllwoman and by the meanys that she made, the moste party

---

1–2 *C* ferther for she byganne   3 but *not in C*   7 *C* that depe   10 *C* saw
that ther was none other bote thenne she made   14 *C* gist loue   23 *C* I charge
the gentylwoman that thou pray   29 *C*† for cold   30 of kynge Melyodas
not in C   32 that *not in C*

of the barowns wolde nat assente thereto. But than they latte
cary home the dede quene and muche sorow was made for hir.

Than this meanewhyle Merlyon had delyverde kynge
Melyodas oute of preson on the morne aftir his quene was
dede. And so whan the kynge was com home the moste 5
party of the barowns made grete joy, but the sorow that the
kynge made for his quene there myght no tonge tell. So
than the kynge let entyre hir rychely, and aftir he let crystyn
his chylde as his wyff had commaunded byfore hir deth.
And than he lette calle hym Trystrams, 'the sorowfull-borne 10
chylde'.

Than kynge Melyodas endured aftir that seven yere
withoute a wyff, and all this tyme Trystrams was fostred
well. Than hit befelle that the kynge Melyodas wedded
kynge Howellys of Bretaynes doughter, and anone she had 15
chyldirne by kynge Melyodas. Than was she hevy and wroth
that hir chyldirne sholde nat rejoyse the contrey of Lyonesse, wherefore this quene ordayned for to poyson yong
Trystrams.

So at the laste she let poyson be putt in a pees of sylver 20
in the chambir where Trystrams and hir chyldir were
togydyrs, unto that entente that whan Trystrams were
thirsty he sholde drynke that drynke. And so hit felle uppon
a day the quenys son, as he was in that chambir, aspyed the
pyese with poyson, and he wente hit had bene good drynke; 25
and because the chylde was thirsty he toke the pyese with
poyson and dranke frely, and therewith the chylde suddaynly
braste and was dede.

So whan the quene of Melᵣyodᶫas wyste of the deth of hir
sone, wete you well that she was hevy; but yet the kynge 30
undirstood nothynge of hir treson. Notwythstondynge the
quene wolde not leve by this, but effte she lette ordeyne **150ʳ**
more poyson and putt hit in a pyese. And by fortune kyng
Melᵣyodᶫas, hir husbonde, founde the pyese with wyne
wherein was the poyson, and as he that was thirstelew toke the 35
pyse for to drynke; and as he wolde have drunken thereof the

1 *C* And thenne   2 *C* moche dole   12 aftir that *not in C*   13 *C* was
nourysshed   16 *C* of kynge   20 at the laste *not in C*   21 *C* where as
29 *C*† quene Melyodas*   *W* Melodyas   32 *C* leue this   34 *W* Melodyas
(*see note 29*)   35 *C* and he that was moche thursty   36 *C* drynke ther oute

quene aspyed hym and ran unto hym and pulde the pyse
from hym sodeynly. The kynge mervayled of hir why she
ded so and remembred hym suddaynly how hir son was
slayne with poyson. And than he toke hir by the honde and
5 sayde,

'Thou false traytoures! Thou shalt telle me what maner
of drynke this is, other ellys I shall sle the!' And therewith
he pulde oute his swerde and sware a grete othe that he
sholde sle hir but yf she tolde hym the trouthe.

10 'A! mercy, my lorde,' she seyde, 'and I shall telle you all.'
And than she tolde hym why she wolde have slayne Trystrams, because her chyldir sholde rejoyse his londe.

'Well,' seyde the kynge, 'and therefore ye shall have the
lawe.'

15 And so she was dampned by the assente of the barownes
to be brente. And ryght as she was at the fyre to take hir
excussion this same yonge Trystrams kneled byfore his fadir
kynge Mel⌐yod⌐as and besought hym to gyff hym a done.

'I woll well,' seyde the kynge [ageyne].

20 Than seyde yonge Trystrams, 'Geff me the lyff of your
quene, my stepmodir.'

'That is unryghtfully asked,' seyde the kynge Melyodas,
'for thou oughte of ryght to hate hir, for she wolde have
slayne the with poyson, and for thy sake moste is my cause
25 that she sholde be dede.'

'Sir,' seyde Trystrams, 'as for that, I beseche you of your
mercy that ye woll forgyff hir. And as for my parte, God
forgyff hir and I do. And hit lyked so muche your hyghe-
nesse to graunte me my boone, for Goddis love I requyre you
30 holde your promyse.'

'Sytthen hit is so,' seyde the kynge, 'I woll that ye have
hir lyff,' and sayde: 'I gyff hir you, and go ye to the fyre and
take hir and do with hir what ye woll.'

So thus sir Trystramys wente to the fyre, and by the com-
150ᵛ 35 maundemente of the kynge delyverde hir frome the deth.
But afftir that kynge Mel⌐yod⌐as wolde never have ado with

2 of hir *not in C*   3–4 *C* hym how her sone was sodenly slayne   13 *C* kyng
Melyodas   16 *C** brent and thenne was ther made a grete fyre &   17 this
same *not in C*   his fadir *not in C*   18 *C* a bone   18, 36 *W* Melodyas   24 *C**
with that poyson and she myghte haue hadde her wille And   25 *C* sholde dye
27, 28 *C* forgyue hit her   32 *C* lyf thenne said the kynge I gyue her to you

hir as at bedde and at bourde. But by the meanys of yonge
Trystrams he made the kynge and hir accorded, but than
the kynge wolde nat suffir yonge Trystrams to abyde but
lytyll in his courte.

And than he lett ordayne a jantyllman that was well 5 (3)
lerned and taught, and his name was Governayle, and than
he sente yonge Tristrams with Governayle into Fraunce to
lerne the langage and nurture and dedis of armys. And
there was Trystrams more than seven yere. So whan he
had lerned what he myght in tho contreyes, than he com 10
home to his fadir kynge Melyodas agayne.

And so Trystrams lerned to be an harper passyng all other,
that there was none suche called in no contrey. And so in
harpynge and on instrumentys of musyke in his youthe he
applyed hym for to lerne. And aftir, as he growed in myght 15
and strength, he laboured in huntynge and in hawkynge—
never jantylman more that ever we herde rede of. And as the
booke seyth, he began good mesures of blowynge of beestes
of venery and beestes of chaace and all maner of vermaynes,
and all the tearmys we have yet of hawkynge and huntynge. 20
And therefore the booke of [venery, of hawkynge and
huntynge is called the booke of] sir Trystrams.

Wherefore, as me semyth, all jantyllmen that beryth olde
armys ought of ryght to honoure sir Tristrams for the goodly
tearmys that jantylmen have and use and shall do unto the 25
Day of Dome, that thereby in a maner all men of worshyp
may discever a jantylman frome a yoman and a yoman frome
a vylayne. For he that jantyll is woll drawe hym to jantyll
tacchis and to folow the noble customys of jantylmen.

Thus Trystrams enduryd in Cornewayle unto that he was 30
stronge and bygge, unto the ayge of eyghtene yere. And
than kyng Melyodas had grete joy of yonge Trystrams,
and so had the quene, his wyff, for ever after in hir lyff, because sir Trystrams saved hir frome the fyre: she ded never **151ʳ**
hate hym more afftir, but ever loved hym and gaff hym many 35
grete gyfftys; for every astate loved hym where that he wente.

1 *C* good meanes   3–4 *C* to abyde no lenger in   9–10 *C** yeres And thenne
whanne he wel couthe speke the langage and hadde lerned all that he myght
16–17 *C* haukynge soo that neuer   20 *C* alle these   25 do *not in C*
27–28 *C* and from a yoman a vylayne   29 *C* the custommes of noble
gentylmen   31 *C* of the age   32 yonge *not in C*   35 *C* gaf Trystram

(4)   Than hit befelle that kynge Angwysh of Irelonde sente
unto kynge Marke of Cornwayle for his trwayge that
Cornuayle had payde many wyntyrs, and ⟨at⟩ that tyme
kynge Marke was behynde of the trwayge for seven yerys.

5   And kynge Marke and his barownes gaff unto the messyngers of Irelonde thes wordis and answere that they wolde none
pay, and bade the messyngers go unto their kynge Angwysh,
'and tell hym we woll pay hym no trwayge, but tell youre
lorde, and he woll allwayes have trwayge of us of Cornwayle,
10   bydde hym sende a trusty knyght of his londe that woll fyght
for his ryght, and we shall fynde another for to defende us.'

So the messyngers departed into Irelonde, and whan
kynge Angwysh undyrstoode the answere of the messyngers
he was wrothe. And than he called unto hym sir Marhalt,
15   the good knyght that was nobly proved and a knyght of the
Rounde Table. And this Marhaltt was brother unto the quene
of Irelonde. Than the kyng seyde thus:

'Fayre brother, sir Marhalt, I pray you go unto Cornewayle for my sake to do batayle for oure trwayge that we of
20   ryght ought to have. And whatsomevir ye spende, ye shall
have suffyciauntely more than ye shall nede.'

'Sir,' seyde sir Marhalte, 'wete you well that I shall nat be
loth to do batayle in the ryght of you and your londe with
the beste knyght of Table Rounde, for I know them for the
25   moste party what bene their dedis. And for to avaunce my
dedis and to encrece my worshyp I woll ryght gladly go
unto this journey.'

So in all haste there was made purvyaunce for sir Marhalte, and he had all thynge that hym neded, and so he
151ᵛ 30   departed oute of Irelonde and aryved up in Cornwayle evyn
by Castell of Tyntagyll. And whan kynge Marke undirstood that he was there aryved for to fyght for Irelonde, than
made kynge Marke grete sorow, whan he undirstood that the
good knyght sir Marhalt was com; for they knew no knyght
35   that durste have ado with hym, for at that tyme sir Marhalte
was called one of the famuste knyghtes of the worlde.

3 *W* all *C* alle   7 *C* vnto his   11–12 *C** defende oure ryght With this
ansuer the   14 *C* wonderly wroth   19–20 *W* of ryght that we of ryght
27 *C* journeye for oure ryghte   31 *C* fast by   34 *C* good and noble
36 *C* famosest and renoumed knyghtes

And thus sir Marhalte abode in the see, and every day he
sente unto kynge Marke for to pay the trwayge that was
behynde seven yere, other ellys to fynde a knyght to fyght
with hym for the trewayge. This maner of message sir Marhalte sente unto kynge Marke.   5

Than they of Cornwayle lete make cryes that what knyght
that wolde fyght for to save the trwayge of Cornwayle he
shold be rewarded to fare the bettir, terme of his lyff. Than
som of the barowns seyde to kynge Marke and counceyled
hym to [sende to] the courte of kynge Arthure for to seke   10
sir Launcelott du Lake that was that tyme named for the
mervaylyste knyght of the worlde.

Than there were other barownes [that counceyled the
kynge not to do] ⟨this⟩, and seyde that hit was laboure in
vayne bycause sir Marhalte was a knyght of Rounde Table;   15
therefore ony of hem wolde be loth to have ado with other,
but yf hit were so that ony knyght at his owne rekeyste wolde
fyght disgysed and unknowyn. So the kynge and all his
barownes assentyd that hit was no boote to seke aftir no
knyght of the Rounde Table.   20

This meanewhyle cam the langayge and the noyse unto
kynge Melyodas how that sir Marhalte abode faste by
Tyntagyll, and how kynge Marke cowde fynde no maner of
knyght to fyght for hym. So whan yonge Trystrams herde
of thys he was wroth and sore ashamed that there durste no   25
knyght in Cornwayle have ado with sir Marhalte of Irelonde.
Therewithall Trystrams wente unto his fadir kynge Melyodas **152ʳ** (5)
and asked hym counceyle what was beste to do for to recovir
Cornwayle frome bondage.

'For as me semyth,' seyde Trystrams, 'hit were shame   30
that sir Marhalte, the quenys brother of Irelonde, sholde go
away onles that he were foughtyn withall.'

'As for that,' seyde kynge Melyodas, 'wete you well,
sonne Trystramys, that sir Marhalte ys called one of the
beste knyghtes of the worlde, and therefore I know no   35
knyght in this contrey is able to macche hym.'

3 *C* of seuen   5 *C* sente dayly   6 *C* cryes in euery place   8 *C* rewarded
soo that he sholde fare   12 *C* of alle the   14 *C* doo soo & said   17 so that
not in C   19–20 *C* seke ony knyght   22 *C* abode bataille faste   26 *W*
Cornwayle durste have   29 *C* from truage   35 *C* worlde and knyghte
of the table round And therfore   36 *C* that is able to matche with hym

'Alas,' seyde sir Trystrams, 'that I were nat made knyght!
And yf sir Marhalte sholde thus departe into Irelonde, God
let me never have worshyp: [and I were made knyght I
shold matche hym.] And, sir,' seyde Tristrams, 'I pray you,
5　gyff me leve to ryde to kynge Mark. And so ye woll nat be
displesed, of kynge Marke woll I be made knyght.'

'I woll well,' seyde kynge Melyodas, 'that ye be ruled as
youre corrage woll rule you.'

Than Trystrams thanked his fadir, and than he made hym
10　redy to ryde into Cornwayle.

So in the meanewhyle there com ⌜a messager with⌝ lettyrs
of love fro kynge Faramon of Fraunces doughter unto
syr Trystrams that were peteuous lettyrs, but in no wyse
Trystrams had no joy of hir lettyrs nor regarde unto hir.
15　Also she sente hym a lytyll brachet that was passynge fayre.
But whan the kynges doughter undirstoode that Trystrams
wolde nat love hir, as the booke seyth, she dyed ⌜for sorou⌝.
And than the same squyre that brought the lettyrs and the
brachet cam ayen unto sir Trystrams, as aftir ye shall [here]
20　in the tale folowynge.

So aftir this yonge Trystrames rode unto hys eme, kynge
Marke of Cornwayle, and whan he com there he herde sey
that there wolde no knyght fyght with sir Marhalt.

'Sir,' seyde Trystrams, 'yf ye woll gyff me the Ordir of
25　Knyghthode I woll do batayle with sir Marhalte.'
152ᵛ　'What are ye?' seyde the kynge, 'and frome whens be ye
com?'

'Sir,' seyde Trystrames, 'I com frome kynge Melyodas that
wedded your systir, and a jantylman, wete you welle, I am.'
30　　So kyng Marke behylde Trystrams and saw that he was

---

1 *C* that I am not　　3-4 *Not emended in O¹*　　5 *C* and soo ye be not
9 *C* fader moche　　11 Cf.*F (MS. B.N. fr. 103, f. 32ᵛ, col. 2)* et voient
venir ung escuier tout seul regardant et chevauchant aprés eulx qui portoit *etc.*
13-14 *C** ful pyteous letters & in them were wryten many complayntes of loue but
syre Tristram　　13-15 *W (sidenote):* How the kynge of Fraunsis doughter sente to
sir Trystrames a fayre brachette　　17 *C** dyed for sorou　　*F (MS. B.N. fr. 103,
f. 33ʳ, col. 1)* qui d'amours meurt　　20 folowynge *not in C*　　21 aftir *not in C*
23-24 *C** Marhaus Thenne yede sir Tristram unto his eme and sayd syre　　25-28 (*see
note*) *W* with sir Marhalt what ar ye seyde the kynge and frome whens be ye com sir
seyde Trystrams yf ye woll gyff me the ordir of knyghthode I woll do batayle with
sir Marhalte what ar ye seyde the kynge and frome whens be ye com Sir seyde Trystrames I com frome

but a yonge man of ayge, but he was passyngly well made
and bygge.

'Fayre sir,' seyde the kynge, 'what is your name and where
were ye borne?'

'Sir, my name is Trystrams, and in the contrey of Lyonesse 5
was I borne.'

'Ye sey well,' seyde the kynge, 'and yf ye woll do this
batayle I shall make you knyght.'

'Therefore cam I to you,' seyde Trystrams, 'and for none
other cause.'   10

But than kynge Marke made hym knyght, and therewithall anone as he had made hym knyght he sente unto
sir Marhalte that he had founde a yonge knyght redy for
to take the batayle to the utteraunce.

'Hit may well be so,' seyde sir Marhalte, 'but tell kynge 15
Marke I woll nat fyght with no knyght but he be of blood
royall, that is to seye owther kynges son othir quenys son,
borne of pryncis other of pryncesses.'

Whan kynge Marke undirstoode that, he sente for sir Trystrams de Lyones and tolde hym what was the answere of 20
sir Marhalte. Than seyde sir Trystrams,

'Sytthen that he seyth so, lat hym wete that I am commyn
of fadir syde and modir syde of as noble bloode as he is; for,
sir, now shall ye know that I am kynge Melyodas sonne,
borne of your owne sister dame Elyzabeth that dyed in the 25
foreste in the byrth of me.'

'A, Jesu!' seyde kynge Marke, 'ye ar welcom, fayre
nevew, to me.'

Than in all the haste the kyng horsed sir Trystrams and
armed hym on the beste maner that myght be gotyn for golde 30
othir sylver. And than kynge Marke sente unto sir Marhalte
and dud hym to wete that a bettir man borne than he was
hymself sholde fyght with hym, 'and his name ys sir Trystrams de Lyones, begotyn of kyng Melyodas and borne of **153ʳ**
kynge Markys sistir.' Than was sir Marhalte gladde and 35
blyeth that he sholde feyght with suche a jantylman.

---

5 *C* Syre sayd he ageyne my   12–13 *C** he sente a messager unto syre Marhaus
with letters that said that   14 *C* the vttermest   18 *C* prynce or pryncesse
24 *W* kynge of Melyodas   29 *C* kynge lete horse   30 *C* in the best maner
that myghte be had or goten   32 *C* born mã̄

And so by the assente of kynge Marke they lete ordayne
that they sholde fyght within an ilonde nyghe sir Marhaltes
shyppis. And so was sir Trystrames put into a vessell, bothe
his horse and he and all that to hym longed, bothe for his
body and for his horse, that he lacked nothyng. And whan
kynge Marke and his barownes of Cornwayle behelde how
yonge sir Trystrams departed with suche a caryage to feyght
for the ryght of Cornwayle, there was nother man nother
woman of worshyp but they wepte to se and undirstonde so
yonge a knyght to jouparté hymself for theire ryght.

(6)   So, to shortyn this tale, whan syr Trystrams aryved within
the ilonde he loked to the farther syde, and there he sawe at
an ankyr six othir shyppis nyghe to the londe, and undir the
shadow of the shyppys, uppon the londe, there hoved the
noble knyght sir Marhalte of Irelonde. Than sir Trystrams
commaunded to have his horse uppon the londe. And than
Governayle, his servaunte, dressed hys harneys at all maner
of ryghtes, and than sir Trystrams mounted uppon his
horse.

And whan he was in his sadyll well apparayled, and his
shylde dressed uppon his sholdir, so sir Trystrams asked
Governayle,

'Where is this knyght that I shall have ado withall?'

'Sir,' seyde Governayle, 'se ye hym nat? I wente that ye
had sene hym, for yondir he hovyth undir the umbir of his
shyppys on horseback, with his spere in his honde and his
shylde uppon his sholdyr.'

'That is trouthe,' seyde sir Trystrams, 'now I se hym.'

Than he commaunded Governayle to go to his vessayle
agayne, 'and commaunde me unto myne eme, kynge Marke,
and pray hym, yf that I be slayne in this batayle, for to entere
my body as hym semyth beste. And as for me, lette hym
wete I woll never be yoldyn for cowardyse, and if I be slayne
and fle nat, they have loste no trewayge for me. And yf so
be that I fle other yelde me as recreaunte, bydde myne eme
bury me never in Crystyn buryellys. And uppon thy lyff,'

153ᵛ

1 *C* Mark and of syr Marhaus they   5 *C* horse Syre Trystram lacked
13 othir *not in C*   16–17 *C* commaunded his seruaunt gouernail to brynge his
hors to the land and dresse   18 *C* thenne whan he had soo done he mounted
25 *C* hym yonder   28 *C* see hym wel ynouȝ   29 *C* his seruaunt Gouernayle
33 *C* neuer yelde me   34 *C* not thenne they

seyde sir Trystrams unto Govirnayle, 'that thou com nat
nyghe this ilonde tyll that thou see me overcom or slayne,
other ellis that I wynne yondir knyght.'

So they departed sore wepyng. And than sir Marhalte (7)
avysed sir Trystrames and seyde thus: 5

'Yonge knyght, sir Trystrams, what doste thou here? Me
sore repentys of thy corrayge; for wete thou well, I have
bene assayede with many noble knyghtes, and the beste
knyghtes of this londe have bene assayed of myne hondys,
and also the beste knyghtes of the worlde I have macched 10
them. And therefore, be my counceyle, returne ayen unto
thy vessell.'

'A, fayre knyght and well proved,' seyde sir Trystrams,
'thou shalt well wete I may nat forsake the in this quarell.
For I am for thy sake made knyght, and thou shalt well wete 15
that I am a kynges sonne, borne and gotyn uppon a quene.
And suche promyse I have made at my nevewys requeste and
myne owne sekynge that I shall fyght with the unto the
uttirmuste and delyvir Cornwayle frome the olde trewage.
And also wete thou well, sir Marhalte, that this ys the 20
gretteste cause that thou coragyst me to have ado with the,
for thou arte called one of the moste renomed knyghtes of
the worlde. And bycause of that noyse and fame that thou
haste thou gevyst me corrayge to have ado with the, for
never yett was I proved with good knyght. And sytthen 25
I toke the Order of Knyghthode this day, I am ryght well
pleased, and to me moste worshyp, that I may have ado wyth
suche a knyght as thou arte. And now wete thou well, syr **154ʳ**
Marhalte, that I caste me to geete worshyp on thy body.
And yf that I be nat proved, I truste to God to be worshyp- 30
fully proved uppon thy body, and to delyver the contrey of
Cornwayle for ever fro all maner of trewaygo frome Irelonde
for ever.'

Whan sir Marhalte had herde hym sey what he wolde, he
seyde thus agayne: 35

'Fayre knyght, sytthen hit is so that thou castyste to wynne

---

4 *C* soo eyther departed from other   8 with many noble knyghtes *not in C*
10–11 *C* also I haue matched with the best knyghtes of the world and   13 *C*
And† faire knyght and wel preued knyght   26–27 *C* am wel pleasyd that
28 *C* so good a knyght   30 *C* god that I shal be

worshyp of me, I lette the wete worshyp may thou none
loose by me gyff thou may stonde me three strokys. For
I lat the wete, for my noble dedis proved and seyne kynge
Arthure made me knyght of the Table Rounde!'

5   Than they began to feauter there sperys, and they mette
so fersly togydyrs that they smote aythir other downe, bothe
horse and man. But sir Marhalte smote sir Trystrams a grete
wounde in the syde with his spere.

And than they avoyded their horsis and pulde oute their
10 swerdys, and threwe their shyldis afore them, and than they
laysshed togydyrs as men that were wylde and corrageous.
And whan they had strykyn togydyrs longe, that there
armys fayled, than they leffte their strokys and foyned at
brestys and vysours. And whan they sawe that hit myght
15 nat prevayle them, than they hurteled togedyrs lyke rammys
to beare eythir othir downe.

Thus they fought stylle togydirs more than halffe a day,
and eythir of them were wounded passynge sore, that the
blood ran downe ⌐fresshly⌐ frome them uppon the grounde.
20 By than sir Trystramys wexed more fyerser than he dud,
and sir Marhalte fyebled, and sir Trystramys ever more well-
wynded and bygger. And with a myghty stroke he smote
154ᵛ sir Marhalte uppon the helme suche a buffette that hit wente
thorow his helme and thorow the coyffe of steele and thorow
25 the brayne-panne, and the swerde stake so faste in the helme
and in his brayne-panne that sir Trystramys pulled three
tymes at his swerde or ever he myght pulle hit oute frome his
hede.

And there sir Marhalte felle downe on his kneis, and the
30 edge of his swerde leffte in hys brayne-panne. And suddeynly
sir Marhalte rose grovelynge and threw his swerde and his
shylde frome hym, and so he ran to his shyppys and fledde
his way. And sir Trystramys had ever his shelde and his
swerde, and whan sir Trystramys saw sir Marhalte withdrow
35 hym he seyde,

'A, sir knyght of the Rounde Table! Why withdrawyst

7 *C* hors and all   12–13 *C*† soo to gyder longe thenne they lefte   17 togydirs *not in C*   19 *W* ran downe passynge sore   *F* (*MS. B.N. fr. 103,*
fr. 35ʳ, col. 2) si qu'ilz perdent de leur sang a grant foison   20–22 *C* more
fressher than syr Marhaus and better wynded and bygger   26 *C* pulled thryes
29–30 *C* knees the edge of Tristrams swerd

thou the? Thou doste thyself and thy kynne grete shame,
for I am but a yonge knyght: or now I was never preved.
And rather than I sholde withdraw me frome the, I had
rathir be hewyn in pyese-mealys.'

Sir Marhalte answerde no worde, but yeode his way sore 5
gronynge.

'Well, sir knyght,' seyde sir Trystrams, 'I promyse the
thy swerde and thy shelde shall be myne, and thy shylde
shall I were in all placis where I ryde on myne adventures,
and in the syght of kyng Arthure and all the Rounde Table.' 10

So sir Marhalte and hys felyshyp departed into Irelonde. (8)
And as sone as he com to the kynge, his brother, they serched
his woundis, and whan his hede was serched a pyese of sir
Trystrams swerde was therein founden, and myght never
be had oute of his hede for no lechecraffte. And so he dyed 15
of sir Trystramys swerde, and that pyse of the swerde the
quene, his sistir, she kepte hit for ever with hir, for she
thought to be revenged and she myght.

Now turne we agayne unto sir Trystrames that was sore
wounded and sore forbledde, that he myght nat within a lytyll 20
whyle stonde. Whan he had takyn colde ⟨he coude⟩ unnethe
styrre hym of hys lymmes, and than he sette hym downe
sofftely uppon a lytyll hylle and bledde faste. Than anone **155ᵣ**
com Governayle, his man, with his vessell, and the kynge and
the moste party of his barownes com with procession ayenst 25
sir Trystrames.

And whan he was commyn unto the londe kynge Marke
toke hym in his armys, and he and sir Dynas the Senescyall
lad sir Tristrames into the castell of Tyntagyll; and than
was he cerched in the beste maner and leyde in his bed. 30
And whan kynge Marke saw his woundys he wepte hertely,
and so dud all his lordys.

'So God me helpe,' seyde kynge Marke, 'I wolde nat for
all my londys that my nevew dyed.'

So sir Trystrames lay there a moneth and more, and ever 35
he was lyke to dey of the stroke that sir Marhalte smote hym

4 *C* hewen in *C* pyeces   12 *C* brother he lete serche   13–17 *W* (*sidenote*):
Here is the deth of sir Marhalte knyght of the Table Rounde by sir Trystrames
15 *C* for no surgeons   17 *C* syster kepte   20 *C* ful sore bled   21 *C*† whyle
when he had take cold unnethe   *W* colde &† unnethe (*see note*)   24–25 *C* and
the kynge and his   25–26 *C* ageynst hym   28 *C* and the kynge and

fyrste wyth the spere; for, as the Frenshe booke seyth, the
spere-hede was invenymed, that sir Trystrams myght nat
be hole. Than was kynge Marke and all hys barownes
passynge hevy, for they demed none other but that sir
5 Trystrames sholde nat recover. Than the kynge lette sende
for all maner of lechis and surgeons, bothe unto men and
women, and there was none that wolde behote hym the lyff.

Than cam there a lady that was a wytty lady, and she
seyde playnly unto the kynge Marke and to sir Trystrames
10 and to all his barownes that he sholde never be hole but yf
that sir Trystrames wente into the same contrey that the
venym cam fro, and in that contrey sholde he be holpyn,
other ellys never; thus seyde the lady unto the kynge. So
whan the kynge undirstood hit he lette purvey for syr
15 Trystrames a fayre vessell and well vytayled, and therein
was putt sir Trystrames, and Governayle wyth hym, and sir
Trystrames toke his harpe with hym. And so he was putt
into the see to sayle into Irelonde.

And so by good fortune he aryved up in Irelonde evyn
20 faste by a castell where the kynge and the quene was. And
at his aryvayle he sate and harped in his bedde a merry lay:
155ᵛ suche one herde they never none in Irelonde before that
tyme. And whan hit was tolde the kynge and the quene of
suche a syke knyght that was suche an harper, anone the
25 kynge sente for hym and lette serche hys woundys, and than
he asked hym his name. And than he answerde and seyde,

'I am of the contrey of Lyones, and my name is Tramtryste,
that was thus wounded in a batayle as I fought for a ladyes
ryght.'

30 'So God me helpe,' seyde kynge Angwysh, 'ye shall have all
the helpe in this londe that ye may have here. But in Cornwayle but late I had a grete losse as ever had kynge, for there I
loste the beste knyght of the worlde. His name was sir Marhalte, a full noble knyght and knyght of the Table Rounde.'

35 And there he tolde sir Tramtryste wherefore sir Marhalte
was slayne. So sir Tramtryste made sembelaunte as he had
bene sory, and bettir he knew how hit was than the kynge.

5–6 *C* sende after alle   8 *C* was a ryght wyse lady   10–11 *C* but yf sire
24 syke *not in C*   26 and seyde *not in C*   31–32 *C* But I lete you wete in
Cornewaile I had   35 *C* syr Trystrā   36 *C* Syr Trystram

Than the kynge for grete favour made Tramtryste to be (9)
put in his doughtyrs awarde and kepyng, because she was a
noble surgeon. And whan she had serched hym she founde
in the bottom of his wounde that therein was poyson, and so
she healed hym in a whyle.   5

And therefore sir Tramtryste kyste grete love to La Beale
Isode, for she was at that tyme the fayrest lady and maydyn
of the worlde. And there Tramtryste lerned hir to harpe
and she began to have a grete fantasy unto hym.

And at that tyme sir Palomydes ⌜the Sarasyn⌝ drew unto 10
La Beale Isode and profirde hir many gyfftys, for he loved
hir passyngly welle. All that aspyed Tramtryste, and full
well he knew Palomydes for a noble knyght and a myghty
man. And wete you well sir Tramtryste had grete despyte
at sir Palomydes, for La Beale Isode tolde Tramtryste that 15
Palomydes was in wyll to be crystynde for hir sake. Thus was
the[r] grete envy betwyxte Tramtryste and sir Palomydes.

Than hit befelle that kynge Angwysh lett cry a grete justis
and a grete turnemente for a lady that was called the lady of **156ʳ**
the Laundys, and she was ny cosyn unto the kynge. And 20
what man wanne her, four dayes [after] sholde wedde hir
and have all hir londis. This cry was made in Ingelonde,
Walys, and Scotlonde, and also in Fraunce and in Bretayne.

So hit befelle uppon a day, La Beale Isode com unto
Tramtryste and tolde hym of this turnemente. He answerde 25
and sayde,

'Fayre lady, I am but a feeble knyght, and but late I had
bene dede, had nat your good ladyshyp bene. Now, fayre
lady, what wolde ye that I sholde do in this mater? Well ye
wote, my lady, that I may nat juste.'   30

'A, Tramtryste!' seyde La Beale Isode, 'why woll ye
nat have ado at that turnamente? For well I wote that sir
Palomydes woll be there and to do what he may. And
therefore, sir Tramtryste, I pray you for to be there, for
ellys sir Palomydes ys lyke to wynne the degré.'   35

'Madam, as for that, hit may be so, for he is a proved

---

2 *C* doughters ward   10 *F* (*MS. B.N. fr. 103, f. 39ʳ, col. 1*) c'estoit Palamedes,
le bon chevalier sarrasin, qui onques n'avoit esté chrestien   *C** sir Palamydes the
sarasyn was in that countrey and wel cherysshed with the kynge and the quene
And euery day syr Palamydes drewe   21 *C* thre dayes   33 *C* shall be

knyght and I am but a yonge knyght and late made, and the
fyrste batayle that ever I ded hit myssehapped me to be sore
wounded, as ye se. But and I wyste that ye wolde be my
bettir lady, at that turnemente woll I be, on this covenaunte:
5 so that ye woll kepe my counceyle and lette no creature have
knowlech that I shall juste but yourself and suche as ye
woll to kepe youre counceyle, my poure person shall [I]
jouparté there for youre sake, that peradventure sir Palomydes shall know whan that I com.'
10 Thereto seyde La Beale Isode, 'Do your beste, and as I
can,' seyde La Beale Isode, 'I shall purvey horse and armoure
for you at my devyse.'
'As ye woll, so be hit,' seyde sir Tramtryste, 'I woll be at
your commaundemente.'
15 So at the day of justys there cam sir Palomydes with a
blacke shylde and he ovirthrew many knyghtes, that all
people had mervayle; for he put to the warre sir Gawayne,
156ᵛ Gaherys, Aggravayne, Bagdemagus, Kay, Dodynas le
Savyaige, Sagramour le Desyrous, Guvrete le Petyte, and
20 Gryfflet le Fyse de Du—all thes the fyrste day sir Palomydes
strake downe to the erthe. And than all maner of knyghtes
were adrad of sir Palomydes, and many called hym the
Knyght with the Blacke Shylde; so that [day] sir Palomydes
had grete worshyp.
25 Than cam kynge Angwyshe unto Tramtryste and asked
hym why he wolde nat juste.
'Sir,' he seyde, 'I was but late hurte and as yett I dare nat
aventure.'
Than there cam the same squyre that was sente frome
30 the kynges doughter of Fraunce unto sir Tramtryste, and
whan he had aspyed sir Trystrames he felle flatte to his
feete. And that aspyed La Beale Isode, what curtesy the
squyre made to Tramtryste. And therewithall suddeynly
sir Trystrames ran unto the squyre—his name was called
35 Ebes le Renownys—and prayde hym hartely in no wyse to
telle his name.

---

2 ever *not in* C   4 on this covenaunte *not in* C   17 C merueylle of hym
C putte to the werse   28 C auenture me   29 C came there   30 C syr
Trystram   33 C unto syr Trystram   34–35 C his squyre whos name was
Hebes (S Heles) le renoumes

'Sir,' seyde Hebes, 'I woll nat discovir your name but yf
ye commaunde me.'

Than sir Trystramys asked hym what he dede in this (10)
contreys.

'Sir,' he seyde, 'I com hydir with sir Gawayne for to be 5
made knyght, and yf hit please you of your hondis that I may
be made knyght.'

'Well, awayte on me as to-morne secretly, and in the
fylde I shall make you knyght.'

Than had La Beale Isode grete suspeccion unto Tram- 10
tryste that he was som man of worshyp preved, and therewith she comforted herselfe and kyste more love unto hym,
for well she demed he was som man of worshyp.

And so on the morne sir Palomydes made hym redy to
com into the fylde, as he dud the fyrste day, and there he 15
smote downe the Kynge with the Hondred Knyghtes and the
Kynge of Scottis. Than had La Beale Isode ordayned and
well arayde sir Tramtryste with whyght horse and whyght
armys, and ryght so she lette put hym oute at a prevy postren, **157ʳ**
and he cam so into the felde as hit had bene a bryght angell. 20
And anone sir Palomydes aspyed hym, and therewith he
feautred hys spere unto sir Trystramys and he agayne unto
hym, and there sir Trystrams smote downe sir Palomydes
unto the erthe.

And than there was a grete noyse of people: som seyde 25
sir Palomydes had a fall, som seyde the knyght with the
blacke shylde hath a falle. And wete you well La Beale
Isode was passyng gladde. And than sir Gawayne and his
felowys nine had mervayle who hit myght be that had
smytten downe sir Palomydes. Than wolde there none juste 30
with Tramtryste, but all that there were forsoke hym, moste
and leste.

Than sir Trystramys made Hebes a knyght and caused to
put hymself forth, and dud ryght well that day. So aftir that
sir Hebes helde hym with sir Trystrams. 35

And whan sir Palomydes had reseyved hys falle, wete

---

3 *C* in those   8 Well *not in C*†   12–14 *C*† unto hym than she had done
tofore And soo   18–19 *C*† in whyte hors and harneis And ryght   20 *C* &
soo he came   27 *C* had a   29 *C* what knyghte it myght   33 *C* caused
hym to   34–35 *C* after sir Hebes   36 *C* this falle

ye well that he was sore ashamed, and as prevayly as he
myght he withdrew hym oute of the fylde. All that aspyed
sir Tramtryste, and lyghtly he rode aftir sir Palomydes and
overtoke hym and bade hym turne, for bettir he wolde assay
5 hym or ever he departed. Than sir Palomydes turned hym and
eythir laysshed at other with their swerdys; but at the fyrste
stroke sir Trystrames smote downe sir Palomydes and gaff
hym suche a stroke uppon the hede that he felle to the erthe.

So than sir Trystrams bade hym yelde hym and do his
10 commaundemente, other ellis he wolde sle hym. Whan sir
Palomydes behylde hys countenaunce he drad his buffettes
so that he graunted all his askynges.

'Well,' seyde sir Tramtryste, 'this shall be youre charge:
fyrst, uppon payne of youre lyff, that ye forsake my lady,
157ᵛ 15 La Beale Isode, and in no maner of wyse that ye draw no
more to hir; also, this twelve-monthe and a day that ye bere
none armys nother none harneys of werre. Now promysse
me this, othir here shalt thou dye.'

'Alas,' seyde sir Palomydes, 'for ever I am shamed!'
20 Than he sware as sir Trystrames had commaunded hym.
So for dispyte and angir sir Palomydes kut of his harneyse
and threw them awey.

And so sir Trystrames turned agayne to the castell where
was La Beale Isode, and by the way he mette wyth a damesell
25 that asked aftir sir Launcelot that wan the Dolorous Garde;
and this damesell asked sir Trystrames what he was, for hit
was tolde her that hit was he that smote downe sir Palamydes by whom the ten knyghtes of Arthures were smyttyn
downe. Than the damesell prayde sir Trystrames to telle her
30 what he was and whether that he were sir Launcelot du Lake,
for she demed that there was no knyght in the worlde that
myght do suche dedis of armys but yf hit were sir Launcelot.

'Wete you well that I am nat sir Launcelot, fayre damesell,
for I was never of suche proues. But in God is all: He may
35 make me as good a knyght as that good knyght sir Launcelot
is.'

3 *C* syre Trystram   9 *C* badde yelde   13 *C*† said said sir Tristram   15 of
not in C   15–16 *C* not to   17 *C* none armour   19 *C* ashamed   25 *C* gard
worshipfully   31 *second* that *not in C*   33 *C* Fayre damoysel sayd syr Trystram wete ye well that I am not syr launcelot   34 *C* al that   35 *C* a knyght
as the good   36 is *not in C*

'Now, jantyll knyght, put up thy vyser!'

And whan she behylde his vysage she thought she sawe never a bettir mannys vysayge nothir a bettir-farynge knyght. So whan the damesell knew sertaynly that he was nat sir Launcelot, than she toke hir leve and departed frome hym. 5

And than sir Trystrames rode prevayly unto the posterne where kepte hym La Beale Isode, and there she made hym grete chere and thanked God of his good spede.

So anone within a whyle the kynge and the quene and all the courte undirstood that hit was sir Tramtryste that smote 10 downe sir Palamydes, and than was he muche made of, more **158ʳ** than he was tofore. Thus was sir Tramtryste longe there (11) well cherysshed with the kynge and wyth the quene, and namely with La Beale Isode.

So uppon a day the quene and La Beale Isode made a 15 bayne for sir Tramtryste, and whan he was in his bayne the quene and Isode, hir doughter, romed up and downe in the chambir the whyles Governayle and Hebes attendede uppon Tramtryste. The quene behelde his swerde as hit lay uppon his bedde, and than at unhappis the quene drew oute his 20 swerde and behylde hit a long whyle. And bothe they thought hit a passynge fayre swerde, but within a foote and an halff of the poynte there was a grete pyese thereof oute-brokyn of the edge. And whan the quene had aspyed the gappe in the swerde she remembirde hir of a pyese of a 25 swerde that was founde in the braynne-panne of sir Marhalte that was hir brother.

'Alas!' than seyde she unto hir doughter La Beale Isode, 'this is the same traytoure knyght that slewe my brother, thyne eme.'   30

Whan Isode herde her sey so she was passynge sore abaysshed, for passynge well she loved Tramtryste and full well she knew the crewelnesse of hir modir the quene.

So anone therewithall the quene wente unto hir owne chambir and sought hir cofyr, and there she toke oute the 35 pyese of the swerde that was pulde oute of sir Marhaltys brayne-panne aftir that he was dede. And than she ran wyth

---

1 *C* knyght said she   8 *C* good chere   9-10 and all the courte *not in C*
13 *C* and the quene   18 *C* and there whyles   20 *C* by vnhap   26-27 *C*
Marhaus the good knyght that   36-37 *C* Marhaus hede after

that pyese of iron unto the swerde, ⌜and whanne she putte
that pyese of stele and iron unto the swerde⌝ hit was as
mete as hit myght be as whan hit was newe brokyn.

And than the quene gryped that swerde in hir honde
5 fersely, and with all her myght she ran streyght uppon
158ᵛ Tramtryste where he sate in his bayne. And there she had
ryved hym thorowe, had nat sir Hebes bene: he gate hir in
his armys and pulde the swerde frome her, and ellys she had
thriste hym thorowe. So whan she was lette of hir evyll wyll
10 she ran to the kynge her husbonde and seyde,

'A, my lorde!' On hir kneys knelynge, she seyde, 'Here
have ye in your house that traytoure knyght that slewe my
brother and your servaunte, the noble knyght sir Marhalte!'

'Who is that?' seyde the kynge, 'and where is he?'

15 'Sir,' she seyde, 'hit is sir Tramtryste, the same knyght
that my doughter helyd.'

'Alas!' seyde the kynge, 'therefore I am ryght hevy, for
he is a full noble knyght as ever I sawe in fylde. But I charge
you,' seyde the kynge, 'that ye have nat ado with that knyght,
20 but lette me dele with hym.'

Than the kynge wente into the chambir unto sir Tramtryste, and than was he gone unto his owne chambir, and
the kynge founde hym all redy armed to mownte uppon his
horse. So whan the kynge sawe hym all redy armed to go
25 unto horsebacke, the kynge seyde,

'Nay, Tramtryste, hit woll nat avayle to compare ayenste
me. But thus muche I shall do for my worshyp and for thy
love: in so muche as thou arte wythin my courte, hit were no
worship to sle the; therefore upon this conducion I woll gyff
30 the leve for to departe frome this courte in savyté, so thou
wolte telle me who was thy fadir and what is thy name, and
also yf thou slewe sir Marhalte, my brother.'

(12) 'Sir,' seyde Tramtryste, 'now I shall tell you all the trouthe.

1–2 *C** swerd that laye vpon the bedde And whane she putte that pyece of stele and
yron vnto the swerd hit was F (*MS. B.N. fr. 103, f. 43ʳ, col. 2*) Et la royne si
oeuvre son escrin et desvelope la piece de l'espee qui avoit esté trouvee en la teste du
Morhoult, si lui adjoint, si y fut tout a point comment celle qui en avoit [esté]
esgrunee a l'estendre [esteurdre ?] (*homoeoteleuton in W*) 3 *C* be whan 7 *C*
Hebes goten her 9 *C* lettyd 10 *C* kynge Anguyssh 11–12 *C* sayde
on her knees O my lorde here haue ye 14 *C* said kyng Anguysshe 19 *C* the
kyng to the quene 22 owne *not in C* 26 *C* compare the 32 also *not in C*

My fadyrs name ys sir Melyodas, kyng of Lyonesse, and
my modir hyght Elyzabeth, that was sister unto kynge
Marke of Cornwayle. And my modir dyed of me in the
foreste, and because thereof she commaunded or she dyed
that whan I was crystened they sholde crystyn me Trys- 5
trames. And because I wolde nat be knowyn in this contrey
I turned my name and let calle me Tramtryste. And for the
trwage of Cornwayle I fought, for myne emys sake and for **159ʳ**
the ryght of Cornwayle that ye had be possessed many yerys.
And wete you well,' seyde sir Trystrames unto the kynge, 10
'I dud the batayle for the love of myne uncle kynge Marke
and for the love of the contrey of Cornwayle, and for to
encrece myne honoure: for that same day that I fought with
sir Marhalte I was made knyght, and never or than dud I no
batayle with no knyght. And fro me he wente alyve and 15
leffte his shylde and his swerde behynde hym.'

'So God me helpe!' seyde the kynge, 'I may nat sey but
ye dud as a knyght sholde do and as hit was youre parte to
do for your quarell, and to encrece your worshyp as a knyght
sholde do. Howbehit I may nat mayntayne you in this 20
contrey with my worship but that I sholde displese many of
my barownes and my wyff and my kynne.'

'Sir,' seyde sir Trystrames, 'I thanke you of your good
lordeship that I have had within here with you, and the
grete goodnesse my lady your doughter hath shewed me. 25
And therefore,' seyde sir Trystramys, 'hit may so be that ye
shall wynne more be my lyff than be my deth, for in the
partyes of Ingelonde hit may happyn I may do you servyse
at som season that ye shall be glad that ever ye shewed me
your good lordshyp. Wyth more I promyse you, as I am 30
trewe knyght, that in all placis I shall be my lady your
doughtyrs servaunte and knyght in all ryght and in wronge,
and I shall never fayle her to do as muche as a knyght may do.
Also I beseche your good grace that I may take my leve at my
lady youre doughter and at all the barownes and knyghtes.' 35
'I woll [well],' seyde the kynge.

5 *C* I were   9 *C* had posseded   16 hym *not in C*   18 *C* and it
18, 20 do *not in C*   21 *C* onles that   many of *not in C*   22 *C* her kyn
24 *C* had with you here   26 *C* so happen that   32 all *not in C*   36 *W*
woll woll   *C* wille wel

Than sir Trystrames wente unto La Beale Isode and toke
his leve. And than he tolde what he was, and how a lady tolde
hym that he sholde never be hole 'untyll I cam into this
contrey where the poyson was made, wherethorow I was nere
5 my deth, had nat your ladyshyp bene.'

159ᵛ   'A, janytll knyght!' seyde La Beale Isode, 'full wo I am
of thy departynge, for I saw never man that ever I ought so
good wyll to,' and therewithall she wepte hertyly.

'Madam,' seyde sir Trystramys, 'ye shall undirstonde that
10 my name ys sir Trystrames de Lyones, gotyn of a kynge and
borne of a quene. And I promyse you faythfully, I shall be
all the dayes of my lyff your knyght.'

'Gramercy,' seyde La Beale Isode, 'and I promyse you
there agaynste I shall nat be maryed this seven yerys but by
15 your assente, and whom that ye woll I shall be maryed to
hym and he woll have me, if ye woll consente thereto.'

And than sir Trystrames gaff hir a rynge and she gaff
hym another, and therewith he departed and com into the
courte amonge all the barownes. And there he toke his leve
20 at moste and leste, and opynly he seyde amonge them all,

'Fayre lordys, now hit is so that I muste departe. If there
be ony man here that I have offended unto, or that ony man
be with me greved, lette hym complayne hym here afore me
or that ever I departe, and I shall amende hit unto my power.
25 And yf there be ony man that woll proffir me wronge other
sey me wronge, other shame me behynde my backe, sey hit
now or ellys never, and here is my body to make hit good,
body ayenste body!'

And all they stood stylle—there was nat one that wolde
30 sey one worde. Yett were there som knyghtes that were of
the quenys bloode and of sir Marhaltys blood, but they
wolde nat meddyll wyth hym.

(13)   So sir Trystramys departede and toke the see, and with
good wynde he aryved up at Tyntagyll in Cornwayle. And

2 *C* leue of her   *C** all what he was and how he had chaunged his name by cause
he wold not be knowen & hou a lady   3 *C†* he þᵗ shold neuer be hole tyl he cam
6 *C* O gentyl   10–11 *C* goten of kyng Melyodas and borne of his quene
15–16 *C* to whome that ye wille I shalle be maryed to hym wylle I haue and he
wille haue me yf ye wil consente   18–19 *C** departed fro her leuynge her makynge
grete dole and lamentacion and he streyghte wente vnto the Courte   23 *C* lete
complayne hym   25 man *not in C*   26 *C* say of me   *second* me *not in C*

whan kynge Marke was hole in hys prosperité there cam
tydynges that sir Trystrames was aryved, and hole of his
woundis. Thereof was kynge Marke passynge glad, and so
were all the barownes.

And whan he saw hys tyme he rode unto his fadir, kynge 5
Melyodas, and there he had all the chere that the kynge and
the quene coude make hym. And than largely kynge
Melyodas and his quene departed of their londys and goodys **160^r**
to sir Trystrames. Than by the lysence of his fadir he returned ayen unto the courte of kynge Marke.   10

And there he lyved longe in grete joy longe tyme, untyll
at the laste there befelle a jolesy and an unkyndenesse
betwyxte kyng Marke and sir Trystrames, for they loved
bothe one lady, and she was an erlys wyff that hyght sir
Segwarydes. And this lady loved sir Trystrames passyngly 15
well, and he loved hir agayne, for she was a passynge fayre
lady and that aspyed sir Trystrames well. Than kynge Marke
undirstode that and was jeluse, for kynge Marke loved hir
passyngly welle.

So hit befelle uppon a day, this lady sente a dwarff unto 20
sir Trystrames and bade hym, as he loved hir, that he wolde
be with hir the nexte nyght folowynge:

'Also she charged you that ye com nat to hir but yf ye be
well armed.' For her lorde was called a good knyght.

Sir Trystrames answerde to the dwarff and seyde,   25

'Recommaunde me unto my lady and tell hir I woll nat
fayle, but I shall be with her the terme that she hath sette
me,' and therewith the dwarff departed.

And kyng Marke aspyed that the dwarff was with sir Trystrames uppon message frome Segwarydes wyff. Than 30
kynge Marke sente for the dwarff, and whan he was comyn
he made the dwarff by force to tell hym all why and wherefore
that he cam on message to sir Trystrames, and than he tolde
hym.

'Welle,' seyde kyng Marke, 'go where thou wolte, and 35
uppon payne of deth that thou sey no worde that thou spake
with me.'

5–6 *W* his fadir kynge Melyodas his fadir   9 *C* of Kyng Melyodas his
22 *C* ny3t nexte   25 and seyde *not in C*   27 *C* I wille   28 *C* and
with this ansuer the   33–35 *C* from† sire Tristram Now said kynge Marke

So the dwarff departed ⌜from the kynge⌝, and that same nyght that the steavyn was sette betwyxte Segwarydes wyff and sir Trystrames, so kynge Marke armed and made hym redy and toke two knyghtes of his counceyle with hym.
5 And so he rode byfore for to abyde by the wayes for to wayte uppon sir Trystrames.

And as sir Trystrames cam rydynge uppon his way with
160ᵛ his speare in his hande, kynge Marke cam hurlynge uppon hym and hys two knyghtes suddeynly, and all three smote
10 hym with their sperys, and kynge Marke hurt sir Trystrames on the breste ryght sore. And than sir Trystrames feautred his spere and smote kynge Marke so sore that he russhed hym to the erthe and brused hym, that he lay stylle in a sowne; and longe hit was or he myght welde hymselff. And
15 than he ran to the one knyght and effte to the tothir, and smote hem to the colde erthe, that they lay stylle.

And there[with]all sir Trystrames rode forth sore wounded to the lady and founde hir abydynge hym at a postern, and
(14) there she welcommed hym fayre, and eyther halsed other
20 in armys. And so she lette putt up his horse in the beste wyse, and than she unarmed hym, and so they soupede lyghtly and wente to bedde with grete joy and plesaunce. And so in hys ragynge he toke no kepe of his greve wounde that kynge Marke had gyffyn hym, and so sir Trystrames
25 bledde bothe the over-shete and the neyther-sheete, and the pylowes and the hede-shete.

And within a whyle there cam one before, that warned her that hir lorde sir Segwarydes was nerehonde within a bowe-drawght. So she made sir Trystrames to aryse, and [so he]
30 armed hym and toke his horse and so departed. So by than was sir Segwarydes, hir lorde, com, and whan he founde hys bedde troubled and brokyn he wente nere and loked by candyll-lyght and sawe that there had leyne a wounded knyght.
35 'A, false traytoures!' he seyde, 'why haste thou betrayde

1 F (*MS. B.N. fr. 103, f. 45ʳ, col. 1*) Atant se part le nain de la chambre du roy
5 *C* waye   8 *C* hurtlynge   9 *C* with his   12 *C* his vnkel kynge
14 *C* or euer he   23 *C*† grene wound   25 *C* bebled   25–26 *C* nether &
pelowes   28 sir Segwarydes *not in C*   31 *C* was come segwarydes her
lord and   32 *C* her bedde troubled & broken and wente nere and beheld it by
W brokyn And so he wente

me?' And therewithall he swange oute a swerde and seyde,
'But yf thou telle me all ⌜who hath bene here⌝, now shalt
thou dey!'

'A, my lorde, mercy!' seyde the lady, and helde up hir
hondys, 'and sle me nat, and I shall tell you all who hath ₅
bene here.'

Than anone seyde Segwarydes, 'Sey and tell me the
trouthe.'

Anone for drede she seyde,

'Here was sir Trystrames with me, and by the way, as he ₁₀
come to me-warde, he was sore wounded.'   **161ʳ**

'A, false traytoures! Where is he becom?'

'Sir,' she seyde, 'he is armed and departed on horsebacke
nat yett hens halff a myle.'

'Ye sey well,' seyde Segwarydes.   ₁₅

Than he armed hym lyghtly and gate his horse and rode
aftir sir Trystrames the streyght wey unto Tyntagyll, and
within a whyle he overtoke sir Trystrams. And than he
[b]ade hym 'turne, false traytoure knyght!' And therewithall Segwarydes smote sir Trystrames with a speare, that hit ₂₀
all to-braste, and than he swange oute hys swerde and smote
faste at sir Trystrames.

'Sir knyght,' seyde sir Trystrames, 'I counceyle you smyte
no more! Howbehit for the wrongys that I have done you
I woll forbere you as longe as I may.'   ₂₅

'Nay,' seyde Segwarydes, 'that shall nat be, for other thou
shalt dye othir ellys I.'

Than sir Trystrames drew oute his swerde and hurled his
horse unto hym freysshely, and thorow the waste of the
body he smote sir Segwarydes, that he felle to the erthe in ₃₀
sowne.

And so sir Trystrames departed and leffte hym there.
And so he rode unto Tyntagyll and toke hys lodgynge
secretely, for he wolde nat be know that he was hurte. Also
sir Segwarydes men rode aftir theire master and brought ₃₅

2 *W* me all now   *F* (*MS. B.N. fr. 103, f. 45ʳ, col. 2*) 'Dites moy qui il est'
5 *C* handes sayeng slee   7–8 *C* Telle anone said segwarydes to me alle the
trouthe   12 *C* traitresse said segwarides   17 *C* Tristram that rode streyght
18–19 *W* he made hym   19 *C** Knyghte and syr Tristram anon torned hym
ageynst hym And   28 *C* hurtled   29 *C* fyersly   35 *C** maister whome
they fond lyenge in the feld sore wounded and

hym home on his shylde; and there he lay longe or he were
hole, but at the laste he recoverde.

Also kynge Marke wolde nat be a-knowyn of that he had
done unto sir Trystramys whan he mette that nyght; and
5 as for sir Trystramys, he knew nat that kynge Marke had
mette with hym. And so the kynge com ascawnce to sir Trystrames to comforte hym as he lay syke in his bedde. But
as longe as kynge Marke lyved he loved never aftir sir Trystramys. So aftir that, thoughe there were fayre speche, love
10 was there none.

And thus hit paste on many wykes and dayes, and all was
forgyffyn and forgetyn, for sir Segwarydes durste nat have
161ᵛ ado with sir Trystrames because of his noble proues, and
also because he was nevew unto kynge Marke. Therefore he
15 lette hit overslyppe, for he that hath a prevy hurte is loth to
have a shame outewarde.

(15)   Than hit befelle uppon a day that the good knyghte sir Bleoberys de Ganys, brother unto sir Blamore de Ganys and nye
cosyne unto the good knyght syr Launcelot de Lake, so
20 this sir Bleoberys cam unto the courte of kyng Marke, and
there he asked kynge Marke to gyff hym a bone, 'what
gyffte that I woll aske in this courte'.

Whan the kynge herde hym aske so he mervayled of his
askynge, but bycause he was a knyght of the Round Table
25 and of a grete renowne, kynge Marke graunted hym his
hole askynge. Than seyde sir Bleoberys,

'I woll have the fayreste lady in your courte that me lyste
to chose.'

'I may nat say nay,' seyde kynge Marke. 'Now chose hir
30 at your adventure.'

And so sir Bleoberys dud chose sir Segwarydes wyff, and
toke hir by the honde, and so he wente his way with her.
And so he toke his horse, and made sette her behynde his
squyer and rode uppon hys way.

35   Whan sir Segwarydes herde telle that his lady was gone
with a knyght of kynge Arthures courte, than he armed

3–4 *C* of that sir Tristram and he hadde mette   6 *W* com ascawnce com
C kynges astaunce† (*see note*)   8–9 *C* neuer sire Trystram after that though
9 *C* there was   11 on *not in C*   21 *C* of kynge Marke   22 *C* that he
wold aske in his courte   29 hir *not in C*   33 *C* gart sette

hym and rode after that knyght to rescow his lady. So whan
sir Bleoberys was gone with this lady kynge Marke and alle
the courte was wroth that she was had away.

Than were there sertayne ladyes that knew that there was
grete love betwene sir Trystrames and her, and also that 5
lady loved sir Trystrames abovyn all othyr knyghtes. Than
there was one lady that rebuked sir Trystrams in the horry-
belyst wyse, and called hym cowarde knyght, that he wolde
for shame of hys knyghthode to se a lady so shamefully
takyn away fro his uncklys courte; but she mente that eythir 10
of hem loved other with entyre herte. But sir Trystrames **162ʳ**
answered her thus:

'Fayre lady, hit is nat my parte to have ado in suche maters
whyle her lorde and husbonde ys presente here. And yf so
be that hir lorde had nat bene here in this courte, than for the 15
worshyp of this courte peraventure I wold have bene hir
champyon. And yf so be sir Segwarydes spede nat well, hit
may happyn that I woll speke with that good knyght or ever
he passe far fro this contrey.'

Than within a whyle com sir Segwarydes squyres and 20
tolde in the [courte that] theyre master was betyn sore and
wounded at the poynte of deth: as he wolde have rescowed
his lady, sir Bleoberys overthrewe hym and sore hath wounded
hym. Than was kynge Marke hevy thereof and all the
courte. Whan sir Trystrames herde of this he was ashamed 25
and sore agreved, and anone he armed hym and yeode to
horsebacke, and Governayle, his servaunte, bare his shylde
and his spere.

And so as syr Trystrames rode faste he mette with sir
Andret, his cosyn, that by the commaundement of kynge 30
Marke was sente to brynge forth two knyghtes of Arthures
courte that rode by the contrey to seke their adventures.
Whan sir Trystrames sawe sir Andret he asked hym,

'What tydynges?'

'So God me helpe,' seyde sir Andret, 'there was never 35
worse with me, for here by the commaundemente of kynge

---

3 *C* was awey   9 to *not in C*   10 *C* be taken   14–15 *C* And yf hit hadde
ben that   20 *C* one of sir   21 *C** court that sir segwarides was   22 *C* to
the poynte   26–27 *C* And thenne was he soone armed and on horsbak   31 *W*
Marke that was   *C* forth & ever it laye in his power ii knyghtes

Marke I was sente to fecche two knyghtes of kynge Arthurs courte, and the tone bete me and wounded me and sette nought be my messayge.'

'Fayre cosyn,' seyde sir Trystrames, 'ryde on your way,
5 and yf I may mete them hit may happyn I shall revenge you.'

So sir Andret rode into Cornwayle and sir Trystrames rode aftir the two knyghtes, whyche that one hyght sir Sagramoure le Desyrous and that othir hyght sir Dodynas le Sa-
162ᵛ(16) vyayge. So within a whyle sir Trystrames saw hem byfore
10 hym, two lykly knyghtys.

'Sir,' seyde Governayle unto his maystir, 'I wolde counceyle you nat to have ado with hem, for they be two proved knyghtes of Arthures courte.'

'As for that,' seyde sir Trystrames, 'have ye no doute
15 but I woll have ado with them bothe to encrece my worshyp, for hit is many day sytthen I dud any armys.'

'Do as ye lyste,' seyde Governayle.

And therewythall anone sir Trystrames asked them from whens they come and whothir they wolde, and what they
20 dud in those marchis. So sir Sagramoure loked uppon sir Trystrames and had scorne of his wordys, and seyde to hym agayne,

'Sir, be ye a knyght of Cornwayle?'

'Whereby askyste thou?' seyde sir Trystrames.
25 'For hit is seldom seyne,' seyde sir Sagramoure, 'that ye Cornysshe knyghtes bene valyaunte men in armys, for within thes two owres there mette with us one of your Cornysshe knyghtes, and grete wordys he spake, and anone with lytyll myght he was leyde to the erthe. And as I trow,' seyde sir
30 Sagramoure, 'that ye wolde have the same hansell.'

'Fayre lordys,' seyde sir Trystrames, 'hit may so happe that I may bettir wythstonde you than he ded, and whether ye woll or nylle, I woll have ado with you, because he was my cosyn that ye bete. And therefore here do your beste! And
35 wete you well: but yf ye quyte you the bettir here uppon this grounde, one knyght of Cornwayle shall beate you bothe.'

---

7 *C* the whiche one   11 *C* maister sir I   15 bothe *not in C*   16 *C** ony
dedes of armes   21–23 *C* & asked hym ageyne Fair knyghte be ye   26 *C* of
armes   27 *C* of you   30 Sagramore ye shal haue the same handsel that he
hadde   32 you *not in C*

Whan sir Dodynas le Savyaige herde hym sey so he gate
a speare in hys honde and seyde, 'Sir knyght, kepe thyselff!'
And than they departed and com togydirs as hit had bene
thundir. And sir Dodynas spere braste in sundir, but sir
Trystrames smote hym with a more myght, that he smote   5
hym clene over the horse croupyr, and nyghe he had brokyn
his necke.

Whan sir Sagramoure saw hys felow have suche a falle he
mervayled what knyght he was, but so he dressed his speare **163ʳ**
with all his myght, and sir Trystrames ayenste hym, and so   10
they cam togydir as thundir. And there sir Trystrames
smote sir Sagramour a stronge buffette, that he bare hys
horse and hym to the erthe, and in the fallynge he brake his
thyghe.

So whan this was done sir Trystrames asked them,   15
  'Fayre knyghtes, wyll ye ony more? Be there ony bygger
knyghtys in the courte of kynge Arthure? Hit is to you
shame to sey us knyghtes of Cornwayle dishonour, for hit
may happyn a Cornysh knyght may macche you.'

  'That is trouthe,' seyde sir Sagramoure, 'that have we well   20
proved. But I requyre you,' seyde sir Sagramour, 'telle us
your name, be your feyth and trouthe that ye owghe to the
Hyghe Order of Knyghthode.'

  'Ye charge me with a grete thynge,' seyde sir Trystrames,
'and sytthyn ye lyste to wete, ye shall know and undirstonde   25
that my name ys sir Trystrames de Lyones, kynge Melyodas
son, and nevew unto kynge Marke.'

Than were they two knyghtes fayne that they had mette
with sir Trystrames, and so they prayde hym to abyde in
their felyshyp.   30

  'Nay,' seyde sir Trystrames, 'for I muste have ado wyth
one of your felawys. His name is sir Bleoberys de Ganys.'

  'God spede you well,' seyde sir Sagramoure and sir Dodynas.

So sir Trystrames departed and rode onwarde on his way.   35
And than was he ware before hym in a valay where rode
sir Bleoberys wyth sir Segwarydes lady that rode behynde
his squyre uppon a palfrey.

2 kepe *not in* C†   9 *C* he myght be   16 *C* no bygger   18 *C* say of vs
22 *C* your ryght name by the feythe   25 wete hit

(17)　　　Than sir Trystrames rode more than a pace untyll that he
had overtake hym. Than spake sir Trystrames:

'Abyde', he seyde, 'knyght of Arthures courte! Brynge
agayne that lady or delyver hir to me!'

5　　　'I woll do neyther nother,' seyde sir Bleoberys, 'for I drede
no Cornysshe knyght so sore that me lyste to delyver her.'

'Why,' seyde sir Trystrames, 'may nat a Cornysshe knyght
do as well as another knyght? Yes, this same day two
163ᵛ knyghtes of youre courte wythin this three myle mette with
10　me, and or ever we departed they founde a Cornysshe knyght
good inowe for them bothe.'

'What were their namys?' seyde sir Bleobrys.

'Sir, they tolde me that one hyght sir Sagramoure le
Desyrous and that other hyght sir Dodynas le Saveayge.'

15　　　'A,' seyde sir Bleoberys, 'have ye mette with them? So
God me helpe, they were two good knyghtes and men of
grete worshyp, and yf ye have betyn them bothe ye muste
nedis be a good knyght. Yf hit be so ye have beatyn them
bothe, yet shall ye nat feare me, but ye shall beate me or ever
20　ye have this lady.'

'Than defende you!' seyde sir Trystrames.

So they departed and com togydir lyke thundir, and
eyther bare other downe, horse and man, to the erthe. Than
they avoyded their horsys and lasshed togydyrs egerly with
25　swerdys and myghtyly, now here now there, trasyng and
traversynge on the ryght honde and on the lyffte honde more
than two owres. And somtyme they rowysshed togydir
with suche a myght that they lay bothe grovelynge on the
erthe. Than sir Bleoberys de Ganys sterte abacke and seyde
30　thus:

'Now, jantyll knyght, a whyle holde your hondes and let
us speke togydyrs.'

'Sey on what ye woll,' seyde sir Trystrames, 'and I woll
answere you and I can.'

35　　　'Sir,' seyde Bleoberys, 'I wolde wete of whens ye were and
of whom ye be com and what is your name.'

'So God me helpe,' seyde sir Trystrames, 'I feare nat to

---

5 nother *not in C*　　　8 Yes *not in C*　　　12–13 *C* Bleoberis they told me said syr
Trystram that one of them hyght　　　23 *C* hors and alle　　　25 here now there
not in C†　　　28–29 *C* on the gro und　　　33 on *not in C*　　　34 and I can *not in C*

telle you my name. Wete you well, I am kynge Melyodas
son, and my mother is kynge Markys sistir, and my name is
sir Trystrames de Lyones, and kynge Marke ys myne
uncle.'

'Truly,' seyde sir Bleoberys, 'I am ryght glad of you, for 5
ye ar he that slewe [Marhalte] the knyght honde for honde
in the ilonde for the trwayge of Cornwayle. Also ye overcom
sir Palomydes, the good knyght, at the turnemente in Irelonde where he bete sir Gawayne and his nine felowys.'

'So God me helpe,' seyde sir Trystrames, 'wete you well 10 **164ʳ**
I am the same knyght. Now I have tolde you my name,
telle me yourys.'

'With good wyll. [Wete ye well] that my name is sir
Bleoberys de Ganys, and my brother hyght sir Blamoure de
Ganys that is callyd a good knyght, and we be sistyrs 15
chyldyrn unto my lorde sir Launcelot de Lake that we calle
one of the beste knyghtes of the worlde.'

'That is trouthe,' seyde sir Trystrames, 'sir Launcelot ys
called pereles of curtesy and of knyghthode, and for his
sake,' seyde sir Trystramys, 'I wyll nat with my good wylle 20
feyght no more with you, for the grete love I have to sir
Launcelot.'

'In good feyth,' seyde sir Bleoberys, 'as for me, I wold
be loth to fyght with you, but sytthen ye folow me here to
have thys lady I shall proffir you kyndenes and curtesy ryght 25
here uppon this grounde. Thys lady shall be sette betwyxte
us bothe, and who that she woll go unto of you and me, lette
hym have hir in pees.'

'I woll well,' seyde sir Trystrames, 'for as I deme she woll
leve you and com to me.'   30

'Ye shall preve anone,' seyde sir Bleoberys.

So whan she was sette betwyxte them she seyde thes (18)
wordys unto sir Trystrames:

'Wete thou well, sir Trystrames de Lyones, that but late
thou was the man in the worlde that I moste loved and 35
trusted, and I wente ye had loved me agayne above all
ladyes. But whan thou sawyste this knyght lede me away

6 *C** slewe marhaus the knyght   8–9 *C†* turnement in an Iland   9 *C* where
ye† bete (*see note*)   25 *C* kyndenys curtosy and gentilnes   26 sette *not in C†*
27 *C* to whome that she wille go lete   31 *C* preue hit anone

thou madist no chere to rescow me, but suffirdyst my lorde
sir Segwarydes to ryde after me. But untyll that tyme I
wente ye had loved me. And therefore now I forsake the
and never to love the more.'

5 And therewithall she wente unto sir Bleoberys. Whan sir
Trystrames saw her do so he was wondirly wroth with that
lady and ashamed to come to the courte. But sir Bleoberys
seyde unto sir Trystrames,

'Ye ar in the blame, for I hyre by this ladyes wordis that she
10 trusted you abovyn all erthely knyghtes, and, as she seyth,
ye have dysseyved hir. Therefore wete you well, there may
164ᵛ no man holde that woll away, and rathir than ye sholde
hertely be displesed with me, I wolde ye had her, and she
wolde abyde with you.'

15 'Nay,' seyde the lady, 'so Jesu me helpe, I woll never go
wyth hym, f[or] he that I loved and wente that he had loved
me forsoke me at my nede. And therefore, sir Trystrames,'
she seyde, 'ryde as thou com, for though thou haddyste overcom this knyght as thou were lykly, with the never wolde
20 I have gone. And I shall pray thys knyght so fayre of his
knyghthode that or evir he passe thys contrey that he woll
lede me to the abbey there my lorde sir Segwarydes lyggys.'

'So God me helpe,' seyde sir Bleoberys, 'I latte you wete
this, good knyght sir Trystrames: because kynge Marke
25 gaff me the choyse of a gyffte in this courte, and so this
lady lyked me beste—natwythstondynge she is wedded and
hath a lorde—and I have also fulfylled my queste, she shall
be sente unto hir husbande agayne, and in especiall moste
for your sake, sir Trystrames. And she wolde go with you,
30 I wolde ye had her.'

'I thanke you,' seyde sir Trystrames, 'but for her sake
I shall beware what maner of lady I shall love or truste. For
had her lorde sir Segwarydes bene away from the courte, I
sholde have bene the fyrste that sholde a folowed you. But
35 syth ye have refused me, as I am a trew knyght, I shall know
hir passyngly well that I shall love other truste.'

3–4 *C* I wille leue the and neuer loue   7–10 *C* courte sir Tristram said sir
Bleoberys ye ar in the defaute for I here by these ladyes wordes she before this day
trusted   15 *C* so god me help   16–17 *C*† I loued most I wende he had loued
me And therfore   24 *W* that this (*not in C*)   27 *C* I haue fulfylled   29 *C*
And yf   31 *C* but for her loue   35–36 *C* her knowe (*see note*)

And so they toke their leve and departed, and so sir Trystrames rode unto Tyntagyll, and sir Bleoberys rode unto
the abbey where sir Segwarydes lay sore wounded, and there
he delyverde his lady and departed as a noble knyght.

So whan sir Segwarydes saw his lady he was gretly com- 5
forted; and than she tolde hym that sir Trystrames had done
grete batayle with sir Bleoberys and caused hym to bryng her
agayne. So that wordis pleased sir Segwarydes gretly, that
sir Trystrames wolde do so muche; and so that lady tolde all **165ʳ**
the batayle unto kynge Marke betwexte sir Trystramys and 10
sir Bleoberys.

So whan this was done kynge Marke caste all the wayes (19)
that he myght to dystroy sir Trystrames, and than imagened
in hymsellff to sende sir Trystramys into Irelonde for La
Beale Isode. For sir Trystrames had so preysed her for hir 15
beauté and hir goodnesse that kynge Marke seyde he wolde
wedde hir; whereuppon he prayde sir Trystramys to take
his way into Irelonde for hym on message. And all this was
done to the entente to sle sir Trystramys. Natwithstondynge
he wolde nat refuse the messayge for no daunger nother 20
perell that myght falle, for the pleasure of his uncle. So to go
he made hym redy in the moste goodlyest wyse that myght
be devysed, for he toke with hym the moste goodlyeste
knyghtes that he myght fynde in the courte, and they were
arayed aftir the gyse that was used that tyme in the moste 25
goodlyeste maner.

So sir Trystrames departed and toke the see with all his
felyshyp. And anone as he was in the see a tempeste toke
them and drove them into the coste of Ingelonde. And
there they aryved faste by Camelot, and full fayne they were 30
to take the londe. And whan they were londed sir Trystrames sette up his pavylyon uppon the londe of Camelot,
and there he lete hange his shylde uppon the pavylyon.

And that same day cam two knyghtes of kynge Arthures:
that one was sir Ector de Marys, and that other was sir 35

1 *C* leue one fro thother and   8 *C* ageyne These wordes pleasyd sir segwarydes
ryght wel that   12–13 *C** cast alweyes in his hert how he myght   F (*MS.
B.N. fr. 103, f. 49ᵛ, col. 2*) en nulle maniere   17–18 *W* to take thist† way
C to take his* wey   25–26 *C* was thenne vsed in the goodlyest maner
28 *C* the brode see   28–29 *C* toke hym and his felauship and drofe them bak in to
35 that other was *not in C†*

Morganoure. And thes two touched the shylde and bade hym com oute of the pavylyon for to juste and he wolde.

'Anone ye shall be answeryd,' seyde sir Trystramys, 'and ye woll tary a lytyll whyle.'

5 So he made hym redy, and fyrste he smote downe sir Ector and than sir Morganoure, all with one speare, and sore brused them. And whan they lay uppon the erthe they
165ᵛ asked sir Trystramys what he was and of what contrey he was knyght.

10 'Fayre lordis,' seyde sir Trystrames, 'wete you well that I am of Cornwayle.'

'Alas!' seyde sir Ector, 'now am I ashamed that ever ony Cornysshe knyght sholde overcom me!' And than for dispyte sir Ector put of his armoure fro hym and wente on
15 foot and wolde nat ryde.

(20) Than hit befelle that sir Bleoberys and sir Blamour de Ganys that were brethyrn, they had assomned kynge Angwysshe of Irelonde for to com to kynge Arthurs courte uppon payne of forfeture of kyng Arthurs good grace; and
20 yf the kynge of Irelonde come nat into that day assygned and sette, the kynge sholde lose his londys.

So by kynge Arthure hit was happened that day that nother he neythir sir Launcelot myght nat be there where the jugemente sholde be yevyn, for kynge Arthure was with sir
25 Launcelot at Joyous Garde. And so kynge Arthure assygned kynge Carados and the Kynge of Scottis to be there that day as juges.

So whan thes kynges were at Camelot kynge Angwysshe of Irelonde was com to know hys accusers. Than was sir
30 Blamour de Ganys there that appeled the kynge of Irelonde of treson, that he had slayne a cosyn of thers in his courte in Irelonde by treson. Than the kynge was sore abaysshed of his accusacion for why he was at the sommons of kyng Arthure, and or that he com at Camelot he wyste nat where-
35 fore he was sente fore.

So whan the kynge herde hym sey his wyll he undirstood

---

1 *C* And they touched   6 *C* Ector de marys and after he smote doune sir
20 *C* in at the   22–23 *C* So by hit happened that at the day assigned kyng Arthur
neither   23–24 *C* there for to gyue the Iugement for kynge Arthur   25 *C* the
castel ioyous   31 *C* of his   35 *C* sente after   36 *C* herd sir Blamor saye

well there was none other remedy but to answere hym knyghtly.
For the custom was suche tho dayes that and ony man were
appealed of ony treson othir of murthure he sholde fyght
body for body, other ellys to fynde another knyght for hym.
And alle maner of murthers in tho dayes were called treson.   5

So whan kynge Angwysshe undirstood his accusyng he   **166ʳ**
was passynge hevy, for he knew sir Blamoure de Ganys that
he was a noble knyght, and of noble knyghtes comyn. So the
kynge of Irelonde was but symply purveyede of his answere.
Therefore the juges gaff hym respyte by the thirde day to 10
gyff his answere. So the kynge departed unto his lodgynge.

The meanewhyle there com a lady by sir Trystrames
pavylyon makynge grete dole.

'What aylyth you,' seyde sir Trystrames, 'that ye make
suche dole?'   15

'A, fayre knyght!' seyde the lady, 'I am shamed onles
that som good knyght helpe me, for a grete lady of worshyp
sent by me a fayre chylde and a ryche unto sir Launcelot,
and hereby there mette with me a knyght and threw me
downe of my palfrey and toke away the chylde frome me.'   20

'Well, my lady,' seyde sir Trystramys, 'and for my lorde
sir Launcelotes sake I shall gete you that chylde agayne,
othir he shall beate me.'

And so sir Trystramys toke his horse and asked the lady
whyche way the knyght yoode. Anone she tolde hym, and he 25
rode aftir. So within a whyle he overtoke that knyght and
bade hym turne and brynge agayne the chylde.

Anone the knyght turned his horse and made hym redy (21)
to fyght, and than sir Trystramys smote hym with a swerde
such a buffet that he tumbled to the erthe, and than he yelded 30
hym unto sir Trystramys.

'Than com thy way,' seyde syr Trystrames, 'and brynge
the chylde to the lady agayne!'

So he toke his horse weykely and rode wyth sir Trystrames,
and so by the way he asked his name.   35

9 but *not in* C   12 *Wh* mean whyle   *P* meane whyle   18 *C* launcelot du lake
20 *Wh* palfray   *P* palfroy   22–23 *C* ageyne or els I shalle be beten for hit
25 *C* knyght rode And thenne she   26 *C* after hym   26–27 *C* and thenne
syr Tristram badde   27 *Wh* hym corne   *P* hym torne   *C* gyue ageyne
28 *Wh* Capitulum xi *P* Capitulum xxii   28 *C* he made   35 *C* waye syr
Trystram asked

'Sir,' he seyde, 'my name is Breunys Sanze Pyté.'

So whan he had delyverde that chylde to the lady [he seyde],

'Sir, as in this the chylde is well remedyed.'

Than sir Trystramys lete hym go agayne, that sore repented hym aftir, for he was a grete foo unto many good knyghtes of kyng Arthures courte.

Than whan sir Trystrames was in his pavylyon Governayle, his man com and tolde hym how that kynge Angwysh of Irelonde was com thydir, and he was in grete dystresse; and there he tolde hym how he was somned and appeled of murthur.

'So God me helpe,' seyde sir Trystrames, 'this is the beste tydynges that ever com to me this seven yere, for now shall the kynge of Irelonde have nede of my helpe. For I dere say there is no knyght in this contrey that is nat in Arthures courte that dare do batayle wyth sir Blamoure de Ganys. And for to wynne the love of the kynge of Irelonde I woll take the batayle uppon me. And therefore, Governayle, bere me this worde, I charge the, to the kynge.'

Than Governayle wente unto kynge Angwyshe of Irelonde and salewed hym full fayre. So the kynge welcommed hym and asked what he wolde.

'Sir,' he seyde, 'here is a knyght nerehonde that desyryth to speke wyth you, for he bade me sey that he wolde do you servyse.'

'What knyght is he?' seyde the kynge.

'Sir, hit [is] sir Trystrames de Lyones, that for the good grace ye shewed hym in your londys he woll rewarde [you] in thys contreys.'

'Com on, felow,' seyde the kynge, 'with me anone, and brynge me unto sir Trystramys.'

So the kynge toke a lytyll hackeney and but fewe felyshyp with hym tyll that he cam unto sir Trystramys pavylyon. And whan sir Trystrames saw the kynge he ran unto hym

---

1 *C* Thenne he said   *P* saunce pyte   *Wh* saunte pyte   2–3 *C** lady he said
6 *Wh* reyentyd   10 *C* was putte in   11 *C* there gouernaile told sir Trystram
how kynge anguysshe was   16 *C* of arthurs   19–20 *C†* brynge me I charge the
to the kyng   22 *Wh* sal wed   23 *C* asked hym what   24 *C* saide Gouernaile   28 *C* syr he said hit is   *P* du lyonas   *Wh* du fyonas   *C* your good
32 *C* shewe me unto

and wolde have holdyn his styrope, but the kynge lepe frome
his horse lyghtly, and eythir halsed othir in armys.

'My gracious lorde,' seyde sir Trystrames, 'grauntemercy
of your grete goodnesse that ye shewed me in your marchys
and landys! And at that tyme I promysed you to do you   5 **167ʳ**
servyse and ever hit lay in my power.'

'A, jantyll knyght,' seyde the kynge unto sir Trystrames,
'now have I grete nede of you, never had I so grete nede of no
knyghtys helpe.'

'How so, my good lorde?' seyde sir Trystramys.   10

'I shall tyll you,' seyde the kynge. 'I am assummed and
appeled fro my contrey for the deth of a knyght that was
kynne unto the good knyght sir Launcelot, wherefore sir
Blamour de Ganys, sir Bleoberys his brother, hath appeled
me to fyght wyth hym other for to fynde a knyght in my   15
stede. And well I wote,' seyde the kynge, 'thes that ar comyn
of kynge Banys bloode, as sir Launcelot and thes othir, ar
passynge good harde knyghtes and harde men for to wynne
in batayle as ony that I know now lyvyng.'

'Sir,' seyde sir Trystrames, 'for the good lordeshyp ye   20
shewed unto me in Irelonde and for my lady youre doughtirs
sake, La Beale Isode, I woll take the batayle for you uppon
this conducion, that ye shall graunte me two thynges: one
is that ye shall swere unto me that ye ar in the ryght and
that ye were never consentynge to the knyghtis deth. Sir,'   25
than seyde sir Trystramys, 'whan I have done this batayle,
yf God gyff me grace to spede, that ye shall gyff me a rewarde
what thynge resonable that I woll aske you.'

'So God me helpe,' seyde the kynge, 'ye shall have whatsomever ye woll.'   30

'Ye sey well,' seyde sir Trystramys, 'now make your   (22)
answere that your champyon is redy, for I shall dye in your
quarell rathir than to be recreaunte.'

'I have no doute of you,' seyde the kynge, 'that and ye
sholde have ado with sir Launcelot de Lake.'   35

5–6 *C* doo my seruyse   7 *C*† & gentyl   14 *W* Ganys and sir Bleoberys his
C* Blamor de ganys broder to sir Bleoberys   *F* (*MS. B.N. fr. 103, f. 51ᵛ, col. 2*)
l'un d'eux qui avoit nom Blanor et estoit frere Blioberis   18 *C* good knyghtes
23 *C* thynges that one   24 and *not in C*   27 *C* grace that I spede   28 *C*
of you   30–31 *C* ye will aske It is wel said said   33 *Wh* racreaunt   *P*
recreaunt   35–p. 408, l. 1 *C* lake Syr said sir Tristram as for sire Launcelot he

'As for sir Launcelot, he is called the noblyst of the worlde of knyghtes, and wete you well that the knyghtes of

167ᵛ hys bloode ar noble men and drede shame. And as for sir Bleoberys, brother unto sir Blamour, I have done batayle wyth
5 hym; therefore, uppon my hede, hit is no shame to calle hym a good knyght.'

'Sir, hit is noysed,' seyde the kynge, 'that sir Blamour is the hardyer knyght.'

'As for that, lat hym be! He shall nat be refused and he
10 were the beste knyght that beryth shylde or spere.'

So kynge Angwysh departed unto kyng Carados and the kynges that were that tyme as juges, and tolde them how that he had founde his champyon redy. Than by the commaundementes of the kynges sir Blamour de Ganys and sir Trys-
15 tramys de Lyones were sente fore to hyre their charge, and whan they were com before the juges there were many kynges and knyghtes that behylde sir Trystrames and muche speche they had of hym, because he slew sir Marhalte the good knyght and because he forjusted sir Palomydes the good knyght.

20 So whan they had takyn their charge they withdrew hem to make hem redy to do batayle. Than seyde sir Bleoberys to his brother sir Blamoure,

'Fayre dere brother,' seyde he, 'remembir of what kynne we be com of, and what a man is sir Launcelot de Lake,
25 nother farther ne nere but brethyrne chyldirne. And there was never none of oure kynne that ever was shamed in batayle, but rathir, brothir, suffir deth than to be shamed!'

'Brothir,' seyde sir Blamour, 'have ye no doute of me, for I shall never shame none of my bloode. Howbe[it] I am
30 sure that yondir knyght ys called a passynge good knyght as of his tyme as ony in the worlde, yett shall I never yelde me nother sey the lothe worde. Well may he happyn to smyte me downe with his grete myght of chevalry, but rather shall he sle me than I shall yelde me recreaunte.'

168ʳ 35 'God spede you well,' seyde sir Bleoberys, 'for ye shall fynde hym the myghtyest knyght that ever ye had ado withall: I knowe hym, for I have had ado with hym.'

---

2 *Wh* worlde And   *P* world And   9 *C* sire as   9–10 *C* as he were
23 seyde he *not in C*   27 *C* rather suffre deth broder   31 *C*† his tyme one of the
34 *C* as recreaunt   37 *C* for I knowe

'God me spede!' seyde sir Blamour.

And therewith he toke his horse at the one ende of the lystes, and sir Trystramys at the othir ende of the lystes, and so they feautred their sperys and com togedyrs as hit had be thundir, and there sir Trystrames thorow 5 grete myght smote doune sir Blamour and his horse to the erthe.

Than anone sir Blamour avoyded his horse and pulled oute his swerde and toke his shylde before hym and bade sir Trystrames alyght, 'for thoughe my horse hath fayled, 10 I truste to God the erthe woll nat fayle me!'

And than sir Trystrames alyght and dressed hym unto batayle, and there they laysshed togedir strongely, rasynge, foynynge and daysshynge many sad strokes, that the kynges and knyghtes had grete wondir that they myght stonde, for 15 they evir fought lyke woode men. There was never seyne of two knyghtes that fought more ferselyer, for sir Blamour was so hasty he wolde have no reste, that all men wondirde that they had brethe to stonde on their feete, that all the place was bloodé that they fought in. And at the laste sir Trys- 20 tramys smote sir Blamour suche a buffette uppon the helme that he there synked downe uppon his syde, and sir Trys- tramys stood stylle and behylde hym.

So whan sir Blamour myght speke he seyde thus: (23)

'Sir Trystrames de Lyones, I requyre the, as thou art 25 a noble knyght and the beste knyght that ever I founde, that thou wolt sle me oute, for I wolde nat lyve to be made lorde of all the erthe; for I had lever dye here with worshyp than lyve here with shame. And nedis, sir Trystrames, thou muste sle me, other ellys thou shalt never wynne the fylde, 30 **168ᵛ** for I woll never sey the lothe worde. And therefore, yf [thou] dare sle me, sle me, I requyre the!'

Whan sir Trystrames herde hym sey so knyghtly, in his herte he wyste nat what to do with hym. Remembryng hym of bothe partyes, of what bloode he was commyn of, and for 35 sir Launcelottis sake, he wolde be loth to sle hym; and in

---

9 *C* and threwe his   10 *C* an hors   13–14 *C* strongly as racyng and tracyng foynynge   16–17 *C* neuer knyghtes sene fyghte more fyersly than they dyd 22 *C* there felle doune   23 stylle *not in C*   28 *C* I haue   28, 29 here *not in C*   33–34 in his herte *not in C*   34 *C* he remembryng

the other party, in no wyse he myght nat chose but to make hym sey the lothe worde, othir ellys to sle hym.

Than sir Trystrames sterte abacke and wente to the kynges that were juges, and there he kneled downe tofore
5 them and besought them of their worshyppis, and for kynge Arthurs love and for sir Launcellottis sake, that they wolde take this mater in their hondis.

'For, my fayre lordys,' seyde sir Trystrames, 'hit were shame and pyté that this noble knyght that yondir lyeth
10 sholde be slayne, for ye hyre well, shamed woll he nat be. And I pray to God that he never be slayne nother shamed for me. And as for the kynge whom I fyght fore, I shall requyre hym, as I am hys trew champyon and trew knyght in this fylde, that he woll have mercy uppon this knyght.'

15 'So God me helpe,' seyde kyng Angwyshe, 'I woll for your sake, sir Trystrames, be ruled as ye woll have me, and I woll hartely pray the kynges that be here juges to take hit in there hondys.'

Than the kynges that were juges called sir Bleoberys to
20 them and asked his advyce.

'My lordys,' seyde sir Bleoberys, 'thoughe my brother be beatyn and have the worse thorow myght of armys in his body, [I dare sey, though sir Trystrames hath beatyn his body], he hath nat beatyn his harte, and thanke God he is nat
25 shamed this day; and rathir than he be shamed I requyre you,' seyde sir Bleoberys, 'lat sir Trystrames sle hym oute.'

'Hit shall nat be so,' seyde the kynges, 'for his parte his adversary, both the kynge and the champyon, have pyté on sir Blamoure his knyghthode.'

30 'My lordys,' seyde sir Bleoberys, 'I woll ryght as ye woll.'

169ʳ Than the kynges called the kynge of Irelonde and founde hym goodly and tretable, and than by all their advyces sir Trystrames and sir Bleoberys toke up sir Blamoure, and the

1 *C* but that he must take   2 *C* to saye   6 love *not in C*   16–17 *C** me For I knowe you for my true knyghte And therfore I wylle   17 *C* as Iuges 22–24 *W* have the worse in his body thorow myght of armys he hath nat beatyn his harte   *C* hath the wers thorou myghte of armes I dare saye though syre Tryst- ram hath beten his body he hath not beten his herte and I thanke (*see note*) 27–28 *C* his parte aduersary   28–29 *C* pyte of syre Blamors knyghthode 30 *C* ryght wel as

two bretherne were made accorded wyth kynge Angwyshe
and kyssed togydir and made frendys for ever.

And than sir Blamoure and sir Trystrames kyssed togedirs,
and there they made their othis that they wolde never none
of them two brethirne fyght wyth sir Trystrames, and sir   5
Trystramys made them the same othe. And for that jantyll
batayle all the bloode of sir Launcelott loved sir Trystrames
for ever.

Than kynge Angwyshe and sir Trystrames toke their
leve, and so he sayled into Irelonde wyth grete nobles and   10
joy. So whan they were in Irelonde the kynge lete make hit
knowyn thorowoute all the londe how and in what maner sir
Trystrames had done for hym. Than the quene and all that
there were made the moste of hym that they myght. But the
joy that La Beale Isode made of sir Trystrames there myght   15
no tunge telle, for of all men erthely she loved hym moste.

Than uppon a day kynge Angwyshe asked sir Trystrames   (24)
why he asked nat his bone. Than seyde sir Trystrames,
'Now hit is tyme. Sir, this is all that I woll desyre, that
ye woll gyff La Beale Isode, youre doughter, nat for myself,   20
but for myne uncle, kyng Marke, [that] shall have her to
wyff, for so have I promysed hym.'

'Alas!' seyde the kynge, 'I had lever than all the londe
that I have that ye wolde have wedded hir yourself.'

'Sir, and I dud so, I were shamed for ever in this worlde   25
and false to my promyse. Therefore,' seyde sir Trystrames,
'I requyre you, holde your promyse that ye promysed me,
for this is my desyre: that ye woll gyff me La Beale Isode to
go with me into Cornwayle for to be wedded unto kynge
Marke, myne uncle.'   30

'As for that,' kynge Angwysshe seyde, 'ye shall have her
with yow to do with hir what hit please you, that is for to
sey, if that ye lyste to wedde hir yourselff, that is me leveste;   **169ᵛ**
and yf ye woll gyff hir unto kyng Marke your uncle, that is
in your choyse.'   35

So, to make shorte conclusyon, La Beale Isode was made
redy to go with sir Trystrames. And dame Brangwayne

---

2 togydir *not in C*   10 so he *not in C*   18 *C** bone For what somever he
had promysed hym he shold haue hit withoute fayle   Syre said sire Trystram
20 *C* gyue me   24 *C* wold wedde   26 *C* fals of   27 *C* I praye you

wente with hir for hir chyff jantyllwoman with many other.
Than [the] quene, Isodes modir, gaff dame Brangwayne
unto hir to be hir jantyllwoman.

And also she and Governayle had a drynke of the quene,
5 and she charged them that where kynge Marke sholde
wedde, that same day they sholde gyff them that drynke that
kynge Marke sholde drynke to La Beale Isode. 'And than,'
seyde the quene, 'ayther shall love other dayes of their lyff.'

So this drynke was gyvyn unto dame Brangwayne and
10 unto Governayle. So sir Trystrames toke the see, and La
Beale Isode. [And whan they] were in their caban, hit
happed so they were thyrsty. And than they saw a lytyll
flakette of golde stonde by them, and hit semed by the coloure
and the taste that hit was noble wyne. So sir Trystrames toke
15 the flaket in his honde and seyde,

'Madame Isode, here is a draught of good wyne that dame
Brangwayne, your maydyn, and Governayle, my servaunte,
hath kepte for hemselff.'

Than they lowghe and made good chere and eyther dranke
20 to other frely, and they thought never drynke that ever they
dranke so swete nother so good to them. But by that drynke
was in their bodyes they loved aythir other so well that never
hir love departed, for well nother for woo. And thus hit happed
fyrst, the love betwyxte sir Trystrames and La Beale Isode,
25 the whyche love never departed dayes of their lyff.

So than they sayled tyll that by fortune they com nye a
castell that hyght Plewre, and there they aryved for to repose
them, wenynge to them to have had good herborow.

But anone as sir Trystrames was within the castell they
30 were takyn presoners, for the custom of that castell was suche
that who that rode by that castell and brought ony lady wyth
170ʳ hym he muste nedys fyght with the lorde that hyght
Brewnour. And yf hit so were that Brewnor wan the fylde,
than sholde the knyght straunger and his lady be put to deth,

---

2 *C*† gaf to her and dame Bragwayne her doughters gentilwoman and vnto
Gouernaile a drynke and charged them that what day kynge (*see note*)   8 *C*
said the Quene I vndertake eyther shall loue other the dayes   10 *C* Gouernaile
And thenne anone syre   16–17 *C* here is the beste drynke that euer ye drank
that dame Bragwayne   18 *C* haue   21 *C* dranke to other was soo swete nor
soo good But by that theyr drynke   23–24 *C* happed the loue fyrste betwixe
30–31 *C* suche who   31–32 wyth hym *not in C*

what that ever they were. And yf hit were so that the
straunge knyght wan the fylde of sir Brewnor, than sholde
he dye and hys lady bothe. So this custom was used many
wyntyrs, wherefore hit was called the Castell Plewre, that
is to sey 'the wepynge castell'.   5

Thus as sir Trystrames and La Beale Isode were in preson, (25)
hit happynd a knyghte [and] a lady com unto them where
they were to chere them. Than seyde sir Trystrames unto
the knyght and to the lady,

'What is the cause the lorde of this castell holdyth us in 10
preson? For hit was never the custom of placis of worshyp
that ever I cam in, whan a knyght and a lady asked herborow,
and they to receyve them, and aftir to dystres them that be
his gestys.'

'Sir,' seyde the knyght, 'this is the olde custom of this   15
castell, that whan a knyght commyth here he muste nedis
fyght with oure lorde, and he that is the wayker muste lose
his hede. And whan that is done, if his lady that he bryngyth
be fowler than is oure lordys wyff, she muste lose hir hede.
And yf she be fayrer preved than is oure lady, than shall the 20
lady of this castell lose her hede.'

'So God me helpe,' seyde sir Trystrames, 'this is a foule
custom and a shamefull custom. But one avauntage have I,'
seyde sir Trystrames, 'I have a lady is fayre ynowe, and I
doute nat for lacke of beauté she shall nat lose her hede.   25
And rathir than I shall lose myne hede I woll fyght for hit
on a fayre fylde. Sir knyght and your fayre lady, I pray you,
tell your lorde that I woll be redy as to-morne, wyth my
lady and myselff, to do batayle if hit be so I may have my **170ᵛ**
horse and myne armoure.'   30

'Sir,' seyde the knyght, 'I undirtake for youre desyre shall
be spedde, and therefore take your reste and loke that ye be
up betymes, and make you redy and your lady, for ye shall
wante nothynge that you behovyth.'

And therewith he departed, and so on the morne betymys 35

4 *C* wynters for hit   6–7 *W* were in preson hit happynd a knyghte were in
preson hit happed a lady com   *C** were in pryson hit happed a knyght and
a lady came   8 *C** them I haue merueille said   13 *C* to destroye them
23 *C* shameful But   24 *C** ynouȝ fayrer sawe I neuer in alle my lyfe dayes And
27 *C* Wherfore Syre knyght I pray   31 *C* said that knyght   31–32 *C* that
your desyre shalle be spedde ryght wel And thenne he sayd take

that same knyght com to sir Trystramys and fecched hym
oute and his lady, and brought hym horse and armoure that
was his owne, and bade hym make hym redy to the fylde,
for all the astatis and comyns of that lordshyp were there
5 redy to beholde that batayle and jugemente.

Than cam sir Brewnor, the lorde of the castell, with his
lady in his honde muffeled, and asked sir Trystrames where
was his lady, 'for and thy lady be feyrar than myne, with thy
swerde smyte of my ladyes hede, and yf my lady be fayrer
10 than thyne, with my swerde I muste stryke of hir hede.
And if I may wynne the, yette shall thy lady be myne, and
thow shalt lese thy hede.'

'Sir,' seyde sir Trystrames, 'this is a foule custom and an
horryble, and rather than my lady sholde lose hir hede yett
15 had I lever lose myne hede.'

'Nay, nay!' seyde sir Brewnor, 'the ladyes shall be fyrste
shewed togydir, and that one shall have hir jugemente.'

'Nay, I wyll nat so,' seyde sir Trystrames, 'for here is
none that woll gyff ryghtuous jugemente. But I doute nat,'
20 seyde sir Trystrames, 'my lady is fayrer than youres, and
that woll I make good with my hondys, and who that woll
sey the contrary, I woll preve hit on his hede!'

And therewyth sir Trystrames shewed forth La Beale
Isode and turned hir thryse aboute with his naked swerde
25 in his honde. And so dud sir Brewnor the same wyse to his
171ʳ lady. But whan sir Brewnor behelde La Beale Isode hym
thought he saw never a fayrer lady, and than he drad his
ladyes hede sholde off. And so all the people that were
there presente gaff jugement that La Beale Isode was the
30 fayrer lady and the better made.

'How now?' seyde syr Trystrames. ' Mesemyth hit were
pyté that my lady sholde lose hir hede, but bycause thou
and she of longe tyme have used this wycked custom and by
you bothe hath many good knyghtes and fayre ladyes bene de-
35 stroyed, for that cause hit were no losse to destroy you bothe.'

'So God me helpe,' seyde sir Brewnor, 'for to sey the
sothe, thy lady is fayrer than myne, and that me sore repentys,

---

9–10 *C*† fayrer than myn   21 *C* I preue and make   who someuer he be that
wille   23 forth *not in C*†   25–26 *C** And whanne syre Breunor sawe that he
dyd the same wyse torne his lady But   28 *C* shold be of   34 *C* and ladyes

and so I hyre the people pryvyly sey, for of all women I sawe
never none so fayre. And therefore, and thou wolt sle my
lady, I doute nat I shall sle the and have thy lady.'

'Well, thou shalt wyn her,' seyde sir Trystrames, 'as dere
as ever knyght wanne lady. And bycause of thyne owne 5
jugemente thou woldist have done to my lady if that she had
bene fowler, and bycause of the evyll custom, gyff me thy
lady,' seyde syr Trystrames.

And therewithall sir Trystrames strode unto hym and toke
his lady frome hym, and with an awke stroke he smote of hir 10
hede clene.

'Well, knyght,' seyde sir Brewnor, 'now haste thou done
me a grete dispyte. Now take thyne horse, and sytthen that (26)
I am ladyles, I woll wynne thy lady and I may.'

Than they toke their horsis and cam togydir as hit had 15
bene thundir, and sir Trystrames smote sir Brewnor clene
frome his horse. And lyghtly he rose up, and as sir Trystrames com agayne by hym he threste his horse thorowoute
bothe shuldyrs, that his horse hurled here and there and
felle dede to the grounde. And ever sir Brewnor ran aftir to 20
have slayne sir Trystrames, but he was lyght and nymell and **171ᵛ**
voyded his horse. Yett, or ever sir Trystrames myght dresse
his shylde and his swerde, he gaff hym three or four strokys.

Than they russhed togydyrs lyke two borys, trasynge and
traversynge myghtyly and wysely as two noble knyghtes, 25
for this sir Brewnor was a proved knyght and had bene or
than the deth of many good knyghtes. Soo thus they fought
hurlynge here and there nyghe two owres, and aythir were
wounded sore. Than at the laste sir Brewnor russhed uppon
sir Trystrames and toke hym in his armys, for he trusted 30
much to his strengthe. (Than was sir Trystrames called the
strengyst knyght of the worlde, for he was called bygger
than sir Launcelotte, but sir Launcelot was bettir brethid.)
So anone sir Trystrames threste sir Brewnor downe grovelyng,
and than he unlaced his helme and strake of his hede. 35

2 never *not in* C   3 *C* not but I   4 Well *not in* C   6 *C* as thou
13 *C* a despyte   22 *C* hors lightely And or   23 *C* the other gaf   *C* sadde
strokes   27 *C** knyghtes that it was pyte that he had to long endured Thus
they fought   32 *C** the strengest and the hyest knyght   34–p. 416, l. 2 *W*
(*sidenote*) . . . Sir Trystra . . . slew sir . . . unor and . . . vyff of . . . el Pleu . . .
(*margin torn*)

And than all they [that] longed to the castell com to hym and dud hym homage and feauté, prayng hym that he wolde abyde stylle there a lytyll whyle to fordo that foule custom. So this sir Trystrames graunted thereto.

5 So the meanewhyle one of the knyghtes rode unto sir Galahalte the Haute Prynce whyche was sir Brewnors son, a noble knyght, and tolde hym what mysadventure his fadir had and his modir.

(27) Than cam sir Galahalt and the Kynge with the Hondred
10 Knyghtes with hym, and this sir Galahalte profyrde to fyght wyth sir Trystrames hande for hande. And so they made hem redy to go unto batayle on horsebacke wyth grete corrayge. So anone they mette togydyrs so hard that aythir bare othir adowne, horse and man, to the erthe. And whan
15 they avoyded their horsis, as noble knyghtes they dressed
172ʳ their shyldis and drewe their swerdys wyth yre and rancoure, and they laysshed togydyr many sad strokys. And one whyle strykynge and another whyle foynynge, tracynge and traversynge as noble knyghtes.

20 Thus they fought longe, nerehonde halff a day, and aythir were sore wounded. So at the laste sir Trystrames wexed lyght and bygge, and doubled his strokys and drove sir Galahalt abacke on the tone sy[d]e and on the tothir, that he was nye myscheved, lyke to be slayne. So wyth that cam the
25 Kynge wyth the Hondred Knyghtes, and all that felyshyp wente freyshly uppon sir Trystrames. But whan sir Trystramys saw them comynge uppon hym, than he wyste well he myght nat endure, so as a wyse knyght of warre he seyde unto sir Galahalt the Haute Prynce,

30 'Syr, ye shew to me no kyndenesse for to suffir all your men to have ado wyth me, and ye seme a noble knyght of your hondys. Hit is grete shame to you!'

'So God me helpe,' seyde sir Galahalt, 'there is none other way but thou muste yelde the to me other ellys to dye,
35 sir Trystrames.'

---

3 *W* customys   4 So this *not in C*   5 *C* knyghtes of the castel   6 *C*† Galahad   *F* Galehout (*var.* Galehoult)   *C* the which   6–7 *C* sone whiche was a   13 *C* Thenne sir Galahad and sir Trystram mette   14 *C* hors and alle   20 *C* nere half   23 *W* syne   24 nye myscheved *not in C*   26 *C* fyersly vpon   30 *C* no knyghthode for   31 *C* me al at ones And as me semeth ye be a noble   34–35 *C* to dye said sir Galahad to sir Trystram

'Sir, as for that, I woll rather yelde me to you than dye, for hit is more for the myght of thy men than of thyne handys.'

And therewithall sir Trystrames toke his swerde by the poynte and put the pomell in his honde, and therewithall com the Kynge with the Hondred Knyghtes and harde began 5 to assayle sir Trystrames.

'Lat be,' seyde sir Galahalt, 'that ye be nat so hardy to towche hym, for I have gyffyn this knyght his lyff.'

'That ys your shame,' seyde the kynge, 'for he hath slayne youre fadir and your modir.' 10

'As for that,' seyde sir Galahalte, 'I may nat wyght hym gretly, for my fadir had hym in [preson] and inforsed hym **172ᵛ** to do batayle with hym. And my fadir hadde suche a custom, that was a shamefull custom, that what knyght and lady com thydir to aske herberow, his lady [must] nedis dye but yf 15 she were fayrer than my modir; and if my fadir overcom that knyght he muste nedis dye. For sothe, this was a shamefull custom and usage, a knyght, for his herborow askynge, to have suche herborage. And for this custom I wolde never draw aboute hym.' 20

'So God me helpe,' seyde the kynge, 'this was a shamefull custom.'

'Truly,' seyde sir Galahalt, 'so semyth me. And me-semyth hit had bene grete pyté that this knyght sholde have bene slayne, for I dare sey he is one of the noblyst knyghtes 25 that beryth lyff but yf hit be sir Launcelot du Lake.'

'Now, fayre knyght,' seyde sir Galahalte, 'I requyre you, telle me youre name and of whens ye ar and whethir thou wolte.'

'Sir,' he seyde, 'my name is sir Trystrames de Lyones, 30 and frome kynge Marke of Cornwayle I was sente on messayge unto kyng Angwyshe of Irelonde for to fecche his doughtyr to be his wyff, and here she is redy to go wyth me into Cornwayle, and her name is La Beale Isode.'

Than seyde sir Galahalte unto sir Trystramys, 35

'Well be ye founde in this marchis! And so ye woll

---

1 Sir, as for that *not in C*   3 *C* his owne   4 *C* in the hand of sir Galahad
9 *C* the kynge with the C knyghtes hath he not   14 and lady *not in C*
17 For sothe *not in C*   23, 24 *C* semed   25 *C* is the noblest man   27–28 *C*
requyre the . . . thy name . . . thou art   34–36 *C*† Isoud and sir Trystram said
sir Galahad the haut prynce wel be ye

917.44   E e

promyse me to go unto sir Launcelot and accompany wyth
hym, ye shall go where ye woll and youre fayre lady wyth
you. And I shall promyse you never in all my dayes shall
none suche custom be used in this castell as hath bene used
5 heretofore.'

'Sir,' seyde sir Trystrames, 'now I late you wete, so God
me helpe, I wente ye had bene sir Launcelot du Lake whan
173ʳ I sawe you fyrste, and therefore I dred you the more. And,
sir, I promyse you,' seyde sir Trystrames, 'as sone as I may
10 I woll se sir Launcelot and infelyshyp me with hym, for of
all the knyghtes in the worlde I moste desyre his felyshyp.'

(28) And than sir Trystramys toke his leve whan he sawe his
tyme, and toke the see.

And meanewhyle worde com to sir Launcelot and to sir
15 Trystramys that kynge Carados, the myghty kynge that was
made lyke a gyaunte why(ght), fought wyth sir Gawayne
and gaff hym suche strokys that he sowned in his sadyll. And
after that he toke hym by the coler and pulled hym oute of his
sadyll and bounde hym faste to the sadyll-bowghe, and so
20 rode his way with hym towarde his castell. And as he rode,
sir Launcelot by fortune mette with kynge Carados, and
anone he knew sir Gawayne that lay bounde before hym.

'A!' seyde syr Launcelot unto sir Gawayne, 'how stondyth
hit wyth you?'
25 'Never so harde,' seyde sir Gawayne, 'onles that ye helpe
me. For, so God me helpe, withoute ye rescow me I know
no knyght that may but you other sir Trystrames,' where-
for sir Launcelot was hevy at sir Gawaynes wordys. And than
sir Launcelot bade sir Carados,
30 'Ley downe that knyght and fyght with me!'

'Thow arte but a foole,' seyde sir Carados, 'for I woll serve
the in the same wyse.'

'As for that,' seyde sir Launcelot, 'spare me nat, for I
warne the, I woll nat spare the.'
35 And than he bounde hym hand and foote and so threw
hym to the grounde, and than he gate his speare in his honde

4 none *not in C*   5 heretofore *not in C*   15 *C* sire Carados   16 *W* gyaunte
whyche fought   *C* gyaunt that fought (*see note*)   19 *C* fast bounde hym
21 *C* by fortune sir Launcelot   sir Carados   22 *C* bounde after hym   27 *C*
outher you or   28 *C* heuy of   35 *C** bond sir Gawayne   36 in his
honde *not in C*

of his squyre and departed frome sir Launcelot to fecche his
course. And so ayther mette with other and brake their
speares to theire hondys. And than they pulled oute their
swerdys and hurled togydyrs on horsebacke more than an
owre. And at the laste sir Launcelot smote sir Carados suche 5
a buffet on the helme that hit perysshed his brayne-panne.
So than syr Launcelot toke sir Carados by the coler and
pulled hym undir his horse fete, and than he alyght and pulled **173ᵛ**
of his helme and strake offe his hede. Than sir Launcelot
unbownde sir Gawayne.   10

So this same tale was tolde to sir Galahalte and to syr
Trystrames, and sayde, 'Now may ye hyre the nobles that
folowyth sir Launcelot.'

'Alas!' seyde sir Trystrames, 'and I had nat this messayge
in hande with this fayre lady, truly I wolde never stynte or 15
I had founde sir Launcelot.'

Than syr Trystrames and La Beale Isode yeode to the
see and cam into Cornwayle, and anone all the barownes
mette with hym. And anone they were rychely wedded wyth (29)
grete nobley. But evir, as the Frenshe booke seyth, sir Trys- 20
trames and La Beale Isode loved ever togedyrs.

Than was there grete joustys and grete turnayynge, and
many lordys and ladyes were at that feyste, and sir Trystrames was moste praysed of all other. So thus dured the
feste longe.   25

And aftir that feste was done, within a lytyll whyle aftir,
by the assente of two ladyes that were with the quene they
ordayned for hate and envye for to distroy dame Brangwayne
that was mayden and lady unto La Beale Isode. And she
was sente into the foreste for to fecche herbys, and there 30
she was [mette] and bounde honde and foote to a tre, and
so she was bounden three dayes. And by fortune sir Palomydes founde dame Brangwayne, and there he delyverde hir
from the deth and brought hir to a nunry there besyde for
to be recoverde.   35

Whan Isode the quene myssed hir mayden, wete you well

6 *C*† it perched   9–12 *W* (*sidenote*): How sir Launcelot slew kyng Carados
of the dolerous towre   12 *C* Trystram here maye   17 *C* Isoud wente
19 *C* mette hem   *C*† Capitulum XIX   27 with quene Isoud   31 *O*¹ was
she *C* feete and hand

she was ryght hevy as evir any quene myght be, for of all erthely women she loved hir beste and moste, cause why she cam with her oute of her contrey. And so uppon a day quene Isode walked into the foreste and put away hir thoughtes,
5 and there she wente hirselff unto a welle and made grete moone. And suddey[n]ly there cam sir Palomydes unto her, and herde all hir complaynte and seyde,

174ʳ 'Madame Isode, and ye wolde graunte me my boone I shall brynge agayne to you dame Brangwayne sauff and sounde.'
10 Than the quene was so glad of his profyr that suddaynly unavysed she graunte all his askynge.

'Well, madame,' seyde sir Palomydes, 'I truste to youre promyse, and yf ye woll abyde halff an owre here I shall brynge hir to you.'
15 'Sir, I shall abyde you,' seyde the quene.

Than sir Palomydes rode forth his way to that nunry, and lyghtly he cam agayne with dame Brangwayne; but by hir good wylle she wolde nat have comyn to the quene, for cause she stoode in adventure of hir lyff. Natwythstondynge,
20 halff agayne hir wyll, she cam wyth sir Palomydes unto the quene, and whan the quene sawe her she was passyng glad.

'Now, madame,' seyde sir Palomydes, 'remembir uppon your promyse, for I have fulfylled my promyse.'

'Sir Palomydes,' seyde the quene, 'I wote nat what is your
25 desyre, but I woll that ye wete, howbehit that I profyrde you largely, I thought none evyll, nother, I warne you, none evyll woll I do.'

'Madame,' seyde sir Palomydes, 'as at this tyme ye shall nat know my desyre.'
30 'But byfore my lorde, myne husbande, there shall ye know that ye shall have your desyre that I promysed you.'

And than the quene rode home unto the kynge, and sir Palomydes rode with hir, and whan sir Palomydes com before the kynge he seyde,

1 *C* euer was ony quene for   2 *C* best the cause was for she   4 *C* to putte
7 *C** had herd   8 *C* ye wille   9 agayne *not in C*   13 *C* abyde here half
15 *C* said la beale Isoud   18–19 *C* comen ageyne by cause for loue of the quene
she stood   20 *C* ageynst her   25 *C* I promysed   30–32 *C** but bifore
my lord your husband there shalle ye knowe that I wil haue my desyre that ye
haue promysed me And therwith the quene departed and rode home   33 *C* rode
after her

'Sir kynge, I requyre the, as thou arte ryghtuous kynge,
that ye woll juge me the ryght.'

'Telle me your cause,' seyde the kynge, 'and ye shall
have ryght.'

'Sir,' seyde sir Palomydes, 'I promysed youre quene, my   5 (30)
lady dame Isode, to brynge agayne dame Brangwayne that
she had loste, uppon this covenaunte, that she sholde graunte
me a boone that I wolde aske, and withoute grucchynge
othir advysemente she graunted me.'

'What sey ye, my lady?' seyde the kynge.   10 **174ᵛ**

'Hit is as he seyth, so God me helpe! To sey the soth,'
seyde the quene, 'I promysed hym his askynge for love and
joy I had to se her.'

'Welle, madame,' seyde the kynge, 'and yf [ye] were
hasty to graunte what boone he wolde aske, I wolde well that 15
[ye] perfourmed [your] promyse.'

Than seyde sir Palomydes, 'I woll that ye wete that I woll
have youre quene to lede hir and to governe her whereas me
lyste.'

Therewyth the kynge stoode stylle and unbethought hym   20
of sir Trystrames and demed that he wolde rescowe her.
And than hastely the kynge answered and seyde,

'Take hir to the and the adventures withall that woll falle
of hit, for, as I suppose, thou wolt nat enjoy her no whyle.'

'As for that,' seyde sir Palomydes, 'I dare ryght well abyde 25
the adventure.'

And so, to make shorte tale, sir Palomydes toke hir by the
honde and seyde,

'Madame, grucche nat to go with me, for I desyre nothynge
but youre owne promyse.'   30

'As for that,' seyde the quene, 'wete thou well, I feare nat
gretely to go with the, howbehit thou haste me at avauntage
uppon my promyse. For I doute nat I shall be worshypfully
rescowed fro the.'

'As for that,' seyde sir Palomydes, 'be as hit be may.'   35

So quene Isode was sette behynde sir Palomydes and rode

---

1 *C* as ye be a   5–6 *C* Quene Isoud to   11–12 *C* help said the quene to
saye the sothe I promysed   13 *C* that I   14 *W* if I   16 *W* she perfourmed
her   20 *C* bethought hym   22, 28 and seyde *not in C*   23 *C* her with
the aduētures that shal falle   31 wete thou well *not in C*   34 *C* fro *S* from
35 *C* it as

his way. And anone the kynge sente unto sir Trystrames, but in no wyse he wolde nat be founde, for he was in the foreste an-huntynge; for that was allwayes hys custom, but yf he used armes, to chace and to hunte in the forestes.

5 'Alas!' seyde the kynge, 'now am I shamed forever, that be myne owne assente my lady and my quene shall be devoured.'

Than cam there forth a knyght that hyght Lambegus, and he was a knyght of sir Trystrames.

10 'My lorde,' seyde the knyght, 'syth that ye have suche
175ʳ truste in my lorde sir Trystrames, wete yow well for his sake I woll ryde aftir your quene and rescow her, other ellys shall I be beatyn.'

'Grauntemercy!' seyde the kynge. 'And I lyve, sir Lam-
15 begus, I shall deserve hit.'

And than sir Lambegus armed hym and rode aftir them as faste as he myght, and than wythin a whyle he overtoke hem. And than sir Palomydes lefte the quene and seyde,

'What arte thou?' seyde sir Palomydes, 'arte thou sir Trys-
20 trames?'

'Nay,' he seyde, 'I am his servaunte, and my name is sir Lambegus.'

'That me repentys,' seyde sir Palomydes, 'I had lever thou had bene sir Trystrames.'

25 'I leve you well,' seyde sir Lambegus, 'but whan thou metyste with sir Trystrames thou shalt have bothe thy hondys full!'

And than they hurteled togydyrs and all to-braste their sperys, and than they pulled oute their swerdys and hewed
30 on there helmys and hawbirkes. At the laste sir Palomydes gaff sir Lambegus suche a wounde that he felle doune lyke a dede man to the erthe. Than he loked aftir La Beale Isode, and than she was gone he woste nat where. Wete you well that sir Palomydes was never so hevy!

35 So the quene ran into the foreste, and there she founde a welle and therein she had thought to have drowned herselff.

1 *C* sente after syr 2 *C* he coude be foũde 5 *C* I am 8 *C* knyght his name was lambegus 10 suche *not in C* 12–13 *C* or els I shal be 16 them *not in C* 17 *W* as she 17–18 *C* ouertoke sir Palamydes And 18 and seyde *not in C* 25 *C* I bileue you 26 bothe *not in C* 30 there *not in C* 32 *C* dede knyghte to 33 *C* he nyst where 34 that *not in C*

And as good fortune wolde, there cam a knyght to her that
had a castell there besyde, and his name was sir Adtherpe.
And whan he founde the quene in that myscheff he rescowed
her and brought hir to his castell. And whan he wyste what
[s]he was he armed hym and toke his horse, and seyde he 5
wolde be avenged uppon sir Palomydes.

And so he rode unto the tyme he mette with hym, and
there sir Palomydes wounded hym sore. And by force he
made hym to telle the cause why he dud batayle wyth hym,
and he tolde hym how he ladde the quene La Beale Isode into 10
hys owne castel.

'Now brynge me there,' seyde sir Palamydes, 'or thou **175ᵛ**
shalt of myne handis die!'

'Sir,' seyde sir Adtherpe, 'I am so sore wounded I may
nat folow, but ryde you this way and hit shall bryng you to 15
my castell, and therein is the quene.'

Sir Palomydes rode tyll that he cam to the castell. And
at a wyndow La Beale Isode saw sir Palomydes, than she
made the yatys to be shutte strongely. And whan he sawe
he myght nat entir into the castell he put of his horse brydyll 20
and his sadyll, and so put his horse to pasture and sette
hymselff downe at the gate, lyke a man that was oute of his
wytt that recked nat of hymselff.

Now turne we unto sir Trystrames, that whan he was com (31)
home and wyste that La Beale Isode was gone with sir Palo- 25
mydes, wete you well he was wrothe oute of mesure.

'Alas!' seyde sir Trystrames, 'I am this day shamed!'
Than he called Gavernayle, his man, and seyde,

'Haste the that I were armed and on horsebacke, for well
I wote sir Lambegus hath no myght nor strength to wyth- 30
stonde sir Palomydes. Alas I had nat bene in his stede!'

So anone he was armed and horsed and rode aftir into the
foreyste, and within a whyle he founde his knyght sir Lambegus allmoste to deth wounded. And sir Trystrames bare
hym to a foster and charged hym to kepe hym welle. 35

2 *C* therby his name　　　7 *C* rode on tyll he　　　9 *C* telle hym the　　　10 and
how he had ladde the quene vnto　　13 *C* dye of my handes　　14 sore *not in C†*
16 *C* and there within　　17 *C* rode styll tyl he　　20 *C* not come within the
20 horse *not in C*　　23 *C* retchyd　　28 *C* he cryed to Gouernaile　and seyde
not in C　　31 *C* Allas that I haue not　　32 *C* as he was armed and horsed
sir Tristram and Gouernaile rode　　34 *C* woūded to the dethe

And than he rode forth and founde sir Adtherpe sore wounded; and he tolde all, and how the quene had drowned herselff 'had nat I bene, and how for her sake I toke uppon me to do batayle with sir Palomydes'.

5 'Where is my lady?' seyde sir Trystrames.

'Sir,' seyde the knyght, 'she is sure inowe wythin my castell, and she can holde her within hit.'

'Grauntemercy,' seyde sir Trystrames, 'of thy grete goodnesse.'

176ʳ 10 And so he rode tyll that he cam nyghe his castell. And than sir Palomydes sate at the gate and sawe where sir Trystrames cam, and he sate as he had slepe, and his horse pastured afore hym.

'Now go thou, Governayle,' seyde sir Trystrames, 'and 15 bydde hym awake and make hym redy.'

So Governayle rode unto hym and seyde,

'Sir Palomydes! aryse and take to thyne harneys!'

But he was in suche a study he herde nat what he seyde. So Governayle com agayne to sir Trystrames and tolde hym 20 he slepe ellys he was madde.

'Go thou agayne,' seyde sir Trystrames, 'and bydde hym aryse, and telle hym I am here, his mortal foo.'

So Governayle rode agayne, and putte uppon hym with the but of his spere and seyde,

25 'Sir Palomydes, make the redy, for wete thou welle sir Trystrames hovyth yondir and sendyth the worde he is thy mortall foo.'

And therewithall sir Palomydes arose stylly withoute ony wordys, and gate hys horse anone and sadylled hym and 30 brydylled hym; and lyghtly he lepe uppon hym and gate his spere in his honde. And aythir feautred their spearys and hurled faste togedyrs, and anone sir Trystrames smote downe sir Palomydes over his horse tayle. Than lyghtly sir Palomydes put his shylde before hym and drew 35 his swerde.

2 all and *not in C*   3 *C* not he ben   3–4 *C* her sake & loue he had taken vpon hym to doo   10 that *not in C*   10–13 *C* nyghe to that Castel and thenne syr Trystram saw where syr Palamydes sat at the gate slepynge and his hors pastured fast afore hym   17 *C* to the thyn   18–20 *C* what Gouernayle said So Gouernaile came ageyne and told syre Trystram he slepte or els   23 with *not in C* 28 ony *not in C*   30 *first* hym *not in C*   32 *C* hurtled   and there Tristram

And there began stronge batayle on bothe partyes, for
bothe they fought for the love of on[e] lady. And ever she
lay on the wallys and behylde them how they fought oute of
mesure. And aythir were wounded passynge sore, but sir
Palomydes was muche sorer wounded; for they fought thus 5
trasynge and traversynge more than two owres, that well
nyghe for doole and sorow La Beale Isode sowned, and seyde,
'Alas! that one I loved and yet do, and the other I love **176ᵛ**
nat, that they sholde fyght! And yett hit were grete pyté
that I sholde se sir Palomydes slayne, for well I know by 10
that the ende be done sir Palomydes is but a dede man, bycause that he is nat crystened, and I wolde be loth that he
sholde dye a Sarezen.' And therewithall she cam downe and
besought hem for her love to fyght no more.

'A, madame,' seyde sir Trystrames, 'what meane you? 15
Woll ye have me shamed? For well ye know that I woll be
ruled by you.'

'A, myne awne lorde,' seyde La Beale Isode, 'full well ye
wote I wolde nat your dyshonour, but I wolde that ye wolde
for my sake spare this unhappy Sarezen, sir Palomydes.' 20

'Madame,' seyde sir Trystrames, 'I woll leve for youre sake.'

Than seyde she to sir Palomydes, 'This shall be thy charge:
thou shalt go oute of this contrey whyle I am ⌐therin⌐.'

'Madame, I woll obey your commaundemente,' seyde
sir Palomydes, 'whyche is sore ayenste my wylle.' 25

'Than take thy way,' seyde La Beale Isode, 'unto the
courte of kynge Arthure, and there recommaunde me
unto quene Gwenyvere and tell her that I sende her worde
that there be within this londe but four lovers, and that is
sir Launcelot and dame Gwenyver, and sir Trystrames and 30
quene Isode.'

And so sir Palomydes departed with grete hevynesse, and (32)

7–8 *C* swouned Allas she said   9 that they sholde fyght And *not in C*†   10–11 *C*
by that tyme the   11–12 *C* dede knyȝt by cause he is not crystened I wold be
14 *C* bisought sire Tristram to fyghte no more (for her love *not in C*)   15 *C*
saide he   16 For *not in C*   18 A myne awne lorde *not in C*   19 *C* I
wylle not your dishonour saide la beale Isoud but   21 *C* leue fyghtynge at this
tyme for   22 *C* she said   *C* your charge   23 *W* I am quene thereoff
*C** therin *F* (*MS. B.N. fr. 103, f. 69ᵛ, col. 1*) Et si vous command que vous jamais ne venés en lieu ou je soye   24 Madame *not in C*   25 *C* the whiche
29–31 *C* louers that is sire Launcelot du lake and Quene Gueneuer and sire Trystram
de lyonas and quene Isoud

sir Trystrames toke the quene and brought her agayne unto
kynge Marke. And than was there made grete joy of hir
home-commynge. Than who was cheryshed but sir Trystrames!

5 Than sir Trystrames latte fecche home sir Lambegus, his
knyght, frome the forsters house; and hit was longe or he was
hole, but so at the laste he recovered. And thus they lyved
with joy and play a longe whyle. But ever sir Andret, that
was nye cosyn unto sir Trystrams, lay in a [watche to] wayte
177ʳ 10 betwyxte sir Trystrames and La Beale Isode for to take
hym and devoure hym.

So uppon a day sir Trystrames talked with La Beale Isode
in a wyndowe, and that aspyed sir Andred and tolde the
kynge. Than kyng Marke toke a swerde in his honde and
15 cam to sir Trystrames and called hym 'false traytowre', and
wolde have stryken hym, but sir Trystrames was nyghe hym
and ran undir his swerde and toke hit oute of his honde.
And than the kynge cryed:

'Where ar my knyghtes and my men? I charge you, sle
20 this traytowre!'

But at that tyme there was nat one that wolde meve for
his wordys.

Whan sir Trystrames sawe there was none that wolde be
ayenste hym he shoke hys swerde to the kynge and made
25 countenaunce as he wolde have strykyn hym. And than
kynge Marke fledde, and sir Trystrames folowed hym and
smote hym fyve or six strokys flatlynge in the necke, that
he made hym falle on the nose.

And than sir Trystrames yode his way and armed hym
30 and toke his horse and his men, and so he rode into the
foreste. And there uppon a day sir Trystrames mette with
two bretherne that were wyth kynge Marke knyghtes, and
there he strake of the hede of the tone brother and wounded
that other to the deth, and he made hym to bere the hede in
35 his helme. And thirty mo he there wounded. And whan

5 home *not in* C   7 *W* recovered thus And thus   *C* he was wel recouered thus
they   9 *Not emended in* O¹   10–11 *C** take hem and sklaundre hem
13 *C* told it to the   23 *C* sawe that there was not one wold   24 *C* the swerd
25 *C* as though he   27 *C* smote vpon hym   *C* on the neck   28 *C* hym to
falle   32 *C* were knyghtes with kynge Marke and   33–34 *C* the one &
wounded the other   34–35 *C** bere his broders hede in his helme vnto the kynge and

that knyght com before the kynge to say hys message he
dyed there before the kynge and the quene. Than kyng
Marke called his counceyle unto hym and asked avyce of his
barownes, what were beste to do with sir Trystrames.

'Sir,' seyde the barowns, and in especiall sir Dynas the 5
Senesciall, 'we woll gyff you counceyle for to sende for sir
Trystrames, for we woll that ye wete many men woll holde
with sir Trystrames and he were harde bestadde. And, sir,'
seyde sir Dynas the Senesciall, 'ye shall undirstonde that sir
Trystrames ys called peereless and makeles of ony Crystyn 10 **177ᵛ**
knyght, and of his myght and hardynes we know none so
good a knyght but yf hit be sir Launcelot du Lake. And yff
he departe frome your courte and go to kyng Arthurs courte,
wete you well he woll so frende hym there that he woll nat
sette by your malyce. And therefore, sir, I counceyle you to 15
take hym to your grace.'

'I woll well,' seyde the kynge, 'that he be sent fore, that
we may be frendys.'

Than the barounes sente for sir Trystrames undir theire
conduyte, and so whan sir Trystrames com to the kynge he 20
was wellcom, and no rehersall was made, and than there was
game and play.

And than the kynge and the quene wente an-huntynge,
and sir Trystrames. So the kynge and the quene made their (33)
pavylons and their tentes in the foreste besyde a ryver, and 25
there was dayly justyng and huntyng, for there was ever
redy thirty knyghtes to juste unto all that cam at that tyme.
And there by fortune com sir Lamorak de Galis and sir
Dryaunte. And sir Dryaunte justed well, but at the laste
he had a falle. Than sir Lamorak profyrde, and whan he 30
began he fared so wyth the thirty knyghtes that there was
nat one off them but he gaff a falle, and som of them were
sore hurte.

'I mervayle,' seyde kynge Marke, 'what knyght he is that
doth suche dedis of armys.'   35

'Sir,' seyde sir Trystrames, 'I know hym well for a noble

2 *C* dyed afore the   5 and *not in C*   6 *C* syr we   9 the Senesciall *not in C*
11 *C* we knewe none   13 *S* ye departe   14 *C* he wille gete hym such frendes
there   19–20 *C* vnder a sauf conduyte   27 *C* knyghtes redy to Iuste vnto
alle them that   29 *C* Dryaunt and there syre Dryaunte Iusted ryght wel
30 *C* profered to Iuste   32 *C* gaf hym a falle

knyght as fewe now be lyvynge, and his name is sir Lamerake de Galys.'

'Hit were shame,' seyde the kynge, 'that he sholde go thus away onles that he were manne-handled.'

5 'Sir,' seyde sir Trystrames, 'mesemyth hit were no worshyp for a nobleman to have ado with hym, and for this cause: for at this tyme he hath done overmuche for ony meane knyght lyvynge. And as me semyth,' seyde sir Trys-
178ʳ trames, 'hit were shame to tempte hym ony more, for
10 his horse is wery and hymselff both [for the dedes of armes he hath] done this day. Welle concidered, hit were inow for sir Launcelot du Lake.'

'As for that,' seyde kynge Marke, 'I requyre you, as ye love me and my lady the quene La Beale Isode, take youre
15 armys and juste with sir Lameroke de Galis.'

'Sir,' seyde sir Trystrames, 'ye bydde me do a thynge that is ayenste knyghthode. And well I can thynke that I shall gyff hym a falle, for hit is no maystry: for my horse and y be freysshe, and so is nat his horse and he. And wete you
20 well that he woll take hit for grete unkyndenes, for ever one good knyght is loth to take anothir at avauntage. But bycause I woll nat displase, as ye requyre me so muste I do and obey youre commaundemente.'

And so sir Trystrames armed hym and toke his horse and
25 putte hym forth, and there sir Lameroke mette hym myghtyly. And what with the myght of his owne spere and of syr Trystrames spere sir Lameroke his horse felle to the erthe, and he syttynge in the sadyll.

So as sone as he myght he avoyded the sadyll and his horse,
30 and put his shylde afore hym, and drewe his swerde. And than he bade sir Trystrames, 'alyght, thou knyght, and thou darste!'

'Nay, sir!' seyde sir Trystrames, 'I woll no more have ado

---

1 *C* ben lyuynge   3 *C* grete shame   4 *C* that somme of you mette with hym better   6–7 *C* for by cause at   8–11 *C** knyghte (*S* knyght) lyuynge therfore as me semeth hit were grete shame and vylony to tempte hym ony more at this tyme in soo moche as he and his horse are wery bothe For the dedes of armes that he hath done this daye and they be wel   10 *W* bothe   17 *C* knygthode *S* knyghthode   *C* I can deme   19 *C* ben fresshe bothe and   21 knyght *not in C†*   *C* at disauauntage   22 *C* displease yow as   *C* soo will I do (*S* doo)   29 *C* Thenne anone as lyghtly as he myghte   33 *C* Nay said

wyth you, for I have done the overmuche unto my dys-
honoure and to thy worshyppe.'

'As for that,' seyde sir Lamerok, 'I can the no thanke; syn
thou haste forjusted me on horsebacke I requyre the and
I beseche the, and thou be sir Trystrames de Lyones, feyght 5
with me on foote.'

'I woll nat,' seyde sir Trystrames, 'and wete you well my
name is sir Trystrames de Lyones, and well I know that ye **178ᵛ**
be sir Lameroke de Galis. And this have I done to you
ayenst my wyll, but I was requyred thereto. But to sey that 10
I woll do at your requeste as at this tyme, I woll nat have no
more ado with you at this tyme, for me shamyth of that
I have done.'

'As for the shame,' seyde sir Lamerake, 'on thy party or
on myne, beare thou hit and thou wyll: for thoughe a marys 15
sonne hath fayled me now, yette a quenys sonne shall nat
fayle the! And therefore, and thou be suche a knyght as men
calle the, I requyre the alyght and fyght with me!'

'Sir Lameroke,' seyde sir Trystrames, 'I undirstonde your
harte is grete, and cause why ye have to sey the soth, for hit 20
wolde greve me and ony good knyght sholde kepe hym
freyssh and than to stryke downe a wery knyght; for that
knyght nother horse was never fourmed that allway may
endure. And therefore,' seyde sir Trystrames, 'I woll nat
have ado with you, for me forthynkes of that I have done.' 25

'As for that,' seyde sir Lameroke, 'I shall quyte you and
ever I se my tyme.'

So he departed frome hym with sir Dryaunte, and by the (34)
way they mette with a knyght that was sente fro dame
Morgan le Fay unto kynge Arthure. And this knyght had a 30
fayre horne harneyste with golde, and the horne had suche a
vertu that there myght no lady nothir jantyllwoman drynke
of that horne but yf she were trew to her husbande; and if
she were false she sholde spylle all the drynke, and if she
were trew to her lorde she myght drynke thereof pesiblé. 35
And because of the quene Gwenyvere and in the dispyte of

---

1 *C* with the   *C* done to the   5 de Lyones *not in C*   7 *C* not soo said ore†
Tristram   9–10 *C* this that I haue done to you was ageynst   12 at this
tyme *not in C**   16 yette *not in C*   23–24 *C** myght städe or endure
28 *C* Noo† he   *C*† Dryaun   35 thereof *not in C*

sir Launcelot this horne was sente unto kynge Arthure.
And so by forse sir Lameroke made that knyght to telle all the
cause why he bare the horne, and so he tolde hym all hole.

'Now shalt thou bere this horne,' seyde sir Lamerok, 'to
5 kynge Marke, othir chose to dye. For in the dyspyte of sir
179ʳ Trystrames thou shalt bere hit hym, that horne, and sey that
I sente hit hym for to assay his lady, and yf she be trew he
shall preve her.'

So this knyght wente his way unte kynge Marke and
10 brought hym that ryche horne, and seyde that sir Lamerok
sente hit hym, and so he tolde hym the vertu of that horne.

Than the kynge made his quene to drynke thereof, and an
hondred ladyes with her, and there were but four ladyes of
all tho that dranke clene.

15 'Alas!' seyde kynge Marke, 'this is a grete dyspyte,' and
swore a grete othe that she sholde be brente and the other
ladyes also.

Than the barowns gadred them togedyrs and seyde
playnly they wolde nat have tho ladyes brente for an horne
20 made by sorsery that cam 'frome the false sorseres and wycche
moste that is now lyvyng'. For that horne dud never good,
but caused stryff and bate, and allway in her dayes she was an
enemy to all trew lovers.

So there were many knyghtes made their avowe that and
25 ever they mette wyth Morgan le Fay that they wolde shew
her shorte curtesy. Also syr Trystrames was passyng wroth
that sir Lamerok sent that horne unto kynge Marke, for welle
he knew that hit was done in the dispyte of hym, and therefore he thought to quyte sir Lameroke.

30 Than sir Trystrames used dayly and nyghtly to go to
quene Isode evir whan he myght, and ever sir Andret, his
cosyn, wacched hym nyght by nyght for to take hym with
La Beale Isode.

---

3 *C* that horne   and so he tolde hym all hole *not in C*†   5–6 *C** or els chese
to dye for it For I telle the playnly in despyte and repreef of sire Tristrams thou
shalte bere that horne vnto kynge Marke his vnkel and say thou to hym that
F (MS. B.N. fr. 103, f. 73ʳ, col. 1) et presenteras ce cor au roy Marc   7 *C* true
to hym he   11 *C* and there to he   12 *C* maade Quene Isoud to   13 *C* with
her *not in C*   17 also *not in C*   20–21 *C* from as fals a sorceresse and wytche
as tho was lyuynge   22 *C* stryf and debate   *C* she had ben an   24 that
not in C   31 evir *not in C*   32 *C* nyght and daye for

And so uppon a nyght sir Andret aspyed his owre and
the tyme whan sir Trystrames went to his lady. Than sir
Andret gate unto hym twelve knyghtis, and at mydnyght he
sette uppon sir Trystrames secretly and suddeynly. And
there sir Trystrames was takyn nakyd a-bed with La Beale 5
Isode, and so was he bounde hande and foote and kepte tyll
day.

And than by the assent of kynge Marke and of sir Andret
and of som of the barownes sir Trystramys was lad unto a
chapell that stood uppon the see rockys, there for to take his 10 **179ᵛ**
jugemente. And so he was lad bounden with forty knyghtes,
and whan sir Trystrames saw that there was none other boote
but nedis he muste dye, than seyde he,

'Fayre lordis! Remembir what I have done for the contrey
of Cornwayle, and what jouparté I have bene in for the wele 15
of you all. For whan I fought ⸢for the trewage of Cornwayle⸣
with sir Marhalte, the good knyght, I was promysed to be
bettir rewarded, whan ye all refused to take the batayle.
Therefore, as ye be good jantyll knyghtes, se me nat thus
shamfully to dye, for hit is shame to all knyghthode thus to 20
se me dye. For I dare sey,' seyde sir Trystrams, 'that I mette
never with no knyght but I was as good as he or better.'

'Fye uppon the!' seyde sir Andrete, 'false traytur thou
arte with thyne advauntage! For all thy boste thou shalt dye
this day!'   25

'A, Andrete, Andrete!' seyde sir Trystrames, 'thou
sholdyst be my kynnysman, and now arte to me full un-
frendely. But and there were no more but thou and I, thou
woldyst nat put me to deth.'

'No?' seyde sir Andred, and therewith he drew his swerde 30
and wolde have slayne hym.

So whan sir Trystrames sye hym make that countenaunce
he loked uppon bothe his hondis that were faste boundyn
unto two knyghtes, and suddeynly he pulde them bothe
unto hym and unwrayste his hondis, and lepe unto his cosyn 35

6 *C* and thenne was . . . and soo was kepte   13 *C* nedes that he   15 *C* in
what Ieopardy   16 *C** for the truage of cornewaile   *F* (*MS. B.N. fr. 103*,
f. 75ᵛ, col. 2) encontre le Morhoult pour la franchise de Cornouaille   17 *C* for
to be   23 *C* traitour that thou   24 *C* auaũcynge   26 *C* O Andred
27 *C* now thou art   32 *C* suche countenaunce   35 *C* vnwrast   *C* and
thenne he lepte

sir Andred, and wroth his swerde oute of his hondis. And
than he smote sir Andret, that he felle downe to the erthe,
and so he fought that he kylde ten knyghtys.

So than sir Trystrames gate the chapell and kepte hyt
5 myghtyly. Than the crye was grete, and peple drew faste
unto sir Andret, mo than an hondred. So whan sir Trystramys saw the peple draw unto hym he remembyrd he was
naked, and sparde faste the chapell dore and brake the
barrys of a wyndow, and so he lepe oute and felle uppon the
10 craggys in the see.

180ᴿ And so at that tyme sir Andret nothir none of his felowys
(35) myght nat gete hym. But whan they were departed, Governayle and sir Lambegus and sir Sentrayle de Lushon, that
were sir Trystrames men, sought sore aftir their maystir
15 whan they herde he was ascaped. And so on the rokkys
they founde hym, and with towels pulde hym up. And than
sir Trystrames asked where was La Beale Isode.

'Sir,' seyde Governayle, 'she is put in a lazar-cote.'

'Alas!' seyde sir Trystrames, 'that is a full ungoodly place
20 for suche a fayre lady, and yf I may she shall nat be longe
there.'

And so he toke hys men and wente thereas was La Beale
Isode, and fette her away, and brought her into a fayre foreste
to a fayre maner; and so he abode there with hir. So now this
25 good knyght bade his men departe, for at that tyme he myght
nat helpe them, and so they departed all save Governayle.

And so uppon a day sir Trystrames yode into the foroste
for to disporte hym, and there he felle on slepe. And so
happynde there cam to sir Trystrames a man that he had
30 slayne his brothir. And so whan this man had founde hym
he shotte hym thorow the sholdir ⌜with an arow⌝, and anone
sir Trystrames sterte up and kylde that man.

2 downe *not in* C   3 *C* sir Tristram foughte tyl that   5 *C* the peple
10 *C* crackys   12 *C* gete to hym at that tyme   Capitulum XXXV Soo whanne
14 sore aftir *not in* C   15 *C** escaped thenne they were passynge gladde
16 *C* with tuels   17-18 *C** asked hem where was la beale Isoud for he wende
she had ben had aweye of Andreds peple Sir   23 *C* a foreste   24 *C* and
sire Tristram there abode   now *not in* C   25-26 *C* men goo from hym For
at this tyme I maye not helpe you soo   28-29 *C* and thenne hit happend
that there he felle on slepe And there came a man that sire Tristram afore hand had
31-32 *C** sholder with an arow and sir Tristram lepte vp   F (*MS. B.N. fr. 103,
f. 78ʳ, col. 1*) cil le fiert d'une saiette envenimee

And in the meanetyme hit was tolde unto kynge Marke
how sir Trystrames and La Beale Isode were in that same
maner, and thydir he cam with many knyghtes to sle sir
Trystrames. And whan he cam there he founde hym gone,
and anone he toke La Beale Isode home with hym and kepte 5
her strayte, that by no meane she myght never wryght nor
sende.

And whan sir Trystrames com toward the maner he
founde the tracke of many horse, and loked aboute in the
place and knew that his lady was gone. And than sir Trys- 10
trames toke grete sorow and endured with grete sorow and
payne longe tyme, for the arow that he was hurte wythall was
envenomed.

So by the meane of La Beale Isode she ⟨b⟩ade a lady that   **180ᵛ**
was cosyn unto dame Brangwayne, and she cam unto sir 15
Trystrames and tolde hym that he myght nat be hole by no
meanys, 'for thy lady Isode may nat helpe the; therefore she
byddyth you, haste you into Bretayne unto kynge Howell,
and there shall ye fynde his doughter that is called Isode le
Blaunche Maynes, and there shall ye fynde that she shall 20
helpe you.'

Than sir Trystrames and Governayle gate them shyppyng,
and so sayled into Bretayne. And whan kyng Howell knew
that hit was sir Trystrames he was full glad of hym.

'Sir,' seyde sir Trystrames, 'I am com unto this contrey to 25
have helpe of youre doughter, ⌜for hit is tolde me that there
is none other may hele me but she⌝.'

And so ⌜within a whyle⌝ she heled hym.   (36)

There was an erle that hyght Grype, and thys erle made
grete warre uppon ⌜the kynge and putte hym⌝ to the worse 30
and beseged hym. And on a tyme sir Keyhydyns that was
sonne to the kynge Howell, as he issewed oute he was sore

1 unto *not in C*   3 *C* and as soone as euer he myght thyder   5 *C* and
there he   6–7 *C* neuer she myght wete† nor sende vnto Trystram nor he vnto her
8 *C* old manoir   9–10 *C*† horses and ther by he wiste his lady was gone
11–12 *C* with grete payne   14 *W* she made   *C* she told   18 *C* haste in to
19 that is called *not in C*   20–21 *C* maynys and she shal helpe the   23 *C*
Thenne Howel wist   25 *C* he said   26–27 *F (MS. B.N. fr. 103, f. 78ᵛ,
col. 1)* si m'a on dit que vous avés une fille qui tost m'aroit gari s'elle vouloit
28 *Not emended in O*¹   30–31 *C** vpon the kynge and putte the kynge to the werse
W vppon hym and putte the kynge   *F (loc. cit.)* Le roy Hoel y fu desconfit et perdi
grant partie de ses gens et de ses chevaliers   32 *W* and as he   *C** as he

917.44   F f

wounded nyghe to the deth. Than Governayle wente to the
kynge and seyde,

'Sir, I counceyle you to desyre my lorde sir Trystrames
as in your nede to helpe you.'

5   'I woll do by youre counceyle,' seyde the kynge. And so
he yode unto sir Trystrames and prayde hym as in his warrys
to helpe hym, 'for my sonne sir Keyhidyns may nat go unto
the fylde'.

'Sir', seyde sir Trystrames, 'I woll go to the fylde and do
10 what I may.'

So sir Trystrames issued oute of the towne wyth suche
felyshyp as he myght make, and ded suche dedys that all
Bretayne spake of hym. And than at the laste by grete force
he slew the erle Grype his owne hondys, and mo than an
15 hondred knyghtes he slew that day.

And than sir Trystrames was resceyved into the cyté
181^r worshypfully with procession. Than kyng Howell enbraced
hym in his armys and seyde,

'Sir Trystrames, all my kyngedom I woll resygne to
20 you.'

'God defende!' seyde sir Trystrames, 'for I am beholdyn
thereto for your doughtyrs sake to do for you more than
that.'

So by the grete meanes of the kynge and his sonne there
25 grewe grete love betwyxte Isode and sir Trystrames, for that
lady was bothe goode and fayre, and a woman of noble
bloode and fame. And for because that sir Trystrames had
suche chere and ryches and all other plesaunce that he had
allmoste forsakyn La Beale Isode.

30   And so uppon a tyme sir Trystrames aggreed to wed this
Isode le Blaunche Maynes. And so at the laste they were
wedded and solemply hylde their maryayge.

And so whan they were a-bed bothe, sir Trystrames remembirde hym of his olde lady, La Beale Isode, and than
35 he toke suche a thoughte suddeynly that he was all dismayed,
and other chere made he none ⌈but⌉ with clyppynge and

6 as *not in* C   13 C grete myghte and force   16 into the cyté *not in* C
19–20 C to the   21–22 C beholden vnto you for   22–23 more than that *not
in* C†   24 C of kynge Howel & kehydyns his sone by grete profers* there
27 that *not in* C   28–29 C hadde all moost he hadde forsaken   30 this *not
in* C   36 C* none but with   W† none nother with

kyssynge. As for ⌐other⌐ fleyshely lustys, sir Trystrames had
never ado with hir: suche mencion makyth the Freynshe
booke. Also hit makyth mencion that the lady wente there
had be no plesure but kyssynge and clyppynge.

And in the meanetyme there was a knyght in Bretayne, 5
his name was sir Suppynabyles, and he com over the see into
Inglonde, and so he com into the courte of kynge Arthure.
And there he mette with sir Launcelot du Lake and tolde
hym of the maryayge of sir Trystrames. Than seyde sir
Launcelot,   10

'Fye uppon hym, untrew knyght to his lady! That so
noble a knyght as sir Trystrames is sholde be founde to his
fyrst lady and love untrew, that is the quene of Cornwayle!
But sey ye to hym thus,' seyde sir Launcelot, 'that of all
knyghtes in the worlde I have loved hym [most and had 15
most joye of hym], and all was for his noble dedys. And **181ᵛ**
lette hym wete that the love betwene hym and me is done
for ever, and that I gyff hym warnyng: from this day forthe
I woll be his mortall enemy.'

So departed sir Suppynabiles unto Bretayne agayne, and 20 (37)
there he founde sir Trystrames and tolde hym that he had
bene in kynge Arthures courte. Than sir Trystrames seyde,

'Herd ye onythynge of me?'

'So God me helpe,' seyde sir Suppynabyles, 'there I harde
sir Launcelot speke of you grete shame, and that ye ar 25
a false knyght to youre lady. And he bade me do you to
wyte that he woll be youre mortal foo in every place where
he may mete you.'

'That me repentyth,' seyde sir Trystrames, 'for of all
knyghtes I loved moste to be in his felyshyp.'   30

Than sir Trystrames was ashamed and made grete mone that
ever any knyghtes sholde defame hym for the sake of his lady.

And so in this meanewhyle La Beale Isode made a lettir
unto quene Gwenyvere complaynyng her of the untrouthe of

1–2 *C** other flesshly lustes sire Trystram neuer thoughte nor hadde adoo   F (MS.
B.N. fr. 103, f. 80ʳ, col. 1) L'autre Yseult ly deffent qu'il ne gise a sa femme
charnellement. Mais l'acoler ne le baiser ne lui deffend elle mie. . . . Et Tristan la
baise et l'acole   13 *C* lady fals la beale Isoud quene   14 to *not in C*   *C*
hym this   15–16 *C** loued hym moost and had moost ioye of hym and alle
18–19 *C* forth as his mortal   27 *C* mortal enemy   31–32 *C* made grete mone
and was ashamed that noble knyghtes

sir Trystrames, how he had wedded the kynges doughter of
Bretayne. So quene Gwenyver sente her another letter and
bade her be of goode comforte, for she sholde have joy aftir
sorow: for sir Trystrames was so noble a knyght called that
5 by craftes of sorsery ladyes wolde make suche noble [men]
to wedde them. 'But the ende', quene Gwenyver seyde,
'shulde be thus, that he shall hate her and love you bettir than
ever he dud.'

1 *C* and how   3 *C* good chere   6–7 *C* but in the ende Quene Gueneuer said
hit shal be   7–8 *C* better than euer he dyd to fore

II

LAMEROK DE GALYS

[Winchester MS., ff. 181ᵛ–187ʳ;
Caxton, Book VIII, chs. 37–41]

SO leve we sir Trystrames in Bretayne, and speke we of
sir Lameroke de Galys, that as he sayled his shyppe felle
on a rocke and disperysshed all save sir Lameroke and his
squyer; for he swamme so myghtyly that fysshers of the Ile
of Servayge toke hym up, and his squyer was drowned. And 5
the shypmen had grete laboure to save sir Lameroke his lyff **182ʳ**
for all the comforte that they coude do.

And the lorde of that ile hyght sir Nabon le Noyre, a grete
myghty gyaunte, and thys sir Nabon hated all the knyghtes
of kynge Arthures, and in no wyse he wolde do hem no 10
favoure. And thes fysshers tolde sir Lameroke all the gyse
of syr Nabon, how there com never knyght of kynge Arthurs
but he distroyed hym. And the laste batayle that ever he
ded was wyth sir Nanowne le Petyte, and whan he had
wonne hym he put hym to a shamefull deth in the despyte of 15
kynge Arthure: he was drawyn lym-meale.

'That forthynkes me,' seyde sir Lamerok, 'for that
knyghtes deth, for he was my cosyn, and yf I were at myne
ease as well as ever I was, I wolde revenge his deth.'

'Pease,' seyde the fysshers, 'and make here no wordys! 20
For or ever ye departe frome hens sir Nabon muste know
that ye have bene here, othir ellis we shall dye for your sake.'

'So that I be hole,' seyde sir Lameroke, 'of my mysse-ease
that I have takyn in the see, I woll that ye telle hym that I am
a knyght of kynge Arthures, for I was never ferde to renayne 25
my lorde.'

Now turne we unto sir Trystrams, that uppon a day he (38)
toke a lytyll barget and hys wyff Isode le Blaunche Maynys
wyth syr Keyhydyns, her brother, to sporte hem on the costis.
And whan they were frome the londe there was a wynde that 30
drove hem into the coste of Walys uppon this Ile of Servage
whereas was sir Lameroke.

And there the barget all to-rove, and there dame Isode

---

3 *C* and perysshed   4 *C* squyer and there he swam myghtely and fysshers
7 they *omitted in S*   10-11 *C* hem fauoure   13 ever *not in C*   14-15 *C*
was slayne syre Nanowne le petyte the which he put to   15 *C* in despyte   16 *C*
Arthur for he was drawen lymme meale   22 *C* we shold   23 *C* disease   25 *C*
to reneye   28 *W* and and   29 *C* to playe hem in the   30-31 *C* wynde
drofe   33 *C* rofe   *S*† rose

was hurte, and as well as they myght they gate into the
forest. And there by a welle he sye sir Segwarydes, and a
damesell with hym, and than aythir salewed other.

'Sir,' seyde sir Segwarydes, 'I know you well for sir Trystrames de Lyones, the man in the worlde that I have moste
cause to hate, bycause ye departed the love betwene me
and my wyff. But as for that,' seyde sir Segwarydes, 'I woll
never hate a noble knyght for a lyght lady, and therefore I
pray you to be my frende, and I woll be yourys unto my
power. For wete you well ye ar harde bestadde in this
valey, and we shall have inowe ado ayther to succoure
other.'

And so sir Segwarydes brought sir Trystrames to a lady
thereby that was borne in Cornwayle, and she tolde hym
all the perels of that valay, how there cam never knyght
there but he were takyn presonere or slayne.

'Wete you well, fayre lady,' seyde sir Trystrames, 'that
I slewe sir Marhalte and delyverde Cornwayle frome the
trewage of Irelonde. And I am he that delyverde the kynge
of Irelonde frome sir Blamoure de Ganys, and I am he that
bete sir Palomydes, and wete you welle that I am sir Trystrames de Lyones that by the grace of God shall delyver this
wofull Ile of Servage.'

So sir Trystrames was well eased that nyght. Than one
tolde hym there was a knyght of kynge Arthurs that wrakked
on the rockes.

'What is his name?' seyde sir Trystrames.

'We wote nat,' seyde the fysshers, 'but he kepyth hit no
counsel that he is a knyght of kynge Arthurs, and by the
myghty lorde [of this yle] he settyth nought.'

'I pray you,' seyde sir Trystrames, 'and ye may, brynge
hym hydir that I may se hym. And if he be ony of the noble
knyghtes I know hym.'

Than the good lady prayde the fysshers to brynge hym
to hir place. So on the morne they brought hym thydir in a
fysshers garmente, and as sone as sir Trystrames sy hym he

---

3 with hym *not in C*   4 well *not in C*   9 to *not in C*   11 *C* eyther of vs to
15 *C* and how   24 that nyght *not in C*†   30 *Not emended 'n* O¹   *C* nought by
31 *C* Tdestram†   32–33 *C* of the Knyghtes of Arthurs I shalle* knowe
34 good *not in C*   35 *C* morowe   36 *C* fysshers rayment And

smyled uppon hym and knew hym well. But he knew nat
sir Trystrams.

'Fayre sir,' seyde sir Trystrams, 'mesemyth be youre chere
that ye have bene desesed but late, and also methynkyth I
sholde know you heretoforne.'   5

'I woll well,' seyde sir Lamerok, 'that ye have seyne me,
for the nobelyst knyghtes of the Table Rownde have seyne
me and mette with me.'

'Fayre sir,' seyde sir Trystrames, 'telle me youre name.'

'Sir, uppon a covenaunte I woll tell you, so that ye telle me   10
whether that ye be lorde of thys ilonde or no, that is callyd
sir Nabon le Noyre.'

'I am nat, nother I holde nat of hym, but I am his foo as
well as ye be, and so shall I be founde or I departe of this ile.'

'Well,' seyde sir Lamerok, 'syn ye have seyde so largely   15
unto me, my name is syr Lamerok de Galys, son unto kynge
Pellynore.'

'Forsothe, I trow well,' seyde sir Trystrams, 'for and ye
seyde other I know the contrary.'

'What ar ye,' seyde sir Lamerok, 'that knowith so me?'   20

'Forsothe, sir, I am sir Trystrames de Lyones.'

'A, sir, remembir ye nat of the fall ye dud gyff me onys,
and aftir that ye refused to fyght on foote with me?'

'Sir, that was nat for no feare that [I had] of you, but me
shamed at that tyme to have more ado with you, for as me   25
semed ye had inowe ado. But, sir, wete you well, for my
kyndenesse ye put many ladyes to a repreff whan ye sent the
horne from Morgan le Fay unto kynge Marke. And hit
sholde have gone to kynge Arthure, whereas ye dud that in   **183ᵛ**
dispyte of me.'   30

'Well,' seyde he, 'and hit were to do agayne, so wolde
I do, for I had lever stryff and debate felle in kyng Markys
courte rether than in kynge Arthurs courte, for the honour
of bothe courtes be nat lyke.'

7–8 for the nobelyst knyghtes of the Table Rownde have seyne me *not in* C† (*homoeoteleuton*)   10 *C* you said sir Lamorak that is that ye wil telle   13 *C* For sothe
said sir tristram I am not he nor I hold not of hym I am his   14 *C* out of
21 Forsothe *not in C*   23 *C* after ye refused me   with me *not in C*   24 *W* feare
that of you   *C** fere I had of you said sire Tristram but   26 *C* ynough but
sire Lamorack for my   27 *C* many ladyes ye putte to a repreef   28–29 And
hit sholde have gone to kynge Arthure *not in* C† (*see note*)   34 *C* y lyke

'As to that,' seyde sir Trystrams, 'I know well; but that,
that was done for dispyte of me. But all youre malyce, I
thanke God, hurte nat gretly. Therefore,' seyde sir Trystrames, 'ye shall leve all youre malyce and so woll I, and lette
5 us assay how we may wynne worshyp betwene you and me
uppon this gyaunte sir Nabon le Noyre, that is lorde of this
ilonde, to destroy hym.'

'Sir,' seyde sir Lameroke, 'now I undirstonde youre
knyghthode. Hit may nat be false that all men sey, for of
10 youre bounté, nobles, and worshyp of all knyghtes ye ar
pereles. And for your curtesy and jantylnes I shewed you
unkyndnesse, and that now me repentyth.'

(39)   So in the meanetyme cam worde that sir Nabon had made
a cry that all people sholde be at his castell the fifth day aftir,
15 and the same day the sonne of Nabon sholde be made
knyght, and all the knyghtes of that valey and thereaboute
sholde be there to juste, and all tho of the realme of Logrys
sholde be there to juste wyth them of Northe Walys.

And thydir cam fyve hondred knyghtes. And so they of
20 the contrey brought thydir sir Lamerok and sir Trystrames
and sir Keyhydyns and sir Segwarydes, for they durste none
otherwyse do. And than Nabon lente sir Lamerok horse
and armour at his owne desyre. And so sir Lamerok justed
and dud suche dedis of armys that sir Nabon and all the
25 people seyde there was never knyght that ever they sie that
dud such dedis of armys. For, as the booke seyth, he forjusted all that were there for the moste party of fyve hondred
knyghtes, that none abode hym in his sadyll.

184ʳ   Than sir Nabon profirde sir Lamerok to play his play
30 with hym, 'for I saw never one knyght do so muche uppon
one day.'

'I woll well,' seyde sir Lameroke, 'play as I may, but I am
wery and sore brused.'

And there aythir gate a speare, but this sir Nabone wolde
35 nat encountir with sir Lameroke, but smote his horse in the
forhede and so slew hym. And than sir Lameroke yode on

2 *W* was done was done   *C* done it was for   11–12 *C* you vngentilnesse
14 *C* alle the peple of that yle* shold   23 *C** at sire Lamoraks desyre   25–26
C they sawe do suche   26 *C* the Frensshe book   29–30 *C* profered to playe
with hym his playe for I sawe neuer no knyghte   31 *C* a day   34 this sir
not in C

foote, and turned his shylde and drew his swerde, and there began stronge batayle on foote. But sir Lameroke was so sore brused and shorte brethid that he traced and traversed somwhat abacke.

'Fayre felow,' seyde sir Nabone, 'holde thy honde, and I shall shewe the more curtesy than ever I shewyd knyght, because I have sene this day thy noble knyghthode. And therefore stonde thou by, and I woll wete whethir ony of thy felowys woll have ado with me.'

Whan sir Trystrames harde that he seyde,

'Sir Nabone, lende me horse and sure armoure, and I woll have ado with you.'

'Well, felow,' seyde sir Nabone, 'go thou to yondir pavylyon and arme the of the beste thou fyndyst there, and I shall play sone a mervayles pley wyth the.'

Than seyde sir Trystrames,

'Loke ye play well, other ellys peraventure I shall lerne you a new play.'

'That is well seyde,' seyde sir Nabone.

So whan sir Trystrames was armed as hym lyked beste and well shylded and swerded, he dressed to hym on foote, 'for well I know that sir Nabone wolde nat abyde a stroke with a speare, and therefore he woll sle all knyghtes horse.'

'Now, fayre felow,' seyde sir Nabone, 'latte us play!'

And so they fought longe on foote, trasynge and traversynge, smytynge and foynynge longe withoute ony reste. So at the laste sir Nabone prayde hym to tell hym his name.

'Sir,' seyde he, 'my name ys sir Trystrames de Lyones, a knyght of Cornwayle, whyche am undir kynge Marke.'

'A, thou arte wellcom!' seyde sir Nabone, 'for of all knyghtes I have moste desyred to fyght wyth [the] othir ellys wyth sir Launcelot.'

And so they wente than egerly togydir, that at the laste

10

15

20

25

30

184ᵛ

10–11 *C* Theune (*S* Thenne) whan sir Tristram herd that he stepte forth and and said Nabon   12 *C* with the   15 sone *not in C*   19 *C* said felawe said   22 *C* wel he knew syr   23 and *not in C*   *C* he wold   27–32 *W* (*sidenote*): How sir Nabone and his son were slayne by the hondis of sir Trystramys in the Ile of Servage   29 *C* Syre Nabon I telle the my name is   30 whyche am *not in C†*   31 A *not in C*   32–33 *W* wyth all othir ellys wyth   *C* with the or with   34–p. 446, l. 1 *C* Soo thenne they went (*S* wente) egerly to gyders and sire tristram sir Trystrames slew sir Nabone. And so forthwithall he lepe to his sonne and strake of his hede.

Than all the contrey seyde they wolde holde of sir Trystrames all the whole valay of Servage.

5 'Nay,' seyde sir Trystrames, 'I woll nat so, for here is a worshypfull knyght, sir Lameroke de Galys, that for me he shall be lorde of this ile: for he hath done here grete dedis of armys.'

'Nay,' seyde sir Lameroke, 'I woll nat be lorde of this
10 contrey, for I have nat deserved hit as well as ye. Therefore gyff ye hit where ye woll, for I woll [none] have.'

'Well,' seyde sir Trystrames, 'syn ye nother I woll nat have hit, lett us gyff hit unto hym that hath nat so well deserved hit.'

15 'Sir, do as ye lyste, for the gyffte is owres, for I woll none and I had deserved hit.'

And so by assente hit was yevyn unto sir Segwarydes. And he thanked them, and so was he lorde, and worshypfully he dud governe hem. And than sir Segwarydes delyvirde all
20 the presoners and sette good governaunce in that valey.

And so he turned into Cornwayle and tolde kynge Marke and La Beale Isode how sir Trystrames had avaunced hym in the Ile of Servayge. And there he proclaymed in all Cornwayle of all the aventures of thes two knyghtes, and so was
25 hit opynly knowyn. But full wo was La Beale Isode whan she herde telle that sir Trystrames had with hym Isode le Blaunche Maynys.

(40) So turne we unto sir Lamerok that rode towarde kynge Arthures courte.

30 (And so sir Trystramys wyff and sir Keyhydyns toke a vessel and sayled into Bretayne unto kynge Howell where they were wellcom. And whan they herde of thes adventures they mervayled of his noble dedys.)

---

1 *C* forth with he lepte   4 all the whole valay of Servage *not in C*† *F* (*MS. B.N. fr. 103, f. 90ʳ, col. 2*) 'Sire, dient tous, vous l'avés conquise, droit est que vous l'ayés.'   5 for *not in C*   7 *C* of this countreye   12 *C* ye nor I wille   15–16 *C* Doo as ye lyst said Segwarydes† for the yefte is yours† for I wil none haue   17 by assente *not in C*   17–18 *C* segwarydes wherof he   19 *C* gouerne hit   22 *C* hym to   26 *C* herd *S* herde   *C** Tristram was wedded to Isoud   32 *C* he was welcome   *C* whan he herd

Now turne we unto sir Lameroke that whan he was **185ʳ**
departed frome sir Trystrames he rode oute of the foreste
tyll he cam to an ermytage. And whan the ermyte sawe hym
he asked frome whens he com.

'Sir, I am com frome this valey.'	5

'That mervayle we off, for this twenty wyntir,' seyde the
ermyte, 'I saw never knyght passe this contrey but he was other
slayne other vylansely wounded or passe as a poore presonere.'

'Sir, tho evyll customys are fordone,' seyde sir Lameroke,
'for sir Trystrames hath slayne youre lorde sir Nabone and	10
his sonne.'

Than was the ermyte glade and all his brethirne, for he
seyde there was never suche a tirraunte amonge Crystyn
men. 'And therefore,' seyde the ermyte, 'this valey and
fraunchyse shall ever holde of sir Trystrames.'	15

So on the morne sir Lameroke departed, and as he rode he
sawe four knyghtes fyght ayenste one, and that one knyght
defended hym well, but at the laste the four knyghtes had
hym downe. And than sir Lameroke wente betwexte them
and asked them why they wolde sle that one knyght, and	20
seyde hit was shame, four ayenste one.

'Thow shalt well wete,' seyde the four knyghtes, 'that he
is false.'

'So that is your tale,' seyde sir Lameroke, 'and whan I
here hym speke I woll sey as ye sey. Sir,' seyde sir Lameroke,	25
'how sey you? Can ye nat excuse you none otherwyse but
that ye ar a false knyght?'

'Sir, yett can I excuse me bothe with my worde and with
my hondys, and that woll I make good uppon one of the
beste of them, my body to his body.'	30

Than spake they all at onys: 'We woll nat jouparté oure
bodyes, but wete thou welle,' they seyde, 'and kynge Arthure
were here hymselff, hit sholde nat lye in his power to save his
lyff.'

'That is seyde to largely,' seyde sir Lamerok, 'but many	35
spekyth behynde a man more than he woll seye to his face. **185ᵛ**

5 *C* sir said sir Lamorak	6–7 *C* sir said the hermyte therof I merueille For this
xx wynter I sawe	9 Sir *not in C*	10 *C* slewe	15 *C* fraūceis we wille
holde	25 *C* also* speke	25–26 *C* saye Thenne said Lamorak a knyght
can ye not excuse you but	28 *C* Syr said he	32 *C* bodyes as for the But
35 *C* is to moche said said sir	36 *C* they wylle

And for because of youre wordis ye shall undirstonde that
I am one of the symplyst of kynge Arthures courte, and in
the worshyp of my lorde now do your beste, and in the dispyte of you I shall rescow hym!'

5 And than they layshed all at onys to syr Lameroke, but at
two strokis he had slayne two of them. Than the other two
fled. So than sir Lamerok turned agayne unto that knyght
and horsed hym and asked hym his name.

'Sir, my name is sir Froll of the Oute Ilys.'

10 And so he rode with sir Lameroke and bare hym company. And as they rode by the way they sawe a semely
knyght rydynge and commynge ayenst them, and all in
whyght.

'A,' seyde sir Froll, 'yondir knyght justed but late wyth
15 me and smote me downe, therefore I woll juste with hym.'

'Ye shall nat do so,' seyde sir Lamerok, 'be my counceyle.
And ye woll tell me your quarell, where ye justed at his
requeste other he at youres.'

'Nay,' seyde sir Froll, 'I justed with hym at my requeste.'

20 'Sir, than woll I counceyle you, deale no more with hym,
for, lyke his countenaunce, he sholde be a noble knyght and
no japer: for methynkys he sholde be of the Rounde Table.'

'As for that, I woll nat spare,' seyde sir Froll.

Than he cryed and seyde,

25 'Sir knyght, make the redy to juste!'

'That nedyth nat,' seyde the whyghte knyght, 'for I have
no luste to jape nother juste.'

So they feautred their sperys, and the whyght knyght
overthrewe sir Froll and than he rode his way a soffte pace.

30 Than sir Lameroke rode aftir hym and prayde hym to telle
his name, 'for mesemyth ye sholde be of the felyshyp of the
Rounde Table.'

186ʳ 'Sir, upon a covenaunte, that ye woll nat telle my name,
and also that ye woll tell me youres.'

1 for *not in* C   3–4 *C* in despyte   5–6 *C* but anone at two strokes syre
Lamorak had   8 and horsed hym *not in* C†   F (MS. B.N. fr. 103, f. 92ʳ,
col. 1) Lors va querre le cheval au chevalier tant qu'il lui ramena et cil monte
9 *C* syre he sayde   12 and commynge *not in* C   20 *C* Syr said Lamorak
thēne   21 *C* for me semeth by his   23 *C* therfor I wil   27 *C* no luste to Iuste
with the   33 *C** Vpon a couenaunt said he I wille telle you my name soo that
ye wylle not discouer my   34–p. 449, l. 1 *C* yours Thenne said he my name

'Sir, my name is sir Lamerok de Galis.'

'And my name is sir Launcelot du Lake.'

Than they putt up their swerdys and kyssed hertely togydirs, and aythir made grete joy of other.

'Sir,' seyde sir Lameroke, 'and hit please you I woll do you 5 servyse.'

'God deffende, sir, that ony of so noble a blood as ye be sholde do me servyse.' Than seyde sir Launcelot, 'I am in a queste that I muste do myselff alone.'

'Now God spede you!' seyde sir Lameroke.   10

And so they departed. Than sir Lamerok com to sir Froll and horsed hym agayne.

'Sir, what knyght is that?' seyde sir Froll.

'Sir, hit is nat for you to know, nother is no poynte of youre charge.'   15

'Ye ar the more uncurteyse,' seyde sir Froll, 'and therefore I woll departe felyshyp.'

'Ye may do as ye lyste, and yett be my company ye have savid the fayryst floure of your garlonde.'

So they departed. Than wythin ⌈two or⌉ three dayes sir 20 (41) Lamerok founde a knyght at a welle slepynge, and his lady sate with hym and waked. Ryght so com sir Gawayne and toke the knyghtes lady and sette hir up behynde hys squyer. So sir Lamerok rode aftir sir Gawayne and seyde,

'Sir, turne ayen!'   25

Than seyde sir Gawayne,

'What woll ye do with me? I am nevew unto kynge Arthure.'

'Sir, for that cause I woll forbeare you: othir ellys that lady sholde abyde with me, ⟨other⟩ [els ye sholde juste with 30 me].'

Than sir Gawayne turned hym and ran to hym that ought the lady with his speare, but the knyght wyth pure myght smote downe sir Gawayne and toke his lady with hym.

8 *C* Thenne he saide more I am   12–13 *W* agayne and seyde sir what knyght is that seyde sir Froll   *C** ageyne what knyght is that said sir Frol   17 *C* departe fro yow   18 *C* lyst said sir Lamorak and yet   20 *C** two or thre dayes *F* (*MS. B.N. fr. 103, f. 93, col.* 2): Lamourat . . . vint la nuit en la maison d'un chevalier . . . A l'andemain se leva et se mist au chemin et chevaucha tant qu'il vint a une fontaine   26 *C* sire Gawayne   27 *C* for I am   29 *C* syre said he   *C* wil spare you els   30 *C* or els   *Not emended in* O¹   33 *W* the the lady

And all this sye sir Lamerok and seyde to hymselff, 'but I revenge my felow he woll sey me dishonoure in kynge Arthurs courte.' Than sir Lamerok returned and profyrde that knyght to fyght.

186ᵛ 5   'Sir, I am redy,' seyde he.

And there they cam togedyrs with all theire myght, and sir Lamerok smote the knyght thorow bothe sydis that he fylle to the erthe dede.

Than that lady rode to that knyghtis brothir that hyght
10 sir Bellyaunce le Orgulus that dwelled faste thereby and tolde hym how his brother was slayne.

'Alas!' seyde he, 'I woll be revenged.'

And so he horsed hym and armed hym, and within a whyle he overtoke sir Lamerok and bade hym turne, 'and
15 leve that lady, for thou and I muste play a new play: for thow haste slayne my brother sir Froll that was a bettir knyght than ever was thou.'

'Ye may well sey hit,' seyde sir Lamerok, 'but this day in the playne fylde I was founde the bettir knyght.'

20 So they rode togydyrs and unhorsed eche other, and turned their shyldis and drew their swerdys, and fought myghtyly as noble knyghtes preved the space of two owres. So than sir Bellyaunce prayde hym to telle hym his name.

'Sir, my name is sir Lameroke de Galys.'

25   'A,' seyde sir Bellyaunce, 'thou arte the man in the worlde that I moste hate, for I slew my sunnys for thy sake where I saved thy lyff, and now thou haste slayne my brothir sir Froll. Alas, how sholde I be accorded with the? Therefore defende the! Thou shalt dye! There is none other way nor
30 remedy.'

'Alas!' seyde sir Lameroke, 'full well me ought to know you, for ye ar the man that moste have done for me.' And therewithall sir Lamerok kneled adowne and besought hym of grace.

35   'Aryse up!' seyde sir Bellyaunce, 'othir ellys thereas thou knelyste I shall sle the!'

1 *C* sir Lamorak saw   2 *C* say of me   4 *C* knyght to Iuste   5 *C* Syr said he   11 *C* thenne she told   17 *C* were thou   18 *C* It myghte wel be said sir   19 playne *not in C*   knyght *not in C*   20 eche *not in C*   22 *C* by the space   24 *C* Syr said he   29 *C* for thou   way nor *not in C*   33 *C* knelyd doune   35 up *not in C*

'That shall nat nede,' seyde sir Lameroke, 'for I woll yelde me to you, nat for no feare of you nor of youre strength, but youre goodnesse makyth me to lothe to have ado with you. Wherefore I requyre you, for Goddis sake and for the honour of knyghthode, forgyff me all that I have offended unto you.'   5 187ʳ

'Alas!' seyde sir Bellyaunce, 'leve thy knelynge, other ellys I shall sle the withoute mercy.'

Than they yode agayne to batayle and aythir woundèd othir, that all the grounde was blody thereas they fought. And at the laste sir Bellyaunce withdrew hym abacke and 10 sette hym downe a lytyll uppon an hylle, for he was faynte for bledynge, that he myght nat stonde.

Than sir Lameroke threw his shylde uppon his backe and cam unto hym and asked hym what chere.

'Well,' seyde sir Bellyaunce.   15

'A, sir, yett shall I shew you favoure in youre male ease.'

'A, knyght,' seyde sir Bellyaunce unto sir Lamerok, 'thou arte a foole, for and I had the at suche avauntage as thou haste me, I sholde sle the. But thy jantylnesse is so good and so large that I muste nedys forgyff the myne evyll wyll.'   20

And than sir Lameroke kneled adowne and unlaced fyrst his umbrere and than his owne, and than aythir kyssed othir with wepynge tearys. Than sir Lamerok led sir Bellyaunce to an abbey faste by, and there sir Lamerok wolde nat departe from sir Bellyaunce tylle he was hole. And than they 25 were sworne togydyrs that none of hem sholde never fyght ayenste other.

So sir Lamerok departed and wente to the courte of Arthur.

HERE LEVYTH OF THE TALE OF SIR LAMEROK AND OF SYR TRYSTRAMYS, AND HERE BEGYNNYTH THE TALE OF SYR LA COTE 30 MALE TAYLE THAT WAS A GOOD KNYGHT.

---

2 *C* not for fere of you   3 *C* me ful loth   11 *C* doune softely vpon a lytil hylle   14 and cam unto hym *not in C*†   17 *C*† A knyght syr Belliaunce said syr Lamorak   *F (MS. B.N. fr. 103, f. 95ʳ, col. 2):* Et Belynas lui respont: 'Comment, Amourat, tu sceis que je te vueil mal de mort et tu me paroles de garir? Certes, se je fusse aussi au dessus de toy comme tu es de moy, tout le monde ne te garantiroit mie que je ne t'occeisse   18 *C* had had   25–26 *C* they sware to gyders   28 *C* of kynge Arthur   29 *C* Here leue we of   30–31 *C* the historye of La cote male tayle   31 that was a good knyght *not in C*

PRINTED IN GREAT BRITAIN
AT THE UNIVERSITY PRESS, OXFORD
BY VIVIAN RIDLER
PRINTER TO THE UNIVERSITY